# ROAD
# THE OCEAN

by

## LEONID LEONOV

1944

L. B. FISCHER · NEW YORK

BOOKS ARE WEAPONS IN THE WAR OF IDEAS

## A WARTIME BOOK

THIS COMPLETE EDITION IS PRODUCED
IN FULL COMPLIANCE WITH THE GOVERN-
MENT'S REGULATIONS FOR CONSERVING
PAPER AND OTHER ESSENTIAL MATERIALS.

MANUFACTURED IN THE UNITED STATES OF AMERICA

AMERICAN BOOK—STRATFORD PRESS, INC., NEW YORK

# Table of Contents

# ROAD TO THE OCEAN

# CHAPTER 1

# A Conversation with Kurilov

CHATTING WITH A FRIEND does not bring back one's youth. The treacherous flame of reminiscence warms you up a bit, stirs you, makes you hold your head up again and then wears you out. This chat did not develop into a real heart-to-heart talk: the friend related only what Kurilov himself remembered. And nothing more could be expected from this particular friend, an old weather-beaten railway car, even though it was now equipped with Diesel motors, soft seats and little window curtains that gave it an unexpected coziness, and though its floor was covered with the soft pile of a good carpet. The compartment that only yesterday had stunk of the hot sheepskins of political workers now shone coolly in neat linen slip covers. . . . A whole generation was growing old, and inanimate objects themselves were hurriedly changing in order to escape the fate of humans.

Kurilov looked in vain for a sign of the old days, but not even a scar was left on the wall once torn by a shell. In this four-axled box our hero had once knocked around the entire south-east, clinging to the tails of lazy, typhus-contaminated trains. But the former member of the Revolutionary Military Committee was now Chief of the Political Bureau of the whole railway line, a title abbreviated, after the fashion of the times, to *nachpodor*. Once again it was his fate to wear a leather overcoat and tight officer's boots.

He pulled out his pipe and rummaged for matches. The box was empty. The last match had been used by the dispatcher of a nearby station, whom he had severely reprimanded at the preceding stop. For a moment Kurilov carefully scrutinized his big, veiny hands. Suddenly he shouted for matches. His secretary took the occasion to report that the party leaders were waiting for him near the car. Kurilov gave orders that the conference be started.

Seven men pushed into the narrow corridor. The first was brazen enough to report that everything was going nicely in the Cheremshansk district, and Kurilov smiled at the childish ease with which the man lied. Without raising his head from his papers, he waved his hand. They all sat down. Dusk was falling, but all of them had managed to size up their new chief. He was big and glum; only rarely did a smile stir his greying, drooping mustache. He raised his head, and they saw that his eyes were not unfriendly. They guessed that he had come to chide the negligent, and all were equally curious to know how he would begin. After one short month in this job, they thought, he could not have grasped the complex science of railroading.

Their fears proved vain. The meeting began with a lesson in elementary politics. The chief inquired in a subdued voice what was the role of Communists in any Soviet enterprise. In chorus they recited the correct answer as stated in the regulations. Kurilov queried whether it was desirable to delay paying the workers their wages, and again the question pleased everyone by its extraordinary simplicity. Alexei Nikitich also asked them whether there was God. The party organizer answered in a booming voice that God had not existed for sixteen years—that is, not since the revolution. Kurilov expressed mild astonishment that a drunken engineer who had fallen out of his cab while the train was in motion had not been hurt. Someone burst out laughing; the case was really remarkable. . . . The new chief seemed to be quite a kindly man, perhaps one might even call him by his first name, Aliosha. Then Kurilov asked the director of the engine-repair shop to remove his galoshes: slush was running off them all over the floor. With burning ears the man went out into the corridor.

Kurilov again filled his pipe. The blue smoke mingled with his mustache and curled into every corner of the parlor car. Then he began to shoot questions like a machine-gun. The meeting was transformed into a rapid cross-examination, and the book of regulations seemed to be open at every page at once. They were seven and he was one, yet they were in the minority because behind Kurilov was the party. And suddenly all of them realized that his simplicity was an expression of his furious anger. So it was not for nothing that the new chief had spent forty-eight hours at the station refusing to receive anyone. And they recalled that at Revizan this man with the shoulders of a stevedore and the forehead of Socrates had handed one employee over to justice and suspended three others on his own authority; that his past was that of a grey-haired soldier whom the times had taught to be pitiless; that his sister, the almost legendary Klavdia Kurilova, had been entrusted with the purge of their railroad. The order of the day unexpectedly took on longer dimensions.

"Is the yard master here?" snapped Kurilov.

"No. He's gone to Putma for supplies."

"Did he know I was here?"

"The whole line was informed of your arrival."

"A non-party man?"

"No, he is a member of the party."

Kurilov picked up his pencil, ready to make a note: "His name?"

"Protoklitov."

Kurilov appeared taken aback. For a moment he played with his pencil; his expression was thoughtful. Doubtless he was relying on his memory, for he did not write down the name of this rash fellow. The others were expecting a surprise solution to the riddle, when the telephone buzzed. Feshkin, the secretary, picked up the receiver. For a long time he roared out questions, his head stuck between the engine compartment and the old-fashioned phone box. The gathering grew absolutely still. The chief's pipe was going out, making a sort of whimpering sound. Feshkin asked permission to report, but everyone already knew what had happened. The tragedy had occurred at the 201st kilometer, Sakonikha siding. Sixty-six cars had been smashed and eighteen of them had rolled down the slope. The causes of the accident, the nature of the freight and the number of victims were still unknown. A salvage train had left Ulgan-Urman an hour ago. . . . Kurilov went to the window which was sweating from the breath of seven men. He wiped off the glass with one stroke of his sleeve. His face looked old and grim.

It was dusk now. An early autumn drizzle, almost a mist, was falling on the roads. Plump hens walked among the cars picking up scattered particles of grain. Two sooty-faced boys were playing near an axle-box. The older was explaining to the younger how to pour sand into it. Even from his gestures one could sense that this child had unusual pedagogic gifts. With childish scooping motions the boys gathered earth from under their feet and shook it down into the axle-box. It was a freight car from another line, which was going to the repair shop.

"Feshkin, how far is it to Sakonikha?" asked Kurilov; now the children seemed to him devils disguised as innocents.

He was answered by several voices. Sakonikha was an hour and a quarter away if one were not held up at Basmanov. At that junction a great deal of traffic started in the opposite direction. Moreover, the new harvest of grain was on its way. Kurilov repeated the mighty word grain, aloud.

"Include our car in the schedule! . . . We're leaving!" He looked under his cuff; it was exactly 7:00 P.M.

Once again, narrowing his black Kuban eyes, Feshkin asked permission to report. His voice sounded cracked. The Diesel car could not leave at once. Despite a number of reminders the fuel oil had not yet been delivered from the depot. Kurilov remained silent for a while.

"Very well then, I'll go on the locomotive. Attend to the oil. . . ." He turned on his heel and was surprised to find the man still there. "Well, you may all go now. The meeting is adjourned. I embrace you mentally. . . ." and his gesture made clear the real meaning of his salute.

He put on his overcoat. The switchmen were calling to each other. It was six minutes' walk to the control post. The stoker stirred up the fire. The handkerchief in the mechanic's hand seemed a piece of flame. The floorboards shook. A solitary green semaphore flashed overhead like a star. Kurilov went out on the front platform of the engine. It was gathering speed, the handrails throbbed against his palms till they ached. He stood there for an entire hour, watching the darkness come toward him between sheaves of light in which dying moths whirled crazily. The engine began to slow down, and the autumnal woods echoed its whistle one octave lower. Kurilov climbed down and went straight toward the back signal lights of the salvage train. The sharp cold wind of disaster blew in his face.

# CHAPTER 2

# The Wreck

THE NIGHT WAS CHILLY, sad, still. Behind the sheds of the repair crew lay the first twisted piece of rail. From this point on the salvage train moved directly on the embankment, crushing the ties with the rims of its wheels.

A man was running toward the train waving a lantern, his wet galoshes glistening in the beams of light. He asked in a panicky voice whether the *nachpodor* had not yet arrived. Kurilov identified himself. They walked along together. The man turned out to be the director of the local railroad zone. Kurilov asked the obvious questions. It was hoped that traffic would be resumed by noon the next day. This extremely long delay was an index of the dimensions of the disaster. It seemed that the head of the rail had broken off. This was an old neglected branch of the road, with rails built on the 1901 model, that is, with a base 108 millimeters wide. The zone director added picturesquely that this branch was not a railroad, but an historic monument. Kurilov gave him an unfriendly glance, but said nothing. A minute later he asked whether the train crew had been warned. The answer was as indistinct as the gesture accompanying it was vague. The swinging lantern began to describe extremely complicated figures. He remarked that the requirements for labor power and repair materials on this road were never completely fulfilled. But the zone director knew that under these circumstances he could have closed traffic. He lost countenance and fell silent for a moment. However, this sinister silence had to be filled in with something. . . . And so, he remarked, the salvage train had left half an hour ago. No, there were not very many injured! (And here he took full advantage of Kurilov's not having insisted on knowing the exact figure.) There were only four passenger cars in the whole train, all four of them of the light type, with two axles. Naturally, they had folded up, one upon the other, like match boxes. . . .

Kurilov quietly asked him not to wave his lantern. "You'll end up by swatting me with it, citizen," he said shortly. But his companion could barely hear even his own remarks: ". . . when we arrived here, imagine, near the wreckage there was a separate . . . a completely severed foot in a bast shoe. I was so stunned by the spectacle that I almost

5

picked it up to look at it. But the person himself, the individual to
whom it belonged, we could not find, although we searched everywhere for him. . . ."

"You're talking nonsense!" said Kurilov.

"Not at all, comrade chief. . . ." The wind, an invisible wind, seemed
to clutch his throat, and he had now no strength left to resist the inevitable. "This means that under the piles of wreckage there may still be
passengers!"

They walked a few more steps in silence.

"A proper place for passengers, . . ." the *nachpodor* said in a low
voice. "I don't need you now. You may go!"

But the man did not withdraw. Now more than ever it was frightening to leave this chief alone with his thoughts. Kurilov hardly heard
the rest of his chatter. Soon they reached the place of the crash. Mountains of tangled scrap were piled up on the embankment. Crumpled
car frames twisted together by a terrible force formed the foundation
for this barbaric altar. The victim was still smoking. The oil tank,
thrown up on the very top, seemed the carcass of some gigantic animal. Streaks of torch light flickered hysterically upon its greasy sides.
The stump of the tank's neck was an unforgettable sight. The murder
weapon was still on the spot: two twisted rails had pierced its under-
belly. From the wound, dense black sap was still dripping. And as
though in order to prevent anyone from witnessing the death agony, a
little plywood sign warned all comers against the danger of fire. Kurilov came nearer. The scratched casing of the railway cars bristled in
the dirty and uncertain twilight, and the red stain of disaster spread a
faint glare over the whole spectacle.

"Very well, . . ." said the *nachpodor* hoarsely.

Mighty bonfires blazed far below on the sides of the embankment.
There were several of them, perhaps as many as seven. The flames
reached the top level of the woods. From the charred branches
streamed thin ribbons of smoke spangled with sparks. For a long time
they tossed restlessly in the sky overhead, then died away. These erratic and weak flames only intensified the impression of ruin and disaster. It was impossible to go any further: an overturned car barred the
way. Kurilov climbed down the slope. His boots sank deep into drifts
of a strangely crisp substance. It was this substance that gave such a
bumpy outline to the embankment and that now, rustling lightly, was
rolling down toward the bonfires.

Trying to avoid stepping even on Kurilov's shadow, the zone director walked behind him: ". . . The circumstances of the crash are as follows. The declivity here is 6/1000, that is to say, a drop of six meters

loes such a binder last a long time?" Kurilov asked with life-

the zone director creaked his galoshes and gave a shake of his
May I report. . . . A three-millimeter plate is good for eighteen
have checked personally. . . ."

*nachpodor* winced with an expression of disgust. So the crime
s based on scientific study. Its exactitude was guaranteed by
ineer's badge on the zone director's cap.

et go of you only to hand you over to the court," said the *nach-*
looking at those new galoshes that seemed to be prancing in
f him. He was still warm, but he did not realize it and began to
up his overcoat; his fingers were sliding through the button-
"You're a shameless fellow. . . ."

hurried away from this human cesspool. The number of chiefs
d him dwindled. And at once the spectacle became more cheer-
undreds of skilful and undistinguished people were moving about
e wreckage, and it was as though a whole shop committee had ap-
d. But the clatter of pickaxes, the whimpering howl of the screw-
. . . even these were insufficient to drown out the rustle underfoot
he had just heard again! Below, past the bonfires, kolkhoz [1]
en with pails were filing by. They scooped up the grain and
ed it into temporary piles. The chairman of the kolkhoz in person
directing this human stream, and over his face, strained and pur-
from the fire, passed the shadows of these five hundred muzhiks.
re was no need to urge them on, for they knew the real value of
ad better than anyone. They were saving the grain.

From time to time a vigorous throaty cry came from above: "On the
les!" A full-cheeked little fellow, sticking his hands into his side-
ckets, kept intoning a long and not very complicated song. It spoke
how "the Soviet power was saved by Melenko kulaks" and of how
s own sweetheart was wooed by a "black-mustached bandy-legs, a
erchant from Sarapul." No one laughed, although everyone knew it
as very funny. He turned his head from side to side as he sang, to
llow everyone to get some of his song, and the torch flame quivered
rom the shrill intensity of his voice. The peasants below listened to
him in respectful silence. Then there was a lonely cry; a heavy car
rame reared up and, tearing the sod to shreds, spattering earth in all
directions, losing windows and doors in its fall, crashed down the
slope. Thus, painfully, they cleared the tracks.

Kurilov walked on further. The silence of the woods grew thicker.
The chiefs were far behind now.

[1] Collective farm.

per kilometer of track. The engineer made the twenty-seven-minute
stretch in eighteen minutes, to make up time. We found that the delay
had been caused by beets—I mean to say," he corrected himself in a
muted voice, "that the crew stopped at Basmanov to buy two baskets
of beets, which in this region are very sweet. . . ."

"Question the senior conductor."

"Impossible. He was killed. When we arrived, he hung flattened out
on the jenny. We tried with hammers to knock the weight off him in
order to be able to question him in greater detail, but he . . . look out,
bend down, comrade chief!"

A twisted rail protruded in the air across the road. A car door swung
from it, in marvellous equilibrium. People silently crawled toward it
from below. A vertiginous entanglement of roofs, axles and twisted
iron was suspended overhead. Kurilov unbuttoned his overcoat; he felt
hot. Desperate shouts came from above: "Pyriev and Teteshin on the
jacks, the others on ropes!" And as though a valve had been opened in
the silence, voices, the crackle of wood and metallic knocks were now
distinctly heard, but the plaintive rustle underfoot could not be dead-
ened by all the other crashing and rustling sounds of the night.

". . . Under the circumstances his speed should not have been above
thirty kilometers, but fearing to upset the timetable as a result of his
stop for beets, the engineer hurried and reached that very spot near
the flag post. He signalled the brakeman, and began to pull the train in
on the bridge in order to take the hill at full speed. . . ."

"Give me some light and go about your business!" said the *nachpodor.* This man had a gift for making himself unpleasant.

Bending down Kurilov scooped the earth from the embankment with
his hand. As he did this he felt a gnawing pain in his back: the ride on
the engine's open platform was beginning to make itself felt. But this
was no time to catch cold. All his attention was absorbed by the
tickling oily stuff in his hand, which rustled so insistently.

"What's this, grain?"

"Yes, that's what it is, wheat."

He was sifting it through his fingers, and the handful was visibly
decreasing.

"How much of it is here?"

"Sixty-two cars carried a load of grain. Of these . . . almost all are
smashed!" the zone director confessed with the courage of utter despair. "To make a long story short, we have formed a committee of
which I am the chairman and resolved. . . . You want to ask a question,
comrade chief?"

Kurilov raised his head. It was doubtless the dust and soot from his ride on the engine that distorted his features so horribly. Like fate itself he kept his eyes fixed on the face of this man whose lot he knew in advance. The director was not young; a dark and sticky lock of hair, that resembled a scar from an axe blow, cut across his sweaty brow. Kurilov could not see his deep-sunken eyes.

"Do you have any children?"

The man understood the question in his own way: in his plight even charity was welcome.

"Yes, comrade, two. Moreover, I pay alimony. . . ." And this unsolicited piece of information had the smell of a bribe.

"Apparently, you're more successful in *those* things!"

. . . And so, what was involved was bread. This was the most crucial word of the day. The political significance of bread had long since outgrown its commodity value. At bottom, the new era was beginning with this first socialist bread. . . . All around them was grain. A blanket of it covered the embankment, and trees were growing on hills of wheat. Grain rolled into the bonfires, crackled in it and stank. No one had ever scattered seed so generously. "There'll be some fine wheat sprouting in the spring!" someone behind them said dully.

Now it was no longer one man but a whole retinue that accompanied the *nachpodor,* and as though by design it was composed entirely of leading personnel. Next to Kurilov, by right of seniority, walked the zone director. Panting angrily, he stopped from time to time to pour out the grain that had got into his galoshes. . . . With measured, soldierly steps marched the overseer of the workshop, who was also the chief of the repair crew, an old man of monumental build with a pitch-black beard that seemed to grow down from his very eyes. The manager of the Ulgan-Urman yard had come to have a look at an accident of region-wide importance. ("Isn't your name Protoklitov?" the *nachpodor* asked him, just to make sure. "Not at all, comrade, it's Kusin.") Another person in authority with a long coat joined this unusual procession. And finally a dashing sturdy fellow with a serious and devoted mien wound up the procession, holding high a little torch which hissed and dripped kerosene sparks; he too was in charge of something—he was the chief of the torch. And so they marched amid the detonations of the bonfires, into which huge wet logs continually crashed.

Kurilov bent down again, and immediately all the others imitated him.

On a displaced rail lay an old, flattened-out sheet of iron. Barely squeezed in under the joining bolt it covered a broken head of rail that had been put back in its old place. The lid was rather loose, it could be torn off for good and all without much difficulty. The *nachpodor* or-

dered that a measurement be taken of th  
nail of the workshop overseer struck into t  
teen. The old man did not dare say this fi  
few hands pushed forward a not too alert-lo  
little old man in a tattered Red Army cap. Al  
be trying to run away, everyone held onto so  
of his clothes. Kurilov inquired who this local  
of voices shouted into his ears that this was th  
son immediately responsible for the crash.

Stammering and casting a fascinated glance a  
behind the lapel of the *nachpodor's* open coat, tl  
plain the purpose of the iron plate  It was not his  
permitted on other lines too as an emergency me  
up an incoming train; and it was not his fault tha  
a matter of routine. Kurilov smiled limply at this  
suddenly everyone interpreted his smile as one of  
sounded, at first not in unison, but all implying tha  
terrible in this trick, that it was called a binder and  
der the bolt and tied with a nut, and that the wheel  
it rolled by, and the result was good, and even usefu  
"We are, so to speak, a poor man's country, and mu  
little things!" the man with the scrawny neck cried  
fellow with a duck's nose turned up in time to add tha  
isn't any worse than in the old days, only there's muc  
was also revealed then and there that there was not  
binders and that the workshop overseer had to steal all  
and had removed all the roofs from damaged cars in  
traffic moving.

"It's a damn bad road!" the scrawny-necked man cr  
tically. "Sometimes the rails break at eleven places out  
age! I can hardly keep up with it, dear comrade. Every n  
run and put down iron plates."

"Are you a track star or what, running like that all th  
zone director inquired curiously.

"No, I'm from Zhitomir, a refugee. I've got a family ther  
So the scapegoat was found. Everyone came to cast a gla  
before he was handed over to the prosecutor. The torch-bear  
his light closer. Its yellow flame illuminated a pair of caulke  
cheeks that looked as though they were covered with popla  
his poor barbaric bast shoes, with a tuft of cotton from his torn  
jacket sticking up on his shoulders, the muzhik looked frighte  
he was smiling, smiling at everyone.

# CHAPTER 3

# The Man on the Bridge

THE LAW OF railway accidents asserted itself. The area affected by the crash was in inverse ratio to its violence. The tracks were cut and scattered for a stretch of only eighty meters; immediately after the turn the rails were intact. Striking a match from time to time, Kurilov looked underfoot. The quality of the track was the same everywhere. He found another little binder, similar to the previous one. The chief folded it in four, like a sheet of paper, and put it in his pocket to show it at the People's Commissariat. There was an intoxicating sharp smell of decaying leaves after the first autumn frosts. The crowd, the bustle, the huge bonfires of hell—all that had been left behind. The inane, confused and jangled noises of this night did not reach here. Everything was asleep, even the wind.

Kurilov thought a great deal about these people, because he looked at them from the point of view not of yesterday, but of tomorrow. Hundreds of men had passed before him during the last month: signalmen, conductors, engineers, traffic- and road-inspectors. All of them were competing for high indices of output, all of them were members of various voluntary organizations, all of them took the floor at meetings and talked to the point of exhaustion, all of them repeated the same things that he himself had said. The station buildings, restaurants, administration buildings and even the dispatchers' offices were covered with wall newspapers, trade-union announcements, slogans, placards and a multitude of other grey papers on which something was written in small letters, hurriedly, with a bad pencil. But the quality of transportation remained the same as before, and the periodic accidents reminded one of ancient mass sacrifices to the gods. The party expected an answer from him, but for the time being Kurilov was silent. He did not yet know. . . . His lumbago prevented him from concentrating. Having stuck his hand under his overcoat he rubbed with his fist the spot that had been chilled; the pain subsided, and he went on further.

A moist cold struck him in the face. Through an opening in the woods there came into view a deserted river with a bridge across it. The space was growing wider, and although a few drops fell from time to time, the western rim of the sky shone bewitchingly. Far in the distance a village was ablaze. The redness of the sky was streaked with dull yellow flounces like those depicting dawn on tavern engravings. On the bridge was the black, thick-set silhouette of a man. With his elbows on the railing he stood looking down at the cold river. It was quiet and lazy; at the very foot of the wooden piles, lilac-colored billows of water were swelling. Kurilov silently approached the man from behind. And although the heart always feels before the eyes have seen, the man did not turn around.

"Strangers are forbidden to stand on the bridge," said Kurilov.

The man started, turned around, and at once his body recoiled against the iron railing. They recognized each other at first glance. "Hello, President of the Republic," was on Kurilov's tongue.

The meeting was unexpected for both of them. But this whole night had been full of unusual happenings. It had begun with the name of Protoklitov, the death agony of the oil tank, the wantonly scattered grain; and the end was not yet in sight. The very nature of the event that brought Kurilov here distorted all reality beyond recognition.

"I'm a watchman here," said the man in a low voice and straightened himself a little. "I'm here on duty."

"If you're a watchman, your business is to make your rounds, to watch and to see to it that everything is in order. Have you heard what happened over there?" Kurilov nodded in the direction whence he had come.

The man said calmly: "That section is not mine. There is no connection between us and them."

"Yes . . . but you also go in for these tricks!" He drew the iron sheet out of his pocket. "I found this one on your section of the tracks. You can be shot for this. . . ."

The man took the piece of evidence from Kurilov's hands, bent it one way, then the other; rusty, it yielded even without a metallic click. He returned it with a smile.

"It's a bad one! . . . And one can always be shot. We're all sailing in the same wind. We've got used to it. . . ."

His insolence was sharp, crisp with insinuation, but it was not worth while to get angry until the rules of the game they had started became clear.

"That's a strange way to talk. What's your name?"

"My name?" He stroked the wet iron of the railing. "Khozhatkin. Rodion Khozhatkin, that's my name."

He lied without faltering and all the more smoothly because Kurilov had no reason to contradict him. Actually the real name of this man, famous all over the Kama, was impossible to forget. And the immense, black-haired Holophernes head on a broad, thick-set torso was also memorable. Kurilov knew that Pavel Stepanych Omelichev had no living brothers; his older brother had died during the war, and his funeral was engraved in the memory of his provincial little town as a model of ugly, merchant vanity. So there was some reason for the transformation of Omelichev into Khozhatkin. He was perhaps ashamed of his present wretchedness and had deliberately donned a new and cacophonous name.

His dirty quilted cotton coat and worn-out, battered-down three-flapped cap harmonized with his name. By the huge awkwardness of his barrel-like feet, with the blotches of string, Kurilov realized that he wore peasant bast shoes. In brief, the chief saw before him a little weather-beaten muzhik, who had been induced by the troubled farm conditions of the day to sell his poor little holding and to leave his merry trade for a lonely hermit's existence. Everything, including his chanting broad-accented speech, had been skilfully thought out. Fourteen years were quite enough for that.

To exchange greetings with his former acquaintance would have meant for him to confess his fall and defeat, to accept the superiority of Kurilov, whom he had last seen in a different, less dignified situation, and whom he had once had almost in his power; to extend a hand to him—would not that have seemed to be fawning to win his favor or, even more ignoble, reminding him to repay an old debt? Kurilov too understood all this and for that reason decided to keep to the original tone of the conversation.

"So you're enjoying the fire, Khozhatkin?"

The redness in the sky was moving to the right; no doubt the wind had given it fresh fuel.

"I'm looking: there's a fire, a fuss, I suppose; women groaning, cows mooing, children staring with empty eyes. It doesn't touch me any more: it's remote. Just another memory: it'll smoke and die out! I myself am all burned out. And so I live like an owl with a little chink in the middle of my soul. And I don't even know which is bigger: the chink or the soul. Only, from that time on I've been drawn to fires as to vodka. . . ."

"And did you have a big house, Khozhatkin?" asked Kurilov, puffing at his pipe. He was well acquainted with Omelichev's vast apartments, the crowning masterpiece of the Kama architects, but he was not referring to them.

The fire cast illuminated spots on the man's face. No, this was not the old Omelichev, with his gypsy features and typical Russian temperament. This one looked much older, and yet he was almost the same age as Kurilov. In his eyebrows, one lower than the other, there were silvery strands; his eyes had sunk deeper, closer to the source of reason, and their wisdom had become mournful. His tufty beard grew in semi-circles, giving him somewhat the air of a screech owl. But the fur-lined vizor of his three-flapped cap did not cover his high forehead with its protruding bumps. The falcon had flown away, the gypsy had vanished, but the malicious and bitter mind remained. . . . Kurilov stood rekindling his pipe, for an excessively long time.

"All right, you've had your look, that'll do now! Blow out your match, else you'll burn your fingers," Khozhatkin observed in a dull voice, turning away. "You've asked about my house. My house was a good one, somewhat crowded—but it's warmer in a crowded house. And what a lot of wealth was piled up in it!"

"Do you regret it?"

"No, not the house. Because I was unaccustomed to my condition at first I felt cold, and ashamed, and afraid to knock about in ditches, but later it was fine. My dad used to say: Fire is God's kindness. He doesn't know how to be kind in a weaker way, God doesn't!"

"Are you living here alone?"

"Alone as a finger. Trimmed of everything. I'm a truncated limb, dear citizen. . . ."

"Is Frosia alive?" Kurilov asked, unexpectedly to himself.

Khozhatkin bit his lip in annoyance.

"I don't know. Seven years is a long time."

Both fell silent, irked by the slip of the tongue that each had permitted himself. At this point a dog ran toward them, a gaunt hound that seemed in tatters, the proper dog for a beggar. He sniffed at Kurilov's boots; the smell was familiar, a smell of stale iron and oil. Lightly, without resentment, Khozhatkin kicked him. The dog sat down and also stared at the red sky. His look was wooden and sorrowful. To each his own troubles: dogs too might be involved in the fire.

"Your dog?"

"My own. His name is Egorka. I picked him up in a frost; it's easy to buy a dog's friendship. He lost one eye recently, some village boys whipped him. As everyone knows, children are the flower of life!" He stroked the dog on the neck; Egorka licked the hand, sensing his owner's thought. "I come to this bridge every night, as to a club. There's a man who sings on the river. Sometimes he sings for an hour after midnight, sometimes more. After all, these are woods here, there's no settlement." And he waved defiantly in the direction of the round, shaggy, empty space in front of him.

"A fisherman, or what?"

"I don't know. Perhaps a saint, or maybe just someone watching horses. And perhaps another old owl. There are droves of them nowadays. You know, he's even wise, even in solitude he seeks an echo for company. Some people would have a lion or a snake or a bird for a pet, but this one gets his pleasure from a song. Not an old voice, his words are indistinct, but he sings with tenderness and understanding. . . ."

Kurilov was listening, shaking his head, unable to get the meaning of Khozhatkin's hints.

"I would have gone down to find out who he is. But maybe he has no papers? I'm a watchman, am I not?" He deliberately made his speech provocative in order to goad this nocturnal visitor to quarrel, for a man shows his hand in a quarrel.

But already Khozhatkin had abandoned the tone he had at first assumed; muzhiks do not speak as he did.

"A song needs no identification papers. It stands by itself. And this man too sings for himself. I take advantage of him like a thief. If you're not in a hurry, wait a while, he'll soon begin to sing. It's interesting: listening to another man's song is like gazing at the stars. . . ."

"I've got to go now, Khozhatkin. Walk me to the turn."

He reluctantly tore himself from the railing. "Why, we're used to walking. Come on, Egorka!"

All three started in a row. And again they could not find the right words. Khozhatkin was hiding. Soon, smelling some prey, the dog rushed down the slope. And sure enough, a moment later there resounded the heavy splash of a bird's wings. Then the dog's luck slipped away. One could hear him lapping water from the ditch, having despaired of success in the hunt.

"Don't put too much faith in saints, Khozhatkin. Have a look at that fellow, ask him for his passport. . . . That's the way they are! When they're ashamed to face people, they hide in God's bosom!" Kurilov insisted. "And what do you think of the accident?"

"You know better, you've been sent from above," the other said evasively. "You know better than I whether the cause produces the people or the people produce the cause."

"You speak in parables! I know, you'll say there are no rails, not enough manpower. But here they're making a temporary stoppage into the law of a system. That's not right, Khozhatkin, we're rich."

"That's true. Through universal poverty to universal wealth!"

"Again a parable," Kurilov said angrily, although he knew what Khozhatkin was aiming at. "And why didn't they issue warnings to the crews?"

"What good would it have done? The trains have to pass. Look how much freight they piled up! In the old days, when I was appointed here, the station master with his family would go for mushrooms on the locomotive. They'd set up a samovar in the woods, the children chased quails, and meanwhile the coachman took a nap on the tender. . . ."

"So you admit we've grown up since that time?" And from this point they resumed a conversation they had once begun in a merchant's attic.

"We're not saying there's no progress these days. There is. The nations are amazed at us, and will be more amazed in the future! One day the nations will tremble and shake their heads, that is, the ones that survive. But . . ." He rolled heavily as he walked, almost like his boats in olden times with the grain-laden barges behind them. He walked and walked and suddenly he laughed in a low voice. "We've had a funny incident here. One young lass, a lively little minx, gave herself to the food store manager for a large cheese. Fine commotion that made. The manager was kicked out, the stores were checked (they found that a pig's head and a *pud* of margarine were missing!), the administration was torn to shreds in the newspapers. But the point isn't the manager, but the young girl. For the manager, you see, is one-eyed, like my Egorka. It gives one a rasping feeling in the throat just to look at him. And the young lady has her mother and a younger brother living with her. Not that I pity her, she's a priest's daughter, why pity her! My dad used to say: 'Not every mother cares for the blood of a stranger's son.' The same is true in reverse, too. . . ."

All this seemed incredible. This man, even if he had not read the newspapers that reprinted the decree appointing Kurilov, could easily guess his rank from his cap and the stars on his lapel. He was not drunk—so should one conclude that he just did not give a damn about his job? And that the persecutions he had undergone and his present wretched lot had not crushed his former insolence? Like a bird of prey he circled above the carrion of great battles and seemed to be inviting Kurilov to sniff at the same terrible repast. All his speeches were only festerings of his old wound.

"Been on the road long?"

"This is the twenty-sixth year."

"Member of the trade union?"

"I pay my dues."

"You've become even more spiteful, Pavel Stepanych!"

The man started. Kurilov shuffled the cards. The hermit had hurried to find an echo for himself and now repented.

"You questioned me, and I gave you my answers, chief. If you had given me a wink, I'd have answered in your way. Well, let me go now. My section ends here. I should have asked you to drop in at my place, but I've only one little stool. One of us would have to sit on the floor, and you wouldn't sit there. And it's awkward for you to be with me. They might crack down on you, too. . . ." He doffed his cap in sign of farewell.

One had to know a great deal about past events not to be surprised by the strange wisdom of this talk. Kurilov went on in silence. After a few steps he looked back. In the darkness one could guess that Khozhatkin was still bareheaded; his forehead shimmered in the mist of the autumn night. And one could still see the dog scratching itself: it was plagued by ticks.

## CHAPTER 4

# Pokhvisnev Is Drawn into the Story

THE BONFIRE EMERGED from behind the turn. A car frame had just been thrown into it. Whole sheaves of sparks spattered forth from the crushed burning wood. Kurilov went on, past the smashed wreckage, past lakes of grain, past telephone-men who had set themselves up right there on tarpaulins, having leaned their poles against the wires. Buzzers droned, the fires crackled, fresh logs were constantly being tossed into them. Near an unwieldy, cumbersome object bearing the name 509-A Kurilov stopped and was immediately surrounded again by the chiefs. A knot of people bustled around the engine. Hauled up on jacks it looked helplessly straight ahead, with one smashed eye. About thirty cross ties, which it had dug up as it buried itself in the ground, barred the way in a disorderly stack. Something was still smoking inside: steam was coming out of the warm boiler. All its geometric insides were spilled upon the sand. The front piston-rod was bent. The right piston chamber had been blown aside by the shock. A wheel torn from a front truck was lying there too. Granular sparks flew about in the newly fractured steel. Under the belly of the boiler, lying on their backs in the sandy ditch, men were silently working. They were trying to push a fresh, still rusty rail under the grade.

"Careful, don't hit yourself!"

"I've done this before. . . ."

Accompanied by the local executives, Kurilov went down to the passenger cars. Four two-axled carriages with numbered berths were clogged up with car scrap, tangled with grass, covered with clay, their sides hole-riddled as with bedsores. Overhead were the half-moons of the wheels. From one window grew a tattered little birch tree that had miraculously made its way through both panes. Beside it, on the detached wall of the carriage, was a stagnant black puddle with a lacquery sheen. The reflection of the torch in it was round and circled with many rings.

"Is that blood, or what?" the *nachpodor* asked dully.

"No, it's heavy oil." The torch-bearer touched the liquid with his finger, withdrew it superstitiously and wiped it on the grass. "They're

18

expecting the higher-ups, but they didn't have the brains to clean this up, the devils!"

A fiery drop fell into the stagnant puddle, crackled and died out. Someone touched Kurilov's elbow. The chief did not turn around at once. Had Omelichev returned to say publicly what he had not dared say to him alone? Kurilov was doubly pleased that he was mistaken.

It was a little old man of old-fashioned appearance who had completely lost his mind. His wide-brimmed hat had dropped down on the back of his neck, the flaps of his enormous canvas coat waved in the air, his hands that seemed four times larger than ordinary dazzled one's eyes. His head was shaking, and his hairless cheeks were trembling. He was like a furiously rotating top. With his eyes clinging to the tall chief, too weak to utter even an ejaculation, he rummaged frenziedly in his pockets. Several men stopped working and gloomily watched his hysteria. They too were somewhat infected by it; all of them felt equally nauseated and as though standing on shifty ground. He was a passenger from the smashed train. Somebody whispered to the *nachpodor* that the old man had sat two hours amidst the wreckage until a floor was cut through and he could be dragged out.

"Take him away," one of the higher-ups ordered with a curse. "Put him any place, in a shed. . . ."

Determined hands were already reaching out, but at this point the old man's little face brightened up and grew lively. He tore his hat off his head and twirled it on one finger with lightning rapidity. It looked as though his fate were being decided at that moment. He cried out, and on all the faces around him his smile was reflected many times. The lost thing he sought was in its place, under his tattered hat-band.

"Ah, I've always been lucky!" And he rushed toward Kurilov. Just in time someone caught the small bundle wrapped up in a pillow-slip that had dropped out of his hand "I've no reason for grumbling against fate! You know, I can even catch flies without ever missing. And I guessed about you right away. Ha, at all ages it's easy to recognize a chief by the atmosphere of apprehension and subordination that emanates from him. I noticed you from a distance when I was still. . . ."

"No so loud, or I'll give orders for you to be removed," Kurilov said sharply, because the man's shrill voice was causing the work to stop. "What do you want of me?"

The old man was nonplussed. This time Providence had assumed too severe an aspect.

"Here," he said in bewilderment, extending a tiny piece of cardboard. "Take it! My name is Pokhvisnev. There was once a Senator

Pokhvisnev who in my day was one of the judges in the trial of Nechaev, but I. . . ."

"Let's see that. . . ."

It was a ticket for a reserved seat from Moscow to Cheremshansk. The ticket looked perfectly regular: it bore a number, and the date of sale was stamped on it. It explained how Pokhvisnev had managed to get here through the cordon of guards. Kurilov gave him back this indisputable bill of passengers' rights.

"No," said Kurilov dryly. "I won't be able to take you with me. I came here on the locomotive." He might also have added that the Diesel car of the Political Bureau was not supposed to be used for the transportation of the victims of railway accidents.

He went back, passing people who were still shouting hypnotically as if to recharge each other with courage and perseverance. On his way he met Feshkin: the oil had arrived at last. Elated by the encounter with his chief, the secretary began to give him a summary of the day's work on the road. Kurilov did not listen to the end; he had changed his mind about the old man and turned back. Pokhvisnev was still on the same spot, pressing his bundle to his chest and looking like a guilty schoolboy. More offended than crushed by his misfortune he was still smiling. Some charitable mechanic with a piece of brake-hose in his hands was at his side explaining that if he reported his case to the management and submitted the proper documents he would undoubtedly be refunded the cost of his ticket.

"Come on," said Kurilov, taking the old man by the hand. "I think my Diesel car has arrived."

Pokhvisnev obeyed; and all the time he spent in the *nachpodor's* car he preserved the same expression of fear and bewilderment. Feshkin, who combined his secretarial duties with executive ones, assigned him a free compartment. With the same fear in his eyes and a look of expecting even greater misfortunes the old man sat down on the plush seat. "I don't like metal . . ." he murmured in various tones, but in his condition this was a natural reaction to what he had experienced. He did not even hear the higher-ups come into the car, nor see how the engineer, singed and unjustly arrested, was taken away under guard, how Kurilov gave him a glass of vodka and an apple and how the zone director left escorted by the same guard. Before daybreak, when Kurilov entered the compartment, he found the old man asleep.

Grey and not too shabby he slept sitting up. His cheeks with their youthful pink skin lay in folds on the coarse collar of his raincoat. He reminded one of something botanical, disembodied, of the genus of cryptogamous plants, and gave the impression that seen from certain angles he might even be transparent. To put this fragile plant into a canvas cover with cocoanut buttons seemed pure mockery.

He jumped and, having cast a glance around him, instantly recalled all the events of the past twenty-four hours. He frowned, bent his head to one side, listening. From underfoot came the dull drone of engines.

"What's this, are we moving?" he said with supercilious surprise.

"Sit down, sit down," Kurilov encouraged him. "We start in two minutes."

Citizen Pokhvisnev narrowed his eyes, and his lower lip drooped in indignation: "So you've decided to take you with me, hi, hi . . . as a trophy of your exploits?" he sneered.

"But you yourself asked me to take you to Cheremshansk!"

"I beg your pardon, you didn't let me finish . . . you even threatened to handcuff me. I wanted to protest to you about the state of your railway. Yes, your passengers are arriving at their destination in far from perfect condition. . . . Yes, they are being delivered in pieces! That's what gangsters call a *wet* business. But while they kill first and then take your money, you do it the other way round!" He seized his hat and paused for a moment so that his sarcasm would have time to penetrate to the very marrow of the dumbfounded chief. "No, I won't be able to . . . I won't take the risk of continuing my journey in your company. Some time later, in an urn . . . yes, then, with pleasure. Now, let me go!"

And in a rather Jacobin manner, venomously and with his hat cocked on one side, he stalked past Kurilov. All the latter could do was to make room for him. The outside door banged. Kurilov rushed to the back window and raised the curtain. Day was breaking. The sky looked swept and clean. The stars were dying, swallowed by the greenish, windless dawn. A crumpled, sleepy cloud was rising in the east. Dew lay on the rails. . . . Tangled in the flaps of his raincoat the old man was walking on the cross ties. From time to time he adjusted his hat with both hands to prevent it from falling. He doubtless suspected that he was being observed from behind, and his gait was almost stately. He no longer had his bundle with him.

"What a gander," Kurilov smiled to himself. "A cranky old fellow, isn't he?"

He stood at the window until the first ray of the sun shone. Autumn that year was ruddy and intense. The country was beautiful.

# CHAPTER 5

# Kurilov and Others

ALEXEI NIKITICH KURILOV did not approve of railroads. It was comical to think that the long road from ocean to ocean was laid out with wooden blocks on top of which were nailed pretentious and expensive strips of rolled steel. The locomotive, itself an inconvenient, parasitic machine, seemed to him a clearer and apter symbol of the capitalist system than the water-mill cited by Marx. In his mind's eye he saw this road differently: its employees would speak a dozen dissimilar dialects, its cross ties would be made of different kinds of wood, and snow-ploughs would crawl on its northern tracks while graceful Chamedorea palms would blossom at its southern terminal. A man of his time, Kurilov always tried to visualize the distant goal toward which his party was moving. This was his only method of spending his leisure time. It goes without saying that he could indulge in fantasies only within the narrow limits of the books for which he managed to steal time from work or sleep. And this imagined world, more material and more adapted to human needs than the Christian paradise, was in his speculation crowned by the summit of knowledge—freedom from death. Like most of his contemporaries, he feared that he was not fated to hold in his hands the ripened fruit of the tree that was growing before his very eyes, ramifying and tearing the earth asunder with mighty roots. He did not fear death, but he did not want it.

Thoughts of death—these were not for Kurilov. A soldier smelted by the war and forged by the revolution, he had a right to smile at other people's fears. That period of life when reason first rebels at the idea of the inevitable, he had spent at the front. He had then barely passed his thirtieth year and had just succeeded in escaping court-martial. He was young, aggressive and had a sound constitution—the main prerequisites for the fruitfulness of such meditations. Apart from that, so many people died around him in so many different ways that the incredulous astonishment with which every investigation of death begins was dulled in him. . . .

However, during recent months he had had an opportunity to observe dying at very close quarters, and not on the trampled battlefield where even fear was quelled by the irresistible whirlwind of death and

22

destruction. Here the experiment was arranged with scientific meticulousness. The hospital he visited was for responsible workers. Little stylized flowers were painted on the dull-surfaced, ochre-colored panelled wall. When the patients requested it, the radio was turned on, and the long hospital evenings were saturated with melodies as blissful as the apparitions of a dream. Professors came like Magi scattering gifts of hope, wise bitterness or resignation. In this refuge of the unfortunate, death itself seemed a mysterious medical remedy indispensable for final recovery.

Twice every ten days, at first even more frequently, Kurilov visited this place. There were two beds; the second one remained unoccupied until the very end. In the one nearer the window there lay a sharp-nosed woman who had never been pampered by fate or her husband. She felt embarrassed before the nurse because of Kurilov's visits; she feared most of all that she might be suspected of being sentimental. And while he sat relating whatever news was accessible to her (and never before during all their life in common had they learned so much about each other!), she ever so often reminded him of a meeting he had no right to miss or sent him out to have a smoke on the staircase; his pipe was second in his attachments. And he would leave, solemnly stroking his mustache, moved as only a man can be by the generosity of this gift. He exaggerated Catherine's kind-heartedness—this magnanimous self-delusion flattered him.

He could see the details of this process of dying, prolonged in time, as though through a magnifying glass. Even after she had left her work, Catherine refused to go south. She sat by the window all day long pulling at the strings of a guitar. And that desiccated little hand on the resounding wooden board was deeply graven on Kurilov's memory. . . . Kurilov had brought his wife here in the spring when consumptives always feel worse. The ice was breaking and Catherine constantly begged him to take her out in the car to have a look at the dirty, drifting floes. They grew increasingly bluer (no—azure, more transparent) as they approached their native sea. He did not understand her and considered her last wish a ridiculous whim. . . . At every visit he found her different. Her eyes were more alien and hollow, the little earth-colored wrinkle between her brows grew deeper: night and day forces incomprehensible to him worked on this woman. Finally Catherine's hands seemed to grow smaller. He would ask her gently how she felt, but he was aware only of the restless drumming of her fingers. . . . Oh, at that time, a whole railroad, with stations, stops and sidings could be placed in the narrow space between them. They stood at the opposite ends of it, and the husband's voice could hardly reach the wife. To be there was more and more oppressive. It was as though the process had stopped. It seemed that in a little more time the doctors would prevail. Kurilov began to skip visiting days; he sat till late at his work.

Those were the busy days of the organization of the Political Bureau. There was a shortage of men and of indispensable technical knowledge. Still unable clearly to understand the logical steps by which iron, coal, men and water constitute the higher kind of engineering economy, spread over a thousand kilometers, he was already responsible before the country for the index of railroad transportation. There were not enough days, and he wasted nights as though he possessed a countless number. . . .

After an absence of three weeks, immediately before leaving for the line, he dropped in at the hospital. It was the first time he had come there in his railroad uniform. The cloth tunic made for him without a fitting was baggy, but—"How elegant you are today, all in black!" Catherine whispered. She wanted to touch the stars on his lapel, but Kurilov sat motionless, frightened by this unusual tenderness. Her hand could not reach him and dropped. Suddenly Catherine jerked back her head and hid her guilty hands under the blanket. "Ah, Alioshka, Alioshka," she said, but in such a low voice now, that he guessed her meaning only by the motions of her lips. And there was such a burning radiance in her glance that he felt almost embarrassed. And he had supposed that it took place imperceptibly, just as one silently draws the curtain not to awaken a child who has fallen asleep. . . . Catherine's words, her very tone resounded in him all night, as he sat in his office at the Political Bureau. His work did not go well.

He packed his pipe tightly, stuck his papers all speckled with tobacco into his briefcase and opened the window. A tree stood close by, dishevelled, in a cracked armor of bark—quite like the fairy-tale hero Ruslan, who threw down his helmet. Over its curly, leafy top spread the moonlight, smooth as oil. (The Political Bureau's offices were situated on the third floor.) Two shadows, tightly pressed against one another, thickened somewhat the shadow of the tree itself. They were not thieves, and it was easy to guess that the thinner of the two shadows belonged to a girl. It even seemed to Kurilov that snow was falling, for her shoulders seemed to grow white. But this too was the moonlight, that lovely moonlight! . . . They were whispering; stupid embarrassed words by means of which lovers grope at each other like blind people. And although all these were trifles unworthy of a serious-minded man, Kurilov unconsciously put his pipe into his pocket (its sparks might be noticed below) and leaned back against the window-

box. The door to his office was unlocked, and he thought of this continually.

The story was at its very beginning; they still did not dare to embrace.

". . . You're afraid?"

"Yes."

"You're afraid of me?"

"Of myself . . . of both of us."

There were occasional light gusts of wind, and the moonlight grew
more intense. The thick branch above the heads of the young people
seemed the snake of Biblical antiquity. Their whispers merged with
the rustle of the leaves, and the couple themselves became a leaf
hunted through the world by necessity. And once again the philoso-
pher with the incorruptible and zealous face of a censor listened to the
mysterious circulation of sap in matter. . . .

At this point it would have been good to whistle out, with two fingers in one's mouth—just what the Lord had once done when faced
with two such organisms. The famous sentence of exile would have
been repeated, the charm of the garden would have been extinguished,
and not they, but Kurilov himself, would have been that much poorer.
. . . A curiosity about something he had never experienced arose in
him. With Catherine his relations had always been those of honest and
sober friendship. He quietly closed the window and left the room.

It was late. An unknown girl sat at Feshkin's table. She was turning
the pages of some old files and writing excerpts on a long strip of
paper. No, she did not resemble the instructor who was to accompany
him on his trip; her nose was more fleshy and somehow like a dot.
Kurilov stood biting his mustache. It occurred to him that here was
an example of the new socialist attitude toward work: no one compelled the girl to work on into the night. Surprising himself, Kurilov
offered to drive her home. She accepted gratefully. The trolley car was
no longer running, and that morning there had been a distribution of
potatoes at her office; without Kurilov she would have had to drag her
bag all the way to her home in the suburbs. In the car he asked her
whether she was not a shock-brigader. She explained bashfully that
she worked in a propaganda group and had to move from town to
town, wherever she was sent, explaining literature, moving pictures,
and also singing to the masses. "I have specially selected works that
make a tremendous impression on the audience." She only felt sorry
because the authors' moods so rarely tallied with the political blueprint. She cited as an example Giovanolli, whose Spartacus, the leader
of the slave uprising, turns out to be a prince.

"Life is more complex than all the blueprints! Just think, for instance, what enormous mechanisms nature creates to set the simplest things in motion," Kurilov observed wisely, remembering the couple under his window.

"I understand what life is. Sometimes one feels like crawling away from it into a bottle," she confessed with annoyance.

He smiled at the naïveté of her talk. Although he had never had children of his own, he liked and easily made friends with children. She cautiously inquired whether he was not acquainted with Giovanolli. Considering his high position Kurilov could easily learn the author's intentions at first hand. (Her respect for the leadership of the Political Bureau of the Railroad was so great that she believed the fate of the whole world was decided in his office.) Alexei Nikitich replied no, that he had not met Giovanolli. . . . Now they had arrived. Kurilov helped her to load the bast bag on to her back. (She lived on the third floor of a ramshackle frame building.) More, to make his attentiveness perfect, he even left his car to open the front door for her. Never before had he been so amiable with a woman other than his wife.

The night was quiet, and the moon still shone. Against the background of a little grey cloud the chimney of a factory was silhouetted. There was a thick odor of fennel; gardens began right beyond the house. Throwing down her bag the girl said she would call a neighbor from an adjoining room to help her. Kurilov did not object, but he did not want to leave so soon. The ray of moonlight of a little while ago that had got stuck inside him broke, its splinters hurt him. Suddenly she asked in a low voice whether it was true that his wife had died. . . .

He frowned in annoyance. The question contained an unpleasant prophecy. The curiosity of this railroad employee seemed to him insolent. . . . Yes, she aspired to take the place of his wife and was now stealthily feeling him out with her little claws! He had heard enough of that species: they quickly acquire the simple art of travelling on government cars with all kinds of distributors of worldly goods, gossiping and generally leading what the Philistines considered an aristocratic life. As for her childishness, wasn't there too much sumptuous flesh on her for a mere child? Incidentally (and this was an ironic surprise to him) he recalled that the girl's name was Marina Sabelnikova (he had decided on an earlier occasion that either a soldier or a gunsmith must have been her ancestor), that two months before she was about to be sent to work at a yard near Penza, but that she had obtained a furlough and then just stayed on at the main office. . . . In brief, by the time he reached home he had thought of dozens of ways of getting rid of this temptation. Climbing out of his car he said, "To

Penza, to Penza with her!" so resolutely that his chauffeur even asked him what he meant by this unusual address. (Concerning the anonymous couple on the vacant plot he had decided to reprimand the superintendent as a result of whose negligence the court-yard of a government institution had been turned into a garden for rendezvous.)

Except for colds, Kurilov had never been ill; his wounds did not count. As one of his closest friends, Sashka Tiutchev, remarked, Alexei Nikitich was perfectly capable of operating a hand water-pump in a Central Asiatic desert. The sickly and quiet Catherine had never been enough for him. Even the very beginnings of their marital life passed without amorous play, without frolics or excesses, but also without the unleashing of that sinful force which gives the soul primitive satiety. With time he got used to his starveling's love ration, tried to spare his wife's pride and only recently had begun to realize that he remembered all the young women he happened to encounter on the road.

A day later it was clear to him that the idea of Marina pleased him. He had read somewhere a long time ago that women who earn their own living respect the time of their lovers and do not demand special attentions. Oh, Catherine would not have condemned him if this good-looking, rather simple-minded girl with a round face visited him once in a ten-day period and left a little later than usual, barely languid and with her eyes turned inward. And once again he magnanimously attributed to Catherine a supposedly motherly generosity. All the circumstances conspired to that very end. One day Sabelnikova timidly came to ask him for some material for his biography: she had been commissioned to write a number of instructive life-stories of prominent transportation workers, and Kurilov was one of the first on her list.

The summer was at its very height. Outside the window on the vast saucer-like square the hot dusty wind was cooling off at last. The weak little breezes from the river were not strong enough to dispel the oppressive sultriness. Kurilov blushed when she entered. "It's come true!" Marina silently crossed the apartment; the number of books amazed her. Standing before the shelves she read the titles aloud. "That's *good*, all about the war, about cities, the Far East. . . ." Frightened by her own ignorance, she clutched her briefcase. She had scarcely written ten lines, half of which only expressed the degree of her confusion, when she caught Kurilov's staring, narrowed glance upon her and jumped up from the chair. All her papers fluttered off her knees with a crisp rustle. This event sobered him up. With closed eyes he sat on the sofa blindly stuffing his pipe with tobacco.

Only for a moment had he looked at her with the eyes of a lover and although he had never experienced how *it* began (in fact he had always been amazed by the inventiveness of lovers who somehow fill up the interval between the engagement and the wedding night), he already knew everything in advance. Surely, Marina would be submissive and yielding. She would not have the triumphant eyes of a conqueror. She would not ask him about the next day, about anything. Of course, he would be ashamed of his cheaply laundered linen and his sky-blue pullover. . . . He realized that there was no one except them in the apartment, nevertheless, he felt an imperious need to close the door to Catherine's empty room. Slowly, as if asleep, Marina walked across the room. She caught sight of Catherine's orphaned guitar. As she passed it she sharply twangled out a fifth. The sound made Kurilov wince, it was an untimely reminder of his forgotten wife.

He dully called Marina by her name; she shook her head negatively: "I don't want you to have to repent, Kurilov."

She stood at the window scratching the cracked woodwork of the sill. Below her extended a bottomless pit twelve stories deep; Kurilov lived high up. A solitary yellow star was rising above the Vorobyev Hills. For Kurilov, who remained on the sofa, the star was standing exactly above the crown of Marina's head.

"Haven't you noticed how hot it is today?" he asked as if to justify himself.

She said in a low voice: "During the day it was ninety degrees in the shade," and then suddenly, "Tell me, *was* your wife beautiful?"

Now he was no longer indignant that the still living Catherine was mentioned in the past tense.

"She was gentle."

"Don't you have a picture of her?"

"She did not like to be photographed."

"Then describe her to me!"

All this was not very comprehensible to him, but now he respected Marina for the very things he did not understand in her. He yielded to the imperiousness of her command.

"She was very honest with people and considered everyone better than herself. She was a simple worker. During the years of imprisonment she did a great deal for me and my comrades. All those who knew her called her simply Catherine. . . ."

Marina bowed her head, as one does in memory of the dead. A breeze coming from the window stirred a strand of hair above her small burning ear. Kurilov buttoned the collar of his tunic. His torpor was passing away, the heat was subsiding. And suddenly he noticed everything about Marina; including her pink elbows for some reason stained with ink, and her worn shoes down at the heels. And although beside him in a box in the closet were all of Catherine's unworn shoes, and although in his opinion there would have been nothing reprehensible in letting Marina choose the best pair for herself, he did not dare propose this to her. Furthermore, he decided that he had received this artless guest too unceremoniously. It seemed to him that to offer her tea was an absolutely indispensable act of courtesy. And while he puttered in the kitchen, lighting the gas, Marina silently left. Having decided that she had hidden, he looked for her everywhere and was angry that in his old age he was compelled to play hide-and-seek. . . . An hour later he was still thinking of her. At night he missed her. In the morning he was aware that he was afraid of losing her forever. People of his type are rather constant in their attachments. Since Catherine had been taken away, his apartment seemed to him enormous and uncomfortable; after Marina left, it seemed to him uninhabited as well.

Here, in the sunset of life, men like Kurilov always experience confusion, an entanglement of their feelings, a surge of the heart from which perhaps only monuments and stupid people are preserved. Tiutchev once had happened to mention to him that from this biological parting of the ways between old age and woman the final boundary comes into sight. False! . . . He did not fear death, but only the process of dying: losing the possibility of influencing the world, becoming an object of ridicule for his enemies and an object of pity and a burden for his friends! Hastiness and oversimplification characterized his deductions.

In the people down below, in the unskilled laborers who tend the ordinary parts of the social machine, this foul scum and rust of the sedentary life never form. At such moments he recalled his former teacher and friend, the foundryman Efim Demin, with enthusiasm and envy. Many years before, at the dawn of a great life, he had initiated Alioshka into the high mysteries of the art of casting. Later Kurilov grasped the marvellous laws of motion of ideas, commodities, masses; he came to know who Shakespeare was, and how property began on earth, but he never learned all of Efim Arsentyich's secrets. Demin was thirteen years his senior. He had already jumped across the boundaries of Kurilov's doubts. He now wore a good jacket and carried a cane. In the days of great technical victories the newspapers mentioned him side by side with the heroes of labor. Every summer his factory sent him to be reconditioned in Kislovodsk.

Only a year before he had sat at table in Kurilov's home; Catherine set salmon before him for a special treat. His visit happened to take place on Kurilov's free day. The old man had drunk a bit, became

flustered, and his face shone with faded senile rainbows. In his cups
he was touchy and ambitious with the noble pride of a toiler whose
stooped shoulders earned him the right to be honored. "I am a man
whom everyone knows. Recently I went to the *Pravda*, and there too
I'm known." He was stirred, he re-experienced his old exploits, boasted
of his successes and dangers and told how he had begun his destitute
youth at the Baltic Works (a fi-irst-class establishment!) at twenty-five
kopeks a day, how he had knocked about during his life and once even
visited a *starets*, a saintly old man (and that *starets*, hi-hi, told me to—
go into trade!), how later he organized a foundry at Motovilikha after
Kolchak had taken the founders away with him; how in the Putilov
Works he had cast the first rotor in the Union for the Volkhov power
station, and at Kolpin the famous stern-posts for lumber vessels, and
steering frames and screw propellers for seagoing ships. Intelligent
steel children created by his hand were living and moving now on all
the seas and roads of Russia. . . . He was perfectly pleased—with life
in Moscow as a whole, and with the view from the window, and with
Soviet power (a fi-irst class government, one must say!), and he was
pleased because for him alone so much food and wine had been served
and because Catherine had donned for him a new knitted blouse and
because his former pupil Kurilov (although he had not been too talented an apprentice!), was now on an equal footing with People's
Commissars. His discourse was somewhat noisy, he waved his hands,
threatened someone (himself!) with leaving everything and breeding
thrushes as soon as he was past sixty-five. He did not quiet down until
he upset his glass. . . . Kurilov gazed at him with narrowed eyes, puffed
his pipe and thought that doubtless under socialism only such masters
would live, in love with their art and their apprentices and their pupils. And he thought that although he himself had climbed high on
the social ladder he would never experience Demin's unsophisticated
satisfactions deriving from his closeness to the very furnaces of life.

"Take me back as an apprentice," said Alexei Nikítich teasingly, examining his hands, which had long since lost their workman's coarse-
ness.

Arsentyich laughed out loud and began to cough; blue veins swelled
on his temples. "What's the matter, does the dignitary feel too tight in
his official strait-jacket?" Occasionally he had a poisonous tongue. "I
can understand you, you're doing *long-range* things, while I'm doing
*short-range* ones, isn't that so?"

"Well, yours too are long-range. Take for instance the lump of sugar
you're holding in your hand," Kurilov went on. "It's a simple thing,
sweet, sawed into little cubes. Yet it must be planted, and grown, and

threshed, and gathered properly and washed, and boiled . . . and then directed into the stream of world economy!"

Arsentyich was still smiling, but now an unfamiliar stern old man sat before Kurilov.

"You'd better choose less strenuous work. For instance, watching an overcoat. A fi-irst class job! The coat hangs on a peg and you sit opposite it and watch it lovingly. And you and it both feel fine." He went on scolding thus for a long while, and finally pitying his confused pupil, reduced the dose of his poison: "Have a drink, Alexei, at your age it's not dangerous. You don't walk enough in your life." And right off he began to speak about the bloomery that had been ordered from his plant. This must have been the most triumphant word of his sunset. The tale was long, with digressions inevitable in such emotion: how a ditch was dug for the concrete coffer-dam, how subsoil water was discovered, how he fought with the stone-masons when they built a drain of brick rubble, and, in conclusion, how their, the experts', hearts pounded when the many-streamed lava poured out of the buckets. The casting of a second mount was scheduled in a month.

"We'll light such bonfires that we'll set the grey Ural sky afire!" His venturesome hands trembled like a gambler's, and Kurilov listened greedily: fearlessness is as contagious as fear.

Alexei did not go back to study casting. Everything turned out differently: he was given a responsible mission, then his wife fell ill, then the decree setting up political bureaus in transportation was enacted. His new appointment turned out to be the best medicine against doubts. This railroad was one of the longest, the most important and the worst in the country. Built in separate sections by enterprising businessmen for the purpose of serving the adjoining Russian provinces, it had always had difficulties in managing its freight turnover. The condition of the railroad, of the rolling stock, the discipline and training of the personnel, had deteriorated every year. This railroad was notorious for its classical accidents; it supplied inexhaustible material for witticisms; it was said to be used mainly by simpletons.

An enormous establishment now depended upon him; it comprised factories, yards, hundreds of stations; everything else in it was computed in numbers with many zeroes. The political and economic importance of this railroad went much further, and Alexei Nikitich had always wanted to spend some time at its real terminal point. He had never taken a furlough and, before his departure, succeeded in reaching an agreement with the proper authorities about his monthly leave. In brief, this time Kurilov's old dream of being on the Ocean seemed about to come true.

# CHAPTER 6

# He Goes to His Ocean

HIS DREAM WAS DOUBTLESS characteristic of every landlubber; it was a mark upon his soul that had remained from a book he had spelled out as a small child. The writer had been clumsy, and for that reason his sincere emotion had not been devoured by the requirements of high art. The book dealt with the various seas of the earth. Scattered illustrations alternated with the text—a sailing-ship with a mysterious and tempting name, a very young cabin-boy swinging on the sailyard above a billowing wave, a good-for-nothing boatswain who bared teeth worn out by rubbing against his pipe and summoned other people to share his wanderer's fate. And even the cover of the book was of a piercing blue. . . . The boy had been captivated by this book, although he did not fully understand the fascination of Ocean's free treasures, which belong to no one. He read it, not with his understanding, but with his heart. And so it had left a scar upon him, an indelible mark. . . . One had only to look more attentively into the evolution of this childish craving to grasp all the rest of Kurilov. (Thus, in a petrified piece of amber, the fibres of the plant imprisoned in it, the tiny bubbles of primeval air, the alternation of the golden stràta, permit you to read the story of the marvellous youth of the world.)

The boy dreamed of being a sailor. Even in his sleep he saw rounded, blue expanses, with fabulous cities on their shores and winged vessels in their bays. During the rainy season, near the small town in which Kurilov grew up, the river overflowed; on this river the children of the suburb organized model battles of amateur squadrons; and their permanent admiral and ship-builder was Lioshka Kurilov. But the time most favorable for visiting this primitive native land of the world, as the book had mysteriously and incomprehensibly called it, had passed. Kurilov's spring rushed by as though under a lash. He went to work in the capital. The foreman showed the boy vises and a box with instruments. He was given a number on the rolls and taught how to polish the heads of pressing screws. For the first time Alexei earned money to buy boots for himself. His dream did not come back. . . .

The summer of his life was at its height when once again he recalled the Ocean. This recollection found him in a cart. Its bottom was covered with hot, rotting straw. The Russian Imperial Army was retreating, German long-range guns were firing at the rearguard, the wounded were being carried to the rear. It was in July. The sun finished off those who had not been killed. Somewhere, halfway, Kurilov was placed in the house of a Polish priest. Wheels were screeching outside the windows, and the surviving cocks were crowing. On the wooden ceiling he saw the confused gabled reflection of a puddle. The old dream attacked him suddenly, as he lay dishevelled, torn by fever. A transparent wave rose and fell; he himself was on its crest. Then the sharp, straight pain in his chest was appeased, and his weakened body was filled with a sensation of majestic, oceanic silence.

With time, the childhood scratch healed into a scar. His very idea of the Ocean, as of a free multitude of waters, disintegrated. In life, water was present in its lowest form; it was poured into the bathtub, into the tender of the locomotive, into a glass with lemon juice; sometimes it even fell untidily from a cloud. Yet of a sudden he was sick once again with longing for the Ocean. This happened at a meeting about fuel. A decrease in the production of coal and oil coincided with a complete stoppage of deliveries of peat and wood; the factories of an entire region had failed to meet the requirements of the Plan.

His head ached after a night spent in preparing the report. The shedlike room was never ventilated. Everything in it, even the ink, was impregnated with the stench of stale tobacco. Kurilov, who was chairman, opened the window. A wet, restless wind irrupted into the meeting. The curtains began to whirl, the papers came alive and fluttered like birds, somewhere a glass door banged and crashed, messenger girls rushed along the corridors. Raindrops fell on cardboard files leaving fat, yellow circles. . . . The Ocean was autumnal now, it was aging. Ships were torn from their moorings; everything in sight was astir; the greenish, disintegrating waves had no time to reflect the smoky, running clouds. The opposition delegate demonstratively raised the collar of his coat, four Furies irrupted through different doors, and the Ocean was shut out.

Now for the last time he had an opportunity to spend some time on its shores. In Kurilov's car there was a map of the country. He followed on it the course of his Diesel. . . . His car had covered two-thirds of the Volga-Revizan line, when a message from Moscow overtook him. Catherine was in a desperate condition. The telegram was signed by his sister. Kurilov was afraid of this old woman, and he was not the only one in the party who was. Dry, self-willed, straightforward, she did not tolerate contradiction. Klavdia Kurilova had no personal biography; its various stages were marked by social dates. And if she had ever loved anyone living, it was Catherine.

The telegram was brought to him at a siding where Alexei Nikitich had gone out to see what kind of life was being built in this remote place. The local saw-mill was ablaze with activity. A juicy pock-marked girl in a white Mordvin shirt was carrying two boards on her back; they danced and bent in measure with her steps. There was also a pregnant woman hanging out wash on a hedge, and some birds were twittering. Kurilov stuck the paper into his pocket and returned, stooping, to his car.

Stopping nowhere, filling district dispatchers with alarm, the Diesel rushed back. The faded Chuvash woods flew by with him. Once again Kurilov's Ocean remained behind. The telegram had been transmitted along the railroad wire, and at the stations the change in the *nach-podor's* family situation was already known. The chiefs were at their posts; they put their hands to their caps in salute as the impetuous car with drawn curtains rushed by like a rocket. The door to Alexei Niki-tich's compartment was closed. The day in the transportation system began at 6:00 P.M. At about nine-thirty the senior traffic inspector came in with a bundle of telegrams. He asked permission to give the chief a preliminary summary of the operations.

"What's the amount of the load?"

"Two thousand seven hundred." And he looked through the narrow crack under the curtain at the burnt, autumnal ribbon of the embankment, which was rushing by.

"That's bad. How much was received from other lines?"

"Four thousand three hundred. Exactly five thousand was delivered, Alexei Nikitich."

"Fine." He was becoming quite a railroadman; the failures of his neighbors helped him put his own rolling stock in order. "Why are we going so slowly?"

"We're not going slowly, comrade chief. If we stepped on it, we'd soon smash up. . . ." The inspector was a former engineer.

"In the old days I made better time in this car. Call my secretary."

Feshkin emerged from the door, hiding his cigarette in his sleeve.

"Take this down, Feshkin: One, Find out how long Khozhatkin has been a watchman on Section 6; two, Summon to Moscow Protoklitov, chief of the Cheremshansk depot. Incidentally, make inquiries about him at the proper place. . . . Have you got that? Bring me a package of tobacco from my table."

Thus he sat locked up, staring at a point before him. The newspaper reports were getting more out of date with every kilometer of the road.

There were no books. Feshkin found a set of Dumas in his travelling library, but Kurilov had no mind for musketeers. The guard discovered a bundle in a pillow case behind the chair: citizen Pokhvisnev's luggage had got lost there in the confusion. The find lay in front of Kurilov, teasing him with its dirty wrapping. By chance he felt in it a towel, a soapdish and books. He cheered up: books—like wells in a desert they belong to everyone! . . . The topmost and the thickest turned out to be a history of religions. Out of boredom Kurilov thumbed through it. Half a thousand pages, it was thorough in the German manner, with illustrations. This was the longest possible catalogue of gods, with mentions of the pedigree, age and date of death of each one. It turned out that their agony was protracted for centuries. Here one could see how slowly man sloughed off his primitive fleece, how he tried to encompass nature with his unskilled hands, how difficult it was for the future master of the earth to rise from all fours. All these were self-portraits of long since vanished peoples. The gods were invented out of fear, flattery and despair; in each epoch the material conditions determined the face of the god. There were winged ones with frantic eyes placed in the back of the head to prevent man from attacking from behind; some were in the image of an indifferent woman graced with an armor of breasts; some in the shape of a hairy nostril inhaling sacrificial smoke, or, on the contrary, in the form of a misty sphere full of slanting and constantly moving eyes. There were gods with thirty hands, according to the number of human trades, gods with dogs' heads, bulls, Cyclops, elephants with a sacred spot on their foreheads (and it is interesting to see the shape this image assumed for the space of a few months in Kurilov's consciousness), she-wolves, snake-headed, four-handed monsters, prickly African Euphorbias with a poisonous milky sap, and, finally, plain unimaginative clods; on these chinky Ostiak eyes and a greedy mouth big enough to swallow itself were painted with sacrificial blood.

In former times at big army meetings Kurilov more than once had found by simple ballot an answer to the question: Is there a God, or not? There were never any complications or arguments. In those years, the soldier Kurilov did not think that religion could be the object of serious scientific investigation. True, he had always been surprised at the fact that barbarians invariably considered hunger and plague gifts of the god, while they ascribed the compass, medicine and the printing shop to the devil; that temples were erected and orders founded in honor of the weak-minded, while mankind threw its geniuses into deep dungeons or burned them at stakes; that Giordano Bruno had been declared a cynic, and Evans a madman; that Salomon de Caus had been locked up in an insane asylum, and Simpson, who used chloroform to ease childbirth pains, and Jenner, who introduced vaccination, had been declared to be servants of the Evil One. No doubt man was always possessed by the dark and greedy hope of winning truth through intuition, by the shortest route. Suddenly Alexei Nikitich imagined that some day this book would include pages written about himself. He smiled, became really interested and continued reading.

The gloomy night of mankind was followed by Hellas. The sun rose from the pages of the book. Before having learned how to think, people learned how to smile. Kurilov was absolutely charmed by the illustrations of the Greek cosmogony. In laurel groves pink-heeled goddesses disported themselves; in the middle of the land, on a tall mountain, in the company of various relatives and parvenus, creatures of Homer's playful imagination feasted, drunkard gods, swindler gods and gods of the military profession. With naïve and secure preciseness the universe was delimited, and only Charon, the ferryman of another, windless shore, cast a shadow over the bright story of Hellas. Out of the luxuriant animal chaos came by degrees the first sad knowledge of oneself. Having known the smile, people learned to fear its absence. Unfamiliar with the living conditions of antiquity, Kurilov imagined Charon upon the Russian model. Stinking, with a round, pockmarked face and soldier's puttees on his legs, he sat in the stern of a leaky boat, with a pile of hemp spread under him, rolling a cigarette of cheap tobacco; a shabby army tin, for scooping the water that leaked through, lay at his feet. Kurilov closed the book, and just as he was, in shirtsleeves and slippers, went out to drink some mineral water.

The dark smoke of this image persecuted him until night. After all, this picture was a fit companion for this journey. Kurilov knew he was returning for his wife's funeral. He was hastening to give his last salute to a human being with whom he had spent twenty-three honest, untroubled years. This woman had taken friendly care of him, she was his last *good* woman. It was easy to imagine how together with Klavdia he would follow the long box; she would draw in her lips tighter than usual and would not say a word about anything. During her more than thirty years of underground work she had buried many others! A stinging grippe-laden wind would blow little papers and dust in their faces. . . . He rang up his sister from the station. In a scolding voice she reproached him for being late. Catherine had been cremated the day before. The details were the usual ones. Moreover, Klavdia had a meeting at her place; she hung up the receiver. The brother and sister knew, however, that they would meet that night in the restaurant of the party committee.

She sat down at his table simply, as though they had seen each other not later than the day before. There was a smell of food in the place; everyone was in a hurry. Once again Klavdia failed to tell him anything about Catherine's last days. They ate their borshch in silence. After that their choices were different, for the sister was not allowed to eat meat. Kurilov cast occasional glances at Klavdia, at her dry hands thin as bird's claws and accurate in their gestures, at her hair drawn up into a small tight knot such as village schoolteachers used to wear. She had not cut her hair, for she would not follow the fashion; but at the same time she pinned it back tightly as though she feared she might be suspected of womanliness. Tiutchev was unjustly malicious when he maintained that she reminded one of Fouquier-Tinville. Possibly Tiutchev had in mind the French revolutionary prosecutor's acid and cutting rectitude, but not his yellow bookish face. The youthful freshness of her hollow cheeks was striking.

"Why are you staring at me; do I take your fancy?"

"How little you change, sister. You're like the Russian women of the people. They have only three ages: ten, twenty-three and fifty. And the change takes place overnight." He caught her ironic look and by a complicated detour took up another subject: "I had several interesting encounters this trip."

She raised her eyes, waiting.

"In the first place, I found Protoklitov . . . I think he is the son of that general who sentenced both of us at different times, you remember?"

"The presiding judge?" She was not surprised: the struggle in the country was still going on. Her face remained indifferent, not because she was reconciled to the fact, but simply because it did not occur to her to take revenge on an enemy's offspring for the crimes of a whole political system. "Well, what about him?"

"He is in the yard. Apparently, not a bad worker. But he'll go wrong at some point, of course. . . . I'll have a talk with him one of these days. I wonder whether the son has his father's long yellow teeth."

"Oh yes, Protoklitov's teeth!" A bitter smile stirred Klavdia's lips.

Alexei Nikitich examined his cutlet for a long time, as though he could not understand its purpose.

"Then I met Omelichev. He is a watchman. . . . Calls himself by another name: his is a *new* life too! He has turned sour, but his wound is still festering. That reminds me, have you had any letters from Efrosinia?"

"Why should she begin writing to me?"

"After all, she is our sister. . . ."

"Don't make me angry, Alexei." She did not speak again until she had finished her *kisel*. "Why don't you ask about *her?*"

"I know all about it, Klavdia."

With squinting eyes his sister looked somewhere past him.

"The day before her death she complained that you had never taken her to see the ice floes. . . ."

She asked him to drive her home. Her own old-fashioned open car was always being repaired. They went toward the door. A fat man in an open shirt, who had been guffawing with a friend, grew considerably less gay. Klavdia could not abide those who repeated Soviet jokes. The waitress respectfully stepped aside near the door. Invisible under her long skirt, the old woman's shoes creaked a little. In the car she said, looking straight ahead of her: "You'll get married again?"

No, he simply had not had time to think about that.

She explained: "Men are always restless at your age."

"I suppose it doesn't matter to Catherine, now, does it?"

His sister did not like to have her own weapons used against her.

"You don't look well. Are you tired?"

No, he wasn't tired! But the harvest had come, and the railroad could not manage to supply enough empty cars. During the last ten days two hundred and sixty engines had not been delivered on time. Of five hundred cars sent to Ulgan-Urmansk to take loads of grain, sixty-two per cent were roofless and twenty per cent had a layer of coal dust one inch thick. Engines released from repair shops showed as many as seventy defects. The director of the locomotive repair shop had his arm tattooed with a two-headed eagle. . . . "For some time the trains have been getting on my nerves." But all this would have been too long to enumerate. He only said that he had caught a cold, as a punishment for yielding to a childish impulse to take a ride on the engine platform.

"You should take care of yourself. Even your coat is too thin," Klavdia said reproachfully.

"Never mind, I've got fur-lined buttons."

She understood his joke because she wanted to.

"Very well, then, I'm glad for you. Keep well." And without waiting for an answer, she slammed the door of the car.

## CHAPTER 7

# Blind Man's Buff

THE KURILOVS LIVED in seclusion and did not see anyone for long periods of time. Their friends were dispersed over Russia: Kurilov was sent to a new place almost every year. He had made two wide circuits around the capital before receiving his last assignment. Like the majority of their contemporaries, the Kurilovs obtained news of their friends from the newspapers. At that time an important and extraneous circumstance compelled them all to gather in Moscow. Immediately after Alexei Nikitich's return, friends telephoned him at his office, one after another. They wanted to hear his voice, to know whether he had become melancholy since Catherine's death. But no one asked him anything specific, and Kurilov avoided answering questions that he was not asked. He postponed seeing his closest friends for a few days. Let them come if they wanted to, let them make some noise in his enormous, empty home!

Nothing had changed there, but the very echo of the rooms was different. He had become accustomed to the emptiness of his apartment during his wife's illness, but now the emptiness of death itself seemed to be here. And although Catherine in departing from life had not left any traces in her apartment, no more than in the mirror into which she had so often and inquiringly looked, at the beginning of her illness (her husband had made fun of her then: she seemed suddenly to have become concerned about her looks), everything here reminded one of her. He had actually nothing to do at home, but in his office he had nothing to sleep on. He came home only for the sake of his bed. Fortunately, he never suffered from insomnia.

Meanwhile the image of the dead had become as though veiled. And only one person reminded him of Catherine, through a remote connection. One day this man entered, announced himself to Kurilov and leaned with his dirty fists on the table.

"My name is Protoklitov. You sent for me, chief."

"As a matter of fact, I sent for you twice! . . . I have the impression you are avoiding me."

"That is not true, I have no reason to avoid you. I returned to

39

Sakonikha one hour after you left," he explained with dignity and without servility. "Here I am. I'm listening, chief."

"Sit down, I'll be with you in a moment," said Kurilov without raising his head, sucking at his cold pipe.

Before him lay the railroad's financial blueprint, which was to be discussed that night at a meeting of the People's Commissariat. Such meetings were always particularly stormy. The railroad was running at a deficit. Kurilov was going over the report for the last time, writing in the margins with a red pencil. His attention was distracted. He heard the striking of a match and then smelt smoke from bad tobacco. And immediately afterwards he saw a blazing match in close-up. At first he did not even realize that he was being offered a light. The match was burning to its end, the black-pointed stem was bending to one side, the flame was licking Protoklitov's fingers, but they remained motionless. There was old, black engine soot in the cracks of his skin.

"*Merci,*" said Kurilov. "My matches are always being stolen from me."

He raised his head.

In the greyish autumn light he was able to examine his visitor only superficially. Protoklitov could hardly have been older than thirty-nine. He was fairly well built for his size. His broad chest in a checked sports shirt hung over the table like a threat. Two deep wrinkles like incisions were cut into his forehead, which was low, very hollow at the temples and protruding over the brows; his mouth was a third, a shorter wrinkle. And this mouth was just big enough to speak a few words and take in food. A calm, calculating will shone in his eyes. This man could have been an excellent flyer, a good chess-player, an intelligent interviewer. There are no accidents in the life of such a man. He was playing a tremendous game.

Kurilov knew very little about him. Soon after the decree setting up political bureaus in transportation, Protoklitov had asked to leave the railroad. He had probably failed to foresee that his application would fall into the hands of the *nachpodor*, as the highest party authority on the road. A clash was inevitable. Protoklitov accepted the challenge.

"Well, I've read your application," Kurilov began and leaned back in his chair. "You want to leave the railroad?"

"Yes, I have my reasons."

"Are they secret?"

Protoklitov raised his eyebrows in surprise. "I should answer that as it deserves to be answered if you were not the chief. I am a party member." He flung a thin lock of dark hair somewhere into the cavity of his temple. "Actually I want to change my profession. I have a talent for inventions. I intend to study and take up mechanics seriously."

Energetically, with the back of his hand, Kurilov swept some scattered crumbs of tobacco off the table.

"You're a lucky man," he said gently. "Our transportation is the very field in which you can use your talents to good advantage."

"I thought that a man in your position would have a broader view of such matters."

"No, I can't boast that I have. We're living in a turbulent period. The turnabout time of a freight car has now reached six days, and"— he slammed the report with the flat of his hand—"we're getting out of the fray with an annual loss of eleven millions. Morally, you and I are equally responsible for this. Don't be distressed, you're still young, you have time to prove yourself in the transportation department!" Apparently Kurilov did not wish to allow Protoklitov to leave the boundaries of his supervision and power.

The yard master crushed his cigarette between his fingers; little sparks scattered. He shook them off his knees and rose.

"It's a pity. But fundamentally, you're right, comrade chief!" He took his hat.

On his head he wore a Cossack *kubanka* with a leather top; it was becoming to him.

"Wait, I'm not through yet." Kurilov stopped him as he was on his way out, and did not continue until he had sat down again. "I wanted to get acquainted with you more thoroughly. It's strange that being a party man you take these things so lightly: to leave, or to stay. How long have you been in the party?"

"Six years."

"All that time in the yard?"

"No, for three years I was an engineer. Later I worked as an instructor-mechanic. I came to the station a year and a half ago."

"You're not liked there."

"That's right, I'm feared," Protoklitov agreed coldly and succinctly. "I am a commander, and our business is almost military: it's the road to the east. The people are intractable. Throughout history they've been massacred, burned and drowned, yet how hard it has always been to push them forward! This country loves to take orders. And it would have been possible to make things go three times faster. People are helpless creatures, they don't even know how to starve. . . ."

"Well, they're not obliged to, either!"

"Of course. I'm made of the same dough. . . ."

"You're dissatisfied with yourself, too?"

Protoklitov had the right not to continue a conversation of this kind.

Kurilov gave him a friendly nod. "Tell me, are you from Altai?" he asked. The question was a fake, designed to baffle his interlocutor.

"No."

". . . And not from the Kama either?"

"These regions aren't exactly adjoining, comrade chief. I see your ruse, but I can't understand why it is so clumsy. No, I am not a native of the Volga region."

His answers were praiseworthy for their dry clarity and accuracy. Strangers whom Kurilov had had occasion to unmask before were usually less direct. There was a short respite. The conversation turned to the work of the yard. The indices of repairs, cleaning and delivery of engines in Cheremshansk were quite creditable. Kurilov had words of praise for it. "We're serving the revolution," Protoklitov echoed, smiling.

"Peresypkin told me that you had opposed having your picture published in the newspapers."

"I consider such a distinction superfluous, comrade chief. I am not doing anything that others couldn't do. To my regret, of course!"

"True . . . but we educate the laggards by showing them good examples."

"I've heard about that, but I have my own point of view when I'm involved personally. In short, I'm not every inch a proletarian. And let me also say that this is not a business conversation."

Kurilov looked at him attentively, and Protoklitov fearlessly bore his scrutiny. "Go ahead, stare at me, old man, get used to me," his eyes seemed to say.

"Your tobacco is bad, take some of mine." Kurilov threw his pouch to his visitor and it was as though he were saying: 'You're a brave man, why should you hide? Let me respect you.' "Have you worked in transportation before, too?" The chief asked.

"What do you mean—before?"

"Before the revolution, for instance."

Protoklitov was rolling his own; not even a crumb dropped from his long, clever fingers.

"Apparently you're really interested in me, comrade chief." He laughed, pretending to be embarrassed by so much attention. "But my life is made up of events that have nothing remarkable about them. My childhood doesn't stand up ideologically. I hardly remember my father, my mother was very pious. By the way, were it not for her religion she would long since have hanged herself on one of those hooks to which she tied her laundry lines. Constant association with a rope, as with a knife, makes one think all sorts of things, comrade chief . . .

have you observed that? She was a laundress in a provincial hospital. She would wake me up at night, dishevelled, screaming, terrifying. . . ."

"Was she sick?"

"She was drunk: she sometimes took liquor. Then she would shriek at me demanding that I read to her all kinds of Lives of the Fathers, legends of saints and other religious stuff. It was dark, windy, our basement was blocked up with snow, there was an awful stench—the public toilet was in the corridor next door—I would read to her from a certain Abbot Dorotheus; or about Maxim the Great. I would be all swallowed up in yawns, neither of us understood what I was reading, but she would sit opposite me and weep. I've never seen so much water streaming from human eyes! But, you know, Kurilov, all mothers are wonderful women. I would have smashed the face of anyone who said something bad about mine. By now I've forgiven her everything— my nightly fright and those sleepless sessions. And it happens that I liked much of what I read to her. I too wanted to live in the woods, in the hollow of some cedar tree, to have chats with the Mother of God, to swallow wild beasts with a glance . . . in brief, to earn that king- dom which, you remember, is mentioned in Johannes Climacus. . . ."

"Yes, of course, of course," Kurilov hastened to agree with him, as if hypnotized. "And there is a beautiful saying in his *Ladder:* 'By the place where I find you I shall judge you.'"

And he looked him right in the face; but Protoklitov continued im- perturbably: ". . . after my mother's death (she upset a boiler full of washing on herself) I left for Siberia. I had long been attracted by it. We've built it up now, but formerly people went there for adventure." He spread his hands out comically: "Now I have a whole engine plant on my hands, and I still feel like pushing my way through the taiga till I reach the ocean."

"We were all children once," Kurilov said sympathetically, inhaling in little doses the sweet bitterness of tobacco.

"Then 'life' began. I'm not particularly versed in Marxism, I learned dialectics chiefly from life. I knocked about for a long time and became quite lousy; then an official undertook to educate me. All in all he in- tended to make of me the same kind of scoundrel he was himself. A bribe-taker, an informer . . . and what things he forced his wife to do! However, thanks to him I attended the Irkutsk high school for three years. Ever been to Irkutsk? Too bad, visit it by all means. . . . I ran away from him; took his new coat, and cigar-case and ran away. I worked in a restaurant, idled my time away in white duck trousers, then I knocked about in mines. Much later I got a job on the Ussur railroad as part of a repair crew. I helped to drive in spikes. There a book was once dropped from a train, and I picked it up. I read it, and was seized by a desire for experience. . . . But soon I got in with a gang of good fellows and was fired for drinking. My mother's weakness turned up in me! . . ." He cast a worried look at Kurilov. "That was before I joined the party. Now I don't take a drop. You don't mind my being so sketchy?"

He stuck his hands between his knees, as though to warm them, he smiled pitifully, and Kurilov was enchanted by this clever cross-section of a man, mathematically demonstrated. Yes, this man had seen much, learned even more and had certainly paid a high price for his fearless glance. "Never mind, I can crack this nut, too!" Kurilov thought to himself, refusing to surrender.

"And your higher education—you got it later?"

"No, I'm almost completely self-taught. Stubbornness is my salient quality, and books were always the biggest item in my budget. I've got no relatives closer than my books."

"But why then? . . ." Kurilov assumed a doubtful expression. "Such a cultured family, and they did not give their son an education? . . . Your father, I was told, was a prominent official on the governor's staff, wasn't he?"

Protoklitov had expected that Kurilov would employ some sort of counter-manoeuvre, but he had not thought it would come so soon. The pipe tobacco did not smoke well in a cigarette. The silence lasted exactly as long as it took to tighten his self-rolled cigarette with a match. Then the visitor smiled, and Kurilov recognized the familiar yellowish grin of his teeth.

"I am not particularly pleased with the whole tone of this conversation, chief," Protoklitov remarked calmly, but the leather of the chair cracked under him. "This is the first time I've ever seen you." (And this was true!) "We're not friends and we're not sitting over a bottle of wine. Apparently I haven't knocked around; I don't know what's what. Do you give every employee such a cross-examination, or do I alone fail to inspire your confidence? You think you recognize—my face, my words, my name?"

"Well, that's no reason to get angry!" Kurilov said with a friendly laugh.

He rose, walked across the room, opened a window, looked out. The puddles in men's and horse's tracks were shuddering as drops of sleet struck them. The tree had faded. The couple was no longer there— very good!

"I'm not touchy," said Protoklitov, "but you insist on mixing me up with somebody else. You're not fooling me, I understand why you began this talk. Either I'm extremely clever, or your memory has begun to go to pieces. Would you like to hear the rest of my story?" He no longer tried his previous method of piling up details till the other got tired. "My name is Protoklitov, and you're making an effort to recognize it! It's a rather rare name; I'm told that it even stems from a Greek root. But there is another Protoklitov in Moscow, a gynecologist or artist . . . quite well known, I think. Then, one of the Chernigov bishops was also a Protoklitov, Gerasim or Iona, I can't recall. And my initials are the same as those of that gynecologist. I checked on it. But no living males are left in our family except myself. Make yourself clear, you strange man; otherwise I won't know what to think!"

It was evident that he was eaten up by simple curiosity as to whom Kurilov had confused him with, and Kurilov readily met him halfway: "You see," he said, "you remind me of a certain official of Tsarist days. . . ."

"Why can't you get it into your head, my man, that I could not be a Tsarist official?" He went around the table and gave Kurilov a friendly tap on the shoulders. "The year war was declared, I was eighteen!"

It was more polite for both of them to explain Kurilov's interest in him by his personal sympathy for a party man of more than average culture. But the meaning of Kurilov's last smile was: "You would have gone places, Protoklitov, had it not been for me!"

"Comrade chief, have you any more questions to ask the defendant? They're waiting for me at the yard."

Yes, he had more questions. No less than in all that had just passed, Kurilov was interested in the competition for the banner of merit and also in the way the Cheremshansk yard was carrying out the Central Committee's resolution concerning the reorganization of transportation. The chief very skilfully showed how sorry he was for his unfounded suspicions, and Protoklitov believed him somewhat too quickly. The whole thing resembled an unwritten truce, and ten minutes later, after Protoklitov had left, Kurilov was in no doubt about the correctness of his original surmise.

Then he listened to what went on in the waiting room. The broken door between it and the office never closed tightly. Someone asked the secretary (and his voice was like Peresypkin's):

"Listen, Feshkin, what's this?"

"A piece of paper, can't you see?" Feshkin answered. "Don't bother me."

"But what kind of paper?"

All of Kurilov's secretaries were impatient with strangers.

"I'll explain it to you in simple terms: some old man left his books in

Alexei Nikitich's car. I was told to find out his address, and I found it. Got it? Move on now. . . ." And suddenly: "Hey there, comrade, private conversations are forbidden on this phone!"

"It's an official matter." This time the voice was Protoklitov's.

The yard master was ringing up the Cheremshansk switchboard. He was informing the man on duty that he had completed his business in the central office and was about to leave. Slightly bending toward the door, Kurilov listened to that dullish voice and deliberate speech. Now the voice too was like his father's. And had it not been for his fear that he had shown his hand too early, merely to think of Protoklitov would have given him the dark and stirring satisfaction that comes to fishermen, hunters and bird-catchers when their prey comes into range. The voice reminded Kurilov of a wonderful time in his life; he had had the courage to listen to a sentence condemning him to Siberia with a song on his lips and such a smile that the presiding judge had a headache from it until late at night. And into his memory came Catherine's story of how she had gone to old Protoklitov to obtain permission to visit her husband and how obscenely he had suggested replacing her absent companion.

The insult was more than twenty years old, and the poison of its indifferent and cynical mockery had completely evaporated. It was not the habit of Kurilov, always careless with his enemies, to seek a late and cold revenge. But the gun had to be fired independently of his will were it only for the fact that the prey had begun to move into the range. All that was needed was to establish the kinship of this railroad employee with that high dignitary of old. The coincidence of the names, Protoklitov's intelligence, unusual for a man in his position, and, finally, the fact that it had occurred to him to flee from the road at the exact moment of Kurilov's appearance argued in favor of such a hypothesis. This last incident confused Kurilov. Too many convict types had passed through the hands of the presiding judge for him to remember one quarrelsome, dishevelled fellow and to tell his son about him six years later when this son had grown up. In brief, Kurilov pursued Protoklitov only because the latter was fleeing.

If this Protoklitov had been a non-party man, Kurilov would have found a way of getting rid of him on the quiet. To be in the same party with him pleased him less. At that moment he happened to notice an open telephone directory on the window sill. Yielding to a still unconscious impulse Kurilov paged it through lazily. An individual with the same name as the suspect was actually listed there, a professor in the suburb of Clear Ponds. Kurilov decided to investigate; he closed the door tightly and called the professor's number. He was seduced by the simplicity of the device by which this victim had trapped himself. All he needed was to find out whether the professor had a brother in the railroads. If Protoklitov had lied on this one point his whole biography was proved false. . . . For a long time there was no answer. Then a voice, solemn and booming, as though coming from a Gothic cathedral, asked him who he was and what he wanted.

Kurilov was in luck, his man's namesake was home.

"My name is Petrokovsky," Kurilov lied quickly, awaiting the result. "We've met casually and, busy as you are, you probably don't remember me."

The professor did not answer at once. In the receiver their breathing hissed and stirred. Then a clock began to strike. Automatically Kurilov checked it with his own clock. The professor's was four minutes slow.

"No, I remember perfectly. At first I didn't recognize your voice. You're calling about your father?"

They were getting acquainted with surprising ease.

"Yes, about my father," Kurilov said haphazardly hoping to stick in his question somewhere at the end of the conversation.

"He died this morning at daybreak," the namesake said sternly. "Two days ago he was operated on by Zemel himself. My diagnosis was confirmed at the autopsy. His disease had been neglected . . . he died from symptoms usual in cases of uremia."

The professor expected additional questions, relatives are curious, but Kurilov forgot to ask for the details. The news of the death of the imaginary Petrokovsky did more than make him prick up his ears. True, it did not frighten him. (Once he had gone to search a house and found a dead man in it; he had made the search.) But this news somehow weakened him. He did not put his receiver down. For half a minute Protoklitov listened to the other's breathing, then he said in a comforting tone that this unfortunate event was to be expected. They were cut off. Kurilov looked absent-mindedly at his watch. There was just enough time left to listen to a report on the day's activities, receive the editor of the railroad newspaper, Aliosha Peresypkin (who was already in a rage in the waiting room) and to go to the Commissariat.

Feshkin came in to say that the car was waiting.

# CHAPTER 8

# The Protoklitov Brothers

In the first phase of Protoklitov's life, which had followed the conventional pattern of men of his class and education, there was indeed much that was damaging. These things had not been sufficiently important to kill him, physically, after so many years, but enough to make him stumble all his life. Of course, it was only an accident that once, when Gleb came to spend his vacation with his father, their small town had been cut off by the Whites, and the students of the Institute of Ways and Means of Communication had been mobilized to help "restore order" which the Bolsheviks had overturned. Even in his youth Gleb was distinguished from his comrades by the sobriety of his outlook. When his career as a railroad engineer was interrupted, he decided to try another field. Gleb took a serious fancy to the career of a national hero. Some of his former friends might have told a great deal about the young lieutenant's exploits and plans, which fortunately had never materialized. He was fated in his own life to discover the inconstancy of political success, to have a taste of power, to give a taste of it to others and to experience later the bitterness of defeat and disappointment.

The peaceful town suddenly changed from a speck in the deep hinterland to a forward position on the most formidable of all the fronts. It became the capital of the Ural region, and its citizens had some practical lessons in counter-revolution. Later they learned by experience the nature of partisan warfare and the stern logic of popular wrath. The White lines wavered and cracked. Having been informed that his unit was being withdrawn, Gleb came to say goodbye to his father. The councillor of state was sitting on a little stool in the lavatory busy throwing papers down into the toilet He was glancing through them quickly while he worked and was talking to himself in a low voice.

"So you're putting everything in order, father?"

"Each to his own task. 'The ant crawls with its burden, the bee flies after its honey,'" the old man recited grumbling without turning to his son. "I heard you were beaten near Kazan? What's going on there, are you all in flight?"

"General evacuation was ordered, father."

"Ah, it's high time we put an end to all this, I'm fed up. There was shooting last night, I couldn't sleep."

"Sailors . . . they ran right into our barrage. Many of them were captured alive."

"Yes, I saw them being led away this morning. Always keep in mind that you mustn't allow the offended to remain alive. Our generation didn't understand that. Here, I'm going over all kinds of papers. . . ." With voluptuous hatred he sank his hands into the bundle of records that was to be destroyed next. "How many of them passed through my hands. . . . It's bitter to discover in one's old age that one was such a humanist, such a searcher after truth, in other words, a piece of Russian filth!"

The father was very old. With eyes that had grown sharper Gleb looked first at the yellow, sparse-haired folds of his senile neck and then at his crooked paralyzed fingers. The old man had retired only four years before; now he was drawing up the balance of his many years' activity. The Protoklitovs never had any illusions about anything. Besides, everything was now clear. The town was already ablaze. The state of siege had been proclaimed three days earlier. From outside came neither laughter nor human speech—only the screeching of carts and gun-carriages. The old man did not speak again until he had finished reading a paper.

"Directly to its destination!" he said, flushing the toilet. "Ideas evolve in an interesting way. Every lofty title that people strive for at the risk of their lives becomes some day a term of abuse. I'm sorry, what did you say?"

"I asked you whether you wished to come with me? I'll try to fix you up in the baggage train. To save anything else, I'm sorry to say, is beyond my power. . . ."

"It isn't worth it, my son. There's a shorter route to get *there*," the old man grumbled; deeply moved, as he ripped open another package. However, he embraced his son. "Forgive me for receiving you here. Are you sad?"

"Yes, you're leaving us a world in a lousy state . . . and we can't refuse to accept the heritage. I wanted to build railroads, invent engines, and now I'm forced to . . ."

". . . fight the epidemics?" The old man laughed. "Never mind. Remember: fear the rescued and the offended. Go. . . . If you meet Ilya, tell him he is an intellectual, an imbecile and, in addition, a turncoat. Imagine in whom this blockhead has put his faith, the Bolsheviks! And if the Lord does not do him the favor of sending a bullet into his neck, he will be given a kick and driven out. . . . Well, let me make the sign of the cross on you. Go. . . ." He poked at his son's back in an impotent caress. He too was in a hurry: his personal records were voluminous, and in about two hours the Red units were expected to enter the town.

Gleb took part in one of the cruellest retreats in history. The soil of Siberia exploded at every step. When the winged, almost berserk, Soviet detachments began to approach, he jumped off his armored train and fled into the night. His own people fired at him. Having foreseen everything he voluntarily renounced the sledges and saddle horse to which his rank entitled him. With ripped-off shoulder straps, distorted speech and features, in shoes torn to shreds because his feet were swollen from constantly fleeing, Gleb retreated together with the military rabble. . . . Then he looked around for new friends and tried to think up some way of taking a hand in his destiny. It was much harder to create oneself for the third time. He polished every detail of his new biography, painstakingly, under a magnifying glass. At that time his hands were often covered with bleeding calluses, because he was unaccustomed to heavy work.

Having started as an unskilled laborer in a repair brigade, he soon became a rail inspector and in two years completed a course for engineers. Like many others in those years he concealed his extensive technical training. His rapid progress was considered the result of his natural gifts all the more readily because this confirmed a belief, widespread at that time, that the culture of a whole generation could be manufactured in the course of one Five Year Plan. Nothing barred his way to further promotion. Sometimes he even feared the speed with which he had advanced and thought that he ought to go more slowly. But those who remembered him as he had been before his last reincarnation had either been shot by firing squads or, like Kurilov, rolled into old age at a terrific rate of speed. Oh, this generation was burning up fast!

Then suddenly came a letter from a friend who had escaped destruction by miracle, just as had he himself. This occurred after Protoklitov had been showered with praise in the newspapers for having initiated kolkhoz battalions to remove snowdrifts from the tracks. A very sincere letter it was, containing, in addition to friendly effusions explainable on the grounds of former intimacy, a request for five hundred rubles. ". . . You must understand that I would not have appealed to you if I had needed the money for myself alone. These wretched *chervontsy* are for my aged mother. Of course you remember her, for it was in her home that we spent a week during the attack on Kotlas. Ever since then she has looked upon you as her own son and has prayed for you every night. Her health, as a result of understandable worries, has been shattered in recent years; she has accumulated some debts, and I want so much to help her. It will be even better if you can take her the money in person. I'm sorry to say that my affairs are in a mess, but you as a railroadman have of course the right to a free ticket. You'll be able to stay with her and take a rest. Her name is Polina Petrovna, in case you've forgotten. Naturally, Glebushka, if parting with this sum will ruin you, send her three hundred to begin with and the rest later. . . ."

No, the sum did not frighten Gleb, although he did not have it on hand; but to respond to Kormilitsin's request would mean admitting that he was his accomplice. However, for the moment this affair did not look like blackmail but only like an act of stupidity on the part of a simple-minded and vulgar person. Gleb evoked the image of the inoffensive, fair-haired, tall and clumsy fellow of mediocre military rank, whose head was disproportionately small for his enormous body. He also recalled that this dunce was a great lover of solitaire, pickled herring, wrestling and discussions on sex; moreover, he used to strum on something with strings and like to tell tall stories that were the butt of his comrades' mockery.

Protoklitov's salary was only four hundred a month, but he left the letter unanswered for entirely different reasons. Enmity with a blockhead is just as inadvisable as friendship with one, and Kormilitsin's letter might have gone to the wrong address. . . . About a month and a half later, another letter arrived. The friend complained of Gleb's forgetfulness and recalled in great detail that he was the same lieutenant Kormilitsin, Evgeni Lvovich (Zhenka) whom Gleb had once rescued from a certain unpleasant pickle. "My aged mother wrote me that she had not received any money from you. I don't know how to explain your callousness; and I thought you had a heart on the pre-war model! But if you have climbed so high that I can compromise you, I, a fallen man, here's a verse for you on that subject: 'You don't love me, it's a shame before God, the devil will punish thee with sulphuric acid!'" Apparently the blockhead was of the dangerous kind. Fortunately for the time being no third person was interested in the correspondence of the manager of the Cheremshansk yard. Gleb borrowed five hundred rubles from his brother and under an assumed name sent them to the old woman, feeling all the time that he was dropping money into a sewer. Kormilitsin was silent from then on, and that was the end of the matter.

Now his own brother might give evidence against him. Gleb went straight from Kurilov's office to the professor's bachelor apartment. Every minute was precious to him. If Ilya were out he had made up his mind to call on him at his clinic. The brothers had not seen each other for two years. It was an unwritten law for both of them not to bother each other with questions. Both were bachelors. Gleb judiciously avoided placing an enemy or double at his side; to share one's bed meant to share one's food, and there was only one step from that to sharing one's soul. Ilya lived alone with his collection of clocks and his books; he had no room for a wife. . . . Both brothers were rather tall, fussy about details and marked by restraint up to the point at which some kind of explosive mechanism hidden in each of them began to operate. Both were distinguished by excellent health, both were self-exacting and had great will power.

Despite all this, and although there was only four years' difference between them, the brothers had no resemblance to each other. All the qualities we have seen in Gleb were distorted, grotesquely exaggerated in Ilya. The professor was not so much tall as long, not thick-set, but bony; Gleb's ruddy complexion had degenerated in him into a disagreeable redness of skin constantly peeling from his cheekbones. The famous teeth were too big in Ilya to be merely the Protoklitov teeth. His hollow temples elongated his head, which was lumpy, clean-shaven and set on a massive neck. In brief, all his Protoklitov features were indicated in such excess that the ironical old Ignatyi had said, "God was angry and put too much of us in Ilya when he moulded him. Hence the result was not a Protoklitov." His father disliked and feared Ilya, Gleb respected and was careful with his brother, Ilya found them both a burden.

In the doorway Gleb asked whether the professor was in. An old woman in a kitchen smock cast a glance at his dirty boots and said that the professor did not receive patients at home. The visitor insisted that he wanted to see not the professor, but Ilya Ignatievich. . . . He pushed the old woman back before she had had time to inquire how to announce him. For some time now life in this house had followed a strict etiquette. . . . The door to the dining room (two years ago it had been a library) was half-ajar. Gleb at once caught sight of Ilya's long legs in tight shoes; in the twilight, their reflection shone upon the floor.

"Ha, the Flying Dutchman!" said Ilya, without particular animation and without rising from his low chair.

"I'm in a hurry and won't detain you," Gleb called to him from the entrance hall. He removed his overcoat, trying all the time to put his finger on exactly what change had taken place here. "Hello . . . I see you're not particularly overjoyed to see me."

Ilya shook his head, his eyebrows rose with deliberate slowness.

"It would have been fine if you had dropped in half an hour later. But it's a good thing, too, that you didn't come half an hour earlier. No, don't turn on the light!" He jerked when Gleb moved toward the switch.

It was too late to take the visitor into the adjoining room: he had already seen everything.

The floor was littered with white petals of irregular shape; a rose as big as a head of cabbage had faded and crumbled half an hour before. The petals were of porcelain. They did not ring, but broke underfoot with a clay crackle. The smashed thing had been large and not particularly valuable.

"I'm not asking you any questions, but I can see you're leading a noisy life. Who did this, your dog?"

"No, my wife," the professor said in a bored voice, and although it was twilight he began to examine his nails. " 'This is the rubbish in my house,' " he quoted.

Gleb seized his brother by the shoulder.

"Listen, old man, two years ago you warned me against marriage in the most insistent terms. What was yours, an accident, love, a blunder?"

The older Protoklitov stroked his sharp knees. Through his hands, the experienced hands of a surgeon, hundreds of patients passed every month. If anyone knew to what accidents the uncautious are exposed, he did.

"Don't talk so loud. The old woman might repeat it to her. And be more indulgent with your elders!" he answered, making an embarrassed effort to be facetious.

Gleb closed the door. All this was incredible. His own trouble assumed small proportions when compared to such a catastrophe.

"Is she one of your assistants? . . . That always seems to happen to professors." He meant that very often scientists absent-mindedly marry whomever they find around them. "Forgive my question. . . ."

"No, not at all! Oh, she's an actress."

"Are you trying to increase our family's notoriety by adding to it the glory of a famous actress?"

"Oh, she is not the least bit famous. Oh-h, one might rather describe her as being in the transitional state between a cocoon and a butterfly. . . ." He did not explain his words and kept looking at Gleb's wet boots. "Is it raining outside?"

"Yes, it has been, since this morning. What a day . . . like an inconsolable grief. Haven't you been out yet?"

"No, I finished early today. But yesterday was a hard day. Two classical cases of hypernephroma . . . and I also made a new nose for some blackguard. The result was excellent. Any woman will notice it, but not the local trade union committee, for instance."

"What's that word you used, hypernephroma?" Gleb asked.

"Yes, that means the kidneys are diseased. In fact, the two patients were doomed." The fingers of the professor's hand, lightly discolored by faded iodine, stirred. "Open the cupboard, please. There's some cognac in there. No, not that one. . . . Wait, I'll do it myself!"

He bent, straightened out again and went to the cupboard. A chip loudly cracked under his foot. In extreme irritation Ilya kicked it with the tip of his shoe, he kicked it a second and a third time, until he drove it under the cupboard.

"What a queer fellow you are! Have the room swept!"

"No, not yet. This is my medicine!"

Suddenly he went into the corridor, and Gleb heard Ilya at the further end asking the cook in a low voice whether his wife had put on her galoshes. He was a lost man, he was in love. . . . Here and there clocks began to strike: it was 6:00 P.M. Time was making his rounds in the apartment. Ilya had a vast collection of clocks. He returned a minute later.

"So you still have a mania for clocks?" Gleb commented with a smile. "I read a story that will interest you. You know, Charles V was a great lover of those things. Once a clumsy attendant dropped his collection on the floor. The emperor said calmly: 'Fine, now they'll all tell the same time.'"

"Ha, that's funny," Ilya observed unsmilingly and yawned. "Want some? This is good cognac."

"No, you know I never take liquor."

"That's true, you never could. I had forgotten."

He filled a coffee cup that he happened to catch sight of and drank the cognac in long slow draughts, as one drinks milk.

"Who are you now?" he asked during an interval.

"You're referring to my uniform. That's a railroad uniform."

"I don't mean that. But judging from the fact that you have begun to shave, you're climbing fast. Have you stopped pretending that you're illiterate? Don't look so distressed, I'm not accusing you of anything. But do me a favor, don't lie to me. I'm all keyed up to know what you've come about!"

"This time I have a great favor to ask you . . . but I swear it's the last!"

"If it's money, don't count on me. I'm a poor man. Of course, the Soviet government won't let me starve, but the period of high earnings is over. What's needed now is epidemic specialists, insurance physicians . . . and I'm still treating individual cases. But do you need much?"

"No, I'm in debt to you anyhow. My business is somewhat unusual. You see, Ilyusha, I've always been successful in everything, although I never believed in my luck. I've always thought that fate lures me on only to trap me more cruelly afterward. But now I've reached a turning point. You see, I'm squirming before you. . . ." He was verbose from fear of meeting with an immediate refusal. "In brief, what I need is for you to forget me. . . ."

"But I remember you only because you force me to!" Ilya said ironically.

That was true. The two brothers had long been cool to each other. Childhood emotions and common adventures in youth, kinship and supposedly similar political interests . . . all this fuel had not sufficed for long. Usually Gleb blew in once a year, whispered just as he did now, gratefully shook his brother's hand and again dissolved into the unknown. When Ilya's wife once asked him about his relatives, he answered that he had none left. People of his stamp have a too lofty idea of kinship; his answer expressed the measure of his disappointment rather than the truth.

"Imagine, Ilya, that I never existed."

Ilya unhurriedly finished his cognac. "Aha," he said, "you've decided to commit suicide. I'm not trying to dissuade you . . . but why tell me about it? Do you want me to stop you?"

"No . . . I just no longer exist as your brother. You'll have only a namesake."

"You must admit that our relationship was never closer."

"Then it will be all the easier for you to do as I ask. I am even assuming that you will be questioned about me. . . ."

Beginning to understand, Ilya interrupted him: "Yes . . . but our middle initials are the same!"

"I don't deny that. But whatever you say will be believed! You have an excellent reputation."

The hands of the older brother hung long between his knees. He raised one and opened the fingers like a fan. This was his characteristic gesture whenever he was perplexed and wary.

"You mean you want me to lie for you, Gleb Ignatyich?"

"You'll have to do it only once. I'm really hurt that we have to speak about it at such length. . . . You see, I can't explain everything, but I shouldn't like to fall into the ditch prematurely. Help me! Why are you silent; are you afraid?"

"I'm not afraid of anything." The professor jerked forward on his chair, and one could believe this cold and hard affirmation. "So, it's I who am compromising you?" The professor's mouth was stretched into a long smile. "I didn't know that kinship with me was such a crime. Fifteen years ago I cut off soldiers' feet in a field hospital and chewed my oil-cakes like everyone else. True, I don't make engines and blast furnaces, but I repair people, the makers of these machines . . . and as much as I can, I correct God's mistakes. That isn't a bad profession, Gleb. Don't be ashamed of me!"

"You don't understand me, Ilyusha," his brother threw in, very pleased with the other's anger; only in such a state could one expect a Protoklitov to be accommodating. "That's not what was in my mind. . . ."

"No, just wait a minute! I'm not very pleased with our relationship. What do I know about you? Only that you're an engineer and my brother. You want to take even this from me. But how does our kinship manifest itself? Let's count our meetings! Once after a silence of six years you came one evening to borrow five hundred rubles from me. . . ."

"I'll send them back to you by the next mail!" Gleb cried in an irritated voice.

"It's not the money that bothers me, I'm very well off. I'm trying to point out something else. You're a tight fellow: you don't drink or smoke or play cards . . . what do you need money for? Then, half a year later you rushed in to ask me whether sciatica was a good disease. I remember how animated you became when I told you about the symptoms under the knee. Of course, that's not a state secret, but I've a strange feeling. . . ."

"You're just out of sorts. When one's wife smashes vases. . . ."

"Not at all. But if you had been really ill you'd have found out all about your disease. You wanted to cheat someone, that's what!"

"I don't see anything queer in the fact that I came to you with a medical question. It would be ridiculous to question you about silk-worms or smoke-pots . . ."

". . . and it would be awful to learn that you're always lying," Ilya finished for him wryly. "I'm disgusted, everybody's lying, my friends of yesterday . . . even things!" A second wave of anger was surging in him, but suddenly he softened and came toward his brother: "Listen, Gleb, are you ashamed of father?"

"Yes," Gleb confessed, lowering his head.

"It's true that Providence gave us a mediocre papa. A clown and a

convinced reactionary. That reminds me, you've never told me about
him. The Reds let him alone, didn't they?"

Gleb did not answer for a moment. He was tempted to lie, to say
that his father had been shot. That would have made sense and passed
well in the dusk, but he thought better of it.

"He died in good time, before they arrived . . . I think by his own
hand. . . ."

The brothers fell silent. Ilya's fingers pressed together, pulling at the
velvet tablecloth. The cognac bottle was perceptibly moving to the
very edge. Unexpectedly Ilya bent down and stroked a speckled lump
at his feet. It was a cat, a magnificent one, with a pedigree. Apparently refusing to believe in Ilya's caress he left the room in a hurt and
solemn manner. Of course, he too knew that he was expensive and had
a pedigree.

"I thought you had disliked cats since your childhood, Ilya."

"Lately I have discovered a peculiar charm in them!" And Gleb understood that it was *her* cat.

"Is your wife giving a performance today?"

Ilya did not answer. Gleb took a photograph in a leather frame from
the table. This was no doubt his brother's wife. A very simple girl was
smiling from the picture. No doubt the grey photographic tones failed
to render the fascination that had ruined Ilya. Gleb put the picture
back without a word. And now he was already repenting of having
ventured to take this precaution, excessive even in his position. It was
unlikely that Kurilov would ever run into his brother! . . . Gleb rose
irresolutely: he did not wish to meet his brother's wife. Moreover,
he always felt bored in the company of insipid, truth-loving people.
Yet he spent a long time putting on his raincoat, waiting for the moment to resume his attack on his brother.

Finally Ilya asked: "What's the matter, are you being persecuted,
hunted?"

"For the present, no, but if they learn. . . ." He paused. "Although
maybe you're right! I couldn't have lied either to a man I respect. But
when it is a man who arouses in you. . . ."

"Well, you and I have different ideas of amorality. I'm profoundly
old-fashioned, Gleb. And I advise you not to give a damn! Every man
accounts for himself by his work for society. And so, I won't. . . . I
don't want to lie even for your sake, Gleb. You know, my nose swells
when I do such things, I begin to resemble Moussorgsky, and I'm not
good-looking without that. And I have a young wife, you know. . . ."

Gleb took his cap.

"You always had this haughty icy honesty, Ilyusha. You're cautious.

... In your youth you even avoided women lest you catch a disease....
You. ..." He gasped for breath.

"Come to see me when it's all over. We'll finish our conversation in
a more peaceful atmosphere." Ilya smiled conciliatingly, and it was his
first smile of that kind during the whole conversation.

The door slammed. Ilya stood in the hall leaning with his hand
against the clothes-rack. His wife's winter coat was hanging there. A
fur cuff touched his hand. It was squirrel fur, insinuating, soft. A tender, disturbing warmth enveloped his fingers. He went back and once
again picked up the bottle. But this time Ilya Ignatyich confined himself to examining the ruddy little fires that flickered in the liquid.

# CHAPTER 9

# Adventure

THE PROFESSOR'S INTERESTS never went beyond his clinic, his lectures and his collections. His passion for collecting began when he was still a schoolboy, and his age determined the nature of his collections. At first, it was all sorts of pens adjusted to various human peculiarities. Ilya did not write with them, but swapped breakfast for them with poor schoolmates and locked them up in a sacred box. Eighteen years later he gave this collection to a ten-year-old boy, his first patient.

The pens were followed by stamps. They bore the pictures of giraffes, lagoons of coral islands drawn in the form of a horseshoe, palms, black-mustached South American generals, pyramids and yachts with sails. All these were symbols of the boyish countries of Cooper, Jacoliot and Boussenard. . . . As an adolescent he was captivated by weapons, and for his age he had a fairly good collection, Indian and Persian, wrought and engraved Damascus blades. An ancient Afghan rifle, with leather tassels, remained forever on his wall. As years went by he also paid tribute to engravings and was particularly attached to the romantic Piranesi, who erected on paper everything he had not succeeded in constructing in reality. Ilya Ignatyich liked the desert solitude of these ruins entwined with ivy, the piles of stony arches, towers and staircases, all the architectural extravagances of this failure of genius. In any of these collections he might have followed the history of ideas as it expressed the evolution of human needs, but Ilya was attracted by something else too: the post office seal on a stamp with a date that would never come again; a jagged dent in a Malay blade, by which one could guess the strength of the blow; the first unsigned rough sketch of an engraving with the fingermarks of the exacting artist. . . . His feeling for all this was not distorted by any form of greed; object after object passed through his understanding and his hands, leaving neither regret nor heartache behind.

After he had improved his material circumstances, he developed a passion for clocks. In his apartment there accumulated a multitude of all kinds of wooden, leather and bronze boxes filled with singing steel voices. He was as well informed in this field as in that of the scalpel and catgut. Upon his previous visit Gleb had said jokingly that only tower clocks were missing to make the collection complete. And once again Ilya stored up this ringing and ticking mass of furniture, not because he wanted to study the stages of the clock industry, but because from the different forms of his clocks he tried to understand the differences in people's attitude toward time, that sepulchre of ideas, passions and heroes; his body had begun to notice the inexorable flight of the years, and in this case the collector's aspirations coincided with the scientist's habit of arranging things in a logical, graphic pattern. His collection contained carved eighteenth century bulb-shaped clocks (tiny bells almost the size of wheat grains played a carefree minuet in them); there were also Masonic clocks of gloomy German invention (three black-clad figures nailed up a long coffin; the number of their hammer blows indicated the hours, quarter-hours and minutes). Some day this fad would end, but a combination of a dozen people and a hundred circumstances would be required to achieve it.

It had begun with a newspaper advertisement. Protoklitov read somewhere that an antique, bulb-shaped Caron clock was for sale. He pricked up his ears like a hunter at the rustle of game. That splendid object twice described in literature, in itself a literary relic, had vanished from the connoisseurs' horizon about forty years before, and now it was returning from non-existence like a comet that had accomplished its mysterious parabola.

On his first free day Ilya Ignatyich went to the address indicated in the advertisement. It was somewhere near the Lefort Gate, by a deserted churchyard. An elongated building of ancient construction, squat and resembling a corn-chandler's shop, stood there. It had cracked slantwise and, judging from two iron fastenings and stains of a limy solution, an attempt had been made twenty years before to hold it together by homemade means. Two gnarled young lilac trees, in blossom, but pitilessly stripped, graced this completely withered place.

And so destiny had made Piranesi's dimmed dream come alive and real and brought Protoklitov into its backyard. The treasure seller lived in a pit, after the manner of hermits. One had to climb down ramshackle, worm-eaten steps (young nettles grew from the fissures in the stones!) to the basement and then turn around the corner of this catacomb of the old regime. As Ilya Ignatyich groped his way along the corridor something made a smacking noise under his feet. He did not smoke and did not carry matches. The tepid, moist stench grew stronger as the visitor advanced: the corridor ended in a water-closet, and soon Ilya Ignatievich smelt the proximity of the hole and saw a paneless little window at the level of his head; a branch of lilac that had remained intact had penetrated here from outside, only to be suffocated by the filth; the weak light of a street lamp shimmered on the faded, dying petals. . . . His passion for collecting had often led Ilya Ignatyich into all sorts of queer corners, but this was the first time he had ever been in such a slum, too gloomy even for an underworld haunt. The connoisseur of rare mechanisms turned back, feeling the slippery wall. Some sort of sticky muck crept under his nails. He knocked haphazardly at a door, which he had recognized as such by two rust-covered holes, part of a lock and a tattered baize curtain. Not even a whisper came from inside. Oh, the treasure was skilfully hidden both from thieves and the Department of Museums!

Protoklitov had had occasion to observe how wastefully, often unskilfully, but always with a nuance of truly moving grandeur, the new age was being born. A month before he had performed a surgical operation at one of the large, newly constructed hospitals. Dusty mountains of rubble and broken scaffolding lay in the yard, but the hospital was fitted up with garish luxury, and the surgeon-in-chief expressed regret that he did not always have at his disposal such equipment glittering with ceramic and nickel. While at the front Ilya had observed how the age of yesterday defended itself, but only here could he see how the defeated and evil old creature was departing life. And he thought with regret that in his rushing between daily meetings and operations he had completely lost sight of the exaggeratedly extreme forms that life assumed in those years.

He knocked again, and this time the door swung open suddenly. If he had not withdrawn in time the prison-like structure made of dampened gun-carriage boards would have crushed his shoulder. The low bluish gap of light in the doorway was filled by an enormous and indistinct silhouette whose head was behind the other side of the lintel. One could just make out an old man, untidy, excitable and with a fantastic beard.

"Who the devil is trying to get in?" the proprietor cried out in a tone of irritation, but without defiance or violence. Having listened to Protoklitov's explanations he swore and moved aside: "Pull in . . . the sill is high. If you have galoshes you may keep them on. In short, anything goes, spades are trumps!"

Ilya Ignatyich cast a glance around him to make sure no one was going to knife him from behind a corner. The place was obviously wretched. Above a round marble-topped table hung a meagre little lamp on a worn-out cord; wrapped several times in a colored rag, it illuminated only itself and what was directly underneath it: a shoehorn and a glass containing some dark concoction (long grey hairs were stuck around this latter like a sugary stain!). One felt not repulsion but shame at seeing this vile example of human slovenliness. Having got accustomed to the half-light Ilya Ignatyich noticed a classical cobweb on the dirty stained wall, medicine phials and soda water bottles in a corner and, finally, an oval mirror lying flat on the floor; from time to time, at some turn, one's eyes caught a tenuous trembling ray of starlight coming from it. This was the most astounding detail of all: the walls were in place, but instead of the ceiling, over at least half the room there was a patch of dark evening sky already spotted with a whitish rash of stars. In one corner, at the right, there were two or three black rafters. The left side of the room was completely lost in darkness. Protoklitov felt as though he had descended into the bottom of an abandoned well.

"What are you staring at?" the proprietor grumbled in a dull and jeering voice. "That's Orion—spades are trumps—ever heard of it? It's a kind of star. In clear weather it's not a bad spectacle; the most voluminous of all books, so to speak. How much nonsense the nations have written about it during the past centuries! They've written and written and I've got nothing to cover the roof with! . . ." He cast a side glance at his respectable and bewildered visitor. "See, the roof—it went pouff! It caved in, they were about to repair it, then it turned out there were no nails. I was the only tenant left, and the Tenants' Association decided" (he almost spat out these words and made a disgusting smacking sound in the air) "that it wasn't worth while to make a fuss for the sake of one individual. They're waiting for me too, to vanish. But I'm not dying; spades are trumps! I walk about in my den and sing like John of Damascus!" And he burst out laughing, not very gaily, but boisterously, threateningly, heartrendingly; at last, as though suffocating in the acid fumes of his own anguish, he abruptly stopped and turned away.

Protoklitov kept silent; he did not know how to behave in such cases. To discuss seriously the absence of the roof would have meant sympathizing with this man, and sympathy in turn led to an inevitable alliance, even complicity, with this miserable and doomed underground. The only thing he could do was to pass the whole thing off with a joke, and that was what he did, though not particularly cleverly: "So you live like the Chaldean sages of old, don't you?"

Once this decrepit giant had been beautiful, even majestic, but all his beauty had now evaporated. The flaps of his lustrine coat hung as though from a mannequin, and no miracle could have restored the former comeliness of this emaciated, hole-ridden bag of bones with a soul. His face, swollen and unhealthy, was big and round as though carved by a child's fingers out of a gigantic pumpkin. Ilya Ignatyich even thought for a moment that he had met him somewhere before, perhaps fairly frequently—but the cobweb of his recollection broke at once. Those still smouldering eyes had an irreconcilable and savage look. They slanted suspiciously toward Protoklitov.

"You're an educated man," he said reproachfully and in a much lower voice. "Today no one remembers the Chaldeans. Today they think more and more of jam and trousers. They don't overwork the upper part of the body. . . . Spades are trumps!" Once again his throat clicked with a raspy, angry laughter; the air whistled with the modulations in his thickened bronchi. "An educated man, but you're buying clocks. That means you've got money. So you're being paid? Never mind, don't get offended: these days all of us are brothers. Nothing brings people so close as grief! Well, sit down, have a chat with me. . . . One gets fed up sitting with a dummy"—the old man pointed his finger at the unlighted part of his dwelling, but despite Ilya's efforts to see he could not distinguish anything there except a little Greek statue and a heap of crumpled laundry on a chair. "It makes your brains rot, and your hair begins to grow inside your head. Eh, it would be good to offer you some tea, spades are trumps," he observed, half inquiringly, but there was nothing to sit on, and even if there had been Protoklitov would not have ventured to drink tea in such a place.

In addition, the proprietor of this horrible hole kept scraping his heels against the floor and coughing—he was tormented by emphysema. Then he would scratch himself and remove something from underneath his beard. He did this so often that Ilya was certain it was unconsciously, out of habit. His speech was spiced with a soured philosophic mixture and so much bile that objects seemed to shrivel up when he spoke of them. Protoklitov began to feel bored and disgusted. Very politely, not indeed without a certain amiability characteristic of the old intelligentsia, he reminded the old man of the object of his visit. In reply the man angrily muttered something, raking his beard with five fingers, and continued booming for a long time, without any coherence or apparent sense.

". . . And so," he seemed to be saying when his muttering began to become intelligible, "you've dragged yourself here to get my Caron. Of course, one doesn't climb down to a grave for nothing. And so my fortune is flowing away! Last week I gave away a Godunov box with amethysts for nothing (and it's even mentioned in the chronicles!). And a month ago someone took from here a copy of *Emile* with the author's dedication to Catherine II. Have you been asleep all this time, Mr. Engineer? There's a Greek who comes to see me . . . or maybe an

Italian or a Jew. Polite, he talks German . . . he talks as though he were cutting glass with a saw. He buys everything and takes it abroad. You'd better hurry, or else he'll pick me clean little by little, you won't even get a small rib!" He stretched out his hand at random into sepulchral space, drew from it two little vases of a corrupt shape, shook some sort of seeds and a dried-up moth out of each, blew the dust off them straight onto his customer and handed them to him. "Have you seen these? Pure Directoire style, if you please! Yes. And the armless wench of Milo, naked, won't pass either? Not at all, spades are trumps. Wouldn't you take something of that kind?"

Perhaps he intended to talk all night long with the "connoisseur" who had descended into his pit. He was rearranging things in the darkness, moving them from place to place, wiping them with his sleeves, showing them with a round arclike gesture and whistling, always whistling. Deeply perturbed for some reason, Protoklitov once again, more insistently now, but still politely, pointed out that he was not an old-clothes-man and aside from the advertised clock had no reason for abusing the proprietor's hospitality. This was said with such circumlocutions that the old man did not understand him at once. Having dug into his beard for some time he scrutinized his long yellow nails. His brows rose in disappointment. Suddenly, having thought of something, he carefully took from the sill one of the flower pots wrapped in thick white mould. A great many such pots stood there; in some green plants were still glimmering, while brown clogs of damp rot protruded from others.

"Wait, we'll come to an agreement, spades are trumps. You're not a botanist? It's a pity, I'd have given you those little orchids for nothing: I don't know how to dispose of them. I live here in seclusion, I never go out. No botanical gardens are left in Russia: they're all ploughed under. And what's left of Mother Russia anyway? Vassily the Blessed on the square and I myself, in ignominy. . . ." He again cooed something long and incomprehensible into his beard, but Protoklitov made up his mind to suffer until the end: a Caron clock was worth a talk with a maniac gone native. "And once all this flourished, Mr. Chemist . . . *oncidium Cavendishianum,* some word isn't it? That word alone is worth about twelve rubles! . . . and now some kind of colored spiders have bred under the leaves, with such enterprising faces. They sit there, the villains, and make a pie of flies. . . . Just have one look to remember, just a look, that's free!" He bent a segmented stem aside, and pointed at a completely empty place: apparently the spiders were meant as an allegory. "Everything's gone to pot, and that's the way the road leads. Rats devoured my library . . . and so I sold *Emile* for my sins. And

please note, Mr. Botanist, that the rats, too, preferred pre-war books of
an idealistic content. They refused to eat your Lafargues: the glue's
not as good! And who wants such things, anyhow?" From the same
darkness, like a country fair magician, he kept snatching book after
book, shook them and threw them back into something soft. Protoklitov fancied that in the darkness someone caught them as they whizzed
by with monkey-like agility. The dimmed gilding of the bindings
gleamed, the opened pages whimpered, and again the books were
drowned in the shadowy pit. "Here are the works of the Dutch soldier
Descartes who travelled to fulfil his vow to Notre Dame de Lorette.
Or look at the Book of Numbers by Galileo who appropriated the invention of a spectacle-maker of Middleburgh. Or again, the pamphlets
of a friend of the Duc de Villeroy, your unforgettable Marat, who,
after beheading the great living mathematician Bailly, immediately
began to go after the great dead one, Newton. . . . You've forgotten all
that, hey, spades are trumps? Except for a dozen of these dubious,
righteous men, history is for you only the criminal archives of mankind . . . and no songs are there, no immortal books, only a motley
crowd of prattlers, grabbers and phantoms! You people always boast
that you've built new ships to sail unexplored oceans, but you've forgotten that there behind you in the mist was a blessed, su-unny dawn"
—and with a contracted finger he threatened some one—"when Ves-
pucci's ships were just approaching the shores of the most marvellous
of continents. Ha, and you've forgotten, too, what it was turned into
afterward. Forgetfulness is the highest social virtue, Mr. Musician!"

At this point it was definitely clear that he was mixing up the visitor's profession solely out of contempt. Spite had prevented the old
man from crossing that ultimate boundary which is called serene and
perfect wisdom; in him the frenzy of boredom had set in at once. The
new era appeared to him only as a dishonest and senseless bustle of
ignoramuses . . . but he could still hear the songs of the youth surging
above his den and he envied them with all the passion of his enormous
and progressively colder body. Something made him shy away from
the only means with the help of which he could avoid growing still
more unsociable and shorten the torments of complete disintegration.
He already attacked every living thing that committed the imprudence
of catching his eye. Without any apparent coherence he hurled at
Protoklitov some dubious historical facts, perhaps addressing himself
to the Chaldean stars, waving his hands, raking up the air beneath
him, threatening to crush an imaginary opponent by his sheer mass.
He asked how the atoms got the idea of sticking together to form a
man or a tree, he shouted about some gigantic, trampled, bloody shoes

in which mankind of yesterday marched, while the physician, forgetting about the Caron clock in the face of such an obvious clinical case, ascribed all this to the weakening of associative thinking and the extreme agitation to which the memory is subject before it is extinguished forever.

"No go, Mr. Flutist. I've changed my mind about selling my Caron. I don't want to, get it? I'll give it to my Greek fellow . . . let him carry it away . . . on a motorcycle . . . to hell!"

The deal was off, and of course there was no point in starting a fight with the gesticulating old man over the physician's lost time. Ilya Ignatyich began imperceptibly to retreat along the wall, starting each time his shoulder caught a half-torn tuft of wall-paper. At that moment something stirred in the depths of the room (the same thing that Protoklitov had thought was a pile of laundry on the chair), but it was not immediately clear to whom the new whining, piercing voice belonged: "Forgive me for meddling into what's not my business, Nikolai Aristarkhovich . . . but look into what a state you've put your visitor. Although he is a stranger, I feel mortified on his account! . . . And who is interested in your confidences? Whose fault is it that when they overthrew century-old idols the people shook the ground under you too? You recall the sins of the great as though they justified your own. Why don't you recall Bakunin whom you tried to destroy? He was a saint . . . and he too, for instance, borrowed money and . . . didn't pay it back!"

The proprietor waved him off jeeringly: "Be quiet, my righteous friend!" he snapped back with incomprehensible bitterness. "You've always suffered from sweaty feet and a liking for scaring young girls with your Jacobin ideas. You've always played the part both of the sage and the virtuous and were tormented by not knowing which of the two you were. And do you remember the incident on the Psnia? . . ."

Again a creaking of furniture could be heard, and, oh miracle! the pile of wash stood up. A man took form and moved one step forward. In the twilight emerged a clean, wrinkled little face with drooping, grey eyebrows.

"I'm indignant at your trick, Nikolai Aristarkhovich," he declared in a cracked and solemn voice. "I regret my trust in you. You're an aged man, yet you're not ashamed of joking about such matters in the presence of strangers!"

And at that point a fierce explosion completed the incredible adventure of our collector. Obviously these men were old, never reconciled rivals. The century had long since stepped across their quarrel, but they continued living on it because they had no other interests. They were now kept together solely by their mutual hatred, which had become stronger than any other tie. But now this hatred too was fated to come to an end.

"I'm fed up with your immortal love, you rascal, you stinking little mouse, you goblin!" the large old man thundered. "I'm fed up looking at that dried-up nettle leaf you've put on instead of a face. Harlequin! . . . Hey, devils, take him, pour ashes on him! She lived with me, your immortal love. Every night I crawled up to her mezzanine, spades are trumps. I slept with her, while you composed your foolish little verses in her honor. . . ."

"I'm not listening, not listening to your brazenness, Nikolai Aristarkhovich!" the small old man whispered, stuttering and prudently moving toward the exit like Protoklitov. "You're a slanderer, Nikolai Aristarkhovich, you dishonor the dead. . . . That never happened, never!"

"You lived under our bed . . . and when we tossed on it we could hear you sneezing from the dust, you painted weakling! Coffin-makers . . . come to take my measure! . . . Out with you, all of you! Let me croak alone, alone . . . make me the gift at least . . ."—his voice almost broke—"at least of your squeamishness toward a corpse!"

And at that moment—let us be fair to the end!—Ilya Ignatyich was not very eager to leave. The cockfight between the two old men was intensely interesting. In everything they seemed complete contrasts. They were a lion and a mouse, but at an age when the disparate beauty and might of these beasts are reconciled. Stopping his ears with his fingers, the small one was now making his way toward the door, getting entangled as he tottered in a loose canvas raincoat the size of a piano. He had a clear chance of getting out before Protoklitov, whose passage was barred by a disembowelled, bandy-legged chair. A wordless, chaotic scene, such as occurs only during a fire, followed. Ilya Ignatyich got into the corridor at the same time as the little old man, and immediately afterward something hit the slammed door behind them with a bang and crash. (The little Directoire vases had at last found suitable use.) Protoklitov succeeded in jumping out of the basement labyrinth first, but the spring slush gave way under his heel; he slipped, and a moment later the old man fell on top of him.

". . . Don't believe him, don't believe him," he rustled plaintively, barely catching his breath and clinging to Protoklitov's sleeve. "He lied, he has been lying all his life! I'll explain everything. . . ."

"Let me get up!" Protoklitov growled, purple with indignation.

"Yes, yes . . . you didn't hurt yourself, I hope?" Suddenly he grasped his head in bewilderment. "It's terrible . . . I left my hat there. Help me, don't abandon me!"

But no one would have ventured back there. . . . They stood confused in the yard, listening to the solemn noises of the frantic pogrom
inside. The impotent man was raging in the darkness amidst his foul
crumbling walls. Judging by a tenuous, glassy screech the mirror was
smashed—the sacred Chaldean star was dimmed! The din grew
weaker. Now the final rustle dissolved in the cool May silence. Only
the heart could still guess the still unfinished frenzy of that enormous,
matured and fading body. No particular knowledge was needed to
diagnose what was happening. It was the death agony, and the social
had preceded the physical one.

They made their way to the window. On his knees, without letting
go of Protoklitov's hand, the small one looked into the basement.
Nikolai Aristarkhovich's room was dark. The little one got up; a childish fear made his eyes round.

". . . You know, he had veronal, he got it from the Greek in exchange
for his *Emile*. Two phials . . . he even boasted that it was imported
stuff, good stuff. . . ." he whispered dejectedly. (Protoklitov clearly
evoked this buyer, insinuating and polite, in a velour hat, with ghostly,
blue-shaven cheeks, swapping death for a precious book; the universal
notion of the buyer of souls was undergoing an amusing evolution in
this country.)

Protoklitov silently led his new acquaintance out of the yard; it
would have been cruel to restore to life what remained behind. The
old man resisted slightly; he regretted his lost hat. Suddenly he
wrenched himself away and, skipping along, ran back. Ilya Ignatyich
thought that he must have had a burning need to see his rival for the
last time. A full quarter of an hour passed before the old man re-
emerged. He tottered, holding his recovered property, broad-brimmed,
crumpled, as though someone had been lying on it. Aside from this, he
had not brought anything away and had perhaps left a part of himself.

So that was how the new life relieved the old, in terrible relay. The
merchants, officials, monks and stock exchange people had gone; even
the words designating them had vanished with them. But it seemed
that some group still remained whose turn was coming only now. And
as though answering the question Protoklitov was putting to himself,
the old man muttered colorlessly and articulately, as in former times
psalms were read over the dead: ". . . And I envied this man for more
than forty years. He rose above me like a star, but we began together.
Without noticing it himself, he swallowed my life. He was successful.
He had healthy, beautiful children and a tall proud wife. He was the
principal of a classical *gymnasium,* a mainstay of the reactionary

cabinet. . . ." His grief was after all understandable: people have always been terrified by the destruction of a luminary.

"Look here . . . what was his name?" Protoklitov cried out like a boy, shaking the little old man by the shoulder.

The old man turned toward him his unseeing, vacant eyes. "Dudnikov!" he said, shrivelling from cold and the grandeur of the name.

Ilya Ignatyich removed his hand. It was as though a musty, stuffy wind had breathed upon him. Dudnikov was the principal of the school he had attended. This haughty man with a big forehead was unforgettable—he lacked only an aura around his head. He wore a blue uniform tunic with a general's red lining and heraldic buttons. Pupils in the upper grades used to say that even when caressing his wife he did not remove his gala uniform lest she forget herself! A talented history teacher, he had an amazing career, which was interrupted by the revolution. His office resembled a temple of which he himself was both the priest and the divinity. From the richly painted ceiling looked down the gilded symbols of the arts and sciences. His liveried attendants possessed the sarcasm of Voltaire and the appearance and bearing of Roman legionaries. And when he himself walked along the corridor, the plaster statues of the ancients reflected in the abysses of the waxed floor accompanied and devoured him with their eyes, as soldiers do a general on review.

"Ah, so that was Dudnikov!" Ilya Ignatyich repeated aloud.

He wished to know the fate of this man in great detail. He was motivated by the almost childish desire to discover the teacher's secret, to look behind a curtained window, to read a forbidden book. He asked questions, but the old man was not in a condition to answer them. Then Ilya Ignatyich asked permission to visit him. He readily gave his address and was even glad of the opportunity to make an acquaintance. His name was Arkadyi Hermogenovich Pokhvisnev.

Around them was spread a dense odor of opening buds, backyard dampness and undried rubble.

Protoklitov accompanied the old man to the trolley car.

CHAPTER 10

# The Actress

THE VISIT DID NOT take place until two months later. So much work had piled up that it was as though all Moscow were standing in line to be cut open by Protoklitov. And this time he dropped in only because he happened to be in the neighborhood. The old man was out; he was expected to return from the queue any minute—there was a distribution of kitchen soap. Ilya Ignatyich was received by Arkadyi Hermogenovich's niece. She was an actress, twenty-one years old; her name was Liza and her eyes were red with weeping. Protoklitov became interested in her, as a physician. He learned that she found it difficult to master her part; she was about to play Angélique in *Le Malade Imaginaire* which her company had long been planning to produce. Ilya Ignatyich offered to listen to her monologue, and he himself read the part of Argand for her. Liza criticized his bad, somewhat stilted diction; he for his part gave her a number of valuable practical suggestions. Among other things, he pointed out the plausibility of Molière's plot, agreed with the author's caustic criticism of contemporary physicians and, as for the conditions of French hospitals in the eighteenth century, he recommended that Liza read the report of that same Bailly mentioned by the deceased Dudnikov. (The fact that this name came back to him showed that he still remembered the purpose of his visit to Arkadyi Hermogenovich.)

He had so much respect for the theatre and the profession of actress, he was so sincere and knew women so little, that he assumed that all this interested her very much: ". . . the patients were put six in one bed, and in such a manner that the feet of one touched the neck of another. Ha, that was some medical science! . . . A dead man on his back occupies half a yard. Those who ventured to fall ill in the Paris of the kings were entitled to only ten inches. The lucky ones lay on their sides, unable to stir; the others waited their turn under the bed. Judge for yourself, Liza—you won't mind an old man calling you by your first name?" (he threw in with the clumsy coquetry of a bachelor) "—what was going on in the backyard of the brilliant court of Versailles! . . . People afflicted with contagious diseases, chronic diseases, pregnant women—all lay together like matches in a box; con-

70

sumption and scurvy were treated in the same way; smallpox patients walked around among the beds looking for a place to lie down. There were two methods of treatment: the enema—ha, forgive this detail! . . . and the saw. Operations were performed on the spot, in front of the other patients. You really ought to read that honest fellow when you have an opportunity; he makes you shudder!"

Somewhat embarrassed by his animation, she looked at him with intense curiosity: "Yes, I'll certainly read it. Wait a minute, let me write down the author's name. Thank you for your suggestion. However, this book won't be in the theatre library!"

"Oh, I'll bring it to you myself if you wish," Protoklitov said, pleased by the young girl's responsiveness to his weighty scientific discourse.

The Pokhvisnevs occupied a heated glass gallery. Two of its transparent walls gave on to a tiny dusty garden composed of a bed of carrots, two little bushes and a tree of some ordinary kind. Liza explained that in bad weather the tree scratched at the glass with all its paws, as though begging for permission to come closer to the stove. "Look, it fawns upon people like a big intelligent watchdog." She added naïvely: "Since my childhood I've loved dogs and cats . . . do you?"

"Cats . . . they're pleasant animals," said Ilya Ignatyich judiciously.

A chintz curtain divided this narrow room in two. (Liza's uncle occupied the other half.) Flame-colored cocks were pecking beetles on it. "There are so many of them when one looks through the glass pendant of the chandelier, aren't there?" Liza remarked. It was just a miserable hole, but Protoklitov liked everything here: the abundance of greenish light reflected from the foliage and the masses of books (indeed a stack of books replaced the missing fourth leg of an oilcloth-covered chair) and the cot with a baize cover full of holes, and the very smallness of the place that seemed saturated with the pure freshness of this girl. Liza grazed Protoklitov every minute with her elbow or a fold of her dress or her breath.

"Uncle told me about how you met at Dudnikov's. He was ill for a whole week afterward. That reminds me, are you a watchmaker?"

"No, not quite."

"Then what do you want with an old clock? A new one is better, it's more accurate."

"Oh, that's hard to explain. It's a hobby of mine."

"Ah, a hobby!" Liza drawled, and her intonation expressed a wonderment much greater than the cause that had provoked it.

. . . Apparently it was impossible to learn all of Dudnikov's biography at one sitting. Ilya Ignatyich became a frequent visitor at the Pokhvisnevs. He began to like other things too—the girl's forehead, open as though swept by winds, her way of smiling, which raised the very wings of her eyebrows, her pure eyes without any small lie in them, and even her habit of speaking a great deal, rapidly, with never a word about herself. He too was reticent and that was why he was doubly attracted by Liza's reserve, the cause of which he could not fathom. In brief, even Liza's shortcomings caught his fancy. (He never learned the second half of this truth—that love has gone when even the good qualities of the beloved become irritating. But so much has been said on this theme that it would be senseless for us to add new variations.)

Ilya Ignatyich wanted this girl for a long time, and in his circlings around her there was something of a child whose fancy is caught by a pretty piece of candy that his elders have forgotten on the table. Unfamiliar with the technique of his time, he resorted to artifices and made efforts three times more elaborate than necessary. This extremely busy man invented all kinds of complicated gifts and trips to the country in the uncle's company, and wrote letters full of dignity, learning and embarrassment. The courtship dragged out for almost a year. The uncle, who at first declared that "the shyness of a man in love is the only kind of cowardice that deserves indulgence," began to be upset. He had secretly worked out a plan for having an explanation with this "young man" (at his age all mankind seemed to him guilty and youthful), when Liza herself, disregarding the conventions, facetiously and naïvely hinted her consent to Protoklitov.

"One condition, Ilya: you must never importune me with questions."

"I love in advance even your childish secrets, Liza!"

She moved to her husband's apartment only after a dealer in old books had been there. Protoklitov's library was mercilessly liquidated, an operation insisted upon by his wife and in which he concurred. The curtains were thoroughly dusted and the new disposition of the rooms was roughly planned. Liza opened a window, and sitting on the window-sill with dangling feet examined her dirty fingers: she had put in a good deal of work that day! A lukewarm summer rain was falling, water dripped from the roof on the pink curve of her nape. . . . Protoklitov's wedding gift was truly lavish. For the space of six weeks the secondhand booksellers of Moscow scoured all the book graveyards on his behalf. They collected a whole library on dramatic art, including the classics of world drama, a many-volumed history of the theatre and monographs on famous actors and theatrical institutions. Ilya Ignatyich spread all this out in his home and summoned his wife, who had already guessed the cause of his excitement. She entered, she was astonished, she refused to believe that so much could be written about *that*. Anxiously and guiltily, standing up, she leafed through one thick notebook. Stately frowning old men in lace ruffles, elaborate wigs and jackets, wrinkled old women in long cloaks peered at her from the past. Her eyes caught only one thing: the variety of beards and coiffures that had been invented in the course of centuries. She was overwhelmed by a confusion resembling the despair of an artist who visits for the first time a museum full of first-rate works; it seemed absurd to enter into competition with all this. She looked at her husband's hands, they were empty. With an embarrassed nod she walked to the window. He was simple-minded, this poor husband of a beginning actress!

At last he held his piece of candy. For an entire six months Ilya Ignatyich chewed it to the measure of his health and strength: one does not get to the filling immediately in this sort of sweet! Absorbed in his work, he did not notice how his regime was changing. Protoklitov went to bed at eleven—the Protoklitovs supped at one in the morning. Protoklitov could not stand cats—at the Protoklitovs' a striped animal of a most unpleasant character nestled at one's feet at night. Protoklitov received his colleagues to discuss the latest developments in urological surgery once every six months—at the Protoklitovs' visitors began to drop in at any time. For the most part they were easy-mannered young men of a skeptical turn of mind, who wore foreign-looking sweaters. Visiting, they made themselves at home, while Protoklitov even at home behaved like a guest among them. Old men no longer came to see Ilya Ignatyich, and now, the youngest of these, he was himself in the position of an old man. Only his constant love for this sonorous-voiced, hazel-eyed woman reconciled him to the discomforts of marital existence.

To his professional cares were added new ones, for the time being still inconspicuous and pleasant. The little woman was inclined to big activity. Liza was not content with being a second-rate actress in an unimportant theatre. She was not permitted to go nearer the footlights than the exit door. It seemed that the stage managers and directors feared in her a rival of their untalented wives. She was envied, she said, the managers took revenge on her, because they feared her potentialities. . . . All this, accompanied by his wife's meaningful silence, was extremely convincing to Ilya Ignatyich. He was puzzled, wondering whether he should not write a long letter to the People's Commissariat or set out and do battle with the director. But he himself had not found the time to see his wife on the stage. She often invited him to her dressing-room backstage. Protoklitov's heavy-weight appearance, his name, his profession were supposed to frighten her enemies. In brief, she wanted to use her husband's profession as a threat against *them*. Not one of those who built bridges or led parades or wrote books exposing evil-doers could be sure that the next day he would not have to take his place on Ilya's enamelled table. In the heat of her resentment she exaggerated the importance of her weapon. In reality, Protoklitov's power was no greater than that of a dispatcher directing trains or a baker who mixes the day's bread.

Before coming forward to defend his actress, Ilya Ignatyich secretly bought a ticket and told Liza that he had to see an American neurologist. The theatre in which she exercised her talent was a long way off. Her husband had to take a twenty-kopek ride on a trolley car and walk down one street on foot. The temple of art turned out to be a former merchant's two-storey private house. A homely whiff of ammonia struck one at the gate, and a flock of local bohemians with fluttering neckties promenaded on the sidewalk. All in all, the establishment was rather forlorn, people came there in felt boots, and before the performance there was a lecture on the usefulness of Shakespeare. An elderly woman in a knitted dress led Ilya Ignatyich to his place with motherly solicitude and sold him a piece of paper which among other names bore that of his wife. A ventilator overhead sucked out the fetid air. It stopped whirring as soon as the curtain went up and the boots under the curtain had vanished. There was a moment of rush and bustle, some late-comers scurried to the vacant front rows. When everything settled down, Protoklitov saw his wife.

At that time imported plays portraying life abroad were all the rage. Staging them gave the director an opportunity to show his refined taste and provided a plausible excuse for exhibiting forbidden dances and elegant costumes. This time the scene represented a commonplace American home. Covered by a piece of sackcloth Liza slept in the background until she was awakened by an unattractive old woman. She began to bawl out the good-for-nothing girl for not having lit the heater and swept the room. It was clear that the old woman oppressed the younger. Liza wore the same kind of rags and wig as her odious aunt. Some people came in, bringing the news of the death of the old woman's husband. With a tense face Liza wielded her broom, waiting for the time when she would at last say her line. Meanwhile Vasiliev appeared dressed as a cowboy. And if only this Vasiliev had been in love with her! But no, Vasiliev was in love with another woman!

A conventional boundary of footlights separated Ilya from his beloved Liza, and whether he liked it or not he could look at her only with the eyes of a spectator. Liza's part in the play was unimportant. She was merely a screen designed to reflect the ball that was caught by someone else. And of a sudden Ignatyich forgot about the mole known only to him on Liza's half-childish back near the muscle, *pectoralis major*, which conceals the deep cavity of the clavicle. The other credulous spectators were captivated, not by his wife's talent, but by the vigorous back-handed humor of the famous pamphleteer playwright. A red flush stained Protoklitov's damp cheeks. It seemed to him that he had been recognized and was being stared at—without scoffing, but without particular sympathy either. He felt that some of the audience found it more interesting to observe the husband's confusion than the wife's antics. Moreover, something was dripping on his head. He leaned to one side and it began to drip on his shoulder, he rubbed it with his finger and sniffed it—to his surprise it had no odor. And during all this act his knees were pressed against the seat in front of him, while from behind someone breathed regularly on his neck like an oven drawing. The theatre was not made for such long-legged patrons as himself. . . . Finally, the surgeon rose and, getting entangled in other people's legs, clinging to the number plates on the chair, ran to the exit. The woman in the knitted dress chided him familiarly as he left: "You should do such things at home before you come, little father, instead of. . . ."

When Liza returned from the theatre she found her husband at home. In shirtsleeves and slippers, ready to turn in, he was reading in his room. The light from a table lamp fell on him from the side, and the angular shadow of his nose was drowned in the cavity of his cheek. Ilya did not raise his eyes when the door quietly opened. Liza whistled: she knew how to make a tenuous, alarming sound like the call of a grouse. Her husband did not notice her. Dancing and circling she crossed the room and peered from behind at the text he was reading. It was a foreign magazine; on the page he was studying there was an exact reproduction of a kidney cyst resembling a human embryo; next to it was a picture of the wrinkled sack which contained it, quite like a *stratostat* before taking off (the newspapers had just given this a great deal of publicity).

"Phew, what a loathsome thing!" Liza whispered superstitiously.

Ilya Ignatyich went on reading. Liza felt hurt and withdrew. Oh, how fed up she was with all those books about cysts, papillomas, excisions . . . terrifying terms for human misfortune! (Once, at the very beginning, she had been terribly afraid of these words. She placed her husband's profession somewhere between that of a miracle-maker and a butcher. On one occasion, with the aid of an assistant of her husband's, she had been admitted to the clinic. She was dressed in a white gown, and a canvas beret was fixed on her head with a safety pin. She refused to follow a patient the whole way from the bathtub to the operating room. She had her own ideas about all this: wards with men who looked like blocks of wood and women who looked like convalescent soldiers. She wanted to see the main thing, and that was why she went straight to the operating room. Nothing surprised or horrified her. A number of people in white stood near a high table, and the surgeon's fingers fished out something from a square, dark, quite bloodless space. For her there was not even a trace of mystery in her husband's profession. Indeed, she thought the business of the graphologist who sat on a little stool in the lobby of the theatre was a hundred times more complicated!) Now she caught sight of her reflection in the glass of the library door. There was a greasy shine on her cheeks and the tip of her nose. She hurriedly opened her bag, to put some powder on her face.

"You were at the theatre today, weren't you?" she asked in a drawl, with her back to her husband.

Ilya Ignatyich was reading. The article was by a world luminary in the field of surgery, although his mortality statistics did not seem to justify his reputation.

"But why didn't you stay to the end?" Liza insisted in a monotonous and all the more sinister voice. "I saw you leave. Didn't you like the play?"

"I had to visit a patient. He's nervous, tomorrow he goes on the table."

"The same one you hacked up two days ago? . . . Is he still alive?"

"No, not the same one . . . and that one is recovering."

She squinted ironically: "You're lying, Ilya, and you're a bad actor. Why did you leave the theatre?"

Ilya Ignatyich put his magazine on his knee and looked at his wife. She seemed to him twice as unhappy as when he had first known her. Her resources did not exceed those of a savage, fascinating but insignificant, and it occurred to him that to describe her one would have to use only diminutive epithets. Her figure was small. Her hazel eyes, had it not been for the wandering little fires in them, were ordinary, a little sad, like those one often sees in failures. Her little face, not too regular, with a small, lightly squashed nose, was appealing only for the hot and helpless flabbiness of her lips. Her behavior was so simple that one would have been ashamed to hurt her. But one had to make a woman angry to see what she would become several years later. Now, hostile and alien, she was advancing upon him. . . . And suddenly bursting into laughter just as she was, in her fur coat, she jumped onto his knees. Through his thin shirt his skin felt the wintry cold of her buttons. The article of the world-famous urologist lay crumpled at his feet. One of Liza's slippers had slipped from her foot and fallen on the horrid, gashed kidney.

"Oh, you didn't like Kagorlitskaya, did you?" And she threatened him with a finger so pink that it cast almost no shadow. "You remember her, she has such a sharp little face, like a penknife? But she's rising fast, that terrible woman, although everyone knows how she made her way. She used to put on her step-ins, hide in a closet and cry 'coo-coo.' And Anatolyi Petrovich would look for her and of course . . . find her at once!" (She all the more readily accused Kagorlitskaya of the sins of her friend Galka Gromova because Protoklitov did not know either of them.) "That reminds me, I saw you at the very beginning of the play and pointed you out to my friends. We took turns looking at you through the hole in the curtain. What were you chewing, something good? . . . Zoyka Ershova said you looked like a dinosaur, and Kagorlitskaya thought you were like the Stone Guest in *Don Giovanni*. But all this is silly talk and you won't strangle me, of course! It's a pity that you left: all the first act I played only for you, did you notice it? But you left, and after that I played badly, I know I did. By the way, do you remember what was Béranger's social origin? There was an argument about it, and I had to keep silent. You don't know? But what if they ask you at the conference, and you. . . . But did you like the way I played? Why are you silent?"

With her cheek she felt his slow breathing, like two dark winds. How she had studied him! (And yet she feared some line in him that she had never been able to read.) And so she went on tousling her husband, petting him, and the chair under them panted and blew like a fat man.

"So you still won't say anything?"

"What shall I say, Liza?" He recalled with a shudder the unpleasant dripping from the ceiling, the naïve joke of the ticket-seller and the simplified acting that was sold to the masses in guise of art. He tried to find excuses for all that: all the famous theatres had begun like that, with two or three enthusiasts, a barn, penniless young people. "You're young, everything is ahead of you. Come, take your coat off, child, and let's have supper!"

"You're not answering my question."

"I'm very hungry, Liza, and I'm tired. I've had a hard day. Your hairdresser came. I made an appointment with him for tomorrow. . . . Are you free?"

Her eyebrows came closer at the bridge of her nose; she was losing her patience. Thus, amidst the chirping of birds and under a clear sky, a storm suddenly growls. Oh, he should have found this out long ago —whether she was a physician's wife or he an actress's husband. The attack was continuing: a Copenhagen vase, the gift of an enthusiastic patient, was uncertainly shaking on the whatnot. But once again a roguish smile illumined her face grown sullen a moment before, the cloud passed away, and a gay sun shone in the clear space. He pressed her to him and in a very low voice asked her how she felt, for they were expecting a baby. She said, in a childish manner, that it was growing.

". . . Oh, I'd almost forgotten. Hurry and get dressed. Victor Adolfovich came home with me . . . you never heard of him before? I'll introduce you, let's go. He is our chief stage manager. Remember that he has a very, very high opinion of you. I think he has appendicitis, and he wants to consult you. . . ."

"Oh, but it's late, Liza . . . and this is not a consulting room. Let him come tomorrow!"

She stared at him: "So you don't care about my success? There's a rumor in the theatre that we're going to stage *Mary Stuart,* do you know that? Can you understand what that means to me? Well, put on your coat. It's strange that you have no friends! How you lived before you had me, how you lived! A great tumultuous life is going on around us, new masses are emerging on the stage of history, and you . . . you lock yourself up, like a wretched individualist and admire your ureters!"

"Liza. . . ."

"Be quiet! Victor is a gentleman from top to toe, and I'm sure you'll like each other. He mentioned that he wanted to work with me. You know, he has his own system . . . he made one elderly actor hang suspended on a string during an entire act: he's Leftist, very Leftist! Incidentally, he resisted coming here a long time, but I told him that you had always wanted to meet him. And he likes me very much too. . . ."

"But tell me, what productions has he to his credit?" asked Ilya, infected by her air of mystery.

"Well, *Frédéric* and some other things, in clubs. . . . That's unimportant, you must just praise him. . . ."

She kept on babbling as she arranged his necktie. Since her childhood she had wanted to play Mary, he was the first person to whom she had ever confessed it. Kagorlitskaya would die of envy if she were successful. Victor Adolfovich was terribly frightened about his disease. . . . He would produce *Mary* in a new way, from a social point of view.

The action would take place in the pit, and the audience would be on the stage. Music was being written for the play by Vlasov, who had won an automobile in some lottery or other. They were planning to print posters in the form of excerpts, and in the center of the lobby there would be a block and the executioner's dummy, life size. It would be an educational, exciting production, it would inevitably give rise to attempts at imitation, to competition and dozens of useful discussions.

"Well, everything's ready!" She pushed her husband—oh, what a stubborn man he was—to the door.

In the former library a sturdy fellow in leggings, deathly-pale, sat at the table. He was no longer young and his face showed symptoms, not of appendicitis, but of obvious liver trouble. He cast an inquiring glance at Protoklitov, wondering whether this new acquaintance would bring him friendship or enmity. His glance was tired and lifeless. Ilya Ignatyich apologized for his slippers. The visitor first pricked up his ears, then brightened: "Why, don't mention it, at this hour! . . . but Liza insisted that you should examine me, and I decided to take advantage of her amiability. She is right; if I am to be hacked open, it ought to be by you. But tell me frankly, don't hesitate to frighten me, does it hurt much?"

# CHAPTER 11

# Liza

A TALENT FOR PLANTING her roots solidly, even in the poorest soil, had always distinguished Liza from her playmates and companions. When she wondered about herself, whether she was pretty or ugly, intelligent or merely greedy, she would unconsciously shift her attention to one detail of her childhood that she came really to know only after many years. . . . There was a certain ravine in Porozhensk, full of mounds of rubble and hardy bushes, enormous as something out of the Bible or a dream. Broken glass, bottomless pails, horseshoes and gigantic, rotting boots littered the place pell-mell, and among these piles of stuff swayed the stems of fertile wild plants with dull-colored blossoms. Only dodders could really thrive here. Their flexible parasitic roots clung like a disease to the coarse soldier-like bodies of the weeds. The tansies, quitches and thistles were probably glad to have their ugliness covered with the fragile beauty of the dodders' tiny delicate flowers.

Liza's father, an insignificant government official, had moved to good old Porozhensk during the war, when it became clear that the world would not be able to get away with all that bloodshed, unscathed. This was before the period of the stop-you-on-your-way brigades and the decree against leaving the cities. The old man brought all his possessions to this small town and bought a little house surrounded by cherry trees. Soon he took to hiding from life even more completely, and only at his funeral dinner did his widow meet their neighbors, who considered them proud and uppish. The Pokhvisnevs had been taken in by the rumors that described Porozhensk as an abundant and carefree paradise and, it must be said, by the legend that some time in the past an ancient tribe had lived there, a tribe without soaring ambitions, but also without promissory notes, medicines and useless palpitations of the heart. The town started to decay after the railroads made their appearance in Russia; Liza opened its not very cheerful chronicle on the last page.

What she found written there was poverty and an ungracious, provincial vulgarity. Soon the Pokhvisnevs experienced this themselves. Their house went to pieces, local wiseacres put a needle into their dog's food and the neighbors, guided by the ancient rule that a stranger's tree burns hotter than one's own log, cut down their cherry trees for firewood. The official's household furniture grew shabby, and all that remained of the family's fortune was about thirty yards of hoarded cloth, which in those days was as good as currency, and a pair of gold earrings—a souvenir of some ridiculous birthday celebration. The mother began to have foot trouble, and her little girl had to find food for both of them. At first she begged; she stretched out her hand, and her eyes were so pure that out of sheer embarrassment people hastened to give her something. She never had enough bread for her mother and herself; some time later she learned to steal it. Every morning she would set out to the ravine, in the Basurmanka suburb. She did not do this out of pity for her mother—poverty is not sentimental; for the time being, it was blind instinct that drove the orphaned little animal out of its lair to seek prey.

At that time there was plenty to steal, the first N.E.P. markets were making their appearance, still timid, still worried about the obsolete decree abolishing private trade. These markets made people's mouths water in floods, they reminded one of the feasts of ancient Rome, the paintings of Snyders and Jordaens, they showed all the treasures disgorged by the charitable earth. Life underwent a magical transformation. From pits, basements and iron chests salesmen crawled out with their merchandise. They looked like the goods they offered; young fellows with sturgeon-like faces drummed on the counters with their fins. Tantalizing apparitions of the dethroned past teased the gloomy older generation so deeply undermined by the war. On yellow rivers of boiled milk with a reddish fat sediment, between shores of smoking edibles, sailed dazzling loaves of porous home-made bread. It was like a splendid funeral of the period of saccharine, rotten herring and potato peelings. People were gorging themselves everywhere, in silence, hiding from their relatives, as though committing a crime. There appeared commodities whose use was only described in dictionaries, that is, whether they were to be swallowed or put on or only smelt after cooking. Professors of the culinary art, with hatred in their fishy eyes, prepared this alluring poison. One could travel all over the country for weeks and without having to leave one's train observe a thousand-mile-long still-life of steaming viands. This Flemish fury, this flagrant orgy of poverty, these temptations made up of all the edible animals that inhabit the air, the water and the earth, was crowned by cakes with icing of paradisiac colors made of butter, sugar and almonds—here were the infamous theses of the old world expressed in the laconic language of the pastry-cook. And it was terrifying and exciting to look into the narrow, ruthless eyes of the enemy who had now approached for a hand-to-hand fight.

Never before had poverty dictated so imperiously the nature of private human relationships. Charity was the only possible form of compromise with the social revolution. In the eyes of the Philistines theft was at that time a sacrilege, a manifestation of insane impudence bordering on heroism.

The people of Basurmanka soon discovered the little girl thief. Jeeringly, with half-closed eyes, they watched her clumsy ruses and, although they knew that she would come to a bad end, they did not arrest her at once; they even encouraged her by pretended indifference —they wanted the fruit to ripen. Thus misers hoard, sacrificing satiety every day; thus children gather strawberries from one patch after another and later stuff themselves in a fit of blissful and cruel wastefulness. The whole market participated in the game with the little ten-year-old sloven, and what she could squeeze into her childish fist was her beggarly compensation for the approaching dénouement.

A truck-farmer from Usterma spoiled the whole game. The people who live there are handsome: the women are like towers as high as the clouds. This particular farmer was like a ruddy-bearded pine tree, in a drab overcoat of a burnt color; he kept peering from one side to another lest he be attacked and robbed of his riches. For the first time after a long interruption he was offering for sale the gifts of Usterma's sandy soil fed by his sweat. Marvellous turnips with pink flanks lay side by side with long-faced carrots of that amusing color which sextons have in the bathhouse; high-cheekboned beets, lilac-colored at the abrasions, affectionately shared their bed with over-ripe cucumbers whose bald, whitish skulls made them look like village elders—they had already acquired a yellowish tint when struck by an early autumn frost. And all this had a sweetly intoxicating smell of fennel, a smell of matter-of-fact plenty, of solid well-being, of a strange but cozy home. Liza felt an irresistible craving for a turnip, and having filched one, she started to jump away from the narrow circle of the carts; but some nuns who had come to beg and who depended entirely on market benefactors stopped her in a narrow lane. She was seized, felt out cynically like a captured beast and brought back. The market moved closer, stood up on its chests and tubs and stared silently at the spectacle.

"Aha, now you're going to be punished, dearie," said the owner of the stolen turnip. "I have some girls at home like you!" And lifting the little thief's dirty skirts he lazily raised his knout. He was about to hit her, using only half his strength, so as not to kill her.

Liza did not cry out or weep, nor did she experience fear; she felt only childish curiosity about these people who in their threatening puerility took her for a grown-up. The red-bearded man did not hit her. "I myself have little ones," the muzhik repeated pensively, with a quite different meaning now. He gave her a slap with his hand, rough from the crust of earth on it, just to abide by the law, and pushed her away. Still holding her turnip Liza fell face downwards, rose and darted off; and everything around her, all those fishes, birds and dead pigs' heads, laughed out excitedly, exulted and clapped hands, as when a bird is released on Annunciation Day.

An enormous huckstress in a man's jacket piped tenderly: "Her little feet, they're so ba-a-are!" and one could see that the pardon had given her a pleasure greater than could any chastisement.

The stolen goods remained in the girl's hands; she ate the turnip—it happened to be a bitter turnip. . . . Thus, little by little, Liza gained experience.

Her school education consisted of the sparse knowledge of two local teachers, sisters; one of them was a hunchback, which had saved her from ferocious officers' caresses when the town was captured by the Whites. The fate of the other sister, who truly loved Liza, was sadder. . . . All her other knowledge Liza got from her mother. The life of this woman had shaped itself in a whimsical and instructive way: she had gone to the Institute, knew languages and music, translated George Sand, travelled abroad—all this only to end up as the wife of an assiduous and luckless dullard, who resorted to all kinds of ventures and was invariably unsuccessful. This prematurely aged, completely disillusioned woman had once dreamed of great passions, but the conditions of her life gradually transformed her good, creative anger into vindictiveness, her love into weak-willed, enthusiastic adoration and the despair that moves the strong to valor into boredom. Her health deteriorated year by year, and since she had no time to educate her daughter gradually, she hastily communicated to her what she had learned directly from life—crumbling, putrid, intellectual raw material, from which an honest, weak or deceitful person could have drawn different and contradictory inferences.

Imperiously holding her frightened little daughter by the hand, she led her through the most extraordinary experiences, now taking her to an imaginary museum full of indescribable treasures, which she herself had never understood, now dragging her to a morgue where corpses of human hearts were displayed in the most unexpected cross-sections and deformities. She brought the child close to the black pits of her former life, the very breath of which was defiling. Whatever she looked at shrivelled and blackened. However, her dubious wisdom was many-sided. From her words it appeared that life was a slow and merciful killing; that three darknesses—those of youth, health and joy—veil the light of truth; that men betray out of slovenliness, and women out of grandeur and grief. Since she had to leave her daughter prematurely to other people's mercy, she injected the poison of her disillusionment into the young girl so as to protect her from being destroyed by evil at the very outset. Her lessons were memorized all the more readily because the disgusting life of the small town served as a graphic illustration. And when Liza could not grasp a thing at once, her mother had enough patience to explain it to her twice and even thrice.

Thus, sitting on a stool at her mother's swollen, almost elephantine feet, the eleven-year-old Liza learned the rudiments of the art of handling people. True, her mother also taught her the superficial, spineless culture she herself had; the daughter uncritically absorbed all this motley inheritance of uneven value. Her mother's stories about historical events were strangely captivating when their subject-matter even remotely reminded the aging woman of her own fate. The story of Mary Stuart—this queen too was transformed to resemble the narrator —remained forever in Liza's memory as her first childhood trauma. Her mother told it, as though looking at herself in a mirror, it was the sad tale of a beautiful and unfortunate woman betrayed by her partisans, insulted by her lovers and erased from the memory of her kin. An almost insignificant event fixed this romantic image in Liza's mind.

That summer the Pokhvisnevs had as a boarder the stage manager of a stock company; he was also its director and acted all kinds of character parts. It was he who took the little Porozhensk sloven to her first theatrical performance. The sunset, which covered half the sky, was red and silent as after an execution, and only the scaffold was lacking to make the impression complete. Evening fires were burning. On the wooden sign swollen from rain and splashed with red paint there were pictures of an axe and a crown, and an inscription in parentheses read: "incident in the life of a queen." The author's name was not mentioned; and Schiller could hardly claim the parentage of this provincial melodramatic rehash with songs, dances and additional "attractions" introduced by the impresario. And the poor .actors! . . . Dressed in brightly colored rags they grimaced before a half empty hall, shamelessly listening for every rustle of approval. In the middle of their monologues their noses broke off, pillars collapsed upon them and the box-office treasurer peeped out from backstage to get an idea of the house. But even amidst the ruins, and under the treasurer's jaundiced eye, these young people continued reigning, fighting and loving. Thus had also been born the comedy of masks! . . . Sir Dudley called the state secretary an arse and a lazy dog, and the latter kicked His Highness' behind. As for Liza, she was equally captivated by the rhythmic speech of the actors, the picture-postcard sufferings of the queen, the cheap tricks of the low farce comedian and even the muddled plot which no one in Porozhensk could make head or tail of.

For an entire week Liza lived in a kind of pensive torpor. . . . Porozhensk grew too tight for her; and although the ancient walls around the town had not been preserved, it seemed impossible to get out of it. Suddenly she disappeared. . . . Here one might tell a long and marvellous story of a child who all alone and unaided wandered through the abysses and wolves' dens of life, and how all evil shied away from her calm and innocent eyes. By long circuitous routes she reached Oblono. Travelling troupes, vestiges of the days of war communism, still existed. As a child without kin Liza was admitted to a travelling theatre. Thus her independent experience as an actress began. She played children's parts. From village to village, over endless frozen dirt roads, she was driven on a peasant's sledge, miserable and happy in her misery, wrapped in whatever happened to be on hand, and the benevolent greenish star, guardian of the homeless, accompanied her in the sky.

She returned home three years later; her mother was still alive, but bedridden. Poverty is terrible in Porozhensk. The daughter entered and squatted down near the door. She was fifteen years old. Her mother passed a finger over her face. Her daughter was alive, that was the main thing.

"What have you been doing?" she asked.

"We gave plays . . . about the life in capitalist countries." Her pupils darkened and the tips of her fingers began to tremble. "In a peasant house . . . crowds of people . . . everyone wants to get in, and there's no room. Once some boys began to smash the windows out of spite. I was so scared. . . ."

"What have you been eating?"

"Oh, everything!"

"Where did you sleep?"

She had slept on a theatre curtain: one can sleep quite well on them!

"No one hurt you?"

Liza shook her head uncertainly: "Oh, I was everyone's pet!"

Her mother smiled at her reticence. Everyone's—that meant no one's. Oh, surely, the child must have had her reasons for fleeing from this happiness back to the dark hole of Porozhensk! Her mother ordered her to undress and began to patch up her rags. Liza's sortie was a fail-

ure, and the mean Porozhensk life began again. Six months later Liza
was an orphan; the house had to be sold.

For the next three years Liza impatiently awaited the return of the
troupe, but the old theatre had failed with such a bang that no new
theatrical daredevils risked a venture in Porozhensk. The dramatic
Muse avoided this place with fear. The local artisans and tough N.E.P.
merchants were not Maecenases or idlers. They preferred to attend the
free spectacles of the "living" church of St. Simeon-the-God-Receiver-
on-the-Precipice, which had acquired a powerful tenor. All the summer he single-handedly and quite successfully competed with the
gypsy circuses that camped in the suburbs. During the third year,
thanks to the efforts of the bored authorities, there finally arrived a
theatre composed half of youthful enthusiasts and half of old-time,
penniless actors. The local newspaper loudly publicized this cultural
undertaking, and their success was enormous and inexplicable. The
plain board walls of the temporary theatre almost broke down from
the pressure of the crowds. . . . Liza went to see almost every performance and learned the whole repertoire by heart. She had reasons for
making such efforts to obtain passes: she was taking the range carefully before making a new jump into life.

Among the members of the company, supercilious and without talent, there was one actor with a resounding, almost fanfare-like name,
which sounded like a title. He was Ksaveryi Valerianovich Dnestrov-
Zakurdaev the Second. On the bill this name was put at the head of
the list, like a luxurious sample, a hint of the survival of the ancient
theatrical dynasties. He was deeply respected by the authorities, lived
in a hotel and walked about in a tailcoat of demoniac model scaring
all the nuns and goats in Porozhensk. Liza chose him as her patron.
One day she came to see him, like the heroine of one of their plays,
with a little bouquet of late cornflowers in her hand, timid, radiant, an
angel of good tidings. Her thin collar-bones protruded from her dress.
. . . As she approached the great artist's temple she did not know what
she would say to him. In the doorway her dress caught on a hook;
something ripped. Her head drooped, she became completely flustered.

The genius sat at an open window, absent-mindedly staring at the
clock-tower now reddened by a watery sunset. He was sipping an
alcoholic concoction he had invented himself. That was his way of
preparing for the performance. That night he was scheduled to lose his
mind in *Arbenin.*

". . . I have something to tell you," said Liza, her head still drooping
and her hands hanging humbly down the sides of her baize skirt.

He turned his head with a regal air. This girl had appeared at a moment of headache and melancholy. Fat black flies buzzed above him, behind him and in front of him, they crawled on his hands; insensitive and magnanimous, he did not chase them away.

"Speak, maiden." Zakurdaev encouraged the little one and patronizingly waved his hand. He was rehearsing a gesture from *Masquerade* which he found hard to master.

As truthfully as she could Liza explained that she loved the theatre with all her heart, that she had tried to get parts in amateur productions, that she had not made any headway, that she wanted to die on the stage, that she had a job as secretary in the Transport Union, that she had come to ask his advice and finally that she was in love with him. Zakurdaev staunchly withstood this barrage and only at her last words recoiled from her as from the devil. However, something like exaltation surged up from the very depths of his soul. His little visitor's look was intent and sorrowful, as though she knew the emptiness of his wandering life and understood the wrinkles on his face, seamed like the crossroads at Basurmanka on market day. She loved him with the ridiculous love of an innocent, stage-struck provincial girl. He was frightened: he imagined that death itself dressed as a virgin had come to visit him. He shuddered, but the chill down the spine was pleasurable.

"Me? . . . Impossible!" And he laughed for a long time, impressively and artificially, and pushed his Oriental skullcap down over one eye. "And how long have you loved me?" He kept laughing and looked askance at her with his triangular pupils faded from alcohol. "Well . . . and what exactly do you feel?"

She blushed. No, her feelings could not yet be defined! They were a product of fear, rapture, adoration and obedience to a higher power. She enumerated his parts, quoting excerpts verbatim; she evaluated each in a naïve, but apt manner. A woman praising an artist to his face always seems to him a paragon of intelligence and tact—and this one praised even his weaknesses. Zakurdaev fidgeted, stroked his eyebrows, twisted their ends into little circles and cast an occasional glance at his ring, set with an opal of convulsive hue. This simple girl with her penny bouquet flattered his vanity more than the baskets of roses he had dreamed of at the beginning of his career. For the first time in his life he was afraid of a woman, he was embarrassed and mistrustful, he wanted confirmation.

"Do you drink port wine?" he shouted suddenly at the top of his voice. "Local vintage, by special order grade A, *for export*. The manager sent me some."

She smiled a perplexed little smile, and throwing back her head slowly drank what he poured for her from a bottle black as sin. The liquor spread to her very heart, and the furniture danced before her eyes; the game had begun, retreat was now impossible. A thick and muddy feeling took possession of her; she was slightly nauseated. The port was mixed with substances that were Zakurdaev's secret. Drops of its spicy bitterness smouldered on her lips for a long time. An hour remained before the show. Zakurdaev told her to tell him everything she knew. He needed time to think over this encounter. She said she did not understand what he wanted.

"I want you to tell me what life is like here. What are its characteristic manifestations?"

Liza nodded her head and smiled. "Life here is free, but dull," she began, spreading her little fingers wide.

"Speak louder. The acoustics are bad here. Ah? . . . And I'll listen to your diction."

The poison she had absorbed must have begun to operate. Now her eyes were brilliant, and incisive words came easily. She began with her childhood and instead of giving him all the details methodically, she told only picturesque bits and then went on to the next thing. Her tale included the description of a flock of jackdaws that settled like soot on the trees at nightfall. ("The boys would knock them down with sticks to have something to play funerals with. We used to wrap them in silver-foil and bury them like bishops. I like sad games!") She also related a visit to the Schengin dunes with some girl friends. Here, rumor had it, was a common grave containing a hundred White gangsters who had been executed. ("Night was falling when we arrived. Something black was sticking out of the mound. I fancied it was the black arm of the man who did a vile thing to my teacher, Aunt Glasha —she was so nice to me. I took a big stone and threw it. The arm, seemed to break at its root and drop. It turned out to be only a stick, and there was no grave there at all; the bodies had all been taken to Moscow. I was in my eleventh year then.") Her story touched upon the nuns from the many closed convents in the neighborhood. ("When will the devil finally take you all, fleas that you are, swarming wood termites!" the chief of the local militia would exclaim, horrified by the tremendous numbers of these creatures. But the old women only bowed to the ground and replied maddeningly in chorus: "We are always ready to receive the crown of martyrdom, little father commissar!") And she concluded her story by mentioning the marvellous, abundant lilacs of Porozhensk, which the small town thought an excuse for its numerous rats, its muddy streets and the drunken rioting of its inhabitants.

"It's called skylac here," Liza said with a childish smile (she had not dropped one word about her first independent sortie in life), and the genius growled and closed his eyes like a beast, as though the last bright ray of sunset had fallen on his now decrepit paw.

"You tell your story with style," Zakurdaev said solemnly and thunderously in his raucous voice. "An electric current seems to emanate from you. A liturgy! Aha! let's have more of it, Lizenok!"

She went on to the provincial gossip, the secrets and monstrous happenings of the little town. Her stories reminded one of frescoes on a church wall. Dark, shrivelled, sinful bodies, singed in the fire of their own evil deeds, piled up fantastically before Zakurdaev. And she herself, squeezed in among them, was striving to break away from this terrifying ring, to be taken out by any saviour into some other kind of life. Oh, what things the ancient Russian devil had piled up in that infamous box that was Porozhensk! An old woman murdered her son for joining the Komsomols. ("With an axe!" Liza's eyes gleamed.) A merchant who sold tape at the dry goods stalls ("You know, springs, hair, sofa stuffings!") took up with a young nun and abandoned his family. ("And he has eight sons, all of them little boys!") The cow belonging to the militia gave birth to a five-legged calf. ("The fifth leg was cut off . . . and the animal died.") The chief priest of the cathedral hanged himself in his vestments at the altar when informed that the cathedral was to be closed. ("And underneath him all the scraps of his torn-up Bible were scattered.") Zakurdaev listened, taking little sips, now smiling, now shuddering when physically excited by some word of Liza's. His skullcap kept slipping on his head.

"The earth like water contains gases. . . . These were the bubbles of the earth!" he intoned in a profound voice.

And this erotic pirate, this cuttlefish in a jacket, this soured cucumber made up to look like Mirabeau, began to believe that the provincial girl was really in love with his booming voice, his hair all grey from dandruff, his golden studs and cockish-like Adam's apple. This conviction came to him all the more easily because in former times his professional tours in the provinces had been accompanied by extraordinary successes with women. He picked them out like a sniper and seduced them methodically. Rarely did one withstand his pressure. His tempo surpassed all previous records. By his own admission his exploits were second only to those of Pietro Luigi Farnese, the son of the pope, who once took advantage of an archbishop lost in contemplation. He was a merciless scourge of virgins, a terror of husbands, a devourer of innocence and good repute. It was said that even abandoned mistresses who had no hope of renewing their relations with him nevertheless preserved a warm and grateful feeling for him, mingled with wonderment. It was clear that Ksaveryi had been very handsome in his youth.

But all that was far behind him now. The monster was becoming decrepit, heavier and, something that no one knew, deaf. He shouted his parts almost by rote. His ephemeral fame as a homebreaker was fading. New names and records were coming up. He had to use more and more effort to conquer fortresses that formerly had surrendered at his approach. In addition, his salary was cut, his physicians forbade him to drink and that ancient institution of benefit performances, the sweetest jewel in the crown of the provincial theatre, was replaced by jubilee shows for the whole company; it was no longer possible to celebrate oneself twice a year! The walls of custom were beginning to crumble. Old age with a dirty broom in its hand was peeping in at the doorway. This explains why Zakurdaev so cordially received the pure little savage who with her gift of laurels brought back to him his youth.

"What a wheedler you are! . . . Say again that you love me. Again . . . three times is not enough! Shout it in my ear, more loudly. God will punish you if you lie at such a moment. . . ."

For him this was an hour of rapture mingled with horror. As never before he was burned by a fleshly desire to possess this woman: but his desire remained unsatisfied. Everything became mixed up in his mind. Thus, in the sunset of his life, love was destroying him. In his confusion he told Liza that a woman's tears shed at his request sufficed for him: he did not want to ruin his "last love." He removed his opal ring and almost dropped it on the young girl's thin finger. Scarcely concealing her fright she gave the jewel back to him. "Only in fairytales does one become betrothed to a dragon!" And although she trembled and felt sick at her stomach, on the way home she laughed at Zakurdaev's forced magnanimity. Her mother's lessons proved useful. She carried out her designs to the last detail. She did not come back to see him for a whole week. He was tormented by his fear of losing a treasure that was inaccessible and that yet belonged to him alone. He waited for Liza, frankly scanned the audience from the stage, questioned the people of Porozhensk about her; and when he was alone he repeated her name in a singing voice. She returned when he had become completely hollow-cheeked with yearning for her. When he saw her, his eyebrows contorted like stung caterpillars. With deep emotion he asked her what was her dearest wish. She told him. Then he swore that within six years she would play Mary Stuart on a stage in the capital. He accepted the proposal of a new company that he take a second-rank position at a reduced salary, only in order not to lose Liza.

He cunningly tried to prove to her that it took time to acquire the very first rudiments of the high art of acting. The season was ending; Liza agreed to go to Moscow. Zakurdaev had friends there more successful than himself. For Liza it was a matter of indifference who would begin moulding her into a great actress.

The day before her departure, she made the rounds of the small town. "But whence came the name of Porozhensk?" She visited Aunt Glasha's sister. The little hunchback was still alive and teaching; her face had acquired a dried-up air of saintliness, which made Liza feel ashamed. The schoolmistress did not approve of the trip but . . . "So be it!" she said. Liza also passed her own old house—a cobbler had moved into it; a pair of dashing boots, the symbol of his trade, were stuck in the window where once she had sat her home-made rag dolls. Yellow leaves covered her mother's grave. The days were growing shorter. The season of fires, gossip, amateur theatricals and drunken brawls with knife-plays in Basurmanka was approaching. It seemed to Liza that no power on earth could ever bring her back here.

Cautiously putting her feet down so as not to leave her shoes behind in the drenched clay soil Liza went out to the Basurmanka suburb. With cold curiosity she walked amid unwieldy primitive carts used for transporting bread and dung, the dead and the newly married. From all the stalls spiteful, hostile eyes followed her. They were beginning to be squeezed, the merchants of Basurmanka. . . . Everything was soaking wet. The late sun could not conquer the mire of Porozhensk. Weary from her walk, Liza climbed out of her old ravine on its further side and sat down on the slippery protruding roots of a birch. She could see everything from here. Near the church pigskins were being delivered. An enthusiastic cyclist was pushing his way down the crowded street, still astride his bicycle. Chickens were picking a path in the wet red clay. From the market, carts were leaving in all directions; their thin matchlike shafts gleamed. The mound was a high one. Liza felt as if she were looking out of the window of a dirigible 'cutting through eternity. Above the distant woods hung fringes of raindrops like a tattered theatre curtain. It swayed and came down quickly. The first act of her drama was ending.

Until it began to rain in earnest she sat there singing all the songs she knew. She wanted to guess at least in outline the content of the second act. She did not yet know that very soon this jabbering old man would become burdensome and useless to her; that she would throw him out, calling him a deaf monster. And all this would come about so naturally that their neighbors would not even suspect they had quarrelled, although Zakurdaev would leave in a state almost of apoplexy.

Even now she was tired of his confessions about the battalions of girls he had kissed and the gallons of wine he had drunk. His own deafness would complete the work of poetic justice on Zakurdaev. (She had already seen how in the middle of a performance he had once forgotten his part; turning his back to the audience he had convulsively twisted the napkin in his hand and stamped the floor in a rage.) As things turned out, the Moscow public did not take to Ksaveryi. He wanted his old fame and easy life, he did not want to have to work and be young. He would be dismissed from his last position for drunkenness and debauchery. All his connections would break up. . . .

Thus, before climbing the second rung of the enormous ladder leading to life, Liza took farewell of her childhood, ironically thankful for the lessons she had received in this practical school of dishonesty, humiliation and minor affliction.

# CHAPTER 12

# Friends

AT A MEETING OF regional chiefs in November, Kurilov again met Marina. She came in at the very end of the session and sat down in a corner on the window-sill. And for some reason the second half of Kurilov's concluding speech had a harsh note addressed to no one in particular. Despite slight fluctuations the railroad was climbing out of the slump; however, all other economic indices were reaching record figures at that period. The newspapers spoke of the profound interdependence of all the sections of the economic organism; the objective was now that the workers' newly acquired good qualities should become habitual. . . . Kurilov did not wish to see Marina. Immediately after his speech he went to his office, hoping that she would leave in the meanwhile. He lit his pipe and walked back and forth in the darkness.

At home his friends had been waiting for him for more than an hour; he had at last invited them to sit down with him over a bottle of wine, to recall the past and discuss the future. But somewhere near the door Marina was watching for him, and he was annoyed at himself for having become intimate with an employee of his own organization, even in conversation. He began to remember how it had happened, and his very thoughts compelled him to approach the window. Drops of rain were hanging on the glass outside. The overcast autumn sky was lilac-colored with a yellowish light in it; the wind was blowing, and the air was frosty. Noiselessly he opened the window and looked out. The denuded trees rustled and groaned. Ruslan was naked, his curved ribs were swaying. A gust of wind blew the big drops of rain against Kurilov's forehead. . . . He closed his eyes, accustomed them to the darkness. Underneath the window the yard was not empty, a couple was there again. Their silhouettes could be accurately divined against the background of dappled autumn puddles. More, in the darkness a patch of the girl's neck shone, and "he" kissed it protractedly and soundlessly. . . . This vacant plot was probably known to all the lovers of the district.

Kurilov imagined that under the patter of the rain he could distinguish their whisper:

"How it's pounding . . . even through your blouse."

"It's young, and you're a fool. . . . Let go."

"Your mouth smells of caramel candy! Give me your ear . . . I'll tell you something."

And a moment later: "Let me go, I'm cold."

Oh, Kurilov heard even the things they did not say. His coat was damp now, his mustache had grown heavy and moist. He had a bitterish taste on his lips as though they had touched the girl's moist cheeks. Surely, Marina must have left long ago, despairing of finding an opportunity to speak to him, and yet, although he felt ashamed to steal from these poor children, some magnetic force kept him there. He had a feeling akin to envy for that intoxicating freedom that is part of any youth. This time once more he could not make up his mind to drive them away, but only. . . . He must have that window tightly plastered to protect himself from temptations!

He went downstairs. All the employees had gone. The watchwoman was making the rounds of the deserted corridors. And there, in the cloak-room, Marina approached him. She did not know how to begin.

"Haven't you left yet?" he said sternly, thinking of Penza.

"Yes, I've already come back."

To be sure, he had forgotten that three months had passed since the night he had taken her home with her potatoes.

"I was told that you wanted to leave the railroad. I have no objections."

"I cannot leave until I finish your biography."

"What do you want of me, Sabelnikova?"

She was obviously losing courage and at the same time was pleased at her own perseverance.

"I have done a great deal of work on it . . . I have a lot of interesting propaganda material on the leading personalities of your railroad. But without you, Alexei Nikitich, the list would be incomplete. I could drop in any time and take some notes. All I need is dates, the rest I can develop myself. A proletarian childhood, the factory, revolutionary activity, persecution, hard labor. . . ."

He burst out laughing. "Well, if by hard labor you mean our railroad, go ahead. . . ." Kurilov had never been sentenced to hard labor. "Isn't your name Marina?"

Marina lowered her eyes. "You have a good memory," she said, smiling.

Kurilov looked at her from the side, he fancied that her last remark was a hint. No, she was not reminding him of anything. She was an unassuming rank-and-file worker, one of many, uncomplicated, without curls or frills, round-cheeked, with straightly parted, smooth hair; and only her eyes, her shining, all-comprehensive, feminine eyes compensated for this excessive simplicity. She had a red scratch on her nose; she embarrassedly covered it with her fingers. They were red, her knitted blouse was not very warm. Now and then Marina stuck her hands into her pockets trying to warm them or to give her knitted garment at least some form, but then she remembered about her nose. . . . And so, she lacked gestures for talking with Kurilov!

"Fine," he said angrily. Every minute another icy draft from the door enveloped them. "Let's do it at the end of the week. How about the twenty-fourth, in the morning?"

He had not yet put on his coat when his secretary took Marina's place.

"Have mercy on me, Feshkin, I'm in a hurry. Fifteen people are waiting for me. Aha, the figures, let's have them!"

Monotonously, following his chief's face, Feshkin reported the summary of the day's activities. The curve showed a tendency to drop. The first frosts were having their effect: subsoil waters loosened the ballast layer, the cars shook more than before, the number of alarms was increasing, the index of commercial traffic was down. It was November.

". . . And you asked me to inquire" (he checked on his piece of paper) "about Khozhatkin. There is no such person employed on the road. The watchman of the fourth sector is Omelichev, Pavel Stepanovich. He did two years' compulsory labor and was released as having proved his social usefulness. He was formerly a shipowner and. . . ."

"Go on!"

"But there are reports that he has changed his cabin into a kind of inn, that he charges ten rubles for a bed and sells wine. As for Protoklitov, his party organization gave him quite a good reference. Rather coarse, but careful and punctual; he has asked to be allowed to study. He has never been punished, tried or suspected. The inquiry about him caused surprise. . . ." Feshkin's face was sympathetic, but at heart he shared Kurilov's exaggerated vigilance. As a rule, secretaries are not very liberal; they play the role of breakwaters before safe havens. "No, Alexei Nikitich, I'm sorry to say, he seems to be irreproachable."

"I know. Has he gone through the party cleansing yet? Aha, then find out when his case is to be taken up. Is that all?"

". . . And I found the name and address of the old man who forgot his books. They were from the lending library and such places keep accurate lists of their customers. His name is Pokhvisnev. . . ." Once more he looked at his paper.

"Let me have it, thank you. And another thing, don't plaster my window this winter. It usually makes it stick and . . . there's no other way to ventilate the room. . . ."

Almost in the doorway the chief of the Regional Political Bureau tried to detain him; the commission for making economies had taken a car away from him, but Kurilov decided that this case could wait until the next morning. He drove home. Halfway to the apartment he took out the key to his English lock. The door opened noiselessly. "Hello, friends!" he said in the doorway to announce his presence. He was met noisily; some of the men whistled at him for his lateness and there was an outburst of comradely affectionate ejaculations. They called him "a handsome railroadman," "the terror of the redcaps" (because before the revolution the station masters had worn red caps) and even "chief-wrecker." No one called him a walrus, as in the old times: that nickname had been Catherine's. This friendly rumpus had been prepared by common agreement. And while Kurilov rummaged in his pockets for his pipe and went out to change and wash his hands, a respectful silence prevailed at the table.

Hiding a smile in his mustache, Kurilov circled around to press a dozen hands that were stretched out to him. Dealing out joke for joke, he asked Tiutchev whether he had not been fired from the theatre he directed because of his usual "tricks"; he wondered whether Arkind had exported his once abundant head of hair; he asked Ivanov, a public health inspector in a Volga district, whether he had at least learned to order alcohol from a drugstore; he reminded Vaska Ananiev, a friend from his days of exile, how they had once caught fish together by torchlight on the Angara and how Vaska's son Fedoska had fallen into the water. It appeared that Fedosyi Vasilievich was now an engineer in the Donbas and had a ten-year-old daughter. The young generation was inconspicuously filling the gaps in the fighting ranks. "The children are growing up, they're getting calluses and mustaches," Vasilyi Ananiev said with virile approval.

Kurilov promised Stesha, an old machine-gunner and friend of Catherine's, to find a husband for her, a dashing Ingush in a long Caucasian coat with silver braid, and when he came to Arsentyich he simply squeezed him in a close and wordless embrace. Panting, the old fellow defended himself from this rough caress.

"Well, how are your birds, old man?"

"I'm going to cast another one . . ."—he did not even utter the word "bloomery"; it was implied—"and that will be that! They make a great fuss about them." (Arsentyich's birds were no doubt living on Kurilov's Ocean.)

Efim Arsentyich happened to be sitting in a corner, apart from the general gaiety. All evening he was solemn and inaccessible. He was meeting most of these men for the first time and, in an old man's way, he envied Kurilov his friends. He took no part in the conversation and found fault with little details. The table was just what you would expect from a widower: it had no tablecloth; it was crowded with bottles and all sorts of tin cans but there were more bottles than tins. The old man knitted his brows heavily; Arsentyich himself had been a widower for years. Now a hand entered his field of vision; on the cuff above it hung a mother-of-pearl stud. "May I start serving?" someone asked. Arsentyich raised stern eyes. The hand and voice belonged to Sashka Tiutchev. However, before beginning to pass the dishes Sashka asked casually whether Kurilov often received a visit from his redoubtable sister. "Oh, she does not like me!" he whispered. "Nor me!" said Tabuntsov. "Nor me, . . ." Savva joined in bitterly. Kurilov set his friends at ease. Even before his misfortune Klavdia had not visited her brother more than once a month, yet her attachment to Catherine was known to everyone.

The mention of this name made everyone fall silent for a moment. During the hard years Catherine had been a laundress, a cook, a comrade and a mother to all of them.

"She was a handy woman!" said Arsentyich and suddenly he raised his voice, turning purple in the face. "Eh, they burned themselves up, they didn't spare themselves! Open a bottle, bald young man!"

The feast began. The big pitcher with a heavy black Caucasian liquid went around. Slightly stooped over the table Kurilov ate earnestly, from each side dish in turn. But before they had drunk to this reunion of friends, Kutenko rose from his seat. It happened to be Kurilov's birthday, and Kutenko was given the floor on the assumption that his speech would be devoted to the achievements of the host. Some of those present were already laughing up their sleeves; Kutenko, a non-party man, had the reputation of being a heretic and a poet. The apprehensions of the cynics were confirmed; in a high, cocklike voice, he began to speak about friendship, which is carried away and smashed against the stones by the stream of time with its fearsome rapids. In addition, he stuttered; his words tormented him for a long time before seeing the light of day, as her infant torments a woman in travail. No one looked at him. The subject of his speech was the honor and valor of his generation, ready to fight to the last man and die without grumbling, so that on this ladder of heroic dead young phalanxes of fighters might climb ever higher and scale the greatest peaks.

In his emotion he made slips of the tongue: ". . . We started out in life as young and ungainly fellows. You, Aliosha, in a factory; I, in a factory office. The road was long. We sang to keep up our spirits on the way. Let us admit that at first our song had a purely folk character ... but a fair wind struck it like a sail, it straightened out and acquired a new resonance. We were lifted, whirled and hurled against the citadel. Our youth exploded, and into the breach irrupted the assault troops of our class. We had no time to do the things we wanted to do; we have done much roughly and hastily. But let us rest easy on this score; those who will come after us will put out enormous, often slovenly and rough plans into a harmonious order. . . ."

Kutenko was lanky and tall. Those who sat near him could see the passionate play of the muscles in his neck and face. Now he had almost stopped stuttering. Occasionally, as though to reassure himself, he cast a glance at Kurilov, who continued eating.

"Go on talking," Kurilov encouraged the orator, winking at him. "I haven't had any dinner today. I had to survey the condition of the whole railroad, it was a terrific day. Go on talking!"

". . . The breach we made was wreathed around with branches, decorated with flags: it became a triumphal arch leading to the future. Under it our successors pass with a springy athletic stride. Let us glance at their faces: we shall not flatter ourselves, fundamental things are at stake now. But orchestras are thundering, and the parade continues. We did not march that way, Kurilov! They sing of a locomotive flying like an arrow and scheduled to stop at a Communist society. But although we are all self-taught we know this much of Hegel and Heraclitus: the stream does not stop, and it always carries in itself everything that is needed for the realization of life."

Apparently he wished to express the idea that new, hitherto untried economic and technological phases may produce unknown social forms. Trying to outshout the fanfare with which the new era was being built, he asked the youth whether they knew from what sewers and graveyards the generation that was aging had rescued them. Did they know at what price these breaches in the wall of centuries had been opened? What great achievements were slowed up by no less respectable errors? How often the best of the insurgents perished because their élan was not guided by reason and knowledge, but expressed itself only in momentary outbursts of hunger, wrath or despair? And did they also know that the last drive for the transformation of the planet would be accompanied by unprecedented civil wars, epidemics and terrible uprisings? He did not ask: "Are you with us?" but: "Are you ready?" And he was forgetting that the beginning had already been made, that people enter into productive relations the moment they are born.

"Don't wear us out; finish, Kostia!" said Tiutchev, whose face had become flushed.

"Kutenko, our birthday child has bribed you to prevent us from drinking his wine," Arkind remarked with a cold smile.

Kutenko acknowledged the reproach as though it had been uttered by a million voices. "I understand you, Matvey. No, it is not doubt that speaks through me. The world is a motor that youth sets in motion. The new generation learned the social value of bread and joy at an early date. The title of man, which formerly we took for granted, many of them have earned by supreme courage and work. But remember, it is in them that the sprouts of future classless relations are maturing, of tomorrow's morality and a new, Socialist humanity. . . . And so, let us drink to the example of higher social friendship that binds together two successive generations! To youth, to our future which certainly neither you nor I will see!"

He drank almost alone, cleared his throat and sat down. Before him there was a plate of sausage, he moved it closer. He happened to pick up a piece of cartilage.

"Don't scrape your knife, Kostia," Stesha said, "the sound grates on my very fingernails!"

"You're a good man, Kutenko, but a provincial," Tiutchev remarked casually. "I still have a book of your early poems. They're bad! You've changed very little since that time. What has frightened you, old man?"

Kutenko kept an annoyed silence without raising his eyes. Everyone felt somewhat ashamed of the doubts expressed by the orator. But this was the same Kutenko who had once been in prison with Arkind, who together with Savva had robbed a bank and together with Kurilov had fled from court-martial. That time Kurilov had been arrested first, but his captors would have strung up Kutenko before him to shut his mouth as soon as possible. Passionate human warmth had always emanated from him. He had once been attacked for maintaining that the social maturity of a class in art is acquired through tragedy, and he assumed that the tragedy of the future might consist in biological extinction.

It was necessary to erase the bad impression created by their comrade's mistake, and Tiutchev was the first to realize this. With the stony face of a tavern actor he began to demonstrate all kinds of magic tricks to Stesha and Arsentyich. He stuck a dessert knife into his chest and with a mystical whistle extracted it from the back of his neck. Or taking a glass he struck its bottom with pretended strength, and a worn silver coin emerged from under it. Laughing and baring her gold teeth (which replaced the ones that had once been knocked out while she served in the Intelligence Department), Stesha gathered together a whole pile of coins, and Tiutchev pretended to stamp them. Raising himself a little, Arsentyich shook his head in distress: the records of his bloomeries were being left far behind.

"Come on, you Philistines!" cried Tiutchev, perspiring and puffing his cheeks. "Give me some gold and diamond objects . . . I will drop them into myself and return them in the shape of any domestic utensils you desire. What, you have no gold? . . . No diamonds grace your necks? Then I'll a-ask. . . ."

And although it was a shame to interrupt the gaiety, Kurilov rose now. "Give him the floor!" resounded from all sides. Only Stesha went on laughing at Ananiev, who, competing with Sashka, pulled himself up from his seat by his greying hair.

"And so, Kutenko, in your opinion, socialism is for those who will survive. You even spoke of friendship from the point of view of our common fate, rather than our community of social interests," Kurilov began, and everyone understood how he was going to take his friend to task. "But now, as I look at your faces, those dear familiar old beans, I see myself multiplied in them. All of you are fragments of my own life; that is because we made our lives together, guided by the same purpose. Each of you separately is my friend. I did not bring you together, I did not introduce you to each other, and yet you are each other's friends, too. And if I fall out of this circle, your friendship will remain unchanged. It binds you by an iron and rational discipline, it does not spoil or disintegrate—let us not even mention those who betrayed it! Of this friendship you should have spoken, not of the dead or the unborn ones, Kostia."

"Now hold on, Kutenko!" Arkind threatened him facetiously.

"I see all of myself in you. I made friends with you, Arsentyich, at Lessner's. You were younger then, and your hair was thicker. You were already getting a ruble, while I had to sell myself for forty kopeks a day. You liked to talk with me and one day, to crown our talks, you brought me to a place on the Peterhof highway. It was a Sunday. The house belonged to an undertaker. In the window stood a showy pyramid of coffins; on the very top, I recall, there was a lady's coffin, all made of silver and lace. We sat down; someone strummed on a mandolin; there was vodka on the table. Then Lenin came in. He wore an alpaca coat with wet stains on the back. It had been a rainy month, and now and then a little shower came down. At that time life was very simple. Lenin read us a report on fines in the factories. I didn't understand much of it—I suppose I was satisfied with my forty kopeks. Moreover, I was proud: the day before I had beaten up a police inspector, Gagin, and taken to my heels. Two faces merge in my mind: yours, Arsentyich, and Lenin's. And I still remember that he dropped a pencil, and both of you bent down to pick it up and gave each other a hard bump on the head. . . ."

"But he didn't let me pick up his pencil," Arsentyich interrupted him in a low and firm voice.

"After that I spoke with him only once, when I came as a representative from the Committee of Military Delegates. It was in the Smolny, a tremendous amount of work was being done. A plywood screen was set up in the reception room, and the Social Revolutionaries jeered that with it the construction of socialism had begun. Lenin didn't recognize me, and I didn't dare remind him of our first meeting. Those were interesting days! I had only just opened Pushkin, I tried to attend school on Sundays and draw Laocoön. Shakespeare was still ahead. I struggled hard over Engels, and lots of things simply could not penetrate my dull brain at all. . . ."

A telephone ring interrupted him. Savva, who sat nearest the receiver, picked it up.

"It's from the railroad, Alexei," he said.

Kurilov apologized to his friends and bent over the little table. He listened, gloomily twisting one side of his mustache around his finger. ". . . How many? . . . fifteen meters high?" he said emphasizing this number in a surprised tone. "Very well, I'm leaving. Attach my car to the night express to Revizan. Has the salvage train gone out?" He turned to his guests. "Go on, eat and enjoy yourselves without me. I've received an urgent call from somewhere . . ."

His secretiveness was useless, everyone had guessed the nature of this emergency. Having said a hurried farewell, Kurilov walked toward the door amid general silence. He stopped halfway, and his face looked as though he had forgotten something but could not remember exactly what. He caught sight of Sashka; gritting his teeth and stretching himself in a strange way, Kurilov stared at him. Confused, Tiutchev moved to another place, but Kurilov continued staring at the spot, at an impersonal and dusty wall. His friends surrounded him, took his hands, but he remained silent and repeated the same gesture as though asking for quiet.

"Wh-a-at . . . it's drilling in my back," he said finally with wonder and effort. "Now, it's coming again . . . and again. . . ."

All through the fall his lumbago had not left him. Now his pain came in waves, cut across his back diagonally and got stuck somewhere under his knee. Kurilov recalled his deceased mother, how she pined away from lumbago, which the village quack had treated with an axe and incantations. . . . His friends cast furtive glances at his ashen face. A chair was pushed under him and at first he did not understand what was expected of him. His pain absorbed all his attention. The toast remained untouched; Kutenko was forgotten.

"Will you please phone the railroad," Alexei Nikitich said hoarsely to no one in particular, "and tell them that I won't be able to leave in *this* condition. Let Martinson go." (Martinson was his deputy.)

Alexei Nikitich looked at each of his friends in turn, with a pitiable and guilty expression. He bashfully told them of his unfortunate ride on the engine. At once a kind of medical council was formed around the *nachpodor* of the Volga-Revizan line. Everyone knew the surest and quickest way of curing lumbago. No one doubted that this was the trouble. In addition to aspirin, they recommended gentle massage, ultra-violet rays, a Russian steam bath and alcohol compresses. Stesha, a simple soul, even suggested that Alexei wear a woollen binder. Finally the conservative Volga public health inspector won the day. Inspector Ivanov was an ardent partisan of mustard plasters. Two packages of the yellow powder were found in the kitchen. Stesha acted as apothecary. The bitter mixture was spread on a sheet of newspaper. Alexei Nikitich was carried to the sofa and, although he resisted, his coat was removed.

"You've got a constitution like a young man, little brother," said Ivanov, applying the mustard-poultice to his back in a businesslike way. "It's as though you'd never lived. Wait, you'll still show your mettle. You're a runner after skirts, and a secret one, too: such men are the worst! Well, sit up. Why are you trembling?"

"You have fingers like a corpse. . . ." Alexei Nikitich complained through his teeth.

"Be patient, it's for your own good!" Suddenly a thought crossed his mind. "Eh, isn't it perhaps gout that you have, Alexei?"

This word associated with old age had a threatening sound.

With a grey face, staring at the ceiling, Alexei lay amidst them, equally surprised and weakened by his attack. The pain was subsiding, he wanted to go to the place of the accident, but nobody would let him. His friends vied with one another in trying to cheer him up. Tabuntsev pretended to take a picture of him with a whole cheese held in his lap; Tiutchev, slightly drunk, stuck a cucumber under his arm instead of a thermometer. Alexei Nikitich smiled, but he was listening to something else. The drain-pipe from the gutter was right outside the window. Rain kept pouring down. And if one listened carefully it was as though at the other end of the pipe a hoarse broken phonograph were playing. . . .

He did not hear any of them except Efim Demin go home.

# CHAPTER 13

# *Morning*

NOW SLEEP IS BECOMING LIGHTER, and the faint creak of wood being planed awakens Kurilov. Arsentyich is fixing the window. The frames swollen from the dampness do not close tightly; in bad weather drafts sweep through the apartment. Kurilov cautiously moves his shoulder: no, there's no pain, it was nothing at all! Pain has gone together with the night. He is annoyed with himself for his weakness of yesterday— things that tormented one yesterday always seem insignificant. This illness cured by two packages of mustard powder is ridiculous. Who spoke of gout? That foul word offends more than it scares. It is associated in his mind with leisure and over-indulgence, which he has never known. You lied, you half-educated Volga medic!

It's simply his general health that he has never taken care of and that now needs some attention. It would be good to take advantage of the winter and buy a pair of skates or spend a month in a rest home, at Borschnia, for example. The manager of the estate once assured him that during a food shortage the whole population of the neighboring villages had lived exclusively on hare meat. It would be grand to do some hunting! Following the manager's hints Alexei Nikitich conscientiously studied the topography of the place. Directly beyond the knobby hill which, according to the local legend, was dragged there by the obscure brigand Spirka, an uncut, leafy forest extends for a hundred kilometers. Didn't Tuitchev boast of his little rifle? . . . And now imagination puts Alexei Nikitich on skis and sends him down the steep snowy Spirka hill; snow dust envelops him from top to toe and he rushes at a furious pace toward the woods that first vanish and then suddenly soar above his head in a white whirl. He feels tingling and elated from the wet cold streaming behind his collar. . . . The early morning is chary of color. Everything, the woods and the fields, is painted blue as if by a child's hand, and even the low winter sun, red, flat and round, seems to have been traced by a child.

He opens his eyes. Fresh bread in a basket gleams on the tidy little table, and vapor flows in a delicate stream from the tea-kettle. "Oh, Arsentyich, you're like ancient Midas in Pokhvisnev's book! Everything you touch turns to gold. You touched my youth and it rang out like a song. You built machines and all kinds of instruments with which man changes the face of the world. During the period of the N.E.P. you revived abandoned workshops. From knowing you, people become more human and more understanding. You know not only bloomeries and stern posts: you know life!" (It's a good thing I didn't finish my speech yesterday. I would have inevitably ended it by a toast to the Ocean. Arsentyich would have laughed, Kutenko would have imagined I was his ally.) "My friends, my beloved, living companion-in-arms, I give you the very greatest river of Ocean, whither all of us are sailing!"

He signalled to me to wait, jumped out of his bed and barefoot ran into the bathroom. The resilient November water splashed against his hands; he mercilessly poured it on himself as a punishment for his faint-heartedness of last night. (Catherine had always chided him for those splotches on the chalk walls.) Then, as the temporary house-keeper, Arsentyich invited me to the table. Donning his professional spectacles, the old man opened the newspaper. The room became lighter. As usual, he read aloud. Japan was stirring up something in Mongolia, Litvinov had gone to America, a French squadron had flown to Moscow. And again not a word was said about Catherine: dead, she was still here!

After tea Arsentyich said goodbye. For the holidays he was going to his people in the Urals. Both men excused themselves and in the hall I heard the old founder scolding his pupil for having boasted the night before about his own life. Immediately after that he began to boast about himself, saying that his factory would send a car to meet him at the station—("a fi-irst-class car!"). As he said this, his face doubtless had a bashful wrinkle. Kurilov took his head in his hands, no one was watching them, they prickled each other with their mustaches. Arsentyich was very old. Tightly, still more tightly hug your friend, Kurilov. You will never see each other again! . . . The old man grumbled, protested loudly and slammed the door.

We look out of the window. The house is tall. If you press your cheek to the outside frame you can see a corner of the Kremlin from Kurilov's window. Today the mass of old buildings is round-shouldered, somehow small. The sky is overcast, although there was a frost last night. A gigantic streamer of black smoke from the nearby electrical plant stretches out toward the faded gold of the Kremlin. Snow-flakes flutter and slowly choose a place to fall on. It is winter, and the passers-by in the street smell of mothballs. Among them I recognize Arsentyich by his yellow plywood suitcase, the companion of his travels. The old man crosses the bridge springily. He is hurrying to his bloomery and his birds. He is overtaken by a chest maker, who holds two chests of different sizes in his hands and a third, the largest, on his head.

"It's like a drawing of the theorem of Pythagoras," I say, but Alexei Nikitich does not answer.

Both of us can see how Arsentyich, stepping toward the handrail of the bridge, lets the Pythagorean dummy pass. Then the old man seems to split in two; one Arsentyich jumps on a moving trolley car, the other turns around the corner of a building with a moving picture theatre. A crow, enormous as a glider, drops from the roof and veers with the wind past the window. We feel shaky and chilly. And suddenly, as though a black hood is being put over the city, everything vanishes under the crow's wing.

"It's a nice morning," I say. "Let's take a walk!"

"Where did we stop the last time?"

"We began to build a railroad across the desert and brought it as far as the Ulug-Mergen station. We'll walk the rest of the way on foot: it's not far. Three thousand and a half kilometers to Shanghai, ten minutes' walk!"

And so we enter an immense sandy space. A caravan of people and machines is moving across the boundless expanse before us. Alexei Nikitich complains that the rattle of picks and shovels deafens him. . . . Your ears are too insensitive and realistic, comrade! . . . Look, transportation combines of a kind never seen before are paving the way to *your* Ocean. They move in an enormous row, their very weight seems to fuse the sands and behind them the broad-gauge Emerson tracks are ready. They chew everything under them, an old Mongolian temple and the bones of a two-humped animal that once fell here during a sandstorm. The caterpillar treads creak and the excavators' chains rattle. There is a parching heat and stench in the shadow of these dragons working as unskilled laborers. This is like ploughing, and the stratum looks like dazzling little glass combs. We cannot ask anyone about the causes of all this haste and the sources of this energy. We do not wish to importune these people gone berserk. They speak in ejaculations, as though in the midst of battle. Pitying my perplexity Kurilov shouts into my ear the news that Socialist China has been a reality for six years. . . . He nevertheless insists on his pick axes, because this simplified method of laying a road brings the longed-for events closer by a couple of decades. We engage in our customary controversy. . . . However, all this requires some supplementary explanation.

My friendship with this man is quite different from the usual relations of humdrum acquaintance. From time to time we meet and, just for the fun of it, engage in imaginary travels beyond the boundaries of the visible horizons. (The builder of our time is formed by dreams; [1] the art of living has always been essentially the ability to look forward.) Our ways happened to go along together as far as the ocean itself. At rare stops we got off to meet people whom we are fated never to see. In such moments we noticed several interesting things. When our eyes were insufficient, and the insight of the poet equalled the perspicacity of the statesman, we also resorted to fiction. It served as an unsteady bridge across the abyss, where the torrents rush—in an unknown direction.

This is difficult because in planning history rationally one must always leave something to chance, to geniuses and to imbeciles. Our surmises are invariably characterized by hastiness and incomplete knowledge, but let those who will correct our inadvertent errors. In brief, this is our chess-game, and a schoolroom globe with tattered continents and seas serves us as the chess-board. The better parts of the game belong to Alexei Nikitich; only the inexactitudes, the fantastic little images and the omissions that are unavoidable when a story is retold, are mine. . . .

We took ourselves out of the present; we destroyed the moving partition between the future and the past, and then both these non-beings acquired equal reality. We entered into a four-dimensional world; everything became accessible to us, and the marvellous contemporaneousness of events was clear. I faint-heartedly hurried forward to the gates of the garden of which the best children of earth have dreamed in so many different forms; I wanted to break through the blood and flames of the inevitable disasters, but my ironical Vergil inexorably led me through all the upheavals that take place at the junctions of history. Sometimes we burrowed so deeply that we could not determine where was good and where was evil. But at the spot where the next-to-the-last round of world wars began [2] we reconciled ourselves to the role of spectators, although deeply grieved at the necessity of doing this, for on many occasions the health and strength of two additional soldiers would have been useful. I regret that I lack Kurilov's gift for clear and exact constructions. True, some of them are too much like

---

[1] "Inexact, you man of letters," Kurilov corrects me. "The builder does not realize a dream, but an iron necessity!"—I readily agree with him.

[2] At that time, aside from A. N. Kurilov, and occasionally Aliosha Peresypkin, P. I. Smirnov took part in our vigils and helped us to clarify the details of the next to the last conflict.

pamphlets, and others are more daring than plausible, but one cannot deny their order and purposefulness. Thus I shall not be able to reconstitute from memory the chronological succession of the uprisings of the Hungarian and Galician peasants, supported by the social revolution in the center of Europe, but my heart remembers the ardent response of the Sierra Nevada to them; and while one great power hurriedly, with all her skirts, extinguished and trampled this human fire, which was burning her sides, she received a mortal stab in the back from her vigilant neighbor.

An indescribable free-for-all fight followed. All the peoples, whether they would or no, were harnessed to the plough of penal servitude, which was digging up the whole map of the planet. No one could have said whether this inhuman tragedy had more of grandeur or of baseness. (And how good it is that the most redeeming quality of memory is its ability to forget!) These wars were long and devastating. With time, their very horror degenerated into oppressive boredom. Their prologues followed the rules of gangster duels, as though the demon of war protected those who first reached for their pistols. The battles resembled the whirling of primitive melted matter, and we were struck by the capacity of human consciousness to endure such terrible ordeals. Finally the conflict became so bitter that it was necessary to throw away altogether the tattered fig leaf of bourgeois humanism. (By the way, humanism was invented at a time when a field-gun fired less than one shot per minute!) The obsolete records of the Nebuchadnezzars and Vasily Bolgaroktonovs, of Hulaga and Alba, of all the Mahmuds and Omars, were surpassed. Leaders appeared who asserted that it was good to do as their long-bearded ancestors had done, to devour during battle the smoking, bleeding heart of the enemy. At certain critical moments belligerent countries turned into cemeteries overnight, and maggots crawling in corpses became the sole population of valleys once blessed. Sometimes madness visited two armed friendly powers spending the night together: one, trembling slightly with surprise, awakened within the belly of the other. Short-lived respites and peaceful dreams no longer deceived anyone: the devil likes to pose as kindly. From time to time there were epidemics of mass migration to the Soviet Union, and cordons had to be thrown along the frontiers to stop the stream of frenzied people from the blazing house on the other side of the border. The old era was dying hard, and the ancient bed of the earth shook beneath it.

Asia underwent the deepest changes. The great yellow land, which for centuries defended herself only by impassable roads and non-resistance against the armored evil, took into her own hands the reins of destiny that she had dropped so long ago.[3] This poverty-stricken seat of colonial plunder and unscrupulous hoarding underwent an almost physical resmelting and reforging. The gigantic peoples who never before knew how numerous they were began to stir. And never before in history had the law of numbers played such a great role. Judging by the legends we found there fifteen years after the events, the great national war leader [4] called the roll of his insurgent hordes by the tried method of Genghis Khan's mother. He ascended a hill, and if everything as far as the horizon was filled with living, stirring lava, he inferred that his troops were all present. This kind of computation became established: the first circle of the heavens, the second, the fifth. . . . There was no way of making more regular subdivisions of this countless multitude of angered people. Yang Tze gave a sign, and they set forth. Clouds of flying loess and *huan tu* veiled the sun. Popular singers exclaimed that Wan Sui Yang Tze had summoned the night to prevent the exploiters from seeing their army from the sky. For many years they fought within the country, then they crossed its borders. In the most primitive fashion everything that dropped from the air or landed from the sea was slain. The punitive coalition, which, with the exception of the Soviet Union, all the nations down to the smallest had joined, retreated. Supreme heroism has always characterized wars of liberation, but there was nothing rational or comprehensible in Yang Tze's elemental assault. The people who had always known how to work, starve and contemn danger, gave freely of themselves during their heroic decade of resurgence.[5]

This century was more eager for sensation than any other, and the most unexpected sensations had a humdrum taste. After an interval of time, which posterity will shorten or lengthen, there came one night: the cock moved his treasures to Central Africa, and the lion on

[3] An eastern power had completely swallowed China and even transferred its own capital to her territory, but the bitten-off piece was enormous; it exploded, the usurping power's belly cracked asunder at the seams and the organism changed its social form. This, of course, did not happen at one stroke, and one could observe the different stages of this instructive process.

[4] His grateful people rewarded him with so many poetic epithets that his own earthly name was lost among them, as the morning star in the sky. But this *min jen*, man of the people, came from the upper reaches, seamed with rapids, of the Yang Tze Kiang and in common parlance he was called by the name of the great Chinese River.

[5] Striving to join her culture with that of the west, young China built that road to the northwest that I visited with Kurilov at the beginning of this chapter. Because the problem of communications between the East and the West was complicated by the piracy of enemy armadas that roamed the oceans, the need for this interior highway had become urgent.

the island of Mauritius licked his stumps with a growl. Everything got mixed up. No one protested when, during this period of convulsive search for support, the Dutch Indies, moving slowly as an oyster, entered the great insular empire; no one was surprised when the Malayan revolution threw that empire out, too. It seemed that the historical role of the Atlantic as a citadel for despots had ended. Our ocean had long since become the arena of the peaceful activities of nations. The hemispheres changed places, and the Old World began to be called the New. At one point the Old World served as an inn for fugitive kingdoms and republics. Their imperilled position and enforced proximity compelled them to seek rapprochement among themselves, but the unity of the bourgeoisies was not realized. A reorganization of the imperialistic continents followed; some of the colonies, without particular pride, assumed the names of their former mother countries. Life in these countries took on an extremely peculiar character.[6] As in the life of an individual, old age strengthened and emphasized the features of youth. And because this instrument for oppressing the masses operated infallibly and uninterruptedly, the Western hemisphere moved all the time as if with an overheated boiler. . . . In brief, at the time of the first decisive clash the frontier between the two worlds ran from Kamchatka past Formosa toward Java, Delhi and Aden, along a bent-in curve, through sands, toward Monrovia, and further up the eighth meridian, considering the one passing through the Cape Verde Islands as zero.[7]

For a long time we did not know whether this formidable clash would take place or whether the reorganization of the planet would

[6] Scientific investigators will some day throw more detailed light on the history of the rise and development of the most popular Old World institution: the General Providence Trust. In its original form—a private detective agency—it rendered the financial rulers of the double continent certain secret services, was legalized and transformed into a very large organization which was given all sorts of missions. This thousand-armed Leviathan undertook any job—from organized kidnapping of child-laborers to crushing tiny states that had survived somewhere on the continent. The president of the firm, Mr. D. Mackenzie, had a very thick conscience and because people's secret designs are always sinful, he took upon himself all the sins of the world for comparatively low fees. (A war of the South American type, for instance, commanded in the catalogue a price only two hundred times higher than tearing off the nostrils of a competitor.) In my notebook there are still a few excerpts from the advertisements of this firm: "Twenty-four per cent of our shares are held by clergymen. Read the Bible and you'll know who are your accomplices!"—"By entrusting your money to us, you become investors in Paradise!" and so on.

[7] On an international geographical conference that took place eight years before the Great War, this meridian was accepted as the zero meridian, since it equally divided the continents into hemispheres.

result from a hundred smaller social explosions. For some reason Alexei Nikitich was a partisan of this "fragmentation" theory—"Hello, don't be scared, men and women. The big event has already taken place!" [8] I rebelled: the poet just as much as the statesman needs the prophetic gift for predictions at such distance. However, we agreed that what was important was the final goal, not the preliminary variations. . . . And so the difference of class potentials moved the two worlds ever closer to each other, even though the mechanism of physical attraction had not begun to operate. Despite the skilful hypocrisy of the ambassadors, the relations between the continents were unfriendly.[9] The government of the Northern Federation of Socialist Republics remained peaceful until the end. This was not out of fear: her rear and reserves were inexhaustible. Her restraint was born of her certainty that every day that passed weakened the enemy and facilitated his eventual rout. Moreover, not only defeat but an incomplete success would have brought an excessive deterioration of civilization in its train. The man-killing industry flourished, and the army staffs had not yet made known their secret achievements. The creators of the latest doctrines of "cheap" wars had long since ridiculed our own methods of scattering mountains of metal merely for the purpose of mechanically defeating the enemy with the fragments.[10] The size of the armies grew incessantly. Under modern conditions of spatial strategy, which struck the enemy all over his territory, even mechanized warfare demanded the participation of enormous masses, and the masters feared their slaves all the more because they maintained a stubborn silence. Rumors circulated that certain devices were being used in the Old World, which stultified the soldiers and thus turned

[8] He got angry when I ascribed this idea to him in order to lure him into a secret admission. He said that neither Marx nor Lenin had ever lulled anyone regarding the unpleasant prospects of capitalism.

[9] More than once the territory of the Federation was the scene of strange and unbecoming disasters; three years before the Malaya incident a Homeric invasion of lice took place in the region of Bordeaux. Of an excellent breed, the fruit of many years' selection, deservedly named after Montecucolli, the inventor of bacteriological warfare, they crawled against the population in closed ranks, movable tubes full of typhus, not subject to the redoubtable accidents of insect fate. On some of the bigger ones microscopic stamps were revealed, bearing the inscription: "May God punish your dullness!" The high level of public health techniques prevented this diversion, justly appraised by contemporaries as a hooligan's tap on the shoulder, from having any serious consequences.

[10] In the Verdun operation (during the introductory war of the penultimate imperialist round of 1914–1918) a ton and a half of metal was required to put one combatant out of action. The cost of killing a man in ancient Rome was only 12 kopeks (the energy of 3 kilowatts, the amount needed for a good swing with a sword).

them into beasts.[11] A method was also discovered of directing from a distance instruments of destruction that could see and record what was happening around them and send their owners visual representations of the battlefield. A synchronized, swing-like scale of wavelengths precluded every possibility of interference from strangers. The receiving instrument, called a "mechanical general," had the outward structure of a fly's eye; very thin nerves put together separate and coded tele-messages. Another terrifying weapon was the special shell called the "winged eye"; it found its own range, and its aim did not need to be corrected. Thus, although in the presence of many industrial buildings, one could not miss, even when firing blindly; the enemy could choose his objectives.[12] Finally, almost on the eve of the conflict, at the Edgewood Arsenal, in the native land of old-fashioned Lewisite gas, was born the very patriarch of murders, jellifying gas. It had the capacity of growing on rain moisture and the blood of its own victims.[13] No container could be made for its transportation; a way was found to create it on the battlefield by means of combined barrages. This gas was named "subdevilite," as though to imply the threat that an even sharper knife was being kept in readiness.[14] She was approaching inexorably, the smiling witch of war.

[11] See an editorial in the *Canton Soviet News*, printed on the day of our arrival there. These devices were later known as the Detter Chambers.

[12] For some time Alexei Nikitich and myself turned into laboratories and experimental factories. We did not shrink from the most startling innovations. We built guns for firing from hemisphere to hemisphere, special hardened bullets that could pierce an entire regiment if it were stood up in one column, submarine battleships with fantastic speeds, of which one might have said that they travelled in fish soup, considering the huge number of fish killed by the water they heated. (Interior coolers regulated the temperature on board ship.) We devised atomic dispersers of matter under the impact of which a man, feeling something like a tickle, dissolved into a bit of smiling nothingness; we sent out invading tanks fed by gases made of all kinds of wooden refuse (they moved on the fuel they found underfoot, devouring forests, tearing out the boards of stone houses, cutting the terrible lanes of war through the planet); we inserted special gas-resistant stoppers into mankind's nostrils and ears so that something might survive, and smeared the girls of the earth with a fire-resistant clay dirt to preserve some mothers for the continuation of the human race. . . . This went on until our occupation seemed disgusting to us, and we erased everything we had done. On an equal footing with technology, we made vigorous human ideas the main weapon of the Federation.

[13] It is notable that the chemists of the New World denied the very feasibility of making the so-called "colloidal gases," while the Old World was already using them for crushing uprisings. Later "subdevilite" was held to be as revolutionary as, for instance, the invention of the alizarine dye in 1869.

[14] We saw it in action in a bamboo grove near Tacao. From a distance its faint spectral gleam was visible, as though a thousand tangled rainbows had dropped on the place. We entered into the depths of this instructive herbarium. Everything swayed around us. We had the feeling that "He" was watching us, convulsed with laughter.

Dream weather is always favorable for voyages. Our predecessors gave us poetic descriptions of marvellous, ethereal lands, sunlit, with blessed valleys full of sages, children and apple trees. Some people dreamed of our era! And so, more than once, together with Kurilov we toured these sad ruins, centers of yesterday's civilization. Europe had had a blood-letting, and for a long time the continent lay lifeless, like a gigantic, badly butchered, one-legged animal with its nose on Gibraltar. We visited abandoned cities built after the latest fashion of capitalism;[15] we descended into underground cities where people hid from terror and the sun; finally we saw cities swept entirely out of existence by the storms of war, resembling from above sections of an enormous brain in whose convolutions madness raged for a long time. Not even a Jeremiah was left to lament over these abject bricks. Amidst wormwood herbs and scattered flagstones little lizards ran, treasure-seekers wandered, looking for buried riches, and archeologists dug, trying to reconstruct their ancestors' gangster relations from remnants of cathedrals, prisons and palaces. In winter snow smoked from the rubble, in summer, stony dust. All this irritated our eyes, so that they streamed tears. . . . The capitals of the young Soviet republics arose far from the former centers, as though the new thought feared to live in the houses in which such murders had taken place. . . . (We also visited Moscow. The new capital had long since moved eastward, but Moscow still lived, pensioned by the centuries, a respectable old woman full of museums, the Mecca of scientific socialism, the underground worker of the rebirth of the world. We surrounded her with a belt of gardens and new city quarters, like old Canton and mediaeval London. We tenderly loved this city. . . .)

We made the tour of many shores in search of a place for the principal of the four capitals of the new world. We put it near Shanghai,[16] near the site of the two last duels. Historically and geographically this was the greatest crossroads of the world.[17] We gave this city the im-

---

[15] That is, with artificial rain antennae along the streets for the purpose of de-gasing, with hundreds of mechanical eyes and ears on the roofs, with automatic batteries that spontaneously responded with fire to the heat waves of airplane engines, with capacious balloons of artificial fog, which almost instantaneously wrapped a city in a blanket colored like the ground or, if it was a city near the sea, like the water. That year the newspapers reported that a fierce barrage had been opened on a flock of jackdaws and all Nibelungenstadt immediately buried itself in a vile greenish smoke. The incident no longer seems ridiculous.

[16] Most cities had been renamed after heroes or events or climatic characteristics. We use the old names so as not to confuse travellers who rely on our charts.

[17] We intended to plant its quays with magnolias and palms; posterity, however, independently of our will planted *hei sun, baigo* and arrow-shaped *nang moo* there. We must agree that the effect is not bad.

personal name of Ocean, because this spacious word has a motherly
meaning with regard to the seas of all ranks, which are in turn united
by the brotherly ties of canals and rivers. . . . Often, like ridiculous pro-
vincials, we visited this place. We lodged in a temporary fisherman's
shack on the shore, but our address had a proud romantic sound:
"1035 Yang Tze Quay, Ocean." Frightened of the monsters we ourselves had invented, we went out only by night. . . . I am at a loss as
to how to begin the description of this city. It was above all the capital
of people who fly naturally and effortlessly; the ancient architectural
urge to see that the view from above is beautiful was here finally and
harmoniously satisfied. There were many flying apparatuses in the
shape of winged canoes, the very sight of which made one feel giddy;
there were buildings with varnished hooks on their doors resembling
moorings for ocean liners; many-storied streets in the official part of
the city, streets with a third dimension; toilets with the names of all
the hangmen of the Chinese people in the drainage sewers, beginning
with Sun Chuan Fang, Yang Hu and Chiang Chui Chang; enormous
moons of high frequency disks that destroyed all kinds of insects—and
many other things that encumber my memory. There were doubtless
also a large number of curiosities, but we did not notice them, because
all the marvels served man as faithfully as dogs.

But, just as the savage when creating gods cannot fail to endow
them with human qualities, we were unable to create a race different
from our contemporaries. Again we found lazy-bones, envious men
and blockheads in the proper quantities. (I must say in defense of
Kurilov that he emphatically denied in the city of the future the presence of dust, flies, accidents and even the normal amount of minor
filth that is inevitable in any human community.) Both of us noted
that boys of all times are equally unbearable (although sometimes
they served us as guides, and they accepted our enthusiasm as a generous reward for this not very strenuous work.) In brief, there were
hours when we considered ourselves above the law.

Once having become scientifically interested in a humming coming
from an unattractive manhole, I was drawn into a gigantic magnetic
dust pump. For twenty-seven minutes I lay crucified on a wire net
covered with the foulest refuse. My hands prickled, and a salty taste
remained for a long time on my tongue. Kurilov, who tried to rescue
me, found himself at my side like Barabbas. A crowd of street urchins,
photographers and such surrounded us. In vain did I shout to them
that my friend, Alexei Nikitich, was the chief of the Political Bureau
of an important railroad line and that the aura of his holiness also
illuminated me. Nothing was of any avail. Nursemaids pointed us out

to their charges, as if we were captive monkeys. Other children, older, whizzed by us on some kind of little buzzing machines resembling our scooters. They spat at us, aiming rather badly at my hat. (It was amusing to learn later that not my hat, but Kurilov's smoking pipe provoked their excursions to the place of our common humiliation. Oh, that old pipe of Kurilov's, charred on one side, the constant companion of our voyages!) Here, while we were still on that terrible net, my regular controversy with Kurilov took place. He emphatically rejected this incident. I think he hoped to turn these flying children into neat, well-bred little students.

"But don't you see that you're trying to make a Christian paradise out of your Ocean!" I cried, spitting out the whirling filth. "You intend to stuff it with Cherubim and monuments. Let them brawl, suffer, mellow . . . after all, that's life!"

"You slander the children of the future, scribbler! . . . Furthermore, why do you look for garbage everywhere?"

"If only for the reason that it reveals the presence of *living* man! Aren't you suspended on a net? . . . Aren't boys spitting at your pipe to put it out? And perhaps this is the luckiest incident that has happened to us *here*. . . ."

"But couldn't we be warned against approaching this devilish thing?"

"There was no one to warn us, dear friend! They have no time to bother with us. As human relations are simplified, an even greater number of objects will require constant alertness. . . ." And I expounded many other ideas on the same subject.

He began to puff at his pipe angrily, and I left him, fully convinced that people argue less to change their opponents' ideas than to prove to themselves the correctness of their own beliefs.

# CHAPTER 14

# Marina Prepares Kurilov's Biography

EVERY MORNING THE landscape outside the window changed; thus a capricious artist rubs out the work of the day before and begins again. One day, while still in bed, Kurilov saw a snowy border on the window-transom. The ceiling shone with an even, dove-colored whiteness. The apartment was damp and fresh: the ventilator had been open since the night before. The freezing river did not stir near the banks, the Kremlin was decked in ermine tatters. The snow dulled the jangle of trolley cars and the wintry cawing of the crows. The bell rang. Removing the tea kettle from the stove on his way, Alexei Nikitich went to open the door. In the doorway stood Sabelnikova, shivering with cold.

"Today is the twenty-fourth," she said, removing her worn knitted gloves with her teeth. "Can I keep my galoshes and my coat on? It won't take me long to finish now. . . ."

"Why hurry? . . . Take off your rubbers!" He turned the tea kettle in his hands; a steam of vapor from under the lid burnt his fingers.

He realized too late that to remove her galoshes was a difficult job. Marina's shoes had gone completely to pieces and before getting new shoes she was wearing her galoshes all the time. At home she apparently removed them together with her shoes, so as not to tear the soles off completely.

"They're slightly stuck," she explained, wrinkling her face in a shamefaced smile and picking up her bulging briefcase from the floor.

"Come in, sit down, come, move. . . . Had your tea today?"

No, she had not had time. Her street had been dug up for the construction of the subway, and there had been no trolley cars since this morning. Moreover, she had been told at the administration building that Kurilov would not come to the office today and she had hurried so as not to miss him at home. Alexei Nikitich had intended to spend the day writing a report for the Central Committee, but . . . the day was long!

"Do you like it stronger? I should have been a bad housewife. Wait a minute—I did have some jam." He went to the cupboard, but found that the jam had been eaten up by his friends; there remained only a package of long toffee in individual wrappings. They had been there since the days of Catherine. "Take these instead of jam. Surely you like candy?" He threatened her facetiously with his finger.

She thought for a while, her face became flushed, and she quickly began to rummage in her briefcase for her notebook. She had to take advantage of Alexei Nikitich's good mood. Big shots are sometimes absent-minded and as inconsistent as women.

"No, let's get on to our biography instead." However, she unwrapped a candy and stuck it into her mouth. "I'm ready!"

He burst out laughing; the candy was too big for her mouth, and she looked like a schoolgirl caught with stolen sweets.

"Fine, take notes then!" he began warming his fingers on his glass of tea. "There's a town called Porozhensk. They say that the fame of a town can be measured by the amount of human bones laid at its foundations. And so Porozhensk is an extremely historical town. But the chief claim to glory of this little hole is its famous Russia leather. Of course, you don't know what Russia leather is!"

"No . . . and I chose a difficult candy."

"Bite it in two!"

"It's too hard to crack. . . ."

He did not understand her hint. "Russia leather—take notes!— Imagine the skin of a yearling ox dressed clean with pitch. Some time ago there were a lot of small leather factories there, but later they shut down. Now it's just a shabby little spot, all overgrown with lilacs and apple trees. And you know the apples there are about the size of a walnut; they turn your mouth inside out, they are used for tea instead of lemons. They taste quite nice that way." (He smacked his tongue so noisily that Marina felt a sharp tartness on her gums.) "All that remains of its old fame is various handicrafts and lace-making. Woman, have you ever heard of Porozhensk lace?"

Marina lost her countenance; she did not know exactly where this town was situated, but its very name somehow smelt of leather and in addition evoked endless expanses of woods, the proximity of the Chuvash region, the notorious kulak uprisings. As for lace, because of her small means she never bought any. Therefore, she hastened to say: "Porozhensk lace? . . . Why, of course!"

He began in a tone of a teller of edifying tales: "And so I was born fifty years ago of honest and pious parents. My father worked as a trimmer in a leather factory. His coarse life is quite uninteresting. Mainly he labored, and I disliked him for his severity. It was from him that all of us fled. Klavdia ran away from home at the age of fifteen;

my sister Efrosinia, an impetuous tom-boy, married a big industrialist, and I went to work in Petersburg. Generally I had no luck with my family. My maternal uncle was a merchant; he had a stall for wooden-ware at the market. He died when I was still a little boy, but I liked his merchandise and, probably because of his merchandise, himself. Shaft-bows, sleighs with painted fronts, decorated tubs, carved ladles—and all this painted with fir-trees, horses, rabbits' feet. On every object —all the equipment of a muzhik's dream! . . . During holidays he would knock about town, drunk, picking up crying children and giving them mints or gingerbread. 'Don't hurt children!' was his favorite saying. He was a sort of 'original,' and he drank himself to death." (He pushed bread and butter toward her.) "Eat something, Marina. Biography is hard work. I am not in a hurry . . . and why don't you take notes?"

Strange, how he failed to understand her confusion! She would have been kicked out of any office with a bang if she had taken down what he said word for word. She needed something heroic, a concrete exploit, an escape, an episode involving self-sacrifice. Like all her generation she romanticized the past; as the difference between the old and new worlds grew greater in the eyes of today, the masters of the Russia of yesterday less and less resembled human beings. If only he would speak about them! . . . Marina felt really embarrassed and her cheeks grew pink. She had only written one line on her page. Apparently Kurilov was bored, rummaging in the dusty pile of his memories for her sake. From the very beginning she had not had much confidence in the success of her undertaking. Naturally Kurilov had long since discovered her helplessness, her torn soles, her ridiculous briefcase and her winter jacket with a rabbit-fur collar dyed to look like leopard. No, he didn't respect her. . . . She looked about, seeking the guitar; she recalled how a voice had resounded in it. But there was no more guitar; probably he had hidden it so that it would tell no tales about one silly summer night. And the candy stuck in one piece on her lips. It did not dissolve, but seemed to be constantly swelling, filling her entire mouth. With a wooden tongue Marina said: "All this isn't enough for a biography. How about your uncle? . . . Perhaps he was arrested?" There was a note of faint hope in her voice.

"No, I can't recall that he was. But after all he never started any riots. Children liked him, escorted him in crowds. However, I understand what you want. But! I'm sorry to say, there was nothing of *that* kind. I'm completely human. Anyone else in the same circumstances could have done twice as much. Drink your tea before it turns into ice cream. So you don't like the candy?" He bit into one to try it, tore it off his teeth, and violently stuck it in the ash tray. "Hm, one could break safes with these. . . ."

Taking courage she bent toward him. "I was told, for instance, that you were imprisoned at Izhevsk during the rebellion!"

He answered dryly: "Yes, that's true. . . . So what?"

"If you would give me some details about that. . . ."

Alexei Nikitich lit his pipe, and when it began to pull well he recalled the incident. He disliked to think of it, and the fact that the participants at that time were unable to determine the connections between forces, or find their way in the sequence of events, was not the only cause of his distaste.

It was the summer of 1918, the period when the front had formed itself spontaneously and what was then called the eastern front constituted a vast, overheated cauldron in which the bubbles of rebellion exploded from time to time. The counter-revolution was advancing on all sides, and the strategy of the revolution consisted in attempts to prevent the deadly ring from closing. It would have been hard to find neat military logic in the summer operations of that year, when panic was just as important a factor as heroism, when the mighty displacements of great armed masses were explainable, not by the perfection of their technical means or the skill of their captains, not by cowardice or valor, but, above all, by the deep idealism of one camp and the spiritual poverty of the other.

Meanwhile the strangling net was being drawn ever more tightly. The territory of the republic was contracting till it was no larger than the possessions of Ivan Kalita. The Second Army of the Soviets, formed of broken-up partisan and Red Guard units, was retreating toward Kazan. Those who escaped the Whites were wiped out by starvation and typhus. The situation was considered catastrophic. At the Izhevsk and Votkinsk plants rebellion was rife. Long before the explosion White officers began to gather there; they had united under the name of the Front Fighters Union. During those tragic June days Kurilov was sent there from Sarapul, to organize workers' volunteer units for the front.

The Whites struck their main blow from the direction of Simbirsk. On August 6, with the help of an underground organization and Kappel's two-thousand strong officers' brigade, they captured Kazan. Two days later, when the nucleus of the Izhevsk Communists was thrown toward Kazan, the notorious Izhevsk rebellion took place. Its technique followed the usual lines. The rebels rushed upon the armaments stores, seized power and began to liquidate their enemies. Kurilov was not taken in the first catch; he was found a month later, after the revolutionary underground had completely collapsed. He was taken by night to a cell crowded with commissars, workers, chairmen of committees of poor peasants and other so-called "enemies of the people." He was the thirteenth man to be locked up there. . . .

As he told it, this sad incident sounded dry, abrupt, colorless. Possibly Alexei Nikitich could not really evoke it for Marina. He was telling it as though looking into a fragment of a bloody little mirror and as though when he probed his heart he found himself no longer the same. He saw behind himself, alive, the heaps of his comrades massacred, shot and cut down, and he refused to reconcile himself to what he had seen.

". . . It's bitter to have to confess, Marina, that I'm forgetting the dates and the faces of many of those who were imprisoned with me. Even the noteworthy places I haunted in my youth (ah, it's a pity you weren't here the other day when my friends got together!) are vanishing from my memory, yet that prison set up on Seventh Street in Izhevsk and the dark faces of our hangmen, Yakovlev and Oshkurov, I see them now before me, more distinctly than your own face, Marina. I remember especially Oshkurov, a resourceful fellow in boots with straps and some kind of semi-Cossack uniform. We thought he was a drunkard, but he was really a cocaine addict; now and then he would turn his face away to 'powder his soul.' And after that he would think it very funny to stick his gun through the hole in the door and fire at the prisoners, 'hit or miss.' Or he would drive all thirteen of us to our plank-beds, order us to raise our hands and shoot at us blindly. Also noteworthy was his favorite weapon—a long leather lash mounted on a zinc wire with a lump of lead as big as a match box at the end; if he struck you with it across your shoulder he reached the small of your back. My comrades told me that he also liked to put prisoners astride his muzzle-loader, and in all fairness it must be said that he did this with childlike enthusiasm. He knew me well, and would often drop in for a talk. 'Well, hello, Aliosha. You threatened to have me brought to court, but God has judged the case!' He would twirl his lash for a while and then ask: 'Well, how would you characterize the situation?' Licking my lips, I simply answered that I was in a gloomy mood, although sometimes my teeth ached from the words I didn't say. 'Do you want a bullet in your head?'—'Not yet,' I answered, 'first you must be hanged, you piece of carrion!' There would be just a gleam in his eyes, as though from a dose of cocaine. 'I get you, Aliosha, but you'd better not count on it. Your people are running like rabbits. We've made contact with the Czechs and now, with the help of the Mother of God, we'll smash the Bolsheviks together!' My comrades would listen to this, groaning with anger, and one of them even bit his hand till it bled, so as not to scream. . . . In the end we got fed up with this terrible life; several of the men's bodies began to rot under their shirts from the blows. It was hard hearing the nightly tortures, when the hangmen made the rounds of the cells—make a note, there's a special sound that I can't describe when a bayonet enters the body of a living man!—then a noose would be thrown around their legs and all of them would be dragged into one cell. We decided to escape. There were no locks on the doors, they were just fastened with boards from outside. We agreed to smash the doors in all the cells at once; the first to break out was to release the others. We collected dust, ashes from the stove ventilator, and about a quarter of a pound of salt, to throw into the eyes of the first guard that entered. And it so happened that the first to come in was Oshkurov . . . we knocked him down . . . and began to cut him up with his own saber . . . but we were unable to finish him. We broke out, tore the barbed wire fences with our bare hands, and we made our escape, losing half our number under machine-gun fire at the pond. . . ."

This was indeed the time to think of the "inevitable," but he did not think of it, as though he had a thousand years ahead of him! He himself now wondered how a defeated and emaciated soldier had been able to show so much resilience. An incomprehensible force had lifted him, and if he had encountered a bottomless pit he would have jumped into it without thinking, believing in his success as in a god.

"I was good at running then. I wouldn't dare to slip away like that now."

Marina was working fast. The lines leapt and rushed under her hand. Her pencil tore and crumbled the cheap paper until at last the lead broke. She cast an embarrassed glance at Kurilov as though the description of his final crowning exploit were to follow, but once again she had nothing but a tattered fragment of life. Alexei Nikitich had turned away and was looking toward the window. His pipe had gone out; he vainly drew on it to rekindle the last remaining spark. Now he seemed older than his age. In his mind he was turning page after page of the subsequent events of his life, things inaccessible to Marina's childish understanding. The reflection of the first snow from the ceiling gave his silhouette an indistinct outline. Taking advantage of the respite, Marina pulled her briefcase onto her lap and began to rummage in it for a penknife or perhaps another little blue stick with lead in it.

"And you . . ." she asked with knitted brows, "were you, too, beaten up by that infamous creature?"

"One doesn't ask such questions, Marina . . . and there's no use writing all this stuff down."

"But after all, it's life," she objected, in his own words.

"It's what happens in every struggle. . . . I'll tell you what, I'll find a ready-made biography for you. I have a copy of it somewhere."

Marina did not argue with him, because she did not feel capable of reproducing all the complexity of Kurilov's life. In fact, she had learned that people's real life stories are completely unlike the biographies that are published.

"I have great respect for you, Kurilov," she said in a low voice.

He turned to her with surprise. She became flustered and covered the lower part of her face with her hand.

"Why do you hide your smile? You have beautiful teeth. . . ." He could also have praised her skin, so fresh and clean, and as though drawn tightly over her temples, even her big, not very feminine hands, even her many freckles, even the way she laughed, showing the tip of her pink tongue between her teeth. "I may say your trip to Penza has done you a great deal of good!"

"Before going to Penza I spent two weeks at Borschnia."

"What is it like?"

"It's a big estate with a park . . ."—she kept rummaging for a pencil—"and a river. . . . I spent whole days in the water. I can swim like a fish!" (Where on earth did I put that thing?) She picked up her brief-case and buried her hand in it. It would have been much simpler to spread out the contents of the bag on the table, but apparently she did not wish to reveal her riches. "And in a lodge in the woods there is still an old woman related to the former owners of the estate. She is shown to all the visitors like a museum piece. And it's true that when you look at her you begin to understand the purpose of death. She still remembers Tsar Alexander II. . . ." (But there *was* a pencil there, and now it's gone!)

Alexei Nikitich went behind her and gazed at the downy, pink hollow of her neck. Since her last visit he had been tormented by amorous dreams, like a young boy. And Marina, as though oppressed by his look, blushed and bent forward. Apparently she was trying to cover her briefcase with her body. Kurilov looked into it from the side. On top there was a big hunk of bread and a warty apple. At the bottom he saw a book, a chipped mirror and some rags. But these objects did not exhaust the contents of the enormous beggar's satchel. It would certainly have burst had it not been held together by a steel rod and sewn with black waxed thread. Suddenly something alive squeaked in it; Marina convulsively squeezed the briefcase between her knees, but once again a comical metallic sound popped out of it.

"What have you got in there?"

All was lost, she could no longer defend herself.

"It's a musical instrument," she said, and suddenly she looked twice as small.

"What kind. . . . Let me see it. . . ."

"A toy."

"Never mind . . . I won't break it, show it to me!"

At the very bottom of the briefcase lay a toy harmonica. Marina pulled it out by its handle, and it sang out in a dissonant and irritable chord. The apple fell out and rolled on the floor. The toy was a little box with slanting sides and bellows pasted with colored calico. Tin stops were fixed on it with tacks, and the whole thing smelled more of paste than of music. Alexei Nikitich shook the bread crumbs off it and examined it with a seriousness born of surprise. He felt in advance friendly interest in the future owner of this toy.

"You see we have no luck in working together . . ." said Marina, biting her lips and flushing. "Well, give me back that thing! Thanks for the story. . . ." She had made up her mind to get additional material about Kurilov in some revolutionary archives.

Kurilov did not hear her, he was busy. "Look here, your harmonica refuses to play for me," he said.

"But it's only a toy. There's a little hole in the bellows. Stop it with one finger and then pull. . . ."

Marina would have been unable to explain why she had bought this thing. She was passing a children's store when an accidental and hasty ray of sunlight fell on the showcase. And so many flamboyant colors glowed suddenly behind the dusty glass that she was tempted to spend half her funds on the spot. . . . Kurilov was still preoccupied. With a concentrated look he took a bottle of something yellow and gluey, cut a strip from a rag and pasted it over the hole.

"So you've already got a child?" The harmonica began to play, and it was like a triumphal march in honor of this third person who introduced a human note into their relationship.

"Yes . . . a boy."

"And it's because of him that you postponed your trip to Penza?" He recalled the scratch on her nose and the ridiculous gesture with which she tried to cover it.

"Yes, it's difficult to go on official missions when one has a child. I can't leave him with his aunt, because she has attacks of liver trouble. I was assigned a damp room, and my Ziamka fell ill. . . . Well, give it back to me, you'll end up by breaking it!" She stuck the toy in its old place, under the bread.

Alexei Nikitich looked at her with gloomy and mistrustful eyes. A completely different woman was before him, a woman to whom Kurilov's friendliness or hostility was a matter of indifference.

"Why didn't you tell me you had a child? I could have sent someone else in your place."

"Oh, please!" She smiled coldly. "It's my fault that I have a child. The railroad doesn't have to be penalized for it. . . ."

"That's wrong, Marina. We aren't automata, we are building our society for living people. . . ."

"I know . . . that's what I'm trying to explain to others!" She rose to go. "Thanks for the tea. Give your biography to Feshkin, will you?"

No longer embarrassed about her shoes, she was leaving, stern, calm and erect. Alexei Nikitich caught up with her in the hall. "You act as though you were angry with me, Marina," he said. "You're just tired, and it seems to me that you're not having a very easy time of it." He felt a great desire to do something especially pleasant for her. "If you're not in a hurry, let's take a ride into the country. It's the first snow . . . didn't you play snowballs as a little girl?"

She stood still like a big, bewildered child; this temptation was almost equal in intensity to her inexplicable feeling of being hurt—no, it was even greater! The last time she had travelled in a car was three months before, when a truck had come to take some books, a projection machine and herself on some propaganda mission.

"And how old is your son?"

She said proudly (and it seemed to Kurilov that she grew more intelligent and upright as she spoke of him): "The day after tomorrow he'll be six. He is jolly and very independent." She smiled and added in a dull voice as though talking in her sleep: "At first he wanted to be a parachutist, but now he has changed his mind and wants to be a street-car conductor. . . ."

"That's fine. I'll drive you home and get acquainted with your Ziamka. I must say I love street-car conductors!" And he thought that he had not spoken to a child for a long time and that this was not right. "So, shall we go?"

"But only for a little while . . ." she said; and now the indefinable offense was forgiven.

"Good. Go on downstairs, I'll join you in a minute." He wanted to take Pokhvisnev's books with him; he might not have another opportunity to return the queer old fellow's baggage.

He did not overtake Marina until the fifth floor landing. Both were in a cheerful mood again. The staircase was filled with Marina's laughter and Kurilov's booming bass. Suddenly Alexei Nikitich stopped at a door and, having split open a match, stuck it into the narrow crack between the plaster and the bell.

"Why are you doing that, Alexei Nikitich?"

"The fellow who lives there is awfully touchy. He has a dog that looks like a lawyer! Run! . . ."

Holding hands they rushed downstairs like two schoolboys. On the last landing they almost knocked over a tall old woman wearing the same kind of leather overcoat as Kurilov. She stepped aside in a surprised fashion, turned her head and followed them with her eyes. Alexei Nikitich involuntarily let go of Marina's hand. This encounter was unpleasant to him.

"I wanted to get some air: it's the first snow!" he said in confusion, and unexpectedly made a sort of boyish gesture. "I was going to call you up. . . . Were you coming to see me?"

It was an idle question. Kurilov lived on the top floor, the twelfth: if she had been coming to see him, Klavdia would have used the elevator. The old woman glanced attentively and sadly at Kurilov's companion, and under this glance the still smouldering sparks of laughter on Marina's lips died. Then, in the same calm, inflexible gait, springier than one would have expected in a woman of her age, she began to walk upstairs. Marina realized in confusion that this was Kurilov's famous sister.

# CHAPTER 15

# First Snow, First Snow . . .

FOR A LONG TIME they remained silent, as though Klavdia might still return.

"How she scared me!" confessed Marina, when the car had entered the stream of street traffic.

"Oh," he said, raising a finger, "she is a very severe woman."

"Are you afraid of her too?" she asked him, entrusting herself to his strength and kindness.

He fancied he detected a note of complicity in her question; he did not wish to pass Klavdia off with a joke. "No," he said, "it is not fear I feel, Marina. It's more—something difficult to understand perhaps. She makes you want to check up on yourself constantly. You know, Marina, she is a very good old woman. She never raises her voice; nor have I ever seen her in tears, although she is chary of smiles, too. She is a human being with a heroic destiny." Something compelled him to be truthful to the end. "You see, when she was young her fiancé was hanged—he was an excellent man and an excellent Bolshevik, so strong he could crush nuts with his fingers, and everyone, even children, called him simply Semenushka. Later it was learned that he had remained alive in the noose for eleven whole minutes. I think she was in love with him. Don't ever mention this to anyone, she couldn't bear people to know. . . ." He fell silent, and there was tenderness in his silence. "Our biographies give too much space to consequences, they should discuss the causes that produce them. That would be shorter and more intelligent. . . . And by the way, have you cooked up many biographies, dear Plutarch?"

For a long time she did not answer. "I still have to write yours, and that is the most difficult of all," she said at last. "It's embarrassing to write about you in the usual manner. But it's always difficult to cope with grown-ups; they're sceptical toward me, they ask me tricky questions. At a meeting in Penza I was asked whether in our time it was not immoral to give charity to the poor. . . . Of course, it's immoral, but suppose they, too, want to eat? I am afraid of making mistakes. I have starved myself on occasion and I understood this question quite well. A note was sent me at the meeting asking me whether I had

eaten my fill that day. . . . And there was a nasty word at the end."
She bit her lip and turned her face away from Kurilov. "I'll just finish
this job, I guess, and leave the railroad!"

A wet wind slashed in at the open window. They were now on the
outskirts of the city all painted with soot against a sullen overcast sky.
The highway climbed up an embankment. Marina looked pensively at
the little silver bird that sat on the radiator cap straight ahead of her.
Its two sharp raised wings furrowed the street like a plough; houses
fell on either side of it, and trucks going the other way, and passers-by;
following the bird, attached to its feet, almost rising in the air, flew the
heavy car. It was wonderful to drive this way, into the nowhere that
is the land of surprises and happiness.

"Where will you go? Life is difficult everywhere."

"I'll work with children. I've done that before. It's simpler with
them, and they don't lie."

"It's hard with children too, Marina. They are laboratories of the
new social relations. This generation is growing on the ruins of old
forms, and you will have to be the catalyst of a very complicated process. Do you get along well with your Ziamka?"

"Oh, we're friends. Ziamka is short for Izmail. I like proud names!
Twenty years hence people will be very proud, without little afflictions
and scars on their spirit. Every grief weakens or embitters . . . certainly
it makes a man maladjusted for a long time. But a proud man never
complains, or lies, or steals. . . . We have very few proud people at
present; only the submissive ones are liked!"

"Pride is anti-social, Marina; it makes people straightforward, but it
also spreads dissension among them."

"Do you think that, too?"

"No," said Kurilov frankly, and laughed.

She did not try to take advantage of her victory; the pleasure of the
drive was stronger than any other feeling. The magic little bird carried
them farther and farther, into the boundless Russian winter. The snow
on the fields was increasingly whiter, and its gleam more mysterious.
Barely touched by the thaw, it rounded out the lines of the landscape
and lent nature a simplified contour without details. Sometimes they
passed a village, and the car irrupted into a cheerful, long-drawn-out
clatter. There were cries of cocks, cranes, dogs; crows cawed in tree
branches, scattering white flakes as they flew from twig to twig; children on sleds were trying out the first snow. Life bustled, somersaulted
and screamed in every key. Wet snowballs hurled by bad marksmen
flew after them. Some friendly little old men tottered swaying from
the drink they had just had to celebrate the first snow; women in their

winter clothes gossiped near the wells, their pails on arm. The turnips were disguised as chrysanthemums; little huts covered with sugar-icing were dancing. It was the gingerbread kingdom of the lovely first snow! . . .

Suddenly a wood approached them. Shaking its white mane it ran along the side of the car, trying to outrun the machine, and it was fun to watch the multiple gleam of its nimble and innumerable feet. It ran until it dropped the car, lagged behind, then spread out as a patch of little shrubs, then pretended to be a little dog, a river, then hid com-pletely in a tiny chapel, in a ditch, in nothing. . . . And they very much regretted that they had not stopped to pick up Ziamka. The boy adored machines and felt suppressed reverence before a car. (And he would have seen that Kurilov's was an old one, that it had travelled a great deal! He knew by heart the makes of all the cars that passed through the outskirts of Moscow, he never missed. And, of course, if the old hairy god of whom his aunt had told him had come again down on earth he would have dropped in a parachute, in leather gloves, all smeared with oil and with a monkey wrench in his hands.)

". . . Scrape a submissive person, and if he is not just plain stupid, you will certainly discover a bad man under the crust. Pride should motivate human actions. Let it be the pride of the master, the pride of the hero, the pride of the mother who has given birth to both of them. Of course, a beautiful life will come—I know it better than anyone! I've thought out everything about it, every corner of it. I visit it every morning, and touch it. . . . Everything is cheap there, and beautiful . . . shoes and white bread! (I'll live long, I know; my father died at sev-enty, stooping to pick up a little piece of paper: he was extremely meticulous.) I'll live to see a quite *clean* life! I know it, I know that the Moscow is the biggest river in the world!"

"You don't live well, Marina?"

She could not at once think of the formula that so well and fully explained life to her. "Oh, my troubles are too small to bother me, really. I like to live . . . even when it's raining and I have to walk three blocks for some kerosene. Difficulties only harden me . . . as for in-stance, recently in Penza. I owed fifty rubles to the boarding house and I was afraid to show myself there lest my books be confiscated. Life is so mixed up. (Is it true that Marx, too, was poor?) So I went to see Ziamka's father; he works at Penza. He was glad to see me (he's al-ready bored with his new wife!), and took me to the movies to see the 'White Spot of the Arctic.' As soon as it grew dark (and less embar-rassing) I said: 'Listen, I'm in a tough spot. Ziamka is sick (it would be a pity if he died!), and I've spent all my coupons for dinners. As a comrade personally close to me you should help me! I'll pay you back on my next pay day. . . .' He said: 'No, I can't; I'm having an overcoat made.' I was silent for a while (I didn't even notice what was on the screen). 'Well, then,' I said, 'at least buy a white roll for Ziamka.' He bought him a roll. . . ."

They raced ahead; fountains of slush were thrown up from under the wheels of the car in front of them.

"You never loved your husband?"

"I realized that I didn't love him shortly before the birth of my child, when he forced me to transfer my savings to his name (to be on the safe side). He is provident! . . . And at that time I was still younger, quite green!"

"He should have been beaten up well, just once, to sober him. . . ."

"That's immoral, Alexei Nikitich. Furthermore, he's busy, he is a responsible worker: he really needs an overcoat! No, perhaps not . . . he doesn't need it so much. But I can't sue him after all; you know, I'm almost ashamed, because of Ziamka. . . . 'Why weren't you careful, mother?' he would say . . . 'you chose a villain.' . . ." She caught herself and fell silent.

How often she repented of ill-advised confessions (you chatterbox, you chatterbox!). That's how friends are lost, when pity sneaks into a relationship. And all this because of that harmonica, that stupid, squeaky little box, pasted with stinking rags. (However, she stealthily touched the toy in the briefcase to make sure that it had not fallen to pieces from the shaking of the car. No, it was intact!) Marina did not notice by what road they returned to the city. And as though in confirmation of her fears the car stopped in a deserted crooked lane.

Kurilov touched her hand in a friendly gesture. "I'll leave you only for a minute; I have to return a few books. Wait for me here, Marina. . . ."

His voice sounded soothing. He slammed the door and vanished into the misty, snowy silence. Nestled in her seat Marina waited for him. Snowflakes were falling, and it seemed to her that they were wooing each other. Kurilov did not return. The monotonous humming of the engine made her feel sleepy. She blissfully closed her eyes, and the only thing she wanted was that the peaceful silence of this forlorn lane should continue forever. . . . She dozed, and dreamed that Klavdia came, very extraordinary-looking, slow and solemn. She pulled the young woman out of the car by her ear. Marina opened her eyes and did not realize at once where she was. The street was unrecognizable. White wet flakes were flying in all directions. Everything had become snowy. Fluffy mushrooms had formed at the edge of the sidewalk. A sleigh passed by, driven by a snowdrift; from under it protruded mournfully a horse's tail, as though sewed on. A snowy muzhik of the kind so often manufactured by Ziamka huddled on the front seat. The snow did not succeed in melting even on the radiator cover. The driver got down to put a blanket over it. A wet gruel at once began to drip on his face. The wind was subsiding, but the snow was growing thicker, falling endlessly. All around her it rose noiselessly to an alarming height. Kurilov still had not come back.

Fearing to doze off again, Marina tried to imagine what could have detained Alexei Nikitich in one of these ugly, grey private houses. She often had to invent unusual stories for Ziamka. First she saw military boots. With their tops bending to either side they stood near a simple field hospital bed, dusty, but not because someone had walked in them along a hot summer road. On yellow, crumpled pillows lay Kurilov's sick friend; with his hollow cheeks he resembled Nekrasov—when Nekrasov was dying. Kurilov was persuading Nekrasov to consent to an operation. Both knew that it was useless, but they had nothing else to talk about. . . . She didn't like this, she crossed it out. Much more likely Kurilov's mother lived here. A woman of the old-fashioned kind, she does not go to see her son; as the oldest male in the family he visits her once every month. It is his custom to sit for a certain time in this shack permeated with the smell of wood oil and camphor. The son, wrapped in tobacco smoke, sits leaning against the wall, his chin pressed into his chest. His dry and small mother sits before him; she wears a black three-cornered neckerchief and has faded eyes. Long before he was exiled she had lamented over him and escorted him to his incomprehensible life as to a grave. From the corner, icons look down gloomily, like relatives who have not received their fair share. . . . Once again Marina dismissed this fantasy: he would not have taken books to his mother! She could not think of a third variation.

A powerful landlady with a basket of wet laundry on her shoulders had opened the door for Kurilov and showed him the way. He went past a little table with four kerosene stoves, according to the number of families, past four doors, behind three of which in turn a child was wailing, a man was playing a mandolin out of tune and burning logs were crackling. Without knocking he entered the fourth room; he was in a hurry. He was dazzled by the abundance of light, although all the glass walls at the Pokhvisnevs were covered with snow. A little old man immediately jumped out from behind the curtain printed with flamboyant cocks. Kurilov said that he was glad to find him recovered from his shock and, handing him his bundle, added facetiously that his railroad was so efficient it even returned unclaimed property. The old man nodded, stroking his trousers that were baggy at the knees. His eyes jumped in his face with the friskiness of playful fleas; apparently the very apparition of a ghost connected with the incident near Sakonikha put him into a state.

His loquacity was enough to madden a strong man, but Kurilov was prevented from leaving immediately by an obscure feeling of guilt toward him.

"Oh, you're right," the old man was saying, scattering his words like seeds. "Fate has often placed me, eh, in various kinds of conflicts, but such a one as this had never happened to me before. We old men, I'm sorry to say, aren't very suited to being shaken up like that in railroad cars. . . . And when I awoke I had a little pain in my shoulder, and the windows were smashed; and everything was in its place. Only the spittoon had moved to the very middle of the floor; it was of an unusual shape, eh, with a lid. I kicked it, but it remained motionless. In despair, even shouting, I began to push it, but it turned out to be screwed to the floor! Actually it was the ventilator, and to make a long story short, I was really sitting on the ceiling. And do you imagine, my friend, that at my age, ah . . . I could spend the rest of my life on a ceiling? Then I . . ."

Kurilov said that he was in a hurry and he was about to reach for the doorknob, when the old man, almost knocking his visitor down in his desire to reach his ear, told him that an hour before his niece had shot herself. . . . (Arkadyi Hermogenovich was himself surprised at the naturalness with which he improvised this story.)

"Is she alive?"

Pokhvisnev waved his hands, and his gestures were almost more comprehensible than his intermittent, senile whispers. The bullet had pierced only the soft flesh of her leg, a homemade bandage could take care of the wound. But the mishap was accompanied by a number of secondary mishaps. The only telephone in the house had been removed a month before because the bills had not been paid; his niece's husband was away on a mission; and cabs were not to be had any longer. . . . Oh, no doctor was needed, but if only his injured niece could be driven home. An important chief like Kurilov had certainly come in a car. . . .

Kurilov was silent. All this was not very plausible. A shot would have caused a tumult in the house. And even the washed floor, still wet, and the pail of pinkish snow in the corner, failed to dispel his suspicions. Then, as though fearing that Kurilov would change his mind, Arkadyi Hermogenovich ostentatiously drew the curtain aside.

Almost all the other half of the room was occupied by an enormous chair covered with black oil cloth, and on it, stretching her legs in an unnatural fashion, Liza was reclining. She was pale, without a drop of blood in her bitten lips; her uncle had wrapped her shoulders in a tattered old fur coat. Despite the rattling fire in the stove, a wintry freshness pervaded this part of the room. Liza made an effort to smile; her eyes expressed impotent hostility.

"You shouldn't bother a stranger," she said sternly as she nestled helplessly against the oil-cloth upholstery.

"Don't teach me the rules of human intercourse, Liza," the old man said heatedly. "You're a little animal! You didn't even cry from pain. I've always suspected that you were inhuman. . . ."

"But I won't be able to walk to the car, anyhow. . . ."

At this point Alexei Nikitich lifted the heap of crumpled human matter in his arms and without a word carried it toward the door. She looked indifferently, somewhere beyond his cap. Only her eyebrows, which rose in an arc on her forehead from time to time, seemed to indicate that her pain had not yet died down.

"Does it burn?" He recalled his first bullet wound.

"No, only I w-as very frightened. . . ." she answered, enjoying the ease with which he carried her.

Marina was awakened by the cold. A silhouette in a canvas coat was getting into the car (and in her half-sleep the crackle of the canvas seemed to her like the gritting of teeth). She was still dreaming and she could not understand why Klavdia needed such a big black hat. And Arkadyi Hermogenovich was already tugging at her knee and with dubious kindness asking the "little citizeness to leave the car for a moment." Marina jumped straight out into a snowdrift that had formed near the footboard; her feet were enveloped in snowy wetness. Her briefcase had fallen out in front of her. She could only guess that some mishap had occurred. And while Kurilov arranged Liza's exhausted body on the seat, the two women looked at each other; Liza winced and turned her face away the first. The little old man nimbly jumped into the seat beside the driver and slammed the door. Marina leaped aside to avoid being struck by it. The headlights went on; the wheels began to turn, spattering snowy mud into the air. Then the body of the car listed, the magic little bird started, snorted, and the red tail light began rapidly to grow smaller. The dream about Klavdia was coming true. . . .

The janitor came out for a single-handed combat with the results of the snowstorm. He pulled down his cap over his eyes and for a long while scratched the back of his head. The first lamp was lit in a basement window. How fast night was falling! . . . Marina felt chilly, her ankle, which she had bumped against the running-board, ached. She was hungry. She broke off a piece of bread and hesitatingly took out her apple (but Ziamka liked just such warty apples, and it went back into the briefcase). She was barely able to read the name of the street. It was time for her to go home. Neither her wet stockings nor the distance could frighten her: this was just another of those "life tangles." And now all of a sudden she recalled the maxim she had vainly tried to remember when talking to Kurilov: man lives on the joy of mastered misfortunes!

A quarter of an hour later, Kurilov's car rushed back into the street. Streams of light searched among the squatty buildings. The janitor shied away toward the wall. The street was empty. . . . Kurilov jumped out of the car and ran past it, looking into the alley-ways. What had happened seemed to him extremely unfair toward his companion. Marina was gone. . . .

"Marina . . . Marinka!"

A few blocks away she was trudging doggedly. The city was miry. The icy gruel yielded under her steps, and she left little black patches of water in her tracks. She was glad that Ziamka was not with her. Everything around her was crumbling, falling. Water thundered on the roofs, crawled down the pipes into the gutters, coughed hoarsely in the drains. And now she could no longer believe that this was the first snow, the lovely first snow!

# CHAPTER 16

# Arkadyi Hermogenovich: His Stuffing

EVERYONE WHO knew Arkadyi Hermogenovich personally ascribed his remarkable longevity to his sensible abstinence. He neither drank nor smoked and, following the Roman prescription for a long life, never indulged in emotions. An iron constitution resided in his dried-up organism. Nor could anyone say that in his youth he had exhausted himself from loving. His biography was perfect, as though designed to edify disobedient children. In his own words, he had drunk his life with unhurried delight, like a glass of cranberry juice at a sultry crossroads between one desert and another; judging by the color of his cheeks, the sediment at the bottom was as saturated as the rainbow-colored foam at the edges. A modest teacher of high-school Latin, he had taught reading at sight to more than five thousand pupils, and the knowledge that he had thus even to a small extent embellished their existence gave him the tranquillity of mind he needed. Moreover, throughout his life he had never had any doubts about anything, had met remarkable people, had been a friend of Bakunin's, had had an apartment in Moscow, and had outlived his enemies. Wherever fate threw him, there were people capable of understanding his spiritual charm and appreciating the quality of his fine velour hat. It had a high crown, and under its broad brim there was always twilight. It cast a romantic shade not only over Arkadyi Hermogenovich's appearance, but also over his thoughts and indeed his actions. Verily, his hat was a part of his character and perhaps of his physical person as well, considering that for its sake he had ventured to descend even into Dudni-kov's grave. This strange object had a history of its own.

In the past it too had known misfortune. Three years before it had almost been destroyed by the explosion of a kerosene stove, and eight years before it had almost been lost at sea. This happened in the Crimea, in a remote Tartar village where he had stopped on his way to Feodosia. He was returning in excellent health from a rest-home. The coachmen usually stopped at that village to water their horses, and Arkadyi Hermogenovich had an opportunity to visit a little of the surrounding country. The day was a cool one, the snowy white crests of the waves rippled unceasingly—an orgy of wind rages in this place all the year round. Arkadyi Hermogenovich's hat was blown off his head and rolled with the speed of a bicycle wheel along the deserted beach. He ran after it, the wind billowing his raincoat about him like a sail. The old man sometimes lagged behind and sometimes ran in front of the fugitive object, and now and then it was unclear which was running after which.

Close to the surf someone at last had the presence of mind to step on the runaway property. Arkadyi Hermogenovich raised his eyes toward the rescuer. . . . Before him stood an obese, prematurely senile man wearing worn-out trousers stuck into knitted gaiters and a woven grey shirt as vast as the sea. His grey mane, held close to the forehead by a leather strap, was streaming in the wind. The enraptured Pokhvisnev in a loud voice compared this man with Ovid wandering near the mouth of the Danube and composing his Epistles from Pontus. The comparison hit the bull's eye. The man smiled and pointed to a two-storey house; he invited his new acquaintance to dry off and dine with him. Meanwhile the last carriage from Otuz had left.

Pokhvisnev's new friend had more than once likened himself to an exiled poet. Indeed he even compared himself to Ovid. Yet no one had deliberately sent him into oblivion. Once a member of an exuberant poetic Pleiade, he was dying here without fame and literary posterity. This was the time when prophets were born among the people—the poet fancied himself one of them, but his well-composed prophecies did not come true. Occasional guests, all solemn, intelligent and insincere, were the only audience for his works. These guests were mediocre artists and professors, aged followers of the arts, and just kindly sick people whose physicians had ordered them to die on southern shores. They paid for a room and for proximity to the Muses with supreme enthusiasm for the poet's dying star. Out of sheer boredom they loved queer people. The proprietor introduced Arkadyi Hermogenovich to his guests as a friend of Bakunin's and the author of many unpublished Latin verses. . . . The poet's hospitality extended beyond the number of rooms in his house so that for the night Arkadyi Hermogenovich was moved to the library, in the blissful shadow of dusty, bronze-colored folios. The next morning the proprietor took his guest to see the Karadag canyons and, in the evening, the ancient Cimmerian plateau; he knew every corner of the country and thought that the sea itself was one of his own creations. . . . Arkadyi Hermogenovich got along very well with him. The proprietor appreciated friends who shared his stale bread and mournful, Ovidian solitude.

In this house a constant poetic excitement was maintained. To the measure of his capacities everyone composed something. Someone once expressed the conjecture that Pokhvisnev might have anonymously fought against the *Rhine Journal* to defend the outraged name of his friend Bakunin. Arkadyi Hermogenovich made no comment. He was mystery itself, smiling in order to remain inscrutable. This was hardly a deliberate ruse; he simply did not understand what was wanted of him. Occasionally he sent off letters, and one idler discovered that the old man was petitioning for a pension and was looking for one Dudnikov, his old physician. It goes without saying that Arkadyi Hermogenovich was interested not so much in the modest sum of his pension as in obtaining the government's official recognition of his previous activity. He had always been deeply and sincerely moved by the idea of freedom. True, he had not supposed that all "this" would take place in such a sweeping fashion; he had got accustomed to the revolution slowly and with difficulty, but at heart he felt himself to be a misunderstood rebel; he had almost run away with Bakunin to join Garibaldi, and. . . . In brief, on the brass plate of history he wished to place his name, too, although in the margin and in small letters. . . . Thus he lived quite well, the Tartars respected his hat, the guests called him "professor," and he himself, after the fashion of coquettish old men, began to add years to his age.

The poet's villa stood on the beach. In fresh weather the house was filled with the salty bitterness of the sea and the scraping sound of wet sand. Pokhvisnev could not sleep on such nights. He would go out and sit on a one-legged stone bench near the gate; its other end was fixed into a hole cut in a large, melancholy tree. (Arkadyi Hermogenovich maintained that this tree was a black poplar; the others assumed he was right because they never contradicted him on any question.) Light waves surged toward the shore and perished in the sand. The tree was shrivelling; through its lancet-like, tamarisk leaves the stars shone more brilliantly. Arkadyi Hermogenovich snuggled into his cotton wrapper. Then the great space in front of him assumed the shape of a feminine face, transparent and azure. The woman wore her hair in the style of the Eighties, when this solemn little old man with plastered-down whiskers was alive and developing. She called him to her. Her brilliant, dewy eyelashes gleamed and breathed a frightening chill upon his forehead. Arkadyi Hermogenovich persuaded himself that he was seeing Eternity, and this was just as pleasant as eating ice cream.

The apparition could be explained by his lyrical mood rather than by his weakened retina. (Everything in the world gave him lofty impressions; he was always somewhat capricious and whimsical; once he boasted absent-mindedly that at Karadag the wind had torn a button

off his coat; he despotically forced everyone present to believe him.
. . .) The outward appearance of Eternity reminded him of Taniechka
Blankenhagel; he had preserved her tender and obscure image through
years of disappointment and fussing over petty things. This girl, dark
and pensive, could never be replaced by another. To be sure, she died
young, but a poem about her remained. (Once again the old man was
lucky: in these days the daughter of a big, although enlightened land-
owner, would have had a hard time, and it would have been infamous
on the part of Arkadyi Hermogenovich not to help her in her need.)
At this very place, by the sea, he acquired the habit of mentally visiting the imagined village cemetery once a week. . . .

The day was dying, the shadows grew twice as long as the objects
that cast them. His black lustrine jacket gleamed with orange gold. . . .
Arkadyi Hermogenovich entered the cemetery, following a path known
only to him. In his sweaty hand a little bouquet of field flowers sticky
with sap was fading. Respectfully and solemnly, kneeling on one knee,
the old man placed it at the foot of the grave. For the hundredth time
he read the inscription on the greenish, jagged, mossy stone, a quotation from Ezekiel who had eaten his own bitter book and had not been
sated with his own knowledge. Taniechka was beside him. She had
dissolved without a trace in the birds' chirping, in the glimmer of the
evening star, in the green rustle of bare-headed birch trees. . . . In
brief, this ancient oleograph filled him with joy as a child is filled with
joy over a new toy and a sparrow over a loathsome lump of dung on
the snow.

You are right, old Roman Ovid: sleeplessness is the mother of apparitions! . . . And now the curtain of his memory drew open, and the
sleeping actors awakened. Arkadyi Hermogenovich saw the lavender
edge of the woods whence there breathed freshness and a smell of
mushrooms. On a wide and smooth clearing, emerald like the cloth top
of a card-table, Taniechka Blankenhagel and Arkadyi Pokhvisnev, the
young student, were starting out to ride. They took the same route day
after day: along a by-road through the woods to Balakino, next to
Borschnia and thence, along the new railroad embankment, to the
Psna River valley with its enchanted water-lilies and swamp duckweed
in the backwaters. The railroad was being built in an almost magic
silence. From the distance one saw a reddish, lustrous mound of dug-
up clay and scattered groups of people, but neither the whistling of
the foremen nor the bang of shovels and hoes reached them from
there. The rounded peal of evening bells shook the silence and covered
the coarse sounds which disfigured the charm of the landscape.

Taniechka longed for a closer look at the "people" of whom there was so much half-frightened talk at the estate. They left the lane in the woods, and Pokhvisnev was the first to approach a group of laborers who were about to start their supper. Amidst them, untidily spitting sparks and talking to itself like an old man, a bonfire was blazing. Fallen-off pieces of wood smoked, and the little spot on the fire gurgled rather appetizingly. The people themselves seemed to Taniechka hump-backed, lopsided and somehow hollowed out in the chest by their pick-axes. A prematurely aged woman in coarse hemp cloth and miserable bast shoes was feeding a baby at her breast. With long-drawn-out, earth-colored lips it chewed a nipple equally earth-colored and long. The men guessed the identity of the visitors. (Taniechka's father visited the road every day.) Some rose, removing their *gresh-neviks,* high woollen hats, others remained seated; none bowed to the guests. But one mischievous old fellow moved closer to have a look at the aristocratic beauty of Taniechka, her fluffy hat with a blue veil and her tight-fitting riding-habit. . . . (So many years had passed, and Arkadyi Hermogenovich was still tormented by the remembrance of the glossy fabric over her chaste, sharp little knees!)

"How goes it, boys?" Arkadyi Hermogenovich asked familiarly, sitting down on a mound of cut turf, and for some reason the baby began to cry at that very moment, and everyone shushed him as if he were a grown-up.

"Oh, we're doing well, we melt fat from fleas," joked a squat and sturdy muzhik, apparently the foreman of the crew and, turning to the woman, he ordered her to "cover herself": "Silly, don't you see the young lady's looking!" (But even before he had finished, the mother had jealously covered her child with a flap of her coat.)

"Look out, he might suffocate!" warned Arkadyi Hermogenovich, well informed of the accidents of peasant life. Then he went on: "Are you strangers here?"

No one answered him, but some of them grew visibly tense. Once again the baby whimpered in a thin voice, and for some reason, now, half a century later, in Arkadyi Hermogenovich's mind this whimper was connected with the choking stream of smoke that emanated from the fallen pieces of wood. No matter how much his mother hugged and rocked him, the tiny, slow-witted muzhik kept on yelling and whining.

"Why is he crying?" asked Taniechka, bending toward them from her saddle, and she regretted that she had not brought an apple or a piece of candy with her.

Then one of the laborers, a scrawny fellow of about forty, with copper-colored, hollow temples, came forward. His eyes were gloomy, and his tow-colored hair above them was stiff; the foreman leered at him, coughed once to caution him and immediately lowered his head. He knew this man, Spiridon Matochkin.

"This baby's father, gracious lady, well, the Frenchie recently gave him a kick," said Spirka, listening to all his own words to see how they sounded and not looking at anything except the young girl's eyes. "You see, he aimed at his belly but he hit him in the very parts. The little boy is no doubt crying because he'll have to go through life without any little brothers or sisters. Ha, the little rascal!" And with his finger, straight and inflexible as an animal's horn, he familiarly poked the little body hidden under the coat. But this deliberate coarse gesture was more friendly than his courtesy toward the guests.

("Stop the show!" Arkadyi Hermogenovich cried to his memory, but no force could have dispersed the actors now.)

Wide-eyed, Taniechka stared at this indescribable poverty; and she would have burst into tears if she had not been put on her guard by Spiridon's bitter sneer. She knew that the culprit in question was Pommier, the engineer and contractor, a very amiable and witty talker, whom Blankenhagel particularly valued for his inflexibility and harshness with the workers. Of course, the backyard of great exploits is always loathsome. . . . She became confused.

"They are so. . . ." She did not finish her whisper to the young man. "But look, he has an ear missing!"

True enough, one of his ears was missing.

"And where's your ear, little brother?" Pokhvisnev asked sternly, and touched his own ear so that his question could more easily penetrate Spiridon's dark mind.

". . . My ear?" Calmly, lazily even, Spiridon touched a dirty fragment above the hole. "That too was eaten up by fleas. It's a kind of blind flea, so to speak. It doesn't care what it eats, if only its food has the smell of bread. . . ." And once again no one, not even he himself, laughed at this insolence unprecedented at that period.

Nettled, Taniechka lashed her Bunny. The old man swerved backwards in an odd way and the beautiful horsewoman galloped out of the camp. Oh, Arkadyi had always lied to her about the people's magnanimity and wisdom! . . . As for Pokhvisnev, following the call of his conscience and desiring to strengthen his social feelings, he ventured to visit the hut where the injured muzhik lay. It was only a little distance away. Spiridon undertook to accompany him. Pokhvisnev bent down as he entered, in order not to bump his head. Through the turf roof set on shaky poles the sky was shining in a few places. A trestle draped with a saddle cloth stood near the centre. On top, in a shirt rolled up to the very neck, lay a still human body taut with pain. The

head was thrown back; Arkadyi Hermogenovich was unable to distinguish the face, only the teeth gleamed once in the darkness. But the
oblique orange rays of the sun painted the injured man's heels and his
hand that hung down in mortal exhaustion (one finger now pressed
the palm and now with terrifying slowness straightened out again).
The muzhik's naked belly was abundantly covered with clayey earth
directly from the quarry; slightly rising, it lay there as in a cup, and
the wound itself was thus concealed from the curiosity of strangers.

"We've put earth on him, see, it draws the burning pain away,"
Spiridon said with indifference, and cast a side glance at the guest's
frightened face. "He was a fine fellow. He would go out in the meadow
and stand straight as a glass: he was solid! . . . Please, just look, master, see how Pommier banged him in the 'bite.' . . ." And casually, as
though digging a grave, he began to dig up this live mound of earth,
throwing it down right on Pokhvisnev's boots.

The young man's face flushed red in bewilderment; he grasped the
muzhik's long veiny hand and begged him to be careful, and the
muzhik resisted effortlessly as though saying: Don't touch, that's *ours*.
. . . Now master of his emotions, Pokhvisnev in a warm voice forbade
him to address him as master; as though reading verses he declared
that he, too, was *of the people*, that he, too, hated the *oppressors* (and
he cast a stealthy look behind him as he uttered this word), that for
the time being one must suffer and *sharpen one's axe*, that the hour of
*revenge* was close . . . and a mass of other such knavish and vague
words that made him feel hot and loathsome. And Spiridon squinted
at the remaining half of the sun behind a distant transparent bush, and
his countenance was inscrutable—still waters are blackest at sunset.

". . . And for the time being you must learn; read books!" Pokhvisnev
stammered. "The people must understand what act they are performing when they take power into their hands. I'll give you something I
have . . . at first the simplest things, about geography, chemistry. Do
you know the hollow tree on the edge of the woods near Balakinsk?
I ll put it there, and you can come for it. . . . Read it aloud, a little bit
at a time, explain it to one another. I'll drop in to see you, to see
whether you've understood it. . . ." And he shook Spiridon's hand,
urging him to agree and secretly fearing that he might suddenly strike
him, sensing his own slippery and confused insincerity.

"Eh, I don't know how to call you. . . . Anyhow, no hard feelings!"

Without a frown or a smile the muzhik waved his hand, and left the
hut first. Pokhvisnev ran after him. Fortunately no one saw them together. The laborers were standing stock still in their amazement at
the young lady. His horse darted off. . . . It was pleasant, fragrant in
the meadow lands! . . . He rode for a long time; there was no greater

pleasure on earth than to rush toward the first evening star and be aware of one's youth, one's health and the terrifying closeness to the people he had just experienced. The shadows merged with the objects that cast them, and the dampening road was as soft to gallop over as a carpet. . . .

He overtook Taniechka in the woods; she had dropped her reins, and her horse was ambling along. The tip of his boot resiliently struck Bunny's croup. Thigh grazed thigh. The girl shuddered as though overtaken by dark phantoms and thoughts. First cautiously, then gradually in a bolder and less restrained manner, Arkadyi Pokhvisnev spoke of the imminent all-peasant revolt, of the overthrow of the ridiculous Tsar with whiskers, that deceiver and villain, of how the master's blood, heavy, redder and thicker than unrefined quicksilver, would be shed on the estates. . . . At heart he doubted whether this harassed race, marked with the weals of recent floggings, was capable of anything worse than looting, but as a poor intellectual not belonging to the upper classes he enjoyed uttering such words. They satisfied some dark, deadly itch in his soul and at the same time made the girl he was frightening closer and more accessible to him. True, he did not propose that she run away with him (although in his opinion this step would have saved her from the people's wrath); he feared that Blankenhagel, so quick with his hands, might beat him up. Nevertheless, he tried to put his arm around the girl's waist; considering his bad horsemanship, this was almost a heroic deed. Taniechka lowered her head still farther. . . . And now there followed that sole kiss they ever exchanged, the kiss that still burned his lips. In the middle of it they were suddenly attacked by mosquitoes, with a particularly loud buzzing and of zebra-like colors. The young people dashed toward Borschnia. On the terrace, handsome and sneering, sat Dudnikov, devouring cherries. Edmoshka, Taniechka's younger brother, was reciting for him a lesson about the Merovingians, while his eyes followed the trajectory of the pits that flew out of Dudnikov's mean and fleshy mouth.

Here the performance ended; the actors went home to sleep until the next one. Sighing and snarling, the sea shook as though suspended on chains; the waves thundered in their depths. Nightly clouds, ashes of a consumed day, stretched over the boundless expanses of the sea. Each of them was reminiscent of objects that once were in use, or of people as unrecognizable as a reflection in rippling water. Arkadyi Hermogenovich, imperceptibly to himself, joined the ghostly dance of shadows and stars. Thus by long circuitous paths the unrefreshing sleep of the aged finally came to him.

# CHAPTER 17

# A. H. Pokhvisnev: His Skin

AFTER THE DEATH OF THE POET, who was buried in the salty Cimmerian sands, Arkadyi Hermogenovich recalled the existence of his niece and, without informing her of his coming, went to Moscow. Liza had not the heart to refuse a place for the night to the old man who stood with his bundle in the doorway; by the next day, here as everywhere, he was already at home. He stood in queues for her, darned her stockings, cooked their dinner with particular enthusiasm on a Primus stove, and planted a whole little garden on the window-sill. In plywood boxes he grew onions and salad greens; bunches of dried dill, which he hung on threads from the ceiling, made the room look like a sorcerer's den. Liza did not repent of her kindness; soon fate rewarded her by giving her Protoklitov. Arkadyi Hermogenovich remained the sole possessor of the room. He sent for his books, which had been left somewhere in the provinces, and began to teach Latin to some half-trained pharmacists. His life began to have a pattern, and that same year he accidentally ran into Dudnikov.

Pokhvisnev had long been tormented by the suspicion that Dudnikov too had been in love with Taniechka, and perhaps with greater success than he himself. And so he began to haunt Dudnikov's basement, trying gradually to unravel the meaning of his frank and impious insinuations. Now when all their other ties with life were broken, this ancient enmity drew the rivals together. The two old men met to spend the evening in silence: everything had already been said before. Sitting opposite each other, they evoked in great detail Borschnia as it had been half a century before: the house built on terraces, the carpet-like flower beds, the tall hothouses with orange trees crucified against the walls, the linden-tree park and the slimy twilight of its alleys. . . . Large as life, Orest Romualdovich Blankenhagel appeared before them, with royal sideburns, wearing a lavender dressing gown; his son Edmoshka, a thirteen-year-old boy, nicknamed "the pinches" by the servant girls; Nikodim Petrovich, the manager, humpbacked like a seahorse; Taniechka petrified in a half-élan, as though she had heard a summons, imperious and inexorable; Spirka. . . . And then another scene of the long-dead spectacle comes to life.

Foul weather is raging, the wind is banging a loosened shutter. The dogs are stamping on the lower terrace and barking at the silence like howitzers. In the house, Nikodim Petrovich passes by with a candle in his hand. Pokhvisnev waits patiently for a weak yellow ray from the keyhole to pierce the darkness of the night. But there is no ray, and sleep does not come. The watchman pounds his rattle, or perhaps it is his own heart. . . . He is frightened. Patrols are still driving along the embankment of the unopened road. The guards sent by Police Inspector Rynda-Rozhnovsky are fattening in the servants' quarters. The village police commissioners are certainly not asleep. The whole district is restless. Somewhere in the vicinity Spirka is knocking about with his crowd. He is willing to be bought off by the merchants, but as for the upper classes, he threatens to clean them out altogether. No doubt till the end of time the undying blood of Pugachev would flow in the Volga muzhiks. . . . Then a sound, dulled and melodious, of three different keys reaches the young man's ears. He interprets it in his own way: Taniechka, too, cannot sleep; she has got up and pensively touches the piano. The musical phrase sounds like a question. Then she opens the window. Falling over each other, bustling shadows move in the darkness. Autumn is peeling the oaks and lindens in the park, and they weep like Marsyas in Apollo's merciless hands. The sky is as though wrapped in bandages. The sound is repeated, and Pokhvisnev can almost see Taniechka's fingers gleaming indistinctly on the keyboard. . . .

Dudnikov's crime, confessed before his death and left unpunished, changed the text of the whole play. Impotent senile jealousy, the new stage director, destroyed, then rearranged the setting. Once again Arkadyi Hermogenovich awakens in the middle of the night. Someone's hand moves along the wooden partition near which his bed is placed. The rustling comes closer, and once again he likes to think it is the steward. But by this time Nikodim Petrovich is asleep in his room. It is Dudnikov, in shorts only, red-faced, self-assured, creeping up to Taniechka's rooms. A layer of wood one inch thick prevents the young man from biting those cautious, exploring fingers. Trying to step on the outside of the stairs, in order to avoid making the floor creak, Dudnikov steals alone. Taniechka meets her lover in the doorway. In the darkness their hands seek each other. Dudnikov's attack is impetuous. The nocturnal horror and the closeness of Spirka's knife only intensify the coarse physical joy of the rendezvous. And then the tender sounds of the strings acquire a new and terrible explanation.

"Stop!" Arkadyi Hermogenovich cries out to them mentally. "You're not alone, I'm here . . . I can hear everything!"

Not a keyboard but a string mattress is ringing realistically over-head, pushed up and down by the rhythm of two bodies. The rug on the floor of Taniechka's bedroom softens the sound, but jealousy, like a pedal, accentuates it till it is like volcanic thunder. Arkadyi Hermo-genovich is choking. "Air!" He opens the window, and the leaves heavy with nocturnal dew break into his room, to come to his aid. "Not enough. . . ." Undressed, he runs outside. On the croquet ground a fallen oak leaf twirls hissing by, and there is something sinister in its centrifugal impetus. Madness seizes the jealous man, the wet wind fails to sober him. Forgetting Spirka, he wanders haphazardly, crush-ing the tall, late autumn flowers. Nothing can interrupt their tryst. Beaten and frozen he returns and hides his head under his blanket. They are still busy breaking the springs. "Stop them, he'll kill her!" No doubt in the next variation the unlucky rival will awaken the whole house, the servants will flock together, and Blankenhagel himself, armed with a gnarled stick, will climb the stairs to Taniechka's bed-room.

The happy lovers no longer existed, but this did not satisfy the third, the deceived one. More, with Dudnikov's departure the last meaning of existence was lost; Arkadyi Hermogenovich seemed to shrivel and fade. The chaste girl of whom he demanded nothing except that she know that he loved her, to whom he by stealth confided the dreams of Saint-Simon, Fourier and himself, was now becoming even more se-ductive. He began to grasp the meaning of that veiled gleam in Taniechka's eyes, open in a manner suggesting that she had just dis-covered the world and all its sinful joys. So it was not very difficult to explain Dudnikov's sudden disappearance from Borschnia and, two weeks later, Taniechka's hasty departure for the Crimea. . . . A fit of belated anger impelled the old man to undertake a risky trip to Borschnia, which was interrupted halfway, near Sakonikha. He was going there to walk upon Taniechka's grave, which in his mind he had reverently been visiting for thirty years. He interpreted the railroad ac-cident as a sign that destiny does not permit anyone to read its books ahead of time. He returned ashamed and subdued, like a child that has been threatened with a whip heavy enough to smite a bull. . . .

Like all old men he thought that he stood on the threshold of old age when it was already behind him. Actually, he no longer under-stood very much of what was going on. His generation had long since departed from life, and he alone, like an experienced antique speci-men, remained amidst the bustle of the new age. Everything was mov-ing, being displaced; one thing pushed another away, only to be forced to yield under the pressure of a third. Arkadyi Hermogenovich would go to a barber shop to have himself made younger and would find a grocery in its place. Reconciling himself to the change, he decided to buy some cabbage for his soup, and the lovely salesgirl was metamorphosed in the midst of a sentence into a tall clumsy fellow in a Russian shirt. Shaken, he would go outside and suddenly discover that he could take a bus home, although he had had to walk thither. Certain ingenious forces deliberately teased him to make him run out on the public square and scream with fear; and he had to be vigilant in order not to have someone else substituted for himself on his way. He needed to cling to someone—hence he saluted the appearance of Protoklitov on his horizon as a favor of fate and a timely interference of posterity.

Thus, in a few sessions with his new uncle, Ilya Ignatyich learned the complete biography of his old high-school principal. In their youth, Pokhvisnev and Dudnikov tutored together on the estate of a certain Blankenhagel, a philanthropist of the Gorigoretsk district; they separated when the younger Blankenhagel went to the Cadet School in Petersburg; they met again only after nine years. Dudnikov's specialty was history; for the next six years he was the principal of the *gymnasium* in which Pokhvisnev taught Latin; at that time Dudnikov was married to the daughter of an important administrator, owned real estate and conducted himself like a grandee in public education; later, having become a school district inspector, he kept Arkadyi Hermogenovich down, deliberately refrained from recommending him for promotions and, in 1906, almost kicked him out with a dishonorable discharge because he supported the abolition of uniforms for pupils of secondary schools. This dignitary held that the foundation of order was morality, but once he sinned out of curiosity and had to be treated by a men's specialist for two and a half months. Nikolai Aristarkhovich Dudnikov had had two daughters, and a son who was shot while trying to flee to the Ukraine, then under the rule of a German puppet; his wife had burned to death when a kerosene stove exploded, during the year of hunger, and his daughters had been dispersed by fate into foreign night clubs; recently he had been living with some priest who had gone to pot, whom he nicknamed the *Pecheneg* and who died in his arms. He had never been a beggar, was irreconcilable to the very end. . . .

Ilya Ignatyich's curiosity was satisfied after the first half-hour, but he rebelled against Pokhvisnev's conversation only after the first six months. Arkadyi Hermogenovich never separated now from that impressive dead body; for half a century it had barred his way to distinction and fame like a toll gate. Now at least once a week he came to

Protoklitov's study with Dudnikov on his shoulders and would begin by unmasking the deceased until he was completely naked, then he would disembowel him, argue violently against him and belabor him with his tiny fists. Little by little Ilya Ignatyich became almost the biographer of that important Tsarist official. The odor of decay was growing increasingly stronger with every page of Pokhvisnev's tale. Finally it was as though Pokhvisnev had dragged Dudnikov's corpse to Protoklitov's apartment, with the intention of displaying it there for all time to come. All this was understandable; for in reality the rotten belly of the corpse, like a sacred box, now contained the whole life of Arkadyi Hermogenovich.

Sometimes they touched on other subjects (while Dudnikov lay at their feet waiting his turn), such as popular medicine (he cited the testimony of the classics about the famous Pirré cure of a disease of the spleen by rubbing his big toe on his right foot) and even politics. For instance, he condemned the destruction of the Romanovs. He was horrified by the casualness of that nocturnal deed; he would have preferred a sumptuous trial, the blood-thirsty cries of a fanatical nation (but fortunately restrained in good time!), an historical speech by the prosecutor, in which eloquence would struggle against justice, with magnanimity winning the day. . . . On one occasion he even expanded upon the possibility of the moon's falling down upon the earth and sketched for the amazed Protoklitov a complete picture of this event. Euler's abstract mathematical formulae were combined in his tale with almost hallucinatory visions. The narrative was accompanied by senile sighs and many grimaces and gestures to which he resorted in order to heighten the effect.

In an abridged form it went more or less like this:

". . . One day the moon will turn some two degrees, and mankind will have a look at the other half of the earth's satellite. The crater of Copernicus will move to the very edge, and the new blackness emerging from non-being will be named the Sea of Suddenness. The law of falling bodies and the attraction of stars will begin to operate. The prelude to the catastrophe will last for months, and the scientists will have time to discuss to what extent the shortening of the moon day will affect many secondary circumstances of human existence. The moon will begin its fall on a slowed-up, elliptical spiral, gradually accelerating and diminishing the circles. Every night, every night, it will rise bigger and bigger! This will be a period of great discoveries, amazing physical phenomena and great social upheavals. The astronomers will make brilliant observations—completely useless. The newspapers, before being forbidden to discuss the question, will print hypothetical information about the fall of the first moon in prehistoric times, when Australia was born. 'Was not this event the origin of the myth of Aphrodite born from the sea foam?' The enormous globe, now visible also in daytime, will begin to turn faster and faster. And when the edge of the immense caulked disc rises above the horizon, people will experience the same feeling one has when a murderer looks into one's window. . . .

". . . The number of unshaven men in the streets will become striking. A period of confusion and uprisings will precede the ultimate commotion. The appeals of the governments for everyone to remain at his place will go unheeded; the producer no longer will need the consumer, on the contrary. No one will stay at home, cook dinner or pet children. Man will throw off everything he has donned in the preceding centuries. Reason will deliberately hide behind savagery. Ancient witchcraft sects, worshipping carrion, debauchery and non-being, will be reborn; new sects will be formed, comparable only to epidemics in the speed of their extension. They will be called the Dilaniators or Lacerators; thus they will be defined in a special papal bull. They will reek of dogs. They will never have enough of women and wine. They will be lynched at every crossroads; clusters of them will hang in nooses, but their number will increase as the moon begins to rise in the middle of the day, three times every twenty-four hours, then five, eight times, in monstrous phases, completely unshining, a lazy, hilly mass. It will be said that in a day it 'waxes' three times. One will have to turn one's head to see all of it. This will be the talk between cynics: 'It has entered the atmosphere . . . don't you feel something like a breeze on your face?'—'Oh, something is even falling from it!'—'Oh, one might even say it stinks!'—'What do you expect? It's a corpse!' Appeasers at broadcasting stations will in vain play popular dances on balalaikas or chant psalms through their noses. . . .

". . . Street loudspeakers will announce that only eighteen thousand kilometers now separate the moon from the earth. Eighteen thousand, no more, only one and one-half times the radius of the earth. The newspapers will cease publication. Three times a day the preliminary findings of an international committee concerning the coordinates of the expected event will be broadcast: the velocity of the fall, its time and place. The computations will oscillate within such limits that all confidence in them will be undermined: they will oscillate between madness and ignorance. 'They're lying! A cosine was never equal to a tangent!' a voice cries in falsetto from the street loudspeakers. 'The rich people are building flying machines so as not to be on the planet at the moment of the collision!' At first the world will hear a strange tumult on the radio, the sound of broken glass, a shot and a death rattle near the microphone. No war that destroyed millions has ever so infuriated the mob as the killing of that simpleton. It is this murder of an anonymous man that will arouse the lower depths. 'To the air!' they will scream, smashing government buildings. 'We too want to be in the air!' (as though flight were still possible). Gun battles in the streets will become frequent. The decree forbidding suicide in public places will be constantly violated. Despair will revive the memory of another terrible date, 1456, when Pope Calixtus III issued a bull banishing and cursing Halley's comet; it turned around and took to its heels! And now the chief Roman priest, escorted by the whole Conclave of Cardinals, drives in an automobile to Central Europe. There he is going to officiate at an Extraordinary High Mass on the largest, the very largest field to be found on the continent—a few centuries earlier Zizka gave battle to the Germans here from his baggage-train. Praying people filling every inch of space as far as the horizon hoarsely intone a Te Deum in Latin. With a thunderous radio voice, which even Moses on Mount Sinai would have envied, the Pope will converse with God. And although it will be maintained that the transubstantiation of the holy Sacrament, the gage of Heaven's blessing, has taken place in the sight of everyone, the moon that day will rise for the ninth time. For the ninth time the murderer's snout will peep in through the window of the clouds! . . . A rumor will arise that the Dilaniators are resuming their murders. The crowd rushes across the field, tumbling over itself, an enormous lump of animal plasma, just as the dark body illumined by the sunset at its edges will begin to cover the sky and unhurriedly descend behind the firing grounds of the famous cannon factories. Once again the stars will shine, piercing and motionless, 'evil-living angels dwelling in flames look upon the dead.'

". . . Suddenly a new name resounds throughout the world. This man rose from obscurity to fame in half an hour. He is a professor of chiromancy at an Albanian university, born somewhere in the Balkans, with the eye of a miracle-maker and the bushy mustache of a retired army major. People believe him; hope is more intoxicating than a drug. According to his computations, the heavenly body upon reaching what the astronomers call the 'danger zone' will blow up into little fragments, as was the case with Saturn's satellites and will be the case with the satellites of Jupiter. Those who are not afraid of a stone rain will witness a unique spectacle. Only a small part of the moon, about one-third of it, will slide along a tangent to the planet in the region between the Hawaiian Islands and Alabama; tearing off a piece of the earth's flesh it will rush at an accelerated speed to the remotest of the

Galactic provinces. '. . . And so, wrap up your china, keep your children and valuables near you, store up provisions for a week. Let us meet the cosmic storm with good cheer! In the worst case our planet will be split in two: science is familiar with such cases. The two hemispheres will revolve about each other. Communication between the separated relatives will be maintained by special rocket ships construction of which is already under way. . . .' And although his computations contain even arithmetical errors, the declaration of this maniac will cause a migration from America that will never end . . .

". . . All night long heavenly bodies will shoot through the sky. . . . The fall of meteors will evoke the bitter fate of Gomorrah. It will be accompanied by fires, avalanches and floods on a Biblical scale. Hurricanes will tear up trees, many objects will lose all weight. The radio will be out of order, and only one future Noah will sleep in his provincial hole in Arzamass. He is a shoeworker named Gavrila. The day before will be pay-day, and he will be sleeping off his liquor. The blow will come at daybreak, striking the Atlantic Ocean. The Iberian Peninsula will collapse, and the air above it will seem to take fire. The smoking waters mixed with fire from the entrails of the earth will rise up, burying nations and empires. . . . Noah imagines that a tree is embracing him with all its hands and hurling him at something not very soft. By morning he will get up and go to look for his leather-lined tub. He makes the rounds of his place, but his tub has disappeared. He can find nothing to help him get over his hangover. He infers that the co-operatives have been closed during the night. The earth looks unattractive; moreover, his insides are burning and his dislocated shoulder aches. The ancestor of future generations will then sit down and weep. An hour later he will catch a cat and eat it. Three days later he will meet a middle-aged woman with a scratched face; she tells him that an angel of impressive dimensions has protected her from the disaster of the previous night. They will marry. Their children, eighteeen in number, will take their father's stories about matches, the samovar and the gun, for the revelation of God Almighty. Lest he be exposed to the jeers of his offspring, Noah will refrain from telling them about the other things. . . . Everything turns out well. Hence will come the sacred expression: 'Spill it, Gavrila!'."

Arkadyi Hermogenovich, having recited all this in one breath, was exhausted and fell back in his chair. Ilya Ignatyich had the choice of deciding whether this was a prophetic vision or a routine case of senile dementia. At any rate, the old man had symptoms of angina pectoris: he was groaning faintly and clutching at his breast.

"Well, aren't you a visionary, little uncle!" Ilya Ignatyich remarked with bewilderment, and then in his capacity as a physician he warned him to refrain from such strenuous exercise in the future. "Why, you're all worked up!"

"I hate to admit it," Pokhvisnev replied in a stern and significant tone, "but this story isn't mine. It's author was Bakunin. . . . He loved to ponder over the future of this planet. Unfortunately, though, he drank. Hence the tenor of his ideas was gloomy . . . and perhaps it was my intercourse with him that taught me to be so taciturn!"

Ilya Ignatyich began to choke with repressed laughter, and this laughter helped him recover his own mental balance. Bakunin's name on Arkadyi Hermogenovich's lips always made him prick up his ears. It was difficult to believe that the famous anarchist, the member of international congresses and opponent of Marx, the respectable old gentleman with the appearance of a heresiarch in an antique frock-coat was capable of producing such bad fiction. However, the study of memoirs had taught Protoklitov not to be surprised at the various weaknesses of great men. Yet even in this light, Ilya Ignatyich considered the friendship between these two men, so completely dissimilar, a most peculiar phenomenon. And he was about to be treated to some other unpublished facts about Bakunin, when Liza, just back from the theatre, asked them to come in to supper.

# CHAPTER 18

# Ksaveryi Receives a Tip

LIZA'S SHORT ILLNESS was explained in as many ways as there were people who asked questions about it. The version Pokhvisnev invented for Kurilov could not be seriously considered: Pokhvisnev grew pale when he even saw a gun in a picture. . . . To an old man who came to see his niece he said that she had sprained an ankle. To Protoklitov, when he returned from his trip, Liza explained her indisposition as "carbonic gas poisoning" owing to the primitive "Dutch" stoves with which the theatre was heated. There was no way of checking up on what she said and no purpose in doing so; a day later she returned to work. Only Galka Gromova, Liza's old friend, who shared with her many hopes that had never materialized, knew the truth.

Galka had long suspected that Liza was pregnant. She threw her arms around her friend on the slightest pretext and with an affected respectfulness touched Liza's forehead with her lips. One day she happened to enter Protoklitov's apartment at the same time as the cook, who had a key. She quietly walked down the hall and looked into a room. The occupation at which she caught her friend completely confirmed her suspicions. Liza was walking back and forth in front of a big mirror, leaning backward with a round sofa pillow inside of her dress. She wanted to know what she would look like six months hence.

". . . And he kissed Elizabeth. And it came about that Elizabeth heard the kiss. . . . What's that from?" the visitor chanted, embracing her friend. She always had ready an appropriate quotation, but could never remember its source. "You should keep your door closed, child!" she reproached Liza.

It was too late to hide, anger would have been ridiculous and denials would not have guaranteed that the secret would be kept. Liza smiled a cold and twisted smile.

"Is this the way one looks?"

Galka's delicacy first of all manifested itself in her exaggeratedly realistic attitude: "Stuff in another pillow, the little one over there. Then it'll be just right."

By their combined efforts they tried to achieve the proper effect, but the addition of a cushion did not work: the seams of the dress were bursting. Liza had a hurt and melancholy smile. Then Galka asked her whether she felt nauseated yet and whether her husband knew about "it." Oh, it was he who had imposed this disfigurement upon her! He seemed to hope that a child would draw his wife away from the theatre.

"After all, he is earning enough for both of us," Liza said sarcastically.

"Doesn't he like your acting?" And because Liza did not answer, she went on: "What a dirty trick to give an actress a big belly just to have one's own way. Of course, you'll lose all your parts. What does he want you to do with yourself?"

"He wants me to study."

"Study what?"

"Life!"

And both of them, not very gaily, but in unison, laughed at this ridiculous husband. Then, noticing a nuance of squeamishness in the way Liza referred to her still unnamed and unborn child, Galka suggested that her friend try her own, oft-tested method. She called it "getting clean."

". . . You just go and come. It's like a dentist. I don't remember the address exactly, but it's near the theatre, the second house next to the church. There is a picture of a bearded, very attractive man in a bathrobe with little crosses on it. I think it's Gregory the Theologian. It's a frame house, and there are dogs in the courtyard. Some sort of throat-specialist lives there . . . but don't pay any attention to him. A lady who has a nimble hand visits him very often. I'd advise you to have an 'incomplete one.' Well, how about it, to be or not to be? What's that from?"

Liza listened, shuddering; her friend's very vocabulary froze her blood. For some reason she imagined a sofa covered with oil cloth dirty and stained, and an instrument—a nail on a wooden handle with the head flattened out into a little shovel. And they'd lay her down on someone else's blood. . . . Her face flushed red with shame and horror: "This thing . . . is it very unpleasant?" she asked.

"My girl, it's not only unpleasant, it's very painful," Galka said in the tone of a grown-up speaking to a child; she was glad of this opportunity to act in real life like the worldly sinner she was always supposed to be on the stage.

. . . It proved to be disgusting. The house itself looked shadier than any other on the block. The dogs barked once, then turned away. The door at the head of the wooden staircase reminded one of a big death notice. Eye charts hung on the walls. Liza read the letters superstitiously, while the lady, letting out a thin stream of smoke from her cigarette, gave her instructions: "And refrain from crying: there are sick children in the house. . . ."

The sofa resembled the back of a scrawny mare with cut-off legs. Liza felt a great desire to buck. "Quiet, quiet!" said madame. It all happened quickly, as in a dream. However, her pain was followed not by the joy of liberation, but by a feeling of defilement. The lady suggested that Liza take down her telephone number for any of her acquaintances who might need such services. Liza left an hour later, reeling. The dogs had hidden. Gregory the Theologian shook his beard and seemed to be saying: you bitch, you bitch! . . . A blizzard was beginning, the first blizzard of the year. There was almost no one in the street. Suddenly she began to bleed and felt twice as weak as when she had left that room. Arkadyi Hermogenovich understood only that something horrible and feminine had happened, when Liza with vacant eyes staggered into his place. Her old apartment happened to be on the way home.

The feeling of liberation came later, but with an admixture of emptiness, unhappiness and incomprehensible pity, so intense that she almost failed to experience the promised lightness. Her husband was away. Probably he was still cutting and sewing, "tailoring for the glory of God," as he had joked before his departure. . . . Those two languid days seemed an eternity. Galka brought her the latest news. The company had definitely decided to stage *Mary Stuart*. It was to be directed by Victor Adolfovich. Vlasov, the composer, was writing music for four drums. Kagorlitskaya, as a partisan of Piotr Fedorovich, would probably not get a part.

"You'd better get well soon, or you'll miss your chance!"

"I won't be given the part . . . and I won't be able to play it, anyway. I'm frightened, as though I had to climb up a tower from which it is impossible to descend. . . ."

"How silly, Lizka! Everything depends on the stage manager. . . ." And she cited all the untalented actresses who had been pushed forward by their stage-manager husbands. "Well, do you still have any pains? Have you thought of what to tell your husband? Never mind, kiss him hard so he won't have time to be surprised. . . ."

"But Galka, I don't know how to lie!"

"Nonsense, you can do anything, you're an actress. But your mouth is bigger than your stomach. You're only a girl, yet you want a part like that. What do you see in it?"

Liza was silent for a while, then she asked her friend to go to her husband's study and get a thick book bound in white leather with bronze clasps from the lower shelf of the book case. They leafed together through this treasure of Protoklitov's. The pages crackled, black Gothic characters stood in rows as solemn as burghers or guildsmen. It was as though the text of this mediaeval German chronicle, a history of battles, revolts and crimes, had been written with ichor that had darkened from age.

"You see, Galka, in olden times this chronicle served as a newspaper," Liza almost literally repeated her husband's explanations. "Here was recorded all the news, the latest items, although sometimes the interval that had elapsed since they occurred was ten years. Some are illustrated by engravings. Here Huss is being burnt in a paper cap with devils painted on it. Here is the battle of Grandson" (bands of Swiss archers were shown falling upon the Burgundians dressed in armor and almost completely hidden by a hail of flying arrows) "and this is the portrait of the *new* doge of Venice, Niccolo Sponte. He was an orator and navigator." (A long-nosed old man with a ruby clasp on his shoulders and a unicorn cap looked superciliously from the page.) "See?"

"How gloomy he is, and thin and pale. . . . What's that from?"

"And now the main thing I want to show you. Here's Mary!"

(The engraving had no documentary value; it was a naïve recording of the chronicler's reaction to the famous execution. On a quilted satin rug there rose a headsman's block. With her head lowered upon it, a middle-aged woman was kneeling. She was dressed after the fashion of city dwellers of that time, in a gown with a square collar edged in gold lace. Sixteen elderly Scottish earls, looking all alike, knelt and with raised hands prayed to the All-Highest to sanctify the last breath of this woman who had murdered her husband. The executioner swung his axe with a strength that would have sufficed to split the execution block itself. Leaning backward, he kept his eyes on his assistant who held the queen by her hair lest she move aside. . . .)

The old engraving was not too detailed, but Protoklitov had taught his wife to notice with the meticulousness of a physician the heavy chains on the courtiers' necks, the jagged axe of the hangman and the leather apron of his assistant. . . . For the tenth time Liza was holding this solemn book on her knees for the sake of one artless little picture. She was fascinated, not by the bouquet of dark passions in Mary's history, nor the grim madness of the lust for power in all its dramatis personae, nor the ardent heart too lavish in love and revenge, but only by death itself, the tragic postlude that takes place only behind the stage of art. And it did not occur to Liza to check on herself by wondering whether Schiller would have even written about Mary if her rival had spared her.

"Was she a great sinner, that Mary? You say she killed her husband?" Galka asked. "What a terrible thing to do!"

"But if she hated him?"

And as though fearing that Galka would suspect her of evil intentions she hurriedly began to tell the story of her heroine. She knew almost everything about her except what an actress should feel. At the age of seven she was a queen, at sixteen she married the future French king, as a nineteen-year-old widow she returned to Scotland, bringing the banner of Catholic reaction with her. She refused to recognize Elizabeth as legitimate ruler and herself assumed the title of queen. She married her cousin, and after he had been slain, married his murderer. Civil war drove her out of Scotland. At the age of twenty-six she fell into Elizabeth's hands and spent the eighteen years that followed in prison, wasting her time on intrigues, plots and love. In her forty-fifth year she was beheaded. She was unattractive; she invented the famous Stuart cap to cover her tall elongated forehead. Her books were bound in black morocco, a coat of arms with a crowned lion was stamped on the bindings. She never removed from her finger a ring with a furze branch on a stone, the ancient emblem of Scottish chiefs. . . .

It was clear from all this that not Liza herself, but Ilya Ignatyich was working on this part, collecting all sorts of information on the would-be Queen of England. All Liza had done was to memorize a mass of details she would never use. She belonged to the unfortunate species of artists who pin all their hopes on their inborn talents and a marvellous, short-lived triumph. By ascribing the circumstances of Mary's struggle to the personal relation between the two queens she robbed herself, because she made banal events of which the real stage was all contemporary Europe. She was infatuated not even with the personality of the queen but only with the bookish melodrama, with her mother's old tale of a guilty and unhappy woman.

"Mary! . . . She wanted too much, she couldn't get it, and so her head was cut off."

Liza's confused explanations were interrupted by a quarrel in the hall. Two persons were shouting at the top of their voices, and one might have thought that they were calling to each other across a ravine. Galka rushed out to see what it was about; when she returned she collapsed at Liza's feet, shaking with silent laughter. Liza threw a wrapper around her shoulders and went out into the hall where two deaf people were conversing. The cook was trying to get rid of a ridiculous old man in a tattered, short winter overcoat with candle-drippings on it and an old-fashioned Caucasian hood with gold tassels. Brandishing his arms in a warlike fashion, he obviously intended to hold his ground. Light from the opened door fell into the half-obscurity, and the old man turned around: "Tell her. . . ." he said in a whimpering voice, seeking Liza's protection.

Her fright was soon gone. This was no longer the old Dnestrov-Zakurdaev, but a moth-eaten scarecrow. He had doubtless dragged himself here to beg some charity, and Liza painfully tried to recall where she had put her money. "Old men, too, have expenses!"

"Here, come in." Stepping aside she showed Ksaveryi into her husband's study. "You see, I'm ill. . . ."

"I'll just take off my hood. I catch cold constantly, you know. Ksaveryi's business is bad, very bad: nothing but the chicory kind of business! I've dropped in only for a minute . . . I felt like having a look at you, Lizushka!"

He threw off his tatters as deftly as he could and ran into the room sideways, so as not to give Liza time to change her mind. His hands were tightly pressed to his belt; he did not greet her formally lest she be tempted to insult him. It was clear that no one any longer tried to spare his feelings. He was somewhat fidgety, but subdued, completely tame. It was hard to believe that this was the same rogue who had once stolen the prompter's pince-nez in the midst of a tragic monologue, the inventor of a liqueur brewed with dry mushrooms, which knocked the most inveterate drunkards off their feet, the braggart and "Samarkandian," as he had been called. Of the legendary Ksaveryi remained only the Adam's apple, the drooping, sensual nose and the colored shirt with an artistic open collar; even the dandruff had vanished from his coat. "Aha, you got cleaned up before coming here. You even removed your skullcap to make your old age more conspicuous. . . ." True enough, it was his grey hair that gave Ksaveryi his neat, respectable appearance.

He cast a glance around him, touched several objects; accustomed to hotel rooms, he was charmed by everything here. "Oh, you have a Shakespeare!" He said this reverently, as though he were seeing the bard in person, and passed his finger over the gilded back of the volume so as to share its sacredness. Liza watched his hands with a vigilant eye: he might steal something in all this sentimental confusion.

"I'm glad for you, Lizushka. You're a practical woman, and I've always feared that type. You've arranged your life cleverly, but look out! It's dangerous to replace force by cunning. . . . But you're a good girl . . . and you're right: one should play with every toy in this world!

Only don't drink. No matter what happens to you in life. . . . And there are still all kinds of things ahead of you in life!"

So he had come here to crow, this crow with broken wings? His miserable unsteady little laugh made Liza prick up her ears. "How did you find me?" she asked.

"I dropped in to see your uncle. He's smart, too, it runs in your family! We sat together on a little chest and whispered like the two old men we are, ear to ear. Oh, no . . . I didn't let anything slip that I shouldn't have . . . I just said I was your teacher. . . . You're married to a doctor now, aren't you?"

"Yes, a surgeon."

Ksaveryi carefully watched her quivering lips. "You said, a surgeon? That's good, very good. Engineers, too, get high salaries these days. They're given bonuses, villas, cars—it's very pleasant. . . . Well, and does he love you?"

"Yes, he seems to. . . ."

With his hand behind his ear, Ksaveryi shook his head in emotion: "That is very good too. Love is the most terrible power, only not a very stable one. Dominate him, dominate him, don't let him go, squeeze him as long as he has not seen through you. You know I came here two days ago, but your old woman wouldn't let me in. She's poisonous . . . it's a pity she doesn't bark! My soul is yearning for you. What's been the matter with you?"

Liza shrugged her shoulders. "Oh, nothing serious. I ate some bad sausage. . . ."

The old man moved closer, together with his chair. His face was insinuating and guilty. "What, what are you saying? Speak louder, I don't hear well. What has become of Zakurdaev! A laughing stock for hens, a piece of chicory, ha?"

"I said I was poisoned by carbonic gas!" Liza shouted into his face.

He nodded, nodded happily, because she was not angry at him. "You must be more careful . . . you're fragile, small. . . . Take care of yourself!" In his voice there was a note of jealous concern for the woman who had thrown him out as useless.

(Oh, Galka is right: one ought to slap their hearts at every opportunity, the cheeks of their hearts!)

Liza began to be bored. It was clear that the old man would ask for something. It would have been insolent on his part to come to her house without any purpose.

"Well, well." He kept mumbling, but she went straight to her goal: "How do you live? I mean, what do you do for a living?"

"I? Oh, I'm all right, I'm not a public charge. I have a corner in

some worker's apartment. I tried to get into our home, but there are
no vacancies: actors die miserably. . . ."

"You're drinking, of course? Ah, you're deaf as a post . . . I say, you
are certainly guzzling vodka as usual?"

"I? Oh, no. I was discharged as an extra, not for drinking, but because I was deaf. I can still hear a little with my left ear, it's been
treated with rays. But they've got no rays to help my right ear. It's a
chicory business! Now I'm putting some archives in order; I put blue
papers to the left and pink ones to the right in a separate pile. Uninteresting work. Comrade Tiutchev promised to give me a job as a
ticket seller; after all, that would be in my line. Ever met Tiutchev?
A great man, Communist, but simple. Sometimes I drop in to have a
talk with him . . . it gives me pleasure. You know I get bored with not
seeing anyone. It's hard to talk with me, it makes people hoarse. You'd
better be silent, spare yourself, Lizushka!" He looked with a smile at
her bare shoulder from which the wrapper had slid down. "Is your
husband strict? Does it matter that we're sitting in his room? You tell
him if he asks that you and I are like Joseph and Mary, Joseph and
Mary . . . eh?"

"It's all right, you may sit here. He isn't at home . . . I say, he is out
of town. Maybe you'd like to have something to eat?"

"No. Why? I just dropped in . . . to see an old acquaintance, to see
how she's getting on. Oh, I'm watching you from a distance. Pakhomov
(once we worked together!) sometimes gives me a pass, and I go to
see you. . . . Such fun, such fun. I know all your parts by heart. . . ."
He laughed himself at this obviously implausible lie. "I just lied; forgive me, Lizushka, it's my weakness!"

"Well, do you like my acting?"

"Not bad, not bad!" And there was a certain satanic gleam in his
eyes. "But you've still got a long way to go to do Mary, it's as far as
England. You like sweets, but you should eat something pickled! One
good thing is that there's a lot of sprightliness in your work. And you
could act. Once in your life, how you acted . . . with deadly effective-
ness!"

She moved forward with her whole body, grasped Zakurdaev's
hand, big as a mass of dough rolled out in kneading: "When? When
was that?"

"That, Lizushka, was when you came to my hotel room." Ksaveryi's
soft, grainy nose grew red. He rummaged in his pockets and blew his
nose so loudly that he almost burst his handkerchief. The remnants of
the old Zakurdaev pathos made his cracked voice tremble. "You were a
child of nature, of our savage Russian nature. You smelled of calico

and were like a little hard turnip just rinsed in a pail of fresh spring water. And your sand has been crackling in my teeth ever since! You acted a girl innocent to the point of shamelessness . . . you acted yourself. You were guided by true passion, if you ventured into a lair littered with the bones of previous victims. Lord, how your shoulderblades stuck out! . . . And I remember your cornflowers were faded, sort of falling apart, like chicory. . . . And even I, even I believed you!"

This man had a right to be cruel to her. Liza winced and drew her wrapper up around her neck.

"Now, that's enough, I'll get angry with you if you say any more."

"Lizushka, I don't mean to be unpleasant. You only paid me back for the tears I myself had caused. One way or another, someone had to destroy Zakurdaev! It is said that the wise hare blesses the wolf who devours him, blesses him and whimpers. Forgive my impertinence: does your husband smoke? Steal a cigarette from him for me, eh? He doesn't smoke . . . your husband is queer . . . if he has enough money to buy tobacco!"

Once more he began to blow his nose. Senile sentimentality is associated with constant colds in the head. Not noticing Liza's yawns, he expanded for a long time upon his feelings. "That, Lizushka, is when I should have played Lear!" Doubtless he rehearsed this part secretly, sitting on a boulevard and reading, reading those lines written for him alone.

"Well, that's that. . . . You bore me. You bore me, I say!"

He jumped up, fidgeted a while, picked up his hood from the floor. "You must forgive me, Lizushka. All old men often importune their juniors. People like me should be put in vinegar for the night and stored in a cold place. I'll be going now. You know, I've important business. . . ."

Liza accompanied him to the hall. Overwhelmed by his emotions, Ksaveryi put on Protoklitov's galoshes, but Liza was silent: let him! To preserve his dignity he mumbled something about unimportant matters. It gave Liza an uncomfortable feeling to let him go empty-handed. She returned to her room and hurriedly rummaged in her bag. The colorful edge of a twenty-ruble bill protruded from a pile of receipts. That would be enough for Ksaveryi!

The old actor drew back; dark red blotches appeared on his face. Crumpling the bill, Liza slipped it into the breast pocket of his overcoat. "Come, don't be silly, take it. But on one condition: don't get drunk! Now, now. . . ."

The old man ran away, covering his face with his hands and even forgetting to tie his hood. He pushed at the wall, not seeing the door.

The gilded tassels dragged after him on the stairs. Liza called the servant to brush the chair in which Ksaveryi had sat: perhaps he had bugs!

Galka entered with an air of understanding and sympathetic seriousness. Everything was clear to her now. "You listened in?" Liza asked with horror.

"Child, after all, I can't stop my ears for your guests. He who has ears to hear, let him eavesdrop . . . what's that from? By the way, how much did you give him?"

Half an hour later Liza regretted having given him so little. "But anyway he'll spend it on drinks!" At twilight she received a telegram: Ilya Ignatyich would be back that night. She had to take a nap so that no symptoms of her illness would be left. She very much wanted to see her heroine in a dream, even if she came out of the Fotheringhay dungeons with her bloody, smiling head under her arm. She had been told that to achieve this it was enough to wish for it very hard and imagine it before falling asleep. (She still labored under the delusion that to know a subject meant to accumulate thousands of details about it!)

Imagination transported her to the deserted road leading from Fotheringhay Castle, the scene of the execution, south-eastwards to Elizabeth's residence. Liza stood nestling close to a tree; a wintry rain was falling. Icy drops gathered on the bare branches and fell on her shoulders. A little wooden bridge, scarcely visible in the darkness, spanned a ravine in front of her. She heard creaking wheels, the stamping of horses and the splash of spattered puddles. Along the miry road, bumping in the ruts, without stops, across all Britain, rushed a cart hermetically closed. A dozen crazy fellows, hoarse and ribald from drinking red wine, escorted this devil's cart, sticking their spurs into their monstrous mounts. The torches flying by struck at the branches and dropped crackling grains of fire. In the cart there sat an unshaven fellow in boots, with a sty in his eye. He was tormented by fleas; from time to time he stuck the tips of his fingers under his waistcoat and scratched himself through his shirt of mail. A little cask wrapped in leather rested on his knees. When the cart passed over ruts one could hear the splash of yellow alcohol and the jerking of the royal burden floating in it. The peace of the whole kingdom now depended on this piece of material evidence: for the cask contained Mary's head. . . . This vision took possession of Liza, leaving a chill on her face and in her body. The wet spokes of the wheels glistened, the paving stones thundered, the sleepless driver lashed his horses, hanging over them like fate.

Liza closed her eyes and in her dream, instead of the visitor she longed for, the drunken Zakurdaev broke in. The twenty-ruble bill had been spent to good purpose. Liza ran away from him, banging and slamming doors, but their number was countless, just as the pursuit itself was endless. Then the beneficent Protoklitov came, destroying all these visions.

"You've been crying, Li . . ." (this was her pet name) ". . . and I thought I'd wake you up."

He kissed her on her forehead like a child and then a little further down, on her bare shoulder. The wind from his nostrils shook and tickled a lock of her hair. With a feeling of boredom Liza recognized this symptom—but this time she would cry if it occurred to her husband to embrace her. To divert him she said the first thing that came into her mind: "How good that you're back. Imagine, last night someone in a railroad uniform got in here. He wanted to see you very urgently, but wouldn't give his name. Grusha noticed that after leaving he went upstairs. . . . We were both so scared!"

All this was very strange. Ilya Ignatyich lived on the top floor, and above him was only the attic. ("If it was Gleb, why didn't he leave a note?") Liza could hear for a long time how Ilya walked back and forth in his room. Then her lids grew heavy, her body grew more and more imponderable, and it seemed to her that all the joy of living in this world consisted in doing foolish things with impunity.

# CHAPTER 19

# The Ring

NEVER BEFORE HAD Ilya Ignatyich been so much interested in his brother's personality. In the last analysis he knew nothing about him. Gleb always arrived at inopportune times, was always upset about something, explained what had brought him, shook his brother's hand and dissolved into the silence outside the door. The street that swallowed him did not reach up here. By the very nature of his profession Ilya was a man of solitary, indoor activities. His work did not tolerate a stranger's interference; and the street, the primitive and noisiest corporation in life, was above all septic. Thus the high art of handling the scalpel earned for the older Protoklitov the dubious right to reticence.

At first Ilya fancied that Gleb simply posed as a mysterious character. Later he conceived of his brother as a restless man who makes a great number of superfluous gestures. The most recent episode concerning Gleb's trip to the attic fell into this category—unless he was an attic thief, it could be disregarded. And this clever doctor with a great reputation, which was at least half due to his inventiveness, was unable to think of the simplest explanation: that Gleb might have had to spend some time in the attic before reappearing in the street. . . .

From all sides ruin threatened Gleb's career, so carefully begun ten years earlier. His fear was born from within and at first had no external causes. It all began with the trivial questionnaire that was sent him to be filled out. Foreseeing all kinds of accidents, Gleb at that time prepared a short, dignified and courageous declaration to the Central Committee, in which he explained the concealment of his social origin by his understandable reluctance to pay for his father's political crimes. But after a week his mood changed completely, and this dangerous document was destroyed. It so happened that one day later he received the third and longest letter from Kormilitsin; it had been put into a second envelope with a note in an unfamiliar hand. According to this note, the address on the first envelope had been written just before the disaster which delayed the sending of the letter for two whole weeks. Evgenyi Lvovich Kormilitsin had been drowned while bathing in the river. No details were known.

Thus sometimes does fate with Herod's wormy smile offer the lucky man his enemy's head. But at the very beginning Gleb's anger was stronger than his joy over the fool's death. He was enraged when he read those six closely written pages, stuffed with gratitude, strewn with many intimate, almost incriminating, confessions and enlivened with exclamations such as: "You're a brave man, Glebushka, our people will get ahead anywhere!" or "We're watching you from afar, we secretly admire you and are proud of you," or "I'm sure that you'll reach the top; but knowing your temperament, we beg you not to go too fast!" The letter differed from its predecessors by its sincerity, its tenderness and occasionally even by gleams of real thought. Kormilitsin himself had foreseen his friend's surprise: "Do not be irked by this barrage of uninvited words. But everyone is entitled to cry out his disappointment once. I have entered my forty-first year and I look at the future now without my old frivolity. Moreover, I see various things and they fill me with shame. It's a strange thing: so many were slain, and yet no desert has formed! Do you remember how horribly the earth stank with murdered men? Not so long ago peasants were dying like flies in our province, and today their children cut capers to the sound of accordeons (I recall how you always hated those fancy tight boots!) and draw up plans for a grand assault upon the whole world. And do you know, Glebushka, I like tractors for themselves, and our sovkhoz with its excellent horses, and even the army—well-fed, intelligent, in good boots (I myself, with my own hands, have felt them). And yesterday, wandering in a little woods and listening to the trill of girls' voices on the river at nightfall, I even frightened away a stranger's love. Life is continuing, very much so, Glebushka. . . ." At this point he began to expatiate on the bitterness of premature old age; these lines were marked with the foreboding of his imminent death.

". . . I was deeply moved when you did what I asked of you. My mother writes me that she finally received your money, although she did not understand why you had suddenly become Grigoriev; I explained it to her in a letter as well as I could. I don't regret having robbed you of that sum. In time I'll pay it back to you with interest, meanwhile consider that you helped your own mother. You are now dearer to this old woman than her own knavish son. Very well, the devil take you, receive your Isaac's blessings; I'm not jealous. (And really it was unnecessary to send her the whole five hundred. I deliberately asked for more than she needed and you didn't bargain with me. I suspect that the old woman is buying up dress materials to put by against a rainy day. Half that sum would have been enough for her!) But as for Zoska, look out! (Did I write you about my marriage, dear friend?) She is a trained nurse, intelligent and pretty, such as a soldier bitten like me by war could only dream of. Quite often she asks after you; apparently my stories about you make you seem particularly attractive. Zoska is everything that has not yet died in me. My honeymoon has now lasted for six months. But if evil people take her, too, away from me, then. . . . But before I forget: I read in the newspaper that a certain Kurilov has been appointed commissar of your railroad. Find out whether he is the same whom we so unsuccessfully hunted during the Kama period. If so, be on your guard. These people know how to revenge themselves and, in all fairness, they do it well. Should it come to the worst, roll up your fishing tackle and hide under my mother's wings. . . ." Gleb burned the letter and damned the naïve friendship that had guided the pen of this accursed exile.

"You should have bathed before writing this letter. Water would have cured your fever, . . ." he said aloud, rubbing the fragile strips of ashes in his hands.

With the force of an explosion everything he had tried to forget came back to him. So the ties had not been broken, the former kinship was still warm! The past extended to Gleb its charred, mangled arms; he hid his hands behind his back, and then, imperiously, it squeezed the very heart with its corny stumps. It was horrible to think that a third person had read this chattering epistle from the other world. Gleb subjected the appearance of the envelope to a detailed examination and discovered that the paste strip had been displaced at one spot. For the space of one week he watched with alarm the faces of his Cheremshansk acquaintances. Every detail, even the casual nod of a neighbor, made him prick up his ears. His childish fears returned, he felt as he had done long ago when he stood in the darkness staring at the bright parlor full of strange people; because of his insecurity he imagined the presence of alien, unkind eyes; he could not distinguish a single pair of them, while they could see him in minutest detail. And all the time he waited to see who would fire at him first. . . . He was obviously becoming ill. At meetings he experienced a painful chill, almost a paralysis of the will, as soon as someone rose behind him and looked at the back of his head. He destroyed everything in his home that might have revealed his education or cultural habits; his room grew empty, but the very nakedness of the wooden walls gave him away. He learned to cut down his needs in everything, so as to be always unencumbered and alert. He expected a salvo to be directed at him and he was already tired of waiting for it.

His mental state affected his activity. The newspapers noted the unevenness in the work of the Cheremshansk engine shed. Simultaneously they forgot that it had twice received honorable mention, and that its yard master had been called an example to laggards. Now he was fall-ing, and the causes of his fall were inherent in himself. Long before the dénouement he let the reins drop from his hands, lost his sure touch and his self-confidence. The yard teemed with people who were little inclined to accept the new order on the railways, and Protok-litov did not dare to call even the most insolent of them a scoundrel, lest he receive a worse insult in reply. Despite the increased fines and penalties that threatened to develop into a routine, by winter the deficiencies of his yard reached almost catastrophic proportions. This took place at the very height of the notorious incident with the Komsomol locomotive. For two months Protoklitov opposed the as-signment of an engine to the Youth group, until the editors of the railroad newspaper took a hand in this budding scandal. The yard master made reference to an article in the regulations that stipulated that every engineer have a year's work as a mechanic. (But Sayfullah, the Komsomol candidate, had skipped this stage and directly passed his examinations for an engineer's license.)

The socially conscious population of the junction refrained from taking part in the struggle: Protoklitov was feared. The party organ-izer recently appointed by the Central Committee had until then been manager of a small shoe factory; he knew as much about railroads as the average passenger. Protoklitov found no difficulty in convincing him of the riskiness of the Komsomol's idea. Suddenly the yard master agreed to give the young people one of the best engines in his stock, a locomotive that was used for long-distance freight trains. Suspecting some ruse, the young people refused the offer and took instead a com-monplace engine with a broken wheel, which had been abandoned after the wreck near Sakonikha. They immediately began to repair it. The scandal seemed to be dying down, but at that point the mysterious incidents involving the Komsomol locomotive occurred, which led to the arrival of the deputy editor of the railroad newspaper, Peresypkin. This person was rumored to be a very disagreeable and meddling fel-low. . . . Chatterboxes may be found everywhere; and at just about that time Protoklitov learned what kind of inquiries Kurilov was mak-ing about him.

So it turned out that Kurilov himself was the chief hunter in this curious chase. Gleb distinctly recalled this grey-mustached man with a high forehead, his first meeting with him, the unskilful tone and crafty friendliness of his adversary, how he had stuffed tobacco in his burnt-out pipe, as industriously as one wads a muzzle-loader. Such beaters-around-the-bush do not give up in case of failure, they dash right across the beast's path. More and more often Gleb was seized by

a wolfish desire to flee from Cheremshansk before the hunters, dead
and alive, had formed a closed circle around him. By methods too circuitous even to be listed Gleb studied his enemy's biography and failed
to discover a single trait that gave any hope of possible complicity or
mercy. He correctly deduced that if his secret were discovered Kurilov,
as a doubly interested person, would be one of the first to be informed.
Then he took a decision that completely revealed his confusion. He
rushed to Moscow intending to demand a point-blank explanation
from Kurilov. This interview was conceived on a note of defiance, as
the direct attack of a despairing hunted man; its purpose was to find
out how much Kurilov knew about him.

"I'm fed up with this spying, can't you understand? Within three
months I've been visited by six brigades of all kinds. They pry into
everything. The last investigators wanted to know whether it was true
that I ate two government dinners a day. You must realize that such
things discredit me as an executive. It would be simpler and cheaper
to dismiss me altogether!"

"Why get so excited? Keep at your job, as long as nothing has happened, and then we'll see, . . ." the imagined Kurilov answered soberly.

"You refused to let me go when I asked you to, and now you are
questioning my enemies about me. Tell me what you suspect me of.
Maybe I roasted nursing babies in a kerosene stove, or sold locomotives to private individuals, or slaughtered my party organizers and
buried their bodies in a well? Tell me, and I'll either confess or try to
prove to you that the accusations are not true!" And although he only
simulated anger, the very danger of the undertaking made him clench
his fists.

Thus worked up, he ran up the stairs to the director's office and
stopped with a feeling of annoyance and bewilderment. From the corridor an extraordinary procession, led by Kurilov, was moving toward
him. Two men held the chief by his hands, one of whom—with an expression of official grief on his face—was Feshkin. Kurilov advanced in
an uncertain, unsteady gait, his belt gone, his features clouded. He
was in great pain. He seemed to Gleb enormous, unhappy, tragic. The
office attendant dragged his chief's leather overcoat behind him, and
a little old man on his right carried his cap and belt, which almost
touched the ground. Gleb pressed himself to the wall, letting the procession go past him. Their eyes met, and Kurilov's remained expres-
sionless. (All that Gleb could learn of what had just happened in the
office was extremely inaccurate and contradictory. This time Kurilov's
attack was accompanied by vomiting, and although the patient complained of sharp pains in the small of his back, the local, recently

graduated physician insisted that it was a case of food poisoning. Gleb had good reason for distrusting the diagnosis of this self-assured young man; Ilya Ignatyich had once been extremely sarcastic about the mistakes of clinic doctors. . . .)

Thus, while bringing them to a duel, destiny made their weapons equal. In this light even Kormilitsin's death acquired a certain providential significance. "Oh, there's no pack of cards without its trumps!" Now everything depended upon the nature and tempo of Kurilov's disease. His enemy's yellowed, aged face remained alive in Gleb's memory. During the war, and later when he visited the scene of railroad accidents in first-aid trains, he learned to recognize victims, not by the disfigurement of their bodies, but by a special look of indifference and resignation in their eyes. At that moment of his still uncertain triumph he experienced a strange confusion, almost shame at his thoughts, and realized that he had been envying Kurilov for a long time, even since their first meeting. And if envy is a scoundrel's respect, he respected him for everything—because Kurilov had no need to hide anything, because beautiful oceanic expanses lay ahead of him, because the straightforwardness of his career was worthy of emulation, because even his blunders and errors were great and human. His envy became a gigantic magnifying lens under which his enemy's virtues could be read in hypertrophic dimensions. But this uncomplicated psychological instrument had all the shortcomings of its material, optical counterpart. It showed an object in fragments—and in each of them Alexei Nikitich was no longer himself, while actually Kurilov was an ordinary human being to whom none of the earthly joys was alien: he liked wine, powerful trees, stately horses, good books and sometimes was absorbed in the contemplation of beautiful and always unknown women. Only this final meeting combined Gleb's fragmentary observations into one whole: even this man, the father of ideas that went far beyond the limits of visible horizons, was mortal!

Gleb went out into the street when, according to his calculations, Kurilov's car would have left. Darkness had fallen; from the height of the buildings flowed the light of nocturnal searchlights. It was the rush hour; Moscow was turning her other, nightly side to the people. After the first frost the first thaw had come. Snowflakes tickled his face. Along enormous damp walls moved streams of pedestrians, now as thin as a tenuous thread, now wide and overflowing into the gutter. Automobile horns cried out in irritation mingling with the traffic policemen's whistles. Gleb joined the general stream without any purpose in mind; at one place someone pulled him back by his shoulder, and immediately afterwards a salvage truck resembling a siege tower glided by him. He did not understand what had happened. From lack of familiarity with this new situation everything swayed in him, and he enjoyed this unsteadiness as a convalescent enjoys his weakness. He turned into an alley and soon emerged on one of Moscow's bridges. Leaning against the rail he looked down into the blackness of the icy pools. Part of the Kremlin wall was reflected in the water. The speckled, snowy mist more and more thickly enveloped this Asiatic heap of gold, ancient temples and white stones. The snowfall was growing more intense. . . . When Gleb raised his head, an old man in a tattered three-flapped cap stood beside him. The gaunt dog at his feet identified him. The old man stared fixedly at Gleb.

". . . Give me ten rubles, son," the old man was saying. "I've been sick, I'm played out, and there are two of us. . . ."

There were two other sentences, before and after, but Gleb could not make them out. He cast a furtive glance at the beggar's swollen hands and thought that charity requires an almost hospital-like cleanliness on the part of the recipient. Dirty, cheerless misery had never touched his heart. He moved away and continued watching the lazy flow of the wintry water.

"I was more kind-hearted when you came to me, sonny. . . . Remember, on the Pushechnaya . . . you were looking for a man who was hiding in my attic. You people are forgetful nowadays!"

The voice was that of a stranger, a tramp, but the insolent tone could not be unintentional. This man was preparing to remind him of something and even put his bluish hand on Protoklitov's leather glove. Gleb was positive that he had never met anyone with such a face, a face as though pasted with soft grey felt . . . but suddenly he tore his hand loose and started to run. The dog darted after him; and the old man himself, fearing to miss his prey, manifested an agility unusual for his age. The simplest road of escape led into a narrow passage, which was always crowded because of the heavy traffic and the proximity of a trolley-car stop. It had just been jammed. Above the throng emerged the head of a cart-horse with bared teeth and its yoke down to its very eyes because its driver had suddenly pulled it up. From under the visor of a Tartar fur cap gleamed a pair of slanting eyes, and someone cried in a cracked voice: "Run over!" People rushed forward from everywhere, and even the windows of the nearby houses showed some animation. A crowd formed instantaneously; those in the back were still screaming, those in front were already silent, having satisfied their curiosity about death.

Within one week fate had presented Gleb with a third head on a platter. Frightened by its generosity, as though the settlement thereby became more inexorable, he turned back, elbowed his way through the crowd, peered from behind someone's back. On the trampled snow, in front of the wheels of a five-ton truck, lay a long shaggy bag flattened in the middle. But this was only the old man's dog. The rainbow reflection from the mirror rim of the headlight was upon the mongrel's head, and one could see that the tail and an ear of Egorushka had been stamped into the snow. In the confusion the driver had backed up, and as a result "it" had happened twice. The militiaman signalled to the traffic to move. The crowd made way, and the round tire for the third time rolled over Omelichev's friend.

The traffic gradually resumed its previous orderliness; only on the hoar-frost-covered screen of the Kremlin wall still tossed the four-handed, double shadows of pedestrians. Gleb felt relieved: only the dog could be chalked up against him now! But then he again noticed the old man at his side. Gleb accelerated his steps, and the other man followed him. If originally he had had no intention of betraying the younger man, now, made desperate by the loss of his dog, he might do anything. Greb jumped into a bus, and for a whole five minutes the old man rubbed himself against his back. They got off at the same stop, and it was now clear that Gleb's pursuer wanted something other than money. It seemed impossible to make one's escape through the crowded evening street. At this point Gleb, in order to get away from the mysterious pursuer, dropped into his brother's apartment, which happened to be on the way.

# CHAPTER 20

# Peresypkin Finds a Subject

In those years the rough drafts of the future history of the epoch were created, hurriedly, while the immediate participants were still alive. The fronts, the factories, the uprisings—everything around which the militant and creative forces of the revolution gathered—were parts of this process. All of them strove to draw up their balance-sheets as though the epoch were already fundamentally completed. . . . Aliosha Peresypkin, deputy editor-in-chief of the railroad newspaper, also decided to join this almost elemental current. True, the Volga-Revizan line could not compare with the main foci of the working-class movement, but it had its heroes nevertheless. Moreover, the road was growing longer every year, and the young man believed that in time it would become something bigger than a part of the Siberian trunkline. Like Alexei Nikitich, he had plans for the future, although on a smaller scale than his chief's. For instance, he assured Alexei Nikitich that the railway cars coming on to their line from the east did not smell at all of fish or timber or raw leather, but above all of the free Ocean wind that future generations would breathe. Sometimes his visions took the form of fantastic projects for the unification of all the railroad lines in the eastern and southeastern regions, as though such a move could contribute to the unification of the wills of millions of youth as impatient as himself and, like him, thirsting for struggle, noisy activity and great exploits. According to him, this was dictated by the special peaceful tasks of the Soviet Union on the above frontiers.

"You're a remarkable fellow, Lioshka!" Kurilov teased him, trying to penetrate his very essence. "True, you're a demagogue and just a little gruff. However, the Spanish say proverbially that a man must be ferocious. And your nose, too, is red, as though run over by a bicycle. You could at least put some powder on it . . . after all, you're an official personality!"

Peresypkin accepted this friendly reproof with the air of an equal.

"Kick me, kick me, old man!" (Alexei Nikitich had never succeeded in eradicating half-slangy phrases from Peresypkin's speech, acquired during his years as a homeless child.) "You're an older comrade, and I, your creature, have complete faith in you . . . but don't let it go to your head, Alexei! I begin where you leave off. Recently, Kostia Strunnikov dropped in to see me at the editorial office. He manages the rest home at Borschnia. A fine fellow; we graduated from school together; once I even won a caliper from him on a bet. . . . He says he's fed up with the glories of his father's generation and further that he's bored counting sheets and cooking soups for the anemic. . . . It's time, he says, for us, too, to study the past. And Kostia isn't the only one!" Speaking thus, he bit his hairless lip, and his eyes were fired with a restrained and defiant smile.

"For the time being, study, Lioshka . . . study everything! Without knowledge there is no true courage!"

Further about Peresypkin: this restless youth represented an important episode in the story of the Kurilov family. Alexei Nikitich had found him in his car near Tsaritsyn—a little frost-bitten savage. The boy had to pay for this trip all through his life: his ears and nose acquired the amazing habit of peeling in any weather. Questioned by Kurilov, he declared that his mummy had died from having eaten clay, that he himself intended to go to Turkey and that his name was Lioshka. For the space of two months he lived in Kurilov's car, sharing all sorts of warlike adventures with its proprietor. After the car was hit by a shell that lightly wounded them both, Alexei Nikitich sent his foundling to Catherine. Taming the boy proved a difficult job: from time to time migratory instincts awakened in him; he ran away and returned, each time quieter and more thoughtful. Because of Kurilov's frequent travels, Peresypkin was placed during his school years with Tiutchev, who never left Moscow. They often met, and Alexei Nikitich watched with interest how the homeless little fellow developed into an excellent young man, capable in his task of building up the new life and, in case of need, capable of firing an automatic rifle, squinting his left eye as he aimed. The last time he had seen Peresypkin, the young man had been taking life seriously; he was hung about with a great number of all kinds of leather straps and at his side he wore a musette bag full of official papers. Kurilov always talked to him in a tone of patronizing irony, and Lioshka repaid him with quick-tempered and devoted friendship. Peresypkin had joined the railroad staff a year before.

The impulse that had set Aliosha working came from a worthless little pamphlet that had been placed on top of a bundle of books in order to save the bindings from being cut by the string. It was a reprint of an anonymous article with a long and very difficult title. Obviously polemical in content, the article discussed certain problems connected with government subsidies to builders of private railroads in the old Russian Empire. The date of its publication was 1876. Editorial footnotes cited the exact figures of the grants made by the government to the Libava-Orel, Feodosia and Petersburg-Warsaw railroads, as compared with the grants received by the founders of the new Volga-Revizan line. This line, a quarter of a century later transformed into the Volga-Moscow line, was the ancestor of the line on which Peresypkin now worked. The article was written in Russian, it did not abound in statistics, it touched upon a familiar subject, but Lioshka read it three times and did not understand a word of it. Assyrian clay tablets would have been just as accessible to him as this archaic hodge-podge from the *Industrial Messenger* of the Seventies. Lioshka's vanity was hurt; for a few days he suffered in silence, then rushed to Kurilov with a proposal.

First he asked the meaning of many terms he was unable to understand. Alexei Nikitich expressed his surprise. The Soviet system had so completely reorganized all legal, financial and other relationships, that it seemed silly to resurrect the barbarous legislation of the past century. He even asserted categorically that the history of the railroad should in the main be the history of the revolutionary movement in it. And at this point Alexei Nikitich gave the young man a brief lecture about how Tsar Alexander II's government, frightened by the failure of the Sevastopol campaign, rushed to support private initiative and made the railroads the guiding principle of that policy in those years. In conclusion he advised Peresypkin to read a number of well-known books on the history of capitalism, to get in touch with the living participants of the revolutionary storms, mentioning Kurilov's name, and to look for an intelligent collaborator capable of organizing the material collected. In brief, he took into consideration comrade Peresypkin's possibilities. The future historian was silent; it was apparent, however, that he was full of a startling story. (After the railroad newspaper had noisily publicized one rather unsuccessful invention concerning automatic control, Alexei Nikitich began to suspect Peresypkin of an excessive fondness for all sorts of sensations.)

"You don't understand me, Alexei," Peresypkin hinted cautiously. "I want to get at the very roots of our history."

"You queer duck! Look for them in the general economic development."

"I want to know what the people themselves were doing while your economy was developing. You see, I smell some machination here. . . ." Peresypkin objected evasively, and then suddenly he poured out a whole bundle of long-forgotten, dead names to his chief.

"But what are you going to do with these, young man? What's the importance of director Melnikov or his Parisian banker, Isaac Péreira."

"My Blankenhagel learned to swindle from Péreira."

"You don't make sense, Lioshka. . . . What Blankenhagel?"

Finally, however, the chief decided that his foster-son had in mind to write an account of certain phases of Russian history in an artistic form. Since he always encouraged literary works on railroad subjects, he helped Peresypkin get access to the archives. But nothing could be found there except old reports on the freight turnover and summaries of fluctuations in the payment of trade-union dues. Peresypkin was faced with having to abandon the project or writing a long memorandum of the kind that already existed by the dozen. Then he recalled that Borschnia had once been the headquarters of the Volga-Revizan adventure. He sent a special delivery letter to Kostia Strunnikov, asking him, in the name of his lost caliper, to collect any fragments of old written papers that could be found in the Borschnia attics. (As a homeless orphan Peresypkin had had occasion to visit provincial attics and had always been struck by their abundance of wasps' nests and old papers.) The young man was so lucky that one might be justified in assuming the existence of a higher justice. Only a month later he received a smoked herring box, 20 x 32", full of old paper. In the corners Kostia had stuck apples from his own orchards, still on their branches (and the smell of apples was stronger than all the other smells!), and in an accompanying note explained that he would have mailed his friend an old woman of museum age, the nurse or perhaps the grandmother of the last landlord, if he had not been afraid that she would crumble into her various component parts on the way. (This old woman lived in a hut near the park and filled all the young population of Borschnia with superstitious terror.)

Without even tasting an apple, our historian rushed to investigate his newly received treasure. He experienced a giddiness familiar only to fortunate hunters of buried treasures. It was unthinkable to grasp Kostia Strunnikov's gigantic gift at one stroke. These documents were the remnants of Orest Romualdovich Blankenhagel's personal papers. They included storehouse ledgers and inventories with complete reports, covering several years, of the estate's business; an album of ruddy, oval daguerreotypes of all those whom Peresypkin now wished to place in the dock; the project and statutes of the Volga-Revizan Company with a copy of a petition signed by Director Chevkin asking for permission to make a preliminary survey of the line; a batch of letters in foreign languages on subjects that for the time being remained mysterious to Aliosha; several reports by the Gorigoretsk Police Inspector Rynda-Rozhnovsky on the measures taken against the bandit Spirka; two complaints lodged by M. Borodulkin, the manager of the estate, concerning damages done by cattle to the buckwheat, the illegal moving of hay and various foolish notions of the muzhiks; the record of the capture of the above-mentioned Spirka at a wedding in the village of Kostritsa on May 12, 1876, and the attached certificate, signed by the local physician Dubiaga and the parish priest, of his death of an undetermined chronic disease; telegrams from Unruhe, the director of the Flug Works in Berlin, concerning the sale and delivery of the first batch of six locomotives to the Volga-Revizan railroad; a pencil sketch of a pretty girl in a riding habit made on the back of a notice from the Ministry of the Court to the effect that the leader of the Gorigoretsk nobility, O. R. Blankenhagel, was to appear for duty on the night vigil over the coffin of Tsar Alexander II; another drawing of the same person, in excellent condition except that a crushed fly had got stuck upon the face; an epistle that had somehow found its way here from Antonyi, Archimandrite of St. Sergius, to the chief priest of Gorigoretsk, supporting the railway because it would facilitate pilgrimages (". . . I can see only advantages in it, most reverend brother, and if sin cometh therewith, may we not fall into confusion, but meet it on the battlefield and combat it!"); an abusive and succinct letter from E. G. Gribbe concerning the arrest of a certain Pafnutyi, certainly a suspicious character—witness his long hair and the fact that he had a suitcase full of books of criminal intent, such as *The History of the French Peasants* and *The Tale of the Four Brothers* (by request of Staff-Captain A. T. Steinpel, deputy commander of the gendarmes, Gribbe also asked that the tutor A. H. Pokhvisnev be put under observation . . .); newspaper clippings describing the opening of the Volga-Revizan railroad, which brought the Gorigoretsk district more fully into the pale of European civilization; a copy made by hand of the part of the "magician Zhezlakovsky" from an unpreserved vaudeville skit, "The Uncle's Kiss," acted on the little stage of the manor at Borschnia on July 19, 1876; a bamboo pencase containing a poster announcing the above-mentioned performance, with a list of the performers. . . . (A picture graced it, painted in Old Slavonic style: yellow Cherubim with the faces of lawyers who, because they had no hands, carried in their teeth a visiting card with a bent corner and the inscription: "The Uncle's Kiss." The part of the Hussar was played by N. A. Dudnikov; that of the uncle by O. R. Blankenhagel; of the lackey Robinot by M. Jacques Pommier; of Aglaë, aged twenty-two, by Tania Blankenhagel; of the magician Agafit Abdul, aged seventy-two, by Mr. Shemadanov; and finally, the part of the booby Mitrofan Spiglazov by a certain Arkadyi P. Near his name the words "three and one-half," followed by a huge exclamation point, were pencilled in parentheses.

Considering that actors of a play given at home could not possibly have been paid, one must surmise that this number was the actor's nickname.) In brief it is absolutely impossible to list in one breath all the treasures that overwhelmed Aliosha Peresypkin. Their contemplation alone would surely produce a new Iliad.

He spent all that evening studying only one of them. It was a large photograph taken on the terrace of the Borschnia manor on the day of the opening of the railroad. On the back were the names of the people in the group and the date. This document was more damaged than the others; some mischievous lad had retouched it to suit his own fancy: he had put skirts on one of the gentlemen, painted another the green color of a waterplant, meticulously transformed a third into a milk-pail. Peresypkin spent a long time washing off with a piece of cotton this frank commentary of a forgotten younger generation. His labors were fully rewarded: he now had an illustrated list of the characters of his future tale. . . . They were all dead now. In front of the high terrace, under the shade of the fine linden trees, they sat with a fore-taste of an abundant dinner in their mouths, those witnesses of the opening of the Volga-Revizan railway, which no longer existed in its previous form. Other dead people were setting the table for them, bringing dead fish soup and sturgeon in aspic prepared by still other dead. Time had died, but the moment engraved upon the photographic plate was preserved. . . . A dead photographer had trained on them the lengthily articulated eye of a Steinheil lens, which had long since become obsolete. Blobs of foam that had evaporated long ago were dropping from the glasses raised to toast the heroic Blankenhagel. The sparkling wine that clouded their reason had long been a cloud and a puddle and wet snow in a child's hands; it rose to the heights to gleam in a rainbow; it was secreted from the eyes of a tormented woman or the bladder of an animal; it trickled into the musty depths of the earth, eroding stones on its way, and a year later insinuatingly crawled back into a cluster of grapes blue from the sun. Thus through a thousand channels hidden from man's reason it flowed into the throbbing, ever-wakeful Ocean. Matter rushed through these phantoms, who in vain spread out their hands to stop it in its flight. And the sun, a half-century younger, warmed these arrogant and business-like corpses.

In the center was a solid, leonine man with impressive sideburns. They were the most important part of his face, the rest being merely a decorative complement. They disappeared behind the turned-down collar of his shirt and probably continued along his entire body to his very heels, like trouser stripes. This was the elder Blankenhagel. Pompous like a Byzantine emperor, he alone sat in a soft chair. At his sides on hard chairs sat other men, still in the prime of life, with silk hats on their knees, in pleasantly ingenuous poses. Only one little old man had wormed himself into the group, a man with a bald skull as pointed as a cockle shell and with senile, fat, drooping cheeks. (The imaginative child had transformed him into a tree covered with yellow flowers resembling dandelions.) He wore a sort of uniform bedecked with so many orders that Aliosha laughed out very, very low. (Was not this Eduard Gavrilovich Gribbe, Blankenhagel's chief accomplice?) Noticeable also were a man who had come to dinner armed with a mighty saber and another in an enormous jacket out of which he peered like St. Tikhon of Kaluga from his hollow tree. Which of the two was P. D. Pestrikov, and which P. P. Khomutov, it was no longer possible to determine. Behind these progressive democrats were four stalwart old men with resolute faces and the aspect of peasants: no doubt they were the founders of some merchant or kulak dynasties. As though by accident, a young student, A. H. P—v, happened to be among the group, in his uniform jacket; but he had moved when the picture was being taken and had passed into history with a blurred face like a pot on a potter's wheel.

The historical pattern of the road was in these documents; it still remained to discover the connections between the events, to label these sonorous bones with dates and, in the manner of Cuvier, to dress them in the pink flesh of facts. Fate itself, foreseeing the judgment of posterity, had stored up these documents in a Borschnia attic. Aliosha had not been pampered by lucky finds of this sort, and aside from Kurilov, whose irony he always feared, he had no mother, sister or intimate friend at hand with whom to share his joy. But: "You have honestly earned your caliper, Kostia!" At that time Aliosha did not yet know that he would have to study the Blankenhagel affair exhaustively; the most experienced ministerial sharpers had become entangled in its cunningly woven cobwebs.

# CHAPTER 21

# New Friends

THE INVESTIGATION OF this case was made difficult by the fact that defendants and witnesses were all dead. But a poet dominated by his idea imagines that there is invaluable material everywhere. He wanders across the earth feeling people, winds and countries with his long fingers; he transforms a tree into a wisp of straw to weave it into his hero's hat, enlarges a grain of sand to the size of a rock against which he will smash this hero a week later, and even in the splash of a raindrop distinguishes the roar of his gigantic fall. In his eyes the world becomes one single palette, and the many-voiced, thousand-handed creature speaks and acts harmoniously. Fate itself, so indulgent to maniacs and children, begins to abuse coincidence. So it was with Aliosha Peresypkin. The little paper with Arkadyi Hermogenovich's address on Feshkin's table tallied miraculously with the initials A. H. P. in the Blankenhagel archives. . . . This last witness was still alive, but his great age made it advisable to see him as soon as possible. The moment was approaching when nature would pick Arkadyi Hermogenovich to pieces, too, and use them as scrap for the formation of new and superior worlds.

Every morning for the space of three weeks Peresypkin had the intention of visiting Pokhvisnev in his little street; but the newspaper was about to change its format, then the chief copyreader fell ill; he had just enough time to refresh his memory about the Blankenhagel papers and to spend an hour or two in the Main Archives. And when everything on the newspaper had settled down, and it was running smoothly, a report arrived from Cheremshansk that disturbed all the young people on the railroad. It concerned the Komsomol locomotive, and touched the young editor himself to the quick. He justly considered himself the initiator of this great undertaking. With the telegram in his hand Peresypkin flew to find Martinson, who, however, was at a dispatcher's meeting. Feshkin was not at his usual post, and no one was guarding Kurilov's door. The young man rushed in without knocking and immediately drew back in confusion.

The chief was not alone, and his visitor was not at all in harmony with the general character of the department. Women who came here on business were usually dressed in the austere fashion of nineteenth-century intellectuals; they were female workers who scurried about in the cells of this immense, overpopulated hive. The lady facing Kurilov stunned the young man's imagination. (He was not only unattractive in appearance, he was quite prone to fall in love!) This woman's fluffy little beret with a blue tassel, her elegant fur coat, which had cost the lives of perhaps a thousand squirrels, appeared to him as the idle refinement of an utterly bourgeois fantasy. The suspicious youth even found her naïve, arc-shaped eyelashes and her bright flabby lips artificial; they cast a sort of inflamed light over her entire face. In brief, she looked pleasant and disturbing. And although in his articles he had never preached asceticism, he did not know that Kurilov had any such acquaintances. . . . He turned to go the moment he saw her, but Kurilov seemed quite pleased at his appearance and would not allow him to leave.

Aliosha thus unintentionally heard a very official conversation which had just begun.

". . . I'm glad you're surprised. If you have so completely forgotten the incident, I feel I cannot have been too great a bother to you!" Her smile was so sincere and trustful that Kurilov felt embarrassed by the business-like, dry tone in which he had received her. He stroked his mustache in confusion. "Well," he said, "so your wound was only trifling?"

"Oh, I was all right," she said evasively. "I phoned you at your apartment, but your wife wasn't home. I wanted to thank you. . . ." She rummaged in a little bag compared to which Marina's briefcase looked like a travelling chest from a camel's back, and Aliosha saw in it a large number of unfamiliar and elegant little objects. Then she placed an unsealed envelope before Kurilov. "This is for you and your wife! She is very sweet. Please tell her for me that I am extremely sorry that she had to be out in the blizzard that day on my account. For some reason I didn't realize at once. . . ."

With an impassive face Kurilov shot a glance at Peresypkin. He was experiencing the unfamiliar uneasiness of a father in the presence of a son who still vividly remembers his deceased mother. But the young man was absorbed in the contemplation of a profile map of the railroad, which hung under the portrait of Lenin. He was studying it with ostentatious diligence. Oh, he was not a bit interested in the amorous adventures of the widower chief!

"What's this?" asked Kurilov sternly.

"These are some tickets. . . ." And guiltily, because she realized her blunder concerning Kurilov's wife, she added that they were tickets for a matinée; that on the next day, which was the theatre's fifth anniversary, they would give the fiftieth performance of *Frederick's Son,* in which she had her best part; and that, finally, this play had been praised even by her husband, who was extremely critical of contemporary authors. She was obviously in a hurry to make it clear that she was married.

"And he, is he an artist, too?" asked Kurilov, playing with his fingers.

"He's an artist but in a different field. His name is different, too. I act under my maiden name—Pokhvisneva."

She looked at him hopefully. No, he had never heard the name before, his face expressed nothing but embarrassment.

"I haven't been on the stage very long, and it's rather difficult to make people remember one!"

"All right, I'll come, without fail." Kurilov now spoke quickly. "And, incidentally, your name was recently mentioned to me by chance."

"By whom?"

"A young and promising journalist." He noticed Liza's impatient gesture. "Come closer, Peresypkin. This is the actress *Pokhvisneva,*" he said, emphasizing her name. "Get acquainted!"

Peresypkin approached in a strange zigzag, struggling against his irresistible desire to flee. He wore enormous shoes made for climbing mountains; they stuck to the floor and knocked against each other when he manfully pushed them forward. And what happened to his nose is unprintable. Aliosha squeezed Liza's hand as though trying his strength on a dynamometer.

"Is your newspaper big?" she asked, rubbing her crumpled fingers.

"Fairly. It's read along a stretch of fifteen hundred kilometers."

"And it has a drama department, too?"

He contritely shrugged his shoulders. "It is called *The Proletarian in Transport.*"

Liza expressed polite surprise; she had not heard the name before. "Ah! . . . I've seen something of the kind. It's a newspaper about locomotives and conductors. Then why did you need my name?" Already her question sounded cold.

Peresypkin's face was tense. His answer, of course, expressed the extreme limit of youthful despair. "I'm glad that my acquaintance with your uncle is beginning so pleasantly," he said.

All the three of them burst out laughing at this brilliant remark. The conversation was finished. Before leaving, Liza added: "Yes, he's amusing, my uncle . . . if you take him in small doses. We live in different apartments. He is bored and poor. Of course, he'd be very grateful if you help him obtain a pension (he lacks some unimportant papers!)

or if you'd print his memoirs or something of the sort. He says he was a friend of Bakunin's. . . ."

She went out, forgetting to invite the young journalist to the performance and leaving behind her a barely perceptible odor of perfume. The two men were silent until its fragrance dissolved in the stench of stale tobacco.

"She smells of poison," observed Peresypkin, still sniffing.

"She's an actress . . . and there is a special perfume industry."

Aliosha did not let him finish. "That industry exists for more rational purposes!" And for a while he was significantly silent. "With age you're growing more indulgent, comrade Kurilov. Fifteen years ago her kind washed floors in your concentration camps. . . ."

"Young man, sometimes it's a very good idea to learn from our enemies!"

"Oh, I have no bad habits at all. But let's not talk about that, old man!"

"You're annoyed because the Moscow theatres don't subscribe to your newspaper. It's up to you to make it more attractive or to introduce a drama department. I can help you get started. . . ." He winked at him. "Take these tickets, call up your girl friend and use them tomorrow. . . ."

"I have no time for girls, Alexei!"

"You're wrong, you shouldn't neglect them. As one gets older, that business becomes more and more difficult and complicated. . . ."

Peresypkin's eyes gleamed, and he rearranged a leather strap on his chest. "You know more about such things than I do, comrade Kurilov!"

He was insolent today; apparently some sensational news had brought him here. Kurilov facetiously asked him to share it with an old man no longer fit for anything.

"Your temper, Alexei—and it's quite understandable!—" (he nodded in the direction of the door through which Liza had left) "is now going to get considerably worse. Some scoundrels have thrown sand into the cylinders of the Komsomol locomotive. Tomorrow I'm taking the train to Cheremshansk. . . ."

As soon as Cheremshansk was mentioned Kurilov reached for his pipe. He filled the air around him with smoke and looked out through the dusky window, rubbing his hands to warm them up. During the last week the production indices in the Cheremshansk engine shed had dropped, but the same figures were lower on the line as a whole. Winter was doing its work. There were snows and thaws, and in the intervals Asiatic frosts set in. Freight loads of fuel piled up, condensers leaked, rails burst during the night, water pipes froze and frost-bitten workers filled the dispensaries. The road had the grippe. . . . And Protoklitov's much-praised engine shed had turned out to be unreliable. Rumors of a hidden struggle were beginning to reach Kurilov; someone's rabid hand stuck out of the silence, and then all was quiet again. True, sometimes such incidents could be explained by ordinary human envy, they expressed the seamy side of socialist competition, and sometimes, as in this case of the handful of sand, they deserved close scrutiny.

"Keep your eye on Protoklitov when you're at Cheremshansk. You like chess and puzzles, you won't be bored. . . ." He contented himself with this hint but did not give Peresypkin any definite instructions. "I don't want to hurry you, young man, but it seems to me you've been sitting here a long time."

An hour later Alexei Nikitich caught sight of the tickets, and now they only annoyed him. He had intended to spend his free day catching up on sleep after two consecutive sleepless nights. Moreover, Alexei Nikitich had never been interested in this form of art. Why should he go to the theatre, when real rivers spread over the surface of the earth and living birds gave concerts in the tops of genuine trees? Moreover, the events of the human heart are reflected in the actors' tears with a different mathematical curve or, at any rate, with a frank violation of the true proportions. He granted the theatre only the didactic right to warn the spectators. But during the thousands of years in which the dramatic art had been practised had even one man been effectively warned by it? How shrewd people are! Even when they leaf through Jeremiah they do not forget that this tearful prophet also was mistaken about a few things.

He tried to get Feshkin to take the tickets, as the secretary was supposed to know something about the theatre. But he had a cold; he was sitting in his office all muffled up, muttering hoarsely into the telephone receiver. Kurilov's friends were scattered throughout the vast expanses of Russia, and only Klavdia was close by. Alexei Nikitich did not like to waste anything. He rang up his sister. She asked him several times to explain what kind of tickets they were, since he was so enthusiastic about them.

He was embarrassed. "Just plain tickets in a box. The name of the play is *The Son* or something. It's supposed to be good."

"Have you become a ticket-seller or what?"

"The tickets are complimentary . . . it would be awkward if the actors saw that the box was empty. . . ."

"But why do you offer them to me, of all people?"

"I thought you'd be interested. It's an historical subject. . . ."

Klavdia was surprised. "Do you think I'm so senile that I have nothing to do but attend historical plays?"

"Of course not. I just wanted to express my interest in you, Klasha," Alexei Nikitich explained gently. "After all, you're not an adding machine either, you need a little recreation sometimes. . . ."

He could hear her sigh with deep annoyance. "Just be frank, Alexei, and realize what a silly thing you're saying. You want to pass those tickets off on me because you can't use them yourself. By the way, we haven't seen each other for a long time, during which you have reverted to your childhood. After all, look at that trick with the bell . . . you stuck a splinter under it, didn't you? You flew down the staircase with that girl so fast that I guessed immediately. . . ."

"Oh, what happened?" Kurilov pricked up his ears.

"What happened was that all the tenants fell upon me, about nine of them, and a little old man with a crutch gave me hell. For some reason they decided that it all was my fault. We had a long and tiring discussion. But, as you know, I don't like to give in. . . ." She stopped laughing the moment she heard her brother laughing, too. "But who was that girl with you?"

"She's an employee of the railroad, she's going to quit. . . ." He suddenly felt guilty toward Marina and immediately decided to take her to the theatre. "She's a very nice person. She was never sentenced, she has never engaged in trade, she has no record of harmful deviations."

"And you find her 'nice'?" asked Klavdia in a changed voice.

"Yes; aren't you jealous, Klasha?"

"I wasn't mistaken: you've become perceptibly stupider, Alioshka. What's bad is that it affects your work. Your railroad is nothing to boast about!"

"It's still better than the other lines, Klasha."

"A blockhead isn't justified in being a blockhead because his neighbor is a blockhead, too."

Then trying to get the better of his formidable sister simply by tiring her out, he began patiently to explain everything about the road, from the causes that accounted for the large turnover to the kolkhoz peasants who refused to clear the tracks unless they received woollen mittens, sugar and calico. He spoke for a long time, using unfamiliar terms such as obsolescence, traction, signal maintenance—and although she understood his manoeuvre, she did not interrupt him. In the end, however, it was he who surrendered.

"I would have jumped into the water, but the rivers are frozen everywhere," he concluded. "Drop in to see me and I'll explain it all in a vivid and interesting fashion."

"Yes, I'll visit you tomorrow," Klavdia promised.

The next morning he went to see Marina. Amidst the suburban snowdrifts he recognized her house only by a long factory chimney at the end of the street. A girl with knees blue from cold led him through the back entrance: the front entrance was boarded up for the winter to save heat. Kurilov was admitted by a fat woman with a face the color of margarine. She wiped her wet hands on the apron over her shaking belly and waited.

"I came to see Sabelnikova. . . ."

The fat woman shook her head with dignity; the glossy wart on her chin spread out and her eyes drowned in margarine. This diabolical trick constituted her smile.

"I'm her aunt, Anfisa Denisovna," the monster said hospitably. "Come in. The floors creak, but don't pay any attention to them."

They passed by a whole string of doors; the floors roared under the aunt's feet while she chatted with Alexei Nikitich. "It's true there are a lot of tenants," she said, "but they're all nice tenants. One is an army musician who lives with his mother, he's an educated man, a Latvian; there's also Grishin from the water-supply department"—it seems strange that Kurilov doesn't know him because Grishin, too, is an executive. True, a "specialist" lived for some time in the corner room to the left, but thank God he was arrested and tried. "Imagine, he threw a cat into the army musician's pot, and he noticed it only at the end of the dinner. Imagine, sometimes he plays something, and my soul comes out of me. . . . Oh, it's such a luxury nowadays to have decent tenants!" she concluded.

She led Alexei Nikitich into a poor room with one window. The prettiest thing there was the ornate hoarfrost relief on the window-pane. Having thawed an opening with his breath, a little boy of about seven was looking out into the street. The stool on which he stood was shaking perilously. He turned around upon hearing a noise.

"Ziamka," said the monster, "come and get acquainted with your mother's friend."

The boy did not answer, and the aunt made a gesture intended to attract the visitor's attention to the young generation. "Perhaps you'll have some influence on him! He's growing up to be a frightful little vagabond. Two days ago he set out for the North Pole, and Marina did not catch him until she got to the trolley-car stop." She was quite pleased with Kurilov's reassuring look, which meant that all this would turn out well. "Where's your mother, Ziamochka? Did she go out for a walk or is she reading?"

Apparently the aunt was trying hard to give the impression that they led a very dignified life.

"She's hanging out wash in the attic," said Ziamka, and reluctantly wresting himself from the window, he hit his knee against the stool. (They're all sceptics and debunkers, these suburban children!)

The monster made another gesture, with a smile, and swam away. The boy alternately rubbed his knee and looked at the window, behind which the thing was standing.

"Ith that your car?" he asked suddenly. "Have you got two cars or only one!"

"Only one, Ziamka!"

"And why did you get a medal?"

"Once the Whites were after me to hang me, but they couldn't find me. And I wasn't scared and stayed on my job."

"That'th good," Ziamka muttered judiciously. "Are you a Communist?"

"Uh-huh, and you?"

"I'm th-till growing up. . . . It takes an awfully long time!"

"Never mind, we'll wait. But try to grow up fast, there are a lot of things to be done. . . . Let's get acquainted. Your name is Ziamka, I knew it from your face. And mine is Alexei. . . ."

They paused to give their new friendship time to strengthen. Meanwhile Kurilov looked around him. Bottles with wicks hung from the window-sill to prevent water from dripping on the floor when the thaw came; a pair of child's half-darned stockings lay on a chair, a cheap clock was on the wall. There was only one bed, and a walnut case above it was empty. Ziamka's treasures were on the table: a crumpled tin tobacco box that bore the traces of all its owners, a bit of china from an electric plug, a torn rubber bulb from an automobile horn and a tooth from some gigantic comb of a beautiful yellow color. Alexei Nikitich also found the toy he had seen before, under the table, and picked it up. The harmonica no longer played a march, but something sad: apparently Ziamka had washed it under the spigot and opened its insides from curiosity. . . .

"My knee doethn't hurt me a bit now."

"That's good. And you showed courage, Ziamka. Always remember to show courage."

"No, it doesn't hurt," he said again. "Ever been on a parachute . . . why not? Marina doesn't let me go becauthe I'm too little. But you're a big man. . . ."

They were clearly getting along famously. Trying to find out whether his new friend was clever, Ziamka inquired in a business-like tone whether thermometers have fever, whether Kalinin could drive a car, whether flies have comrades and whether frogs have bones. Yes, Alexei was clever, although on the score of frogs their opinions differed. Then they began to play, and by the time Marina returned their friendship had assumed proportions dangerous for the tenants. The room now remotely reminded one of the Manchurian mounds.

"Now, you'll be Japan, and I'll be the Far Eatht," said Ziamka. "But you're little and I am big. Well, scream just as I taught you, and attack me!"

And Ziamka rushed headlong, brandishing the handle of a kitchen knife, and chairs fell, and the broken electric plug, replacing an air bomb, exploded with a fracas, and the warrior got entangled in Kurilov's strong arms. He immediately tied the vanquished foe's hands with a red Pioneer necktie. Marina looked on worriedly. Later she explained that her line in the attic had broken and that she had to rerinse a whole basketful of wash, although she knew that Alexei Nikitich was waiting for her.

"Let's go to the theatre. . . . It's getting late," Kurilov said casually, while watching for Japan's next ruse.

"Why, what's on?" (It was as though she still might refuse, and Alexei interpreted her question as a reflection on his recent slight.)

By the end of the next battle Marina was dressed. She wore a tight dress, funnel-shaped at the bottom, with enormous printed flowers, and a patent leather belt; Kurilov noted with pleasure that her shoes were also new. (But he could not even imagine how much they squeezed Marina's big feet over the instep.) And although they were going to an unimportant theatre, to see a mediocre play with second-rate actors, Marina looked like an older sister of Ziamka, she was so happy and excited. Having donned monumental felt boots, Ziamka escorted them to the street. And while Marina took her seat in the car, the boy performed all kinds of complicated figures on one skate, trying to arouse base envy in Kurilov. The delighted Alexei Nikitich promised to send the car for him immediately after the performance. "You'll come to see me; first we'll eat candy and then we'll discuss everything you asked about before, thermometers and flies and so on."

"Fine," said Ziamka. "If I'm not at home, I'll be at Shanka's. . . . Now don't get off on a thpree, mother!" he added in a business-like tone.

(Only a week later did Alexei Nikitich realize the meaning of the round yellow spot, like a large cheese, on the open window that he noticed when his car started. It was Marina's aunt standing on a stool to enjoy her niece's unexpected good luck.)

# CHAPTER 22

# The Attack

MARINA ENTERED THE half-empty box and, with the frightened gesture of a woman who is being looked at and who is not quite certain that her appearance and dress are impeccable, passed her hand over her hair, checking on every lock. The folds of her dress rubbed against her knees as though she were walking in high grass. But she knew that her alarm was vain. From her niche she cast a quick and worried glance at the space in front of her. It was impersonal, alive, slightly hostile. Incomprehensible spots of light gleamed on the ceiling, there was a swarming whisper, and belated spectators stumbled about ludicrously among the seats. Bending her head, she stepped forward more boldly, hoping to find her place as quickly as possible and become inconspicuous. The mysterious musty warmth of the theatre breathed into her face so that her nostrils widened. People in the rows of seats downstairs turned toward her, and she experienced a brief triumph as though standing before a mirror that reflected her whole length. She was frightened and dizzy from this new feeling of looking at herself through the eyes of hundreds of strangers: then the music began to play, and Alexei Nikitich pushed her chair right up to the railing.

And suddenly she began to like everything here (this time the theatre was not a bit like the strange den in which Protoklitov had once watched his wife!): the elegant semi-circular railings of the boxes, finished in polished oak and gilded with reflections of orange light; the simple but majestic circular pit created by the removal of the floor between two consecutive stories of the building; the festive excitement of the spectators—as is always the case in the presence of a still untried wine; the complicated lighting machinery under the ceiling on which an inexperienced electrician played as on a piano; even the simple canvas curtain still drawn (but already a swinging door into the marvellous land of miracles and coincidences—lavender twilight was hidden in its folds, ready to blossom). . . . Marina and Kurilov had arrived just in time: the lights were already half-dimmed. The footlights shone blue. A delicate shiver, as across the night sky before dawn, passed along the curtain. The invisible musicians began to play a sad tune about something that never happens in real life. Marina frowned, and suddenly Vlasov's philosophical meditations were interrupted by a carefree little song that evoked fresh meadows, June breezes playing in the thin-stemmed flowers, hosts of vari-colored and solemn beetles playing on toy 'cellos. . . . Gradually the music dissolved all the whispers, the creak of the seats, the barking January coughs and even all of Marina's recent fears.

But all this was only the cunning ruse of the producers. Instead of the promised banality of idyllic happiness they showed something else, the banality of poverty. Near an arched basement window a cobbler was busy sewing a pair of shoes. He was very industrious, and got up from his bench only at the sight of one young girl; in her presence his tools fell from his hands. Then came his comrades, those who shared his fate and trade, three in number. Their conversation revealed that this excellent master would have become the pride of the whole cobblers' guild if he had not been possessed by the stupid and conceited ambition to become the royal cobbler at all costs. His friends tried to dissuade him, but the man was stubborn and kept silent. And in addition he was trying to win this title at an unfortunate period. His three comrades obscurely hinted at the misery of the people and their right to put an end to conditions that are unfair—at their sacred custom of taking bread if they have no money to buy it with—at their ancient passion for cutting off the heads of royal personages. The girl was feather-brained and cruel; she wanted pretty dresses and such ridiculous honors at least as a cobbler could achieve. All told, the first act consisted of a dozen more or less trenchant phrases on the family, the artisan's right to mastery of his craft, the solemn moments when the people's right to insurrection becomes its civic duty. The text of the play had been expressly simplified till it was only a string of formulas, and the spectators accepted it as a fable easy to remember and not requiring any thought. The content could be easily guessed from the title. Anyone could be called Frederick, but Frederick with a number could only be a king. The cobbler's fate was obvious, too, because in those days plays with ambiguous solutions rarely reached the stage. Marina noted a phrase from the text: the people lives by its stomach, the hero by his heart and the leader by his reason, and she felt relieved at not having to explain the social tendency of work to anyone.

During the intermission Kurilov went out to puff at his pipe and he came back only after the beginning of the second act. On the stage was a very conventional royal bedroom. Under a baldaquin, which rested on carved twisted bronze columns as high as the sky, the king himself was lying, yellow, long and frightfully flat. He was dying. A physician in a black coat, who looked like a grandfather's clock, was mixing a draught necessary to conceal the impotence of court medicine. On the steps beside the bed, shaking with grief, a little woman was weeping. She was too beautiful to be the queen, too insincere to be a daughter, and too young to be a sister. And although the death agony was taking place in reddish twilight, and the lenses of Marina's old opera glasses had long since been somewhat out of commission, she managed to recognize the actress's face. . . . It was Liza, and Kurilov's companion began to feel hostile toward her even before she picked up the mother-of-pearl handle of her shabby opera glasses from her knees. She decided not to look at the stage, and immediately the goatee-bearded chief of the financial section of the railroad came into her field of vision. This fault-finder always chided her in his squeaky voice when she handed him the expense accounts of her trips. He sat alone, in his usual *tolstovka*, a baggy shirt buttoned up to the neck, of which the advantage was that its wearer did not have to change his underwear very often. Petrov was staring at the stage and eating gingerbread mint cakes, crumbling them in his hands and throwing the crumbs under his mustache. This sight was even more distressing than Liza's contortions. Marina again turned to the stage on which Pokhvisneva was lamenting her highly placed lover.

"Surely this woman has never cried in her life. Everything she says sounds so false!" whispered Marina to Kurilov.

She jealously waited for his answer, and when it did not come turned toward him. . . . Alexei Nikitich sat with his chin sunk down on his chest, biting his lips. On his damp forehead dark, deeply shadowed veins were pulsing, and he was trying to conceal the convulsive motions with which he seemed to push something away with his side. Marina grasped his cold hand, and he tried to smile.

"I don't feel well, I want to go home. You stay here, Marina. . . ." And stumbling, almost blinded, he left the box.

Marina darted after him. She found him standing on a step of the staircase, clutching the railing. When she looked into his narrowed, motionless eyes, he made one quite mechanical step forward and straightened out, as though he were walking on crutches. Now he was a different man, a true brother of that mechanical Klavdia who had frightened Marina in her dream. She felt like crying for help, for someone to awaken her. . . .

"The pain—it's eating me alive, . . ." said Kurilov distinctly, and Marina thought he was going to fall down, like a large broken object.

An agonizing quarter of an hour went by before Marina was able to summon the car from the garage. Alexei Nikitich sat in the check-room, helplessly lying on a heap of strangers' fur coats. His face was changed and red as though he had taken the disquieting twilight of the royal bedroom with him. A sudden lonely cry drowned in the thunder of applause brought him back to reality. (The suburb was applauding some clever stage trick that indicated the despot's death.) With an expression of great surprise Kurilov looked at the badly plastered oval window against which snowflakes were whirling. For a few moments the pain subsided. As though just awakening from sleep, Alexei Nikitich cast his eyes all around the empty theatre lobby. At first his attention was attracted by a piece of paper on the dirty floor; then two attendants behind their counter caught his glance. Dreamily, shaking slightly, one of them, a man with long hands, was telling the other how he had killed a wolf in his own home. "On Our Lady's Day, in the same year as the war, a wolf began to visit our farm. Thin, but i-intelligent! What does he want, I thought. One morning I hid in a haystack. . . ." And while he told this his face was kind, and his hands gentle, as though he were petting his child. (The other one counted the receipts, placing the coins in neat piles with an absorbed and austere expression.) Alexei Nikitich listened attentively to the story about the wolf; a childish bewilderment shone in his eyes. And when the beast in the checkroom attendant's story fell and clawed the dead hoary grass with his paws, his pain returned with renewed intensity. Alexei Nikitich rose, to go somewhere whence his voice could not be heard, but at that moment Marina cried to him from upstairs that his car was coming. The check-room attendant ran toward him, threw his overcoat over his shoulders, put his cap on him awry as if on a drunk; he did not allow Marina to take him by the arm. The attendants pushed upon the door with all their hands. A beggar quickly moved aside. The car darted ahead in high gear. Suddenly Kurilov cried shrilly to his chauffeur to drive faster. In the elevator he stood with his back to Marina to prevent her from seeing his face. His pains were growing more severe.

Kurilov lurched across the room and threw himself onto the sofa. He was dominated by the animal certainty that there was some position in which he could cheat his pain, such as lying with his shoulder to the cheek or with his whole body tied up in a knot. And he industriously tried to find this position, twisting, bending, making the springs ring wildly in the hope that he might eliminate, or silence even for a moment, the frightful cutting pain and the fierce spasms and burning in his back. The sofa was narrow, Alexei Nikitich could not lie on it comfortably; he tried the table, the chair, even a low bench that had been ordered by Catherine for a pot with a fig tree (which faded soon after her death). Thus he staggered through every room, trying out all his furniture and for a few minutes his pain retreated. He raised his head, rejoicing at being able to feel another tiny pain in his bitten lip and at hearing Marina's desperate voice calling a doctor on the phone.

She was asked whether a general practitioner or a neurologist was required—and in her confusion she forgot the difference. She was asked the name of the disease or at least the description of the food the patient had taken recently; she was chided and told sarcastically that only angels could diagnose a patient without seeing him. Then she managed to find Klavdia Nikitichna at some meeting—Marina's imperative, sonorous voice reached places that would have been inaccessible to other, ordinary tones. Klavdia's dry surprise did not calm her excitement; her real fright would, much later. Klavdia did not ask any questions, she promised to come at once with a doctor. Marina was still holding the receiver, the dying vibrations of the old woman's voice were still breathing into it, when she was deafened by the sound of a bell ringing in the hall. Oh, only angels could respond that quickly! Marina opened the door and saw Klavdia Kurilova. Her appearance was like a hallucination which makes people jump out of a window from any storey.

"Hello! . . ." Marina whispered in terror.

The visitor looked her over from top to toe, perhaps trying to find some disorder in her dress, and remained silent. The only possible question in this case was eliminated as a matter of course; Alexei Nikitich must be at home if this woman, who was not his wife, was present here. This time Klavdia looked strange: she had grown somewhat fatter during the last month and for some reason wore a black sheepskin with a heavy scarf tied on top of it. Under it was a calico blouse and a long dark skirt. And as a finishing touch she wore felt boots, carrying a basket tied criss-cross with a red coachman's belt.

"Is Catherine home, dearie?"

"No . . . she is dead!" Marina whispered wide-eyed.

"A-ah!" the woman drawled out, and for some reason cast a glance at her reed basket (it contained a present for Catherine).

Soon it began to dawn upon Marina that this woman was not Klavdia; she was heavier, gentler, more deliberate in her gestures. Once she had been beautiful . . . while the other, had she ever been a woman? This sister's name was Efrosinia, she was the middle one of the living Kurilovs. Without waiting for details about Catherine, she entered the apartment uncertainly. Everything here revealed the absence of a housewife; the untidiness, the air poisoned by tobacco, the heaps of dust in the corners, the piles of wrapping paper strewn about. Then her eyes caught her brother's leather cap that had rolled from the sofa on to the floor; she picked it up and shook the dust off it. In an adjoining room, Kurilov's overcoat lay on the desk—it had been thrown there and ink had spilled on it. Wonderingly she hung it on the back of the chair and with a worried air examined the dark stain on the material and her own discolored fingers. In the next to the last room she discovered Kurilov's belt and his tunic that had burst along the seams. (This had been the path taken by Kurilov, who had thrown off his things one by one.) Finally, before the last door she called her brother by his name; not receiving an answer, she pushed open the door and looked inside.

Alexei was lying on his side, across Catherine's bed, bending his legs under him, in the position his pain had thrown him into, his face stuck deep into the dusty pillows. His shirt was pulled up, one could see his body with an old scar below his shoulder and a little roll of fat on the small of his back reddened from the tightly drawn belt. Efrosinia would have thought he was asleep had it not been for his fists clenched so tightly that they were blue and as if wringing the blanket. . . . They had not seen each other for fourteen years. At that time he was quick, young, contemptuous of danger and illness; she addressed his heavy, greying neck.

"Aliosha, what's the matter with you?"

She touched his hand lightly; he shuddered and began to wriggle as though trying to crawl away from her.

"I'm dying, sister . . ." he said in a creaking voice. "I'm dying like the lowest scum. . . ."

After that he did not answer any more questions. Then Efrosinia ran to get somebody—a doctor, Marina, God Himself, to save this man. In the hall doorway she ran into Klavdia and a doctor. The sisters did not embrace, although they had not seen each other for so many years: they did not even shake hands. The older one asked where Alexei was; the younger answered with a nod. Klavdia stepped forward, and with this resolute gesture seemed to take command in Kurilov's apartment. Before seeing the patient, the doctor wanted to wash his hands.

Klavdia returned to the hall where Marina was still sitting in her corner.

"Come here," said the old woman. "Where are the towels? Where does Alexei keep his linen?"

"I don't know," said Marina rising. "I don't know where his towels are. . . ."

"What do you mean, you don't know!" She hated prudery more than anything, and always demanded an immediate confession of guilt from anyone she questioned. "That's strange, to say the least. . . ."

If no one except Catherine could boast of her favor, such insulting and cynical harshness was not customary with Klavdia. But she was upset and she believed that this sumptuous—for the unfastidious—girl was setting her cap at Alexei. Marina, silent and austere, looked into her face, impassive, as though carved from yellow alabaster; Klavdia turned her eyes away. Then she and the doctor went to Kurilov's room. Silence fell. (In the theatre, the insurgents by now had probably overthrown the sickly and faint-hearted son of Frederick, the royal cobbler had seen the light, had broken into the palace tower to avenge his dishonored fiancée, and the royal ermine had become tricolored. At home Ziamka was patiently waiting for the car that would come any moment now to take him into a fairy-tale. . . .) The door opened again. Klavdia approached Marina, and even the furtive touch of her hand seemed a caress. "Why are you sitting here alone, Marina? Are you angry with me? Please don't be: old people are often querulous and unpleasant. Come in, he's asking for you."

Everyone was sitting down. The doctor was putting his things in a little suitcase. The light had been turned on, but the lampshade for some reason was lying on the window-sill. Alexei Nikitich reclined in a chair with a slightly swollen, red and embarrassed face. Without looking at anything he was stuffing his pipe. His left sleeve was pulled up almost to his shoulder. Suddenly his tobacco pouch slid on the floor; Marina picked it up, and Kurilov gave her a friendly nod. He advised her to return to the theatre, she might still see the last act. His speech was mechanical; he got entangled in his words, and it was obvious that he was listening to the strange calm that spread all over his body.

"Your Ziamka is a grand boy. We're certainly going to be friends. Say hello to him for me. . . ." He turned to the doctor. "Was that morphine? It's good stuff. . . ."

The doctor spoke. He suspected that this was worse than an ordinary neuralgia and advised him to consult a surgeon. Because of the pain, detailed investigation with the fingers—he used the term "palpation"—was impossible, but he had the impression that the kidney was not moving. Klavdia quickly approached him, as though fearing that he would say too much before the patient. She looked on gloomily as the thin needle that had relieved her brother was washed, disappearing in the colorless liquid.

"It's good if it isn't moving. . . . What should it move for?" she said nervously and dryly.

"Oh, I don't want it to be any friskier than it should be. . . ." The joke was not appreciated, and he began to say goodbye.

Klavdia accompanied him to the door. She closed it tightly after him, casting a significant look at the other women. For some time everyone was silent.

"How are you, Frosia?" her brother asked her.

She said that little by little her life was returning to normal.

"Any news from your husband? He had a job on my line, but he seems to have run away recently. . . ."

No, she had separated from him long ago, even before he had been deported. "He keeps knocking about, trying to find humility somewhere, but can an Omelichev ever be contented with black bread?" Then she said that she wanted to move to Siberia. An acquaintance had written her from there that a good cook was needed at their project, and from her youth Efrosinia had been noted for her culinary talents.

"It's better for me to go there. Too many people remember how we lived before. . . ."

"That's right, that's right, . . ." Alexei Nikitich approved absent-mindedly: it was obvious that he was thinking of something else. "Now go listen to what they're saying in there!" he suddenly commanded her in a tone of complicity. He winked to his sister in the direction of the hall, where the most important secret of his life was being discussed. Efrosinia hesitated and, while she was busy doing something not very necessary, Klavdia came back. Alexei Nikitich noticed that she avoided his eyes. Marina took advantage of the pause to say goodbye and leave. The telephone rang—Alexei Nikitich was being invited to some party.

"No, I won't take down any addresses, dear comrade Pokhvisneva," Klavdia said in a tone of irritation. "Alexei Nikitich cannot bear parties . . . and please don't telephone him any more!"

Then she expounded her plan in a brief and business-like manner. Alexei, she said, must take care of himself. His disease was almost minor, but for the time being he needed constant supervision. Klavdia caught his inquisitive demanding glance, and for the first time in his memory became confused. Oh, nothing very terrible—only a strict diet and complete rest! The method of treatment would depend on the physician, and Alexei was to see him the very next day. As for a long furlough and all kinds of negotiations with medical committees, she herself would attend to all that.

"Buy me a nipple, too," Kurilov said frowning.

His sister disdained to answer his joke. "Well, how is the pain now?" she asked.

"I felt relieved the moment you entered. You frightened it away, Klavdia!"

Without showing her usual impatience or disapproval, Klavdia shook her head: "When will you grow up, Alioshka?"

She was still keeping something from him; he began to suspect the worst, and sat helpless and suspicious, waiting for his sister to let the secret out. She was worried about how he would spend the night all alone, once the drug wore off. Naturally, Efrosinia had just arrived in time, and she must stay with her brother for some time: she could attend to her own business later. But Efrosinia was loath to agree to this, and Klavdia became angry with her.

"Couldn't you get a residence permit? If you can't, things will be even worse!"

"No, I have a permit. I've been working for myself nine years now. But, you see, I'm not alone here. . . ."

"Your husband?"

No, but she had brought her child. She had left him at the station for a few hours while she came to visit Catherine. "After all, I didn't know how Alexei would receive me. He might have thrown me out. . . ."

"Aren't you ashamed of yourself, Frosia!" Alexei Nikitich said, with annoyance. "After all, we're blood relations!"

"Oh, what blood relations! Your joy and our grief—they're blood relations. . . ." (She laughed briefly and began to wipe the lavender stains from her fingers. How poisonous the ink was nowadays!)

Klavdia decided to show her well-known initiative. "Take my car downstairs," she said, "and get your child. You must stay here for a time . . . and you can take a rest, too." Her voice expressed impatience dictated by fear for her brother.

Half an hour later Efrosinia pushed into Kurilov's room a thin little creature with an old scarf wrapped crosswise over his chest and shabby shoes on his feet. Disencumbered of his clothes, he turned out to be a boy of around ten. His mother pushed him forward to greet his uncle, and her gesture implied her pity for her son, her willingness to stay with Alexei until he recovered, and her embarrassment over her own ill fortune in life.

"His name is Luka," she said in a low voice, bowing for him down to her waist.

A long, awkward pause followed.

"Well, hello, little gypsy!" Kurilov cried out in an effort to be natural.

The boy remained silent. Bending one leg out of shyness, he looked in turn from under his brows at all those present. He was swarthy, big-eyed and not very handsome because he was so sickly and fragile-looking; his non-Russian curls were particularly striking. He looked like a martin taken from under the roof and placed, still frightened, on one's palm.

"Why are you silent, little boy?" Klavdia asked him. "Don't you know you should answer when spoken to? . . ."

His eyes expressed non-childish alarm; he wanted to understand something, but he could not.

"He is a deaf-mute," Efrosinia explained dryly, taking her son by the hand; then something broke in her voice. Her face became grey, aged, and her lips began to tremble. "The children, oh, what the children must answer for, . . ." she said and burst into tears.

CHAPTER 23

# Ilya Ignatyich Takes Steps

AFTER ILYA'S FIRST SURGE OF wedded happiness abated, he began conscientiously to investigate his wife's right to her profession. During the
last month he had tried not to miss a single performance in which she
had a part. And when he had been to see her he was more exhausted
than on any working day (yet he often stayed in the operating room
until nightfall). He was deeply upset, too, as though it were Liza's
début he was watching. At first he felt only shame and pity in watching her—his impulse was to rush backstage, seize and crumple her in
his arms and take her home by force. He felt sorry for his wife, who
fawned upon the directors and deceived her friends in order to retain
her right to defraud the spectators. Falseness, intrigue and spiritual
emptiness seemed to penetrate the very air that Protoklitov breathed:
Liza did everything she could to draw him into her plans. Gradually
he himself became an accomplice in this, according to his view, criminal undertaking; he felt himself equally guilty with the producers who
lured the public into this dubious den, with the directors who substituted acrobatics for real acting and with the box-office clerk who
sold tickets for a product that she knew was inferior.

Later this feeling of complicity was combined with the protest of a
master craftsman accustomed to working precisely and irreproachably,
and who considered idleness far more justifiable than this deliberate
counterfeiting. To remain inactive in such a situation was in his eyes
an act of infamy, a compromise with his conscience, perhaps even a
bribe with which he bought Liza's love. (And it so happened that
every technical term connected with the theatre aroused inexplicable
bitterness in him.)

Once she asked him what he wanted of her—"to leave the theatre
for you? Never, darling."

"I want you to learn your profession."

"You just don't understand the new stage, Ilya."

"But you know so little. Any additional knowledge will teach you to
be critical of yourself and will give you an idea of the world in which
you have lost your way. . . ."

195

"Oh, let me be an average human being," she said coldly.

"But it's criminal—deliberately to make oneself an average human being!"

He was angry; he had long since made up his mind about the numerous group of mediocre artists for whom art is a means of attaining a social position to which they are not entitled. Such artists counted on either the consumer's illiteracy or his kind-heartedness: after all, people sometimes buy matches that don't burn! Even after they realize that their talent is unequal to anything great, they continue to accept their miserable earnings in the hope that some lottery chance will raise them to the same level of fame as prominent strato-navigators, atom-smashers and rescuers of Arctic expeditions. As they grow older they unite to act in common in the back alleys of art after the fashion of the seven lean kine in the Bible.

Liza listened to her husband and her lips grew pale. She felt that "all this" had been maturing in him for a long time, even before he met her, and was coming to the surface only now. In Ilya's voice there no longer sounded the craftsman's protest but the cheated consumer's fury. Indeed, a man of his kidney would not hesitate a moment to hire a dozen loud-mouthed ruffians to hiss her at the next opening.

She assumed that her husband's references to an art in which there was more shell than edible kernel applied to her. "So what? Samarin, the successor of Shchepkin himself, said that nothing good would come of Ermolova. . . . I'm glad that you are so interested in my career. Of course, your opinions are reactionary. There are no secrets in our business, my dear. Anyone who has some social consciousness and intelligence can write a play. Moreover, you can inquire about my work at the theatre. They've changed their opinion of me since my performance in *Frederick!*"

He himself had once questioned a friend of Liza's, who seemed to him a clever girl on this score. According to her, Pokhvisneva was tolerated because everyone in the company liked to think that Protoklitov would be glad to serve him in case of emergency. This revealed to the surgeon some of Liza's backstage manoeuvres.

"I forbid you to use my name in the theatre. It's low, as well as absurd!"

Liza's smile lasted just long enough to veil her furious and threatening reply: "You're losing your self-command. You should be more careful: in such insults even the most ardent attachments can be dissolved without a trace!" She was quoting from a part that had been given to someone else.

Then he recalled that she was pregnant; he came close to her and embraced her, this thin little mother of his future child. (At that time Ilya Ignatyich did not yet know the change that had taken place. She would not allow him to examine her medically: she was embarrassed to appear before her husband otherwise than as a wife.)

"Oh, I'll be quiet, you've outshouted me. After all, there are two of you!"

In her haste she interpreted this sudden gentleness as fear and, consequently, as the recognition that she was right. But her hoped-for peace proved premature. Ilya Ignatyich had long since made up his mind to take extreme measures; that is to say, to speak to the director of the theatre. He went to see him shortly before the end of the jubilee performance, but for a purpose exactly opposite to the one he had had in the early days of their marriage. He was told that the director had left for dinner half an hour ago and would not be back until six o'clock. Ilya Ignatyich was still wondering how to spend the next two and a half hours, when the play ended and the public, as though released from prison, rushed for the check-room. To avoid being knocked off his feet he went to the further end of the corridor, near the pit, and almost immediately Liza came out toward him from the back. She was engaged in friendly conversation with another actress and would have passed him by without noticing him if a new stream of outgoing spectators had not thrown Protoklitov directly against them.

"Oh, how very lovely of you to wait for us," Liza chirped, clinging to his arm and speaking alternately to him and to her friend. (She backed up against the wall in order to let more impetuous legs and bodies pass by—"What dust they raise!") "Let me introduce you; this is Kagorlitskaya, an excellent actress and a lovely person. You know, I have spoken about you so much to my husband that he has a crush on you without knowing you. He's an amorous fellow, but you're the only girl I'm jealous of. You know Jacqueline; today she played the cobbler's fiancée. Wasn't her scene with the captain in the third act effective?"

Protoklitov grimaced a smile at this unconscious, almost naïve depravity. (And he was surprised to note that despite her pregnancy his wife had not lost the singing clarity of her voice.) Kagorlitskaya noticed his grin and said quietly that Liza's childishness was simply charming. She was an almost emaciated woman for her size, with an unpleasantly thin nose; she undoubtedly suffered from some specific gynecological disorder. But she had an attractive expression in her big, restless eyes, compounded of alertness, sensitivity and fear; looking at her one thought of a forest bird alarmed by a strange rustle in the nearby ravine.

Next to Liza she looked like a plain poor relation, and no doubt Liza took her appearance soberly into consideration when she showered all these perfidious compliments upon her.

"We're going with Staska to buy something for our guests. I hope you haven't forgotten that we're giving a party tonight? Vasiliev, Pashka, Trubetskaya and Pakhomov are coming. . . . Have you ever heard of Ellen Arens? A world-famous actress! Well, it's Pakhomov who made her. Alexander Ieronimovich also promised to drop in after his meeting at the Commissariat for Education. Six pounds of sausage, do you think that'll be enough? Pashka will take care of the wine. There'll be about fifteen people. To make it less boring for you I think I'll invite a certain chief of the Political Bureau of . . . oh, never mind, you don't know his name, anyway. We'll lock you both up, give you some cognac . . . and you can discuss the role of the party in medicine, while we dance. But he's an austere man . . . do you think he'll spoil the fun? Today I feel a sort of animal desire to be gay. You're sure you haven't forgotten?" Once more she threatened him with her finger.

No, he remembered. On that day the new theatre was five years old and was celebrating its jubilee. One of the big newspapers had promised to run an article about it, but the editor had changed his mind at the last minute. When the actors conceived the idea of marking the day with an intimate party, Liza's apartment was found to be the only suitable place: the other young actors roosted in all sorts of odd corners. The original plan had been to send Ilya to spend the night with a friend of his, but Liza had insisted that he be present. "If you're there they won't drink too much," she said.

"Are you going home now, too?"

"No, Li, I must drop in at the hospital. . . ."

"What a nuisance! Is someone worried again? . . . A man . . . a woman?"

In Ilya Ignatyich's voice there was real tenderness, barely concealed: "This time it's a little girl, five years old. She's called Eva!" The name had a refreshing sound. "Oh, she's charming, like something out of Dickens. Poor thing, she swallowed a sharp instrument. . . ."

"Do you like children?" Kagorlitskaya asked him in a strange voice, avoiding his eyes.

"Oh, I don't know . . . I respect and fear them."

Liza frowned capriciously. "Well, I see two kindred souls are getting together here! . . . And you know, Staska, you've never seen how he does that business in his clinic. He opens them like watermelons: chi-chick . . . something red. . . . 'The clamps!' he yells . . . and it's done."

"You're saying horrible things, Li," Ilya Ignatyich observed, shrinking in mortification.

"Why? . . . Is it anything to be ashamed of . . . helping people?"

They had no opportunity to continue the discussion; the trolley car arrived. Ilya Ignatyich left in the opposite direction. However, he had decided not to go to the clinic, so that he would certainly be on time for his appointment with the director, and there was no other place to go . . . but now it seemed to him that some while ago he had seen this craggy house on the corner that looked like a ship's prow and cut the square into two adjacent streets. A year before Protoklitov had come here from another direction. He recalled Dudnikov's untidy hermit's beard and, with a feeling of the same boyish curiosity he had experienced the first time, he walked down the little street looking for the familiar courtyard. But nothing remained there: it had been dug up and removed, together with the dead lilac trees. Two subway towers dominated a whole group of new unpainted building sheds. From the dark jaws of the shaft came some sort of vapor, or perhaps it was smoke mixed with snow. Men were digging underneath as though seeking the lost Caron clock.

(This object, which in a roundabout fashion had brought him and Liza together, was now part of Ilya Ignatyich's collection. And if it had not been the gambling demon of the collectors who threw it again into human hands in order to earn interest on the turnover, one might have used it as an example of the law of displacement of such treasures, so different from the motion of other material values. Most frequently during periods of great social landslides, these objects wrest themselves loose from the narrow orbit of connoisseurs and experts and, like comets, move through the most variegated social strata, past amateurs' chests and museum show-cases, not halting till they reach the place where they are fated to perish. Thus, after having been in the pocket of the health officer who had concealed it when Dudnikov was transported to the morgue, the Caron successively passed through the hands of a second-hand dealer, a small speculator in antiques, a professional thief, a fence, an examining magistrate, an appraiser and, finally, a clockmaker who was an old acquaintance of Ilya Ignatyich.

Verily, this elegant masterpiece of the art of the clockmaker deserves an obituary. It was a chronometer with a single-shaft movement, with a repeater and a calendar, manufactured, judging by the watermarks on the dial, by the clockmaker Caron in Besançon, in 1758, the year of the coming of age of his son, Pierre-Augustin Beaumarchais, who later attained the title of "supervisor of the pet dogs and guardian of the royal pleasures"—and who in addition was the author of a few excellent plays. The mechanism itself, a wonder of its age, was enclosed in a beautiful enamel case of a blue so deep and strong that it would have sufficed to cover the entire sky if an appropriate dissolvent had been found. The embossed monogram of the first owner of this jewel remained illegible. It would have been absurd to seek a substitute for this exquisite object if it had been lost; destiny does not smile twice. But the circle was closing: now only one event separated the Caron from destruction. And by hastening to have his talk with the director of Liza's theatre, Protoklitov was bringing this event closer.)

The trolley car turned back at the city gate. The same conductor gave Protoklitov a return ticket. At the theatre people were standing in line for the night performance. The director had not yet returned. Ilya Ignatyich made the round of the establishment and learned from the wall newspaper that the local bookkeeper failed to attend shop meetings and that Trunina, the charwoman, displayed disruptive tendencies. He also lifted a slip-cover from a chair and saw signs of ugly poverty; he spoke to the Methuselah who heated the stove and learned that he had married six months before. . . . Made intensely uncomfortable by his unaccustomed idleness, Ilya Ignatyich entered the pit and sat in a corner of the auditorium. It was cool, the ventilators were singing in the silence. As usual during the intervals between performances, the curtain was open. On a wooden stand in the center of the stage a lamp was burning. Its shadows covered the bare chalk walls with austere silhouettes laid one upon another, and everyone could find his own meaning in the chaos of these unrepeatable frescoes—a fragment of a battle subject or of a Cyclopean structure or the gears of a ship leaving for a voyage into the infinite, or even a garden in bloom.

The theatre now seemed far more enormous than it was in fact. Contemplation of the empty, unadorned stage produced an alarming stillness deepened to the point of unreality. The tall brick wall behind the reflector encumbered with palace mantelpieces, groves and stained-glass windows from mediaeval cathedrals, was imbued with the secretions of the human soul; more strongly than cement they joined the coarse bricks to one another. Surely, if one scraped the wall with a knife, one would hold in one's hands the grey earthy dust of human passions. Here Hamlet wept while tireless Scapin bustled about and the insatiable Don Juan for the millionth time led the yielding Anna to perdition. These apparitions teemed in all the corners of the emptiness, ready at any moment to step out onto the boards.

And now, amidst the silence, unhurried monumental steps could be heard, and the floor, though used to all sorts of loads, creaked under them. The Stone Guest, bored from standing in the cobwebs among the shabby backdrops, had slunk down from his pedestal to stretch his legs. The great event was approaching, the thunder of stone jack-boots was coming closer, the right wing of the curtain stirred threateningly. Ilya Ignatyich was prepared to see something never described before. . . . Then from behind the pile of decorative shield emerged a fantastically tall and thin fireman, in a helmet and greasy boots, capable of turning back a storm of fire by his very appearance. But theatre fires were becoming rarer, and the man on guard, out of sheer boredom, from time to time made the rounds of his domain, perhaps in the hope of discovering a blaze. Having walked across the stage along a curved path he stopped at the footlights and in a business-like manner pressed his right thumb to his nostril. There followed a sound reminiscent of the whimper of a smith's bellows. And overthrowing all of Protoklitov's romantic imaginings, by one stroke he directed the lamp like a spotlight toward the back of the stage. The frescoes were wiped out by darkness, and at that very moment someone called Protoklitov by his name. From the assurance with which the tall, fair-haired man of Scandinavian appearance approached him, he guessed that this was the director.

Ilya Ignatyich began facetiously to apologize for having come in without a ticket to spy upon the most sacred secrets of the theatre. He told about the Stone Guest's prank between office hours, and the two men laughed; both were inclined to see in this incident an example of the relation of life to imaginative thinking about it. Laughter brought them almost as close as the distance of friendship, and Protoklitov no longer doubted the success of his undertaking.

"You don't recognize a former patient of yours, professor," said the director, taking his place beside Protoklitov. "True, we met only casually: I was lying down and you were standing up. I don't quite remember what followed, but I think you cut me open. . . ."

"Yes, last year. How is your liver these days?"

He said that he was quite satisfied with the quality of Protoklitov's work. And closer contact revealed that this man had drunk quite a bit at dinner. He added he would consider it a pleasure to be of service to his doctor. It was difficult to be completely sincere in such an ambiguous and ticklish affair: so Ilya Ignatyich chose a manoeuvre that at any other time he would have considered beneath him.

"I wanted to speak with you about a certain actress."

"I have droves of them here. Are you referring to your wife?"

". . . my former wife!" Protoklitov corrected him emphatically. "We separated about a month ago, but this woman is not indifferent to me, and I wanted to consult you about her future."

The director was visibly surprised by the ease with which this dignified man initiated a stranger into his family affairs. This created an obligation, and he pricked up his ears. Ilya Ignatyich realized that he had made a bad blunder: the director had been invited to Liza's party. It was too late to retreat and too late to explain the meaning of this not very clever manoeuvre. The director's expression was now one of sly and incredulous seriousness.

"This is an important matter. . . ." And, moving forward, he pressed Protoklitov's knee in a strong manly fashion.

"You have a strong hand," Ilya Ignatyich remarked.

"I'm a former tennis-player: that gives you strong hands for the rest of your life!"

". . . and an extremely good heart. Of course, that is not meant as an accusation. . . ."

"Oh, please, don't be embarrassed to speak freely, dear friend. As a piece of your handiwork, I'm listening to you with the greatest attention."

"Don't misunderstand my question, but why do you keep a bad actress in your theatre?"

Only now did the director begin to grasp the reasons for Protoklitov's visit. It was unlikely that he wanted to take revenge on a woman who had once shared her love with him. But the director knew of cases (at this point, like a reminder, the fireman again walked across the stage, but no one noticed him this time) in which love drove people not only to heroism, but also to baseness, and the ineradicable force of one feeling lent a furious impetus to its opposite. The director's face became bored and absent, and the dimensions of the service Protoklitov had rendered him suddenly shrunk to the point that made it negligible in this case. He kept silent in order to give his visitor an opportunity to explain himself further.

"I have watched her carefully," Ilya Ignatyich went on. "This woman does not work or create, she only goes through the motions. Ha, she tries to sing without knowing the music with which life is written. In your theatre she only hums out of tune. In our day, art is the work of unskilled laborers. To determine the course of the future river bed while in it is full flood—is this not to create the course oneself?"

The director smiled; he explained the surgeon's vehemence in his own way. Victor Adolfovich had always liked Pokhvisneva and he knew that the spite of deceived husbands often makes them over-critical.

"I am glad that you make such heavy demands on our theatre. That shows your serious attitude toward it. But our theatre is still young. . . ."

"I'm speaking of only one actress."

"She's almost the same age as the theatre!"

Protoklitov was irritated. "Ha, youth can't justify lack of talent, can it?"

"Can you draw a scientific boundary between genius and mediocrity?"

Protoklitov made an impatient gesture. "So you really think you are getting something for the money you pay her?"

Victor Adolfovich thought he detected a sort of hope in Protoklitov's voice; but a furtive glance at his face revealed only calm and hard expectation, the same expression he had seen in the operating room.

"At any rate I'd be able to prove to any control committee that she fully earns her one hundred and forty a month!" This equivocal formula revealed the director's real opinion. "You see, professor," he went on removing invisible grains of dust from his interlocutor's suit and carefully dropping them in the air, "there's hardly a chance that she will ever develop into a first-class artist . . . and, of course, we wouldn't be any worse off if she left us. But she loves the theatre and would give her soul for it if she had one, damn it! And I must also point out that in every art, not only creators, but also rank-and-file-workers are needed, they are the culture medium in which the genius develops. Moreover, don't you agree that greatness does not come all at once?" And still industriously flicking the non-existent grains of dust off his visitor, he quoted a few well-known maxims to strengthen his position.

"All this is very inexact," Ilya Ignatyich said somewhat more gently. "For the time being, our science of man is only an index of our ignorance. People have never been able to define a phenomenon without incorporating into their definition some of the imperfections of their time. I mean that any idea is influenced by the epoch in which it comes to fruition. . . . But in this case it is clear that Pokhvisneva has only a childish fondness for art, intensified by adolescent vanity."

"You're right only in so far as art has always been an arena for clashes of ambitions!"

"Look. Perhaps I'm an outsider meddling in what is not my business. I cannot ask of you the sincerity I need as I would ask the pharmacist for a medicine. But we surgeons are accustomed to greater courage. It's more pleasant to tell a patient that he is perfectly fine, but the honor of our profession is in the accuracy of our diagnosis. The later a disease is revealed, the more dangerous it is. If neglected, it leads to disaster. I must apologize for having wasted your time."

But the director would not let him go. They finally agreed on a middle-of-the-road opinion. Protoklitov had no intention of playing a dirty trick on his former wife, and the manager accepted his view that she needed the good school of life. After half an hour's discussion the director grasped Protoklitov's real intentions, but the more he agreed with him, the more irreconcilable his tone became.

"We have no legitimate reason for dismissing her."

Protoklitov rose from his seat. "This conversation is beginning to give the impression of a plot; all I wanted to ask of you was to *think* about this woman."

For a few minutes they spoke of new productions and interesting operations. Then a moment of silence followed, which strengthened their alliance.

"I have a project . . ." the director said in conclusion; "it's a big social undertaking . . . you'll read about it in the newspapers. And if only you don't impose a time limit on me. . . ."

"It isn't necessary, I hope, to ask you to keep this conversation between ourselves?"

"I'm just as anxious to do that as you are." He smiled and looked Protoklitov straight in the eyes. "Tell your wife, please, that I won't be able to come to her party tonight. I must go to a meeting . . . we're having such a fuss now about our repertory! They want to kill our *Mary.*"

The director's broad hint that he had fathomed the visitor's motives was a rather clumsy familiarity. Although apparently trying to obtain his wife's dismissal, Ilya Ignatyich secretly hoped to be refused; at any rate the director's ready consent annoyed him. And then Protoklitov realized that he did not respect Victor Adolfovich, neither as a party man nor as a theatre worker.

# CHAPTER 24

# Destruction of the Caron Clock

HE LEFT THE THEATRE and realized suddenly that he had nothing to do that evening. Early in the day he had made up his mind to come home as late as possible. He thought his presence might spoil the party. He visited little Eva, made the rounds of the hospital and caught himself idly paging through the loose-leaf surgical record. Then he left, hungry, and was pleased to think that he could kill some time eating. He drove to the House of Scientists, angry at the speed with which he was able to do all these things.

His car rushed along the dug-up Moscow streets. The waitress brought his order before he had time to change it. He did not meet anyone he knew. He spent the rest of his time reading the newspapers and walking home. Pushed by some diabolical force he found himself on the staircase landing outside his flat. As in all buildings belonging to the cooperatives, the doors were thin; from his apartment came the hoarse jangle of jazz music and a tinkle of indistinct voices. *They* were dancing. Ilya Ignatyich had miscalculated: most of the guests had arrived only after the night performance, and the party was at its height. He went downstairs again, and his next two hours were like those of a man whose possessions have been burned. It was too late to go to the movies, a café closed up right under his nose, and he stood for one and a half wretched hours on the boulevard, watching the life of the town by night. A long stay in the cold always made him feel chilly in the head, so that finally he went home. By now some of the guests had gone, but the party was still on. He rang the bell, but for a long while no one opened the door. Suddenly Liza appeared in the doorway in an extraordinary wrapper printed with flowers and leaves, gold on blue. Her cheeks were aflame. Breathing heavily, she looked at her husband's grey, tired face. Her left eyebrow, lengthened by paint, rose higher and higher in surprise.

"Oh, it's you?" she said in a disappointed tone.

He grasped the meaning of her expression. "I happened to run into your director in the House of Scientists. He asked me to apologize for him—he can't come. . . . I'm sorry to be so late. Is something bothering you?"

She interrupted him: "It's nothing, nothing, take your overcoat off. An old man is here, my first drama teacher . . . don't listen to him! Believe me, everything he says is a lie. When I married you I was as innocent as an unborn baby. How nauseated I feel, how disgusted! Don't look at me, Ilya, I'm completely drunk!"

"But why? . . . You know you shouldn't drink now, it's really criminal. . . ." Thus he again and again reminded her of their child.

"Oh, we drank a toast to our husbands, and I couldn't refuse. All our liquor is gone now, there's only beer left. But don't be afraid, I've outsmarted them all. Only I'm dizzy . . . my head has split open, it's detached, it's swimming. . . . But I can understand everything! Seventeen times seventeen is two hundred and eighty-nine . . . correct? That reminds me—is it true that one drinks beer only to toast horses?" she finished in a worried and guilty tone.

"Ha, that sort of thing isn't up my alley, Liza."

"Nor mine. . . . But where have you been? In the clinic? . . . I've forgotten everything."

Only a few guests remained. On the table under the mirror, made double by the reflection, were a shabby otter cap and a felt beaver; something that Ilya Ignatyich had at first taken to be Kagorlitskaya's little white beret turned out to be a shabby Caucasian hood with a tassel. So only male guests remained. Attracted by the whispers of husband and wife, Victor Adolfovich poked his head out of the door. He was dressed in a fantastic costume made up of bits of clothing from all the plays to the success or failure of which he had contributed. He wore the president's ribbon from *Betrayal and Love* (under which one could see a pair of old suspenders mended by Victor Adolfovich himself) and an open doublet with slashed puffed sleeves from *Don Carlos;* on his chin was a round beard that Protoklitov could not identify although it was maddeningly familiar.

"Aha, here's the man who drenches his hands in blood! How many innocents have you butchered today?" he exclaimed in a tone of playful, tried-and-true friendship, and after crushing Protoklitov in a pretended embrace he passed him on to the others.

Heavy from drink, the guests did not rise from their seats. There were six of them, all dressed just as picturesquely as Victor Adolfovich. One man, whose eyes were close together and who was old enough to make the boorishness of which he was guilty quite surprising, drew his black cloak around him and defiantly introduced himself as Horatio; somehow he looked the part. Another, all lumpy with a crumbling complexion, was easily identified as Falstaff; bowing, he tore off his reddish wig and solemnly waved it like a hat. Two others, just as dishevelled, slept in each other's arms on the couch—perhaps they were Montague and Capulet, now reconciled by the statute of limitations. The collection was completed by a grey, long-haired old man who was rather drunk; he alone was not in costume, but his natural appearance was that of an actor made-up in an exaggerated fashion for a part in the *Lower Depths*. For a long time he submissively shook Ilya Ignatyich's hand, as though hoping to shake something—an additional bottle, perhaps—out of his sleeve, and muttered about the joy it gave him to contemplate Lizushka's prosperity. . . .

The chairs pulled out of place, the stained tablecloth, the pile of bottles in a corner, an aluminum basin placed for some reason on the gramophone and finally a clearly visible and completely inexplicable imprint of a man's foot on the wallpaper—all this untidy chaos laconically told of the youthful passions displayed at the beginning of the party. Everything had now been smoked and drunk, and the merriment was ebbing; liveliness returned, thanks to an intact bottle drawn by Ilya Ignatyich from a secret place. It was met with the same applause as the miraculous water of Cana two thousand years ago. (Ilya Ignatyich was rubbing his hands; he was cold.) Thus there was fuel for another quarter of an hour. The previous conversation was resumed, and only then did Ilya Ignatyich understand the cause of Liza's confusion.

". . . now I shall conclude," the man dressed as Horatio announced in an acid tone. He knocked his glass with a knife to call for silence, and Liza shrank at once as though she knew a blow was coming. "I have only a little left to say . . . and you yourself asked for it!"

"Only speak so that everyone can hear . . . everyone!" said the old man busily, putting his hands curved like horns to his ears; he rose, then sat down and settled himself more comfortably.

"And so you've stolen closer and now you want to take a fling at *Mary*. You are not old enough, you have no temperament, you're not a born actress; you are stubborn out of weakness, perfidious, indifferent toward other people, and you want to jump into a new adventure. And at bottom, no matter what role you're given, you won't know the difference! What right do you have to this part? Answer me, have you ever had an experience in life that made you forget everything except your own grief for three whole days? Was your fiancé killed, did your child die, did your father drive you out of your home? You've never suffered, lived or loved. . . ."

"How dull you are and how cruel, Pakhomov!" Liza interrupted him in a metallic voice.

Pakhomov disregarded this remark intended to stop him. Ilya Ignatyich poured the rest of the cognac into his glass and caught Pakhomov's brief sharp glance. It seemed to him that all of them, six avengers, had deliberately awaited his return in order to complete Liza's destruction in the presence of her husband. The old man was radiant, as though he had known about it all in advance.

". . . I told you: cut yourself to pieces, and if the pieces grow together again, come to see me and we'll have a talk about art. I don't know an infallible remedy, no one does, everyone has his own. In olden times one sold one's soul to the devil, later one fell in love with a scoundrel with dyed mustaches and a worn-out tailcoat. It's also said that killing one's husband helps. . . . Don't take me literally, darling; I am leaving the whole thing up to your taste and inventiveness. You're a capable girl, capable of *anything*." He again leered at Protoklitov, who, having finished his cognac, painstakingly made himself a sandwich of smoked salmon. "But live, move about, fear spiritual fat and remember: what does not burn does not make a fire! So far you've been trying to open the temple of art with the wrong key. We have all developed a rotten need to please our superiors, while real success comes only from below; but our fame is only productive waste, shavings of the soul, refuse, the ticklish and poisonous dust of our corporation. And you imagine that by being close to a few big wigs you'll grow in stature? You'll only grow fatter, darling, only fatter!" (He doubtless thought that Ilya Ignatyich was at least the director of some industrial combine.) "Don't you like the truths I'm telling you?"

"Now, don't overdo it, don't overdo it!" the old man said with an expression of fright, while moving closer, so as not to miss a word. "You're hitting pretty hard. . . ."

"Shut up, Zakurdaev!" Horatio warded him off contemptuously. "Like the *Revizor* you appear only at the end of my speech. Go on eating! Eat what's most expensive: tomorrow you won't have anything. Devour, destroy! Let her pay for our being at her table."

Some incident, intensified by the shortage of wine, must have irritated him profoundly to make him upbraid Liza with such insolence in the presence of her husband. He interrupted the stream of his abuse only to clink glasses with Falstaff. "To the poor comedians!" the fat man roared defiantly, showing his cards, and this reply sounded like the watchword of a brand of conspirators. He drank and with comical horror stared at his belly that moved and trembled. His swollen fingers ran along the emptied plates; a painter would have invented just such a scene to create the portrait of the famous glutton and brawler. Taking advantage of the pause, Liza ran out to the kitchen, and after four minutes of forced silence three cutlets, Ignatyich's dinner, hissed and stank in the pan. By this housewifely behavior she was trying to buy the sympathy of her colleagues. No one paid any attention to this frightened bustling, lest it intensify her humiliation; no one except her husband. Then, sitting on the edge of the sofa, she stealthily watched Horatio capriciously pick the meat he had been given.

Only yesterday, only yesterday, how she had wanted to lure this cold, spiteful, easily offended man to her house! By winning his favor she would force recognition from all her enemies who feared him. And now how she regretted her enterprise! She recalled the director's recent wisecrack about him: "Shut that man up, his voice gives me a cold." For three years Liza had studied Pakhomov thoroughly. This actor had never had any luck. Not having enjoyed even simple notoriety, he expatiated on the nature of fame with the biliousness of an expert. When he failed in his profession of actor, he replaced it with the redoubtable profession of failure. The only woman who loved him was struck by the same fate as Komissarzhevska: she died of smallpox. This woman, who had the temperament of a great actress, was called Ellen Arens. Her memory was preserved in Liza's theatre, for like every young organization this theatre needed its own saints. Pakhomov's former intimacy with Ellen Arens enormously heightened his prestige in the eyes of his colleagues; such is the gratitude of the dead. And it was true that he had made great efforts to help his mistress discipline her talent. But when the creature dies, its fate is inevitably shared by the creator. Without realizing it himself, Pakhomov had been living on the interest of his secret for four years. By now people were becoming forgetful; more and more often he had to draw upon his capital. He was temporarily saved from attack by his pretense of being an incorruptible judge. To spare Liza would have meant to waste his reputation for maliciousness—all that he had left. Everyone knew that he would soon mention Ellen, and it would be interesting to see how he would bring her in this time.

"And so, let us analyze in detail one fragment of your biography, my dear. . . ."

"Too late, Pakhomov! . . . It's time to go home!" Victor Adolfovich said hastily. "And today you seem to be filled with some sort of destructive genius. . . ."

"Chew your ration and don't pinch my knee," Horatio went on in a creaking voice, growing excited. "You're a modern stage manager, you've been forgiven even for letting a 'governor' come on in shorts, but I am an old actor and a friend of Ksaveryi Zakurdaev's. I have earned the right to speak in every house where an actor lives. For eighteen years we dragged ourselves with him through the provinces, from town to town, half-starved, or, inversely, suffering from over-loaded stomachs, which is one and the same thing! We were poorer than church mice, in boots reminiscent of the apostles' sandals, but with hats, those greasy fig leaves of noble poverty! And we wasted our youth on drink, not because our parents begot us in a wanton moment, but because the old Russian actor is an engine that runs on heavy fuel. Throughout the Russian provinces, where the moral code was dictated by the priest and the policeman, we dragged our cumbersome wagon full of Shakespeare, Ostrovsky and other Holy Fathers of the world repertory. On our own flesh we learned the geography of this country—the sweep of its absurd expanses, the harshness of its cold, the floods of its truly epic rivers, the importunate hospitality of its inhabitants, which alone teaches you how poisonous a stranger's bread can be. Well, you present-day generation in shorts, why don't you take a walk across this country? . . . And who among those shepherds who have now become Deputy People's Commissars, and among the village schoolmasters who now determine the fate of the world, does not remember us, the peddlers of a great art? Hah, applaud us; even if we did not deserve to have our fill of food and a secure old age, he and I at least deserve a little vibration of air!" He stopped for a while, his eyes grew damp, then self-pity again opened his lips. Now he was Ksaveryi's own brother, remembering their homeless youth.

"We weren't strong enough to reach our goal, we weren't strong enough," Zakurdaev whispered amid sobs, and kept demanding that Pakhomov relate a remarkable incident that had taken place in Saratov.

"Shut up, they won't understand Saratov!" Horatio shouted angrily. "And now before you is Zakurdaev, deaf, drunk, and getting on everyone's nerves. Hide yourself, you unkempt repulsive old man, don't disgrace the history of the Russian theatre! This woman is ashamed of you and hates me because I dragged you here like a ghost, like her conscience, like the plague. Never mind, darling, don't spare him, to the devil with him! The Russian actor has always *loved* to die on a hospital cot. He'll lie in a big, vaulted, musty room with a birch log under his head; young men with little scissors in their hands will cut out his heart with its traces of alcoholic degeneration. They won't know that this scarecrow made of rags and a handful of grey hair was once an actor, an experienced master of his art, with an honest, naïve, although primitive talent. He was ridiculous, he broke balustrades when he played *Othello*, the actors had scratches, cuts and black eyes, for the thirty years that he made exits and entrances. He had a respite only at night when, full of liquor, he slept until the next performance.

His was not the modern audience, which goes to museums, public libraries, night schools. . . . Our audience was unshaven, illiterate and savage; they knew only one book, the Psalter, the book of the dead. One had to explode every night to move those half-human stones. Yes, darling, this insignificant old man gave shudders and thrills of enthusiasm to scarecrows in civil servants' uniforms and wadded peasant coats, to artisans who never saw the sky and who beat up their wives and children! We ploughed up this country just as much as the village schoolteachers and the anonymous propagandists of the truth of the future. This old man is a whole academy! Turn, show us your profile, Zakurdaev; let them remember you forever . . . you're particularly handsome in profile. True, this academy likes a drink, it has always liked a drink. . . ."

"True, true, . . ." cooed Ksaveryi, stirring in his chair as though Pakhomov were complimenting him. "I've seen devils! I've felt them . . . they're bald, with ve-e-ry thin shoulder blades, their hides are bluish like lousy ink. . . ."

". . . And so, for two years you lived with him, every day, every hour . . . and what did you learn from him? Don't be frightened, I'm not speaking of your gratitude. Add another five rubles to the twenty which you had the nerve to give him: it's more than enough! But just show me what mark was left on your soul by Zakurdaev's ridiculous belated love? Look in the mirror: your face is youthful, babyish, intact; and in it genuine childish candor is combined with hard-boiled, mature calculation. . . . It's a great thing in art, to overcome one's youth. . . ."

"But it's just as important to preserve it!" Victor Adolfovich gave an edifying antiphonal response.

Pakhomov's speech now had its full effect. The repulsive spectacle of Zakurdaev drowning in his own self-pity was emphasized by Falstaff's sloppily sentimental groans, the frightened faces of Montague and Capulet, who had waked up, and finally by Protoklitov's concentrated silence. He even seemed to smile, as he drew complicated eights on the tablecloth, and doubtless experienced the feelings of a man whose beloved wife is being undressed on the public square to be flogged by the executioner. Whatever new information he was learning, nothing could have shaken his conviction that Liza's punishment was considerably greater than her guilt toward this old man. Pakhomov intended to continue the torture, and only the mention of Ellen Arens could now divert the avenger's attention and spite.

"Ellen, too, looked youngish, but I remember you had different opinions about her," Liza said in a low voice, while her eyes seemed to shout. "You yourself, like a raven, are feeding on your dead Ellen, and now you're crawling about looking for new carrion!"

". . . It's you who mentioned her name!" Horatio exclaimed, and a passionate hoarseness came into his voice. "Let us recall how *she* did the most insignificant of your parts. No one will ever forget how she played at her trial performance: things were dropping all around her and everyone was sure that the ceiling would collapse on her. Oh, Ellen was first and foremost a woman with a great heart, who knew how to love those who deserved love, and in addition she was intelligent. To the very end she remained young . . . you hear me, not youthful. The French, then visiting Moscow, called her a second Duse, and she would have been, had it not been for her misfortune. (Fate dons every kind of garb to lend variety to its murders!) And I remember Duse . . . in that play by her imbecile husband, which she acted with Ciaboni under Reinhardt. The depth of her voice, the tragic charm of her face. . . ."

"Well, I shouldn't say that Arens was very attractive, . . ." said Falstaff, rolling his oxlike eyes.

Pakhomov was cut short; only four years after her death he, too, remembered her pimply though noble forehead, her ugly ears and her face, rather infantile for a tall powerful woman of her age. But it was too late for him to retreat: "I can see her now with her red locks, twisted in heavy rings and already streaked with thin silver, the price she paid for her short-lived fame. She was a lighthouse, and her hair glowed like the flame of her genius. And the last time I held that beautiful hair, to cut at least one curl. . . ."

At this point Protoklitov raised his head. "Were you her hairdresser?" he asked, and he yawned, covering his mouth with an air of polite and patient boredom.

Ilya Ignatyich's deliberate rudeness might have been interpreted as a stab in the back and, considering that Montague's indiscretion was proverbial, as an attempt on Pakhomov's life. Horatio stumbled over his next word and looked wretchedly about him, seeking help from his friends.

"He was her husband," Victor Adolfovich explained reproachfully.

"Unlikely! Liza told me something about Arens. She seems to have been a meritorious person. But the apology of alcoholism we have just heard. . . ."

"I see you don't like our opinions," Pakhomov, now recovered, interrupted him and, prudently gathering up the flaps of his cloak, went on: "What can I do about it! You yourself sometimes indulge in divination from the insides of your patients, like the augurs. In controversial matters we, too, are forced to practise anatomy. It's true, I have left many things unsaid. . . ."

Ilya Ignatyich rose. "Your analysis of my wife won't be any worse if you stop right now. Moreover, the cognac is finished, it's getting late, and your hosts want to go to bed."

All of a sudden it became uncomfortable in this cozy place. Everyone except Liza got up noisily, as though setting out for an open field to have a duel. And so they scattered, these painted scarecrows, like devils at cock crow. How quickly their fictitious gilding peeled off! Falstaff, whose moral principles differed from those of Shakespeare's Falstaff, rummaged under the table for his oakum hair-do pasted with carpenter's glue, to avoid being fined for losing a stage property. Out in the hall Montague and Capulet were quarrelling over galoshes. Very pale, but hospitable in his own way, Ilya Ignatyich stood near the door with his hands against the lintel, bowing dryly to each departing guest. Zakurdaev obviously amused him; the old man was swaying in the middle of the hall with a wooden expression, flapping his eyelids and wondering who exactly was driving him out of this magic paradise. A scandalmonger and born reveller, his soul was starving for good food (eaten slowly, not in a hurry because one had to go somewhere), for a spotless white tablecloth, with a woman dear to his heart presiding, and for a peaceful, friendly talk.

"Well, we've behaved like pigs, Ksaveryi, and that's that! Noble people live in this place . . . spectators! They don't like gags and other people's noise," Horatio said, shaking the old man by his shoulder. "It's time for you to go sleepy-bye until the beautiful morning comes."

He dragged the resisting Zakurdaev after him, imperiously and cruelly, like an object no longer of use. Zakurdaev did not want to go before shouting some insult, but he could not think of any. "She has grown fat, quite fat!" he babbled without his former gusto and clung to pieces of furniture, to his friends, to everything in his path. Ilya Ignatyich went out to see how Pakhomov would get on his overcoat over his absurd cloak. He found that it was necessary first to pin up the cloak—and that underneath it the actor wore ordinary, half-woollen breeches of a flamboyant material. Flushing with horror and shame, hoping to make up for what had happened, Liza expressed regret over the early departure of her guests. With sinister politeness someone answered that the trolley cars that day stopped running one hour before the usual time.

Victor Adolfovich was the last to leave. "Goodbye, Liza," he said affectedly, and tickled her limp, pallid hand with his beard. "Goodbye, dear professor. You need a wife, we an actress. We won't quarrel over trifles. She herself will know which to choose!"

Horatio-Pakhomov supported him. "Take your instrument and play on it yourself. . . ." And already in the doorway, to be on the safe side, he added something about a violin that sounds equally badly with any bow.

"You haven't stolen any of my things, have you?" Protoklitov cried after him with clenched fists.

He closed the door and untying his necktie, which annoyed him, went to his room. The latest issue of the *Surgical News* lay on his desk. He glanced through it, cutting the pages with his hand and reading only the titles of the articles. Liza's silence worried him. Just as he was about to go to her, expecting to find her resigned and submissive, she broke into his room.

"What have you done?" And everything whirled around her, the air, her words, even the furniture. "How clumsy and tactless you were! You shouted at a man who wanted to help me! You, an aristocrat who have memorized your books, want me to darn your linen and go to market for your cabbage? Now they'll fire me!" She pulled him by the hand, but was unable to move him half an inch. "Run, get them, bring them back!"

"I'm not boundlessly broad-minded, my dear. And it's a good thing that everything has come out. Ha, one way or another you'll have to leave the theatre for a time, and then we'll see. . . ."

He held her hand and listened to her pulse; her hand was still throbbing, but he decided that this unusual patient was by now sufficiently prepared for the operation. Then he began to speak as fast, soberly and succinctly as he could. The operation had to be performed without anesthetic, and however painful it might be, he was in a hurry to get it over. The initial incision had been made, and he did not choose his words; surgical intervention always has an element of harsh and intelligent violence. He told Liza that she could not hold an audience, that to work as a waitress and serve hot tea in clean glasses was more honest than this bustling around in emptiness, that one's usefulness to society is determined by the result of one's activity and not the respectability of one's intentions. He gave Liza the choice between studying, so that in time she might assist him under conditions which would secure her independence, or looking for work now that was suitable to her talents. The imminent birth of her child made necessary her departure from the theatre. Of course it would be a son—that was a wonderful window into the future! His plans in connection with this event were elaborate and enthusiastic. And with the utmost vividness Ilya Ignatyich painted before Liza, crushed and silent, the picture of a tiny little man marching in step with her along the street. "A swarthy little fellow, with chubby pink cheeks!" Not fearing to be ridiculed for his sentimentality, he evoked the fat little face with a chocolate mustache, the comic judiciousness of the little one's comments on the outside world, the odd habits from which an adult with fright and amusement learns to know himself. (Liza listened to him with a shudder; oh, oh, what are they not capable of, those helpless little childish hands!) And Ilya Ignatyich suggested how lofty under socialism would be the sound of that most ancient word on the planet: mother—as for father, it would be only a component part of the single concept of motherhood. The operation was now approaching its end. Liza sat as though unconscious, her head sunk low, and once again Protoklitov was deceived by her apparent submissiveness. He approached her from behind and raised her head by the chin.

"And when it is all over . . ." The long pause contained unsaid words about her temporary disfigurement, about all sorts of hardships and privations, labor pains, etc. ". . . When it is over, all three of us will go to any seaside resort you wish. This time I'll get a furlough. And we, two handsome and loving men, will warm up that cold little nose all quivering with tears. . . ."

Speaking figuratively, this was the last thread of catgut. But suddenly Liza pushed him back by his chest and cried out that there would be no child, that he had no child, that this demanding little man would never enter their lives. . . .

". . . I killed him . . . that time, you remember, when you came back from your trip and I said I was poisoned by carbonic acid in the theatre!"

Fearing most of all that he would think this confession was a lie born of her passionate desire to cause him pain (and that later she would torment him for a long time by seeming to expect a child!), she hastened to name the street, day, hour, price and a thousand other details, to convince him that what had happened was irretrievable. The whole story, told in a voice deliberately raised to shouting pitch, served to cover her horrible confusion before her husband who, according to her morality, was entitled to consider himself robbed. Hiding her face in her hands, swaying, perhaps she was trying to arouse his pity. Through her spread fingers she saw his deaf, solemn face, a dark spot on his neck left by his collar button, which she noticed only now, and his deeply cut nostrils in which black whiskers stirred. . . . And it seemed as if his whole interior was lined with a coarse, curly fur, that he had no warm, human insides, that he was made entirely of logic and machinery. She was all the more terrified because her voice was giving out and because he had not yet uttered a word. Abruptly he said: "I shall wipe you off myself . . . ha, as one wipes off chalk with a sponge!" And turning on his heel, he left the room.

With his hands behind his neck he entered the dining room. Day was breaking in at the windows; someone had turned off the light, and the cigarette stubs scattered on the floor appeared all the whiter. Ilya Ignatyich heard Liza call him in a low, insinuating voice, but he remained standing still. He was amazed when he realized that once the very approach of this woman had thrown him into an embarrassed, almost adolescent confusion. In spite of himself he evoked details of the drunken farce that night and imagined Ksaveryi a hundred times more repulsive than he was in reality. What Ilya felt at this moment was not jealousy but disgust. Then he heard a sound, multiplied and dispersed, as though a handful of coins had been hurled on the floor.

One could hear the last one rolling further away than the others, circling in spirals. He thought that Liza was trying to bring him back by any method at all, only to pass to the attack later. He mechanically recalled all the objects on his table, wondering which of them could make such a brittle and crackling sound. Before his eyes passed a cut blue drinking glass, in which he kept his pens and colored pencils, then a new cystoscope with an enlarged field of vision and magnificent Zeiss lenses, a marvel of optical technique just arrived from abroad, and finally an enamelled Chinese dish in which he stored old razor blades, studs and all sort of trifles from his desk. And he was tormented by his inability to recall the most important thing that he had seen on his table only a quarter of an hour before.

"What has fallen down in there?" he shouted through the apartment.

In three enormous strides he reached the door of his study and looked in. Liza was squatting on the floor, her back to him. One higher than the other, her shoulder blades twisted convulsively. From the chips of blue enamel strewn on the floor Ilya Ignatyich realized that his bulb-shaped Caron clock was gone. (He was in the habit of keeping every new item of his collection on his table for a long time until he got accustomed to it.) Impelled by deep and malicious curiosity, he approached Liza from the side. With scratched and trembling fingers she was trying to push back into the broken case all the little wheels and pinions. Their number seemed doubled. The little parts dropped from her hands over and over and after rolling a while lay again in front of her.

"They don't go in, . . ." she whispered pitifully, and raised her head in despair.

With one word he could have taken possession of her forever, but he did not understand what was taking place within her. His jaws opened like the opening of a cave. He yawned exaggeratedly loudly and went out of his study.

"Lizard, you lizard, . . ." she threw after him in a whisper.

Two hours later, barefoot, she came near his door and looked in. Ilya Ignatyich, in only his shirt, sat near the lighted window, sipping his cognac. This time she could not make up her mind to disturb his meditation, but after an hour she was again awakened by an alarming sensation of loneliness. Her husband was not in the room. She was frightened; in passing by her mirror, she stopped for a moment; the actress in her wanted to remember what her face looked like on such occasions. (Her griefs were quick and stormy and never left any traces.) Ilya Ignatyich was sitting in the same place as before, but for some reason the amount of cognac in the bottle was considerably greater now. (She distinctly remembered that the liquid had before reached only to the lower edge of the label. In her haste she did not realize that this was a second bottle.) Liza approached her husband. Her strategy was extremely simple: her light silk wrapper emphasized every line of the naked body underneath it.

"But it's silly to drink all by yourself," Liza said in confusion.

He silently rose and picked up the telephone receiver. The number he asked for was unknown to Liza; he rang up the hospital, not his own office, but the room of the physician on duty. He questioned him in detail about Eva's condition. The unfamiliar feminine name struck Liza; for a moment she was ready to interpret this conversation as a transparent and trivial ruse resorted to by every husband in similar situations. No, she was not interested in his affairs with his lady patients!

"I am extremely concerned about that sweet child. She smiled at me even on the operating table! . . . Yes, you can let the mother in to see her now," Ilya Ignatyich went on. "Look in on her and call me, will you? I won't be asleep. . . ."

Then Liza remembered that this Eva was only five years old. She felt cold and ashamed, and her own presence here seemed to her an example of the vilest debauchery. With drooping shoulders she returned to her room.

# CHAPTER 25

# I Have a Talk with the Historian A. M. Volchikhin

I MET LITTLE LUKA OMELICHEV ONLY ONCE, during one of my last visits to Kurilov and almost on the eve of the day when sad and irrevocable events took place. Sitting on the floor, he was playing with a model of a locomotive that had been presented to Alexei Nikitich by the railroadmen. I have never seen a child show more passionate enthusiasm for an object. This toy was truly marvellous, like a real locomotive in every detail. Sticking one's finger into the engineer's cab, one could even feel the thin pipes of the injectors. A slight push of the lever made the pistons move and the wheels turn. Then the boy would clap his hands, throw back his head and moo, imitating the sound of a horn. This last branch of the Omelichev tree was not a cheering sight.

When I went to Porozhensk to dig up material about Liza's childhood I had the good luck to meet a certain regional patriot, Andrey Matveich Volchikhin. An excessively polite little old man with a bumpy forehead, as if in two storeys, and agile clutching hands, he would get into a state of poetic frenzy when the subject of his native district was brought up—within a radius of not more than fifty miles. It was he who gave me some information concerning the genealogy of the Omelichev family. I intended to spend an hour with him, but he sat me down in the best chair in the room behind a barricade of tea things and all kinds of pickles and regaled me until morning with his stories of Porozhensk antiquities. He led me through the thick woods of the Burgas land and the ancient Mordia of Constantine Porphyrogenitus, past the shack of the legendary Mordvin, Tesha, through the patrimonies of Pureisha and Purgas, the first Mordvin rulers, through the ungovernable hordes of Bulgars and Polovtsi. I bent over Prince John the Big-Bellied, who was slain by the Kazan warrior, Arapsha, at the Piana River; I watched the pious Dmitri Konstantinovich, who fled from Nizhni without his trousers; I marvelled at the infamy of Simeon Kirdiapa, who induced the Tartars to attack what are now the eastern provinces of contemporary Russia. Out of the dark night, brandishing their crooked swords, marched straight upon me the enormous Ulu-Akhmet with his son Mamluk, the Murza of Nogia, Ahmed-Amin, who captured Governor Khabar Simskoy, buried under the Porozhensk cathedral, the firebrand and burglar Safa-Ghirey at the head of his gangs; finally a certain Ibrahimka came to sit at our table, but I could not make out exactly what this last fellow's historical exploits were.

Tired after one hour from the glimmer of the names of our quiet rivers and boundaries, our tumultuous monasteries and war leaders who drenched with blood the barren local sands, I was beset by doubts as to whether this deafening little old man was not fibbing in order to give bright colors to his desert. His hovel was over-heated; moreover, my stomach was upset by his corned beef, which had awaited a guest too long at the bottom of a deep vat. And he kept poking me in the side to make sure that I remembered this smoking rehash of headless bodies, devastated temples and charred riches. Overwhelmed by all this hospitality, hiccoughing and nauseated, I picked up my hat only to be stopped in my tracks by the magic of his imaginative tales. And once again he hurled me against countless mounds of mushrooms and brittle tartlets of satanic charm washed with oceans of tea.

"Describe us, my boy. Describe our antiquity. Show to all the scholars our Porozhensk humanity, how it struggled, how it grew and how it failed in life. And even if they condemn us it will be all to the good!" And I should be dishonest with regard to this old man if in this story I passed over his tales in silence.

He reminded me of the old-time bazaar merchants who tried to thrust a carriage and a yoke upon every customer who came to buy a harness strap. For the sake of a few pages about the Omelichevs I was forced to listen to entire treatises on the various plagues that had visited Porozhensk—"we used to burn dung in the ravines, but can you put God off with smoke?"—on eleven thousand executions that took place here during the crushing of the Tushinsk rebellion—"most of all they liked to impale people. There was some stench here under the gentlest of the Tsars!"—on many prominent Porozhensk citizens. I tried to draw him on to the subject of the Omelichevs and mentioned the young Luka. Andrey Matveich recoiled from me as though stung. It cost me a certain effort to convince him that this name had unwittingly slipped from my tongue. But later, too, even when the fundamental nature of this garrulous man overcame his distrust, he kept casting suspicious glances at my notebook.

His tale about the Omelichev dynasty contained elements of legend, criminal records and even socio-economic investigations. He used them as an example of the law of decay of such families of merchant-industrialists. Rapidly changing conditions of existence, not connected with the immediate struggle for bread, were reflected in the story of their generations. The initiators and heroes of primitive accumulation were replaced by squanderers of the wealth that had been amassed; they fed on the cream of knowledge and valuables that they themselves had not acquired; the family was consumed within the space of a century, it flared up and died. Concerning the little boy Luka, Andrey Matveich eloquently depicted the beautiful cradle surrounded by all sorts of uncles and kinfolk. Gathered there were fugitive peasants from Count Saltykov's estate, merchants, epileptics, rowdies, philanthropists and plain idiots who had exchanged confinement in one room for the life of beggars under a fence. Every one of them brought this last scion a little part of himself as a gift, and not one of the offerings could be thrown out of the innocent little cradle. Even the admixture of new blood (I could not distinguish whether he had Efrosinia Kurilova in mind or that poor camp gypsy, the mother of the present Omelichev) could not protect the family from extinction.

"Dross is produced at each smelting, the amount of the original metal always grows smaller," said Volchikhin, shoving toward me some sour apples the size of walnuts. "Eat our bitter apples, my boy. They clear your throat and soften your skin!"

And so he began in the distant past, in the ancient golden age when Porozhensk was only accumulating fame and capital. The tiny, enterprising town grasped at everything profitable: it gilded the crosses in all the neighboring dioceses, made coaches for dandies in the capital, fed on laces of a special weave—"the mouse path"—and the glossy linens of Porozhensk were as famous in Russia as the exquisitely flavorful Porozhensk nuts. But it was not for nothing that the town's coat-of-arms represented a resisting bull dragged by two citizens of impressive appearance. To this animal the town owed its prosperity. By many routes horned cattle were driven here from all sides, and after a visit to the Porozhensk slaughter-houses, fat-rendering plants and tanneries, were moved to the Makaryev fair in the form of soap and sheepskins, saddle wares and candles. This was the time when kerosene lamps and lighting gas were unknown. Yellow suet candles filled with their smoke the palace of the Petersburg grandee and the hut of the village sexton.

The main profits, however, came from the famous Porozhensk Russia leather. It sold like hot cakes; the red kind, the *Bulgara,* went to Asia, the white to German lands, and the black half-finished product, the *Mostovye,* to the free Don. Labor was cheap at that time, and the tanneries were extremely primitive. The oak was pounded with pestles in stone mortars, and the skins were sprayed with pitch directly from people's mouths. The little factories were crammed together in the eastern suburb, justly named Pogiblovka (death trap), and the stench in that place was so thick that it had even a specific color. According to Volchikhin it was stratified, so to speak, of a dull indigo color with yellowish streaks like a sort of infernal marble. Fetid pools formed, and in them all kinds of pestilential bacilli probably nested, ready to pounce some day and sweep the planet with a black tornado. Most of these tanneries belonged to enterprising serfs who paid rent to their masters. The law forbade serfs to own serfs, but a way was found to get them in bond at two hundred rubles per soul, and how these slaves of slaves lived can only be imagined.

At that time a man in a rough felt hat and a frayed Circassian coat arrived in Porozhensk. He began to walk about, look around, take his range and be seen quite often: on the high bank of the Mialka he stood with his head thrown back, gazing at the wooded smoky distance, drawing the boundaries of his future conquests or listening to the peculiar silence of Porozhensk: all day the wretched bleating of sheep and mooing of oxen to be slaughtered hung over the town. Sometimes the stranger would visit a shop at the bazaar and ever so often he blinked with his left eyelid. He was nicknamed the Circassian; people feared to chase him and they skirted around him when they met him; he inspired terror because he did not speak, did not brawl, did not drink and did not ask for anything. Everyone, the clergy and the members of the lay professions, marvelled at what different kinds of people it takes to make a world! And at this point the legend comes in. During the high spring waters, at an unseasonable hour of the day, he saw something on the river—three men, saints or fugitives, were sailing in a leaky boat. They were drifting with the ice, whirling crazily. The story goes that he climbed down to them, rescued them from death and conversed with them, while they wept, blue from cold and squatting on the thawing snow. At daybreak he swapped with them half a gallon of vodka, an axe and four handfuls of nails for a pile of gold. In brief, everyone embellished the secret of Omelichev's wealth according to his own imagination. Soon afterwards the newcomer bought a tannery from a childless merchant who wanted to make a pilgrimage to the Holy Land. When the contract was being drawn up he showed a paper, and the credulous Porozhensk citizens learned from it that the Circassian's name was Luka Omelichev, that he was not, thank God, a Circassian, but a village bailiff's son, freed and kindly treated by his master Saltykov as a reward for certain confidential services.

The details were gradually forgotten, and the longer Luka lived in Porozhensk the less was known about him. Behind his high fence, without the slightest crack, chained dogs growled and barked. By night one heard the watchmen's rattles. And even on the brightest days his windows were dark. Someone bored a hole in the fence and through it people could see Luka personally trampling down and paving his yard, laying out ditches for draining the leather impurities and planting trees. "He liked maples best of all!" Volchikhin said. Only at mass did Luka show himself in public, and even then he was escorted by two sturdy tanners, long-armed and taciturn as his shadow. One could also see that the left one had been branded with the executioner's iron on his forehead under a lock of hair. All black, as though tarred, Luka stood motionless in church too; he did not pray, but, leering at the icon, kept on blinking his eye as though threatening Our Pure Lady and her child. . . . No one could boast of having drunk even a penny's worth of Omelichev's hospitality. Only the governor of the town called on him in his fortress, not oftener than twice a year, and half an hour later, all red and contented, returned home.

Omelichev's factory was pushing to the first place in Porozhensk, but his riches increased out of all proportion to his achievements as a tanner. It was conjectured that he sowed money in the ground and that the very next morning, frightened by his blinking, the earth gave birth to a harvest of gold. Four years later, coming from the same unknown, his wife and two grown-up sons joined him; their wide peasant sledges entered through the gates which closed with a coffin-like bang. In the fifth year Luka was found with his throat cut near a vat full of soaking skins. "His blood had all flowed out and made a puddle like rain." His head, almost severed from his body, still kept blinking at all those present. Podsosov, a furrier and neighbor of the Omelichevs, stated at the investigation that on the eve of the crime he had met three tattered men near the chapel in Basurmanka. Since he needed hands he offered them jobs as dressers of rabbit skins, but they merely laughed at him, piercingly, as only saints or fugitives can. The widow did not lament at the funeral, the streets were empty, the dogs howled, the priests trembled. Omelichev Junior—Ivan—took over the inheritance the same year, it seems, in which his older brother, Afanasyi, took the habit in the Vysokogorsk Hermitage, the one on the Mialka.

In those days fortunes were born elementally or pined away as buds without ever flowering. There were too many paths to sudden wealth. This was the result of deep-going changes in the economic system (but the railroads and commercial navigation were still ahead), or a great war and contracts connected with it could bring a fortune to a dishonest and clever dealer; finally, every industrial innovation that cheapened the productive processes could raise its inventor to a position of wealth. At the root of all these methods was the predatory human passion for cornering the treasures of the earth, and the first Omelichevs were filled to excess with austere competitive asceticism. In the middle of the last century the Porozhensk capital investments made complete turnovers as many as five times a year. Ivan's resourcefulness helped him to strengthen his firm and scatter his weaker competitors in the shortest possible time. He dealt in everything, not a single profitable item, neither bristles nor wax nor grey Kalmuk sheepskins, escaped his grasping hands. Like his father, Ivan walked through the town with a lowered head. Soon his fellow citizens understood what he was studying on the ground.

The soil of the lower part of Porozhensk is to this very day mixed with rotting leather refuse. Wherever you dig you find sand, oak wood and cattle horn. Soon after the Crimean campaign, without giving up his father's business, Ivan Omelichev organized the first felt factory in Porozhensk; imitators blindly followed him, trusting the old man's instinct. Every year he personally made a tour of Kazan, Sudislav, Ostashkov and other leather towns. He bought up cow hides and sheep wool from which a good grade of white felt was made. It was transported to his yard on thousands of horse-carts, and the long black man with a sorrowful look, who from morning to night counted the carts in the gates, was the master, Omelichev himself. Later his firm also made glue from sheep's feet as well as from tannery scrapings. This type of glue containing much fat was priced considerably lower than others; there was an enormous demand for it. Kerosene was being introduced into Russia, but there were no iron cisterns yet in which to transport it, or keep it at ports. It was kept in oak barrels covered with glue inside. The demand for this glue many times exceeded the supply. The product was brewed from all kinds of carrion, and people who went by the Omelichev premises held their noses. . . . For the sake of what, they wondered, did this restless old man torture himself and his silent victims? Even at the age of sixty he managed to preserve the vehemence of a twenty-year-old, and his deep-sunken eyes had a sharp gleam, like the eyes of martyrs, lovers and madmen. He owned his own slaughter-house, three factories of considerable size for Porozhensk at that time, five brick houses, several wholesale stores and had about ninety thousand rubles in cash. His power and influence increased every year; he envisaged the foundation of a public bank in Porozhensk; there were plans for making him a municipal alderman—"that might quiet him down." And suddenly a new undertaking of his sent a shiver down the spines of his fellow citizens.

The mainstay of the Porozhensk fur trade was the grey hare. But from the beginning of the Sixties the demand for hare began to decrease. This ordinary fur, too expensive for the lower classes and too cheap for the upper classes, was going out of fashion and use. A suitable substitute for the domestic market had to be found. For the space of five months, in deep secrecy, a new factory was equipped. Ivan Omelichev discovered the cat in Russia. Six months later he extended his long hands for hundreds of miles and gathered up the first catch of three provinces. For the first time in Porozhensk there resounded the plaintive, maddening whimper of cats; according to rumor, it even drowned the sound of the church bells in the evening. And the cat-killer was cursed in Porozhensk, but the machine kept working, and the business, branded as of the devil, flourished. In the second year more than one hundred and fifty thousand head of cats passed through the firm. Killed cat meat in brine was sent here even from Irbit. People murmured, criticized, envied; they looked forward to the time when, having spent his fury, this Omelichev too would shave his head to atone for his father's crimes. For by that time Afanasyi's extravagant behavior in Vysokogorsk was already known. After two years he implored his superior to confine him to a cell, and the superior yielded, despite the monk's youth and the Synod's prohibitions. But three days after the wall had been bricked up, the young hermit broke through the ceiling and like a wild beast ran out into the world. How he quenched his thirst for life is unknown. Six months later he crawled back, sick and broken, in tattered clothes, fouler and worse than the carrion from which Ivan brewed his glue. And the friars turned away from him as from a naked one. Not much was left to God of the former Hercules. The two brothers met behind closed doors; one could hear sobbing and Ivan's shouts, after which Afanasyi remained in the monastery for good.

Having grown older, Ivan sometimes went to the monastery to visit his brother. In the droshky, in front, between his knees, sat his oldest son, Guryi. The most affectionate and gentle of Ivan's five sons, he was the only consolation of the old man's cheerless twilight. The meeting took place after mass. The brothers sat opposite each other and remained silent, because within the walls they had no disagreements. They began to talk only a few minutes before the time came to separate.

"Still strangling cats?" Friar Ananyi, as Afanasyi was called, tooted through his nose and guffawed, rustling his elegant cassock. Since he had entered the angelic ranks, he had become perceptibly less human in appearance; he was fatter, balder, and emanated a kind of rotten benevolence. Squeezing his nephew between his knees, he stroked his hair, and made faces to amuse him, and the little boy laughed in a shrill, birdlike, choking voice.

"Our daddy," Afanasyi began again, "was captured by the mountaineers, he petted Turkish women in Baghdad . . . he skinned people under Buzuluk, and you're skinning cats. We're going down, brother!"

"That's the way it is!" Ivan sighed mournfully, wrapping the skirts of his tunic around him with two broad red fingers. "I brought you some sturgeon and pressed caviar from Nizhni. Have it unpacked. Now I'm keeping my eyes on the Volga. All the capital in Russia is being invested there. . . ."

"Have you enough for everything? . . . Aren't you overreaching yourself?"

"I can't complain, there are seven of us." And suddenly, with anguish: "Eh, brother, I won't have time for anything, I won't have time."

And since he had no one else with whom to share his news and plans, he reported to this pile of decayed flesh how he had opened, near his flaying-house, a dye-mill on the German model, how Blankenhagel was pestering him to get into the railroad construction business and how he had been snubbed in the homes of the Petersburg nobles. "You're lying, your highness. You want my money; and where my cash-box is, am I myself!" Whatever Afanasyi, that deep well of passions, might have been, he was able to understand Ivan's disease of greed better than anyone else. And an irrepressible emotion of fierce envy compelled the monk to wrap himself in folly and exasperate his brother more and more.

"You stink through and through, Vaniusha. Angels shy away from you, you cat strangler! They've got clean noses. They'd be afraid to defile themselves by touching a flower even!"

Ivan nodded to him squeamishly: "My soul won't smell. . . . It's in a bag. Made of skin. Nothing will happen to it!"

"And why did you go to Nizhni?"

"I bought a machine. It's called 'Bova,' forty-eight horsepower. I'll see how it works. . . ."

The old man's strides into the great world were superhuman. Actually he minimized his achievements. He had already leased two tugboats and built three of the barges that made their first appearance at this time. The Porozhensk Russia leather had just begun to decline, and the old man tried, before it was too late, to take root on other free rivers and fertile lands. A momentous change in his activity was partly determined by his family conditions. His numerous poverty-stricken relatives hated him; his sons—except Guryi—were frankly waiting for their father's death; his daughters already during his lifetime began to play around with his sturdy red-faced workers. In the town, despite his generous contributions to various charitable institutions, he was never called anything else than "the cat-killer." And he had not the time to lay his redoubtable hand on the underground whisperers. He rushed to the Volga to escape his solitude and his past, rather than in search of new profits. He often had to deal with Volga shipmasters, who bought cargoes or contracted to transport his loads of skins, and had always been attracted by the power and solidity of these primitive Volga men. Once he happened to take a trip from Elabuga to Samara. The banks of the Kama were deserted at that time; in thatched hovels slumbered foresters, and the trees were mirrored in the dark backwaters, one on top of the other, as if after a battle. Into this virgin forest a frightened monster with wheels was moving, accompanied by streams of smoke, the curses of the river pilots and the thunder of the one-piston beam engine. (This was a delightful steamboat with an iron roof over the deck to protect the passengers from the abundant sparks and charcoal dust. Later the formidable force of the steam was concealed in well-designed and economical boilers, but at that time the whole mechanism was still in the open. Hissing vapor spattered everywhere, the hull shuddered, glass tinkled, and the hair of the superstitious stood up on end.) The old man was captivated by this new force; and watching the foam drifting far behind the stern like the feathers of a shot bird, he shivered as with cold and thought sadly of the things he would never see. And he regretted that he had not enough hands, nor enough time, to seize all these still undiscovered treasures. He did not succeed in moving his enterprises to the Volga. Death felled him at Rybinsk, in the port, and he collapsed on his own short shadow with his hands spread out, just as he used to sleep, face downwards, on the cobblestones heated by the midday sun.

Guryi, the third Omelichev, was famous for the original methods he found for conquering his boredom. The tow-headed, gentle boy developed into a lazy and sickly man. From his father he had inherited only his tormenting and now completely barren restlessness. From his very first independent steps it was clear that he was a playful and whimsical master. He bought and restored the ruins of the palace that had belonged to the governor of the town under Catherine II, a mass of bare walls as thick as those of a fortress, among which grew tall, ungraceful trees, the favorite haunt of the lively little urchins of Porozhensk. His order not to cut down any trees was obeyed so literally that in his study, near his desk, an ash tree grew to its full height, and until it died everyone went to see whether it was true that Omelichev had a tree in his study. At holidays he liked to gather his kin together, get them drunk, and then invite the notables of Porozhensk to admire his assortment of Omelichevs. Legends circulated about his kind-heartedness, and he himself often boasted that "women and dogs" loved him.

"Let any of them loose, they won't touch me!" Three years after Ivan's death Guryi was sent to an asylum following his attempt to open a restaurant in newly conquered Tashkent for the warriors of General Skobelev. Having discovered a clause in Ivan's will which they could use, the whole tribe hurled themselves like a pack of wolves on the family fortune and tore it to shreds. The firm disintegrated, the brothers separated, each taking his share, and the youngest, Stepan, received the Kama holdings.

With him came the period of final decay. The demand for sturdy but coarsely finished Russia leather dropped. Competitors appeared in other Russian cities. Simultaneously the government ordered that tanneries near dwelling houses be closed in order to prevent epidemics. Those who desired it were given a homestead three versts beyond the town, on the banks of the Mialka, downstream. Misfortunes did not come singly. With the development of steamships and the appearance of railroads, the famous Porozhensk post-road lost all importance. Tobacco, plums, millet and groceries, which used to go to the Nizhni Fair in wagons, with a stopover at Porozhensk, now proceeded by a different route. The heart of the province now beat faintly. In less than twenty years this ancient highway from Bokhara, Persia and the lower Volga was completely forgotten. The bustling inns were deserted. The apiaries, whence flowed famous meads for the delectation of the Uriupin coachmen, fell into decay. Hides, the treasure of the province, finally betrayed Porozhensk. It was no longer profitable for them to be dressed there and turned into Russia leather. The necessity of transporting raw materials to the Porozhensk factories by wagon increased the cost of the merchandise by ten per cent, not to mention that the period of processing was prolonged two weeks. . . . Decay also set in elsewhere. The hazel-groves, the source of valuable oil, were cut down; manufacture, with her many-colored shoulders, pushed the famous local hand-woven materials out of the markets. Salesmen's clubs and dental offices appeared in the town. The merchant classes fled from Porozhensk and ruin. By that time Stepan Omelichev had taken root on the Kama. But his path was a new and difficult one. The first in Porozhensk became the last on the Kama. The Volga was then undergoing hectic changes. After a stubborn struggle, the wooden tugboats went down, the thundering steamships with capstans were defeated, and the haulers' long drawn-out cries ceased. The prosperity of the firms depended upon volume of the loads they hauled. The principal cargo was bread, and the irregularity of the Volga harvests caused sudden drops in freight. The great river became almost twice as shallow as in former times. The freight rate dropped to a kopek and a half, and the depth of the river on the sandbanks to four fourths. Dredges were still unknown. . . . "And there are lots of things that we, too, don't know, my boy. Let our grandchildren stir our bones with their feet and recall our labors!" By the end of his life Stepan became almost the exclusive owner of the "Kama Commercial Express Steamship Company."

From that point on, Volchikhin's tale began to be much hazier and duller. Andrey Matveich no longer possessed colors to depict Stepan. One could gather only that he drank and during such periods vanished from his home. After one such flight he brought a gypsy back with him from a camp and married her. This sharp-nosed woman, quick as a gust of wind, bore him his son Pavel and then withered away. "Yes, my boy, that's the way it was, from gypsiness she went straight over to the Old Believers' faith. Worst of all, she caught cold!" And at this point Andrey Matveich yawned.

Volchikhin was every inch a son of his own province and never left its principal town. He was fascinated by the stories of the first two Omelichevs, for this was the heroic epic of Porozhensk; the humdrum bustle of a second-rate steamship company did not interest this chronicler at all. He did not know the river, he confused pilots with boatswains and could judge of Stepan Ivanovich's affairs only by their reflected light on his Porozhensk residence. When he came to speak of the present-day Omelichev, Pavel, the old man displayed inexplicable reticence. Judging by the fact that he referred to Efrosinia Kurilova only as Frosia (and from other observations), I am inclined to surmise that the steamship magnate had taken the historian's fiancée away from him. (Neighbors confirmed my impression that Volchikhin had always been the enemy of Omelichev.) Having forgiven him this blow, and perhaps not wishing to show his grief to a stranger, the old man refused to let an outsider smear his enemy's name all over the Soviet land.

There was a draft from the window. From time to time the chimney howled, and I fancied that apparitions awakened by Volchikhin, the murderers and the murdered, the robbers and their victims, were whirling around the room, chained in a ferocious ring.

"That's the way it goes, my boy. Fame doesn't stay put, and wealth vanishes!"

# CHAPTER 26

# Kurilov Becomes Indebted to Omelichev

THE IZHEVSK-VOTKINSK WHITE rebellion and the simultaneous fall of
Soviet Kazan at the beginning of August, 1918, determined the situation
on the middle and lower Kama. The Red front was like a wedge in
the territory occupied by the White. The Second Soviet Army (Azin's
28th Iron Division) was poised against the lines of communication of
General Chechek's Volga detachment. The Red troops did not have
means adequate to outflank the enemy; moreover from behind, at a
distance of only three days' march, they were threatened by the White
Izhevsk forces. On September 10, by a counterblow from a detachment
of Red sailors, Kazan was recaptured, and this operation was the decisive factor in the formation of the Fifth Soviet Army. The retreating
avalanche of the Whites and Czechs, needing a wide escape corridor,
moved directly eastward. Up to that time the Kama had had no independent strategic significance; its fate was determined by the main
campaigns of the war that was beginning. In fact, only now did the
civil conflict reach the quiet towns of the Kama.

The town in which Pavel Stepanovich Omelichev had solidly established himself had long since been a sort of center for the second-rate
Kama shipowners. It was a picturesque little place situated in a cozy,
circular valley formed by the slopes of the high river banks; two-thirds
of its buildings were made of clapboards, and it abounded in orchards.
The little steamships near the wooden moorings looked like a band of
lizards as a child might paint them. After his flight from Izhevsk and
a short stay in Sarapul, Alexei Nikitich reached this region in the first
days of September. He entered the town only two days before it was
invaded by Colonel Stepanov's unit reinforced by Czech effectives.
On the very second day, he unexpectedly met his sister Frosia in the
street. She was glad to see him and asked him what he was doing
there. Alexei Nikitich lied to her, saying that he had been sick with
typhus for a month and was now on leave. She believed him; Kurilov
looked rather shabby. She suggested that he come to stay with her for
some time. He promised to drop in, and they separated.

The Reds left the town without regret as soon as it began to be bom-
barded from river boats. The barrage was inaccurate high-trajectory

fire; and many of the townsfolk went out to see what this war looked like. Soon rioting broke out, as when any populated place changed hands. Groups of high-school boys and white-collar workers captured the military headquarters. Through the streets was led the first prisoner, still unbeaten, but for some reason in his underwear only; he was a spindle-shanked man, very much embarrassed by his appearance, and he was shivering. (Leaves were already flying, and a harsh wind was blowing from the quays.) The prisoner was killed on the same day, in the ruins of the old town, and this first shot awakened to activity the well-to-do part of the population. All of them tried to do something to assure the rebirth of the old Russia, and those who did not know how to shoot tore down Soviet posters from the walls or looted flour-dealers' shops at the commercial port. These stolen goods were sold in a disorderly fashion, and files of overloaded peasant carts moved out of the town. Two bursts from a machine-gun would have dispersed this rabble. The Whites and Czechs did not enter the town till the following morning.

They walked along the street, blue-eyed, not very cheerful, their yellow leather jackets crackling. There was something about them that made one think of a blade that rips living flesh. They walked and smiled nervously at the flowers that were thrown under their feet. The blare of a brass band mingled with the pealing church bells. On Church Square the conquerors were received by the sweaty, excited fathers of the town and the clergy in their Easter cassocks. The military commanders ascended a platform, a curt order was shouted, and the conquerors removed their caps, which had patent leather visors. In the crowd with the others, Kurilov watched the spectacle. For special reasons he had not left with the Red forces and, taking advantage of the fact that he had never before been seen in this city, did not hide. However, a fellow with a paralyzed right eyelid, dressed in his Sunday best, with boots shining like mirrors, began to cast stealthy glances at him. Just to be on the safe side, Kurilov elbowed his way out of the crowd, but the fellow immediately followed him and soon stood at his side. Apparently he was someone from the port; a thick stench of fish enveloped Kurilov like a cloud.

"It's going to rain, don't you think?" the fellow asked him, anxious to hear his voice.

True enough the wind was blowing up, the banners were twirling on their sticks like weathervanes, and the voices of the choir were carried away by the breeze. White-caps ran along the river. And although for the time being there was no threat in the man's question, Kurilov realized that he had been recognized by some imperceptible sign. He stepped unhurriedly into a side street. The fellow followed him, and this time someone accompanied him. The second one was less tall, with a ruddy mustache so bushy that he seemed to be holding a roll between his teeth. Kurilov lazily cut across the deserted bazaar and began to go downwards in the direction of the match-factory workers' barracks. Meanwhile the number of his pursuers had increased to five. This was a free day anyhow, a holiday, no distractions were in prospect; everyone relished the idea of catching an "outlaw" and seeing what he would look like after ten minutes of terrible and disorderly rapture. Alexei Nikitich turned into Aptechnaya Street, quickly ran to the end of it and walked on as if nothing had happened. But they caught up with him; he saw a dozen men behind him and the same fellow with the paralyzed eyelid was in front. Fearing to approach him in the open, they shouted something from the distance and beckoned to him with twelve fingers.

Then Kurilov ran, looking into the courtyards as he flew by, and everything alive on the street tore after him, even the reddish, sticky clay underfoot clung to his boots. The very thought of a repetition of his Izhevsk adventure made the still store welts on his back burn again. The pursuers fell back, and only one little old man, unusually active for his age, ran nimbly forward to offer his life on the altar of the fatherland. Kurilov awaited him at a corner, and when a loud panting groan revealed the proximity of his foe, he jumped out, striking him with the full weight of his body. The old man rolled on the slippery autumn grass. After a minute of desperate running Kurilov looked around in bewilderment. High plank fences, boundaries of fine merchants' estates, stood on either side. Other people's property surrounded him. With his last strength, pulling himself up by his hands, Kurilov scaled the wall. It seemed to him for a moment that someone had seized him as he climbed; actually one of his boots had got caught in a nail, and Kurilov fell flat on the other side on a pile of rotten leaves. There he lay, squeezing his shirt near his heart. Dogs barked and howled in the garden—he no longer cared. Then he heard steps and realized that there was a witness to his acrobatics.

Beside him stood a youngish man, perhaps six years older than himself, black-haired, gypsy-like, in a short cloth jacket, such as lordly huntsmen wore in olden times. And although they had met only once, in Perm, nine years earlier, Kurilov recognized his sister's husband at first glance. Fate would have been more intelligent if it had sent Frosia here in this cheerless moment, but he was glad to see even Omelichev. He got up, clumsily rubbing his knee; but this gesture was only a feint; his knee did not hurt at all. Omelichev picked his teeth with a match, blinked his eyes, and did not hold out his hand. From the other side of the fence the cries of the pack of pursuers were growing more distinct. It was necessary to begin any sort of conversation. "Now I've spoiled my boots," he said. "They were good boots!" He looked down regretfully. "Frosia asked me to visit her . . . and just see what I look like!"

"These are times when brothers-in-law drop from heaven," the owner of the house answered, pointing with his eyes to the open door of a nearby cellar. "Take a look at my farm; later we'll talk."

"Well, thanks. . . . Your farm is extensive." Kurilov nodded, standing up nonchalantly, despite his hurry to get away.

Omelichev locked up his guest and unchained his dogs. Although there were only four they filled the garden instantaneously. It was high time: suddenly the fellow with the drooping eyelid appeared on top of the fence, but drew back immediately when the four sharp-toothed hell-hounds jumped up at him with a roar. . . .

At night, when all was quiet (except that once in a while there were inexplicable shots on the river), Omelichev led Kurilov into the house situated in the center of the garden. Both of them walked on their tiptoes, hushing each other. The yellow lacquered floors, covered with a home-made strip of carpet, creaked. The bent flame of the candle left a thin stream of soot behind and swam, now in the white tiles of the stoves, now in the glass that covered the firm's certificates of merit that hung on the walls. After two weeks of imprisonment in Izhevsk it was strange to see furniture in uncrumpled, shaggy slip covers, a church lectern in a corner (Grandmother Glafira was still alive) and veritable thickets of green tropical plants in the windows. It was quiet, there was no one in Omelichev's house to make noise or disorder. Only the pendulum of the clock marked the silence like a tambourine. The guest was taken to the attic. Efrosinia made a bed for him on chests, and soon he was eating cold fish soup and listening to the dogs, the guardians of Omelichev's property, prowling in the darkness.

"Why do you shiver all the time?" Frosia asked him, wrapping herself in an ample robe with a vari-colored Turkish design. "Your eyes look hunted. And you're coughing. Are you ill?"

"No, I'm healthy and beautiful. But I had to swim across a river. Must have caught a cold."

She still did not realize what kind of cold bothered her brother.

"Aren't you fed up with all that business, Aliosha? You should spare yourself a little, there's nothing closer to a man than his own kin! Pavel and I are tired. Recently *Vania* again sailed quickly along the river, fired a couple of shots and ran away. . . ." She referred to *Vania* No. 5, a warship of the Volga fleet, which a few days later went down heroically near the village of Piany Bor, having fallen into an ambush between two White batteries. "What's going to happen to us, Alioshenka, tell me, I beg of you!"

"There will be a Soviet government, that's all. Why didn't your Pavel go to the square? . . . Doesn't he like the rebellion? . . . Why shouldn't he? By the way, your soup is excellent. Everyone should have such soup. Have you got a fresh shirt? If you can't spare a new one, an old one will do. And then bring something to rub my back with. I fell here and hit myself in various places. . . ." He was ashamed to complain to a woman about Oshkurov's hateful lash.

In this low-ceilinged, elongated box used for storing all sorts of trash, Alexei Nikitich spent a week and a half: his back was in a sorry state. From the half-round attic window he could see Omelichev's fading garden—which occupied almost an entire town block—a wooden steeple and endless woods on the other side of the river. Kurilov was cold here; it seemed that in the morning a crust of ice formed on the edges of the Kama backwaters. He imagined that his comrades were fighting the Whites somewhere near the Viatskye Poliany; he no longer had an idea of the present position of the front line. In the corner he found a pile of books with their beginnings and endings missing, the works of all sorts of mentors of provincial minds, Xavier de Montepin and Gustav Born, for instance. . . . And he tasted to the point of giddiness the amorous secrets of Madrid and other capitals; he read or, closing his eyes, listened to the rare exchanges of fire on the now quiet river.

During that time Omelichev visited the border only once. Shaking his head, he screened the window with a picture, so that the light could not be seen from the street. In the gilded frame reclined a naked little lady with coarse charms; a thick and for some reason yellow rain poured down on her.

"First have a smoke," said Pavel Stepanovich, and he put some cheap tobacco in Kurilov's box, which had long been empty. "Aren't you disgusted to find yourself sitting with a bourgeois?"

"Not if the bourgeois is smart!" And he rummaged in his pocket for his pipe, then still quite new. "I wish you'd bring me a newspaper!"

"I myself am a newspaper. Recently a second lieutenant knocked down an old woman for saying something impertinent. With one stroke, that's military prowess for you! As for me, it takes me eight minutes to kill a chicken. . . ."

It was clear that he did not rejoice over the occupation of the town by the Whites. He was keen enough to see further into the future; he guessed that the Czechs were only the first of hordes of foreigners who did not give a damn about Omelichev's Russia. (But apparently he did not expect the Soviet power to last, if he was hiding Kurilov in his attic!) At that time Alexei Nikitich could not make out why Omelichev tolerated him here, why he did not get Colonel Stepanov's people to come and slaughter him while he was asleep, like a bear under the snow. No one in those days was able to calculate the relations of forces, although for strategic reasons the White rule on the Kama could only be short-lived. Russian history had always abounded in surprises, and it was to Omelichev's advantage to acquire a friend for a rainy day. True, Frosia was Kurilov's sister, which complicated the situation, but during the bitter civil war kinship had no importance at all. There were no neutrals at that time.

"I'm pining away here, Pavel Stepanych."

"Maybe the food doesn't agree with you. It's always fish and fish. We live on a river."

"So I'm becoming indebted to you, Omelichev . . . eh?"

"Are you afraid that you never will be rich enough to pay me back?" asked the shipowner, and burst out laughing, playing with a heavy bundle of keys. Their tinkle accompanied this nocturnal conversation to the end. "If my bread disagrees with you . . . eat what you will!"

"I should have gone away, but for my back: I can't bend. I'm no good for the time being. . . ." In fact, he felt ashamed to eat Omelichev's bread. Coughing interrupted him at every third word. "Well, do you like the Bolsheviks and their ideas about your property?"

Omelichev correctly understood the question. "No, I'm not on your side, Kurilov," he said, and once again the keys tinkled with a piercing sound. "Your arms are too short: I don't believe, I don't believe in you!"

"We don't need you either. The people will believe in us!"

"The people!" He smiled angrily. "Better not cough so much. The people! . . . On this estate there are twenty men of that people. And they will tear you to pieces as soon as they find out you're here. See what I mean? And you don't know how to handle the people. Take everything away from me, and give me a yard, one yard of land . . . and I'll grow a miracle on it. You'll see a tree, and birds on it building nests amidst golden apples. But this yard must be mine, my son's, my grandson's, my great-grandson's. . . ."

"You seek immortality, Omelichev . . . and property is a rather deceiving ladder to it. And for the time being you don't even have a son. . . ."

Omelichev ignored this pointed remark. "I know man as well as you do. He becomes a magician when he alone has to provide for himself.

No one will give him and his puppies anything on a hungry day, and he knows it, the son of a bitch. So he tries, and racks his brains, and invents things, and is glad. Do you remember Ivan, my grandfather? An explosion of a man! Contemplate him, study him, Alexei Nikitich. Man is man! . . . With what will you replace his joy in solid earthly power? (Don't take the trouble to explain your theories to me. Other people's misery has spoiled my nights, too. . . .) How will you make him work if you don't dangle profits before his eyes? Perhaps for the sake of developing his muscles? . . . Or will fear be the incentive? . . . But fear, too, is a close relative of hatred. Class struggle, class struggle . . . even the words aren't Russian, aren't ours."

"There's another foreign phrase that you don't know, Omelichev. Both of us left the sodden life of Porozhensk . . . only I got angry, while you sat on top of the pile and comforted yourself with the thought that other people's lot was even worse than yours! There in Porozhensk no one ever heard that phrase. If you gave it to one of your ships as a name you'd be the laughing-stock of the Kama, you'd lose your credit. This phrase is: *creative power,* Pavel Stepanych!"

Omelichev's face was red with anger, and his keys jangled in his hands. "You . . . you're a soldier, you're homeless, so keep your mouth shut. So far you've only killed, and what, what have you created?" He stopped speaking as abruptly as he had begun.

Kurilov seemed to do everything possible to force Omelichev to drive him out, but Omelichev did not drive him out; he fed him and protected him from death. And again he picked up the conversation, as though trying to get his fill of the truth Kurilov bore within himself. A light rain was drumming on the roof, and somewhere in the eaves sleepy birds were chirping.

". . . And why do you always carry your keys with you? Do people steal things from you?"

"No one steals here, Alexei Nikitich. My people are well fed."

"Look out, they'll cut your throat. Well-fed people are the readiest for such things. They, too, want to have sons and grandsons. . . . Hm?"

"We'll see which of us will have his throat cut first! Recently they've been looking for you, commissar."

"Who?" and Kurilov's body was all ready to spring.

"Two young fellows, Colonel Stepanov's henchmen, came with a platoon. Someone must have seen you climb over the fence. One of them was just a big dolt, the other is light-footed and handy. He was trying to sneak into the house."

"Well?"

"I told him. . . ." (And the little keys in his hand had a triumphant ring.) "I said I didn't know whether their colonel had many pairs of trousers to spare that he was willing to risk so many in this idiotic fashion . . . and that I had invested a million and a half rubles in the business of Russia. I said: I know better than you, my young falcon, what the Bolsheviks are. Go to the front, fight the sailors, rather than knocking down old women here on the square. . . . And you've become famous, Alexei Nikitich. He knew you by name!"

Apparently Omelichev was amused by this game. His tale was long and amounted to this: The lieutenant had disbelieved Omelichev's claim that Kurilov was not in the house and decided that the fugitive was hiding among Omelichev's servants. He spent two hours searching the rooms, closets and cupboards. What was soft was pierced with bayonets. And when they visited the quarters of the pilot Chernodiadiev, who had gone over to the Reds, his little girl, only five years old, brought her one-eyed doll to the officer, asking him to search her and cut her open with his bayonet. "My doll, I want you to cut my doll!" This went on until the officer with a purple face yelled to her mother to take the child away. (Kurilov noticed that Omelichev had even found a tender word in his coarse vocabulary to describe another man's child.) After that conversation, they did not meet again. Three days later Alexei Nikitich ran away, unable to bear any longer the torture of idleness. He awakened Frosia at night, asked her to give him some food and to accompany him to the gate. . . . It was beginning to rain. Golden rings gleamed in his sister's ears.

"You've got as much gold on you as an icon," Kurilov jested.

"Don't make fun of me, Aliosha."

"Come with me, just as you are . . . want to? Your Pavel has something to die for: he is a partisan of free enterprise, but you? . . ."

She clung to the wet gate post and leaned forward, and Alexei saw her avid teeth. It was black and empty on the river. Somewhere a quick burst from a machine-gun pierced the night. The conquerors imagined that they were being assaulted by people who could not die, people unkillable by any human force! The distant, sudden alarm prevented brother and sister from embracing. They both had had time to repress a minute-long, unconscious impulse. Both listened, but there was nothing, only the wind rustling in the nearby branches. Alexei laughed: "Well . . . goodbye, sister: I may come back and I may not!" he added, quoting a popular song, and at once the wind took him away somewhere downhill, into the homeless and alluring night.

CHAPTER 27

# The Broken Trough

THE GHOST OF the stillborn child was present invisibly in Protoklitov's apartment, and until it ceased to haunt the place, its inhabitants lived silently, thinking only of it. Ilya Ignatyich did not see Liza. His working day began while Liza was still in bed; she returned from the theatre when her husband was already asleep. Once the couple ran into each other in the dining room; correct and withdrawn, Ilya Ignatyich drank his black tea and walked to his study with a military step. Liza followed him with close scrutiny. Sometimes she caught his glance scanning her attentively, without any of his old tenderness; it was as though he were looking for the mark of her criminality in her face and were angry at not finding it. Life in the apartment became quite unpleasant. Liza ventured to upset this oppressive state of equilibrium. One morning she went away to the theatre and did not come back. She had enough pride and taste not to take Protoklitov's gifts with her; she went as poor as she had come. She did not leave any note. . . . She was ashamed to return to her uncle; for a long time she roamed the streets, and was on the point of going to the railroad station to sit there until she was picked up by the authorities. It was a starry night, and Liza was frozen. Finally, sinking into the snow, she dragged herself through the gate to Arkadyi Hermogenovich's window and knocked at it.

Everything was reversed, and now the uncle was compelled to give hospitality to his unfortunate niece. Once again cotton roosters partitioned the small room. The sun no sooner appeared than they revived and twisted their necks: this was the old man beginning his bustling day. While dressing he muttered something, and suddenly Dudnikov's name exploded on his lips.

"Forget him, after all he's dead, . . ." said Liza sadly.

"Oh, does death free one from the hatred of the living?"

Hatred! He spent it little by little so as to savor it for a long time. It was now the fuel on which his senile organism moved. He set the sooty coffee pot on the kerosene stove, went out to get bread and brought back a newspaper. They drank a thin concoction made of oats, and the old man read the news aloud. The *Chelyuskin* was cutting her

237

way through the ice, the Araks had staged a revolt on their islands. Arkadyi Hermogenovich liked disturbances that no longer endangered his own life. His professional habits made him read accidental dactyls in the text with special feeling. Liza warmed her fingers against the empty glass and looked out of the window. She never got enough sleep because of this bustling old man.

Arkadyi Hermogenovich simply adored silent company. Their number was constantly decreasing: the younger generation had no use for philosophical idleness. And, once he had been officially notified that his pension had been granted, he became even more talkative.

"Did you ever happen, Liza, to look at life as though you were observing it from outside? Look carefully, and you'll see countless variations on an identical theme. Eh, doubtless . . . the world will last until all the possible combinations of these material elements have been realized. Everything must be reflected in everything else and, after having been reflected, must shudder and recoil. Everything flies, everything whirls in all directions and from everywhere. Everything passes through us, and we pass through everything. We are only provisional vessels in which nature preserves its idea. How understandable everything becomes when you look back upon it from the vantage point of old age! How simple everything is! . . . And just think of the monstrous blast furnaces in which these blessed worlds and abysses were forged! Count how many efforts matter had to make to produce, say, this tree, a poor botanical variety, from which you cannot even gather a wreath in summer. Was it worth all the toil spent on it? . . . Or would you say that man, the master of the earth, is fated to correct and crown with wisdom God's preliminary work?"

He expected Liza to take up this cue, but she was silent and sat looking through the window-pane scratched by frost. The old man's voice resembled the annoying gurgle of rain in the gutter. Liza thought of her own troubles. . . . Active preparations were going on for the production with which her company expected to attract public attention. A week earlier, when the director summoned Liza to inform her that she would be included in the Uzbek kolkhoz brigade, she had seen sketches for the *Mary Stuart* costumes on his desk. With envy doubled by resentment she looked at that motley assembly of mediaeval ministers and ambassadors in hats resembling a garden illuminated by fireworks, jailers with keys that had human profiles, buffoons with soft drooping noses, sceptre-bearers in fur-trimmed brocade robes . . . and even Elizabeth herself was present; her deathly bluish breasts pushed into a basket-corsage would have repelled even the complaisant Dudley. Magic colors glowed on these papers; while the director in a bored tone spoke of self-sacrifice and the need for intensive study of the people's monumental passions, without which no true artist can develop. With burning ears she obediently nodded in agreement, realizing that she was being thrown out of the theatre without any hope of return. (Confused and already broken, she was ready to confess her guilt, the nature of which she did not yet understand with her heart.) Today the brigade composed of actors who were not to take part in the next production was to set out on its way. The train left at half-past ten. She was already late. . . .

The water kept babbling in the gutter—". . . Let us grasp the meaning of these empirical exercises of nature. Don't you think, Liza, eh, that nature seeks some lucky coincidence that might justify its chaos and confusion, some yardstick of its clumsiness? Look, it moves gropingly, it creates monsters and destroys them, because it is ashamed of them; it paints and rubs out its creations before they have had time to become aware of themselves; it hits them on the head shouting—that's not what I want, no, no, no! No industry produces so many imperfect articles. And so, eh, . . . we ourselves are only rough drafts of giants who in their own time will learn that they are only dwarfs. You're yawning; does my chatter bore you?"

"Yesterday you spoke of the same thing. Shall I pour you more coffee?"

"Half a cup." He cast an inquisitive glance at her. "I have the feeling that I'm boring you. . . ."

"I'm chilly, uncle."

He jumped up and brought her his enormous canvas coat; it did not bend; it crackled as though frozen; it was like a shroud.

"The window is drafty. Today it's all pink from the frost. The newspapers predict an arctic February. We must save wood. . . ." With a dissatisfied gesture he poked a newspaper article. "The railroads can't cope with the transportation of fuel. Throw this thing around your shoulders, Liza, and you'll be warm, eh, you'll be warm like a soldier in his sentrybox!"

"I'll put it on a little later. It's too early yet!" she said meaningfully. "Why did our neighbor attack you? Did she read the review in which I was advised to take up sewing as a profession?"

Arkadyi Hermogenovich gloomily lowered his head. "Neighbors are always nasty, and reviewers are only the neighbors of art. You won't be late for your rehearsal, Liza? . . . When does it begin?"

Blushing and hiding her eyes, she said it would begin at twelve. The old man did not guess anything. He was preparing to work, and Liza took out some potatoes to peel for dinner. "It's awful how potato

peels spoil your hands!" Suddenly blood mounted to her face. Stopping
her mouth with her hand, Liza listened to her neighbor making a noise
with her broom, and challenging her to a quarrel. This was the plumber's wife, who was taking revenge on the young actress for having refused her friendship. "You sloven," she shouted behind the door; "and
she even lived with a doctor!" Something had to be done at once. Liza
jumped up and ran to the telephone booth in the drugstore. Frozen
snow hissed under her heels, sparrows hopped about and jumped on
the fence. Liza phoned Galka Gromova twice, but the line was busy.
She threw her last coin into the slot to hear her friend's questioning
alert voice. She was doubtless afraid of Liza: misfortune is contagious.
. . . Yes, the list of the dismissed actors were already posted in the
theatre. Yes, Pokhvisneva's name was on them. No, Galka did not
know what should be done in such cases. She thought that a company
was being formed to go to Oirotia. . . . They were cut off. Distraught,
Liza banged the hook of the receiver: she heard hums. . . . The cashier
looked at her pityingly. Liza was a habitual visitor here. Sometimes
she used up a whole ruble in phone calls. Now, worn out, she returned
home. She no longer wanted to go anywhere, so as not to hear sympathetic murmurs varied only in pitch. She returned slowly, thinking
with fear that today someone had cancelled a lesson with Arkadyi
Hermogenovich. (It's strange—he teaches his pharmacists to read Hor-
ace in the original, as though that were necessary to distinguish aspirin
from purgatives!)

Liza's day grew enormously long, she had nothing with which to fill
it. She began a dozen things and did not finish one. She darned the old
man's underwear, which was kept in his provincial chest. It was of
coarse cloth, and there were more holes to it than underwear. She
stuffed it back into the chest haphazardly. Sitting on the stool she
made a fire in the stove. Warmth enveloped her knees. The fire devoured the crackling logs. Liza turned over the pages of the books from
a pile destined to be sold: the Pokhvisnevs could not make ends meet.

There were Lafargue and Darwin, an Ovid in Russian and separate
volumes of Anatole France. Arkadyi Hermogenovich no longer read
these works. On his table, *Love of Goodness* had made its appearance,
a thick, round-shouldered book on monastic habits, old age and Christian resignation. He read it not because he was looking for faith, but
because he no longer had anything with which to feed his atheism. . . .
On the shelf there was Liza's favorite book, about Mary Stuart. She
read it several times in succession, but it was never enough for her. She
learned about Riccio and Darnley, Mary's lovers, although neither figures in the dramatis personae of Schiller's play. She was surprised at

the names of Norfolk, Walsingham, Mendoza and Philip II, the chief stage managers of the tragedy. She tore through the pretty cover of the picture to look at it more deeply, and it began to wither in her hands. "So that's what you were in reality!"

Her neighbor cried at the door that a "visitor" was asking for Liza. Her voice was suddenly respectful. Liza hesitatingly went out into the entrance hall. In the doorway Protoklitov towered monumentally. He had on such an impressive fur coat that her neighbor would certainly have respect for her for a whole week. ("How quickly desires come true when one wants them no longer!") Liza gave him a half-bow and did not hold out her hand.

"May I come in to see you, Liza."

"No, there are people with me." Only now did she realize why she had wanted him to come: to shout in his face, yes, in his face, that she was free! "Do you have any special business, or did you just want to drop in?"

The doors of all the rooms in the apartment were ajar. Nine tenants who were taking their evening tea listened to them and were pleased.

"Let's go to the staircase," said Liza. "Well?"

A cold wind streamed through the broken glass of the front entrance and one could hear creaking steps.

"I don't think that I was unfair to you, Liza," Protoklitov began with deliberation. "That's the kind of profession I practise. Ha, we do people good, and they fear us like fire. But even disregarding all the things you did. . . ."

She interrupted him impatiently, covering her throat with her hand: "I'm freezing, come to the point!"

"Very well. I want to offer you some money . . . you must be having a hard time?" He was tormented by the fear that his talk with the director might lead to her dismissal. He did not know that this had already taken place. "I'll undertake to send you the same amount every month until you return to me."

"It's funny, the *barin* coming to give me a kopek," she thought. And she said: "Do you want to buy my faithfulness?"

"Oh, she doesn't guess anything," he thought. And he said: "The logic of the offended is always monstrous . . . but I don't see any reason for resentment."

"I agree with you, Ilya: I don't work well, I can't do better. But I eat what I deserve . . . and, the devil take it, I like my food!"

He bowed with an air of satisfaction at having done his duty and moved down a step. "Very well, Liza. Your firmness honors you. I shall return in six months."

"You mustn't! . . . In such a fur coat, to such slums!" And she cried after him: "You'll be robbed in our street!"

The four logs, the ration of fuel supposed to last a whole day, had burned out; the ashes were smouldering and growing blacker. Liza went to the window. Hoar frost was falling; the trees stood stark naked as if charred. Arkadyi Hermogenovich came in. They ate the same soup they had had the day before. Uncle was noisier than ever.

"Something has made you sad, Liza?"

"No . . . but I've been bothering you. There's no way of airing or cleaning the room. . . ."

"You want to hint that old men of my age are difficult to live with? That's true, Liza. . . ." He guiltily patted her hand. "How was your rehearsal? I'm so afraid . . . I won't go to see this performance!"

"Do you know what, uncle . . . I think I'm going to give up my part. I've changed my mind." She put her fingers to her cheeks. "How my cheeks are burning . . . it's from the stove."

Arkadyi Hermogenovich ostentatiously pressed his hand to his ears, rattled the dishes, and recoiled from his niece. And from these clumsy, too transparent manoeuvres, Liza realized that Arkadyi had long since guessed everything.

# CHAPTER 28

# The Body

EFROSINIA'S VIGOROUS HOUSEKEEPING affected Kurilov's whole apartment. The furniture stood solidly where it belonged; the clear, scrubbed window-panes admitted twice as much light as before; on top of the cupboards, where the sickly Catherine had never looked, not a grain of dust remained. Dinner was ready at a fixed hour, and Efrosinia scolded her brother whenever he was late. Klavdia came to see him more often, and each time her visit turned out to be quite accidental. Slowly walking through the rooms, she read from certain elusive signs the events that had occurred during her absence. She opened the side-board in the dining room: new objects were there instead of the old broken, ill-matched bits of china; she looked into the bathroom: the floor shone. Life was returning to this uninhabited barn. Made happy by the waxed floors, the big mirror, the very dimensions of the apartment, little Luka ran in the corridor, quietly slunk along a wall, was suddenly scared by some creature of his own imagination, swerved aside, moo-ing strangely, and again began his assault from a distant corner. Thus he played hide-and-seek with himself. . . . Klavdia told him that good children never, never make any noise—translating her words into the language of gestures and listening attentively to the silence: someone was singing. . . . Pricking up her ears she went in the direction of the voice. It was Frosia singing in the kitchen while she cooked dinner (and this was no longer Frosia's old song). Playing with the cord of her pince-nez, Klavdia watched her nimble-fingered sister paring the vegetables.

"You're singing?" Klavdia asked instead of greeting her, surprised that life had not completely crushed this woman's desire to sing.

"Songs are coming to me, Klavdia," Frosia answered, without inter-rupting her work, and she put aside a cabbage-stump, Luka's favorite delicacy. "Why, don't you like singing? Sick people like to hear songs. . . ."

"No, never mind, sing, . . ." and she added in a scarcely perceptible voice, "if you can. . . ."

Even before this the sisters had not got along. Klavdia never forgave Frosia her marriage. On another occasion they had been brought together by their concern for their younger brother. Klavdia had come to the Omelichevs' house while engaged in carrying out a secret mission for her brother, who was being transported to Siberia, and then the only heart-to-heart talk the two sisters ever had took place: it had ended their relationship. At the same time Klavdia pitied her sister, and this was her last "old-time" feeling of which she felt ashamed and which she perhaps despised in herself. Of course, it would have been better if Frosia had vanished to her Siberia . . . but Alexei was gravely ill, and there was no other reliable person to stay with him.

Another day she entered the kitchen and found Efrosinia wiping off the window-panes. It was thawing, dripping from the roof, all the curtains in the apartment were stirring. Holding the cross-beam of the frame, Frosia stood dangerously on the very edge of the twelve-storey pit and looked down into the snowy twilight of the quay. A languid breeze seemed to draw her there, and her whole body was bent over the abyss. Klavdia brusquely pulled her by the apron: "You're out of your mind, Efrosinia. Get down at once!"

Frosia turned to her sister with a smile that boded no good, and some intense emotion restored her former beauty for a moment. "Are you afraid that I'll jump?" she asked.

"You've jumped enough in your life. You're no longer a young woman, Frosia! But you might catch cold from this draft. . . ."

". . . And then no one would be left to take care of Alexei?" her sister completed Klavdia's thought in the same tone. "Don't worry, in addition to Aliosha, I have my little one. . . ."

Klavdia stopped short, but was unable to leave at once. She stood touching some unfamiliar kitchen utensils, counting the scattered matches on the table.

"There's a smell of tobacco here. I can't bear women who smoke. . . ."

"No, Klasha, I don't smoke. It must be coming from Alexei's room."

Klavdia went to her brother's room.

He now spent most of his time at home, surrounding himself with books, and awaiting the next attack with the nauseated feeling of a doomed man. . . . Klavdia sat beside him and raised her brows with surprise at his pile of literature about the Far East. There were articles about various remote peoples, economic studies, discussions of possible wars between certain Pacific powers, fantastic blueprints of railroads, works by sinologists on Chinese antiquity, statistical tables. Klavdia asked her brother why he was interested in these subjects. He told her that these were only parts of one great subject—the Ocean—that had once taken hold of him for all his life. Klavdia recalled his old love, dating from his childhood, for vast expanses of water. She only said: "But I thought that you'd grown up since that time, Aliosha?"

"The Ocean, too, has grown up, Klasha. . . . Don't you understand? After all, you have a judicious mind, sister!"

She retreated. As always, he was not quite right, but it was not worth while to give battle for such trifles. She tried to give her next question a nuance of casualness: "Did you have any pains last night?"

"You don't want me to ache every day, do you? . . . Good things come only in little doses. . . ."

"I've bought you a cap. I brought it with me. You can try it on later! It's stupid to walk about with a light hat in such cold weather." She moved closer to him and her face had a mysterious expression. "What do you think of Frosia?"

"She's fine, she looks better."

"That's not what I mean. This . . . her husband, does he come to see her?"

"But they're separated! Didn't you know?"

"Yes. . . . But he might come all of a sudden . . . to visit his child!"

"He might. . . . And I won't throw him out."

She frowned. She had always played the part of his guardian to some extent, but now her authority was diminishing in proportion as Kurilov's illness grew more severe. This time she refrained from her usual scolding, and not only because she feared to upset him. After Catherine's death, imperceptibly to herself, she had transferred all the warmth of her old woman's heart to her brother.

"Of course, I don't know what your relations with him are. . . ."

"Why, you ought to know! The revolution did not abolish paternal rights . . . besides, I am indebted to these people. . . ."

Yes, she had heard something of the sort. It appeared that they had not handed him over to the Whites, when they had the opportunity. But after all it was not particularly praiseworthy to refrain from acting like a complete scoundrel. In a soothing tone, as though trying to awaken in him the instinct that guided her own life, she spoke of the need for caution.

"You see, Alioshenka, they were well fed. And well-fed people are always compassionate. A well-fed man wants to sleep, but he is afraid lest he be attacked in his sleep. That explains the Omelichevs' attitude toward you. . . ."

"But this thing happened after October."

"What difference does that make? They never believed in our strength. And do you remember his *sweet* joke at your trial? 'Maybe

I'm an imbecile, but when my son is the president of the republic, he will be an *intelligent* president!' He wanted to use us as stepping stones . . . see? But now, when everything has been taken from them—and I don't refer to Omelichev's barges, Aliosha, but to his broken hopes—now that they have experienced real grief, they're embittered. And even a blade of straw is dangerous in the hands of a cornered enemy! One must be careful: sometimes even the dead rise up to stab you in the back. . . ." She spoke in a low-pitched voice, which grew passionate and hoarse as though she were speaking at a meeting. "At any rate I beg of you not to keep any important documents here. That isn't cowardice, it's only vigilance!" He was silent, and she became angry. Alexei Nikitich watched with curiosity how her genuine anger rejuvenated her. "So you're preparing to pay your debt, Aliosha?"

It was hard to answer her; the new morality was still partly based on the vague norms of the individual conscience.

"Yes . . . but not on the same level, of course! However, I'd help him to get on his feet, if he were willing to give up his old ideas."

"It's too late for him to go back to the cradle, Aliosha. And he would find it narrow, after the Kama. . . . I find it strange that you had to think before answering me. This must be because of your pain. Haven't you seen a surgeon yet?"

"I have no time, Klasha."

"Don't forget that all your symptoms point to kidney stones."

"Nonsense, all my engineers on the road have stones in their kidneys. I don't give jobs to those who don't. . . ."

He was definitely escaping from her power, and she was irritated. "This is what we'll do. . . . I myself will make an appointment for you. What surgeon would you prefer?"

"Show me their pictures, I'll choose. Personally I like small ones with chestnut hair. I think they're gentler. . . ."

"You'll make me prematurely grey, Aliosha!" But she laughed.

She interpreted his facetiousness as an attempt to laugh off his own fear; possibly he already knew everything about his condition. To destroy the danger was not in her power. She lowered her head. Blushes covered her face, and suddenly he saw in her the lanky, bare-legged girl who once rescued his whole toy fleet from capture by the children of the suburb. He tenderly stroked her hand, already bony from old age; he stroked it for a long time, and she did not remove it, only her eyes were more and more lost. She was drawing in her shoulders, as though his caress made her feel older; she was not used to it, she did not know how to react.

"Thank you, little sister," he said almost inaudibly. "You truly like me. I'll feed you to your fill as a reward! Today I have excellent stuffed cabbage, just as you like it, with onion sauce. I'm getting used to such food! . . . It differs from meat only by its taste, color and odor." He formed a horn with his hand and shouted to Frosia: Was dinner ready?

By that time Kurilov sufficiently knew himself to be entitled to such jokes. Before being examined by a famous professor he had to go through a long conveyor belt of all kinds of humiliating—at least so it seemed to him—investigations. His abdomen was auscultated, after his bowels had been pumped full of air; methylene blue was injected into his arm, and then for hours they waited to see what would result from it. For the first time he learned of the existence of the cystoscope, and experienced the peculiar feeling of nakedness that one has when one is looked through with something invisible. He had pains in the small of the back, and doctors looked under his eyelids. Now even he himself no longer thought he had just a cold. Gradually he ceased respecting his body. Accustomed to consider it an obedient and perfect instrument created by nature for many important deeds, he was all the more sensitive to the smallest modifications in it.

From the middle of January his ailment grew more severe and, had it not been for Frosia, Alexei Nikitich would have been quite ill. The attacks were not more frequent than before, but one day after each of them he was overwhelmed by a tormenting fear that another was about to start. Sometimes fear surprised him at night, and sudden sweat appeared on his temples. Lying on his back, Alexei Nikitich listened to the processes in his body. He feared to cry out lest he thus provoke the *beginning* of an attack; when it started he would drop an object. This was a signal agreed upon with his sister. For this purpose the telephone directory was tied with a string to prevent it from falling to pieces when dropped. Then there followed a noiseless bustling routine. Efrosinia opened the drawer of the table where the needle, with Kurilov's only medicine, was kept. Feeling the pain with her brother she hurried, running the risk of breaking the needle in his back. Only by the end of the month did she acquire the habits of a professional nurse.

Then, sitting opposite him, she told him about her life on the Kama, about Omelichev's relatives, about the marriage that had taken place in her brother's absence, about the disappointments that followed it. "It's strange," she once confessed, "as I tell the story I feel as if I were examining the wax flowers used at my wedding. They crumbled away long ago and the wire pricks my fingers. I was greedy, Aliosha. I liked pretty dresses, I always dreamed of carriages and fireworks. Surely man is born for joy, and if he is given sorrows, Aliosha, it's only to enhance his joys. I always looked upon you and Klavdia as people who had renounced the world. You filled me with pity, but also with awe. I've never loved saints. My mother-in-law Glafira (my husband's stepmother) had thirty-six icons hanging in her private chapel, a whole pack of them. She called each by a special name; I nicknamed the one representing the eye of God, the ace of diamonds. And there was my favorite, St. George the Victorious, golden, ardent, thin . . . with a lance like a sonorous string . . . St. George—and also Alexei, the man of God. That was you. After all I don't know your rank, I'm not in your battalion. And to whom else are you as dear as you are to me—as a man, I mean? . . . Name him and he'll be my friend!" And suddenly he realized that she was falling asleep. She opened her eyes with effort, trying to drive her sleepiness away. "Now I've lost the thread. Where was I?"

"You were speaking about yourself. . . . I asked your husband whether he regretted everything he had lost. He said, no. And how about you?"

"He's lying, while I really don't regret. Do you think that grief tastes sweeter in a silver cup?" And she nodded toward the wall behind which slept the boy, her conscience, the curse and the joy of her life, Luka.

"And whose fault is that, Frosia?"

"Whose indeed!" His sister's lips grew thinner. "Do you remember what we ate . . . what we wore . . . where we had to sleep sometimes, remember? It was better to be with Pavel than to fall into the depths of misery, eh? And how I wanted to be with you, Alioshka, that time on the Kama!"

"I thought then that you were pregnant! Was that Luka?"

"No, Luka is my second misfortune," she said, her face darkening.

And she went on, about the same thing, in many troubled nocturnal words. Daybreak was coming, and once again, Alexei Nikitich dragged himself to the hospital, this time to get a paper with a description of his disease.

The examination revealed the presence of a tumor; it had not yet reached the kidney cortex, but a considerable portion of it was below the floating ribs. To the touch it was hard and bumpy like a cartilage, and it caused great pain to the patient when handled. The doctors were confused by these very painful sensations, and the surgeon was to have the last word. The name of this professor was invariably found at the bottom of all official documents. Yielding to Klavdia's demands Kurilov telephoned him. A very quiet feminine voice suggested that he ask for an appointment a week later; the professor had had a heart attack, and for the time being could not see any patients. . . .

Finally the meeting took place. When Kurilov entered, a very thin man, his face covered with red blotches, was hurriedly dressing in the waiting room, not seeing anything, stuffing his feet into his galoshes; apparently Kurilov's predecessor had just learned his fate. The room was furnished in the style of the end of the nineteenth century, when the young physician had rented his office after having received his diploma. Now he was an indifferent old man, the color of paraffin, with obvious symptoms of a cardiac ailment on his face. During more than forty years of activity as a surgeon he had successfully exchanged his health and youth for world fame and many comfortable objects of daily use. . . . Kurilov introduced himself. With the pencil the surgeon pointed at a chair that was shabbier than anything else in his office. He began to take down data about the patient. Kurilov noticed a great deal of furniture, old-fashioned landscapes and two photographs: that of Chekhov (no doubt because he, too, was a physician) and of a stern old man of irreproachable appearance, with a beard like Abraham Lincoln's. From the next floor or behind a wall came the sound of scales timidly executed on a piano.

"Well," said the professor, wrenching himself from his ledger of sorrows, "tell me all about yourself."

Alexei Nikitich told him everything he knew: about his ride on the engine, his pains in the small of the back. "I have lost faith in my body. I have begun thinking about it too often. I think something has become rusty inside." The professor's face remained impassive. His pupils gleamed lifelessly. He ordered Kurilov to undress, and while he pulled his sweater over his head, the doctor read the medical record his patient had brought in a sealed envelope. Without turning his head he told him to remove his trousers too. . . . The examination did not last long. Icy fingers moved along Kurilov's body, so skilfully that Alexei Nikitich perceived the doctor's touch only by a slight sensation of cold. The professor did not question him about bleedings or any other symptoms; he merely said that he could confirm the results of the hospital examination, adding that the swelling was combined with stones, which explained the pain. He advised Kurilov to go to a clinic at once, while his case was "still operable." Kurilov's hand involuntarily moved some round smooth object at the edge of the table, unencumbered by books or papers. He raised his fingers, under them he found a brass ashtray polished to a shine, and in it was somebody's twisted cigarette stub chewed through and through. Mechanically he reached out for his pipe, but he remembered in time that he was not supposed to smoke here.

The professor noticed his gesture. "Never mind, you may smoke," he said expressionlessly and coughed into his fist. "Make up your mind." He explained that next week he was going to a congress in Barcelona and thus would not be able to perform the operation himself.

"Is it a serious operation?" Kurilov asked and thought that the old man might not live long enough to get to Barcelona.

"This disease is more dangerous than any operation." His voice at times was almost as low as a whisper. "Every day the kidney paren-chyma undergoes further modifications. . . ."

The word was unfamiliar, solid, and it contained a sort of sinister comfort. Alexei Nikitich tried to memorize it. "Nevertheless, I'd like to postpone it for a month," he said, disturbed. "One of these days I have a railroad conference, connected with an important party task. Then I intend to take a trip somewhere to the country, to the snow. We have an excellent rest home, and I haven't taken a rest for seventeen years." (He might just as well calculate the interval from his last imprison-ment.) "Meanwhile perhaps some further symptoms of my ailment will manifest themselves? . . ."

He tried to be as shrewd as he could, and the doctor listened to him with half-closed eyes. Patients are always intractable. The professor had long since become used to all kinds of excuses, to attempts to con-fuse him by irrelevant considerations; it bored him to utter again and again the words he had been compelled to utter for forty years. A party task and a rest home in the snow—all this was only another vari-ation on an old theme.

"After all, you don't expect me to pity you!" he said simply, as one speaks only to equals.

And sometimes "they" demand the exact name of their disease, as though this could, if not heal, at least give comfort. Kurilov asked, and now he learned of the existence of the hypernephroma. The word was solemn, sonorous, and evoked in his mind the name of an ancient Ger-man queen. At present it meant only a tumor. Without understanding the nature of his own question, Kurilov asked whether it was malig-nant; the professor answered that the microscope would show that. He looked at his watch as though calling upon his visitor to spare an old man's numbered minutes. Kurilov rose and left his own little pile of charred tobacco beside the stub. Suddenly a horrible thought went through his head. Biting his mustache he asked whether this "thing" could be the result of a "blow . . ." (He was unable to find at once a polite neutral term appropriate to the sacred academic silence of this place.) ". . . let us say, from a piece of lead the size of a match box falling on the back."

"And were you hit with great force?"

"It fell like a bullet . . . and several times."

"But how did it happen to hit there?" the professor asked, this time with frank annoyance.

"Let's say . . . it was a specially constructed lash."

A gleam of life was born in the old man's eyes; it seemed that he was about to say something, to express his indignation, to cry out . . . "A man . . . with a lash!" But everything went out cold, before his first word was formed: the old man had nothing to do with politics.

"The origin of tumors is not accurately known. . . ."

All his plans were upset. His sisters were particularly frightened by the fact that the professor had not even prescribed any powders for him. Alexei Nikitich began to rush about in all directions. His furlough was confirmed; for two weeks now Martinson had actually been directing the work of the Political Bureau. Kurilov had only to busy himself with the railroad conference, and he impatiently awaited its end to go to Borschnia. He still tried to work; he spent two days at the Moscow railroad stations, comparing them with the stations of his own line, and many people interpreted this naïve attempt to hide from himself as an act of self-sacrifice. . . . And when he was overcome by his feeling of loneliness, he went to see Ziamka.

He had become a regular guest there. Marinka's aunt surpassed herself in efforts to arrange a sort of cozy refuge for him. Silent enthusiasm over her niece's future shone in her eyes. She already anticipated the day when she would go to buy mutton chops in a government car. She always kept the samovar ready for him. When he came she unlocked the box of biscuits, the object of Ziamka's greatest desire, served tea and in every glass put a spoon polished till it gleamed like a mirror; Alexei Nikitich was given the shiniest one. Then Anfisa Denisovna sat down at his side and with childlike enthusiasm told him what she had recently experienced in the crematorium. "Imagine, comrade Kurilov, an organ plays, and one wants so much to sob for the grief there is in life!" From time to time she got up and went to the bed to fix the drapery or smooth out a corner of the blanket. She did not explain anything, but Kurilov realized that this nuptial scaffold on which she had slept with her deceased husband for twenty-six years was going to be her contribution to Marina's dowry. To lie on this walnut construction would have been tantamount to lying on a burial mound, on the bones of the departed spouse. Kurilov patiently suffered Anfisa's gushy hints, her sickeningly cordial hospitality (at such moments a special polite

perspicacity appeared in his speech and eyes), winked at Ziamka and
fed him biscuits.

Ziamka exulted, dropped them stealthily in his bosom, stuffed them
into his full cheeks. "You should come more often. The biscuits are
very good," he confided and was suddenly choked with laughter.
"Anfiska recently borrowed money from a tenant to buy biscuits.
And he didn't like it! . . . After you go everything's locked up. But you
eat some, too. Shall I steal one for you?"

"Eat, Ziamka. I'll bring you a whole pound next time!"

"Maybe half a pound will be enough? And later more! . . . Because
otherwise they'd get stale, wouldn't they?"

"All right, comrade, all right!"

It was more than merely amusing to look at the child's worried little
face still blazing with January colors and guess what kind of man he
would develop into; whether he would conquer the Arctic or build
"oceanic central stations" or steer air trains between the capitals of the
world Soviet republic. . . . Sometimes he took Ziamka with him and
they drove through the city. (Anfiska, too, tried to join them. "You
won't believe, comrade Kurilov, that only once in my life, on March 8,
Woman's Day, I drove in a car, and even then I had to stand, in a
truck!" But he always excluded her.) He would put the little boy,
numb with rapture, next to the chauffeur, take him to museums, invent all sorts of stories for him and the boy would break into laughter,
energetically holding his sides or banking with his felt boots on the
floor of the car.

"Don't make me laugh so much," he would sob during a respite.
"Don't you see I'm losing my breath?" And then suddenly: "You're
free, all the time, and yet you probably get money? You must be a
specialist!"

"I'm on furlough, Ziamka. On furlough it's no disgrace not to work."

"Anfiska says you're sick. . . . Is it true? What's sick in you?"

"My body, Ziamka, my body."

"You're old already. . . . Does everything hurt you at once or only
the insides?"

"Everything at once, dear."

The boy fell silent, grew serious, even grim, and neither an orange
nor a funny story could cheer him up.

"Are you afraid of death?"

"Why do you ask that, Ziamka?"

"You surely tremble a bit, don't you?" And stealthily in a whisper:
"I do."

Kurilov's sisters noticed that returning from such rides he looked somehow younger. They were mistaken in ascribing the cause of this change to Marina. Apparently the sisters had reached some secret agreement, but Kurilov was never able to learn which of the two was the author of the monstrous project that was revealed to him one night by Efrosinia. She stopped him as he was going to his bath. "I must speak to you, Alexei," she said.

He was surprised at her urgent tone. "Are you in such a hurry? My water will get cold. . . ."

"Yes. You see, I must go. I've received letters . . . my job won't wait for me. And then . . ."—the main thing apparently was coming now—". . . I met Pavel on the street right near the entrance. It's hard for me! I don't want to see him, I can't stand it."

He spread his hands. "Have I chained you here? Of course, if you must go, go. I myself was going to go to Borschnia for a month." He only asked her, in case her departure had to be sudden, to lock the apartment and leave the key with Klavdia. "Even so I owe you a great deal, Frosia!"

"I've been talking with Klasha. . . . So you like that Marinka? I always thought that you liked girls of the 'lenten' type, Catherine was so thin. . . . And this one. . . ." And in a familiar, almost crude way she softly enumerated Marina's feminine charms. "She'd make things very nice, Aliosha, wouldn't she?"

"But Frosia, I don't understand what you're talking about!"

"Why let slip such an opportunity. . . . You won't find another one like her; *how* she looks at you!"

The proposal stunned him by its wildness. And at the same time there was a nuance of concealed hope in his sisters' project. Frosia's eyes were candid; she offered him Marina's hand with a clear conscience—so they expected his early recovery? He made his idea more precise: "So you have destined Marina to be my widow?"

Misfortune had doubtless taught her to be vulgar. "You're ashamed to give people a ruble," she said, "and they'd be glad to get even a kopek!"

Or perhaps she did not know anything?

"No, Frosia, it won't work. . . . You see, I've got a cancer. . . ." Without an effort he removed her hands with which she had covered her face in fright. "It's all right, the old house is breaking up, that's all. The doctor said that my parenchyma was in a bad state, too . . . see?" And to distract her from gloomy thoughts, he added: "Have a look, won't you, please, and see whether my water is still warm?"

CHAPTER 29

# We Go Through a War

MY MEETINGS WITH Alexei Nikitich became less frequent. I did not wish to disturb his enforced rest and, of course, I could not have taken Ziamka's place. My days grew rather dull. All alone I knocked about our favorite Oceanic quay, visited the suburbs of the great city which was awaiting new upheavals and dropped in at the old Chinese theatre to see how Yang Tze's exploits were reflected in art. Sometimes I stood idly on the shore watching primitive sampans of the olden days swaying on the waves among gigantic floating islands. . . . Left to myself I meditated upon the future stages: the Ocean appeared to me as an endless space enveloped in a rosy mist. (Thus every promised dawn begins in dreams!) A tree stood in the foreground; a long horizontal branch with glittering leaves hid all other details from me. I liked the unfinished landscape, because it freed me from the necessity of extending the framework of my tale, and also because no one knows what events are concealed within the spectral, rain-colored shell of the future! . . . It still moved with the wind, is still dissolved in water and still lies buried in the entrails of the earth: it has not yet coalesced into crystals . . . and who can say what history will do with them!

Then Alexei Nikitich would come to join me. He scornfully discarded my lyrical branch of ignorance and laziness, urging me to look about me and see. In the mist human shadows were born and began to move so fast and so stormily that I had not even time to distinguish the color of these heroes' faces; then I knew the consternation once experienced by the poet of the little island of Patmos. And so I saw. . . .

. . . One day in January, on the nineteenth anniversary of the assassination of Yang Tze, at the season when the Malayan rivers swell and southwest winds scatter fogs over the archipelago, the Old World created a new diversion. In Java, the center of the Malayan People's Republic, an uprising broke out that spread to the adjacent islands. A dictator emerged, calling himself Abong-Abong, after an extinguished

254

volcano in Sumatra.[1] The fame of the great Yang Tze still frightened
some people! Everything that was considered contaminated by ideas
from the mainland, even palm trees, dogs and poor people's hovels,
was destroyed. Native Communists were massacred by hand, and the
Sarawak leader joked with the gloomy candor of Pigafetta that they
had hairy trunks like banana trees and abounded in gluey red sap. The
revolutionary parties and territorial defense units retreated to Sumatra,
carrying with them the bodies of the fallen martyrs.

The whole world looked upon all this in torpor. The newspapers
stained one's fingers red, so bloody were their reports. But the mas-
sacres sent a wave of anger through the whole Northern Federation of
Socialist Republics. Countless crowds stood on squares with bared
heads while on tele-screens red wooden coffins, ten in a row,
passed to their final resting place. The silence was broken by women's
hysterical cries and the roar of the overstrained producers. Grief wiped
out racial differences: the faces of Whites, Negroes and Yellows were
of the same ashen color. These were the most awesome burials in the
history of mankind. Almost a billion and a half men and women invisibly took part in the funeral ceremonies. On the night of mourning
it was forbidden to use the air for the transmission of plays and movies
or for visiting friends by radio, and all the lights of the cities were
turned out. In the primeval mist that descended upon the continent a
white mother in Dublin lamented the death of the brown children of
Borneo. The following morning the masses demanded military intervention. They paraded in the streets, carrying horrible effigies of
severed heads and arms, and they shouted the slogan: "We want to go
to Borneo." In some places portraits of the latest theoreticians of war
who had won fame without ever winning a battle were carried upside

[1] The details are mine. Kurilov frowned at the appearance of Abong: "What
kind of man is he?" he asked.

"He comes of well-to-do citizens of Sarawak. He calls himself Abong to suggest
that the 'Malayan volcano has awakened,'" I explained. "However, the natives call
him Mia, which means orang-outang. His temperament is the result of his
equatorial origin, the bourgeois element that supports him, and a badge bearing
the initials G.P.T. The General Providence Trust, now ripe for world ventures,
received from powerful clients orders for bilithon, lead, Sarawak petrol, gold,
copper, antimony and other imported materials. In brief, he is a stooge."

"Stooges were sent to defeat us too; Wrangel, Kolchak and others, but in vain.
How could all this happen? . . . Lack of vigilance? . . . Breaking of the weakest
links?"

All I could do was to cite examples proving that history had often been a
manual of mistakes.

down. Asia recalled the ancient Mongolian proverb about the camel who did not stir until the wolf [2] had devoured half its thigh. The government postponed action either to save its resources or to allow the popular fury to mount.

This Old World attack took us by surprise: no one would have imagined that Oceania would be the theatre of the next clash. Shortly before, commercial airliners that plied between the Fiji Islands and Lima via Capetown reported that the Old World fleet (the so-called Fleet of Direct Action) was concentrated in the region of New Zealand, but naval manoeuvres of the Checkered Flag ships [3] off the shores of the Federation were an everyday occurrence: the Old World posed as the protector of the sovereignty of the Philippine People's Republic.[4] Events followed one another so quickly that it was as though a scroll had unfolded and stretched down to the ground, revealing all the hieroglyphics of horror.[5] And although diplomatic relations were not yet broken, a continuation of the aggression was to be expected in the form of parachute landing parties, which by capturing bases were to secure the success of landing parties from the sea. On the day of the burials in Sumatra, the ambassador of the Old World, sweating copiously and casting worried glances at the windows behind which a noisy demonstration was taking place, informed the People's Commissar for Foreign Affairs that the Malayan misunderstanding was caused by disorders in the G.P.T.,[6] that the squadron of the Fleet of Direct Action had already set out with the mission of restoring order on the islands,[7] arresting Abong and investigating the whole affair. All this was the sheerest insolence, and the ambassador himself was frightened of it, even though his airplane was at that moment perched on the roof of the embassy, ready to take off. The People's Commissar, a man of Japanese nationality, whose politeness was proverbial, without stopping the interview telephoned to the Supreme

[2] A reference to Jonathan Wolf, vice-president of the G.T.P.

[3] The combined flag of the future coalition had six stripes of different colors, one for each of the participants.

[4] Coconut glycerine for explosives, chromium and iron ores.

[5] January 14: capture of Borneo, Java and Celebes.

January 16: burial of victims in Sumatra.

January 17 (at night): explosion in the Canton embassy.

January 18 (morning): capture of Sumatra by Abong-Mia, sudden attacks on industrial regions in Europe, explosion in Niebelungenstadt, complete destruction of air bases on Formosa, appearance of enemy submarines on European communication routes.

[6] M. Mackenzie, the head of the company, had shortly before gone to his Maker to settle accounts for his crimes.

[7] "And they were going to foreign waters!" Kurilov observed with a smile.

War Council, asking whether the time had not yet come to throw out this obese and stinking hypocrite.[8] On that same night the explosion in the Canton embassy took place. Engineered as a provocation it destroyed several city blocks. The rulers of the two-headed continent did everything possible to bring events to a crisis.

At daybreak on January 18 masses of light bombing planes appeared above the bays of the Gulf of Siam. The night was cold, the sea heavy. During the first salvos of the anti-aircraft batteries, tanks began to crawl toward the shore and, still half submerged in water, opened fire. Rattling their caterpillar threads, fumbling with the mooring hooks in front of them, during the flashes of gunfire they seemed to be shaking the water off before climbing ashore. Although some of them did not stop even after receiving several hits, the first phalanx was disrupted by artillery fire. One moved straight upon a battery; standing on its tail it was smashed by point-blank fire, but inside no human bodies were found, only a mass of twisted mechanisms. . . . The second phalanx was supported by gunfire from cruisers of which the silhouettes could be seen moving lazily in the misty drizzle. Then came a wave of shock planes sowing death and concealing something else in its thick mass. The fighting planes of the defenders dashed to meet them and were crushed by their overwhelming numbers. Swaying on the high waves, bristling with coil-pipes of tommy guns, motorized launches moved toward the shore. As though cut in two the cloud of shock planes opened up, and parachute battalions dropped from the gap; they landed beyond the barbed-wire fences, capturing a half-mile-wide strip within seventeen minutes. A fourth and fifth wave of tanks rolled over, and it was still unknown how many of them were concealed on the bottom of the gulf. The parachute landing party separated the defenders into two parts; resistance was crushed. Sappers were driving the last nails into the gangways when gently rolling on the swell the first oceanic transport, the *President,* approached the beach. From its belly emerged rumbling armored monsters; the air shook, and in comparison with the noise of these machines the roar of a storm would be like the bark of little puppies entangled in one's feet. A second aerial battle took place, with the same result as the first; nothing could now prevent the unloading of new transports with fuel and equipment for building airfields on land. An hour later Pnom-Penkh and Banama-on-Mekong were under bombardment. Similar operations took place on the coastline of Cochin-

[8] The mobilization of the eastern regions of the Federation had already been decided upon, and this telephone conversation served only to express the feelings of the People's Commissar.

China. Shock gunboats acting jointly with aircraft forced all three beds of the Mekong. Indo-China had been occupied, and war broke loose upon a peaceful and flourishing land.[9]

The main forces of the Fleet of Defense and Manoeuvre (and the Federation's eastern squadrons as well) did not leave the Mediterranean where they were stationed. Atop the quarter-mile-high mast on Gibraltar (for direct ultra-short-wave communication with the fleet) the fortress flag hung drooping in the still air. The High Command of the Federation awaited the moment when the main direction of the attack would be disclosed. The straits of the Asiatic seas were blocked, the Sea of Japan became an inland sea. Surface vessels and planes were mobilized for the protection of the coastline. Stratoplanes plied between the continents like phantoms. The newspapers gave a great deal of publicity to the exploits of the commander of a certain flight of planes, a Korean who made a deep fighting reconnaissance in the direction of Polynesia. The Federation silently accepted the blows that were dealt it, and this behavior suited the Old World very well. The Checkered Powers thought that the most advantageous military routes would be opened up by the conquest of Asia. Only thence was it possible to move gradually westward. The density of Europe's industrial enterprises, and its armed working-class population, precluded the possibility of quickly occupying this continent. By carrying on stubborn reconnaissance activities along the western coastline, by launching diversionist landing parties [10] and by creating a number of secondary theatres of war, the Old World painstakingly kept up the fiction that the whole blow against the East was only a deliberate and short-sighted provocation.

Simultaneously with the attack on Indo-China, in order to confuse the adversary, the Checkered Powers planned a heavy flanking blow in Central Africa intended to transfer the operational direction to Europe. Here they concentrated considerable numbers of South American troops. George Shvint, the commander of the Fleet of De-

[9] We borrow the description of this attack from the *Canton Soviet News*, No. 22 (6757).

[10] On March 4, taking advantage of a rainy night, eight amphibian tanks landed from submarines near Newcastle and proceeded along the highway without arousing anyone's suspicions. The guards saluted them, and little children on their way to school peered into their slits. Informed of the disposition of the defensive troops, the enemy set fires near the objectives he wanted to destroy. Two hours later naval squadrons appeared, and worked for only half an hour. Profiting from the confusion, the tanks managed to embark and leave, except one that broke into a hangar and joyfully crushed a number of airplanes and projectors. Similar deep raids against industrial centers were repeated in Le Havre, Hamburg, Riga and Helgoland; later they were completely unsuccessful.

fense and Manoeuvre, under whose very nose the military transports had passed, was dismissed and handed over to the courts. A neutral Central African power, which bore the name of its former motherland, submitted to violence with a merry widow's readiness,[11] though its merchant marine suffered damage from submarines near the Atlantic coast. Even the chief of the expeditionary force, General Gregor, did not know the dimensions and nature of the operation until the completion of the landing. Having reached the ruins of Archambault, he waited for the signal to move on Khartum and further, across the Red Sea. But the objective of this trans-African raid was not the capture of neutral Sudan or Egypt. The real plan was, immediately after a diversion in Suez,[12] to cross over to the adjacent Arabian Peninsula, penetrate northwards with lightning speed,[13] invade the southern Russian steppes and cut off Europe and North Africa from the New World. The fantastic character of the plan was to serve as its camouflage, and it was to be based on the powerful rear guard of the Southeastern African Union. The campaign began; 150-ton land battleships crawled along the electrified Upper Nile directing thousands of tele-automatic tanks.[14] The armies marched within this steel fortress, and the wings of a powerful air fleet served them as a reliable protection against the hazards of war. But the Suez diversion ended in failure (April 26). The 11th squadron of the Fleet of Defense and Manoeuvre sailed around the Red Sea and, leaving a guard of cruisers, returned to Malta.

Then, changing the strategic plan, General Gregor transferred the direction to Cairo, along the famous trunkline of the three C's. An army of three million, sending mobile units from the left flank, that is, from the desert, moved along the Nile, fighting minor engagements; more accurately, the North African army of defense did not interfere with them.[15] The expeditionary hordes were now only at two days' marching distance from Abu-Hammed, when suddenly impressive

[11] However, it managed to utter a widow's "ah-ah" when the two-million-strong army of the Southeastern African Union crossed its territory to join Gregor.

[12] To cut off the Fleet of Defense and Manoeuvres from access to the Indian Ocean.

[13] Part of the plan was to stir up the Moslem world on the way. An explosion in Arabia could first of all become a stimulus to the backward Moslem divisions impressed into service in the Sudan. Thus the ancient path of Mahomet coincided with the oil route from Iraq, Syria and the Caucasus.

[14] They were stuffed with explosives because the very purpose of their creation was to send them to certain destruction.

[15] Even when Gregor began to blow up the locks in order to cut off access to the fleet of river defense, the North African army did not resist, and this fact set him wondering.

units of the Federation's army, led by a certain commander Feisi, appeared near Aden and on the same day crossed to Somaliland, the extreme northern boundary of the Central African power. Its ambassador had diplomatic hysterics in Canton, but incriminating evidence in the form of two million foreign troops prevented him from lending his indignation even a shade of sincerity. The Central African power now had either to enter the war or, taking advantage of the fact that its frontiers were guaranteed by the Federation, to stop supplying the army of occupation through Kabinda. Fearing its friends no less than its foes,[16] the power chose the second course of action, and the Southeastern African Union immediately sent out another army to its frontiers.[17] To avoid encirclement by Feisi, Gregor moved into the Libyan desert. His position became precarious. Regular raids by planes from Cairo broke his communications with South Africa along the eastern coast. All these automatic crocodiles, iron rhinoceroses and mechanical Harpies were stuck in the sand, under furious tropical rains, living on the scanty supplies that were somehow dragged to them from Gambia via Timbuctoo, along the ancient caravan route through the oases of Tintum and Mo-Mo. Discontent broke out among the troops, epidemics started, machines were abandoned. Beasts of prey began to follow in the tracks of the unsuccessful conquerors, and their mangy hides soon recovered the lustre of fatter days. The commander was nervous, he demanded that his soldiers hold out heroically until aid reached them, although it was more sensible to hope for a miracle, which actually did take place. Rumors spread of an internecine struggle in Feisi's armies. Whether the Iranian was seduced by the opportunity to ascend the ancient throne of Axum with its sycamores,[18] or whether he was offended at being commanded by an obscure Uzbek from near Chardjuy, the fact is that he stopped here with his divisions and, until his public trial, spread out among the uplands of the beautiful Kafa. Gregor joined him for support and a rest; their common life flowed like a ballad,[19] and this state of affairs lasted until the northern army of defense once again began to press them.

Then, without weakening the pressure in Indo-China, and multiply-

[16] We recall a cartoon from the Birmingham *Maritime Worker,* representing the discomforts of a proprietor whose apartment was invaded by two million visitors with guns.

[17] To serve as an armed corridor for supplying Gregor.

[18] Feisi bore the name of a once-famous Iranian poet, and it may be correct to assume that he had some imagination. Later the causes of his treachery and double-dealing were found in the social position of his ancestors.

[19] Gregor wrote in his memoirs that this was the happiest period of his life.

ing the raids in Europe, which led to the militarization of a fifty-mile coastal zone,[20] the high command decided to come to Gregor's aid. From Australian ports the largest ocean liners transported six hundred thousand men to Africa, with the most powerful equipment. A caravan surrounded by a mighty convoy was making its way toward Mombasa, reconnaissance squadrons clearing its path. A second group was about to be landed. Shortly before, enemy submarines had moved toward Socotra Island at the entrance to the Gulf of Aden, in order to bar the Fleet of Defense and Manoeuvre from the Indian Ocean. However, our airplanes sank some of these, and the others submerged and were captured when they ran out of fuel. Immediately after that. . . .

(Looking back at these movements of gigantic and still unbroken armies, Kurilov and I vainly tried to discover unconquerable heroes, striking war cries, dizzying battle scenes in the style of Uccello or Salvator Rosa—all the tinsel which used to adorn the bloody chaos of war. True, we encountered amazing warriors, and memorized many heroic incidents, but thirty-six million armed people, killing one another simultaneously, cannot be an object of enthusiasm for the historian or poet. . . .)

For the peoples of the Federation the war was above all humdrum, heavy labor. Our immense fatherland did not send its sons forth to rob weaker neighbors or steal other people's wealth, and for that reason their exploits were only a duty done faithfully to the end. Enormous masses of men dressed in the colors of war crowd my memory. Let us pick out one of them and follow his fate. His name is Samuel Bothead, a Negro, thirty-eight years of age. His biography was not yet completed, but Kurilov and I knew that he would be celebrated by the people, who would say that at Shanghai his face was as black as the sun on a day of wrath.

We had for a long time intended to visit him, and while we prepared to do so he was placed at the head of the Mediterranean Fleet of Defense and Manoeuvre, replacing the disgraced Shvint. As correspondents for the *Canton News* we went to Aden and interviewed him on his flagship *Lenin*. For about an hour we were kept in a well-isolated room while our identity was checked on by the radio.[21] Fortunately

[20] The lighthouses went out, the seas were deserted, the cities plunged into darkness, the people lived stealthily. Kurilov and I walked over armored hills. A wounded moon was shining on the wet concrete. We said sadly to each other: "War; it's war!"

[21] Alexei Nikitich was angry. ". . . Go into that cable box (that is to say the place where the anchor cable is kept, or in other words, the prison) yourself, if you must, and spare me your artistic details!"

I shared his indignation. It was dark and stinking in there; rats scuttled about

for us, in the commentaries to a thick volume published for the use of academicians the names of Krylov and Leontiev, names similar to ours, were discovered. . . . We were led into Bothead's reception room, which contained his library, composed of the old mathematicians of warfare and Shakespeare. A little breeze streaming through the bull's eye stirred the thread shrouds on a model of an ancient frigate. We sat down and I explained what we had come for; Bothead was tactful enough not to be astonished by anything. He shoved water, tobacco and ashtrays toward us. We were often interrupted; and although everything here was automatized, secret reports were handed to the commander in the old way, in a locked iron box.

He began to tell us the story of his life, and I experienced Marina's difficulties when she came to see Kurilov in order to write his biography. The superficial facts he gave us were only the framework of a great destiny; their roots led to the events of a strange and incomprehensible century. Verily, one must create a whole universe to enhance the existence of a grain of sand! . . . Thus his great-grandfather had been bought in the Sudan by a certain British baronet as a gift to his nephews. After they were killed by Hindus, the old slave was sent to the Black Republic to manage the plantation of his inconsolable master. The lives of the second and third Botheads, simple farmhands, do not contain enough adventure to fill even a couple of interesting lines. The great-grandson, like millions of other children, left his family at the age of eleven. For seven years he worked in the port installations of Pernambuco. He was fired for annoying the daughter of a White engineer: too often his admiring and unblinking eyes accompanied her.

An immense greenish space extended in front of the quay; even then there were not enough ships to saturate it completely. Human reason is inclined to fill every emptiness with images; hunger lends them emphatic reality. Pascal, who was horrified by the emptiness of the universe, certainly never starved like Samuel Bothead and never visited Pernambuco! One day, as the Black boy sat there lost in torpor and apathy, a fairy-tale magician approached him, assuming for the sake of variety the shape of a captain of a schooner. A deep scar from

---

and salt water seeped through the walls. Moreover, the same material of which we were created was to serve as the raw material for this descendant of ours. Did not Kurilov demand respect for himself because nature had leased him this material before leasing it to Bothead?

"And how about vigilance?" I reminded Kurilov.

"Let them ask about us in Canton."

"Very well then, we'll do it in a manner more in line with Socialist Realism."

a knife wound crossed his right eye-socket, and from his left one there looked out dangerous archipelagoes, lilac bays, conquered storms and women, the wind and the wine he had drunk; the sea loves good-for-nothing fellows. Having walked all around the bench, he asked the unemployed Negro whether he did not wish to work as a pilot on his sailing boat that plied between Fortaleza and Paranagua.[22]

". . . He was the skeleton and ghost of an old-fashioned pirate. Mornings, he climbed on deck, belching, with a scarf around his neck and a naked belly button. He poked the compass with his finger to ascertain whether it was sitting firmly, uttered a curse that was like an explosion of a rocket and again went down to his cabin to guzzle rum with sarsaparilla. Over his stinking cot, nailed to the wall with a knife, hung the photograph of a long-nosed wench with bared breasts and an enormous bow on her garter; usually he clinked glasses with this prostitute! But I am thankful to him, because first, . . ." Bothead spoke thus, bending his fingers to count, "he taught me not to vomit. Second, he put me in touch with comrades who knew a thing or two about surplus value. Third, he proved to me that the degree of human bestiality is not determined by the color of one's skin. Fourth, he brought me to the sea. . . ."

A year and a half later Bothead signed a contract with a steamship company for a forty-year term, pledging himself not to get married before reaching the rank of captain.[23] He was sent to a school from which he graduated as an ocean-going pilot. At the age of twenty-four he became fourth assistant on a ship travelling between America and the ports of the Federation. During the American-African war he was appointed as midshipman [24] on the old battleship *Alvares Cabral.* When the South American general strike broke out, the crew of this ship mutinied but was not supported by the rest of the fleet. The *Cabral* fled and was overtaken only at night when, having lost speed as a result of air bombardments, she was tossing on heavy seas. Summoned to surrender, the *Cabral* answered by opening fire. A duel between one and many took place. They pelted her with torpedoes; she dodged them as well as she could. Battered, with a smashed stern, scarcely afloat, she still did not run down the battle flag. The crew

[22] All of Bothead's biography is the work of Alexei Nikitich. I followed with interest the evolution of reminiscences from the book he had read in his childhood, enriched by his own personal experience. I recognized the very words, Pernambuco, Fortaleza, Arakaju, resembling bird calls in a tropical forest at noon.

[23] On the two-headed continent there was a law forbidding the poor to marry, so as to avoid producing more beggars and rebels.

[24] Gardia marina.

jumped into the water; they were picked out by searchlights and machine-guns. No one understood how Bothead managed to save himself from hell. . . . For several years he remained on land engaged in the obscure and unsung work of an organizer of the revolutionary forces. Later, after his flight to the Federation, he piloted its merchant ships, was admitted to the naval academy and. . . . At this point another report was brought in. Bothead rose and gave orders that we be given a cutter. Something had happened that overshadowed the importance of our visit. Kurilov had not even had time to pack his pipe with Bothead's tobacco (fi-irst-rate!). Our surmises proved correct: the squadron was getting under way.[25]

By a few vigorous blows Bothead captured the islands near Madagascar, thus securing air and supply bases for his fleet. Another squadron set out for the Cocos Islands transformed into a base for his reconnaissance. This squadron informed Bothead about the movements of his adversary and cut the communications between Africa and Australasia in a zone from the equator to the twentieth parallel south. Bothead surmised that Detter Sr.[26] did not count on a sortie by the Fleet of Defense and Manoeuvre which was only half as strong as the combined fleets of the Checkered Powers; he also knew that even under the most favorable conditions it would take Detter two weeks to get from Java to the meridian of the Seychelles Islands. The weather forecast indicated that the adversary would try landings right now, while Gregor had still not surrendered. The somewhat crude boldness of the Negro admiral compelled his White opponents to steer a southward course and throw adequate protective forces around the Coconut Islands, but nothing remained there except tin cans and other similar traces of former human habitation. Once again the squadron changed its course northwestward, in the direction of the Seychelles and Mombasa. And only when the Fleet of Direct Action moved in amidst the Amirante and Mascarene Islands, did it become clear whither the reconnaissance planes had vanished and what had happened to the neutral ships and cruisers sent ahead of the rest. Detter undertook an active reconnaissance, but Bothead was already busy. . . .

The Checkered Powers' Fleet was dismembered, the transports scattered in all directions, and from those which had not been sunk hostages were taken among the high-ranking officers. When the government order arrived to leave the neutral islands, the batteries were

[25] The secret message reported the departure of Old World convoys from Australian bases.
[26] The commander-in-chief of the Fleet of Direct Action.

already aboard, the aviation was ready to take off, and Bothead himself had had time to thank the governors of the islands with precious
gifts for their forced hospitality. The Indian Ocean was lost to the
Old World for a long time.

After the failure of the African landing, the enemy intensified his attacks in Asia. The attempt to force the Indo-Chinese foothills lasted
six months and developed into fierce positional warfare. Concentration of technical means was of no avail. Everything was thrown into
the balance, including bacteria, albumin poisons, the pollution of the
reservoirs, clouds of termites, the abuse of the white flag. The war
became hysterical: it scratched against concrete walls, seeking a fissure
through which to poke its sting. Subdevilite was tried; its first trophies
remained on the field like mummies, untouched by decay, yet a means
was found to deal with every new instrument of destruction in the
shortest possible time. Ordinary cooling balloons caused the new gas
to disintegrate and flow in lilac puddles into the gutters through the
action of ultra-short currents. The attempt to find a vulnerable spot
in the Federation failed, and the front remained stationary.

Then, trying to bypass the obstacle, the Checkered Powers landed
considerable forces near Canton [27] and, feeling out their way with the
help of their superior aviation, they crawled slowly along the coastline northward and southward. They sought a weak spot in the Federation, which was fighting on numerous fronts; their intention was
to hurl against it a new army of three million men that had just been
formed in South America. By agreement with his government Detter
Sr. intended to direct his main blow through Shanghai into the heart
of Socialist China. The motives for this hasty plan were naïve. The
socialist reorganization of small industries in the Yang Tze valley had
been attended by special difficulties; this fact inspired hope that the
population would largely support the invaders and that it would be
possible for their armies to hold out even if their sea communications
were cut.[28] The commander-in-chief issued orders for the training of

[27] The operations against Macao and Hongkong had previously determined the
fate of the Federation's second capital.

[28] We also visited the *Fraternité*, Detter Sr.'s flagship. We did not get there at
a very pleasant moment. Before the drawn-up ranks of his sailors, the commander
was receiving a delegation of Chinese peasants; we had the impression that their
pigtails were not genuine. The delegates spoke glibly of the "horror of socialist
life" and in one voice promised almost no less than a general popular uprising as
soon as the armies of the Old World entered central China. Detter, a flourishing
old man weighing about two hundred pounds, pressed the hands of these dubious
peasants and mentally tried on the laurels of the "liberator from the socialist yoke."

advance shock battalions destined to effect a landing under conditions of chaos and terror.[29] By that time almost three-quarters of all the transports had come through Australasia, and the emissaries of Detter's reconnaissance failed to note any increase in military traffic on the Lisbon-Shanghai trunk-line.

Suddenly the Indian *Popular Newspaper* of August 5 printed a report that Bothead with a fleet of two hundred and sixty pennants had cast anchor in the Gulf of Peter the Great, at Sasebo, Nagasaki and adjacent ports, that the eastern and western divisions of the Fleet of Defense and Manoeuvre were now combined under his command, that tremendous demonstrations greeted the arrival of his squadrons, that the fleet would scatter in the nearby ports for a "Seamen's two-week excursion to all latitudes," that representatives of neutral powers had been invited to Vladivostok to taste the local cabbage soup and *kasha* and that everyone had seen the Black admiral in a white naval jacket and a red order for his exploits in the Seychelles. A news agency confirmed Bothead's arrival on a stratoplane.[30] Spies reported that the Fleet of Defense and Manoeuvre still occupied its Mediterranean bases in the same numbers as before. If guns and battleships had not been in question, one would have had to assume that supernatural powers had intervened in this situation. In brief, the chief of the intelligence bureau was dismissed with a reprimand, and Admiral Detter himself had a nervous breakdown and resigned.[31] He was replaced by his son, an educated and gifted fleet commander, who did not resemble his father even in his features. Heeding Nelson's recommendation

[29] Groups of noncoms of two hundred men each were placed in special chambers where they were subjected to every conceivable hardship through the use of various machines. Boats loaded with men were thrown into water foaming with exploding shells, shrapnel burst over them, gas lacerated their nostrils and lungs; they were blinded by artificial flashes of guns and projectors, boiling filth was poured over their heads, bullets ricocheted against the buttons of their coats and smashed the oars in their hands; they were submerged under water, strangled by maddened comrades, thrown up to the black and tattered skies by exploding bombs, and they were supposed to row, sing gay songs and keep on rowing. According to secret reports, the number of draftees unable to endure these ordeals reached forty-eight per cent of the total; but those who managed to stand their ground on the edge of healthy idiocy were capable of setting out to conquer hell itself. These methods of training were abandoned after an uprising known as "the noncom mutiny."

[30] But no one had enough imagination to use the same method for transferring almost five million tons of metal: the ships themselves!

[31] His affliction, of a kind never seen before, was accompanied by vomiting, convulsions of the limbs and the disintegration of the memory. It was sad to watch the brave commander sitting in a deep chair and constantly repeating the words: "Black tramp, shoe shine, bought head!"

never to despise the enemy in order not to weaken one's hatred of him, he had for a long time carefully studied the military style and manner of thinking of his future adversary. The son assumed his post at a difficult moment, complicated by the possibility of action on the part of middle-class India.

Detter silently shared the fears of his staff. Gathered into one strong fist, the Federation's fleet was now capable of contesting the Checkered Powers' naval superiority; under these conditions, the landing of a shock army suddenly assumed the character of a wretched adventure. It was clear that, if at the critical moment of the clash Bothead achieved air superiority for twenty minutes, the whole algebra of the war would turn against Detter and that he would have to take a seat in a chair beside his father. Then, having interpreted in his own way the meaning of the "Seamen's two-week excursion," and following the ancient strategists' dubious precept always to finish undertakings once they are begun, he decided to force a landing near Shanghai and obtained the promise of the commander-in-chief of the land forces to accelerate his march northward. As early as August 7 (instead of August 15, as originally planned) Detter seized Formosa and transformed it into a supply base for his future Shanghai front. Acres of tanks awaited only the touch of a living human hand. At daybreak on August 10 the first transports carrying specially trained troops were to approach Shanghai.

The Federation's counter-plans were as different from the plans of the Checkered Powers as their war aims were different from those of their opponents. The technical level of the two adversaries being equal, the socialist world relied on a supplementary weapon inaccessible to the general staffs of the Old World. The tactical value of this weapon was once again tested during the transfer of Bothead's ships from one hemisphere to the other.[32] The Fleet of Defense and Manoeuvre was assigned the task of permitting Detter's shock army to land and later, after its equipment and fuel had been exhausted in three days of stubborn fighting, to cut its sea communications. The enormous hordes, squeezed into a narrow zone between the sea and the line of defense, unable to deploy and manoeuvre, armed only with individual weapons, would then meet the same fate as Gregor.[33]

[32] It took strenuous efforts on Bothead's part to direct into the proper channels the almost elemental courage of his sailors. Kurilov recalls that he ordered the court-martial of a captain of one of his destroyers in the stock-hole of which a mechanic had died from over-exertion.

[33] When expounding his plan to the Supreme Defense Council, Bothead concluded with the following words: "Since the time when the first warship went out

Events revealed to Bothead that the enemy was trying to take advantage of the time he needed for repairs. Under these circumstances even one week of idleness might prove fatal. The commander-in-chief's order containing an analysis of the situation was discussed on the docks, in the workshops and below decks. The fleet challenged the factories to compete with it in efficiency; the sailors hastened to clean the still warm boilers. There was an angry and silent outburst of despair and courage. The two-week rest was reduced by executive order to ten days, but already on the night of August 9, when the enemy began to clear the mines from the approaches to Ning-Bo, Bothead informed his government that his main forces would be ready by the 11th. The impetuousness with which Detter ran into the trap automatically speeded up Bothead's time-table. Long before he had appeared in the East, the Federation's entire Asiatic submarine fleet had been sent to the intermediate and far bases of the Checkered Powers;[34] now a coded message from the *Koloman* [35] urged Bothead to occupy positions astride the communications between the landing forces and Manila and the Australasian ports. Earlier in the war squadrons of bombing planes had been gradually drawn here from the secondary fronts; now they were instructed to concentrate at once near Shanghai, even though the concentration of large numbers of aircraft might induce Detter to change his mind and pull his head out of the trap.

As soon as his preparations were completed, Bothead sent all his aviation for a visit to Detter's airfields on Formosa. At that time the island was one gigantic arsenal of all the conceivable instruments of warfare. The defensive air baggage was wiped out by numerical superiority, but, to tell the truth, the success of the attack was directly proportional to the attackers' losses. In compensation, masses of Old World bombers and tanks were transformed into piles of twisted scrap, into steel blocks, metal shavings and nothingness. Meanwhile the land battle had been going on for two days. The Old World had struck against the suburbs of Ning-Bo, which were encircled by concrete walls. That morning, the commander of the landing party, expressing

---

to sea, no fleet has ever had so simple and honorable a task. In my eyes, this task is to let history and the indignant nations give vent to their just anger and wreak their vengeance undeterred by any outside considerations. Our great mother, our socialist native land, must not be able to reproach us with indifference!"

[34] The Federation's High Command discovered the plans of the Old World concerning the attack on Shanghai, and as a result transferred part of the Mediterranean fleet to the East.

[35] Bothead's flagship.

the mood of his troops, threatened to surrender if he did not receive reinforcements before nightfall; toward the end of the day he reported that he had given the order to distribute all the reserves of shells to his exhausted armies. Late at night, two radiograms crossed each other on the ocean. Detter's instructed his bases to send out a convoy immediately to aid the Shanghai expedition; Bothead's reminded his submarine fleet that upon the accuracy of their destructive operations depended whether the inhuman tortures of this war would be lengthened or shortened.

Half an hour later the *Fraternité* received the first, almost panicky descriptions of the wild attack of Bothead's ships on the Old World convoys.[36] Omitting preliminary mine-sweeping operations, the submarines in chains three ranks deep tore into the ports. Those at the head were doomed to certain destruction.[37] The deeds of the submariners who managed to escape death were epic indeed. . . . In their situation, it was inadvisable to await the safe arrival of the floating store-rooms, and Detter decided to replace his sunken convoys with the guns of his eighty battleships. While the anchors were raised and the powder magazines filled with shells, the general staff worked out the battle order of the squadrons in the forthcoming action.[38] The *Fraternité* had another alarm when patrols of Tsushima reported that Bothead's main forces had put out to sea. Now it was too late to change their plans; if Detter renounced his expedition to the mouth of the Yang Tze Kiang, Bothead would undertake a similar raid, and the landing armies, caught by crisscross fire from the sea and the land fortifications, would be cut to pieces. To discover the location and disposition of Bothead's squadrons, Detter Jr. rushed westward after having executed a sweep in the northern direction.

The East China Sea was divided into twenty meridional zones, and a couple of destroyers accompanied by a flight of planes were assigned to each one. Every unit was instructed to stay within its own zone and to open fire without warning on any ship it met. The warships set out at daybreak. The light ripples of the sea were soon covered by a fog [39]

[36] Detter Jr.'s report contains an interesting sentence in which there is an echo of his unfortunate father: ". . . The strategy of naval warfare and the gentlemanlike traditions of the Fleet of Direct Action were never designed for a struggle against madmen!"

[37] The automatic vessels went first, but there were several rows of mine barrages, too.

[38] Detter's fleet moved in squadrons.

[39] The sea was tragically silent, and it seemed to Kurilov and myself that we were falling with vertiginous speed into an ever-widening black circle.

which seemed expressly created for all kinds of accidents.[40] The "sweep" that ran into Bothead's reconnaissance ended in the famous "massacre of destroyers" and had almost no results. Detter's officer who arranged on a map little flags with the names of the enemy ships was able to determine only fourteen of them during the entire night. Bothead's disposition and location remained secret; only the ultimate goal of his naval expedition was clear. At seven o'clock in the morning the news came from the shore of the first crushing attack by the screening force. It seemed to the Chinese armies that the great Yang Tze had returned to them to complete his work. . . . [41] Detter realized that the second and third attacks might prove decisive if he did not

[40] The first accident occurred on the left flank with the second pair of destroyers. The adversaries, who were sailing without lights, noticed each other when the collision was already inevitable; neither changed his course. Bothead's destroyer had the time to signal its tail destroyer to reduce speed and throw its machine-guns to starboard; the guns were given the angle of firing. The first flashes of disorderly salvos blinded those of the crew who were not killed. Their armor crackling, the ships crashed into each other; they listed, their keels almost touched, then they stopped. The left propeller of Bothead's destroyer broke through the wall of Detter's ship and one blade rummaged around in her enemy's insides until it broke. The tail destroyer's searchlights and guns hit the ship. In twenty seconds Detter's *Garcia* went to the bottom. Left with only one engine, Bothead's head destroyer changed places with the tail destroyer, and sank half an hour later. Ten minutes after that, Detter received reports of the loss of several other patrol boats after a short engagement. The steel broom of the "sweep" was rapidly losing its teeth.

Meanwhile the head destroyer of Bothead's tenth pair attacked four huge silhouettes. It reported to the commander of the flank that it had been repulsed by anti-mine fire and that it was pursuing its prey. A dozen planes took off from the nearest aircraft carrier. Sighting trains of fire from the exhaust pipes, the destroyer gave secret signals and, upon receiving a reply, illumined its victims. Searchlights irrupted into the darkness. In vain did the warships (amidst them crawled the decrepit *Nagato* that the aristocrats had taken away at the very beginning of the Japanese revolution) try to hide behind a smoke screen and change their course. The onrushing planes almost grazed their chimneys, two of the ships shuddered and broke while a fire broke out on the third. Reflections of the flames streamed in the water. In the confusion Bothead's destroyer came closer in a whirl of exploding fragments and exultantly discharged its reserve of torpedoes point-blank, until the *Nagato*, which had listed to one side, succeeded in slightly recovering itself; it opened its searchlights and with a hail of projectiles literally dissolved the heroic destroyer in the water. The tail destroyer, approaching the glow with a plane from its zone, reported that now only three large silhouettes were limping away southeastward. A second air attack did not take place; a flotilla of Detter's destroyers discovered the spy, and the wounded plane, streaking the sky with fire, fell on its own destroyer when it buried its nose in the water.

[41] Kurilov kept nudging me with his elbow and pointing at the heroic countrymen of Yang Tze: "What do you think of these Chinese kolkhoz girls, hm? . . . They get the idea of Soviet power, don't they?"

protect his landing troops by a powerful barrage. Only one report, like Noah's dove, offered some hope. The Federation's submarines, which had for some time shown an energy surpassing the capacities of men and machines and had suffered tremendous losses, were now obviously exhausted. Twenty-two convoys managed to break out of burning Manila; it occurred to Detter that five hundred out of a thousand transports could reach Shanghai and, supported by naval guns, evacuate part of the troops. His armada was approaching the shore at full speed, and three hours later his forward ships could open fire at the attacking screen. In order to bring into battle the largest possible number of guns at the same time, he was beginning to reorganize his lines when a countless number of air squadrons from the shore passed over him; there was something sinister in the fact that not one bomb was hurled at his disposition. Detter sent his own aircraft up, and the planes of the defenders retreated. Fearing that Bothead would appear at his flank, he recalled his planes, but the spear [42] of the Federation once more pierced his air fleet. Again a short engagement took place, and again the defenders' planes repeated their previous manoeuvre of running away. Keeping Detter's aviation busy, Bothead was preparing to deal the crushing knockout blow with his main forces.

His fleet was now proceeding from the north, drawn up in an arc opposite the deployed phalanx of Detter's ships.[43] The secret of his battle disposition was secured from the air and by squadrons of battleships on the flanks. At ten in the morning these broke through the adversary's screen and shooting small vessels on their way cleared the path for the attack. The air battle continued far to the south, when the great rout of the aircraft carriers began; at the same time Bothead's main forces set out to destroy the flanking battleships. This attack alone made all help to the expeditionary forces impossible; Detter had now to fight for his own life. He made convulsive attempts to take parallel courses and straighten out his crumpled flank, but again and again he found himself in the center of the deadly arc, with four hundred guns aimed at his heart.

First to fight were the automata, but the fierce dispute of these incredible, man-killing inventions did not last long; no doubt they lacked human hatred—so quickly did they strive to perish. They were followed by machines whose souls were living people. Everything that

[42] Having taken off in wedges, they had managed to reform into a spear.

[43] It seems incredible that with the highly developed art of fleet manoeuvring it was possible to catch one's adversary in the ancient crossed T. But history does not love the vanquished, and it is always their privilege to appear stupider than their adversaries.

carried planes or torpedoes rushed forward. The advance cutters hit mines and were destroyed at once. It was horrible to see that no one jumped from them into the water. Some of them exploded, smashing all around them and leaving, as on land, a deep funnel above which the water for a long time did not dare close. The two commanders-in-chief without leaving their conning towers saw all the details of the battle on screens, until the moment when complete chaos began.[44]

. . . It would be absurd to relate the further regroupings. Everything became confused; the ocean was crowded. Our memory which is powerless to grasp the whole throws light only on individual episodes.[45] This was the day of reckoning. . . .

A light vapor rose from the surface of the water warmed up by all this fury. Machine fell upon machine, and the affair was no longer being decided by the talent of the commanders, but by the mettle of the fighting masses. Dive bombers fell almost vertically on Detter's dreadnoughts, stung them and flew away, and the twisted smoke of the explosions was drawn into the funnels of their hurried flight. The Old World defended itself. Its ships, littered with wounded men and twisted iron, tried to flee to Macao. Dusk fell three hours before the usual time, the horizon was covered with a stinking mist. . . . Amidst a second of silence there resounded something like a deep sigh, and a shudder ran along the antennae of Detter's monsters when water irrupted into their ripped bottoms. The enemy's broken line crumbled, lost its will power and ceased firing. One could see four dreadnoughts, their decks swept clean, as though they had been transformed into aircraft carriers, smoking, rocking and getting stuck in the swirling

[44] Moving my face close to the tele-screen, I saw with amazement two enormous ships, duellists that had imprudently approached each other, both wounded and with a heavy list, clumsily circling around the same spot.

[45] I recall that above the sea, where masts of sunken ships with wet pennants still protruded from the water, two clouds of planes appeared. Their clash was like the battle of the fallen angels and a multiple collision of airtrains. Thousands of aircraft furiously fought each other; they dived, rammed, cracked into the enemy at full speed, paying with their death for a shortlived moment of heroic rapture. They swarmed, blazed, smoked, merged in full flight and, wrapped in flames, went down. Those that were cautious and retreated were immediately pursued. Rocket throwers and anti-aircraft batteries were silent lest they hit their own fellows. Madness seized the combatants' minds. Suddenly one of Detter's destroyers opened a furious barrage at this howling clot of hole-riddled metal, flying wings and human daring. This broke the hypnotic apathy of the ships. . . .

"Wait a minute," I cried to Kurilov through the deafening noise, trying to bring some kind of order into this rabid confusion, "let's begin from the beginning! Stop. . . ."

And the battle began anew, and we, the stage-managers of events, were unable to direct the forces we ourselves had created.

water. The televisors were out of commission. Bothead took off from a catapult and directed the pursuit in a plane, until an accidental explosion smashed the desk in front of him and wounded him.

The final battle took place on the shore. In many places the destructive machines were destroyed in the battle: their armor was crumpled and their steel fists broken; hand-to-hand fighting finished the engagement. Detter's rapid tanks deserted to the Federation, and his own artillery fired at the fleeing infantrymen. From early morning the armies were locked together as closely as fingers. By noon the whole shore had a heavy smell of men, dead and alive. By night the armies' terrible grip on each other began to weaken. The muscles on the effeminate barbarian hand were broken. . . .

This ended the Asiatic epic of the war, that lasted almost two years. The Old World lost its head and extinguished with human blood the fires which broke out in its rear. The Federation had every opportunity to transfer operations to the two-headed continent; it was clear that the very appearance of the Federation's armies would arouse forces of proletarian gravitation in the masses. (If anyone ever visits Samuel Bothead, let him question him in greater detail about that next-to-the-last clash of the worlds.) [46]

[46] For the last time Kurilov and I visited the mutilated plain. We walked and did not notice the dead. It was a late, cool and very clear evening. A pouring rain had just fallen, a rare event in August in these latitudes. Nature hastened to wash away the traces of its children's fury. On the wet soil bonfires were burning. The patrols no longer needed to take cover. We approached one. Two Japanese sitting on a tattered, worn-out *tatami* silently ate their traditional meal of rice with turnips. A third man, leaning against an enormous solenoid spool, stood absentmindedly at the side, watching the flashing of the chopsticks in his comrades' hands or listening to the crackle of the burning logs. His Russian face, spattered by the mire of battle, seemed familiar to us.

"Hello, war!" Kurilov said to him and with embarrassment added a few words about the joy of victory.

The man did not turn around and did not answer. It seemed to us that, before dropping from exhaustion, he was already thinking—he, the master!—about the tomorrow of the planet.

# CHAPTER 30

# The Third Rung of Her Ladder

SOMETIMES, NOT MORE THAN ONCE A WEEK, Liza was invited to perform at concerts. One of her acquaintances who arranged programs of entertainment came to her when he could get no one better. Liza was not asked whether she wished to perform; she was merely told the time and the place. He paid from fifty to five hundred rubles for an appearance. Of all the caterers in the line of dramatic rehashes he was known as the most generous. But he paid Liza only twenty-five rubles. From time to time, instead of money he gave her a piece of cloth for a blouse or a coupon for a meal. She was announced as an actress in the Moscow theatres, because she was not on the staff of any of them. She had to do her number first, while the audience was getting settled and the front rows were still empty. Having got accustomed to this situation, she always arrived long before the beginning of the program.

Never before had she experienced the need of being alone with herself. Now she went on foot to every cheap play that came along. The dark streets were equally suitable for robbery or rendezvous. That month the street lamps burned with a dimmed light, and the newspapers attacked the inefficiency of the transportation system. Suddenly she recalled that she was going to a concert which had been arranged to wind up a conference on railroads. Its mediocre quality could be inferred from the very fact that she had been included in the program. Oh, surely, this would be a club situated in some former private chapel; the ceiling would have been lowered a little and the place decorated in conformity with the superintendent's taste! She vividly imagined the artists' table with bottles of lemonade and sandwiches. . . . And so it was. She sat listening to the booming voice of the speaker in the adjacent hall. He kept concluding his speech, then warming up again, and the desired end continually slipped away from him. Liza chose one of the most substantial sandwiches and ate it in a corner. . . . It was good, so she took a second one.

Meanwhile the artists began to gather. A lady with a disagreeable, made-up face took a talking doll out of a box, frightening because of its likeness to a human, while a lightning calculator walked from corner to corner alternately touching his Adam's apple and ruffling up his hair so that he would resemble a certain famous mathematician. The entertainment began, but the program had been changed, and Liza's number now came at the very end, so that she could eat the sandwiches at her leisure. . . . As she was finishing her third, she saw a familiar face. She had recalled this man more than once during the days of her humiliation; it often seemed to her that if she told him everything he would listen to her carefully and would be able to point out what she lacked for success. She had invited him to the theatre secretly hoping to win his praise (and now she had an overwhelming desire to ask him whether he had liked her in *Frederick*). It was Kurilov; he stood in the corridor filling his pipe. Liza arranged things in such a way that they met. The light was behind his back, and as a result he looked younger. She told him so frankly.

He laughed. "Well, not to grow older at my age, is tantamount to growing younger. Do you dance, act or sing?"

"I read bad poetry. I'm trying to become famous. . . ."

"Everything is ahead of you, comrade. And how is life going? . . ."

". . . Well!" She shook her head with a professional gesture. "I've had a long furlough. I've read a great deal and, I think for the first time in my life, I've thought hard. . . ."

They were being pushed aside, for they were standing in the passage. Attendants carrying tea passed them. Some second-rate celebrity floated by, with a bosom, covered with two foxes, as solemn and enormous as a birthday cake. They had to go to the reading room, and since there were comfortable chairs here, they sat down. Their conversation came easily; the fact that he had seen Liza at a moment of horrible weakness brought them closer.

"How is your part in the new production coming along?"

Liza flushed: apparently he had not forgotten what she had said to him the last time about *Mary*.

"Thank you."

He did not show that he had noticed her momentary confusion. (Every day, every hour, she had to pay for her garrulity!) He smiled: "I liked what you said the last time. You said . . . I'll remember it exactly in a minute . . . you said that your right to joy is in this part. That is correct: under socialism everyone's activity will be a means of proving his right to joy."

"To joy, or to bread?"

"Don't confuse these two things, you'll get mixed up. Any labor gives us the right to bread; but only creative work, the right to joy. . . . To make a long story short, when does the play open? Put me down for a pass. I am extremely susceptible to things historical."

She had imagined him older and sterner; even now she was struck by the hard steadiness of his eyes, softened only by his smile, friendly, indulgent, utterly simple. It would have been absurd to lie to him, he might suspect the worst. She tried to mask the bad news about herself with a joke: "Didn't I tell you? I've left the theatre."

"Ideological disagreement?" He kept sucking at his unlit pipe: smoking was forbidden in the reading room.

"Yes, this theatre is far removed from the contemporary scene. Moreover, very bad traditions have found shelter there," Liza remarked casually. "And did you notice how uncomfortable it was?"

"It was rather barny!"

She was pleased. "So you noticed it?"

". . . And there's a draft from the floor," Kurilov concluded in the same tone.

His remark about the floor was gratuitous. She fancied he was being ironical. She looked askance at him and realized that he had guessed everything long ago. All she could do was jump downwards; she said, breaking her fingernails: "I fail in everything, Kurilov. I probably have no talent at all. It hurts me to have discovered this so early. . . ."

"Did other people reveal it to you . . . or did it come from inside you?"

"People are malicious, Kurilov."

He laughed and asked her whether she had begun to think so since the day when Klavdia rebuked her over the telephone. That day, he said, he had not felt well, he had caught a cold from a ride on an engine! (This version of his illness was now his favorite, it did not commit anyone to anything.) "You're wrong, comrade!" he concluded. "If there is any good in yourself, you'll find it reflected in others."

"And vice versa?" she asked suddenly.

"Of course, it's possible to cultivate it in oneself too."

Oh, this man knew a way out. Perhaps he was the very man she had been looking for? All the signs were there. He was enormous, pockmarked, magnanimous. And he asked her about everything so simply, as though he had known her since her childhood. "And what are you going to do now?"

"Nothing for the moment, Kurilov!" She smiled. "Perhaps I shall go to work in a seamstress' shop. My mother used to say: one always finds some little backwater close to home."

"And what does your husband say to all this? You said he, too, was an artist. . . ."

"I have separated from him."

"Also ideological differences?"

She shrugged her shoulders, and her face was twisted. "Oh, it was just an unsuccessful professional tour. Let's drop the subject!" She rose. "By the way, I have made a mistake about you. You haven't grown younger. . . ."

"Yes, I'm all tired out. Now I am about to take a rest for the first time in my whole life."

Suddenly he asked her for her mirror, on the pretext that he had a speck of dust in his eye. He scrutinized himself with cruel curiosity, trying to determine the changes in his face. He never looked in the mirror, except perhaps at the barber's, and even then all his attention was absorbed by the master's nimble, almost boneless, hands. This time the glass was as frank as the old man who was going to Barcelona; it refused to lie or flatter. Alexei Nikitich returned the mirror and for a moment held her hand.

"Listen, comrade . . . isn't your name Liza? I was often told that I have an excellent memory. I'll call you Liza. Can you ski?"

"No."

"You should learn. You've begun to be tired prematurely, you were over-confident, you rushed ahead too fast . . . and it didn't work. It's made you blue around the eyes! Now this is what I want to tell you, Liza. I'm taking a month's furlough. To a place about two hundred miles from here. A solitary place, not a grain of soot on the sky . . . and as for the silence, it's good enough to export! The only drawback is that the newspapers are always stale—it takes them three days to get there. The house is called Borschnia. Do you want to come with me to Borschnia?"

"You're quite a poet," Liza said coldly. "What words you find to describe it!"

"Oh, my soul too is of the best quality," Alexei Nikitich said facetiously. "Say yes!"

She abruptly withdrew her hand from his. She was familiar with this kind of attack: Oho, so he, too, has designs on me! She asked rudely, insultingly, directly: "Do you expect me to *live* with you?"

He frowned as though someone had slapped him in the face: did she want to insult herself or him? He put his pipe into his pocket (and it took him some time to do so), then said in his usual voice: "Of course, we'll live in the same house. It has many rooms. And if you wish to organize a dramatic club among the vacationists, you won't have to pay anything. Say yes, if you want to freeze a little, read and think over the things you have not finished thinking over. Borschnia is a lot of snow, books and woods. . . ."

She felt ashamed and shaken; she hesitated. "I'll telephone you."

She was summoned to the stage. (Usually she impersonated a cute provincial girl who made fun of the trolley-car service and the Disarmament Conference in pert childish verses. The audience applauded her, pitying her youth and rewarding her dubious courage in reciting such a number.) Then she went home and thought about Kurilov's proposal. At the bottom of her heart she distrusted him. Kurilov was a Communist, and these people never did anything without a purpose: life is too short, the tasks assigned them are too great. What did he want of her? Or could it be that only the little grain of sand that was she was lacking in the enormous concrete-mixer of the times? . . . And the advantages were obvious. In Borschnia she would have a rest from her uncle's philosophical mutterings and the irritating dance of the curtain with the cocks. To achieve this end she would have moved to any hole in the wall, if only it were heated and had a piece of sky in the window! Moreover, Kurilov could teach her to understand the most mysterious little springs of life; in her opinion it was only such details that had always been wanting in her. Finally, Alexei Nikitich was closely connected with Tiutchev, the director of the Young Theatre. This organization was considered to have a brilliant future. It had introduced an unprecedented reform: the text of each play was read in several interpretations, and the whole season was spent in controversies among the various stage managers. Those who worked in that theatre quickly acquired fame. When she passed the building Liza looked at it with the hidden ecstasy of a Porozhensk Cinderella passing by Omelichev's palace. . . . In a conversation with his friend, Kurilov might mention Pokhvisneva's name. Oh, it is so easy for the great to make a holiday for the small!

He was supposed to leave four days later. On the eve of his departure she telephoned him: "Hello, Kurilov: This is Pokhvisneva. I'm coming." She had the impression that he had forgotten about his invitation; but he then recalled it, for he laughed and said that he was very glad. He promised to stop by for her half an hour before the train left. That evening Arkadyi Hermogenovich learned that his niece was leaving him for a whole month. He assumed that she was afraid of this trip and was asking his permission. "Why not, go! It's an excellent idea; at your age I loved nature, too. Are you going alone?"

"No, uncle."

The old man assumed the pose of one who must answer for his niece before his conscience. "Is he a decent man?"

"You know him. It's Kurilov."

He still shuddered at the mention of this name. Suddenly it turned out that despite his age her uncle still was shrewd and calculating. "That's surprising . . . is he a bachelor?"

Liza blushed, and the old man had never seen her so angry. She tore down the calico cocks and threw them at his feet. The Love of Goodness, like a heavily wounded crow, fluttered into a far corner. She shouted that she forbade him to question her about "that." She was on the verge of tears. ". . . You should be ashamed, ashamed. You're an old man! What you are implying is filthy, filthy!"

In reality she was angry with herself for the tactless remark she had permitted herself when talking with Kurilov; at any rate this outburst revealed everything she had thought during the last three days. Arkadyi Hermogenovich listened to her with increased curiosity. For the first time a dramatic note sounded in his niece's voice. As though attending a rehearsal, he half closed his eyes and from the vibrations of her voice he tried to imagine the dry gleam in her eyes. He waited until Liza had finished her performance. "Not bad, not bad at all, Liza!" he said. "You were wrong to give up your part. But don't be carried away: our neighbors might think we were quarrelling." Two minutes later he resumed his cross-examination. "Where are you going with him?"

"To Borschnia," said Liza, wringing her hands.

Now it was his turn to be upset. Arkadyi Hermogenovich heard this word with extreme distrust; he asked Liza whether she was not mistaken, and all the rest of the evening he sat by the window, subdued and tiny, gazing at his toy gardens. From time to time he raised his head, turning it aside a tiny bit as though listening to voices outside. A long-drawn-out process of his mind was now being completed. They turned in at the usual hour, but the overturned cocks continued stirring a long time after Liza had fallen asleep.

She was awakened in the middle of the night: someone light, almost disembodied, had sat down on her bed. It was her uncle. The canvas raincoat he had thrown around himself instead of his wrapper was crackling. He seemed to Liza drier and sterner than usual.

"Don't be frightened, Liza, it's I. I awoke you to give you a mission that I would entrust only to you. Listen carefully, I don't want to have to repeat myself: there are mirrors into which one does not look twice. . . ."

"Have you been dreaming? . . . What mirrors?"

He did not even shake his head, he simply had not heard her. "Tomorrow morning you're going to Borschnia. In that place the moon rises enormous. In that place I dreamed of my youth. And there, to the best of my knowledge, a woman lies buried to whom I have remained faithful all my life. I learned too late that she betrayed me. It would have been better if the joyous ignorance of my youth had ended in the mournful ignorance of old age. But my enemy told me the truth: after all someone must be under the bed to disclose the love of two others to the world. I won't mention that name again. Don't ask any questions, don't spill it to Kurilov; I don't need him to make fun of me!" He paused.

It was apparent that he had memorized these words many hours before. The street lamp threw the swaying shadows of branches on the frozen window. Arkadyi Hermogenovich was sitting as though in a garden painted upon the bare walls. His brows hung over his eyes. And Liza fancied that her uncle was having a conversation with phantoms surrounding them on all sides.

". . . In Borschnia, there's a graveyard. Once I set out to go there to place my hatred on her grave, but fate stopped me halfway, as it stopped Saul of Tarsus. Now everything has changed, and I'm asking you, Liza, to do something else. Go down from the terrace along the avenue. Go to the ravine and from the arbor turn to the right. Amidst old linden trees you'll see two urns on stone pillars: gates. . . . There, all the owners of the estate for the last century and a half are buried. She, too, is surely lying there; find her grave. Her name is . . ." He whispered the sacred name into Liza's ear. "Bend over it and whisper that I have forgiven them. Say that if this woman who has remained a maiden in my eyes came to me now I would receive her as a sister, I would share everything with her, I would take her to my home, I. . . ."

Liza sat up; she thought all this was very funny. "Well, between you both you would certainly smoke me out of here!" she said, stretching herself and yawning.

"I'm sure you understand me, Liza. You're quite grown-up for your age. I have no possessions, no great ideas. I will depart without burdening you with any will and testament. (Nature demands that I join her. We'll see what use she will find for this decrepit rotten wood! I'll look and laugh!) This is the only thing I'm asking you to do for me. And, believe me, it's not an old man's whim: it's the final result of a whole, although insignificant, life!" And Liza shuddered when with almost feverish fingers he touched her bare elbow. . . .

She dreamed that she was in a moving car. Suddenly a sharp chilling freshness penetrated her body. "This is Cheremshansk," Kurilov said in the middle of the night. And Liza found it strange that he, as enormous as life itself, could fit into the crowded space of a train compartment. He bent over her and lightly raised her, sleepy, warm, in a nightgown only, on the very tips of his fingers, to carry her across the deep snow. "We aren't doing anything bad, are we?" she asked him in a whisper. But she did not tell him that behind the thin partition her husband was spying upon every move they made. Kurilov, invisible, whose presence could only be guessed by the pounding of his heart, carried Liza outside. And all this was not even a dream, but only the obscure presage of the coming turning point in her life.

# CHAPTER 31

# Borschnia

How like her dream! . . . Kurilov knocked at the door of her compartment. Liza had slept with her clothes on. The voices of the engine sounded sad at the various stops. As though washing herself she passed the tips of her fingers across her face. She was still dreaming, she had to tear her dream off her burning cheeks with her hands. The conductor helped her to get down. She went out into the cold. There was a great deal of snow and many stars. A tall man in a leather coat walked with measured steps along the deserted platform.

"Is this Cheremshansk?" Liza asked, yawning.

"This is the station, citizeness. The town itself is a mile and a half away." He walked by her side, staring at her face. There was an insinuating insolence in his voice. "I think I recognize you now. Aren't you an actress?"

A faint hope made her smile. "I suppose you saw me on the stage?"

"I saw you on my friend's desk."

And in her sleepiness it occurred to her that her wretched fame might have reached this remote hole! . . . Liza pressed her poor oilcloth suitcase to her breast and hurried away. But apparently this man wanted to make sure again: he kept walking and staring at her face. He behaved as though he had discovered something, but did not know yet what to do about it.

"You're as pretty in reality as you are on paper. You're as daintily made as a chessman, and your name is Liza. Isn't that so?"

"Are you going to make love to me?"

Kurilov appeared just in time. Liza heard the man report to his chief that everything was going well in the yard. "There was no reason for you to get up so early," Kurilov was saying to him lazily. "I am going on a furlough. The official order will be issued shortly, comrade ——" And he spoke her husband's name. Liza shrank as though she had been discovered doing something shameful. It was tempting to think in her half awakened state that Ilya had split in two and that while one half snored loudly in his Moscow apartment, the other, sleepless and overstrained, followed her. (Ilya was jealous.) The two men talked for a long time. Kurilov laughed incredulously, holding the other by his button. Liza was freezing like a forgotten dog. A snowy smoke spread along the tracks.

"All right, shall we go, Liza?"

"How I want to sleep, Kurilov!"

In the darkness behind the water-tower a comfortable sleigh was awaiting them. Its bast body was powdered with snow, and a granular frost had accumulated under the fur rug. Beside it an enormous driver looking like a house in a fur coat was hopping up and down to keep warm. She got into the sleigh. The runners creaked, the whip snapped. This trip to Borschnia was a repetition of her dream, but now the dream's uncertain symbols acquired solid, material outlines. The cold burned her nostrils. The road shook, and Liza's head shook. Occasionally a snowy branch grazed her sleeve. With a deep sigh, as always when awakening, Liza opened her eyes. In her sleepiness she imagined that her nose was being sawed off with a very thin saw. Glades emerged from behind the coachman's back. The landscape smelled sweetly of fresh hay.

Kurilov should have held her by the shoulder. On the steep descent the sledge was almost carried away, and Liza nearly fell out at full speed. Their legs touched; it was warmer that way. Her knees grew weak. . . .

"Shall we be there soon, Kurilov?"

"Lean on my shoulder and sleep. Children must sleep. . . ." The rest of his words were drowned in slumber.

When she again opened her eyes, she saw a big house standing among trees. It was dark. The snowdrifts at its sides resembled foamy waves breaking against a ship. A green star, big and kind, stood overhead. . . . They walked up creaky steps. There was a homey, warm odor of newly baked bread. A bare-headed woman led the newcomers to their rooms. Their numbers were six and eight. Aha, these two rooms and the one between them gave onto one balcony! Liza tore her clothes off her body. "Good night, good night to all!" Thus little babies fall asleep, crumpling the pillows under them.

The old house cooled down during the night. In the morning Liza jumped up and remembered everything. Icy water wetted the curls on her neck. All day long she would carry this tingling chill with her. Logs snapped in the stoves in the corridors and puddles from bundles of wood formed. Kurilov went out. Liza drank cold tea. The staircase that remembered Blankenhagel's heavy steps sang and sighed under the young woman's light feet. She met no one. The vacationists had all gone off in different directions. Liza pushed open the glass door and blinked as though a shovelful of snow mingled with sun had been thrown into her eyes. Everything sparkled. She found the day at its height. Blue tracks left by skiers ran in all directions from the terrace.

She walked in the clean swept avenue, felt chilly and returned. Just then the bell rang for lunch. Ten men and six women were at table. Liza sat in a corner. The conversation revolved about the relations between transportation and the local party organization. Liza was surprised at the vivacity of this conversation. Kurilov still had not returned. How strange that he had not even left her a note!

"Are you from the central office?" her neighbor at table asked her, passing her the meat platter.

"No, I'm from the theatre, . . ." Liza replied, blushing.

"Ah, you're an instructor!" The woman grew interested and tried to interest the others. "That's good. . . ."

Solid-looking people glanced at her with facetious respect. Liza went up to her room. A young woman dropped in to see her half an hour later, to discuss concrete plans for the dramatic club. She was enthusiastic and impatient. Meanwhile the sunny spectacle outside the window was gone, all that could be seen now was the grey backdrop of the previous set. There were many crickets in the house. When light was turned on, they began to sing behind the stove. The evening was as long as a railroad. Liza again went downstairs. "Well, let's get acquainted. . . ."

One by one she visited the buildings of the estate. None of the doors were closed here. In the pigsty, well-fed edible chunks of meat were squirming and grunting. The frost-covered window had a bluish shine. The sleek horses flapped their ears sleepily. Her feet stepped softly and sonorously on the straw. Cows sighed in narrow stalls. The oldest one seemed to be telling her sisters with a shiver that the day before once again a mouse had run across the trough. The news made her listeners prick up their ears. The warm aroma of dung widened Liza's nostrils; it had the fat, sweetish smell of fresh jam. Smiling, Liza went on farther.

In the long hothouse there was the same silence and twilight as in herself. The familiar greenish star leaked through the steep glass roof. Perhaps it had got frozen outside. Dove-colored, flaky smoke floated above the shelves. A man sitting on a log was heating the stove; orange gleams leapt up on his bony face.

"Hello," said Liza affably. "How smoky it is in here. Doesn't that spoil the flowers?"

". . . But the moths like it," the gardener said without turning around. "If we weren't careful the moths would eat everything nowadays. Bugs have at least some conscience. They don't like to be stared at; they're shy, but these. . . ." And he nodded somewhere in the direction of his riches, a countless number of winter cinerarias and primroses; the greenish light of the star gleamed on the pale crowns of the flowers.

The gardener was silent now. And because his posture, as though he were talking with the fire, was in tune with Liza's mood, this stranger was now closer to her than anyone else.

"I have nothing to do. . . . May I sit here with you?"

"Sit down, why not? . . ." And a second log magically rolled out of the darkness.

The stove heat enveloped Liza's feet imperiously. The man and the girl silently watched the last spurts of the fire. Like everything else in the world, fire is not a thing but a process. An orange muscle rose from the ashes and withered; a flaming spasm ran across the red-hot wood. "How proudly you're dying, fire!"

"So you always sit here all alone?"

"It's winter, everything has faded. And when the season comes, everything will be dressed up again. . . ." He said much more, as though to himself, and the meaning of his confused speech was that in solitude one must draw upon oneself; that then one learns how much has been stored up within. "To be alone—that's like a girl looking into a mirror. . . ."

The brief and bitter experience of the day compelled her to agree without reservation. How many mistakes she had made! You can't soar to the very peak in one breath. Now she fancied that the hothouse was a long hall and that in it lay the dead picked up in the street or people who had committed suicide. Liza mentally walked through them; they lay with their feet turned toward her, and one was marked with an indelible pencil. The numbers tallied: "So it's you, Zakurdaev?" And all her complex feelings, her secret faith in the greenish star, her fear of the unknown, her aversion to Zakurdaev, her terror before Protoklitov's caresses—all this was compressed by some ferocious force into one involuntary tear. . . . The first was followed by a second. Liza's shoulders were convulsed. She wept. No one stopped her.

"Anyone done you wrong?" the gardener asked her without stirring, and Liza had the oppressive feeling that he could see right through her.

"No, only myself."

"You shouldn't cry like that! Everyone has little troubles of his own. Some because they're sick, other's because they're poor. For me, it's my wife. . . ." He rolled a cigarette and with his fingers took a half smouldering piece of coal to light it. From everything, especially from the slowness of his speech, it was clear that for the first time he was putting together, aloud, his dispersed memories. . . . "That was during the war. In the Carpathians our brigade was pounded for three days, like chewed sunflower seeds. The war was only beginning, there were plenty of bullets, and even more people. A hundred and fifty men from various companies were herded together, they were picked from those who were not too badly hit, and were ordered to attack. And the spot was such that no sooner did you show your head than there was firing from every little hill. And I had a friend, Grechishev, Vasil Adryanych, a warrior like myself. 'Let's go,' I say to him, 'we're supposed to attack. Start a hurrah, and I'll support you!' But he stood gloomily: 'I've no strength, I'm dizzy . . . I'd rather sit on a bayonet by myself.' 'If so,' says I, 'we're no good for heroes. Let's get out of here, there's no war without prisoners.' Meanwhile firing had begun, dozens of our men were falling. Our officer, a kind of rash fellow, was already lying on the ground, and his forehead looked as though it were dripping sealing wax, and his face, I'm telling you, it was dead white, like someone in a sanatorium. So he didn't see us. We darted into the bushes, hollered, stuck our bayonets into empty places. We walked until night, no one took us prisoner. In the end one kind fellow, may God give him good health, led us where we wanted to go!"

He poked in the stove and painstakingly collected the dropped pieces of coal. "Our camp was small," he went on, "but the work was tremendous, and we had very little to eat. They made us do all sorts of dirty jobs. It was clear that a prisoner was worse than carrion! And I had a young wife, we'd been living together only three months, hadn't had time to get really acquainted. So I made up my mind to a risky thing—because our guard, well, it was like keeping a bear on a piece of thread. But then one prisoner who tried to escape was shot. I began to think it over—if I ran back, I should be sent to the front, anyway. So I'd better wait until all the others got fed up. With time there were three of us—as they say, a 'conspiracy.' And there was one fellow with us, a very good man, although black (by the way, the inside of his mouth—we looked inside it—was as red as other people's mouths!). He amused us a great deal. He'd draw his Africa on the ground and explain where his home town was on the drawing. It's an island, Madagascar; ever heard of it? He lived on the left side of it, near the sea. Then he'd add a mustache and eyes to his drawing and the result was a kind of a Turk. And it was very much like him, too. And he'd burst out laughing himself, and we'd echo like a choir. I must say their dialect is quite like ours, only they pronounce the words differently. We'd go into a corner, he'd babble about his girl, and I'd boast about Masha. We described every inch of both of them. Anyone who has ever been a prisoner will understand! Our conspiracy soon fell apart. Grechishev died of typhus, and the African was kicked in the face by a horse—right under Madagascar! . . . I didn't return until 1921. . . . We travelled on and on, wherever the train dragged us, for sixty-five days we travelled homeward, sick, disgraced, swollen. At every stop about five corpses were thrown out of the car; some of the soldiers kept repeating the names of their girls with lips so numb it made you shudder to touch them. . . ."

The star was moving outside and as it moved, Liza's tears dried.

"I was a forester. . . . When I got to my glade, my knees trembled. . . . It was a swampy place, there were clouds of man-eating mosquitoes, but at that time even the mosquitoes were my brothers. They thronged and sang around me like dogs: no doubt they recognized me! . . . In the glade there was a cabin, a light was inside. I peered in: I saw a gun on the wall, and Masha about to go to bed. When I left her she was nothing but a slender stem, now she was a little blossoming tree. . . . It's a good thing, I thought, that the gun was at the wall, and that my wife was going to bed. And I in my joy had the idea of playing a joke on my wife. I wore a beard, I was thin, I had strange clothes on. I knocked at the door . . . an unknown dog answered . . . I asked permission to spend the night, I said I lived in the neighborhood. . . . Masha had become an efficient forester; she came out, looked around and said: 'Get in, but at daybreak you must go.' She turned out the light and lay down on a bench. It was hot, she was living amidst wood in abundance. I lay there and felt like laughing: my own wife didn't recognize me! You'll learn to know me soon, I thought. So I went under her sheepskin, dug her up . . . and she didn't even push me away, she let me in readily. I slept with her, but without pleasure: stolen goods. She lay on her back, spoke of her life, her farm, she spoke interestingly. Her husband, she said, had been killed, and she had stupidly sworn that she'd never marry again. 'How many fellows I've sent away!' 'So you kept your oath?' I asked her. 'The trouble is, I did keep it,' she said. It was night, I couldn't see her face; only the gun gleamed on the wall. 'Is it loaded, your shooter?' I asked. 'It's loaded, what's that to you?' Again I crumpled her under me, to dispel suspicions. We were lying there, and I said again: 'So you made an oath, and what am I, not a husband?' 'You're not a husband,' she said, 'you're a sin!' That's all! I felt sick at my stomach. At daybreak I left quietly.

Outside there was the axe, she had forgotten to remove it the night before; I drove it into an ash tree to the very butt end. . . . That was long ago! I remember it as though in a dream. . . ."

His cigarette was finished. The coals were fading in the stove and there was no way of seeing the gardener's face. Liza did not know what to say on such occasions. Drops were falling somewhere. The steaming soil had a stifling smell.

"Thanks for everything, . . ." Liza said in a low voice and shook the light clay dust off her knees. "It's nice here."

"Drop in to see me, if you like it. Come and get some flowers. I don't know what to do with them, anyhow. . . ."

He did not turn around to look at Liza's embarrassed face, he did not care to know with whom he had shared the story of his solitude.

CHAPTER 32

# Jack Frost Paints the Landscape

ALL NIGHT LONG SOMEONE taking long steps walked in the park. By morning everything was covered with hoar-frost. A young woman gave Liza a pair of felt boots. She tried to stand on skis. The estate was situated on a hill and from the gates began a steep descent. The lions on the stone gate-posts were wrapped in hard fur which was pinkish in the sun. The skis slid downward. The snow flattened by runners had been covered during the night with an icy varnish. Everything began to shake. Losing her sticks, Liza rolled down. She succeeded in grasping a tree on her way. Prickly, mother-of-pearl, sparks rained from above. The skis got caught in the bushes. . . . But after that she walked more steadily with every step. The road led to Akhmetovo, and further, to Cheremshansk.

Everything was foamy and pink. How many hands are needed to decorate the forest so splendidly in one night! A pile of horse dung on the road resembled a lost jewel. And even a dropped log looked almost proud, as though the creation of that magnificent morning had begun with it. . . . A plaintive clank and snorting came from the bend of the road. Toward Liza an automobile was coming, the pride of Kostia Strunnikov. It had been newly lined with iron and painted a beautiful brick color like a mummy; it took an energetic blow on the rubber pear to produce a rusty cough. Nature shuddered all around, on the passengers' faces astonishment was written. There were three daredevils inside; except for Kurilov, Liza did not know any of them. Alexei Nikitich shouted something that could not be distinguished above the roar of the engine. The car stopped. Liza discovered that at the steering wheel sat the director of the rest home, Strunnikov, and that the man next to Kurilov was Shamin, the secretary of the regional Youth Committee. Two minutes later the machine was frozen. They pushed it, took turns trying to start it with the crank, but an old car is something like an old horse. It was an act of folly to have stopped it before it reached its destination. Kostia said it was all the fault of the poor gasoline; no one contradicted him, because everybody liked him and it was not far to the house, anyway.

Liza walked on foot in order not to lag behind. She felt genuinely relieved when Shamin offered to carry her skis. He wore a baggy sheepskin all patched up; he was tall, and Liza's neck ached after she had talked with him a little while. She learned that a party conference had been going on in Cheremshansk and that Shamin had persuaded Alexei Nikitich by telephone to come and speak. Kurilov's speech had been excellent; he had found striking images in which to describe the future, images that were all the more interesting because, although fantastic, they were rooted in the production figures already achieved.

"He's a fascinating man," Liza agreed, just to be on the safe side.

"Yes. . . . And you can imagine what happened to our economists and cooperative managers when he sketched the approximate size of our future economy!"

"Our people always limit their dreams to the narrow confines of their daily bread," Liza remarked cautiously, and cast a glance at her companion to see if this remark had offended him. "Will the man of the future need to eat more than he needs to eat today?"

Shamin spoke fluently as though reading from a book: "Not only food is in question," he said. "We want to liberate man from subjection to the blind elements. Long ago he won the right to a better lot by his sufferings; now he only has to conquer it. We're greedy, we want a great deal. The ice of the Arctic and the storms of the ocean, the course of time and death itself will serve man and take orders from him."

To add emphasis to his argument Shamin took hold of Liza by the shoulder, and she liked this. He was excited, uncompromising, inflammable. "It would be nice to have such a man for a brother!" she thought. "But you should have your felt boots fixed," she said, laughing.

He answered quite like a boy: "And your eyelashes are completely white from frost. Incidentally, are they your own eyelashes?"

Liza swept them upwards and looked at him. She guessed by their weight rather than saw that they were just as glittering and furry as everything else around her. He explained his question: "They say that in the west people make eyelashes of fur . . . then they paste them on with something or other. After that you can't wash, you must only use a brush. It would be fun to see that! You must have heard of it; aren't you an actress?"

It was quite easy to talk with this open, long-legged fellow. "I was an actress," she answered, "but I was fired."

"You speak frankly, but I don't quite understand you. Was it for bad acting?"

"It was a combination of circumstances. . . . Rub your nose, it's getting all white!"

Shamin went to work, and although his mittens were as green as grass, his nose grew redder and redder.

"Well, what are you going to do now?" he asked.

"I'm looking for a way to use my misunderstood genius. But for the moment there's no special demand." (Thus I'm sitting inside myself as in a prison. Help me to escape!) She could permit herself that much frankness for once; tomorrow Shamin would drive away, tomorrow he would forget her! (Now I'm poised like a spider, lurking in the back of my web. . . .)

Shamin smiled without answering. The house came into view, smoke was rising from its chimneys. Liza walked, humming some march. A frozen crow, all white, was lying on the road. Shamin's felt boot touched it, and it fluttered away into a snowdrift.

"Why are you so silent?" Shamin asked.

"I'm thinking. And so, first comes bread. Bread in the wide sense of the term. And when does happiness come?"

He shrugged his shoulders in annoyance. "That word always makes me angry. It hasn't any social significance. Some find happiness in having a buttered roll every day, others in collecting shabby antiques. And if happiness is the product of many things that we will soon learn to manufacture in quantity, everyone will soon be happy as a result. But I'm afraid that man still won't be satisfied. Happiness is a variable function."

"Everyone will be happy," Liza repeated mechanically.

"Let us say you need a dress. Please! . . . Get a dress for the owner of work book number such and such. A brown-haired girl, size twelve, eyes. . . . What is the color of your eyes?"

She turned away from his insistent glance and laughed out loud. "What do you need to know the color of my eyes for?"

"I thought women were guided by the color of their eyes in choosing clothes. . . . Or, suppose you've become interested in how the South Pole looks in the moonlight. You go to an airfield, take a seat with other queer people like yourself. 'Lean back on your pillow! We're starting! . . . Please wrap yourself up better. Notice the greenish shine of the icebergs. Watch out, there's a hole in the ocean here!' Then a short lecture on polar cattle-breeding, a cup of coffee or a bear cutlet to make your experience complete—and back home! Has the citizeness a third desire that I have not guessed?" And with the air of a magician retailing miracles he rubbed his hands.

"You're always joking. But I really have a demand on the future."

"Please, place your orders!" He spread his hands comically, as though standing behind the counter of a huge department store of human pleasures. "Our establishment serves its customers well and counts on the public to show order and restraint. By *that* time birdlike hustling around for the sake of oneself will be undignified and superfluous! . . . And so what's your order?"

"Well, this. . . ." And, once expressed aloud, her old desire fell off like a snake's faded skin. "I'd like to play Mary Stuart."

Shamin quickly found himself. "Please, read aloud the second article on the back of your customer's certificate. There it says that no individual's happiness may be secured at the expense of others' happiness. You will be allowed to play Mary if it gives your audience pleasure, if you have something new to say on the subject. But why have you chosen that gloomy mediaeval lady? Look for something closer to hand. . . ."

"For instance?"

"Would you like to come and work with us in Cheremshansk? We need eight leaders of dramatic clubs . . . and where are we to find them? Living is cheap in our town, the fellows are splendid and, as you see, the climate is magnificent. I like your frankness. You're the kind of person we need. . . . Well, what do you say?"

"I'm afraid I shouldn't be able to do anything with the job. I know so little."

"I don't want to hurry you. Give me your answer when you've thought it over." He smiled, ascribing her doubts to caution.

The road ended. As they climbed up to the gate, something like a bundle of rags rushed past them. Frightened eyes gleamed in a dirty face, and about ten hands—he seemed to have that many because he waved them so rapidly—flashed against the snow. He was being pursued and, if Shamin had not moved out of his way, he would have been thrown down into the snow. The scene was as kaleidoscopic as a movie. The boy slipped on the icy snow and floundered in Kurilov's embrace. On the spot in Kurilov's coat where his mouth touched, a hoar-frost stain formed at once. They were immediately surrounded by people. From the rapid exchange of shouts it was clear that this homeless child had robbed the steward of the Borschnia rest home. All the stolen goods were discovered on him except a pair of lady's gloves. The victim of the robbery was present, wearing a warm sweater and a new felt cloak. Everyone made way for him respectfully: the boy was his entirely. A heavy hand, as though uncertain of its rights, moved toward the dirty frost-bitten ears of the little thief. Kurilov with some disgust pushed it away, and the steward looked at him with troubled eyes. "You shouldn't spoil this child, comrade Kurilov," he said. "At this rate he'll steal everything, everything. . . ." Angry blotches stained his face. It was undoubtedly not the first time he had been prevented from doing justice. He wanted to hurt Kurilov. His voice rose till it was out of key: "I'll complain about you to Martinson! . . ."

Alexei Nikitich shot a severe look at the man. Of all the owners he had ever met this was the shrillest. (And so everyone had got wind of Kurilov's possible departure from the road?) Tense, they all waited to see whether the steward would blurt out something about the nature of the chief's offense, but he kept silent, frightened by his own boldness. The spectators scattered in disappointment. Liza was the last to leave. She locked herself up in her room. The old, almost forgotten taste of the stolen turnip was burning her tongue. . . . An hour later she went to find Kurilov. His door was closed, and Liza tried in vain to find out what was going on in his room by the indistinct sounds that came from it. She was frightened by an attendant who came up carrying a bowl of steaming soup. In the brief fraction of a minute, while the door opened, Liza managed to see everything. The boy sat in a corner, crumpled up, as though tied in a knot, and Alexei Nikitich was trying to untie him by every possible means. The prematurely old, ill-washed face of the prisoner expressed rage and stubbornness. In his eyes, Kurilov's ample shirt was probably worse than handcuffs. . . . That was exactly what Liza would have felt in his position.

She went back to her room. She tried to read, but could not. And thinking of the Usterma truck-farmer she did not feel belatedly grateful to him, but was merely ironically surprised that he had not struck her, since he could have done it with impunity. . . .

Before supper Kurilov stopped in for her. He asked how she had arranged her life in Borschnia, and spent a long time lighting his pipe.

"I'm tired," he confessed later. "I learned that that child's name is Gavrila and that he is ten years old. A regular little polecat. You give him bread, and he . . ." With a smile he examined his hands, scratched during the scuffle that morning.

"He treats people just as people treat him. Then he's quits with the world! . . . He'll run away from you, anyhow. You have to make him want to come back of himself. I understand this business quite well."

"You must have had a rather poverty-stricken childhood, Liza!"

"I, too, stole. At that time begging was unprofitable and, what's more, I was ashamed to do it. It's easier to steal, Kurilov."

"Let's go into that question thoroughly! Look around you . . . have you ever met a real person?"

"You mean aside from you?"

He took his mustache in his fist and crumpled it gloomily. "You've formed an opinion about me too hastily," he said. "Did you think I'd lynch that little animal like the others? In the first place, we're strict in such matters. . . . And in the second place . . . tell me, didn't your husband help you change your opinions of people?"

"I've always been afraid of him. I felt like closing my eyes when he came near me. And I kept on chattering and chattering whenever he was with me, just to prove that I existed in spite of his overwhelming presence!"

"But why did you marry him?"

The question disconcerted her. All she could say was: "That's the kind of husband I happened to marry. . . ."

The bell rang for supper. Alexei Nikitich went to see whether "his precious Gavrila was asleep." Liza waited for him in the corridor. Something squeaked in the wall and was immediately echoed from the room opposite. Then two voices took up the song at the other end of the corridor, where the stove was, and the sounds ran down the stairs and came back, awakening in various places. The crickets' evening concert had begun.

# CHAPTER 33

# In Cheremshansk

IN JANUARY THE NUMBER OF railroad accidents increased. On the Volga-Revizan line most of them were caused by snowdrifts. Whatever route was chosen by the storm, the railroad seemed to be on its way. At that period the Cheremshansk executives got up long before daybreak in order to have time to inspect their departments before the seven o'clock siren.

The brick buildings of the repair shops were located at the foot of a wooded hill. Everything around them was saturated with soot and a smell of burning; even the snow, always covered by a thin layer of coal-dust, even the emaciated plants in the barracks windows, even the children, that black-faced tribe of future engineers. But seen from the ridge between two fields above the yard roofs, the station on the hill had a spectral shine, and in the moonlight the window seemed made of mica. A path of fresh-cut, still fragrant timber climbed up the slope amidst sparse pine trees. These passed imperceptibly into Cyclopean accumulations of nightly clouds pierced by moonlight. Then they looked like a simple-minded dreamer's version of the future happy life, a vision nurtured in sulphurous, choking fog. A steep wooden staircase led from there to the busy yard criss-crossed with rails and perpetually resounding with the dull rattle of wheels. And no matter how crowded the day which lay ahead of him, Protoklitov always stopped here for a minute: somewhere below, the hunter, Kurilov, was lying in wait for him.

His hand on the icy handrail, he stared into the smoky valley below, full of the crackling of fires, the frantic puffing of engines and the thunder of rolling wheels—cradling monstrous silhouettes with humps and manes of opaque smoke—saturated with a huge gamut of metallic voices which sounded harsh to unaccustomed ears and, at the same time, with the light crunching of snow which reminded him remotely of his childhood. Dawn was still a long way off, a fire still smouldered in the dispatcher's tower, but from the fifth track, judging by the signal lights and the clanking of couplings, a freight train was leaving for Voronezh; slowly, stopping at each car, crawled a white lantern with one pane; the conductor was taking down the numbers of the cars.

The third track was clear, awaiting the passenger train from Siberia, and on the sixth, a green semaphore like the eye in a peacock's tail was calling the shunting engine (there was no sorting at Cheremshansk). Another train, with an insistent, punctuated whistle was demanding admittance to the second track because the local from Ulgan-Urman threatened to hit its tail any minute. The engineer was angry, but the switchman still delayed. "What's all the screeching for, I'm letting you onto the second, . . ." he said with the notes of his whistle and, with his lantern, traced a double arc close to the ground: the engine was advancing with its tender in front. At that moment, from the fourth and furthest gate of the yard, snorting in a satisfied fashion and jerking at the switches, came forth an enormous locomotive. The deep breathing of its pistons and the powerful torso raised over its truck identified it as belonging to the KU series. The steam was *thundering*, and Gleb made a mental note to reprimand the fireman on duty for having heated his boiler above the prescribed twelve atmospheres. This locomotive was now ready to relieve that of the Siberian express, scheduled to arrive at 6:40; less than half an hour remained till the siren. . . . Thus, from a height of thirty yards, Gleb read the events of the night in the moving fires and the sounds that cut through the silence.

The great train from the Far East always filled him with a tormenting fear. Wherever it found Gleb, its many-voiced steam whistle reminded him of the long way he had once walked on foot, and he could not resist its call, imperious as the call of a friend with whom one has shared joy or disappointment. Every time the engine with steam roaring from its D-valves savagely and reluctantly stopped near the platform, Gleb was seized by an unaccountable compulsion to jump onto the last car and take a ride into the past, to put his finger on the sinister scars, if only to make sure again and again that he had remained alive. . . . Yielding to his desire, which was unconscious and even stronger this time, he began hurriedly to walk down the path. Somewhere far to the left the engine whistle sang out, and lights flashed impetuously. Gleb was running now, leaping over the steps, tearing his mittens against the frozen snow on the handrails. The past was coming closer, and Gleb needed to touch it so that he could then tear his hand away with animal relief. No one could see him; his impulse was stronger than his reason. The station was on the other side of the tracks. Gleb reached it a moment before the cars, their couplings screeching, stopped at the platform.

There, near the snowbound front garden, lay stacks of burlap bags prepared for grain. Leaning against them, Gleb watched the turmoil which always attended the arrival of a train. From the next-to-the-last car, some baskets and then a bag dropped out, followed by four peasants whose faces showed how long they had lain on one side. The same flat mark of the boards on which they had pressed themselves was preserved on their coats. They passed by him, their sheepskins creaking. Two other sleepless passengers came out to get a breath of the frosty air. They looked on impassively while the greaser ran along the whole train and some bales were carried into the baggage car. Then out of the third car, from the front, came a man in a fur jacket, who sauntered along the platform with an air of uneasy idleness. He passed Gleb twice before venturing to speak to him. Very prudently he inquired whether Protoklitov still had his job at the yard. . . .

This encounter was as good as a bullet fired by Kurilov. The past had answered Gleb's call, it had sent its messenger. Before him stood Kormilitsin. There was still a chance to hide, to escape this meeting; Kormilitsin had not at once recognized his friend's face under the *kubanka* drawn down to his eyes; but Gleb's very surprise gave him away.

"But you were drowned!" he stuttered, and with a superstitious feeling, as though warding something off, stretched out his hand.

Kormilitsin laughed aloud excitedly, joyfully—it was the half-howling laugh of an animal that has at last found its master.

"Oho, so you believe in ghosts!" And he gave Gleb a tap on the shoulder to show that his slip of the tongue had not offended him. "Never mind, I'll try to drown the next time. Well, let's have a look at you. Why, you seem quite prosperous, Glebushka. You smell of soot. . . . That's industry for you!" And he laughed artificially, disturbed by his friend's silence.

A lantern high on a pole helped Gleb to examine this grey, unshaven, hollow-cheeked face. Kormilitsin had grown heavier and had begun to stoop during the last few years, but Gleb's fingers still ached from his handshake. Every now and then a sharp, hoarse note of extreme bitterness resounded in his speech. He talked a great deal, tactfully giving his friend time to recover from his surprise; remarked on Gleb's extraordinary youthfulness, sympathized with his loneliness, praised his firm hold on life; then he began to joke rather inanely and in a few minutes Gleb became irritated by his facetiousness.

"Are you going far?"

Kormilitsin spread out his hands. "Everything depends on what happens to me on the way," he said. "I'm single now, Glebushka. My old mother has gone completely to the dogs, and as for Zoska. . . . Didn't I write to you about that viper?" He shrank, covering his face with his hand, and there was such force in this convulsive gesture, that Gleb would not have been surprised if he had burst into tears, burying his head among the cold mat-bags. Trying to forestall a fit of hysterics, Gleb with some squeamishness touched his shoulder, and his forced gesture was received as an expression of sympathy and a caress.

"I don't give a damn about anything now, Glebushka . . . anything except friendship! You see I have no secrets from you. My Zoska got mixed up with an agronomist. A long-nosed fellow, swarthy, and with a hideous name, that sounds almost apocalyptic . . . Eksakustodian— some name, what? He's about one and a half times my height. Oh, my Zoska always had a sweet tooth!" He choked with grief, grasped Gleb's hand and wretchedly, imploringly, stuck five icy fingers into his sleeve, reaching out for living warmth. "I took to drinking, broke out in boils and was fired from my job. Soon I found a boon-companion. He had once had a powerful bass voice and had sung in opera, but in a drunken brawl someone hit his throat with a stick. One of his cartilages must have been damaged. At any rate, his voice was gone. . . . After all, you can't sing with your knee . . . or with any other part of you, can you, Glebushka?"

Gleb was looking in the direction of the head of the train. "Very interesting, if you're not lying, . . ." he said through his teeth, angry because the relief engine had not yet been connected. They might be seen together . . . and yet he kept up the conversation, in order not to part from Kormilitsin as an enemy. "I was very much surprised by your letter, Evgenyi!"

"You mean that story about my drowning? And you believed it, you queer duck! Who'd go bathing in October, dear friend? What do you think I am, a furry animal, or waterproof? . . . Don't be angry, but I thought I was a burden to you. So I decided to die for you, to give you some peace. As for that little note, I asked Zoska to write it for me . . ." (He sniffed—these bags have a smell of violets in the frost!) "but later I was ashamed of having thought so badly of you. In short, consider the very fact that I've come to you now the measure of my repentance and friendship!"

"I didn't mean that, Evgenyi," Gleb said, trying to insure himself against future letters. "But you wrote imprudent things in your letter."

Kormilitsin frowned with the air of a conspirator. "You think so? . . . Perhaps you're right. There are a lot of curious people around, these days. . . ."

Gleb interrupted him impatiently: "Better don't be late, Evgenyi. The train leaves in half a minute. . . ."

The conductor was holding his whistle up to his mouth; the engineer looked out of his cab (and it was horrible to see what his yawn did to his face). And at this point it turned out that Kormilitsin was not in a hurry to get anywhere. Oh, his plans would not be spoiled if he continued his journey later, at night. And more generally it would be nice if Gleb sheltered and fed him for a day, the poor forty-year-old orphan, "without a daddy or a mummy." This was said with the implication that no matter how different their social positions were today, a soldier always has the right to come to another soldier with whom he has once shared a bundle of rotten straw in a trench, if only to spend an hour with him in silence. And there was such imperious insistence in Kormilitsin's furtive and threatening glance that Gleb did not dare irritate this defeated man.

"Of course," he said with insincere animation, "I'd be glad to have a talk with you. But your luggage? . . ."

"It's in my pockets!" And with the pride of a beggar he showed his empty hands.

"Haven't you got anything?"

"Nothing. All treasures have remained with Zoska. Even my razor. I wanted to lodge a complaint, but I was advised not to because I was a former. . . ."

It was better that way; he would have attracted attention by carrying suitcases.

"Fine. Go now, I'll return immediately, as soon as I inspect the yard. . . ." And after the train had gone, he gave him his keys, and with the help of a drawing on the snow, explained where his house was on the hill. "Try to get there without questioning anyone!"

They walked through the sharp morning frost, jumping over brake-beams, exchanging all sorts of remarks—how often they had walked together in old times, the only difference being that no one was afraid to run into them now. However, their attempt to speak with the old warmth was not very successful.

Meanwhile dawn had broken. The cumbersome mechanism of a railroad day was about to start, and machines and men waited for approaching relief. Thick, sleepy smoke floated above the yard; the lanterns covered with soot during the night were still burning, but a low patch of sky the color of dish water was already moving across the darkness; an empty car rattled; station hands—an intractable race that never got enough sleep—ran about amidst altercations; a cat cautiously picked her way among the tracks, and on top of the hill, like a flock of noisy jackdaws, boys were already tying their sleds together to roll them down in a train.

Near the shed, where the engine that had brought Kormilitsin was being cleaned over a pit, the friends separated. For a minute Gleb's eyes followed his visitor as he climbed uphill with a loose gait, slightly stooping. He walked unhurriedly, no doubt feeling out with his hands and eyes this world that was unknown to him, and, as a newcomer, giving everyone the right of way. He slipped on an ice-covered step, but did not fall; he followed with his eyes a gang of children enthusiastically rolling down the slope of the hill. Feeling probably the physical weight of Protoklitov's glance, he turned around and shouted something, amiably waving his cap. With this gesture of friendship and closeness he asked him not to stay at the yard too long. Then Gleb turned away from him and, right in front of the nose of an incoming engine, ducked into the black jaw of the shed.

Immediately afterward, as though it had been waiting for him alone, the dull morning siren began to roar.

CHAPTER 34

# The Engine House

AT THIS EARLY HOUR the engine house seemed an enormous square of darkness surrounded on all sides with black bricks. It was swept by drafts that penetrated even through a leather coat. Like the metallic girders under the ceiling, they unified the scattered impressions of this uninhabitable, vaulted space. The engine house had six sections; drainage pits divided each of these into a number of engine stables, and in them, stuck into the semi-darkness as tightly as pistons, rested the motionless bodies of the locomotives. Some stood without their wheels, raised on jacks for "turning," others yawned from their open smoke boxes, and one could see their black tubular insides streaked with light. The place became animated as the new shift took over. In the sooty funnels on the ceiling an uncertain dirty light was turned on; the eye perceived, not whole objects, as reason is wont to think of them, but only the mutilated parts of them that happened to fall within the dim, swaying cones of light. There were four such fragments, as many as there were lamps, in the first section into which Gleb entered.

We might generalize this remark and show how the aspect of the world changes according to whether it is illumined by a waning moon, a flash of shrapnel or a smouldering bonfire. We could also base our description of this engine house upon its odors, using as paint the corroding stench of burning oakum, the poisonous smoke of engines under repair and the tickling mixture of steam and overheated oil. No less expressively could sounds have given shape to the outlines of the morning in the engine house. In the sonorous confusion, the ear distinguished the noises of various labor processes—the crunch of drills, the insinuating rustle of transmission belts or the howl of files on brass bearings. . . . Gleb's depressed mood, too, gave a definite form to the picture. And although he had done nothing criminal on the station platform, his feelings of guilt had never before been so acute. They lent a sharp novelty to this place with which he was familiar to the point of aversion. Thus he perceived the sulphurous taste of coal gas on his tongue, with heightened bitterness. . . . Of a sudden he threw up his head inquiringly.

He heard a simple tune, held within the limits of one octave, drawn

delicately against the noisy background of the engine house. Somewhere among the slumbering and paralyzed engines a quivering, metallic little tongue was singing. And because he could not at once locate
the instrument and the song itself, Gleb's irritation grew more intense.
Striving to find its source, he entered the nearest circle of light. He
felt a rapid rattle in his legs and his ears. A man with a mallet clung to
the smoke-box grating, rolling the pipes. The booming belly of the
boiler droned—but the little song could be heard more distinctly! The
mechanic exchanged greetings with the yard master, and the yard
master proceeded on his way. Another locomotive surgeon was astride
the hump of another engine, digging into its chimney cowl. A little
torch shaped like a teapot was blazing beside it. The fluid orange reflections of the fire shone in the foreman's greasy trousers, and the
patches in them seemed to be made of red copper. The foreman's face
was hidden in darkness, but at the moment his teeth gleamed, and
Gleb realized that he was smiling.

"They're putting in some work, the Tartars . . . all night long they've
toiled!" He pointed at the next section, whence came the hissing of
steam and a bluish glow. "It's as if they were dressing a bride. But
you won't find a male for such a bride, Gleb Ignatyich, in all Cheremshansk!"

The intention of this remark was malicious, incomprehensible and
obscene.

"I don't like your jokes, Gashin," answered Gleb with restraint.
"I've had my eye on you for a long time!"

The mechanic laughed, tore off his cap with feigned zeal; and it was
strange to see that his hair had been smoothed down flat on his head.
Gashin's laugh meant that he knew the limits of Gleb's authority and
that it was dangerous to quarrel with him, Gashin.

"Of course you've noticed me: the place is rather crowded. I've noticed some things about you, too!" He quietly tapped with his hammer
and did not explain his hint.

It was humiliating to stand near, waiting for him to explain himself,
but Gleb lacked the strength to turn away. With his hands in his
pockets he silently stared at the face of his most dangerous enemy
(so he thought at that moment), trying to recall in what circumstances
they had met before.

". . . And I'll say openly that the boys are being naughty, and for
that reason *something* must happen to them."

It was clear that this man would have done anything to make his
prophecy come true. He was absolutely opposed to the release of the
Komsomol engine. Once this engine had been in his charge; then, as a

result of several train stoppages, he was transferred from the right to
the left wing on the line; later, he was entirely removed from the engine, upon the insistence of the Komsomol group. Gleb knew who had
thrown a handful of sand into the engine's cylinders and how a coal
shovel had happened to get stuck in its smoke stack. But Gashin was
the only man never touched by Protoklitov's punishing hand. Some
people even thought that Gashin was particularly favored by the yard
master and expressed surprise that the latter had not succeeded in
keeping him on his previous job. Gleb felt that he had to go somewhere, away from those unbearably insolent eyes, but he could not
find the final word to save his dignity as yard master. Familiar with
Protoklitov's attitude toward the Komsomols' project, Gashin considered him an accomplice and interpreted his superior's grumbling
restraint only as an indication that he wanted to keep him, Gashin, at
a respectful distance. At this point the tune Gleb had heard a few
minutes earlier resounded again. He mechanically turned to the adjacent section of the engine house and looked in.

Near the window an autogenous welding was taking place. The
protective screen had been removed in order to obtain additional light.
The glare of the burning stream of oxygen was many times stronger
than the dawn twilight. The windows seemed dark although it was
already day. And glittering festively in this pulsating light stood the
Komsomol engine. Only in such a narrow space did the enormous object reveal its mighty dimensions and potentialities. It was a proud and
beautiful engine of series ES. No. 4019, with a newly repaired boiler,
smooth projectors and handrails freshly painted with a piercing red
lead. A gigantic sign, KLM, as though taken from a legendary hero's
chest, graced its broad smoke stack with the cone in front. Its profile
shadow on the wall, thrown slightly backward as though it were moving at full speed, could have been an inspiration for future engine de-
signers. The machine was steaming, and there was something magical
about the way the rattling boiling water from the fire-pump throbbed
in the steel tendons.

The locomotive was being washed; its most serious test was approaching, after a long period of agitation. Soon, very soon, the 4019
was to run its first stretch. About ten silent fellows with rags and
oakum bustled around the body of the engine that was long as a
dragon-fly. Its polished shaft and outer armature already rejoiced the
eye, but these enthusiasts strove to achieve the highest degree of
eternal beauty. (Gleb thought to himself that the wives of these boys
would have a hot and merry time!) The metallic little song resounded
again, this time louder, closer, more assured. The tune was clean and

pleasant; it was good that someone's fresh and impudent tenderness was relieving the austere morning boredom of the engine house. Gleb was older and more experienced than these boys, but his irritation was not caused by any feeling related to his age. He thought continually of Kormilitsin; the very fact of his arrival implied that simple and honest joys were inaccessible to Gleb.

He went behind the engine. Near the damp wall, on a thin layer of oakum, sat a fellow in an old patched sweater, with one knee bent under him; the boot on his other, outstretched leg was soaking in a puddle of water. The music was coming from him. In his left hand he held a still burning cigarette and in his right hand a wooden plate covered with tin and stuffed with a great number of brass voices. Oblivious and ecstatic, he passed his singing toy over his lips, and the impetuous cascade of sounds, now gathered into low trilling sheaves, all running together, sonorous as a bird's twitter, made his frowning sleepless comrades smile. With an air of absorbed indifference Gleb listened to these musical exercises. The fireman Skuriatnikov, a member of the crew of the Komsomol engine, had only recently been admitted to the organization. He was an odd, impudent little fellow, with a stubborn temper; his comrades liked him.

Skuriatnikov opened one, then the other eye, and the music ceased. "What are you playing?" Protoklitov asked in a friendly tone.

"We're playing a march, comrade yard master." He put his harmonica in his pocket.

He was entitled to do anything he liked on his day off; he was not interfering with anyone here in this corner. Protoklitov was about to inquire about the reasons for all this merriment, but at that moment someone noticed him; facetious greetings resounded, and someone brightly called out the name of the still invisible Peresypkin. . . . Their silent stubbornness and zeal had to be remarked upon in some way; Protoklitov said in a low voice that in such a machine one would not be ashamed to drive straight into the Socialist society. He was answered by ten roaring voices: "We're trying!" Then something made a noise in the cab, and soon an unfamiliar young man began to climb down the engine, clinging to the handrail from lack of habit. Gleb found the appearance of this young man amusing: he looked about twenty-three years old, but he stoically bore the burden of his age. He was all tied up with leather straps like a suitcase that has travelled across many lands. One sleeve of his reddish leather coat bore traces of fresh paint, and the young fellow obviously flaunted this stain as a warrior shows his wound. For the space of about a minute he scrutinized the engine anxiously, as though it were his favorite creation, drumming with his fingers on the musette bag at his side. Then he held out his hand to Protoklitov and informed him that he was Peresypkin. "I have been wanting to meet you for a long time!" he said, knitting his brows.

"Well, it's easy to find me. I live on the hill on the ground floor. . . ."

"Then please excuse me," Peresypkin said in a low voice. "I've been trying to find you in the engine house."

Protoklitov did not deserve this pinprick. Peresypkin knew that the other spent the larger part of the day in the engine house, but those discourteous words had slipped out while all his comrades stood listening. He hastened to soften his impertinence by recognizing the difficulties of the work. But his own gentleness seemed excessive to him, and once again he bristled, ready to fight. "Well," he said, tenderly touching the bluish flesh of the steel still warm from steam. "Here is the thing you have opposed so much. You've got excellent boys, Protoklitov! With such boys one can storm any fortress!"

Protoklitov hinted that servicing an engine was a somewhat complicated job for people who only occasionally worked on the line.

"Well, it's not my first year on the railroad!" Peresypkin burst out.

"At any rate, you're well preserved for your age, comrade!"

Peresypkin tossed his head, stung in his most vulnerable spot; it seemed that even the whites of his eyes blushed. And as though he feared to be suspected of ignorance he fired in one breath all the accusations he had had time to collect in the Cheremshansk roundhouse. He mentioned the cases of non-delivery of engines, the frequent need of second repairs, the incorrect alternation of hot and cold cleanings; striving for perfect accuracy, he pointed out that the tender boxes of engine S-64 had loose bolts and were leaking, that the day before engine OV-201 was filled with unsoftened water which was thirty per cent hard. Gently criticizing the work of the shop cells, he also asked why comrade Idrisova had not yet finished her accounts concerning the water-tower for the second half of November? He was warming up—if he fought, he might as well fight to the end! The coal mixture lay for six months under the scaffold bridge, until all the calories evaporated. The engine house did not observe the prescription with regard to temperature, and engines can catch cold just like people. . . .

". . . And they're sneezing like mad in your engine house!" he concluded hotly.

He was not alone; the boys listened to every word of this altercation. Soot deepened the planes of their sullen faces. The yard master pointed out to the young man and esteemed journalist that their discussion was taking place in the presence of people from whom he demanded absolute obedience. He turned his back to Peresypkin, promising to continue this instructive conversation at another place and in a moment of leisure. Then, in a business-like tone, without special tenderness, he thanked the Komsomols for the work they had done and spoke of the responsibility they were about to assume. Immediately the older workers, who had gathered around them, attracted by the noise, became animated, and one of them shouted the prophetic words: "They'll bring her home!" and another promised to give them the dirtiest matting in the place of their banner should they lose this game too difficult for their experience. A third one added in a deep bass that even before reconditioning this engine rolled perfectly well. ". . . Lord! Just give her three shovelfuls of good coal, and the steam will thunder!"

Thus the still unresolved quarrel was ended by a facetious and friendly exchange of words between the old and the young. The Komsomols invited the yard master to come to their meeting after the siren blew. This was a move toward reconciliation. Protoklitov promised to come and, trying to strengthen the ties of friendship, asked who was to drive the engine the next day. A tall, broad-faced youngster in greasy overalls stepped forward. He was the only Tartar mechanic in Cheremshansk, recently transferred from the left to the right wing. His name was Sayfullah, and he was no more than twenty-five years old. He was a distant relative of Badrudtin Ziganshin, commissar of the Moslem battalion, who, it was said, had fallen during the Bashkir uprising near Belebey. In fact, Sayfullah resembled his legendary kinsman: he had the same tall sailor's stature, the same proud head, which he always kept down on his chest, the same keen, hawklike, yellow eyes. And perhaps because Protoklitov had happened once to meet Ziganshin, he disliked this handsome and courageous man.

The boys waited to see what the yard master would say. "Well, I congratulate you, Sayfullah!" he said, and even offered him a cigarette. "Grow up, learn how to run an engine, don't make mistakes. . . ." And suddenly he asked in a casual tone what he would do if a shaft broke while he was driving.

An experienced engineer is not asked such questions; Sayfullah's broad eyebrows, like those of his nomadic ancestors, closed at the bridge of his nose. He began to speak with emotion, and from his very first words it was clear that his notions about the mysteries of steam-distribution were somewhat vague. Gleb nodded with approval, shaking the ashes off his cigarette. Then he extended his hand to the young man, and Sayfullah's whole body seemed to soften in an embarrassed and grateful smile.

"That's good, that's good, boss!" he stammered, dropping a piece of emery paper on the floor.

The boys scattered, and the young man still stood amidst the steaming puddles, his eyes on his sooty rusty fingers. The warmth of his joy was passing away; the morning chill was penetrating him through the overalls that he wore over his shirt. The Tartar raised his head and saw the engine of which he was soon to become the master. His childhood dream was coming true, but now the engine appeared to him different from that of the fantasy of a peasant boy. He looked at this mass of intelligently organized metal that had once overawed his imagination, and it seemed to him that he hastily repeated in his mind everything he knew about engines.

In stone hollows under the roof lived the plump yard pigeons. Crowded like sparrows they sat on jutting bricks brocaded with hoarfrost and chattered about something—no doubt about the incoming transports of grain. Sayfullah absent-mindedly listened to their cooing, which reminded him of his adventures as a boy. He had come a long way from his past. Suddenly he snatched a chamois cloth from the floor and began to wipe the fresh rust off the buffer plates.

# CHAPTER 35

# A Conversation with the Past

KORMILITSIN WAITED FOR GLEB, sitting on his friend's cot. It was a hard cot; through the blanket he could feel the cracked boards. He leaned his elbows on his knees and put his face in his hands. He had no watch and did not know how long he had sat thus, idle and oblivious of the world. He was resting from his trip, from Zoska, from himself. . . .

The house had two storeys. From time to time chairs moved about on the upper floor, and Kormilitsin would start and stare at the ceiling of smooth planks. He felt hungry and got up to look for food. In an unpainted closet lay thread, buttons and all sorts of small objects for the daily use of a bachelor, in orderly arrangement. A stack of books on railroad questions was piled up on the window-sill. Kormilitsin mechanically paged them. The third book from the top, with a flamboyant red cloth back, bore the name of Lenin; he jerked back his hand in fright. In an unlocked, woven basket under the cot were a pair of trousers, some linen, and on top, quite conspicuously, a revolver. The cold burnished steel somehow evoked in his mind the image of Zoska and her new lover, enormous in all his parts. The object almost stuck to his hand, an effort of will power was required to shake it off. There were no other hiding-places here. The room seemed a desert; no mirror and not one fleck of dirt. . . . All this tallied with Kormilitsin's ideas about his friend. This was only Gleb's temporary haven; and here, on the intersection of two roads they were fated to meet. Neither of them had any possessions; Gleb, because he was climbing up, and Kormilitsin, because he was hurrying down, to the "valley of the blessed." So they called in their old, intimate language the last destination of every "leather bag with a soul."

Meanwhile, outside the window the sky had cleared. The smoke was descending, and in the sky a ghostly sun, hardly more than a hint, made its appearance. . . . The visitor began to be angry. He imagined that Gleb's absence was the result of a deliberate and cunning plan to reduce the time of their communion to a minimum. Yet so great was his attachment to Protoklitov that he forgave him these unkind intentions the moment he entered. With a loving and embarrassed smile he watched Gleb cutting some bread in enormous slices and opening tin cans. In addition Gleb drew a handful of candles and a bottle of vodka from his pocket, thus completely dispelling Kormilitsin's suspicions.

"I'm giving you trouble, Glebushka?"

"It's nothing. . . . Sit down, be my guest. I've been detained, excuse me."

"Anything unpleasant at the engine house?"

"No . . . but everybody is shouting about the struggle, they try to convince each other, and forget that one goes to the attack in silence. And first of all one must tell that apathetic rabble sternly: if you want to eat your fill, and live in a heated home, do your job well. In America there are no socialist competitions, but the trains run on the minute and at seventy miles an hour. . . . My arms are too short, Evgenyi!"

He expatiated on this subject, and Kormilitsin nodded in approval, almost with rapture, imitating his expressions as faithfully as a mirror.

"You're intelligent, Glebushka. You know how to express what I can only think. And you like to be conscientious in any job. But don't speak so loudly, we're surrounded by strangers." He pointed at the ceiling. "They're moving all the chairs up there . . . does that matter? Now I understand your hint about my letter . . . forgive an old friend! Incidentally, do you live like this, without a woman? . . . You get along without? . . ." He was about to explain himself by a coarse gesture, but was deterred by a sudden gleam in Gleb's eyes. ". . . I mean: without a family?"

"Yes, I live alone. Drink, drink . . . I ate at the station!" And this sounded as though he meant: Get drunk as fast as possible!

"Don't you want to drink with me? Well, I won't insist! So, to our reunion, dear old man!" the visitor said hoarsely, overcome by emotion. He drank, and apparently the liquor got stuck somewhere; he passed his hand over his throat as though trying to push down a too-big gulp, then sat still, with a confused and swollen face. "I'll pour myself another, if you don't mind."

Gleb attentively studied his guest. He was only the skeleton of the former robust Kormilitsin, covered with an unhealthy and dirty skin. And some demon of inconsolable grief had given him the idea of growing long, priestlike locks!

"Do you drink much, Evgenyi?"

"No, only from time to time . . . as a tonic. You understand, when I see you everything that is buried under us is revived. We walk, and our steps resound sonorously on *their* coffins, eh? So let's drink to those who are now listening to our talk. . . . You don't like me to drink?"

"Why not? . . . You're my guest. Only eat something, too!"

"I drink to *you*, the dead, who died an *undesired* death!" Evgenyi declared, speaking into space. He raised his hand and, as though the liquor had exploded in him, he wrinkled his face and again reached out for the bottle, then thought better of it and hid his hand under the table. He sat stroking his non-existent beard with his left hand. (Apparently, at the beginning of his *new* life he had grown a beard, but had shaven it in a moment of lucidity; however, the habit of stroking it had remained.)

Gleb was silent; he himself had challenged his past to a duel, and it had thrown at him this bone from the grave. He watched with half-closed eyes how some surviving muscle jerked in it. Hiding his eyes from his friend, Kormilitsin dug with his penknife in a tin can.

"Is this shad?" he asked, oppressed by Gleb's silence.

It was as though his question had awakened Protoklitov. "What are you now?" he asked.

"What am I?"

And he burst into a humiliated, ugly and squeaky laugh. "Just like yourself, a non-party tramp. . . ."

"Are you an honest man?"

"I don't kill or steal. . . ."

". . . But you were in prison?"

"Yes. . . . A regimental banner was discovered in my home. I didn't hide it well enough. . . ."

Gleb raised his eyes questioningly: Kormilitsin had never served in the infantry. "How did you happen to have it?" he asked.

"The late Ferapontov had given it to me to keep. . . . Remember him?"

One could not have forgotten that face flattened from underneath, fleshy as a whale's—and in its swarthy, soft cheeks one surmised there were slanting eyes. He had enjoyed special and well-deserved hatred on the part of the Reds.

"You say, he, 'the late'? . . . What did he die of?"

Kormilitsin stuck out his underlip. "Oh, what can a decent fellow die of nowadays? . . . Of the revolution! He was recognized on a train, he jumped out, but broke his leg. We're growing old, gymnastics is no longer for us! You and I also. . . ."

"Well, I should say there's little similarity between us."

"And why?" Kormilitsin exploded; the liquor had begun to affect him. "We too are completely spent. Eh, don't pretend, Glebushka! You were saved by your frantic energy, I, by my laziness—after all I've always remained in the shadow. But it's too late for both of us to begin from the beginning and it's too early for us to finish. . . ." Thus discarding the future he turned to the past: "It's strange to think, Glebushka . . . in the Transbaikal the marsh rosemary must be flowering under the snow. . . . No leaves yet, but there are already crimson flowers on the bare stems!"

"It's too early for flowers."

"What month are we in now? January? Yes, perhaps it's too early." He had correctly foreseen that the rosemary deserved a fifth glass; the third and fourth had come all by themselves in the heat of their talk. "Why do you keep a copy of Lenin here? Is it because strangers come to see you or just to get quotations out of it?"

"No, I read him," said Gleb firmly.

"Hm, his style is somewhat heavy, isn't it? I once borrowed a volume of his works from Zoska's boy friend, but . . . it didn't work out!" He leered at Gleb with curiosity. "Well, and do you like the way he writes?"

Gleb drummed with his fingers on the table; it was high time to put an end to this humiliating game of hide-and-seek.

"You see, Evgenyi . . . I'm a party member."

"So-o-o?" Kormilitsin's eyes goggled, in genuine surprise. "Since when?"

"Seven years."

Kormilitsin rose and energetically pushed back his unfinished glass; the liquor in it splashed. He was pale and more confused than shaken by the stunning cynicism of this confession. His eyes prowled about the room until they found his cap. He stared for a long time at its greasy wadded top, as though unable to understand what this object was for, then he picked it up.

". . . Impossible!" He almost blinked with fright. "You're making fun of me. It's still part of the act you're putting on for me. . . . You've never respected me, Glebushka, have you? . . . How did it come about?"

"I'm afraid it's beyond your comprehension, Evgenyi."

"Yes, you were more gifted than any of *us*. You figured everything out, after all you're a mathematician. But I still remember your threat that anyone who agreed to serve the Soviets should be regarded as a deserter. Did you foresee even then who'd lick whom? I suppose you wanted all of us to be shot so that no one would remain to denounce you . . . isn't that so?" He jumped up and grabbed Gleb, crumpling his coat at the shoulders. "You devil, tell me, is that true? . . . And what about everything that *was*? And what about *us*? What are we to do, applaud you, or what?"

"That's your own business. And don't breathe right at me, Evgenyi, it's nauseating!"

Kormilitsin moved away, mechanically wiping his hands off on the lapels of his woollen shirt. He picked up his cap from the floor: trying tensely to understand exactly what had happened, he pulled hairs out of the fur and threw them all around him. Suddenly he grinned with a hurt expression and very carefully put his cap on the edge of the table.

". . . Well, then I may sit down. Why should I stand before you! What a fool I am! . . ." No longer restraining himself, he poured himself another glass and, following it, still another—he lost count. "It's strange: after all, I don't know anything about you. . . . Have you a sister, a brother or a mother—to spit in your face? Or were you born by immaculate conception? Who are you, who? . . . And how . . . I mean to say, are you devoted to this, this *new* government?"

"I myself am this government," Gleb said, not quite firmly, but he had decided to go the whole way.

"Yes, yes, I get it. What is it, ambition? Judging by your furniture" —his eyes roved sneeringly over the empty walls—"you haven't profited much so far. Do you expect to make up for it in the future? . . . And you're not struggling for socialism, nor for your own system of general happiness, not even for the right to reveal•ourselves later so that people can weep over you as they did over Jean Valjean. . . . In fact, you're a man without an upper storey, without God, without conscience . . . you, completely indifferent to everything, you've joined the big gamblers—but what for? It's interesting, I've seen many things in my life, but never repentant scoundrels. . . . And do you know, I could kill you now, and I'd be tried as the murderer of a Soviet saint, eh?" He guffawed, rocking his chair and waving his arms and legs. "Eh, you, gladiator, son of a bi-i-tch. . . ."

He lost all his previous restraint, threw up his head so that Protoklitov could see in detail his unshaven throat with its protuberant Adam's apple. (Suddenly the chair on the floor above ceased moving.) Having lost his home and wife, Kormilitsin was now losing his only friend. He took revenge upon him, poured salt on his wounds, wanting him to cry out and confess at last that he had indulged in a bad joke. With partly closed eyes Gleb watched these convulsions. This was a living piece of incriminating evidence from the past. Crushed, it squirmed underfoot, if unable to sting him, at least trying to defile him by its touch. . . .

Gleb's mind was veiled by a sudden rage. His hands closed involuntarily, his fingers with hallucinatory reality felt Kormilitsin's prickly unshaven throat. Outwardly motionless, he clenched his fists, and the throat was yielding slowly, was squeezed in, cartilaginous, warm, hateful. . . . And his friend kept roaring with laughter, indulging in complicated trills and runs, waving his hands and stealthily watching Protoklitov's eyes darken. He stopped as unexpectedly as he had begun, and with his earlier, doglike humility poured himself another glass.

"I'll throw you out, Evgenyi, if you have these hysterics again," Protoklitov remarked impassively, frankly examining the traces of his nails on his hands. "I must say, I don't particularly believe in their sincerity."

With a gleam in his eyes, Kormilitsin raised his glass. "I like your fearlessness, my friend," he said. "I take back my vile abuse. I prophesy that you really will go far! Perhaps that is better for both of us. I'm aging, I'm becoming less and less resourceful . . . you won't forget me, will you? And so, to your great future!" The toast sounded like a promise not to spoil his friend's career. "And now I think I can have a bite. You know, I'm quite hungry. . . ."

He ate with considerable appetite, keeping up a polite and quite intelligent conversation. He spoke of all that he had experienced and thought. He described a sovkhoz,[1] gave a picturesque report of his quarrel with Chumko, the bookkeeper, and excerpts of his interesting interviews with the examining judge who had declared at the end of the investigation that Kormilitsin was completely undangerous to the Soviet government. "An impudent fellow he was, but I can't deny that he had a certain sense of humor!" Gleb laughed at the Chekist's perspicacity, and was even about to drink a glass in honor of his reconciliation with his friend, when someone came from the yard asking for Protoklitov. Kormilitsin timorously accompanied him to the door. "Will you be gone for long?" he asked.

'At any rate, I'll see you again before you leave. I advise you to lie down and take a rest, Evgenyi. I'll wake you up. . . ."

Kormilitsin stammered: "You see, I'm afraid I won't be able to get a ticket for the night train. . . ."

"That's nothing, I'll fix you up in a car. I know some people at the station."

He left and remained absent until dusk. Half an hour before the arrival of the train, when Gleb came for Kormilitsin, he was still sitting at the table. The bottle before him was empty. Gleb said that it was time to get going, but Kormilitsin kept muttering incoherently about the bookkeeper, Chumko; apparently the unknown pettifogger

[1] State farm.

had annoyed him. Gleb tried to shout at this piece of carrion, but it began to stir and show its claws. "We keep our coats on, you and I, let's take them off, old pal!" But he immediately repented of his effrontery, burst into tears, asked forgiveness and became utterly insufferable.

"I've put on your felt boots, Glebushka," he said, putting his legs forward from under the table. "My feet were frozen, they hurt me, see?"

These were magnificent buckskin boots, fur-lined, newly soled, warm as an oven; such objects were priceless in Cheremshansk, but Gleb did not mind anything now. "Never mind, take them as a souvenir, Evgenyi!" he said.

Kormilitsin refused; both men began to feel sick at their stomachs from this contest in nobleness, in which every mistaken move could have the exactly opposite meaning. "I'd be ashamed, Glebushka . . . I'm not a robber."

"It isn't worth talking about! By the way, I've arranged for your ticket. You'll have a seat. . . . Get dressed."

Kormilitsin stammered and stroked the edge of the table in confusion. Suddenly he declared frankly that he had not come for a visit, that he had no place to go, that for the time being he had made up his mind to stay with Gleb. "You understand, it would be a pity to take my feet out of these felt boots. They're nice and warm . . . and yet I'm ashamed to take them!"

Kormilitsin's declaration disarmed Gleb at once and for all.

"And . . . do you intend to stay a long time?" he asked lifelessly.

"I'm afraid, yes. . . ." He got up with an effort and tried to look into his friend's eyes. "Do you hate me very much, Glebushka?"

He could barely stand on his feet; it would have been both absurd and dangerous to drag him to the station in this condition. Protoklitov locked him up and went to his post outwardly calmer than ever.

For the night Kormilitsin magnanimously made his bed on the floor. "You're working, Glebushka, you need rest." Until daybreak he was tormented by a cough that shook everything in the room. Twice during the night Gleb got up to see what Harpies were lacerating the chest of this fool. . . .

It goes without saying that of all the different kinds of friends there are, he preferred a dog: at least one can shoot it if necessary.

# CHAPTER 36

# A Corpse Wants to Live

AND SO EVGENYI did not leave the next day, nor any of the following days. . . . Gleb did not express displeasure, he even brought some boards on his shoulder and with his own hands made a cot for Kormilitsin who, distrustful of every favor, sat beside him in the pose of the Tempter, destroying the last remnants of his host's tobacco. Now they shared everything half-and-half, even Gleb's underwear. Kormilitsin accepted his part casually, lived dirtily, behaved importunately, constantly and loudly demanded wine; he expected his host to rebel, and then he would flood him with a hail of dead bones, their common past. Gleb seemed not to notice his unprovoked fits of quarrelsomeness, and Kormilitsin secretly envied his ability to yield without losing patience or dignity. As the visitor more clearly realized his role of uninvited parasite or blackmailer, he began to repent.

One day upon returning from work Gleb found that his floor had been washed and realized that Kormilitsin was tormented by idleness. He himself was very tired that month, and he dropped on his bed without saying a word. The next day he found Kormilitsin darning their underwear. His face was red and strained; the patches looked monstrous; he was angry at his own incapacity and pricked fingers. In confusion he stuck the needle somewhere in the wall and hurriedly walked to the window. "I'm ashamed to eat your bread," he said a minute later in a dull and bitter voice.

This was the first time he had ever said anything of this kind. Usually he liked to pose as an idler in Gleb's presence and only recently had blurted out a sentence that was enough to enrage one: "I shaved this morning, I'm awfully tired. . . ." Gleb lay on his bed staring at the ceiling.

". . . Why? I think I have enough bread. Actually you eat very little for a man your build."

Kormilitsin fancied there was an ironical note in these words. "You think it's funny, Glebushka," he said; ". . . and yet I'm still alive! And I want to be like everyone else. For instance, I . . ." (he sounded as though he were speaking of something impossible) ". . . I even want to buy some sort of little chest and have in it a pair of new trousers, a book I haven't read, my own razor, the picture of a girl . . . she may even be thirty-five years old, I shouldn't mind! You surely have un-friendly ideas about me! Oh, don't pretend, Glebushka. Yesterday you were tactless enough to offer me money to go to some sanatorium. You were perhaps too frank, old pal. I'm afraid you won't get rid of me as quickly as that. The way I understand our friendship is that either we'll both soar to the heights or both drop to the ground. Until I croak I'll follow you like a faithful dog, do you hear me? . . . But I'll bite you to death one minute before you betray me. Remember, a dog can be well-bred like a human being, but it's always ready to snap like a real dog!"

Complaisantly and patiently Gleb awaited the end of the usual fit. When these verbal convulsions were over, he got up, took Kormilitsin by his shoulders, looked bravely and imperiously into his rheumy eyes, called him a fool, and Kormilitsin, all softened, drew in his shoulders, grew yellow and small and accepted Gleb's virile, strong, rude caress.

"Do I try to throw you out or reproach you with anything, Evgenyi?" (And he listened in boredom to a confused tirade about how Kor-militsin wanted to be resuscitated, to go straight, to assume a human appearance.) "But what exactly do you want? Tell me, no one is listening . . . we'll discuss the matter."

Kormilitsin's face showed some animation. "I want . . ." (he was terrified, as though someone might refuse him!) ". . . I want to forget everything, to be tired like you, to dig myself into this mire and soot . . . and that someone, even the smallest man, even ten years hence, should praise me. You're a great strong man . . . help me!" All red from shame, he finally uttered these words: "I want to work."

Gleb let him out of his embrace because his surprise was much stronger than his false tenderness of a minute ago. It was strange to hear someone imploring for work in a country that suffered from a shortage of men in every field every day. . . . At the same time it was the biggest thing Kormilitsin could have asked him. The appearance of a new man in Cheremshansk, particularly a man brought in by the yard master, would attract a great deal of attention. Out of a hundred random guesses, one might hit the bull's eye, and then his collapse was inevitable. Some time later Gleb asked Kormilitsin to show him his papers, and carefully studied them. Among other things he ex-pressed surprise at the fact that Kormilitsin was forty-one years of age; the latter, who was inclined to speak in fancy metaphors, re-marked bitterly that the last twenty years had gone by in one year. Gleb was silent.

"Well!" Kormilitsin urged him, rubbing his hands as though to warm himself. "After all, I've been punished in every possible way. Or do you believe I have committed some special original sin that is sufficient to exclude me from life forever?"

"Are you . . . clean?" Gleb asked suddenly.

"You've already asked me that. I can say that it's hard for me to pretend to be a pig. I'm not afraid of any work and whatever I undertake I do well."

Then Gleb began to list aloud all the possible jobs in Cheremshansk. Kormilitsin could not become a timekeeper or foreman of engine crews without a thorough knowledge of the yard's business. He did not wish to sit in an office, although once before he had worked in such a capacity on a railroad. The only post that remained was that of superintendent of the supply store. The man who had been slated for this job was about to be fired because he had sold five pounds of liquid ammonia on the side. The pay for this not very difficult work was two hundred and fifty a month, and it required nothing except a good memory and honesty.

"Well, make your choice, Evgenyi!" Gleb said coldly.

Kormilitsin grew red in the face and turned away. "I want something lower, Glebushka. Any kind of work, . . ." he said emphatically. "I'm very strong, believe me! Eksakustodian avoided meeting me! . . . I thought that if I began at the very bottom, in the lower depths, like you. . . ."

"Aha, so this bookkeeper wanted to suffer!" The only kind of job of that sort he could offer him was that of an unskilled laborer in the yard; this required equal amounts of muscular strength, modesty and absolute obedience. In this job no nerves at all were required; it was useless to seek another remedy with similar healing powers. A good dose of it did not leave a man any time to be alone with himself; thus there was hope of getting rid of oneself and the painful memory of Zoska. . . . From Gleb's point of view there were other assets, and the first of these consisted in the possibility of keeping Kormilitsin at a distance. At the same time it was no trouble for Gleb to get him this job: the turnover of unskilled laborers at Cheremshansk had more than once been the subject of discussion. The administration itself often confused the names and faces of these people. In brief, one out of fifty attracted less attention than one out of five. The very fact that Gleb was thoughtful showed that he agreed. The affair was being concluded to the satisfaction of both of them. All that evening, Kormilitsin looked absent-minded, did not drink vodka, kept dropping things and, when night came, went out to take a walk in the snowy glades on the road to Borschnia. All that remained now was to play the last act for the benefit of the public. They decided to pretend that they had met before, in the repair crew, and that Gleb was being kind to an old acquaintance who had entered upon a path of repentance and work. But in the meantime peaceful days still alternated with hysterical fits on the part of Kormilitsin. . . . The very next night Gleb was awakened roughly; some sudden force had torn off his blanket from his head; the swish awoke him. Bending toward his head, Kormilitsin stood over him with a burning match, and there was obvious madness in his squinting eyes.

"Why did you remove my blanket?" Gleb asked sternly, but did not venture to bend down for the cover in order not to expose his neck to Kormilitsin in the darkness.

He struck a new match. Squirming and excitedly laughing he explained that he had had a sudden desire to see the son of a bitch undressed: "You want to run away from the wheels, but never mind . . . ha, they'll catch up with you anyhow! Keep wriggling. . . ." Gleb smiled with disgust at this pathological gibberish and next morning got up with a headache as a result of the weird two-hour rumpus with this resurrected ghost. Imagining all kinds of variations and repetitions of this scene he removed his revolver from the basket to a secret hiding-place he alone knew. (He had noticed the signs of a stranger's careless hand.) The second time Kormilitsin woke him up for another reason, mysteriously shaking him by the shoulder. From the feverish speeches one could gather that he had dreamed of the faithless Zoska, his last attachment in this world; and it was unclear whether she had appeared to him in her seductive nakedness or drenched in her own blood. . . . She tormented him even in his dreams. Stuttering and stroking Gleb's hairy wrist, he described Zoska as no one but himself had known her, her lovely height and the proud slope of her shoulders, her throaty, metallic voice, the dark, too regular semi-circles of her brows, as though drawn with a compass, her long full legs, her cheeks unbearably pink as though prickled by the mustache of her present boy friend, her eyes under her laughing eyelashes, slightly greenish like sedgy lake water, all of her, her most intimate feminine secrets. Before Gleb's eyes, he turned her every possible way, lovely, naked, filthy, inviting his friend's hands, his aroused nocturnal imagination, to follow him along all the hollows, sinuosities, ticklish spots and warm dimples of that big, beautiful, insatiable and imaginary body. "Touch her, touch her everywhere! . . ." cried his desolate eyes; and Gleb listened to him, feeling with his back every splinter in the wainscoting of the wall. This woman whom he had never seen began to arouse in him a dark, hidden, masculine feeling. (Only the next morning did it occur to him that Kormilitsin had deliberately made him the accomplice of his secret, his longing and jealousy, and showed him Zoska *alive*, in order to have someone to whom he could transfer his anger and thirst for revenge.)

Kormilitsin's eyes twitched, they were veiled by a red film. Falling and tossing on the ground he groaned out: "With this Eksakustodian she goes . . . everywhere! If I see fallen trees in the woods—it's they. If I enter into a dark room—it's they. I close my eyes—again they, they. What does she call him at night when they embrace—Kuzey, or what?"

He was shaken with fever and chills, and one could only imagine what frantic images of sexual love filled the space around him night and day. The number of his imagined rivals intensified his jealousy tenfold; they already marched in platoons, and in their midst, merrily, always walked Zoska. (Actually she was a quiet woman who had finally got fed up with the gloomy and enthusiastic oaths of Kormilitsin's love!) It was becoming clear that he would have killed her if she had been close at hand. . . .

Having clearly perceived what would follow such a crime, Gleb saw in it a good way to get rid of Kormilitsin. Yes, indeed, Zoska had many more reasons to fear for her life than did Protoklitov. Then Gleb made up his mind to help his friend, to direct his hand in such a manner that it did not miss. He had to hurry: the hatred of a small man requires to be quenched immediately. In the morning Gleb put the revolver back into his basket; thus a net is spread for fish. He left for the yard with the certainty that an hour later Kormilitsin would run into the thing when looking for a fresh shirt and that the very sight of it would give him an idea. And so it was: the next day Gleb saw that the revolver was missing; the bait had been swallowed . . . but the same night the weapon reappeared, only to vanish a day later. Kormilitsin hesitated to shoot his former love, and Gleb decided to intensify his hypnotic suggestion by direct questions about Zoska.

He carried out his plan not too subtly, he was unceremonious with the heart of this tiresome old soldier. He asked for details about Zoska's new love; rudely, almost cynically, he questioned Kormilitsin as to Eksakustodian's physical qualities; he expressed his sympathy for the jilted lover; he screwed his words like corkscrews into Kormilitsin's hardened skin, feeling out the most sensitive nerve in his organism. . . . But Gleb's calculations proved wrong. After his first day at work Kormilitsin came back half dead from fatigue and went to bed at once. He threw himself into work with the frenzy of a starved man; no one demanded such efforts of him. He deliberately spent himself on the heaviest labor, he turned hand jacks raising engines to be repaired, removed shafts, cleaned drainage ditches. His excessive efficiency might even have aroused dangerous suspicions that he had taken a job in the Cheremshansk yard not for the sake of earning his bread alone, that his zeal was a mask for some sinister design.

At the same time Kormilitsin began to visit all kinds of clubs and attended weighty lectures. His virginal ignorance of political questions reliably protected him from other people's alertness. He liked the heat of the yard; he believed that owing to his abundant sweating his former skin was leaving him. Gradually his appearance, speech and habits became indistinguishable from those of his comrades. He looked more sober now, the black air of the yard proved beneficial to his mental health. He postponed moving to the workers' dormitory for various reasons, and Gleb suffered from Kormilitsin's excessive snoring as he had formerly suffered from his cough. This new Cheremshansk worker apparently had no nightmares. Zoska's phantom no longer tried to break into the hermetically closed door of his mind barricaded with fireboxes, cans of grease—with everything that goes through an unskilled laborer's hands during a working day. (And Gleb decided with restrained regret that perhaps Kormilitsin had killed her in his sleep!) Gradually the normal relations between a chief and a subordinate developed between them.

And now he reached the point of attempting to utter the very word "socialism." Gleb was irritated when a shy and subdued Kormilitsin came to question him at length as to what exactly the new world would look like. And not once did Protoklitov succeed in satisfying the burning thirst for knowledge of this savage.

"I watch you, Gleb. You eat grey bread, you know only your engines, you sleep on a hard bed, you never sleep enough. . . ."

Gleb tried to pass this off with a joke. "When socialism comes, I'll eat and sleep for my whole life."

"You refuse to talk with me about it . . . perhaps my tongue defiles this future country? But you, too. . . . After all, it's impossible not to believe in anything!" He expressed his fears in a very confused manner; in his opinion, thinking was always concentrated in one social stratum, just as was capital in the hands of the exploiter; and you can't take thinking away from people together with their property!

Protoklitov answered, yawning: "But why? Thinking will become everyone's property. Everyone will have more than enough time to think about the world and himself."

"That's what I mean!" Kormilitsin plunged in. "But actually no one can determine what should grow on his bones, isn't that so?"

"What do you mean?"

"New people are born from old ones, yet just look into yourself. Is everything clear to you there? It's incomprehensible, but I can't say it better. All right then: who will rule *them?*"

"But why do they have to be ruled? There won't be any government at that time!"

"But who will show them where to go ... or what is good and evil?"

"But who showed all that to primitive man?"

"He did not have such an economy!"

"Nor did he have such a culture!"

Kormilitsin smiled distrustfully; in this chess game he felt like a newcomer.

"Don't hurry, Evgenyi. Read, think." And Gleb proceeded to sketch an approximate picture of what he was trying to believe. "The new man will create iron slaves after his own image and likeness. In brief, he will be a god. He will be the soul of gigantic mechanisms that will prepare sufficient amounts of food, clothing and pleasure. These articulate iron robots will labor, sing songs, plough the earth, dance on holidays like Salome, even reproduce themselves. Man won't have to be exhausted by work, his only duty will be to know. . . ."

"That's interesting," Kormilitsin drawled. "I've always liked to read about the miracles of science and technology. But how about the people themselves?"

"There will be separate associations ... say, a northern or northeastern union of flax producers. The only government organ might be the central statistical office of the planet. It will draw up annual comparative tables."

"And who will draw conclusions from these tables?"

His worry about a future so distant amused Protoklitov. "Well," he said, "Marx doesn't speak about that. It is remote, and it's only a detail!"

"But I'm speaking about the man in whose hands the threads of perfect knowledge will be joined. Don't be angry at me! What if this man is a Protoklitov like you, selfish, secretive, undiscovered by anyone?"

This was an echo of his former, and seemingly dead, hostility.

"Such a man will be powerless to do any harm. Moreover, he himself will be superior. . . ."

"But can you think of any divinity in the past that had no defects? And then why speak of harm? He will do only *good*, but following his own mind. . . . In brief, I don't believe, Glebushka. The revolution killed its enemies and supported its friends . . . but how many of either have remained undiscovered? . . ."

Protoklitov began to be angry. He went to the window. One conversation with Kormilitsin was enough to make him sick. Gleb had never liked provincial simpletons. Night was falling. Someone's shadow passed on the snow; from the leather bag at the side, which gave a characteristic outline to the silhouette, Gleb recognized Peresypkin. The young man was coming to see him, and Gleb went out to meet him in the entrance. Kormilitsin was an involuntary witness of a remarkable interview. The iron latch dropped, and almost at once: "I've come to speak to you about two things, Gleb Ignatyich. First, about the Komsomol locomotive: tomorrow it will at last make its first run . . . and I'm a little worried about it!"

Gleb interrupted him: "You're afraid of your responsibility?"

"I'm afraid that I have done too little to share this responsibility with *them*," Peresypkin retorted superciliously, but then he softened: "Perhaps I should come in and have a talk with you?"

It seemed that he intended to enter the room, but Protoklitov did not feel it necessary to prolong this conversation. "I'm sorry," he said, "but I can't let you in at present, dear comrade. You see, there's a . . ." he whispered now, "I have a girl with me. . . ."

Again the latch banged. Protoklitov returned with an embarrassed and false face. Fortunately, Kormilitsin did not ask why Protoklitov avoided bringing him and Peresypkin together.

"Why didn't you tell me at once that you were expecting a woman?" he said enviously, winking and pushing his shoulder forward in his characteristic manner.

He hurried to leave in order not to spoil Protoklitov's rendezvous; Gleb's confusion now had a natural explanation. This time they separated quite peacefully and, so to speak, satisfied with each other. Gleb went out to see whether Peresypkin was not standing behind a corner. Aware of his almost family closeness to Kurilov, the yard master suspected some hidden motive in the young man's visit.

# CHAPTER 37

# Sayfullah

THEY WANTED IT TO BE the noisiest night in the whole history of the Cheremshansk Komsomol organization.

Soon after nightfall the young people gathered in the club. For the first time the agenda contained only one flaming word: the locomotive. The boys came directly from the shift, and although in the neighboring movie theatre a cowboy picture was playing, non-party people filled the seats long before the beginning; they awaited the continuation of the controversy that had acquired an almost romantic interest. For a long time proceedings did not begin, everyone kept looking at the door, but Protoklitov did not appear. . . . On a little table stood a radio, and it occurred to one of the audience to find out whether people were not dancing somewhere in the world. The indistinct hum soon changed into a definite sound. A lone voice from the Moscow station gave the weather forecast. The Central Meteorological Bureau reported that a cyclone had started somewhere in the region of Hammerfest. The storm was moving along an arc passing through Murmansk, south from the Pechora Sea. Peresypkin, who printed weather reports in his newspaper, understood the meaning of such prophecies; he cast a glance at the carefree Sayfullah, who sat at the chairman's table. The expression in the editor's eyes suggested that some third person was preparing a blow against the young engineer. It was decided to begin the meeting without waiting for Protoklitov.

The secretary of the repair shop cell read the telegraphed reply of the Komsomols of the Third Region, who had been challenged to a competition. In a voice vibrant with emotion, switchwoman Katia Reshotkina enumerated the duties which the girls at the station had voluntarily assumed with regard to the locomotive they patronized. Suddenly she pinned a red bunting rosette on Sayfullah's chest. She bent over him, as it were eye to eye, and Peresypkin saw that at that moment there were only they themselves; for them the others did not exist. . . .

Then the young editor recounted the episodes of his struggle with Protoklitov, whose name, to the great dissatisfaction of the audience, he did not mention; his voice had a note of biting sarcasm when he spoke of the suspicious connivance between the party organizers and the administration. "Sometimes we respect culture so much that we do not even inquire where it comes from. . . ." He assured the gathering that very soon, not only locomotives, but also trains and zones and even whole railway lines would be managed entirely by Komsomols. One bearded coupler in the fourth row, who did not understand rhetoric, asked what this bright young man intended to do with all the old men. The speaker replied that the old men would move out by themselves, just as, for instance, they had moved out of the Red capital.

"In other words, people like us are to be transported!"

"Not at all, only they'll become more cleanly and shave every day. . . ." Peresypkin's retort was greeted by thunderous applause.

When the business of the meeting was finished, they decided to have a little party and discussed where it should be held. The mechanics' dormitory was out of the question. The young people's celebration might be overheard and frowned upon by the stolid muzhiks from the repair shop barracks nearby. And because there was no other place, they decided to go to a famous bar called "The Red East," two miles from the yard, in Cheremshansk itself. They went there in a gang, about a dozen of them, silent as conspirators, all of them wondering whether everything possible had been done to insure success on the morrow. Katia Reshotkina went with them, for she wanted to spend the evening with Sayfullah. . . . The winter weather was erratic: by night the air warmed up and slush gurgled underfoot. Katia Reshotkina sang a song in a high voice about the Komsomol locomotive, but a wet wind choked the sound. Through the woods the sparse kerosene lamps of the Cheremshansk suburbs began to flicker. Very white clouds ran across the nocturnal sky, and the surface of the fields became bluish, speckled, as though covered with bedsores. Everyone heard Sayfullah ask Katia whether she was not cold. . . . The fierce wind almost knocked the young people down.

(Kurilov's sceptical friend Kutenko should have been there to hear their talk. Then he would have realized how the blueprints of the older generation were becoming a reality. True, the new world looked coarser and more material, but the master's hands always fall short of the marvellous might of his dream. And these boys did not even think about far-off world tasks; all their passion was for the time being concentrated around a model engine, which had become their passport to manhood. . . . And the man of little faith should have gone with them to the provincial bar, filled with the dove-colored vapor of thawing snow, where the floors sag unsteadily as you step on them, where withered paper flowers blaze on tablecloths lying askew, where Cheremshansk artisans and street loafers talk noisily and smoke cheap cigarettes, and where from behind the beer barrels peers the pock-marked and copper-faced Abdurakhman!)

"*Insanme!* How do you feel, renowned barman? We've come to taste your fun!"

Baring yellow teeth behind a clipped mustache, Abdurakhman dusted off the glass case in front of him. There he kept his temptations—eggs baked to a deep yellow color, a much martyrized herring with a wreath of onions, peas on little dishes—about twenty grains on each—washed-out sandwiches. Not a very appetizing display, but never mind! Two years before, this glass case had not existed!

"*Hush kiliasez,* brave lads! I have the world-famous beer of the Red East brewery. Everyone comes here, engineers, doctors, technicians! I'm a technician myself, and everyone loves me!" He was very proud, this Bacchus of Cheremshansk; because of the establishment entrusted to him, he respected even himself. "People say that I am like Omar or Hummarshikele, but I say that Omar is like me, ho-ho. . . . Sit down, *djigits.*"

His eyes were alert. People rarely brought a woman here, and now a group of hooligans in a corner were already baring their teeth. But this woman was not alone. A dozen sturdy young fellows with hammers instead of fists surrounded her like a wall. They sat her down first. Abdurakhman poured the heavy, foamy liquid into cups. He liked sumptuous and exquisite words just as he liked fancy food. He said that behind her wall of young men Katia was like the sun behind the stone crenelations of a fortress. He brought her, separately, soda water and syrup and looked into the faces of the boys to find out who was her beloved. The talk consisted of various fragmentary thoughts about the locomotive. Some were apprehensive because the administration had been absent from the meeting, others were worried about Protoklitov's false conciliating attitude. . . . To them Abdurakhman's beer was priceless wine, which in some mysterious fashion strengthened their friendship!

Meanwhile Peresypkin with the air of an explorer made the rounds of this low-ceilinged place. He scrutinized, sniffed and touched with his hands the quality of life in Cheremshansk. A strange piece of furniture resembling a chest of drawers filled a dark corner. On it was painted a mustached fellow, obviously a Tartar, offering a lavender lady a bouquet of tin flowers. Above the lady's head there was a slot with an inscription stating that the coin was to be dropped right there. For scientific purposes Peresypkin dropped an enormous Tsarist five-kopek piece into it and waited. The lisping springs rattled, and then a choir of hoarse metallic voices sang an ancient tune about the Manchurian mounds. (What antiquity, Kutenko! Remember: The Japanese war and Port Arthur, Rozhdestvensky and Kuropatkin. That year you were drafted, top sergeants trained you to march. . . . Then you were sent to Mukden, and a thin-browed accordeonist with a face that would be frightened forever was playing this very tune to amuse all the grey-uniformed fellows. Play on, play on, remind us of the past, you wooden veteran!)

Peresypkin listened, pressing his hands to his chest. He wanted to shout to his comrades about the marvellous countries near the great reservoir, about the future fraternal republics on the shores of the ocean, about everything Kurilov had told him and that he and his friends were thinking. He waved his hand, but he was not allowed even half a word. The beer yeast was fermenting in the young heads unused to liquor, and one of the Tartars was singing the merry song "Bala-Mishkin." . . . Then Abdurakhman rushed toward them like a falling tower. He demanded that the singing be stopped. He wanted to explain to the street ruffians that a mighty decree of the local cooperative forbade singing in his establishment.

"Citizens, *ishtyplar!* . . . Let a literate person read this poster. Mehna!"

Crestfallen, they went to another place. The friendly "feast," as such gay meetings are called in Cheremshansk, was spoiled. They walked aimlessly along the narrow streets. Little mouse-colored houses slept on either side. The wind whistled at the corners, puddles splashed underfoot.

". . . You're not wet?" Sayfullah asked Katia, just to hear her voice. "No, my feet are quite dry. . . ."

The engineer Riabushkin, the only old man who had gone with them on this expedition (it was he who had helped the young people to master the technique of driving locomotives!) remembered Makhub-ebi.

This old woman had a comfortable house, *aulak uy!* In despair they wandered out to the suburbs, to grandmother Makhub's cottage. Their band thinned out, only seven of them reached the place, but Katia was still with them. They knocked at the gate. A dog barked hoarsely. On the edge of the woods the long, tangled bodies of the trees engaged in hand-to-hand fighting. Makhub was asleep, Makhub was old, Makhub was tired.

"Hey, there, get up, granny! We're from the station, and we've got money, eighteen rubles!"

Bare-headed, she looked out of the little window into the night. Wicked people like midnight; they lurk in the shadows of the suburbs!

"*Yiuk*, Makhub has nothing left. It's all been drunk, *vallagi-billagi!* The necks of the bottles have long since been covered with cobwebs, only spiders live in them!"

But she was tractable, if one knew how to talk to her. They entered one by one, stooping in the low narrow doorway. Makhub recoiled: for the first time a woman entered her home. "Never mind, Makhub, we're not going to do anything bad, this girl is a fiancée!" In the dark hall, encumbered with chests and trunks, Sayfullah stumbled over Katia. Hand pressed hand till it ached. He uttered a dull throaty word, and she, although she did not understand his native language, correctly translated the meaning of his loving slip of the tongue. . . .

The old woman was a magician. She lit three kerosene lamps, no less, and (in order to make the wine act more quickly) spread a tablecloth red as a flame on the shaky table. Makhub-ebi's house was clean. A phrase from the Koran, embroidered on canvas and brief as an oath, hung under the window. Hemp towels embroidered with flaming wool, like a July sky crossed by lightning, hung on the walls. She had understood the world, that incomparable anonymous artist! . . . "Do your stuff, get going, Makhub!" Soundlessly she came and went, cut black bread according to the number of her guests, brought a clay jug full of vodka mixed with water and a cup, cracked and glued with putty; the light gathered at its handle. The silent visitors took their places on benches.

Thus passed the priceless minutes of the night. And then Riabushkin, with his reed basket—for his wife had asked him to stop at the cooperative, and he had not expected to go out with the young people —came from behind his table, stepped forward and stamped his foot. The fireman Skuriatnikov began a tune on the harmonica that he always kept in his breast pocket. Shaking his shoulders, Riabushkin performed two rounds of the dance and beckoned to Skuriatnikov not to spend his music for nothing. "No, I can't dance any more," he said and with a confused hand rummaged for the spot on his chest whence came the ailment of old age. "Eh, I'm no longer young! The little ball bearings in my knees must be worn out! Eh, come on, you Tartars!"

Granny Makhub kept her house very warm! . . . The boys were sweaty and restless. Blood pounded in their temples. Then they opened a window, and individual snowflakes began to fly in, to the tune of youth. Skuriatnikov was still playing. . . . And Katia Reshotkina danced the *tsiganka*, and while she danced, Sayfullah followed her with sad, unblinking eyes. Her dark beauty—and not only her beauty, but her shining eyes and irrepressible liveliness—more and more powerfully veiled from him the image of the remote and proud Mariam. And when only a fragment, small as a drop of blood, was left of Mariam, Sayfullah jumped to the middle of the room and in a throaty voice cried out something to the Tartars, and Skuriatnikov's little singing tin toy fell silent. The Tartars intoned a long-drawn-out chant, striking the measure with their hands, swaying, exchanging winks and nudging one another in the ribs. And Sayfullah circled among them, pushing the air around him with his hands, scraping the sodden floor with his enormous boots.

Now it was a pleasant dance, the *apipà*, merry and coarse, which is danced at weddings with one's hands behind one's back. Sayfullah performed it with all the impetuousness of his blood, with restrained and precise passion. His was the grace of a virile body boundlessly self-confident, accustomed to heavy loads and long strain. He danced, and Riabushkin frowned with facetious envy. The cup made a cracked sound as it touched the clay jug, the July storm shivered on the towels, and looking at the youth old Makhub shook her head and waggled her toothless jaws. It seemed that to please Katia, who stood motionless, with narrowed eyes, on the threshold, he was deliberately trampling upon his past, his old infatuation, his heart and his clumsy vows: his beloved Mariam.

> . . . *Along the river sails a boat.*
> *Girls stamp their feet;*
> *Those who love*
> *Dry up and wither.*

And Makhub with half-closed eyes whispered in accompaniment—she knew her way in those ancient lines:

> *Boys look at girls,*
> *And the girls know:*
> *The ground would boil under their oars*
> *If they swam on the ground!*

Without completing the last figure of the dance, Sayfullah rushed headlong out of the room, upset a rattling bucket in the entrance hall, and ran far away until he could no longer hear the applause of his comrades. The night wind began to burn his face. Sinking knee deep in wet snow he stood alone under the stars listening to the dull distant calls of the steam engines. As though set whirling by the rapidity of his flight, the stars turned above him. Clouds like snowdrifts floated weirdly through the sky. And the wintry cold was not enough for Sayfullah—he grabbed up handfuls of snow and applied them to his burning temples. . . . Water rolled down him . . . and he trembled and shivered from the icy trickle that crawled under the collar of his shirt. It was of coarse hemp cloth, Mariam's farewell gift, embroidered with red swans, tiny as spurge-flax berries. And this unconscious wandering about in the woods at night was the most expressive of all the dances of maturing youth, just as the silent stirring of swollen lips is the most artless of love songs! Here the story of one amorous surge was completed.

Memory led Sayfullah far into the depths of Tatarstan, to the window of a poor peasant hut. It is broken and stuffed with a rag. The wind gently sways the straw roof. With his burning forehead Sayfullah touches the cold glass. The light of the oil lamp is dim, and he must make another effort of memory to distinguish the details hidden in the corners. At first only thin threads of smoke stream above the pink arc of the flame. Then the young man sees an enormous loom, *chypta sukkych*, an ingenious tangle of wooden wheels, long crossbeams and combs unvarnished by time.

The village of Aldermesh is asleep, and while it sleeps, two old women are weaving mats. As one of them with a strong push of her hand passes the shuttle heavy as a log through the bast frame, the other, on the floor, bending her head, disentangles the fragrant fibre that stains one's hands. This is the mother, Bibi-Kamal. She sings a song with a *germankie* tune; the father brought it back from the World War. On a plank bed deep in the room he himself is lying, Samigullah, a man broken by the war: for sixteen years he has been resting from its hardships! And now Sayfullah goes through the wall and moves invisibly, a shadow among shadows. He peers into his mother's hard face, which he has never seen smiling. He bends over his father. Cockroaches walk indifferently over these mounds of rags and suffering. The old man's head rests on a worn-out quilted coat folded in four. His face is like a stone on the road, with a thin mustache like *djep*, the coarse Tartar cloth; and there in the hollows, submissive silent eyes. . . . My filial *selam* to you, Samigullah!

Before leaving his father's house, Sayfullah for the last time casts a glance at the walls. The neighbor's little boy (while his grandmother sternly makes the mat) sleeps on a pile of fragrant bast. Through a hole in his shirt he can see the baby's navel big as a wild apple. "Sleep, grow up, with high cheekbones, brave, gay. Dozens of brand-new electrical engines that will cross the deserts to other countries where men speak marvellous tongues are waiting impatiently for their engineers!" And suddenly, turning around, Sayfullah sees Mariam nestling against the glass at the same spot where a minute before he himself had stood. Her face is dark and thin. Golden moons no longer swing in her tiny earlobes. She is jealously looking into Samigullah's hut to see whether her *harmonchidjigit* has not come back for her. . . . "No, don't wait for him, silly girl. He is ashamed of the past, he reads books, in the morning he waits impatiently for the night, and at night he is in a hurry for the morning. . . . He has become the captain of a majestic and mighty machine, and captains are fickle people!" (She was the daughter of a proud and wealthy bey. When they met on the *siu-yula*, the water road that ran from the well, Mariam put down her pails and for a long time looked at Sayfullah. It was only to earn a horse, boots and *maghiar*—the purchase price of his fiancée—that Sayfullah had left for the railroad. He had left stooping, penniless, in trousers not his own. His family escorted him howling, as if he were going to his death; and at first the science of the locomotive came hard to him; but children conceived on a bast bed are said to be lucky. And now, even if a thousand Mariams, inconsolable and tender as widows, tried to lure him back, the path of return was closed for him!)

Here, in the glade, Peresypkin found the engineer. "Look where you're standing, in that water! You're not a child any more!" he chided Sayfullah, pushing at his arm. "You're all wet. Get out of that snowdrift, you Tartar devil! You'll catch a cold; don't you remember what you must do tomorrow?"

He had taken along Sayfullah's leather coat and with almost feminine solicitude covered his damp, chilly shoulders.

"Has Katia gone home?"

"She is still dancing with your Makhub. Although why should she be there without you?" Peresypkin said sagaciously, and Sayfullah smiled, rejoicing at the very sound of her name. "It's time you went to sleep, come on! Here's a ditch full of water, don't stumble. I'll walk you home. . . ."

From the very beginning he had been reluctant to attend this party; it was awkward for him to follow a bad tradition of the engineers. Only one week before he had printed in the wall newspaper a thunderous article against all saloons at stations. But once he had committed this sin, he painstakingly pretended that he, too, was tottering from liquor.

"It's a wonderful night, Alexei!"

"The kind of night in which all kinds of foolish things are done," Peresypkin grumbled like an old man.

"It's a wonderful night," Sayfullah repeated with a full chest, and began to tell about what a giant among men was his remote uncle Badri, that the Soviet government was a spacious and hospitable house and that it had never before happened at Aldermesh that a Tartar should become an engineer. He muttered all the way, mixing the Russian language with hot Tartar words that came boiling from his heart. And although it was out of their way, they went by silent agreement to the engine stable. The Komsomol engine, the 4019, was in its place. A thin lazy stream of soot came out of the flue. About a dozen other slumbering engines were being prepared for tomorrow's runs, the lighter-up on duty barely managed to attend to them all. Near this one a Komsomol stood on guard. He was here not so much to protect the engine from possible sabotage as to express the Komsomol's distrust of the yard administration. They went into the cab, and Sayfullah, touching everything with the tips of his fingers, inspected the machine. . . . Suddenly he stuck his hand into his bosom pocket and drew out a half crumbled letter. The paper was worn out at the creases, it was disintegrating into grey fragments. He did not give it to Peresypkin at once. "Six years—that's a lot of years, isn't it?" he said.

Peresypkin thought of what he himself had been then and agreed that six years was an enormous number of years!

"Take this, Alexei . . . *rakhim itegez!*

"What for?"

"Read it. Tell me what you think. . . . Eh, you don't know our language, 'infidel'!" He took back the letter with an expression of chagrin, and almost without looking began to translate it by heart.

The ink had run and faded from his perspiration, but Sayfullah did not make a single mistake. The letter was from his mother, from the village, in Tartar. The old woman described her life and reported that thank God her days were drawing to a close; more and more often her hands were numb when disentangling bast for fibre. With the bitter and ruthless straightforwardness of old age Bibi-Kamal called her son a renegade, who had lost all filial feelings. She begged him to visit his native village, were it only for a week, before his father was dropped on three towels into the *kabyr,* the grave. And she also wrote that the Khairullin family had been de-kulakized a year and a half ago, that the mother had died of grief and that the head of the family, as a member of the Mosque Council, the *mutavalli,* had been sent to dig some new river that the Lord had forgotten to create. With utter dryness she also reported that an ambulance station and the school had taken over their house for good, and that Mariam was living far away, in Chukurga, with distant relatives. Every sixth day she came to Bibi-Kamal's house, and with a dark face and lowered head, sat on a bench. She never asked about anything, but only waited for her beloved fiancé. . . . The letter also mentioned that the kolkhoz had fulfilled the sowing plan 110 per cent and the mat-weaving quota only 76 per cent: old people's hands are not nimble. And that the snow that year was deep and that the kolkhoz lambs had got frost-bitten and that recently the mullah had gone out into the street, weeping, squatting and scattering ashes over his shoulders, and had shouted that no one wanted to pray any more and that he had neither sheep nor bread to feed his family and himself. . . . Sayfullah read some passages with particular emphasis so that Peresypkin could feel the earthy heaviness of the peasant words. "And now tell me!" And he followed the changing expressions in Aliosha's face. "You know everything now."

Peresypkin scratched his nose in a businesslike way. "Well, I think it's good that the plan of sowing was fulfilled above schedule. Tartarstan . . . your land is good and honorable, Sayfullah! If you write, praise them by all means. But mention that the proletarian government needs mats too . . . and tell them to take better care of the lambs. And as for the father, he should get a furlough!" His lips twitched with bitterness. "Not everyone has a father nowadays!"

Sayfullah listened greedily to every word. He was just as upset as when he had had his engineer's examination before the inspector. "And Mariam?" he asked.

Peresypkin lowered his head and remained silent for a while. "You know, Sayfullah," he said, "I've drunk a little . . . my head is turning. It's hard for me to talk about that!" But he was almost suffocated by Sayfullah's questioning silence and he went on: "You see, I've gone through many things in my life, I've been in railroad accidents, was wounded by a shell, jumped with a parachute, and I saw what happened to people when they ate too much clay. . . . But this I don't know, comrade!" Suddenly he looked at Sayfullah's face with straightforward honest eyes. "Katia is a good girl. She's pretty, she's intelligent, she's *our* girl. . . . That's why, perhaps, you should forget your Mariam?"

". . . Forget," Sayfullah echoed, and his hand, mechanically stretched toward the injector, was trembling.

The engine was warming up. More and more perceptibly it was accumulating hot and driving steam; its strength was growing in the manometer. And surely if the handle of the regulator were turned slightly leftward, a light shiver would have spread over that massive body, like a torpedo ready to be launched. Only eight hours remained to the test. At 9:34 Sayfullah was scheduled to come of age. To think of it was awesome and joyful.

"Never mind, Sayfullah! It is said that Napoleon too was nervous before a battle." This was Aliosha's favorite saying.

Then they went to sleep.

# CHAPTER 38

# Aliosha Peresypkin's Historical Experiments

ALMOST THE WHOLE COLLECTIVE went out in a body to escort Sayfullah and his crew to the locomotive. And four trumpets and one flute tried manfully to sound like a whole orchestra; the other musicians were busy on the shift. The birds, their feathers soggy after the damp night, swerved to one side at the sound of the blaring instruments. Some of the big drifts had melted, but the hard crust of the old snow still remained on the ground. The train was a long one, its tail was lost in a vague grey twilight. The people shouted after the cars, and those who had handkerchiefs waved them. Katia Reshotkina picked at the wet roadbed between the rails with a twig, while Peresypkin quietly went back to his room. The victory had lost its newness; a damp snow was beginning to stick to the fresh paint of the locomotive. And the fact that at this festive moment everyone forgot about Aliosha, who had done so much to defeat Protoklitov, gave the young editor a pleasant little pang. He returned to his room, stooping slightly and raising his eyebrows—even in this he imitated Kurilov. Perhaps this gesture was all that remained in him of the boy of yesterday.

His temporary haven was in the guard room of the conductors' assistants. The stove on which wet clothes were always drying divided this place into two equal parts. The vapor from sodden sheepskins mingled with the smell of cheap tobacco. In the empty space behind the stove, near the window in the dispatcher's tower, stood two tables. Aliosha slept on one of these, using as a pillow the Blankenhagel archives he always carried with him. He worked at the other. He had done a great deal, but the end of his labors was not yet in sight. He had to abandon his original plan to write a history of the railroad. The internal logic of his material imposed upon him the quaint form of a semi-historical genre with certain fantastic elements, a fact which Kurilov had foreseen. In this vast work written on the backs of the sheets of an old railroad report, the young man tried to study certain actions of the rulers of the past century; their photograph now washed clean graced Peresypkin's wall: Aliosha believed that constant contemplation of it would enable him to penetrate more deeply into the life of the nobility of that time, into their interests, their moods and

334

ideas. He had gathered a countless number of documents. The ledgers and inventories that Kostia Strunnikov had sent him from Borschnia in addition to the first batch of papers; the intimate and petty confessions of imperial stewards, archimandrites, tax-farmers, who had profited from their job; the reports of police chiefs, the business correspondence, the illiterate memoranda of technicians and contractors, had all led Peresypkin into deep forests from which he could no longer extricate himself without help. But luck is often on the side of inexperienced gamblers!

He never wrote novels; he had no time; certain important circumstances had prevented him from becoming an erudite historian; and indifference had kept him from investigating such affairs as an economist. Yet his success required a combination of these three related professions. . . . More than that, he realized what old documents turn into when they stay for some time in the careless hands of posterity. He wanted to wipe off the ironical patina which the acceleration of the tempo of living, the development of new creative tasks and the increase of material power gives to obsolete ideas. In brief, he felt that the Soviet government was strong enough for its historians to be objective and even dispassionate with regard to the dead enemy whose ashes now awaited his judgment. . . . Yet Aliosha could not acquire these virtues of old age! He still heard the scraping of Tsarist officials' quill pens and the grating of the iron yoke on the neck of the enslaved people. And so his inkwell was hatred, and his work unwittingly became the portrait of himself.

During that month Kostia came to see him twice from the Borschnia *sovkhoz*. He entered, thin, sharp and tense, smelling of wintry freshness; he threw his gloves onto the table, wiped his steaming glasses and smiled as though presenting his comrade with the glow of the dawn.

"Still scribbling, chronicler?"

"I'm building a scaffold, Kostia. I want to pass judgment in my own way!" And jumping up every minute in poetic excitement, he reported everything that had fallen into his hands assuming the form of the posthumous indictment.

And so, after sleepless nights spent in studying the original project for the Volga-Revizan railway, after several visits to all kinds of archives and, above all, to a certain bookkeeper who bred canaries on Zatsiep Street, after staring at patriarchal pictures of the former life recorded in documents, the conditions and details of this monstrous enterprise appeared to him as follows: It was the time when the nobility, pushed out of important functions by the intelligentsia and enriched merchants, more and more readily took up trade. Frightened by the threat of ruin, they engaged in all sorts of speculations that often led them to criminal acts. But these pampered beasts of prey lacked the tenacity which distrust nourished in the merchants and the impetuous drive that characterized the contemporary intelligentsia. . . . After an unsuccessful war, when there was a pressing need for railroads, all the more enterprising elements rushed into building them, as to a California. And here, too, they followed the principle: if you are going to soil your hands, let it be for something worth while!

In the Seventies, except for a small part of land under allotment, all the Gorigoretsk district constituted a feudal monolith of four very large estates (the peasantry apparently lived in the boundaries between them). Three of them bordering the Volga and its tributaries belonged to Baron Tulubyev, a certain Khomutov (P.P.), and finally to Blankenhagel, who occupied a special place in Peresypkin's investigation. Blankenhagel's land, situated between Tulubyev's fertile fields and the endless forests of the monastery, was largely unprofitable, and soon after 1861 the owner began to look for ways to mend his fallen fortunes. He did not seek offices which might have served as bargaining points, he had no claim to shine in high society; this heroic man contented himself with being the leader of the local nobility and with his reputation as an industrious gentleman farmer. Between 1858 and 1862 he engaged in turn in the acclimatization of rare animals, the publication of a magazine on poultry breeding and, finally, in silkworm breeding. Judging by the receipts preserved in the attic, all his peasants wound silk for him zealously and at reasonable wages. But in 1862, a year after the Emancipation Manifesto, the silkworms were attacked by a disease hitherto unknown in the annals of Russian silk breeding. The larvae turned black before one's eyes and were twisted as though charred; they had to be shaken off into a ditch by the basketful and buried in sand. The large sums invested in the incubators, ovens, hothouses, winding looms and other ingenious devices were lost. Under these conditions the monarch's message to Orest Romualdovich, expressing his satisfaction at the development of a new native industry, sounded like a mockery. Taking advantage of the opportunity, Khomutov (P.P.) bought from his future partner three of the richest stands of trees, a cheese dairy and a distillery. Then Blankenhagel began to meditate upon life, upon its nature and its higher meaning, and why it is the way it is!

The fortune made by Derviz, the famous railroad magnate, on the Moscow-Saratov line, and later the successful sale of the shares in the Volga-Don line, had long since set him dreaming. Still earlier, an article by the famous Pogodin [1] on the usefulness of the Moscow-Sergievsk railway had aroused civic emotions in him. An active correspondence began, as well as visits and secret meetings: Blankenhagel was feeling out possible accomplices in the affair he was planning. But not until July, 1869, did a secret council take place at Borschnia, attended by Blankenhagel's closest neighbors, K. K. Shepeliashin, the cousin of the omnipotent Tsar's equerry who was visiting Tulubyev, and Chamberlain Tufelkin, a close friend of Adlerberg himself. Another man who was invited was the prominent industrialist who had just branched into shipping, I. L. Omelichev; he was vitally interested in the new railroad, because it created for him a supplementary flow of freight for the fleet he was building. He saw further than anyone else. He tore down the road to the manor house in the heat, all covered with horseflies and waving his low-class cap, but upon the insistence of old Tufelkin, he was excluded from the meeting; the chamberlain could not bear the smell of leather. Ivan Lukich refused to sit in the entrance hall, and this ridiculous incident later affected Blankenhagel's enterprise.[2] The council unanimously decided to join the Grigoretsk district to the pale of European civilization by a railway, and accordingly they petitioned the government for permission to make a preliminary survey, float shares and, in the spirit of the times, to grant them privileges and guarantees.

". . . All this was just a big swindle, dear Kostia, and its mechanism consisted in the foundation of a corporation by a group of highly placed scoundrels seeking self-enrichment. They had neither money nor knowledge of the railroad business. Some foreign bank gave them a loan for which their shares served as security, a loan amounting, for instance, to one-half of the real expenditures involved in building the line; this bank did not run any special risks, because the Russian government guaranteed them profits if the railroad turned out to be commercially unprofitable. Now let us determine the cost of the road . . . how much do you think it was?"

"Well . . . let's say five million rubles," said Strunnikov prudently.

"Perfect. . . . They made an estimate and later drew up bills to the amount of ten millions. The five millions thus earned went to the

[1] In the *Russian Journal* of September 23, 1859.

[2] In a subsequent private letter, dated January 21, 1871, and addressed to M. H. Reytern, the Minister of Finance, O. R. Blankenhagel, trying to raise the bogey of a coming influx of unwashed merchants, ascribed to the leather-manufacturer this prophetic utterance: "Noblemen, you refuse to share Russia with us; very well then, we'll tear her from you by the hair!" And he added another peasant expression concerning a woman who chooses her man not for his clean clothes, but for his solid plough.

directors as the first profits of their 'enterprise.' One of them made a contract to supply the cross ties and charged double price; another bought land for a song from owners who did not know about the planned railroad, and through an intermediary person he resold it to the corporation for ten times as much as he had paid for it. A third one signed his own land, which was included in the railroad zone, over to his aunt, for instance, and then in the name of the corporation purchased it from her at a good price. . . . Do you get the idea, Kostia?"

"It's not quite clear yet, but I'm beginning to see the light. Tell me some more, I want to see what you're after!"

"Then comes the stock exchange part. On the ten millions mentioned above, the government guaranteed six hundred thousand in annual profit. It was more advantageous to any investor who wanted to increase his income to buy shares than to deposit his money in the bank. The trick now was to give the public a false idea of the flourishing state of the business by bribing editors of trade newspapers, bank directors and other such low-lifes. Thus they managed to market a capital of ten millions for fifteen millions. This was the second profit. . . . Meanwhile there was no railroad! Thus they enriched themselves behind the slogan of a so-called liberating reform. . . . But the main thing is still coming, Kostia!"

That was the period when subsidies of all kinds were given to the railroad companies at the expense of the mass of the people, for their tax burdens were thereby multiplied. Moreover, the interested officials had apparently good reason to disregard the real economic significance of the new railroad. The Moscow-Saratov line, almost parallel to the planned one, was already under construction, and there was no real need for the Volga-Revizan line. It was obvious to anyone that the projected road passed through the estates of its founders. These people were not guided by the idea of shortening the freight run to a minimum. Only the shrewd chief of the Communication Office, K. V. Chevkin, saw through the speculative character of the newly formed corporation (not one of its mainstays had distinguished himself in the industry of road building, and there was no banker in the group). "You've already divided the profits, your highness?" he grumbled facetiously, and his old man's sneer remained inflexible. In vain did Blankenhagel's henchmen, Tulubyev and Gribbe, the future director of the railroad, rush about in all the lobbies of Petersburg. And an hour and a half later, when the matter was discussed in the Cabinet, Chevkin slyly agreed to guarantee a dividend of four per cent on the stock capital on condition that the cost of the line, including all expenditures, should not exceed 50,700 rubles per verst and that the railroad from the Tyrts port would be extended along the coast to Astrakhan. The founders began to meditate whether it was worth while to join the Caspian regions to civilization. . . . In brief, Blankenhagel failed to obtain money from the government. Then he thought of a strategic device to circumvent this obstacle.

At the very next session of the provincial council, soon after he had been granted a concession with guarantees, Orest Romualdovich got the Zemstvo itself, or the counties, to guarantee a loan for the Volga-Revizan line. The councillors were made to believe, still in the name of the same civilization, that they were guaranteeing an income to the shareholders on only one-fourth of the capital. Although Blankenhagel mentioned Mucius Scaevola and other famous exemplars of civic virtue, some landlords began to protest, suspecting the brazen schemes behind this enterprise. The counties petitioned Petersburg to protect their interests from the enthusiasm of certain influential leaders. The Council of Ministers was shaken . . . but the highly placed nephew paid a visit to his powerful uncle, the grand duke whispered something to his august cousin, and all was well. The government took deep comfort in the fact that some traces of activity remained in consequence of all these fly-by-night corporations.

The last resistance of Archbishop Innokentyi, who saw in the spread of railroads a threat to religion, an encroachment upon the prerogatives of the Church, and the debauch of the faithful, was broken by a personal letter from Blankenhagel. He assured the dignitary that the price for the expropriated lands of the Gorigoretsk and Vasil-Dubniansky monasteries would not be smaller than that paid by Mamontov and Shipov to the St. Sergius monastery. Nevertheless, the cautious archbishop wrote to the archimandrite of St. Sergius, and only after receiving a favorable answer, did he give his approval to the Volga-Revizan project.[3] More than that, roused by progressive impulses, he came in person, with flying banners and a choir of monks among whom the deepest basses predominated,[4] to bless the opening of the works. Amidst a great affluence of worshippers the chief shepherd intoned prayers for the success of the honorable benefactors of the Gorigoretsk region.

[3] A. V. Peresypkin was unable to discover how the original message from the archimandrite happened to be among the papers found in Blankenhagel's attic.

[4] Amidst all sorts of arithmetical calculations and flourishes with his pen, on page 32 of his business notes, Orest Romualdovich with unusual warmth spoke of a certain monk, Job, whose larynx would have been envied by Satan himself.

"Well, Kostia, aren't you weary of being dragged through these excavations?"

"No, but I find too much of *you* in all this: your impatience, your anger, your sarcasm. . . ."

He seemed to want the historian to draw a clearer boundary between reality and his own invention; yet he shied away from hurting his comrade's feelings by directly expressing distrust in his judgment.

"Then prove to me on the basis of these papers that all this didn't happen!" Peresypkin objected heatedly, shoving toward him the whole pile of balance sheets, reports and bills of lading. "The court considers the depositions of witnesses credible, if there are no depositions to contradict them!"

"Where are they, your witnesses? Absent in the unknown! Go down into their graves, wake them up, question them, Aliosha!"

"I'll question books. . . ."

"Eh, books are bones too—bones of ideas, centuries and great men!"

". . . Finally, my last witness is still alive!" the chronicler cried triumphantly, referring to Pokhvisnev, and the conductors in the other half of the room pricked up their ears, as though a quarrel were beginning. "I'll hunt him up, take him by the shoulders, look into his faded eyes and check my statements in them. . . ."

It was enough to glance at Blankenhagel's estimate to grasp the scope of the affair. While the normal value of the rolling stock was two and a half millions, Orest Romualdovich raised this sum to three millions. ("And that was at a time when the Berlin works of Borsig and Flug offered locomotives at prices one and a half times lower than the Hurst Works in Lancashire and the Birmingham Soho!") The diggings were estimated at such figures that one might have thought this was the most mountainous region of Russia. Actually the land was level, the roadbed was laid out on a plain, all that was required was to dig little ditches at the sides of the tracks. Even the cross ties were estimated at a ruble and a quarter, although their highest price on the market was half a ruble, including the price of impregnation with creosote. Thus, 180 versts of single tracks were estimated at 75,000 rubles per verst. The very fact that this estimate was approved revealed the complete ignorance of the Ministers concerning even the geographical peculiarities of the various regions of Russia.

And so, the throaty bass of the monk Job gave the signal for a huge movement of papers, people, capital and wheelbarrows. The first gang of road-builders, as the result of a bad harvest in the Volga region and other circumstances favorable to the entrepreneurs, was ready at once to move to the place of work in return for bread and water. (In the meantime Blankenhagel was trying to get the government's permission to employ Polish prisoners at a reasonable price, as was done during the construction of the Kharkov and other railways.) A certain Mr. Orbek was given the chief contract. . . . In brief, things hummed: directors brandished checks, officials scraped their pens, priests intoned prayers, and little peasants ("those ancient Russian excavators, Kostia!") drew their belts in tightly and set out for the long trip. The whole contemporary social machine was being set in motion.

The shares of the new corporation sold slowly; in a year and a half only one-third of them were bought. Then the government issued five per cent banknotes paying regular dividends, and the smaller brokers began to unload Blankenhagel's speculative stock. By the middle of 1874 the price of a share had gone down to 165 (par value was 225), then it went up a little, as always before the last gasp, and finally dropped for good to 112. The local government subsidies had meanwhile been eaten up. The construction could be continued only if the money that had been stolen from the community were returned or if a large and stupid backer were found to finance the railroad. Under these conditions it was an act of pure childishness to appeal to the famous tax-farmer V. A. Kokorev; and at that point Omelichev, who was a close friend of this influential person, fully repaid the insult he had received. Kokorev informed Tulubyev through one of his employees that it was not fitting for an unwashed merchant's money to lie in the same purse with a nobleman's spotless rubles. The once frisky "Russian" troyka now barely dragged itself; the shaft horse was exhausted, the side-horses were getting entangled in the harness traces. . . . Later, after the completion of the road, when interest had to be paid on the town loan, the provincial council found that to cover its guarantee a levy had to be made amounting to thirty kopeks per acre of land in the province. A great howl went up to the capital from all the taxpayers in the region. This "revolt of the fools" (as Reytem called it) threatened the local government with bankruptcy. Then, against all logic and reason, government millions were thrown into the hole made by the Volga-Revizan line. To save its face, the local government made an additional levy of two kopeks per acre and that was the end of the matter. . . .

"Just have a look at those dusty faces, Kostenka!" Peresypkin snapped his finger against the worn-out cardboard of the picture. "These scoundrels in peasant coats, cassocks and chamberlain's uniforms stole six millions from the Treasury. No ordinary thief ever grabbed as much!"

"Come to Borschnia while our old woman is still alive. She can surely tell you some interesting things. . . . Incidentally, Kurilov too is staying with us now. He came with a girl . . . she's attractive and simple and quite stimulating for people like us!"

Peresypkin looked at his friend severely, but Kostia's eyes were clear without a trace of insinuation.

"Is her name Marina?" Aliosha asked through his teeth.

"No. . . . They were going to a nearby village when I left, to take a walk. I think he called her Liza."

Aliosha Peresypkin, who had unravelled Blankenhagel's ingenious schemes, was nonplussed by this news. . . .

In the estimate for the earthworks the price for a cubic yard was mentioned as twenty kopeks. One might have thought that the construction of the Volga-Revizan line would certainly bring prosperity to the road-building gangs. But this was not the fact. Actually, Pommier, Orbek's right hand, leased his contract to others, to avoid rubbing up against the Russian lower depths, and they, in turn, leased it to others still. Each of these go-betweens got his share of profits, and the peasant, who came fifth or sixth in these deals, made barely five kopeks for a cubic yard of earth dug up, carted off and laid down. The living conditions of the laborers were cruel even for the muzhiks of that day, who were accustomed to terrible hardships. The labor required was enormous; to save a kopek to bring back home demanded real self-denial. And yet the road was built. Verily, the beggar's purse of the sorely taxed Russian people was inexhaustible. . . .

". . . And at this point, dear comrade, emerges the figure of Spiridon Matochkin. He really existed, because I saw the traces of his peasant shoes and his blood on official documents. He died from 'unexplained' causes at your place, Borschnia. And when I wrote about this man, Kostia, I thought of my father: he was beaten to death by the Whites . . . haven't I ever told you about him? So you see it's not I who gave them similar fates."

This was the first time that Aliosha had ever mentioned his father to Strunnikov. Kostia thought to himself that history could learn from studying the biographies of rank-and-filers more than from those of great men, for all the conditions of a period are so truly reflected in them.

# CHAPTER 39

# Spirka Strides Through Aliosha's Pages

On July 16, 1874, almost two years before the opening of the railroad, Ekim Sharvin from Larion Bayushkin's *artel* received a letter from his native village. The same night, the half-literate Spiridon Matochkin read it aloud by the road-gang's bonfire. There was a word for everyone. The wives and fathers of the diggers informed their husbands and sons that conditions had become very bad; they ate whatever they found, the village dogs had stopped barking, there were omens announcing imminent war and destruction, and in a certain village the police-commissioner's wife had taken her child to the pump one morning and what she found there was not water but blood, thin as *kvass*. ... All this had begun when the Surozhinsk tax office took the poor people's belongings away from them, to sell their bread before the grain was reaped, and to drive the cattle from the farms. It was a question of six hundred and eighty rubles of arrears; this sum had long since been sent to the village by the heads of families, but had been lost in the mails. The tax official was shown the postal receipts proving that the money had been sent in payment of taxes, but he refused to be moved either by the peasant's tears or the official seal, and insisted on full payment in cash.

"... We're wa-asting away, poor wretches that we a-are," Spiridon spelled out with great effort. "Our sou-u-ls are lea-ea-ving our boddies. ..."

The letter reported that Kiril Makurin's cow had been sold for eighty rubles and that his hut was foreclosed for twenty-five rubles of taxes, that Bayushkin's wife had been haled into the district court for having said something imprudent; and that Feonia Matochkina had been whipped with gooseberry branches on her bare body (although she was a betrothed girl) for having insulted the mounted guard, Lomonosov. (Feonia was Spiridon's sister.) Thus everyone received his bit of news and greetings. The reader folded the letter and returned it to its owner. ... There was perfect silence. Red lights blinked on the horizon; the moon was rising sideways as though it had a hangover; the bonfire was choking from lack of air; mosquitoes from a nearby swamp trumpeted in the men's ears like angels on Judgment

Day. All day long the sun had been beating down on the laborers. They hoped that by night a heavy shower would water the desert around them. But the storm petered out in thunder and distant flashes of lightning. There was nothing to talk about. Having scraped the remnants of onion and bread crusts from the bottom of the bowl, the *artel* went to sleep.

By morning they learned that similar sad messages had been received at various times in other *artels*. And everywhere the above-mentioned Lomonosov managed to get in the letters. However, they began work early, at daybreak, intending to go to the authorities after the day's work at sunset, when it would be cooler. An excessive number of complaints had piled up. The principal drink and sustenance of the muzhiks—their *kvass*—had invariably turned sour; only one bundle of straw per man a week was given for bedding; people hired originally for earthwork were employed for stone work at the same wages; their boots, the full price of which had been deducted from their wages, turned out to be of the shoddiest kind—"through the soles one can feel every bug with one's toes, if you will excuse the expression!"; instead of baths, they were given five kopeks per person in vodka or cash; the district officer struck Agafon Zimkin of the Sviridov *artel* with a 'chump of wood,' and as a result the laborer was deafened and lay for a week in a mud-hut; his time was deducted from his wages, although he had not been absent by any fault of his own. . . . There were a great number of other complaints, the most important of which concerned the tax-collector. And just for the fun of it, the laborers took with them an earthenware bowl full of the oats that had been given them the day before for their *kasha*. . . .

Large numbers of peasants gathered in a semi-circle near the office of the fourth building section. In the center they placed the incriminating bowl and beside it piled up their digging tools, so that everything might be clear without any explanations. Clearing their throats, decorously as though before prayer, they waited for the authorities to come out. But instead of Mr. Schekotikhin, the assistant engineer who was famous for his amiability as well as for his fondness for cards, M. Pommier himself came out—he was on an inspection tour of the project to check on certain unfavorable rumors. Small and swarthy, he looked like a charred tree trunk in a silk tunic. He knew in Russian only words of abuse, which always filled the workers with distrust. He did not come out alone, but accompanied by a Mr. Shemadanov, an official on a special mission, and Achilles Teofilovich Steinpel, who always played the part of the fox endowed with the lofty human gift of persuasion. They had both been sent to the district for the purpose of

discovering the "trend of thought," [1] and it was a lucky coincidence
that they happened to be here at this very moment.

Mr. Shemadanov, a man of mournful appearance, with a very long,
drooping mustache, stepped forward making strange motions with his
fingers, as though feeling the air, and asked the men the meaning of
the oats and the pile of shovels. He put a great deal of feeling into his
voice, and it seemed to the muzhiks that if he did not die on the spot,
he would certainly burst into tears. Then one birdlike old man answered him that on the left were the "eats" and on the right the
"labor," and that the provisions were not adequate to the labor. In one
breath—for he had been chosen spokesman—he listed the other complaints, while M. Pommier sucked at his gurgling pipe and Steinpel
stared at the dust on his shoes. Mr. Shemadanov gloomily bent down
to the bowl, scooped up a dozen grains and tossed them into his
mouth; they felt like wooden cobblers' nails on his tongue. He spat
them out and shook his head. "Fear God, boys, . . ." he said, mournfully pulling out one of the nails that had got stuck in his mustache
and leering at it.

The muzhiks began to grumble. "God wouldn't be ashamed to complain of this!" sighed one ancient man suffering from scurvy, all
hole-riddled, as though a fire had devoured his clothes, his eyes like
two incurable wounds.

There was a movement in the crowd, and then Mr. Steinpel, quickly
pushing Shemadanov aside, gave them clear and perfectly reasonable
explanations for everything. He had been on the project two days and
knew all about the muzhiks' complaints. Thus, concerning the main
question of tax arrears, he showed the gathering a document bearing
the number of 5591 which had been sent to Surozhin, the tax-collector,
and communication No. 1115 which he, Steinpel, had received in reply.
In view of the obvious obscurity of No. 1115, a second report, No.
5602, had then been sent to the tax administration, and the muzhiks must
now wait for a favorable answer to this latter. Concerning the deafened Zimin he read aloud the findings of the local assistant physician,
Dubiaga, and the parish priest, according to both of whom the above-
mentioned Zimin's organs of hearing were found to be in a normal
condition, although they could not function as a result of the patient's
exhaustion following a previous illness. As for the *kvass*, the baths and
the boots, he proposed a peaceful middle-of-the-road solution, and
finally he promised to double the amount of straw distributed for bed-

[1] A copy of the report by the Gorigoretsk district police chief Rynda-Rozhnovsky
addressed to central police headquarters mentioned conversations overheard in the
*artels* about some sort of "second" freedom and other harmful notions.

ding. In all this he emphasized figures, because, owing to the Russian muzhik's inability to calculate quickly, figures were an old and tested method of persuasion. . . . Thus everything was settled; Mr. Steinpel impressed upon the crowd the sanctity of contracts, and the muzhiks were ready to swear under oath that they were receiving the finest possible treatment—when suddenly something happened.

A blue-eyed young peasant, from the same county as Spiridon, Semyon Shpagin, wanted to show the Frenchman the abscesses and swellings on his Russian feet acquired at the 124th verst of the road while building a dam over the Zakreev swamp. Having untied his rags he courageously walked toward M. Pommier himself. The engineer, ignorant of the Russian language, took Shpagin's action as a piece of deliberate insolence, and without taking his pipe out of his mouth, kicked the peasant in the lower part of his belly. Shpagin fell at once and lay as though tied up in a bundle, his knees drawn under his chin; fearing to cry out he only blinked in the direction of the sky with eyes that had become the color of tar. And although he had not hurt his face in falling, blood appeared on his lips. All of Mr. Steinpel's work was now ruined. The muzhiks rioted, broke into the yard, smashed two carts and Mr. Shemadanov's carriage standing there, wrested the gun from the soldier on guard and broke an icon representing the conception of St. Anne. Soon, however, drops of rain began to fall, and the rioters peacefully dispersed to their mud-huts, taking the unconscious Shpagin with them.[2] That very night Mr. Steinpel had a talk with M. Pommier and urged him, in his quality of Orbek's right hand, to reach a compromise with the peasants according to the spirit of Articles 1534, 2224 and 2226 of Volume X, Part I, of the Civil Code, but Pommier told him in French to go to the devil. Mr. Shemadanov's fears proved justified. The next morning four *artels,* comprising 245 men, failed to report for work, and their mud-huts were found to be empty. The peasants had gone, apparently in a northeastern direction. Then Mr. Steinpel went on horseback to Borschnia where O. R. Blankenhagel was spending his summer vacation. Shemadanov remained at the office to drink his share and finish his card game with Messrs. Schekotikhin and Pommier.

There were present at the council, in addition to the above-named officials, E. G. Gribbe, inspector Rynda-Rozhnovsky and the private tutor A. H. Pokhvisnev. Various people expressed the opinion that the runaway peasant *artels* had gone to appeal to the governor of their

[2] Comparing the dates of this incident and of an unsent letter by Taniechka, Peresypkin surmised that Pokhvisnev's visit to the road builders took place about three hours after this incident.

district, who was famous for his gentleness, for protection against the arbitrary action of the tax-collector. They had apparently taken with them the stricken Shpagin, who could not have left without help. With him in their cortege they would naturally have the effect of a powder charge; the villagers along a stretch of 412 versts would certainly see this procession of wretched muzhiks who had been lured to work at the railroad. One could imagine what would happen when this bare-foot horde appeared on the square before the governor's house. (Pokhvisnev, frightened to death, did not doubt that the soul of this whole affair was Spiridon Matochkin.) A telegram was immediately sent to the commandant of the local garrison with a request for aid against a mutiny of fifteen hundred workers within a radius of twenty versts from Borschnia. A special messenger, carrying a detailed report on the incident, together with a certificate signed by the local assistant physician, Dubiaga, and the parish priest, to the effect that Shpagin's illness was caused by a chronic stomach ailment rather than by M. Pommier's foot, was sent to the provincial capital.

Extremely upset by this incident, Taniechka Blankenhagel related the details of her visit to the laborers' camp, and Mr. Steinpel knitted his brows. Turning to Pokhvisnev he said: "I'd like to question you as to the circumstances of your meeting with Matochkin and as to the person who gave them the idea of quitting work!" And Pokhvisnev experienced a strange feeling of stickiness all over his flesh, merely from the glance of those slippery, reddish eyes.

As a temporary measure, it was decided to remove the bridge, thus cutting the passage across the Zuyka River, but the muzhiks easily got hold of a few rafts and left the boundaries of the province they hated. They moved on and on, and it was clear that they were angry enough to cross all of boundless Russia. Less than two weeks later, all the departments of three adjacent districts engaged in active correspond-ence concerning the riots, the attempt on M. Pommier's life, the flight from the place of work and, finally, the unprecedented blasphemies in which the peasants had indulged, blasphemies that people could not repeat in public. Not to mention the broken icon. . . .

It was beyond Aliosha's powers to depict the disorderly procession of the emaciated and barefooted peasants; they were led by Spiridon Matochkin. In front the older peasants dragged themselves, followed by four younger fellows who carried Shpagin's body, flattened and at last uncrumpled, on a coat attached to four poles. He had died on the third day, but they continued carrying him grimly and savagely; be-cause of the great heat, the bearers were frequently relieved. His body was the most convincing symbol of the crimes of the authorities, and for the sake of the peasants' cause, Shpagin, one of their own, could wait a little for burial. "Suffer a little, brother! . . . Your village asks this of you!" And he floated along, black and obedient, spreading silence and a horrible stench all around him. . . .

Thus they moved ahead, haphazardly, with a concentrated, even fanatical stubbornness, led by their despair, as a flock of migratory birds is led by its instinct to return to its old home in the spring; they walked across meadows, silently climbing the green hills of their beloved "native land" and descending every night into the mists of the river valleys; they walked past ripening fields, past shady estates where life was carefree, past gay village churches set on hills, and at their very approach the bells must have pealed. Larks sang above them; the dead man blinked in the sun; from a distance came the gleam of the round, sun-burnt bald heads of the old men, the color of pink gravel. At night they camped near fires, wherever they happened to be, leaving a guard and covering the anthills with their shirts to protect themselves from the insects—and Shpagin, too, took a rest at some distance from the others. . . . Among them there was one fellow not without imagination: he had taken along the bowl of oats. It was strewn with the dust of the roads and dampened with rain water; soon the grain in the bowl began to grow in coppery poisonous colors. (Did this fellow think that it would shoot up into ears by the time they finally got to the governor's house?)

"Well, my boys," the governor would ask them in a motherly tone, "why do you disgrace your fatherland like this? Who among you has a grievance? Let him step forward and speak out!"

"He can't step forward and speak out," the muzhiks would say in chorus. "He's been hit a little, beloved highness, and he'll never move from his place again. And, see, since that time he's been tanned a little and he's got quite a color. . . ." And they would present the governor with the putrefied "surprise" on the coat, and he, horrified, would dismiss the tax-collector and give orders that the Frenchman be given twenty-five lashes so that he should never again forget himself in a foreign land; furthermore, he would compensate the Shpagin family for the death of its breadwinner. That was what they thought; but things turned out differently.

At first the Gorigoretsk disabled veterans' unit, comprising two non-coms and sixteen privates, were sent after them. The pursuers were instructed to get the runaways to repent by persuasion and gentleness, and only later to flog the ringleaders in order to clinch the results achieved. But whether the peasants walked faster, feeling that they were being followed, or whether the veterans were no longer accus-

tomed to military marches, the procession continued and was now approaching the boundaries of the second district. Then, following an
attempt by Spirka to get the population of a whole village to join him,
a mounted detachment of Nogai Tartars received the order to attack
these self-taught agitators and make an example of them on the spot.
However, in order to avoid bloodshed, A. T. Steinpel, now wearing
the full uniform of a colonel of gendarmes, was sent along with the
troops.[3] Out of humaneness, in order to avoid an investigation, and
because he wished to punish the tutor by psychological means, Mr.
Steinpel took Pokhvisnev along. . . . The troops set out under the
command of Captain Kaznacheev and overtook the fugitives in two
days.

The meeting took place near the Psnia River, on the pastures near
the village of Apraksino, where three sprawling white birches gave
enough shade for the people to labor without getting exhausted. In
order not to frighten the peasants gone wild, the detachment of
mounted men went down into a dell where the soldiers rested and
watered their horses. Loping over the small meadow a little carriage
approached the crowd that had halted. Shpagin had been put down
behind, on the slope of the hill; he refused to go on any further. Mr.
Steinpel resolutely pushed the young tutor forward, and he at once
addressed the peasants on the great importance of railroads for transporting heavy loads and called upon them to renounce their errors and
trust the government to take care of them. He could barely stand on
his feet and, whether as a result of his having been shaken for a long
time on the bad roads, or whether the color of the foliage was reflected on him, his face was completely green. However, he found
enough voice to point to his own fate, the fate of a simple peasant's
grandson who had achieved a certain education and high position
even under the present conditions. (During this speech Achilles Teofilovich smoked a cigarette and remarked through his teeth that probably the grandfather, too, had been a "son of a bitch.")

At this point a little breeze from Shpagin's direction hit the young
man, and now his tearful appearance was such as to demand medical
treatment.

"But, little *barin*," Larion Bayushkin said to him compassionately,

[3] From documents of the 3rd Section, Peresypkin concluded that Steinpel was
only imitating a certain Giolio, a colonel of gendarmes, who had been active only
six years before the events described here. Endowed with an impressive appearance,
a stentorian voice and a deep knowledge of the peasant soul, the latter had often,
single-handed, pacified disorders that arose during the construction of private
railroads.

looking in the direction of the dell, "why do you speak so mournfully. Don't be frightened, it's not you who will be whipped, but us!"

Mr. Pokhvisnev completely lost countenance and, pressing a handkerchief to his nose, gave up any attempt to continue the conversation. Mr. Steinpel put out his cigarette and proceeded to do his part. His uniform was more becoming to him than civilian clothes. Without any circumlocutions he now proclaimed the government's determination to return the fugitives to the mud-huts and to bury the body of Shpagin, who had died of a chronic disease. Furthermore, he demanded that three ringleaders be handed over to him. He started to move along the ranks in order to choose the guilty ones, but the peasants became agitated, and, among other things, the colonel was more than once subjected to physical insults.[4] . . . His demands had touched off the muzhiks' impetuous, hysterical anger; and sober reality now appeared in the shape of Captain Kaznacheev. The course of the negotiations had been watched from the dell. . . . It was beautiful to see how in front of the avalanche of dashing cavalrymen a light breeze rolled over the grass. Having loaded Mr. Pokhvisnev, who had closed his eyes, into the carriage, Achilles Teofilovich drove away in order not to interfere with Captain Kaznacheev's work.

(Peresypkin deliberately omitted the description of the punishment; without it his ink boiled and foamed in his pen!)

The repentant criminals were put in chains and transported to the Gorigoretsk provincial courts, but Spirka managed to escape. However, these facts were not mentioned in any of the papers found in the Blankenhagel archives. Only from private letters of various Borschnia people could one infer what terror Matochkin's subsequent exploits spread in the region. Everyone was surprised that, having won his complete freedom, Spirka did not return to his native village, but continued to operate in the railroad zone.[5] He was possessed by a strange idea: to capture and flog Blankenhagel himself. He had no accomplices in his brigandage, and this perhaps was the reason that he was hunted for more than a year. He was finally seized at a wedding party, and the same troyka that had served the newly married

[4] Judging by Mr. Steinpel's personal report he was hit in the face only twice; but later Matochkin testified that he had struck the victim six times. Peresypkin managed to discover an annotation in the bold handwriting of Prince Dolgorukov, the chief of the gendarmerie, which read: "Official business requires exactitude. Where were the remaining four blows delivered?"

[5] However, his operations were never on a large scale. Mr. Rynda-Rozhnovsky's old wish ("Lord, send us a gruesome crime so that I may become famous!"), expressed in a private conversation with O. R. Blankenhagel, was never fulfilled.

couple, with ribbons on the shaft-bows and the horses' tails, brought
him in an inebriate state to Borschnia. By that time, the official papers
about him weighed almost as much as he did. The Gorigoretsk prison
was closed for repairs, so Matochkin spent the last days of his life in
Borschnia. He is mentioned again only in the documents concerning
the opening of the road.

This was on July 20, 1876. (Peresypkin found some details about
this remarkable celebration in old newspapers.) First a train was
launched carrying soldiers who sang songs appropriate to the occasion; once long before, Noah had let an experimental dove out of his
ark for the same purpose. Then, amid a great crowd of people, benches
were covered with rugs and placed on an open freight car; this was
attached to a two-axled engine with a formidable chimney that smoked
like the devil. On the benches sat the directors, the engineers and the
most important shareholders with their families; also inspectors and
other personages prominent in the province who had been invited to
participate in this family affair. (The official banquet to celebrate the
opening had taken place two days before at Gorigoretsk.) The bishop
also agreed to ride on condition that the engine did not whistle while
he was on the train. Even so, he hesitated for a long time before climbing in. "How sad all this is!" he exclaimed. Blankenhagel waved a
handkerchief, the populace shouted hurrah, the soldiers presented
arms, the train started. Sparks flew in people's faces, then it began
to rain, and many wondered why it was necessary to make all this fuss.
The guests of honor returned all wet, and only a Gargantuan feast for
seventy-five persons rewarded the heroes of the first run. The meal
lasted six and a half hours; blind children from the nearby orphanage
incessantly sang cantatas, and Khomutov (P.P.) made a speech about
culture; he very cleverly and appropriately [6] compared the Borsig
locomotives to the fiery chariot on which, according to the legend,
the prophet Elijah had gone to heaven, to the eternal palaces of the
Creator.

When the storm had passed and the grass began to gleam in a pale
sun that had spent its strength in the battle against the storm, everyone went to see the captured criminal. All the guests were tremen-
dously interested in him. They stood in a semi-circle waiting for him to
be led in; the ladies trembled, and not only because of the evening
dampness, even before Spirka appeared. Ten minutes went by before
Matochkin was brought up out of the cellar. A tattered coat was

[6] It was still thundering, and through a lazy rainbow a lavender evening was
approaching.

thrown around his shoulders. Khomutov (P.P.) asked the guests to make room in order to allow the ladies to see everything without having to come any closer. The bandit stood in the glow of the setting sun; its rays still came obliquely through the branches. He stood silent, his head hanging. His eyes were swollen. For some reason he had been hurriedly splashed with water before being led out, and his wet hair stuck to his forehead. Everyone was struck by the terrible beauty of this face. The bishop stepped forward. "Raise his eyelids!" he commanded.

As an honorary inspector of public schools he encouraged the study of literature and knew all of Gogol by heart. Blankenhagel's henchmen interpreted his words as an order to raise the criminal's head.

"Do you see me, Spirka?" asked the church dignitary in a low voice.

"I see you, but my arms are too short, . . ." Matochkin said with a sigh, and everyone marvelled at the amount of fight left in this beaten man. He was lying, he could not see anything with those purple tumors; he was lying even to a priest.

"You're a merry fellow, Spirka!" the bishop went on, slightly confused; he threatened him with his staff.

The brigand's dark face became animated; he tried to smile to all those present whom he could not see. "I am merry. You should take me into your choir, little old man."

Then for the sake of decorum the bishop made an edifying speech, and the guests saw before their eyes the enormous black body of Barabbas, flabby where the nails and ropes had held him. . . . With deep feeling the man of God expatiated upon the importance of the new railroad for the common people, pointing out that now everyone, after buying a ticket at the window, could visit any monastery in Russia. It was a passionate duel between a silent hardened soul and a preacher unjustly forgotten in the annals of the nineteenth-century church. Spirka began to weep, although his fists remained clenched; he was put against a tree to prevent him from falling blindly to the ground. Orest Romualdovich ordered that he be given a drink, and although it seemed to choke him he emptied it in a second. And the bishop still kept on talking about the conceit of science and the futile pride of mankind. "For instance, everyone chatters, 'Jupiter, Jupiter,' but what that 'is exactly, no one knows!" It was very pleasant. Heartfelt emotions are good for the appetite. The air was fresher. Everyone returned to the table. The guests let themselves go, and half an hour later the father steward of the Vasil-Dubniansky monastery had to be carried out dead drunk, wrapped in the tablecloth. Had it not been for that, and a quarrel between two of the engineers over a question of spiritualism,[7] this day would have marked the perfect union of all the progressive forces.

The business of the railroad, however, went very badly from the very beginning. The Saratov line had cornered the principal freight loads, and the Volga-Revizan line could get only wood. During the first years the freight turnover was so insignificant that it was not worth while to clear the snow off the tracks in winter. The shareholders were completely disillusioned . . . and then it happened that the new director of the Communications Office, P. P. Melnikov, had to travel on the new line. And although this highly placed gentleman was known as a miser,[8] Orest Romualdovich together with Khomutov went to meet him with a petition. The road was still not paying its five per cent, and Blankenhagel wanted to ask for some military loads, soldiers or cannon, or something else that was heavy and government-owned. The meeting took place at Barmalevo station. Melnikov received the guests cordially, remarked on the solitary charm of the place, the wealth of the country and the enterprising spirit of the upper classes. His praise was full of mockery. "I expected to see mountains here!" he concluded, ironically hinting at the high cost of the road per verst. Replying to Blankenhagel's complaints he gave him the friendly advice to open inexpensive brothels at the principal stations in order to attract passengers. Orest Romualdovich stiffly reminded his excellency of his nobleman's dignity, but the high dignitary dryly inquired as to what prices had been paid for the expropriated land.[9] Blankenhagel softened (the director might, for instance, have demanded better bridges to insure the safety of the passengers!), stroked his sideburns and even uttered some compliments about the statesman's wisdom and penetration.

Very soon, however, the exemplary impudence of the "Gorigoretsk brigands," as the railroad entrepreneurs began to be called in the province, was properly punished. A great number of directors and their countless relatives lived off the "wooden" road. The five per cent government subsidy failed to cover even half the thefts committed in the form of salaries and special expenditures. Then Blankenhagel

[7] About a month earlier a certain Mendeleev had published a book on spiritualism (1876), of which the proceeds were supposed to finance the investigation of the upper atmospheric strata in a dirigible. This desperate attempt to wangle 6,000 rubles out of Russian society was a failure, as one might have expected.

[8] There was a rumor that on his days off he did not wind his clocks so as not to wear out their precious mechanisms for nothing.

[9] The founders had received 200 rubles per acre of arable land and 115 per acre of cut woods, that is to say, for stumps of various kinds, while the sheds for the wood cost 3,000 rubles apiece.

mortgaged his shares, hoping to find a way out of his difficulties by the time traffic picked up, but certain experienced people soon found out that the value of his shares still did not cover his loan! The bank demanded that he cover the difference and later took sharp measures against him. The affair fell into the hands of the investigating magistrate for special cases. E. G. Gribbe, the director of the railroad, testified during the first cross-examination that the money had been withdrawn upon Blankenhagel's orders, destined for purposes of public welfare, while the gaps made in the treasury were hurriedly filled with fictitious promissory notes. The entire district held its breath and wise-cracked about the arrest of the enterprising Orest. The new leader of the nobility was a radical, who had served as a mediator during the peasant reform, an irreconcilable enemy of Blankenhagel. Gloom settled over Borschnia. The founder of the railroad was actually under house arrest. Intercessors, spies, queer characters who were mixed up in this unpleasant business, and undistinguished individuals wearing ordinary clothes came to visit him in droshkies. Then the blinds would be lowered, and an hour later an unshaven errand boy would carry secret dispatches to the post office. They remained unanswered. Adlerberg was ill.

Orest Romualdovich read a great deal during those days. The penal code and the Revelation of St. John never left his table. Thus he took his own measure in the first of these books and tasted the bitter antidote in the other. (It happened that the capital began to make inquiries about the disappearance of S. M. Matochkin. Apparently Petersburg, too, wanted to settle its accounts with this criminal.) Sometimes Orest Romualdovich went to Pokhvisnev's little room and played checkers with him until he felt dizzy. . . .

Arkadyi Hermogenovich was bored. Nothing now detained him in this refuge of elegant life, as he called Borschnia. Dudnikov had been sent to the capital together with Blankenhagel's heir, and Taniechka to the Crimea, in order to spare her from being present at the last act of her father's disgrace. The romantic groves were deserted. Yellow leaves littered the paths, and at night the wind howled with Spirka's voice. Pokhvisnev had completely lost faith in Matochkin even before he went with Steinpel to lecture the captured peasants—in fact as soon as he realized that this homespun Spartacus would have cut his throat for one roguish expression in his eyes. He decided to disappear from Borschnia; he did so without even thanking his host for the hospitality he had enjoyed. "I am choking in the stuffy air of this feudal latifundia!" he wrote in the note that he left behind and declared that he intended to seek popular truth elsewhere. (So firm was his assurance that Taniechka would ask about him after her return!) He crowned his epistle with the famous Latin quotation about the necessity of destroying Carthage.

This masterpiece was handed to Blankenhagel one morning while he walked on the terrace waiting for his *kvass*. He read Pokhvisnev's explanations and for a long time stroked his dog, smiling. His dressing-gown had come open, and the chambermaids who were setting the table turned away in fright. The old man was surprised by the contents of the note. No one was trying to catch this blusterer by his coat-tails; since the homespun Fourierist had fed for two whole years on the rich Carthaginian pastures one would have thought he would have had plenty of time to learn some manners.

"What a rat, eh? Three and a half! The fool, . . ." Orest Romual-dovich trumpeted through his nose. "Latifundia, no less! A fine Tacitus he is!"


. . . Peresypkin closed his notebook and began to look out of the window. The first little fire blinked in the mist, flakes of snow clung to the pane. . . .

"Well, Kostia, have you had enough for today?"

Strunnikov reluctantly took his cap. "But what happened in the end?"

"Oh, nothing. That time Adlerberg recovered!"

# CHAPTER 40

# Kurilov Works Out a Course of Treatment

AT THE END OF ONLY ONE WEEK Alexei Nikitich looked much fresher. His mind was clear, and life appeared to him as logical as though the universe were constructed exclusively of straight lines. Everything pointed to his recovery. Since his arrival in Borschnia he had had no attacks. The surgeon's monotonous voice had long since been lost among the other noises of life, and experience had taught Kurilov not to give too much credence to physicians' predictions. All in all, medical science is good for the very reason that it is often mistaken! Like most people who have never been ill, Alexei Nikitich had a childlike faith in the healing power of nature.

He rose as soon as the first vein of day broke in the eastern sky. The chambermaid brought him a basin of water with floating lumps of ice. Believing that no illness likes shaven people, he painstakingly scraped his cheeks every morning. He read a thick book—something about the rivalry of the naval and land powers on the Ocean—and casting periodic glances at his companion, Gavrila, slowly drank his milk. . . . When he left the house the moon was still fading in the sky, a very thin moon, as though sliced by a knife. Everyone was asleep. He walked aimlessly along the crackling, ever more dazzling road. He examined the tracks of the night animals and read their adventures in the snow. He climbed Spirka Hill and stood motionless for a long time contemplating the lovely, melancholy scene stretched out before him. And he breathed and breathed deeply, squeezing into himself every sensation of the snowy air, the straggling morning breeze, the shaggy and slanting little woods sketched against the bluish snow. He thought: how ridiculous that he, a tough sturdy man, should have gone this long way, only to stop here secretly and await a miracle.

Nature was wonderful at this hour. The little clouds in the sky seemed boyish in their beauty, and the transparence of the air made him want to write poetry. Alexei Nikitich would then go down to the dell to smoke, sit on a familiar tree stump and drop his finger into the water of the thawing stream, black with a topaz gleam. The woods were growing ruddier now, they took on the color and sonority of copper as the sun rose; a hunter's shot in the thicket was like a blow against a metallic tambourine. Kurilov rose and went enchanted toward the sound. . . .

During those endless wanderings he found a secret and anonymous friend of about sixty-two years of age. He was a merry old man who might have come out of a popular engraving, a hunter who seemed ethereal, for he walked without skis on the snowy crust as soon as it began to freeze. During the hard years all his family had died, and he now lived alone in a hut, shot all kinds of game, which he sold, and in the summer went to the villages "to listen for water for new wells." He boasted that death itself was afraid to meet him face to face and was instead trying to jump at him from behind a corner. He advised Alexei Nikitich to have himself treated by a village quack (who had gone away to buy yokes for the kolkhoz but would be back next week) and told him peasant stories sharply spiced with laconic peasant humor.

Alexei Nikitich puffed at his pipe and listened to the music of his words: ". . . One day a peasant was about to die and he asked his wife: 'When I'm dead, what will you cover me with?'—'Just die, I'll cover you . . .' his wife said. He died, and his wife wound three threads around him (for the poor woman had nothing else), from his heels to his head; then she got up and began to lament: 'My beloved, what do you look like now?' and he answered: 'Like a balalaika!' "

It was now immaterial to Kurilov what force lifted him up again, back to life. "Cure me, cure me, old man of the woods!"

. . . And so no symptoms of dying remained. But the former piercing attentiveness became even stronger in Kurilov's glance, as though new eyes had opened in him. Suddenly everything became interesting to him: how the little wood beasts went about their winter business, how a squirrel leapt from tree to tree, leaving a toy blizzard behind its tail; how a prismatic crystal of snow fell on his sleeve and grew larger with his breath. He learned that the winter woods have a slight smell of dogs, and that woodpeckers will risk their necks to satisfy their curiosity. And just as from a great height the eye easily penetrates the depth of the sea, so all the smallest psychic motions of people became accessible to him. From a distance he read with new eyes his nephew Luka's flattering, alarmed enthusiasm for him and Ziamka's frank, virile friendship. He also realized that he had taken Gavrila in because of his unquenchable desire to listen to childish speech. . . . Sometimes he visited neighboring kolkhozes to drink milk. He told the peasants about the plans of the Soviet government or listened to their complaints which indicated growing needs, the impatient dreams of increasing prosperity, and, consequently, a passionate striving for the very thing in the name of which all their sacrifices had been made. He divined the seamy side of human behavior (and he laughed with all his heart when the Borschnia steward came to see him and in an ingratiating way asked him where Gavrila had hidden the gloves he had bought for his wife's birthday; the steward's eyes roved around the room as though tied by threads to his thought and he seemed to suspect Kurilov himself of complicity); finally his attention was more and more frequently fixed on Liza.

He put aside his book, stopping for a while the battle between tremendous squadrons, and compared the two women, the living one and the dead. Liza remotely reminded him of Catherine. In his opinion, they were related by their seeming helplessness (although Catherine had had the strength to struggle with the Protoklitov father, and among Liza's trophies was Ksaveryi), their insinuating candour and absence of outward cleverness, their shy ambiguity of speech (beneath their words there always rang other, more important ones) and by everything else that he invented in his search for similarity and continuity. He was mistaken; there was something in Liza's face that had always been lacking in Catherine's; and to tell the truth, all these superficial comparisons rarely turned out to the advantage of the deceased. He had always had too much respect for her, and had been too afraid to cause her pain, to be truly happy with her. Twenty-three years of Catherine's faithfulness and devotion were now re-appraised. In his belated disappointment he committed an injustice toward this uncomplaining friend, as well as to his own work, for he assumed that he had thrown into this work the energy of his all too human passions.

In him the experience of youth was combined with the ironic insight of an old man. He had guessed all of Liza's secrets long since. Surely here was the primitive, imperious greed to dominate the world through creating its image—does not the genuine artist always begin with this greed? He defined this quality as a subconscious desire to fix in the memory the moment with its color and form, its idea and emotional quality, the very play of the reflections of a huge and complex world contained in it. Not to condemn all this was to understand the unskilful self-confidence of youth, the folded petals of a human being grown in chrysalis and developing in the conditions peculiar to those years—the same thing that her husband had discovered in her. In his exaggerated indulgence Kurilov painstakingly sought to remember other cases in which the magnitude of the errors committed determined the scope of future achievements. . . . This woman had everything ahead of her; this was just as true as the fact that he himself had everything behind him. . . . His amiable attentiveness toward her was being replaced by an alarming and unfamiliar feeling.

So that was what it looked like, the present! It seemed that his own youth was coming only now. Verily, he was recovering. Here, at the sunset of his life, love became a powerful and still unexplored means of physiotherapy. At any other time he would have considered such ideas superstitious. For two consecutive days it seemed to him that he had forgotten about his attacks. He now counted the symptoms of his rejuvenation by the dozen. . . .

Wherever he looked in the presence of Liza, she always remained in his field of vision. When he met her in the morning, he carried her touch on his hand until night, like a glove. This feeling prevented him from thinking, but he readily became accustomed to the discomforts of his second youth. He wanted Liza, he fell asleep thinking of her, and Liza, too, by jolts, as though in her sleep, was moving toward him. . . . Rest homes always predispose their inmates to romantic adventures, and in Borschnia there was even a special "moonlight committee" composed of vacationists who kept a facetious register of all the amorous incidents that took place. However, this two-week love affair escaped the committee; its preparation proceeded unknown even to its main participants, and its realization was too tiny an explosion for it to be noticed by the Borschnia gossipers. . . . The actress was attracted by the bigness of this man, although at the beginning she did not understand what it consisted of. But she had always granted Kurilov the great right to condemn and praise, and what she lacked to be happy was no longer to have a conversation with Tiutchev but to win at least a little approval from Kurilov. In addition, she was always aware of the dark cloud that hung over Alexei Nikitich, and she wanted to push it aside, but did not know how. . . .

In a letter to Arkadyi Hermogenovich concerning his secret mission, she wrote: ". . . Forgive my not having written you sooner; I visited the Borschnia graveyard as you asked me. I could barely find it, for it is abandoned; it is just one big snowdrift, and it's a good thing I went there on my skis. By night, in the moonlight, it is beautiful, but the moon here is very small; it must have worn out since you were young. How many lovers have used it! . . . I have been treated very kindly here. One very nice man, Shamin, took me to Cheremshansk to show me the people. It's strange, but when talking to them one feels that one wants to do something big in order to have the right to say 'we.' Don't be surprised if I stay here. It is possible that I will return to Moscow only to get my things. . . .

". . . I keep digressing from the subject that interests you. I twice visited the place, but could not find Taniechka's grave. The tombstones here were used for paving the square of the riding grounds; this particular tombstone must have been used, too. However, your Taniechka may have been buried somewhere else. . . . Remember Mary Stuart— think where she spent her youth and where her bones were laid! . . . By the way, I've definitely renounced my dream of playing her. It was only a childish desire, but I am indebted to it for having made me read many books of which I had not before suspected the existence. . . . An excellent library has been preserved here. I have read a great deal. I am bored by this old dream.

"Again I have digressed, chatterbox that I am! However, we have discovered here a relative of the last Borschnia landlord, possibly his sister. She lives here in a cabin in the park. I shall try, if I have time, to question her about your Taniechka; she must remember her. I went with Alexei Nikitich to have a look at her. . . . And you were wrong to speak so ill of him. His life is just one endless working day, and yet I find that he is constantly afraid he won't have time, time to do the most important thing. Of course he is a big man. I am filled to the brim with him, but I still cannot find enough room for him. Don't imagine things; nothing has happened. I am the same as before. Just realize that your Liza is simply drunk with air, snow and people. . . ."

The most convincing proof of her sincerity was the fact that she was disinterested in finding out whether Tiutchev was really one of Kurilov's intimate friends. More, she very skilfully changed the subject when he himself mentioned it casually. She came to Kurilov without even the false artlessness of a provincial girl that she had used with Zakurdaev. And if this was not an attempt to ascertain whether she was capable of a great passion, it was budding love. Liza was frightened only by the existence of Marina, whose part in Kurilov's life she did not understand. Ascribing to her rival qualities that she actually did not have, she resolved to engage in a struggle with her in her absence. She tried to give these attempts a shade of casualness: "You know, that woman who was in the car that time, is pretty. Drowned women look like her: a little plump, with greenish eyes . . . because they have looked too much at water." She said this with closed eyes, as one recites a poem. "In a July moon . . . she floats with her face up . . . Ophelia . . . all in yellow flowers and broken sedge . . . and everything around her floats together with her. . . ."

He did not even understand that this was jealousy, but he realized that Catherine, for instance, would have disliked Liza's perfidious remarks.

"That woman," he said, respectfully of Marina, "is the mother of a fi-irst-rate son. And she herself is not a bad human being . . . she knows her own limitations." And he thought that in the space of an hour Catherine would have become a friend of a woman like Marina for life!'

Liza fell silent; perhaps it was from shame. They were returning home. Since nightfall it had been snowing without interruption. The road through the woods could be guessed only by the width of the cleared space ahead. Actually, all this conversation took place only because they were unable to see each other's faces because of the falling snow.

"Well, and how is your Gavrila getting on?"

"Oh, he has made a great stride forward. He is learning to smile. You know, children always trust me."

She nodded affirmatively; she doubtless had herself in mind. "That's true. Have you any children yourself?"

"I never had any." He hurriedly sought for an explanation. "At first I had to hide constantly, and then—remember?—the republic did not dismount from its horse for three years. And when life settled down, my wife fell ill. . . ."

"Is she alive?" Liza asked quickly.

"No." And for about twenty steps he walked in silence. "But sometimes I've had a great desire to have a son . . . with broad shoulders, ironical, stern, sort of . . ." (and the impetuousness with which he threw his fist over his head expressed the force of his old desire) ". . . a son who would answer my every word with two. Now he would be a Red soldier. And he would write me letters from the Ocean, not very long ones, quite business-like . . . nothing to weep over, but every page would have a barely perceptible smell of the great watery expanse. 'Come fly to me,' he would write, 'ancient and respectable old man, let us meet once more before you are shoved into the big oven, before we set out with a song on our lips for the last far-flung campaign!' And I would go to see him there and be respected as the father of a Red Army man . . . I would sit on my son's hard cot and would walk with him on the freshly dug earth, smoking his strong Red Army tobacco . . . and I'd watch all the time to see whether there was much of me in him and of him in me. And who knows, perhaps my grandson too would have sent me such a letter. I should have got along well with a grandson: I've never cheated children. . . ."

The snow was falling more and more heavily. The road had been blocked, but someone had passed over it with a broad sledge and left a greasy and winding rut. A twig from a bush cut by the runners lay on the snow. Liza picked it up and walked on ahead of Kurilov. "No doubt animals are fond of you, too—and trees," said Liza and slashed once at a pine tree dressed in blue flakes. "They like masters like you

—generous, with a heavy, assured step. And they want them to be, not compassionate, but intelligent toward everything alive in the world! Then they're not afraid of anything, neither of the night nor of the foe. . . ."

"I haven't noticed that with trees; I have had to deal with them chiefly in the form of lumber," said Alexei Nikitich dryly, angry at himself for this not very clever retort. "Walk faster, it's getting dark . . . one might lose one's way in these devilish woods." He raised his voice. "Don't you see, a snowstorm is blowing up!"

Suddenly she turned toward him, barring his way with raised hands. "Listen, Kurilov . . . I don't need anything from you. I don't need you to be my companion to the end, but . . . look, would you like me to give you a son?" She feared that he might suspect her of some dishonest game: her arms fell down at her sides. "I shall bring him up to be what you said. . . ."

He was silent, scrutinizing her face ironically; through the snow it looked misty, as though seen behind a wedding veil. He suspected that Liza's feeling was momentary, the result of an impulse not deeply rooted in her heart. He wanted to say that she had failed to notice something very essential in the imaginary letter from his son. Liza waited, her head raised. Snowflakes hung from her lashes. Suddenly she asked, frowning: "Have you a disease? . . . Or is it too late for you?"

Then he began hurriedly to recall how all this had been accomplished by the anonymous couple under his office window. Now for the second time youth was being offered him, and the gates to the garden were opening! He raised Liza, small and light, to him, so that she did not have to stretch so hard to reach him. She clung to him, and her heart tightened as though she had climbed onto a high bridge, over an immense river with a distant mouth that flowed into the Ocean. Yes, he was like a bridge, and people passed over him into the future. . . . Her knitted cap fell from her head as she threw it back. Her tangy lips damp from the snow were hard as sealing-wax; but they melted and poured somewhere deep into Kurilov's being.

"You're like a lynx . . . you leap at people," he whispered, confused and alarmed, and he whispered something else, clumsy and strong, holding his amorous prey in his hands.

She tried to free herself. "Let me go, you're pricking me all over. It's like kissing a gooseberry bush. . . ."

He carefully put her down, dug up her cap from the snow and handed it to her. She forgot to put it on and walked stooping forward, her curls white with snow. It was a bad moment, like all sobering moments. Alexei Nikitich caught up with her and asked her whether he had hurt her feelings. She asked sarcastically whether the law did not punish girls like her, who bring disorder into the lives of responsible workers. She felt uncomfortable, as though Ksaveryi were looking at her from behind her shoulder and shaking with a vile, senile guffaw. Then Alexei Nikitich burst out laughing and in a comradely way pressed her cold wet hands.

"People like me must be excused when they lose their heads: we're no longer young! As for you—" Apparently he referred to her actress' professional defensive instinct.

As though nothing had happened they walked back, hand in hand, facetiously discussing the name of their future son. "He'll surely be called Izmail, . . ." Kurilov thought. "That is a good name for the leader of a great liberating armada, isn't it?" Suddenly she stopped him and repeated, as though defending herself from herself: "I don't need anything from you, my dear. . . ."

CHAPTER 41

## We Take Liza with Us

In Ocean we saw and touched many things which filled us with joy. We felt sad when we had to leave, we felt as though we were giving up a trim comfortable house for an unfinished structure, still leaking, with no roof, with black rafters overhead and coarsely laid bricks still showing in the unplastered walls. . . . We had made the round of the transformed planet on foot. We liked everything, even the very different colors of the evening clouds. Sometimes, as though by tacit agreement, we stopped, picked up a handful of the new rich earth, and for a long while, with misty eyes, examined its grain. The combined efforts of excavators, planners, leaders—my contemporaries!—must surely have left some mark on this earth, we thought. Then we looked at the land clothed in forests, from which would come the timber of the future, and we were overwhelmed with pride at belonging to the generation of pioneers.

And though the span of the future is boundless, we had hardly enough time to turn the leaves of his magnificent new edition of the world, corrected and supplemented by the genius of man. But after all we had no intention of writing a Baedeker of the new planet. It would have been as ridiculous as trying to set the brilliance of noon down on a picture postcard. We shall limit ourselves to simple enumeration: reports sent by pioneers are always sketchy and inaccurate. . . .

And so we tried to be in all places at once. We went to the opening of gigantic hydraulic stations; and the morning that the waters of the Mediterranean Dam, boiling and storming, rushed into the Central Sahara setting turbines in motion, will remain in my memory the greatest triumph of reason and of man no longer confined to the prison-like frontiers of ancient states. We went to remote Arctic provinces and ate excellent grapes grown on the seventieth parallel; we became acquainted with the newest methods of wiring electric plants; we visited marvellously complex combines where anything could be manufactured out of anything, because matter is one, and all can be found everywhere. We asked the price of such and such an article and were told that it was cheap, that is to say, uninteresting; we tried to find out how all this had been organized, and I am glad

364

that my ignorance of technology exempts me from the necessity of citing facts and figures.

Not astonished [1] by the technical cunning of our descendants, we looked attentively at the people themselves. It seemed to us that human nature had improved. The people stood more erect, seemed more assured—whether because each one was aware of his neighbor at his side and did not fear him, or because the clean air of the new time did not contain the bacillus of falsehood. . . . I expected them to boast of the perfection of their social order and I should not have condemned their pride, but actually they took no notice of the social order. Here, man's natural state had at last been attained—he was free, he was not exploited and he rejoiced in the work of hand and brain. But although everything was within reach—bread, work and fate itself —we often saw people with careworn faces. We understood that sadness dwelt among them, and that they, too, knew tragedy, though of a kind more worthy of man's dignity.

This struck us particularly when Ocean prepared to honor the first interplanetary explorer. This whole episode is still vivid to me. I remember clearly that for two weeks the newspapers trumpeted the news of the brave traveller's imminent return and announced the exact date. He was the man of the year, and countless photographs of him were scattered over the cities of the earth. Everyone knew his biography and could recite the most important events of his life; girls kept in their favorite books the photographs of his two sons who had accompanied him to the arctic regions of the universe. And that year the mother of the daredevils was the mother of all heroes who dreamed of performing deeds worthy of historical record. The problem of this adventure was not to die "over there" for the glory of human curiosity—death had long ago lost its sensational character and was incapable of stirring the people—but to return alive without causing grief to anyone and to bring back the crown of the unknown as a trophy. To honor the homecomers, on the day they were scheduled to return, their native planet put on its most brilliant best and doubtless floated in the universe like a particle of down struck by a ray of sunlight. . . . One night passed, then a second and a third, and the ship did not return.

On the fifth day the whole world became anxious over the fate of four human beings. A prolonged and bitter discussion was carried on

---

[1] We were not astonished. The ancients spoke with awe of countries wherein wool grew on trees. They were called liars, yet their only mistake was to call cotton wool. Astonishment will always be the lot of those who take the horizon for the frontier of the universe.

over the radio, in which the constructors of all five continents took part. The navigational properties of the ship were subjected to exacting criticism; implausible hypotheses were advanced; the newspapers received hundreds of thousands of letters recommending ways and means of rescuing the explorers from "out there," among the worlds. The reputation of the astroplane's builders hung on a hair. For the time being no one accused them, but these men knew real unhappiness. The failure of the flight was equivalent to moral death for them, because the calling of man had by then been definitely identified with the concept of creativity, that is to say, *mastery.* Under the pressure of public opinion and at the request of the builders a government commission was formed of over two hundred members, charged with subjecting the absent ship to expert analysis, determining the positions of the planets on the day of the ship's departure and the day of its scheduled return, and working out the formulae of interplanetary gravitation, the pressures, velocities, parabolae and everything on which the success of the enterprise depended. The conclusions of the commission were very favorable, but the architect of OCEAN I did not smile upon hearing of his acquittal. His ship had not returned. . . .

One woman—the wife of the captain and the mother of two of the explorers—might be said to have had most at stake in the fate of these brave men. And while Alexei Nikitich and myself should have been glad to comfort her, we did not visit her: sinister rumors had begun to spread among the nations, and in what language other than silence could we address her? We saw her only at the last session of the government commission. . . . The attendants did not leave, they were waiting for someone. Then, through the high door, very simply she entered all alone, the modest little *mother of the giants,* as her contemporaries called her. A stern old man whom we had not noticed before hurried to meet her halfway. All present rose respectfully when, in silence, he stooped to embrace her thin shoulders. The two sat down on the left side of the amphitheatre, where the seats of honor stood, almost like dots in the distance.

The ellipsoid dome hung over the gigantic yet humdrum hall. Its very dimensions conveyed a feeling of emptiness, twilight and coolness. (What ovations must have shaken these walls on the day of the departure of OCEAN I!) And though this was the main hall of the Central Observatory, nowhere did we see the familiar thick pipes with glass lenses, nor the marvellous all-seeing screens of which the radiotechnicians of antiquity had dreamed. At a given signal, a man noiselessly went to his post at the board representing the sky in mercatorial projection; the lights went out. The switching-on of the electronic tele-

scopes was accompanied by an increasing hum. The dull metallic ringing was followed by the roar of remote avalanches, and suddenly
something stirred in the emptiness, something of which we took cog-
nizance with fear and trembling. A formless dark body followed by a
smaller body passed before us. Kurilov covered his mouth, as men
do in a high wind; I thought my shivering was from cold. A feverish
chill touched my forehead. The flashes became more rapid, the stars
began to come up from the darkness . . . and since we had not left the
earth it seemed that the universe was hurtling through us, the paralyzed witnesses of its secret. In the chaos a luminous disc was being
conceived, still naïve, as in a morning dream; it grew, we began to
sense its spherical form; then misty outlines, such as are seen by fortunate voyagers, began to make their way through layers of inert
clouds. I gripped a rail in front of me; it creaked. My confusion passed
into vague anticipation, as happens in disasters—I felt as though we
were falling upon a strange, ghostly and virginal continent, never to
return.

Our sight became sharp as that of a god. No one had known matter
so intimately. For entire minutes we distinguished the very cells of
that aqueous stuff, oblong, almost crystalline, with green pulsating
foam. It seemed that you had only to stretch out our hand to touch
streaming trunks of trees resembling submarine plants; they swayed in
the damp, purplish fog. An armored insect sensing the presence of the
unknown superstitiously sought shelter in a crevice, and a blade of
grass bent under the weight of dew: a quiet evening was descending
upon the evening star. . . . Like gods, and yet, in a way, like intruding
bats, we soared over these hairy hills, now looking attentively, now
shying off, fearful because we were not reflected in the waters over
which we bent our faces. But, though omnipotent, we were powerless
to move so much as a grain of sand; omniscient, we could not find the
tracks of our brave and beloved explorers, the first human tracks on
another planet. We searched everywhere and could not find them, we
could not . . . when suddenly a wail wove itself into the somber hum.
There could be no mistake; it was the cry of a human being. Everyone remarked how the mother jumped from her seat with raised hands
in the direction of the voice: André . . . "No, these are just bolides,"
the man at the board muttered.

When this magic flight through eternity was over, the shadows crept
out of their boxes, and earthly dusk entered the hall. With a guilty expression and an apologetic cough, the mother said goodbye. Her
sunken eyes seemed young to me. What had rejuvenated her? If not
the greatness of her grief, it must have been her proud joy in know-

ing that she had given her immense homeland the dearest of her possessions.

"Search more thoroughly, search every night," the stern old man said as he left. (He was giving orders to *search* the universe. Power! So that's what power is, and such is its price. . . .) But in fact all search was futile. The fourth paragraph of the commission's final report mentioned somewhat vaguely that according to all available data the supplies of energy, gas and provisions carried by the ship would be nearing exhaustion (read: were completely exhausted), and yet the newspapers were forbidden to print obituaries of the lost men. All four were still counted members of their organizations, they were listed as absent on official trips for an indefinite time. Was this not the most perfect form of immortality: *to be treated as living*. . . . Meanwhile new lists of volunteers for a new voyage into the unknown were posted in the streets. Alongside the name of each candidate was the enumeration of his scientific works and sporting achievements, which were to guide the public in the judgment of his merits.

And it was only after a plant had won the competition and was authorized to build OCEAN II, that the landing of OCEAN I in the district of Tarussa, near Moscow, became known; the unbroken interplanetary vigil had missed its arrival. To avoid an influx of the curious, a cordon was thrown around the place and all communication was cut off.

For several days after that the radio broadcasted incomplete fourth-hand reports of the return; something was being concealed. No one, except the doctors, had as yet seen *them*. In daily bulletins issued by the first government secretary there was much about the exhaustion of the navigators, but for some reason only two names were mentioned. Then it was learned that the captain's two sons had perished. Leading editorials written in the language of deep and solemn sorrow were devoted to the first human graves beyond the earth: thus the settlement of newly discovered continents had always begun. . . . That day I walked in the streets of many cities, and it seemed to me that all the girls in the world felt widowed. The mother of the lost wrote a short letter to the newspapers; she shared the grief of her native globe because her children had been good boys and had always tried to justify the love and trust of their friends. She received so many letters—it seemed that all the young men of the earth wanted to be her sons. Nothing had so forcefully demonstrated the unity felt by mankind.

A day was set and a modest ceremony arranged for the entry of the new Columbus into the capital. An unprecedented migration of people from one hemisphere to the other began: and they came, not so much to see him or hear his voice for a little while, as to greet him with thunderous earthly cheers. Kurilov and I took Liza with us to attend the ceremony, to show her how beautiful is man cleansed of original mire.

Everyone who was there must know that when you leave the quay and walk along Stalin and Yang Tze Streets, past Academy Square, turning toward the southwest, you see the two-humped hill of Unity with a gigantic fountain on its second top, the so-called Tree of Water. This is unquestionably the most magnificent spot in Ocean. . . . The glossy walls of the Palace of Statistics covered with Chinese lacquer reflected the bridge across the canal, and it was as though the arches of this bridge, delicate as a complex mathematical equation, pierced the throng of the fantastic ancient ghosts on the porcelain panels. Long before the celebration began, we went up on escalators to our regular café. But the tables had been removed to make room for the influx of people. Every spot was full of noise and laughter. The flocking together began at daybreak, and the immense fields beyond Nantao sparkled with a mass of planettes. It was hot: the sun-coolers were inadequate against June. We drank gingery water with a grainy taste. An immense radius of the city extended before us. How it had changed since the days of rickshaw coolies who ran through the streets and of the unyielding gentlemen who lived opulently in the concessions. . . . Far beyond the bay an island appeared through a greenish mist, and behind, resembling historic inscriptions on faded grey canvas, lay the ancient quarters of Pu-Tung and heroic Chapei.

While Kurilov argued with Liza (at that moment I had not guessed the dénouement), I glanced through a newspaper. The routine news began only on page 10; on page 11, under a flashy title, there was an interview with a homely woman stricken with spotted typhus; her photograph was shown and a picture of the clinic in which she had been placed; I did not understand what it was all about. I also read the verses of a popular poet who wrote in sonorous images about walking. It was a kind of lyrical treatise which showed how walking benefited the function of the heart and the muscles, and at the same time described the sunny spots on the path along which the poet passed. . . . Suddenly the distant thunder of orchestras sounded. I dropped the newspaper.

At once there was silence. The streets below seemed empty because of the quiet and they shone as though rubbed with heavy oil. There was a general stir, everything around us seemed to take wing like a flock of birds. People bared their heads. I rushed forward, and the weight of a mighty unanimous sigh fell on my shoulders. I assumed all the time that I would see a man with a dark face of Lazarus who had spent three days on the other side of life; that he would walk alone, this captain of super-distant voyages, spreading around him the silence and cold eternity. My assumptions collapsed at once. Suddenly on the harbor boom which sloped down to the square three men appeared. And once again I saw the same tall, clean-shaven old man wearing a broad-brimmed black hat—the chairman of the executive committee of this hemisphere. Beside him, arm in arm, walked a solid, well-set man in a dark beret, with the intelligent and virile face of Koloman Wallisch, who long ago, at the dawn of this era, was hanged by the savages of the earth. As he walked he looked straight at the sun with unblinking eyes. The third, the doctor and captain's aide, walked a few steps behind the other two. Eyes and tele-mechanisms followed every one of their movements. The orchestras were silent, no one shouted to greet these men, and a hundred times more impressive was this human speechlessness.

He ascended the platform, and at once a little girl with a bouquet of flowers, which she herself had picked, ran up to him across the square. All the planet, jubilant and laughing, watched the flashing of her sun-tanned knees. Not daring to say a word from rapture and fear, the girl held out the flowers to *him*—once, twice, but he kept standing and staring at the sky. It was a blue sky, a kindly sky, quite unlike that which had killed his sons. The crowd stirred, moved slightly forward, and a rustle of conjectures floated confusedly above their heads. The old man in the immense hat whispered something into the captain's ear. The captain shook himself and bending, with apologetic, cautious hands, began to grope in the air before him. Without noticing it he stepped on the flowers which had fallen to the ground. . . . But he caught the child, tenderly touched her face, and raised her to his head; everyone moved from his place, and at that moment it seemed to me a storm was unleashed with one single blast. . . .

The report did not begin until our hearts were unburdened of all that had gathered in them during the three and a half years of this unprecedented heroic voyage. In a low, almost prosaic, voice (the wise simplicity of this celebration was deeply moving), the man in the beret spoke of his gratitude to the nations of the earth for their sympathy and support; he expressed regret that fate had deprived him of the possibility of repeating this voyage; he told briefly of his companions' death, of the catastrophe during the return trip, of the things he had seen and touched, his memory of which was still warm. These years had aged him, but he had the strength to jest and say a few sharp, unforgettable words. (In time, if my friendship with Alexei Nikitich continues, we shall recall the details of this, the most marvellous adventure that has ever been the lot of man.)

Then came the salutes and speeches, and it was not length but brevity, nay, aphoristic terseness, which the people considered meritorious. On an invisible screen, magnified and almost three-dimensional, appeared the representatives of nations, countries, continents; a boy behind me (perhaps a radio enthusiast of those days?) whispered with a hurried gasp: "Now Africa is going to speak!" And then we saw the famous Samuel Bothead. My heart began to pound, it was as though the stately, grey-haired Negro were my dearest friend. He had greatly aged since we had gone to see him at Aden, and he limped perceptibly as a result of the wound he had received in the battle of Shanghai. His voice, however, had preserved something of its former passionate impetuosity which had so attracted me. In speaking he beat time with the club on which he leaned; he spoke of the infinite spaces of the universe in which from now on the man of the earth, free and a thousand times prouder, would develop. I listened to him to the end and went down, leaving Liza and Kurilov. (She greedily absorbed everything that surrounded us—this noble air of friendship, this magnificent emotion arising from the contemplation of heroic deeds; and there was such childlike enthusiasm in her eyes that I had radically to revise my original opinion of her.)

Night had fallen. High in the sky, brilliant and twice as large as the moon, shone an antique hieroglyph, signifying longevity. In gigantic parks, under trees, people danced; the light wind of their movements still clings to my face. I heard laughter and tender words; it was sad having to leave Ocean on such a night. Making my way through the throng, I felt almost like an old man. . . . Some sort of glittering melodious insects flitted through the air above; I fancied that they, too, were singing. I saw one of them, which had been flying from far off, hit a lantern at full speed and drop with folded wings, sated and dead. (So that was how the problem of death was solved *there!*) I lengthened my steps; I had to hurry, because real and urgent events were tearing me back from my wanderings in the gleaming unknown.

# CHAPTER 42

# The Ferryman Knocks with His Pole at Kurilov's Door

KURILOV MET LIZA at the same spot in the woods many times. No one prevented them from seeing each other in the house, but in the free air their meetings seemed cleaner and more honest. They left the house separately, often stopping on the way to listen to the nocturnal crackling of the branches, and going off the path to confuse those who might have tried to follow their tracks; the omnipotent Borschnia gossipers of the "moonlight committee" had their agents everywhere. Perhaps such fears held for them a sharp, unknown novelty. . . . And so they met, ashamed of the incident in the blizzard, and first wandered at random on the endless winter road. The withered green of the sky faded; the hardened ruts had a faintly orange color. Kurilov spoke of his friends and enemies, and Liza was struck by the importance they acquired as he told of them, as though he had spent his life among a special race of giants. And she began to understand why her own encounters with people had always seemed so wretched and insignificant. Perhaps at this point the hoped-for thrill of the meeting ended. These moments were imbued with a sort of ominous cold.

Sometimes Liza was certain that Alexei Nikitich really possessed the key to life and the universe and that if one entered into the being of this man one would find at the bottom of his soul the potent word that explained everything (Izmail, the name of their never-to-be-born son, was now for her a path to Kurilov's Ocean). Was it then for some hidden reason that she was attracted to this man? . . . For the surge of desire that had once almost brought them together did not recur. Alexei Nikitich, too, caught himself thinking that these meetings in the wintry solitude were only a clumsy imitation of the anonymous couple under the window of his Political Bureau. No, they did not achieve the singing lightness that marks all the actions of lovers—from the mystery of the first handshake to the concluding transport, when in one hour all the tenderness that has been piled up in crumbs is prodigally spent.

The month was drawing to an end, the country around Borschnia was familiar now, and the events of Kurilov's life had all been told; in fact, there were not so many to tell, and all of them were contained in one infinite word: work. The love affair was moving at an ever-slower pace. More and more often Shamin demanded that Liza give him a final answer about working in Cheremshansk. And more and more often Alexei Nikitich, too, spoke of his imminent departure; he began to be hungry for his old bustling activity; Klavdia wrote that the professor had returned from Barcelona; and he found that Gavrila could not replace the quizzical and entertaining Ziamka. . . .

Then something happened that interrupted their meetings. In an-swer to Kostia's repeated invitations Peresypkin came to Borschnia. He wanted to find Spirka's grave and sit beside it for an hour before finishing his epic chapter on the victims of the Volga-Revizan line. No sooner off his sleigh, he ran up to Kurilov's room to embrace the old man and learn of the latest excitement, but he was told that Alexei Nikitich was out for a walk. Aliosha rushed after him and, a quarter of an hour later, came upon a scene that compelled him to revise his ideas about his closest friend.

No further than thirty steps from him two people barred his path. Bending his head down (if the man had been a stranger, the scene might have seemed comical), a man was looking into the face of a woman, considerably shorter than himself; stretching out her arm, almost hanging on him, she stroked his eyes and cheeks with her fingers. And although instead of his overcoat he wore a plain sheepskin for which he had conceived a liking in Borschnia, Aliosha at once recognized Kurilov, just as he recognized Liza's picturesque beret. The former homeless boy to whom life had taught everything was shaken by the indescribable and, as he thought, shamefaced intimacy of this scene, which seemed to be a farewell. His first impulse was to run away as fast as he could (and of course Kurilov would have turned at the noise and cried: Aliosha, Aliosha, where are you running?), but Peresypkin controlled his childish impulse and, having no time to re-treat, hid behind a tree in the crumbling, miry snow to give them a chance to leave. . . . Kurilov and Liza went by, hand in hand; they had passed the tree when Liza noticed Peresypkin's footprints and showed them to Kurilov. He walked back from the road straight into the woods, and at that moment Aliosha emerged from his hiding-place. Now they stood silently facing each other, and never before had Aliosha seen such a cold and unkind expression on Kurilov's face.

"What are you doing here, Alexei?" asked Kurilov sternly.

And although he knew that he could be suspected of having de-liberately rushed from Cheremshansk to spy upon his foster-father, Aliosha stood silent, breaking a twig, and his lips trembled. Alexei Nikitich turned away in disgust and walked after Liza. . . . The same day, not having exchanged one word with him, Peresypkin went back to Cheremshansk.

Even before this, Liza and Kurilov had kept their friendship secret; now at the common table they behaved like strangers. Fortunately, a checkers tournament was being held in the rest home at that time, and the rehearsal of the glee club was in full swing. (And always at the beginning of the evening a solid fellow, a traction inspector with athletic shoulders and a skull shaven like a mirror, sang the same love song; he did this with his whole strength, spreading his legs and booming out each word so loudly that he might have been chanting the disciplinary regulations or trying to make as much noise as a whole broadcasting station.) Kurilov visibly avoided Liza and took his walks alone, while Liza more and more often stayed in the house to listen to the singers. Shamin always sat beside her; he had been a frequent visitor in Borschnia ever since her arrival. "Atten—attention, this is station ERRV, . . ." he would say, facetiously nodding in the direction of the inspector as the latter rose to begin his performance.

One day Liza told him that she had decided to work in Cheremshansk.

"Is that a promise?" asked Shamin. "Remember that this is not 'going to the people.' You'll get something from us in exchange for what you give us."

"Yes, it's a promise!" she said and held out her hand. She asked where she would work; and learned that she was being considered for the Ulgan-Urmansk locomotive yard.

"What does Ulgan-Urmansk stand for?"

"I think: 'dead woods.' "

She repeated, biting her lips: "Aha, dead woods, dead woods. . . ."

"It's up to you, comrade, to change this name, just as we ourselves changed the heavy name of Russia." He almost had to shout, for the one-man radio station was sending out some particularly deafening roars. "And by the way, what's going on between you and Kurilov? It looks as though you'd quarrelled. The old man's gone out to walk alone. You have such a lovely . . . and . . . and I may say, pleasant face, that it's hard to imagine. . . ."

She interrupted him. "Oh, nothing much. He maintained that you would certainly try to make love to me, and I said that you were first and foremost a devoted and intelligent comrade."

He groaned, worriedly ruffled his hair, then laughed and rose from his seat. "Well, thanks for the lesson. I'll go play checkers with the radio station!"

It was true that Alexei Nikitich now took his walks alone. His whole episode with Liza suddenly appeared criminal to him. The meeting with Peresypkin had reminded him of what had almost completely dropped out of his mind; not Catherine (as though at his age faithfulness to his dead wife was not only decent but obligatory), but his illness. Nothing had changed since his arrival in Borschnia; the professor who had returned from Barcelona was sharpening his knife for him, the ferryman was knocking at the door with his pole. He turned from the half-blocked path into the park and for a long time walked through the grounds knee-deep in snow. He came to a spot in the ravine which was overgrown with young aspens like brooms. The gust of wind did not reach here. Kurilov looked back; no one was around. He removed his gloves and, pulling toward him a branch in a furry and flaky overcoat, tried to break it. The needles scratched his face and hands, but the flexible wood refused to yield. He waited for a moment, listening to the howling of the east wind, and again looked around. The place was deserted, there was no sign of a human dwelling-place. And again with an exaggerated effort he attacked the branch, and again during a respite listened to himself to see whether he had not stirred up his illness, whether it was still there. But it was not there . . . and were it not for the whistling wind that reminded him of the twig in Liza's hand, the same silence would have prevailed in nature as in his body. Then the sharp little wedge of the moon broke through the high, smoky clouds. New snowdrifts piled up, and the flakes whirled around him, greenish silver.

He came home late. . . . And if it had been summer time he would have picked an armful of some yellow ravine flowers and entered Liza's room to place the fragrant fading sheaf on the sleeping woman's pillow. But it was winter, and his garden was covered with frost. . . . He wandered into the open but empty hothouse and passed a match along the shelves; leaping black shadows ran along the plants that looked like lettuces or nettles. With empty hands he climbed up the staircase to his room, and the floor under him grumbled like old age itself. He threw his sheepskin through the half open door so as not to awaken Gavrila, and after standing for a moment in hesitation before Liza's door, went to the reading room: all in all he did not know enough about his Ocean, hence the truth in his constructions was liberally sprinkled with errors.

But once he found the door to Liza's room half open, for life in Borschnia was simple. He saw that something had happened in there. Half dressed, on her knees, she was hurriedly fumbling with one hand in her suitcase, which had been thrown on the floor. On her left hand, which hung at her side, he noticed blood. With narrowed eyes he asked her in a low voice whether she needed any help. She said she had cut her finger and asked him to bandage tightly the bleeding wound. He entered, and she held her hand out to him.

"I'm not looking . . . I'm not looking!" he muttered, and the very air of Liza's room, full of vague nocturnal feminine odors, confused him.

She shook the blood off her hand to show him her wound, and immediately a new drop budded in the cut, ripened and dropped to the floor. This bead of blood hypnotized them both and through some feeling of compassion brought them closer. . . . He took her up in his arms and carried her, and she did not resist. She only held her hand away from him so as not to stain him with blood. She was fascinated by the drops of snow on his grey mustache.

Kurilov's exultation was premature. For suddenly it was as though the sky had collapsed on him. Deep wrinkles cut through his face. His head fell forward and his mustache, hard as iron, stabbed Liza's forehead. It seemed to the young woman that her lover was dying. Terrified, she pushed his face up with her palm. Alexei Nikitich staggered out of her room. . . .

And that was when the ferryman knocked at his door. The blood from her cut finger remained on his cheek. To Liza all this was terrifying. Pressing her hand over her mouth to keep from screaming, she watched him struggle, as though blinded, with the door which he was unable to open. . . . Half-dressed as she was, she jumped out on to the balcony. Standing knee deep in snow she clung to Kurilov's window. Behind the glass she saw a large and indistinct shadow rush by, and that was all.

Had it not been for the reflected moonlight on the glass, she would have seen how he rummaged on top of the stove for a box containing a needle and a phial that he had hidden there to escape the curious eyes of the chambermaids; how the chair dropped under him, and how, scraping the wall with his whole body, losing his balance, he collapsed on his bed; how he tore his shirt to bare his arm; how the thin, beneficent needle entered his unhappy body. . . .

The dampness and icy air drove Liza inside again. Shivering with shame and cold, she sat on her crumpled bed with her legs drawn up under her, listening. The crickets hummed in a warning tone; perhaps they were guards. Something made of glass broke somewhere. Ten minutes later compassion again impelled her to go, now fully dressed, to Kurilov. . . . The moon was shining. The sheets and blankets had slipped off his bed to the floor. Formless, as though slain, Alexei Nikitich lay flat on the striped mattress, his legs hanging down. The room was chilly. Liza picked up his sheepskin and carefully covered him. She did not dare to awaken him, but he was not asleep.

As soon as she left he sat up, stunned, his body sagging against the wall. A blissful numbness spread all through him. A minute later he opened his eyes and noticed the chips of the crushed hypodermic on the floor, as sharply as if on a carefully made police photograph. Still not knowing what he wanted, he mechanically rummaged for his pipe. He called his little prisoner by name (it had not occurred to him that if Gavrila had been there he would have long since been awakened by the noise). No one answered. Ziamka's substitute had vanished: his roving instinct had proved stronger than Kurilov's kindness or his own fear of the blizzard. Alexei's overturned suitcase lay in a corner. Apparently the little human beast had gone through it to find something he needed for his trip. With an anxious feeling Alexei Nikitich sought his pipe with his eyes; it always lay somewhere in sight; but it seemed that the thrifty Gavrila had needed the pipe, too.

("What do you need a pipe for, now!" the ferryman Charon, out of Pokhvisnev's book, would have said to Kurilov.)

Upon seeing the suitcase, Kurilov realized that Gavrila had fled. Every other day, before midnight, a cart left Borschnia with the mail. He had to hurry if he wanted to catch it, but only half an hour later did he find the courage to get dressed and gather up the poor remnants of his belongings. By sheer force of will he bent down and picked up the needle so as not to leave anything that might arouse suspicion. This took two long minutes. To carry the suitcase was beyond his strength and he dropped it in the doorway. He wanted to pass Liza's door without being heard. Beads of sweat came out on his forehead when he realized that she might be waiting for him in the corridor.

She was. "Are you ill?" she asked.

"Go away, Liza," he said and waved his hand.

It would have been more sensible and generous to act as if nothing had happened. With a furtive and guilty caress he stroked her sleeve when she tried to take hold of him from under the arm. She insisted, and he yielded; without her help it would have been difficult to get down to the yard. Theirs were the first footsteps on the fresh snow. The blizzard had now completely subsided. The air was magnificently clear; one could count the snow flakes.

"Now you see how nice things would have been for my poor wife," Kurilov said, touching the snowdrifts with his knees. And, to change the subject: "There's been a lot of snow . . . it's hard for engine drivers, watchmen and homeless people!"

Two men in old sheepskins were harnessing the cart, having put their lantern down on the snow. The horse looked gloomily at the snowbound willow. An empty kerosene barrel lay at the bottom of the sleigh.

"Well, make room, citizeness," said Kurilov to the barrel, and settled himself at the side of the cart. Liza saw how much effort his joke cost him. "Don't be angry with me, comrade!"

"I pity you as I pity myself," she whispered.

He told the fellows that he had to go to the station immediately. They recognized him, put some straw under him, and covered him with a piece of cloth to protect him from the cold. He fell silent at once. The sleigh started tracing lines in the fresh snow. Sinking into the deep drifts, Liza ran after him. "I'll come back. We'll still see each other. . . ."

Her promise sounded like forgiveness which he did not need. Liza remained behind, her face grew smaller, then vanished. The phantom procession of the Borschnia birches accompanied Kurilov longer than did Liza. The future was now closer to him than what had rejoiced him only the day before. Something rang all the time, as though in the horse's belly, or perhaps in the barrel that responded to the slightest bumps on the road. When Alexei Nikitich looked out, the birches were behind him; no doubt they had returned to Borschnia.

"Give me something to smoke, comrade. I had a fi-irst class pipe, but. . . ."

The driver handed him an old pouch made out of colored rags. Reclining on his side, Kurilov took a pinch of tobacco and rolled a peasant cigar. He smoked it until the very end, until it began to burn his fingers, and never before had this dove-colored smoke, sweet in the frost, tasted so good. . . . Oblivion was coming to him; Ziamka went by, hand in hand with Arsentyich, and Frosia suddenly began to sob with her head on her sister's lap. ("What have you done to Alioshka while I was away!") He was awakened by a bump; the sleigh scooped some snow, having slipped to the shoulder of the road and struck a hidden tree stump. They lost a quarter of an hour in allowing some enormous, silent wagons pass by. These carried hay and moved slowly like time, for the peasants and the drivers in sheepksins sat high, under the very stars, like silent Christmas Magi. The ancient smells of dry grass and horse dung surrounded Alexei Nikitich . . . the next time he was awakened by girlish laughter, trilling in the moonlight. Sooty faces bent over Kurilov; in sheepskins put on inside-out, rolled in snow, waving birch twigs, they beat on the kerosene barrel as on a tambourine, shouting that probably the traveller was going to his wedding with his round iron bride. Here in the remote provinces, the ancient customs of the Russian after-Christmas season were still preserved, and the young people of the village were looking for companions. Alexei Nikitich rose slightly, and, frightened by the blackness of his eyes, they all vanished in the light, moonlit mist.

They arrived early at the station. The gnawing pain had stopped, whether because the drug was still operating or because the attack itself was over. Kurilov regretted having to leave the warm straw on which he had lain, but a foreboding of a new attack tormented him as sharply as the pain itself. He was shown the way to the infirmary. This time no one accompanied him in his wandering amid the snow-drifts. The people who lived here were very busy; after yesterday's blizzard the station was like an oasis in a desert of snow; it seemed that the rolling stock from the whole line was gathered there. . . . There were very few patients. Kurilov sat on a narrow bench and kept casting stealthy glances at his own picture, which hung on the wall in a good frame; the Kurilov on paper looked fresher and sterner. From other people who were waiting their turn Alexei Nikitich learned that the blizzard had caused a great number of accidents and that Martinson was leaving Cheremshansk that same night. This was good; every cloud has a silver lining, Kurilov decided; he could find a place in the Diesel car. . . .

Then a thick-set doctor, with the reddest hair and complexion that Kurilov had ever seen, appeared in the doorway. His ruddiness shone through his white physician's gown which looked like a piece of muslin wrapped around a pile of bricks. Under the gown a pair of stout shoes of a coppery hue moved impassively. (For some reason you thought as you looked at him that in former times he had treated big animals and had been promoted to the curing of people as a reward for his long years of service.) He cast a glance at Alexei Nikitich, mooed something unintelligible, frankly leered at the portrait, compared them again, cleared his throat and apparently failing to recognize Kurilov, began to let the patients into his office, in order of their arrival. They came out of his room with frightened faces, and Kurilov decided that this sturdy fellow treated illness chiefly by means of fear.

"Let's have a look at you now!" he boomed when Kurilov's turn came.

Medicine appears to be indifferent to ranks and titles. Out of deli-cacy, while relating various episodes from his day-to-day struggle against unworthy seekers after hospital certificates, the doctor covered his mouth with his hand, but at one point he forgot to do so, and Kurilov smelt alcohol: evidently the man did his best to brighten the solitude of his life at the station. . . . Some desperate hope compelled Alexei Nikitich to agree to be examined; the procedure took no more than three minutes.

"*Mauvais*," said the doctor in a deep bass as he went to wash his hands. "Quite *mauvais*," he repeated. It was as though fate wanted to spite Alexei Nikitich, for of all the words in the French language, this was the only one he understood. "Do you drink much?" the doctor asked. (Kurilov decided that the other doubtless wanted to advise him not in his state to bother to abstain from anything!)

"Do you?" Kurilov was about to retort, but could not. "Morphine, . . ." he said hoarsely, biting his lips, and just then the glasses on the table rang out with tenuous, medicinal little voices—as though a wind had swept through them.

# CHAPTER 43

# The Snowstorm

THREE TIMES SAYFULLAH RAN his train exactly on schedule. For the young engine driver this was an important victory. (But Peresypkin, who for hours awaited his arrivals, did not even come near him in order not to spoil the young Tartar with praise. Only after the third run did he go so far as to squeeze the engineer's hand in sign of approval.) And although Sayfullah's temples pounded and his eyes stuck together, he did not get off his locomotive before he had personally brought it to its shed and given the foremen instructions as to the necessary repairs. He unhurriedly returned home and thought about Katia Reshotkina; she was now closer to him by the four hundred miles of the first three runs. Halfway there he was told that his mother had come to see him. He ran at top speed to the dormitory behind the freight platform; there in a stuffy, low-ceilinged room with eight beds, Bibi-Kamal had been waiting for him since noon. Still and quiet, with a small withered mouth, she had settled herself on a stool near her son's cot, now stroking his poor patched blanket, now silently and sternly gazing at Stalin's portrait (and Stalin answered her gaze from the wall with the same steadiness).

"Ah, my heart is pounding! *Kuandyr dyn, anka* . . . I rejoice to see you, mother!"

Her big son burst into the room, and the window-panes trembled; but the very sight of his mother's tattered *beshmet*,[1] bast shoes and calico headkerchief, her thin hand raised as though to bless him, and her sunken faded eyes, stopped him short. ("What has become of her!") Bibi-Kamal had long ceased wearing silver coins at the end of her pigtails. . . . Incredulously, but still smiling with all his being, he drew near her. His mother rose and bowed to him deeply and respectfully: he was quite grown up now, her Sayfullah! The sharp bone of her chin protruded inquiringly. He embraced the old woman, but she wriggled in his arms muttering: "Fie, *astafirula*—my child's going to the dogs!" and burst into tears. Her son was not surprised: that was the way of mothers all over the world. And it was a good thing that

[1] Tartar coat

no stranger was there to interfere with their greedy exploration of
each other with words and fingers.

Crumpling in his palms his mother's calloused hands, he at once
began to tell her about the little griefs and great joys of his success,
about the Komsomols, the locomotive, in short, about everything that
made him different from the old Sayfullah. Very lightly, to quiet him,
she tapped on his shoulder, casting stealthy glances at his thin sooty
face. She did not believe much in his Tartar happiness. True, he was
now the boss of a big machine and was entrusted with many-thousand-
pound loads, but his poor blanket was the same one that he had taken
from Aldermesh six years before. . . . In a hoarse, high-pitched voice
he related the little mishaps of his first run on his own. She swallowed
some air, and staring at the dim bulb on the ceiling informed him that
his father was dead: "*Ziarat*, that's the place where poor people are
well off!" She handed him his inheritance on the spot: Samigullah's
silver pocket watch, a very precious object, which he had received as
a prize for marksmanship while still in the Tsarist army, and an old
worn razor.

"Have it ground, *koyra any!* There's still some use left in it," she said
thriftily, passing her finger along the edge. "You don't drink wine,
do you?"

"No, Lenin told us not to, *ankay!*"

She bowed her head to indicate that this was very good. It was not
for nothing that in Aldermesh Lenin was considered a good Moslem!

Still striving to impress her with his success, or at least to drive
away the black shadow of her grief, Sayfullah told her how well his
comrades liked him—only a few days ago the whole organization had
vouched for him! With a very contented look (and stealthily rubbing
her chest under her blue calico shirt, the place where it always ached
her), the mother replied that their house had at last fallen to pieces
and explained with a gesture how easy it was to stick one's hand into
the ample cracks in the earth walls. The masons wanted two hundred
rubles to replace the rotten beams, and she had no money; her last
pennies had been spent for daddy's funeral and the mullah's *sedak*.
And so she had come to ask the oldest man in the family whether he
thought their wretched hovel ought to be repaired and whether he
had the funds to do it. (She covered her mouth with a corner of her
kerchief as she spoke: after all he was a man, her Sayfuk!) Her son
listened to her with deepening gloom. He correctly understood her
question: it meant, would he ever return home to Aldermesh? Cares
and responsibilities which were now alien to him were crowding upon
him from that direction. It seemed to him that soon his mother would

utter the bitterest of all words: Mariam, whose name evoked worm-wood, the odor of flocks at night and the dry wind of the steppes. He shrugged his shoulders; no, it was unlikely that he would ever return home: his engines did not pass through the place! In a burst of sincerity he almost mentioned Katia, but his mother began hurriedly to nod, because she had now guessed everything: in new places, new flowers blossom! And with the silent tactfulness of the old she began to untie the coarse bag in which she had brought him some presents. . . .

Their talk was interrupted by a messenger from the engine house; it appeared that Sayfullah would have to drive the next train. His mate had fallen ill, and if the young Tartar refused, the engine itself would inevitably be affected. The dispatcher's request was reinforced by an order from the man on duty at the engine house, who was responsible for the schedules. The transit freight train for Sarzan was leaving in forty minutes. There was barely enough time left to inspect the engine and attend to other minor details connected with the departure, and perhaps a minute to splash his face with cold water. Sayfullah's time off was cancelled. "Wait for me, mother, I'll be back, *tis kantermen*. You lie down and sleep as hard as you can, rest yourself. I will be back, *yukla!*" And he dashed out.

This time the Komsomol locomotive went on its run without any ceremony. Sayfullah's crew had long since taken their places. The driving of an engine had not yet become a trade to them; the extra work involved flattered them; it proved to what extent they were needed. Moreover, all of them were at an age when men like to try their strength again and again. The profile of this branch of the road was unfamiliar to them, but Protoklitov refused to add a mechanic-instructor to the crew, because there were only two such mechanics on the freight trains leaving Cheremshansk, and both were now on other runs. This gave the young boys an even greater sense of their own responsibility and they mounted the engine with a pleasant feeling of their own importance. It was 6:20 P.M. Leaning down on the handrail, Sayfullah accepted the "sceptre," a conventional metallic document with a ring, to be thrown to any passing train, and gave a deafening whistle: young engine drivers like to make their signals loud. Then he went through the necessary routines as though the most exacting inspector were following every motion he made.

Having quickly checked everything, he set the D-valves going and pushed the regulator one-third down on the dented screw. The water immediately jumped up in the gauge, and in the firebox ruby-colored flames began to throb as though clipped. Thick flakes of smoke crawled back to the yard. The cast-iron plates underfoot began to jolt, and the station—its night lights and sounds—moved somewhere into the past. The green semaphore star that always gave its blessing to this road into the unknown magically emerged overhead. . . . The station was in a valley. The fireman added coal, and Sayfullah lowered the ash-pan a little. In order not to upset the schedule, the next two stations had to be passed with a gain of twenty-seven minutes. The engine was marvellous, there was not even a draft in the closed cab; one match would have sufficed to light five cigarettes. And Sayfullah thought of what he would tell Katia Reshotkina after returning from this fourth run. "I sing as I drive it!" he would tell her in the tone of an experienced Russian engine driver, and at this understandable boast she would laugh such a sonorous laugh that even Mariam would hear it in her poor Chukurga!

There were three of them, on this trip memorable in the annals of Cheremshansk. The engineer's assistant was Vitia Reshotkin, and it was strange to find that the small and gentle Katia had such an impressive brother, who could barely find room under the iron ceiling of the cab. He must have shaved himself before leaving; a cut on his lip was pasted with a strip of paper. . . . And the firebox was in charge of the same Skuriatnikov who had played the part of a whole orchestra at the unforgettable party in Makhub-ebi's house. The rumor had it that despite his youth he had stoked the boilers of all the factories in the region, that his "dream" had driven him on from each place in turn and that he had been categorically condemned as a drifter. And true enough, unique and unattached as he was, he had an unfortunate tendency to leave suddenly without saying farewell. A tramp by vocation and, consequently, with an innate passion for fire, he had now apparently found a job to his liking: to wander legitimately through the world "with his little fire under the arm"—thus he himself defined his passion. To ride with him was not boring, and it was perhaps even instructive. On the long stretches he liked to recount his adventures until the mechanic scolded him.

Thus it was now. They had no sooner passed Barmalevo than he pretended he had once worked as a fireman in Kaluga. And who can tell stories about fire if it is not a fireman! . . . Moreover, at the very start Reshotkin provoked him: "But you're telling lies, Skuriatnikov, first-class lies, good enough for export!"

"Eh, you won't deny that there were good fires at Kaluga!" Skuriatnikov repeated, gazing at the blinding crack of the furnace door. "The meat market, for instance, or the veterinary hospital! . . . And once I saw a merchant's house ablaze on the Square of the Three Marys . . . it was a beauty!" And by a special insinuating monotony in his voice one could predict that this story would last as far as Kulla. "I had known the house before: an elegant one, with pillars and little galleries. Sometimes as you passed it, you heard a piece of marvellous music, or a many-colored reflection from a chandelier fell on you. And for such things I have a prophetic eye, Solomon's eye! . . . One day I passed by and somehow it looked queer in the windows, spooky. So I thought to myself: you'll be burning soon, with a first-class blaze. And then I'll go in and see what kind of life goes on in you. You know, once you have a fireman's helmet on you can even get into a palace! And imagine, a week went by—and it didn't burn. A month went by, and it still didn't burn. Half a year went by!"

Sayfullah had no mind now for these fiery battles. He had driven on this branch to Sarzan and beyond to Mias, only twice, as assistant driver. Fearing to miss all sorts of low signs on the road, he looked out from behind the canvas curtain, and immediately all the lights went out, as well as Skuriatnikov's voice and the hissing of the injectors. The wind struck him violently in the face, and grains of snow prickled his shaven temples. At first he saw nothing: only the orange glow of the ash-pan skipped along the snowy mounds on the roadbed. After he had looked hard for a while he began to distinguish things: the wavy field was stirring lightly. The wind was rushing along the ground playing with the clumps of grass wherever it found them, and it was as if it did not comb them very gently. Indeed, for about a quarter of an hour, they vanished altogether, and Sayfullah realized that at that place the blanket of snow was deeper. In the hollows the wind was even stronger. He recalled that the map showed a small declivity at the spot where they ought to be, judging by the time. Without looking back he pulled the wire of the whistle and gave one long-drawn-out signal calling for greater alertness; there was more snow and the brakes might be required. A squeaky little cloud of smoke spiraled up, and immediately all the conductors' crew showed their white signal lanterns. There were seven of them, as many as there were brakes on the train. Everything was going well, there were no knocks in the engine. Sayfullah let down the earflaps of his cap to protect his left cheek from the frosty wind, and drew out a frozen apple, that had thawed in his pocket—his mother had brought it to him. It had a pleasant smell of straw. Sweet grainy sap spattered from it as he bit into it.

He decided that his mother had come just in time. According to his ancestors' customs, which no one had abolished, any more than the respect due a mother, he ought to show her his fiancée. Bibi-Kamal was a good woman. (He vividly recalled her raised hands and the ancient abundant warmth of her motherly embrace.) Let her heart be assuaged, let her compare Katia with that proud and half-literate savage! Of course, it would be hard for Katia to carry on the first conversation: Sayfullah's mother could not speak Russian. It was also a pity that Katia did not like beads, that she did not blacken her eyebrows and that she did not wear beautiful hard pigtails with a bluish sheen, *chach tulum*, like his old girl. "But if you saw her, you yourself would retreat into the shadow, you would belong to the past!" He superstitiously avoided pronouncing that name, as though it had now acquired the power to cause a storm or strike him with an incurable disease; at any rate, it interfered with his frank expression of his feeling for Katia. During the previous year (he had carried the letter from Aldermesh in his pocket that long before showing it to Peresypkin) the name "Mariam" had followed him everywhere, ringing mockingly, drowning his joy and giving a bitter taste to his food. Sayfullah imagined what would happen if she conquered her pride and came to Cheremshansk. She would be dressed in sackcloth and would look a thousand times more beautiful and alien than when he had last seen her. She would ask him, smiling and baring her black agate-colored teeth (surely, back *there* girls still painted their teeth after the old fashion, to add femininity and charm to their faces): "Are you glad to see me, Sayfullah?"

Offended by his distant manner, she would raise her arched eyebrows and hand him the letters she had managed to protect from her father's jealous hands. She would say: "Take them, they were written by you; don't be ashamed. *Ut alsyn alarne*—let fire devour them! Otherwise someone will read them, and you'll be driven away from here with an old broom. Take them, I have no better gift for you!" And he would take them, because it is not good to leave incriminating evidence in the hands of a woman one intends to forget. She would also say: "Let us go somewhere to a field, or, in memory of old times, to a *kiug*, a well, else someone might see us together, and that is not necessary!" And he would agree, and every stranger's look would make him feel uncomfortable because he had learned to fear what he had formerly striven for passionately. . . . Laughing because she saw through him, she would strike him in the heart. "You're ashamed of me. Your frightened conscience cries out even before it is touched. I suppose you think you're more honest now because you've memorized how to open a regulator. It's not worth while to respect a kulak's daughter if she hasn't managed to become an engineer's wife!" Very angry at himself for not having driven her away at once, he would bite his lips and remain silent. . . .

"Well, and how does she love you, the Russian woman?"

Oh, if only Katia loved as the women of his race love! "Eh, a heart is more precious than the handshake of a Russian girl: in the darkness hands join all of themselves, they're made that way. Or should one believe simply in two or three of her unguarded glances?" It was not for nothing that Skuriatnikov maintained that such merchandise could be had more easily than galoshes of the right size at the cooperative. The old men of Aldermesh who had had the misfortune to leave the boundaries of their native village often told of the frivolity and fickleness of Russian wives. They burn you like vodka and age you prematurely; they enter your chest like a disease, and your heart pines away in sad songs, it wrinkles and withers away; no honest pleasure will rejoice it after the first scalding night; and after she has had her fill, she will leave you for the first Russian that appeals to her . . . and together they'll make fun of you before they unite in amorous exultation! According to these old men, a drunken god made such women in the joy of Creation, mixing the dough with sweet wine and adding burning poison to give it strength.

"She is a *marza!*" so old Tartar women call Russian women in common parlance.—"Your mother will curse you because of her!"

"That's all right. Even so I'll never return to you."

Then the swarthy girl would bend toward his ear and sear him with her last warning. Sayfullah was cold now; he would violently throw out his arm as though pushing her away: "Go, Mariam, *yugal*, vanish!"

It came to pass that his hand remained in this position. It quickly grew white on the windy side. Sayfullah was surprised; he had not noticed when "it" began. A thick friable snow was blowing against the engine. The wind was stronger; in the illuminated cones of the headlights a snowy chaos was whirling and smoking. Sayfullah raised his brows, listening to his engine to make sure it was in order. There was no trouble; there was only a whistling somewhere in the gears, the siren whined, and at every gust of the storm a rag of tarpaulin struck against the iron support. Sayfullah was somewhat frightened by the thought that he would have to take the accursed Sarzan pass at the very height of the blizzard; judging by the time, it was no more than twenty miles away. In Cheremshansk, old engine drivers used to say facetiously that one wins one's right to drive a locomotive only on the other side of that pass. (They were also hinting at something else: the *old* engine drivers used to visit the accommodating barwomen of Sarzan.) Snowdrifts did not frighten Sayfullah; there was a rule that in case of need one could uncouple the engine and clear the snow without the train. . . . He turned to his crew. In the same pose as two hours before, Skuriatnikov sat on a log, still describing the Kaluga fire.

". . . And from all the chaos I managed to save only a clock with bells . . . but not that devilish young lady, nor the kind old woman! And so I carried the clock through the smoke, weeping from the smell of burning, and it ran strangely in my hands, as though it were alive. . . ."

"Hey, there, more coal!" cried Sayfullah.

The fireman jumped up; actually his tale was finished. Skuriatnikov liked not only to leave without saying farewell, but to stop his stories in the middle of a sentence. He shoved in more coal and, protecting himself from the heat with his shovel, almost lovingly examined the quality of his fire. The flames in the firebox became tousled and taut; a running gold fleece lining appeared amidst the leaping white flames. Skuriatnikov knew whether the amount of coal was sufficient from the hues and behavior of the fire; to satiate this inferno more and more fuel was needed. He was preparing to assault the Sarzan pass, no less, and the whole world was certainly now watching him with bated breath! . . . The fireman went to the tender; he had barely thrown down ten shovelfuls when he was hurled back, all crumpled up into the cab. And the white whirlwind still pursued him. Confusedly leaning on his shovel, he breathed like a fish with his whole mouth— and snow was even in his ears.

"What's the matter, can't you breathe?" Reshotkin asked, laughing. He was strong, his body was designed to overcome heavy loads; manifestations of weakness always evoked sneers from him.

Skuriatnikov guiltily shrugged his shoulders. It was strange to learn that there were elements equal in scope and power to his wonderful fire. He had great respect for fire because he had often observed its exploits at close quarters.

"It's queer, my falcons, my soul is ablaze, yet my feet are cold!" the fireman said. "Some whirlwind! But you're lying, devil. . . ." And angrily he once again rushed toward the tender.

He did this with determination as though he were taking a jump over a precipice. One could hear him curse obscenely, as though this might inspire him in his hand-to-hand battle with the storm. Again lumps of frozen coal rolled down from the tender, and there was so much water on them that it was not even worth while to coke it. And this time the duel lasted for no more than three minutes. Skuriatnikov returned bewildered, without his cap, all pasted with snow. His hair, lashed by the storm, stood up on end straight and wild, as on a devil's head.

"Look, my cap blew off," he said, rubbing his eyes in amazement and licking the thawing, dirty snow from his lips. "And it was still a good cap!"

Exasperated, he generously fed his firebox. He clung to its opening, shaking down the coal along the firebars; he seemed to be coaxing the fire and upbraiding it for having insulted him. Angry black stains began to stir in the liquid mass of the fire; they harnessed themselves completely to their work. Through the crack in the tarpaulin one could see the golden locks of the blaze flying out and scattering in the darkness. . . . And for some reason the loss of the fireman's cap amused the others. The cap was new, a "marvellous" cap, Skuriatnikov loved it. They joked that he even slept with it, that without it he felt uncomfortably naked. . . . At the same time they felt more confident and gay, knowing what kind of blizzard was beating against the hull of their Komsomol ship. Reshotkin even expressed regrets that Peresypkin was not with them in order later to celebrate their Sarzan adventure with an appropriate poem. They had no doubt that they would master those twenty dangerous miles. Never before had a crew felt so completely the iron health of their engine. . . . And so they came to the beginning of the pass. Sayfullah gave two short signals demanding that the brake be released. He stuck his head out of the tarpaulin, trying to distinguish the outlines of this enormous hollow in the plain. He could already feel the snow and the steepness of the gradient; from time to time the wheels tugged; the mighty breath of the boiler was mingled with the exhaust steam from the chimney.

"Give 'er more fuel!" Reshotkin commanded, substituting for the chief.

One could not distinguish anything; not only the track, but even the embankment had vanished from view. More accurately, the eyes saw only what the alarmed mind imagined. The lanterns pasted over with snow gave almost no light. It was as though the engine were moving blindly through an enormous and angry snowdrift. But if one bent out to the waist one could distinguish two or three cars, completely white and round from the snow that was stuck on them. But all this was just the result of imagination; deprived of any point of support, that faculty now acquired unusual flexibility. It painted on this flying canvas now a house, now a tree, now a man, only to obliterate them the next instant. And if one listened intently to the thunder of the wind rollers, it seemed that far away, alone in the midst of a field, the homeless Mariam was singing. . . . Oh, Sayfullah could recognize that voice, so artless and pure in the upper registers, like ringing silver bells. Her refrain led Sayfullah away, beyond the boundaries of the night, into the ghostly twilight of childish visions, joys and fears. And an old fairy tale again passed his blinded eyes, and the howl and impetus of the snowstorm were pregnant with a new meaning.

The young Khasan-Bator is looking for a spot to found Kazan. A gang of mounted *batyrs* in shaggy white Turkman *telpeks,* tall as towers, accompany him in his futile wanderings in the desert. They trot from land to land; a snowy dust smokes under the horses' hoofs. Alas, in all this gloomy steppe there is no place worthy to be the Tartar capital! And when the warriors are exhausted and their tall horses halt, they discover the place where lives the Azhdaga. . . .

The last sister of an ancient Chinese dragon, she dwells in a deep hole, and it is deadly even to step in her footprint. The image of this gigantic serpent haunted the common childhood of Sayfullah and Mariam. In winter, hugging each other in terror, they heard the furious snowy swish of its wings; on summer nights, when meteors gleam in the chilly air, they observed in the sky the fiery glitter of its scales. . . . And now, enormous wings, the size of half the world, spread above the heads of the *batyrs.* It is unconquerable, it kills many of them, only in order to be pierced by Khasan's lance as thin as a splinter.

"Stop singing, Mariam, about what never was. *Erlamah!* The human reason knows that there is no Azhdaga, and that your legendary Khasan is only the invention of a wandering poet, *terche.* You're wrong not to read books, Mariam. . . ."

On nights of storm such as Sayfullah was now experiencing, the memories of childhood are strong; one cannot erase from the heart what has been engraved there by the woods, the lightning, the smell of field flowers. . . . It is no longer the sun but the innocent childish heart that rises above the world. Those hardly visible trees, dried to the marrow by frost and wind, are covered with green, as though the green *chapan* of the mullah had been thrown over the grove. A boy and girl are running along the edge of the woods. They are in a hurry: for a storm is coming. Their knees are full of scratches, but they are still far from home. The green becomes lavender; the leaves turn their grey undersides to the wind. A bird flies by, so quickly that its shadow cannot catch up with it. Thin stems wave something that looks like hands. The grass becomes animated. The modest, creeping asarabacca plant smells as fragrant as though it had tried to absorb all the remaining odors of the earth. . . . Suddenly the roads begin to smoke, the martins circle overhead. The first drops of rain are falling; the dry soil rings out under them. Then a blow, momentary blindness, and Mariam's terrified cry. . . . A solitary tree on a hill is ablaze from the roots to the top. It stands there in a red dress, shriveling before their eyes. It is entirely reflected in Mariam's wide-open eyes. The angry angular shoulders of the fire move from side to side. Falling on their knees, the children press against each other. Primitive man once experienced the same amazement mingled with rapture and terror, before the sun. The clouds embroidered by lightning crackle; the wind tears them into shreds. There is a minute-long downpour, and the vision dies. Somersaulting, the first ray of the sun skips along the meadow. The enormous torch visited by the god is still smoking. Little white fumes on the charred branches look like marvellous flowers. "Oh, let such a day strike you with the foreign woman before her blood joins with yours, Sayfullah!"

He asked aloud, frowning: "Are you threatening me, black, wicked Mariam?"

Suddenly not the lovely refrain about Khasan, but an alarming screech cut his ears. The Sarzan trains are long, there is much snow on the tracks; the engine was sliding, and all three of them listened with narrowed eyes to the desperate, futile turning of the wheels. Apparently they had reached the Shamaev slope. Two figures defined that spot: an elevation of .009 and hundred-yard-high hills at the sides. Between them as into a tunnel the storm was breaking, and the whirlwind of snow acquired physical resilience. Skuriatnikov looked out of the tarpaulin, and it was as though someone had taken his face and pushed it back with mighty strength. It was terrifying to think what would happen beyond the pass when the seventy-five cars in the back pressed on the engine and rushed down the slope.

"Give us sand there . . . hey!" Sayfullah cried and moved the regulator to the last notch.

Skuriatnikov cut the wire, but the sand did not fall under the wheels. The engine kept screeching without advancing. And as soon as they realized that something was wrong with the sandbox, Reshotkin rushed out onto the engine platform. A furious howl struck his ears as though someone were blowing simultaneously into a thousand empty bottles—and snow, snow. . . . Lumps of it stuck together hit the red-hot body of the engine, thawed, ran down and hardened underneath. Fearing that the pumps would freeze, Skuriatnikov added more fuel. The draft grew stronger, and coal dust flew almost intact out of the chimney. Streams of sparks flew up into the sky, and they were Reshotkin's only light. He pulled down his cap and with one bound grasped the "triggers" of the sandbox—screws that hermetically closed its lid. He suddenly felt a gluey warmth in his palm; much later he realized that he had torn off his skin. His booted feet slipped from the boiler. Then he pulled himself up by his hands with all his strength and somehow managed to get astride the engine.

The "triggers" had to be knocked off, for they refused to be un-screwed. The cowl had fallen off, and Reshotkin finally succeeded in finding the chimney under the sand with an iron rod. He spent much precious time pushing the frozen lumps through it. The wind rung his hands and tore his clothes. He felt the stress of its flexible, icy muscles. Sand that stuck to his hands hindered him in his work, his fingers were numb with cold and tried in spite of themselves to get inside his breast pocket to warm themselves. . . . He happened to have some gauze in his pocket; he tried to pull it out to wipe the blood off his hand, but he lost his balance and would have fallen under the wheels if he had not managed to grasp the handrail. He felt frightened and angry. Tearing the snow off his face, shouting curses to deafen the excoriating pain in his whole body, clinging to the steam-supply pipes, he crawled back into the cab. He had to throw the snow out of the sandbox and replace the lid. Ice mixed with sand got under his nails, and Reshotkin almost wept with rage. . . . All this time the engine kept working idly. The rails would have shone if they had not been constantly greased with snow.

"Ah . . . the sons of bitches! They were too lazy to dry the sand!"

Bruised all over, bleeding, shivering perceptibly (even his strip of paper had been torn off his lip!) he returned to the cab. He smiled when the first strong jolt indicated that the engine was moving. Mean-while the wires had been tied together, and Skuriatnikov kept on reddening and fattening his ruddy beast. All the space under the engine was red with sparks. No one said a word; they silently listened to the whistle of the wheels and cast glances at each other. Now they all had equal authority. Very slowly, although the pistons were work-ing full force, at three miles an hour, they climbed up on the Shamaev plateau. All of them remembered distinctly that the gauge glass was only one-quarter full of water. At the same time they could see on the manometer how the vapor had settled. They saved it and did not try to pump additional water, in order to keep up what speed they had. The danger of being snowbound was behind them. So it was not through a glass of beer with friends, but through such an adventure that a master comes of age!

"Well, if we can only get down the slopes now, comrades. . . ."

They washed Reshotkin's hand, put the torn piece of skin back in its place, and bandaged the wound with a handkerchief. He frowned, and probably because of his pain, teased Skuriatnikov. (Everyone knew that in the absence of a certain conductor the fireman visited the man's wife, who was a lewd and crack-brained woman. Everyone sinned more or less in Cheremshansk; as for Skuriatnikov, in view of the husband's character, this adventure was bound to end, if not with a stray child, with a broken rib.) Skuriatnikov answered these quips as best he could, and licked his lips that still preserved the taste of the woman's kisses. . . . Meanwhile the engine gathered speed by jolts. Again they fell silent. Sayfullah looked out, fearing to break his train as a result of the irregular movement of the engine. Reshotkin prepared to turn the tender brakes. And at that moment the disaster occurred.

A strange noise came from the firebox, and a yellowish cloud of steam splashed through the poker hole. There was a thick smell of iron and boiled water. Suddenly the water disappeared in the gauge glass. Reshotkin opened the testing spigot—there was no water in the boiler; he seized the injectors—neither of them pumped. They realized that there was little water in the tender, that during the climb it had fallen back, and that the pumping sleeves of the injectors no longer reached it. Now, as they were descending, it fell forward . . . and never before had the fire thundered and bustled so much as now when it felt its strength.

"Put out the furnace!" they all cried in one voice.

They opened the firebars and beat the fire with shovels to choke it, and no voices could be heard amidst the hissing steam. The locomotive kept advancing on its own momentum, but even then it was only a dead body moving. Soon the pistons died out completely. They did not need to look into the firebox. Unless the worst thing that can happen to an engineer had happened, the "burning" of the firebox, that is to say, the outright murder of the locomotive, one had to presume that the control plugs were melted. Sayfullah's face twitched, little streams of sweat washed out stripes of soot on his cheek. With his remaining steam he gave his crew his last signal—to put on the brakes.

". . . Eh, *kharab buldym byt!*" he cried out in a high-pitched voice, and the gesture with which he threw his cap on the floor meant the same thing: that he had perished because he had believed too early in his own success.

Cheremshansk had to be informed of the disaster. Reshotkin, physically the strongest of them, went to the nearest siding to telephone; he had no sooner got off the engine than he dissolved in the blizzard. Here, on this bare spot, the wind had no obstacles. It kept storming in, and the whistle valve sounded one gloomy note; the wind sought any little chink it could find in order to stick an entire snowdrift through it. Waist-deep in snow the conductors came running to ask what was the cause of the stop, and perhaps the bitterest thing of all was to explain it to them. (One alert greaser took the opportunity to check the axle-bearings of his cars, still unaware of what had happened.)

The train was being covered with snow, the wheels were no longer visible. In two hours all this would surely be buried under a snow that would never, never thaw! The engine was now covered with a thin crust of ice.

Then Skuriatnikov sat down on a pile of coal and lowered his head. About ten minutes later he drew out his harmonica and timidly put it to his lips, looking into the flooded firebox like a conjuror. But the slain divinity did not arise. With an air of complete indifference he put his instrument back into his pocket; he knew now that the next day he would have to find another job. Sayfullah silently, without his cap, sat down beside him on the iron floor. . . .

Thus they awaited their rescue and their punishment.

# CHAPTER 44

## "I Am Returning to You, Mariam!"

BETWEEN CHEREMSHANSK AND SARZAN as many as seventeen pairs of trains ran every day. It is easy to imagine what went on at the stations the next morning. By daybreak the tracks at the entrances were entirely covered with trains. They stood about like chessmen; hordes of sleepless passengers roamed around in the snowdrifts and raged against the authorities; but no one knew when traffic would be resumed. Cheremshansk learned about the disaster very late. The frozen Reshotkin did not reach a siding for three hours after he left the engine; he found that the telephone wires were cut and he was unable to reach Cheremshansk. An alarm was raised by the dispatcher who failed to get word from Kulla confirming the passage of 4019; he summoned the snowplows and the repair crew even before the causes of the stop were known. By midnight the blanket of snow on the tracks was a yard deep. The wind had subsided, but the murderous snowfall continued all night. Meanwhile Protoklitov had gone to Chemsha to inspect a roundhouse; from the man on duty at Savrusha he learned that Sayfullah's train had got stuck. And although this matter concerned the division superintendent rather than himself, he went to the scene of the accident with the salvage train. He arrived there shortly before daybreak when the snow was level with the roofs. Walking carefully on the roofs of the cars, he reached the engine.

The cab was dark and cold. Two men crouched on the floor, leaning against the iron wall. They were cold; some snow had drifted onto the shoulder of Skuriatnikov, who sat close to the passage to the tender. Perhaps he was slumbering, but when the stranger's shadow veiled the opening in the tarpaulin, he flabbily drew one leg under him, and the snowy fold on his shoulder broke in two. . . . Day was breaking. Sayfullah raised his head, but Protoklitov's face was lost in the darkness, so he leaned back again. A bluish reflection of snow from the crack lay on his slightly flattened nose. A terribly long minute went by, but the yard master had not yet spoken; the lantern danced in his hand. "It's hopping about like a hanged man," Skuriatnikov thought, and turned away so as not to see it.

"Is the chief in the engine here?" Protoklitov asked distinctly. It seemed to the two men that he smiled, and both unconsciously imitated this smile of squeamish indulgence. "Get up, I'm not your pal. Now, hold the lantern. . . ."

Protoklitov wore a leather coat tightened with a thin belt for greater warmth; for some reason he felt the need of unbuttoning it at this minute and tightening the belt. Then he rapidly inspected the locomotive. The engineer, who once more had become a boy, with an air of desperate indifference moved the lantern wherever Protoklitov's eyes turned. The yard master was first of all interested in the water and the steam. The water gauge was empty; the manometer still showed two points of steam. Protoklitov also felt the injectors and threw back the handle of the regulator that now had no meaning. Then he picked up a handful of coal and carefully examined it, bending out into the dove-colored light of the dawn; the only conceivable purpose of this examination was his desire to prolong the torture. He spoke very little; he was hoarding his anger, just as only recently they had hoarded their steam. He bent in every conceivable direction while making his examination, he bent lightly and nimbly as though boneless, and Skuriatnikov smiled through his grief, thinking how hatred gives people flexibility and elegance. The ordeal continued. Having placed the lantern in the firebox, Protoklitov rummaged in the firebars, and managed to pick out from the slaggy crust a piece of melted lead. The diagnosis was now definitive.

It was quiet; a dull voice came as though from under the snow. And once again shouts were heard calling for Pyriev and Teteshin, just as a few months before, near Sakonikha. The snow-clearing crew had begun to dig. ·

"Well, who was watching the water level, you tramps?"

The boys remained silent; the question was asked only to humiliate them and did not require an answer. Sayfullah looked at the yard master wearily and apathetically. The muscles of his face had become flabby, and no matter how he tried to raise his heavy eyebrows, they invariably dropped again. He felt chilly; his black lips muttered something, and one might have imagined that he was drunk. Protoklitov put the melted plug into his pocket. His eyes roamed around the frost-covered walls of the cabin. Suddenly he noticed a torn wet wall newspaper. A cartoon in the center of the sheet represented him, the yard master, sleeping on a bed, embracing a hole-riddled locomotive. All his body twitched. He grew even drier and taller. "*Kyrgan,*" he said, the only Tartar insult he knew, and his hand abruptly moved backward, but the cabin space was too narrow for a fight; the bone of his finger painfully hit against something, and this saved him from committing in his fury the greatest possible folly.

Sayfullah did not draw back, he only pressed the lantern to his chest; any punishment would have seemed insignificant to him at that moment. He scarcely even heard what took place in the cabin. Then Skuriatnikov got up, shook the snow off his shoulder and looked hard into Protoklitov's eyes. "Pity a comrade, . . ." he said, and violently turned Protoklitov toward himself by his shoulder. "Pity a Tartar, you beast. He's a proletarian, too!"

Protoklitov jerked and muttering something quickly, left the cab.

Here began the downfall of Sayfullah. His personal misfortune was insignificant as compared with the disgrace of the organization that had prematurely trusted him. He imagined the hostile, reproachful eyes of his comrades and Katia's brilliant jeering glance. Misfortune aged him. . . . Then he sat in a corner of an unfamiliar freight car and kept looking at his hands, which had been burned when he put out the firebox. Strangely enough, they did not hurt at all. . . . Day had broken, but the car was still dark. Workers back from cleaning the snowdrifts were boiling tea on an iron stove and seemed not to notice the guilty engineer. One of them took a log from under Sayfullah and began to cut it up for firewood. He now felt Mariam's proximity almost physically. The stern angry girl again stood before him holding out her hands in a gesture of reconciliation. She was smiling: "Oh, so you've exchanged me for a locomotive, Sayfuk!" A black velvet sleeveless blouse embroidered with glass beads in the city fashion (all that had remained from her family's ruin!) was drawn tight across her little breasts which no one had squeezed in his absence. And Sayfullah felt sorry for her. . . . But one of the crew put a tin cup of tea into his hands. Sayfullah greedily drank this empty, briny beverage, and the icy Mariam melted away for a time, returning to non-being.

He realized suddenly that something had to be done. Upon his arrival in Cheremshansk he was seized by a morbid excitement. He went to find the secretary of his cell, but he was neither at the yard nor at home. All the members of the organization had gone out to help clear the tracks. Half an hour later he found among the cars both the secretary and Peresypkin. Brandishing shovels, sodden with sweat, they were doing their best to show the kolkhoz muzhiks an example of socialist labor. They looked guilty; no doubt they had been informed of the crime committed by the crew of 4019. As though by silent agreement they pretended not to notice Sayfullah's approach. Temporarily, until the organization had judged his case, he had ceased to exist in Cheremshansk. Moreover, time was precious, there was enough work for the whole day, and snow was still dropping from the hole-riddled sky. It seemed to all of them that Sayfullah for a long time lazily rummaged about in his pockets; three Komsomols leaning on their shovels watched him from under their brows.

"Take this," said he, holding out his crumpled Young Communist League book in his fingers. Then it occurred to him that he had other things to return, too. He began hurriedly to ferret in his pockets, and his fear of losing *such* a document, his right to life and his comrades' friendship, for a moment restored a kind of tragic animation to his face. But no, it was in its place, one does not lose such things. This was his shock worker's booklet. "Here!"

The secretary frowned worriedly. "What's the matter, comrade?"

"Take my cards," Sayfullah repeated, patiently and insistently.

"But what am I to do with them? . . ." The boy spread his hands in bewilderment and had not the courage to look into his comrade's ravaged eyes. He was about to put the engineer's very life in his pocket, when suddenly Peresypkin became infuriated and, sticking his shovel into the snow with one stroke, cried out: "Ah, no, my friend . . . you must wait till we ourselves throw you out. That's no way for a Komsomol to behave—to sin and run away. We still have to try your case; yes, yes, we'll try you!" And then he contrived to find a word that hurt: "Are you looking for pity?"

Then he went back to work with the stubbornness of a wound-up mechanism. Snow flew over his head, and the muzhiks looked at him respectfully; he was like a steamship wheel tearing through water. "Such a one makes himself feared!" Sayfullah stood there for a while, then dragged himself away. For a long time he wandered among the cars; a whole city of them had been set up here during the night. At one place Katia crossed his path; he intently followed her with his eyes, and now no longer Mariam, but she herself seemed a distant phantom. Perhaps he was wandering deliberately: at home his mother's searching and all-seeing eyes awaited him.

Sayfullah kicked the door in. A comrade was changing his boots, but—he quickly got up and went away. As though she had not gone to sleep, Bibi-Kamal was sitting in the same place. Like all peasants, she left her cot at daybreak. Sayfullah stretched himself wearily, but did not manage to yawn; his face was shrivelled like an old man's. His mother rose lightly. Misfortune had left its mark on her boy. She ran toward him, led him to his bed, tried to pull his boots off—all her life she had pulled off Samigullah's. "You sit here . . . it's soft here. Sit down. . . ."

Shrinking from her stern motherly solicitude, he dropped her hand. "It's not necessary, *ankay*, I'll do it myself. . . ."

She did not dare to question him. Oh, he had become a complete grown-up, her Sayfuk, he had even learned to stoop. She easily read in his eyes that his suffering was great and tried to transfer at least a little part of it to her own accustomed shoulders. Of course, she would never grasp the complex mechanism of life in a locomotive yard; she had never held a book in her hands, and correct reading of human grief was the only thing she had been taught in her youth.

"Is the snow still falling? Ah, what a snow fell this year on Tatar-stan! And twice as much in Aldermesh. . . ."

Having pulled off his wet boots, he tapped her on the hand. "You've arrived in time, Bibi-Kamal!" His mother watched all his motions. Nor did she fail to notice that the soles on his boots were thin, and his heels worn down. "Somewhere I have a piece of leather. It's a good thing I didn't use it for myself." Her son shrank under her gaze; his grief made him completely transparent to her; she knew everything that was going on inside him. How well she understood at that mo-ment—locomotives, and people, and the endless roads to the Ocean! . . . He was surprised that the dawn had come so soon. It was suddenly light, as though someone had washed the soot-covered windows. He wondered how much time had passed since he had killed himself together with his engine. Samigullah's watch was completely unused; the ailing old man had had no place to go with his watch; it had spent their whole life in a chest. Forgetting his original intention he held it out to his mother. "Take it, *al!* I might lose it. When I return you'll give it back to me. *Minga birersen.* . . ." Then, forgetting to give it to her, he put it back into his pocket.

She began to nod hurriedly. . . . What would happen was now clear to her. Of course, the house must be repaired, so that by the time of his wedding with Mariam life in Aldermesh would be completely or-ganized. She thought that the sharp-nosed Imamutdinov had delib-erately asked too high a price for the job just to make himself seem important. "Carpenters are big people, nowadays!" Moreover, it is al-ways easier to get people to fear you than to love you; and respect is somewhere in between. But she would beg and implore and he would give in, he would do the job for one hundred and fifty. She said: "I think I'll hire Imamutdinov. He is the most reliable carpenter in the Bitaman. And the kolkhoz promised to give me the wood."

Sayfullah agreed absent-mindedly. "Oh, Minur is a good worker. Why, I remember Minur quite well!"

And so the boy was returning to the parental home. Bibi-Kamal had not prayed to God in vain. He would not inflict upon her a lonely old age. The mother's cruel wish was coming true. She would nurse grandsons and, when falling silent forever, she would hear the high-pitched wailing of babies, merrier than a wedding dance. . . . Of course, her Sayfullah was an ordinary Tartar peasant; he was no good for driving those big Russian machines. Mullah Ibrahim would say that God never strikes without first giving a taste of sweet things: in that way it hurts more! "Eh, a poor man finds some advantage even in misfortune," Ibrahim would say patronizingly. . . . And, after all, Mariam was a wonderful girl. She was beautiful, all black like a *suliuk*, a leech; the boys say it makes them hot even to look at her. Poverty had taught her things, but it had not broken her bones. Moreover, in Aldermesh the people have become accustomed to God's ways; He does not like to make people equal in wealth, He likes to make them equal in poverty. Mariam's future husband might become a tractor driver . . . oh, he even might become a bookkeeper! A good Moslem has all paths open to him. "Do you want something to eat, Sayfuk?"

The shrewd Bibi-Kamal had baked a whole stack of sweet cakes in order not to ruin her son by her visit. . . . He hesitatingly took one, broke it, cast a side glance at his mother's small hands that had mixed this dough. It was a sour dough, and the name of the bread that was baked with it was *kabartma*. And with that forgotten word a thousand details—and above all pigeons, pigeons, flocks of them on the Aldermesh minaret!—fluttered up all around him. With utmost clarity his eyes—they even ached with the vividness of the sight—saw his village. ("Eat, eat, Sayfuk; when one has troubles, one must eat well; the troubles eat the food, and you watch them from the side!") He was surprised and felt a chill in his spine in thinking of how fast he had gone back over the path it had taken him six whole years to travel. . . . He wanted more, she happily gave him two at once. He was hungry, he had toiled bitterly. "Ugh, how much he had buried in one night!" They began to discuss the future.

They must not sell anything. Thrifty tones came into Bibi-Kamal's voice. "Buy me material for a skirt, so that I may have something to boast of to the neighbors. Don't spend much, take something cheap. And for Mariam get green calico with blue flowers, young Tartar girls always like that." He nodded, adding up the cost in his mind. . . . But suddenly he felt regret at having to lose the friendship of the comrades with whom he had grown into manhood; regret at having lost the engine the day before, and worst of all, at never being able to return to *his* engine. He pressed his feet under him, as for centuries his fathers and ancestors had done, and swaying back and forth burst into tears; at that moment, his burnt fingers began to hurt. He did not cover his face with his hands, he was no longer ashamed before Bibi-Kamal.

"Are they going to put you in prison, Sayfuk? . . . Never mind, your fingers will heal, Mariam will wait. You'll come back *afterward.* . . ."

Oh, how could he know? This was the first time such a thing had happened to him. Perhaps he would only be dismissed and deprived of his right to work on the same line. "One must assume that somehow this affair will be settled, Sayfuk! Your comrades will soon forget you, hence, forgive you." She put him to bed and covered him with his blanket. In his sleep he continued groaning through clenched teeth, as though someone had bitten through his very heart. Patting him on the hand, Bibi-Kamal in a measured voice chanted a song. She could compose them of any length required, but she was particularly successful with lullabies. . . .

"The fire is weary. It says: I have burned out, I won't shine, I want to sleep. *Yukla sym kiliaz!* The night told him: Sleep and I will keep watch. You don't sleep all night, and in the day you envy the sun. It is out, *siunde.* Good."

Sayfullah fell asleep at once. Bibi-Kamal drew the blanket over his ravaged face, then began to prepare for her trip home. She was in a hurry to get the house and the bride ready for her son's return. From time to time she cast a silent and stern glance at the portrait of Stalin, and Stalin looked back at her just as steadily from the wall.

# CHAPTER 45

# The Cheremshansk Knot

SAYFULLAH AWOKE after Bibi-Kamal had left. Clear daylight was pouring in through the window. His face was burning, his skin was swollen, and his fingers were covered with blisters. Feeling himself over as though he were trying to make sure he was still himself, he went over the details of the day before. Now, in the light of sober analysis, the irretrievable nature of his misfortune was even more obvious. (Someone walked by on the landing, and he quickly imagined that his comrades had come to see him . . . but the steps died out, and just as before the noise of the fire crackling in the stove was heard. He did not want to go to them first, because he, it seemed to him now, would not have forgiven any of them such a crime. . . .) And so first he had to find out with what he would return to Aldermesh. His chest where he kept his money and belongings was unlocked. Suddenly it occurred to him that his money had been stolen. Distraught, he threw all his things around him; the misfortune suddenly became very small. . . .

Once again this desperate, and it seemed last, hope proved false. Everything was intact. Subdued, having wiped his hands off on his trousers so as not to smear the notes, he began lazily to count his savings. There might be enough for a skirt for his mother, but he could not afford a gift for Mariam.

He went out, the snow blinded him, his temples began to throb. And it so happened that instead of going to the cooperative store he found himself in the courtyard of the tavern-keeper, Medvedeva. Perhaps he went there more from curiosity (because in his situation idleness was worse than torture) than from a desire to imitate what old engineers did when singed by grief; at any rate this visit might also postpone his return to Aldermesh. The widow Medvedeva had gone out to get water. Sayfullah waited for her, sitting on the stairs. The weather was warm and windy. Wet washing shook on the lines. Nothing happened; only a well-fed cock looking like a murderer, dashed after a hen, caught up with her and announced this fact to his neighbors.

Medvedeva, in a soldier's fur cap and masculine boots, put her pails down on the snow and looked questioningly at the engineer.

Sayfullah held out to her the pile of bills in his fist, all he had in the world. The widow cast a glance around her to see whether this was a trap, whether witnesses were not hiding around the corners. However, she was not afraid; everyone in Cheremshansk knew about her and kept silent, for everyone might some day urgently need her services. Wetting her fingers with saliva she counted the money; she made mistakes, got angry at herself, and stamped out the number of rubles with her foot. There were only eleven of them.

"I've no pints left, and this isn't enough for a full quart," Medvedeva said with indifference. (She bent down, made a snowball and hurled it at her cock to stop him from sinning with strangers' hens.)

"That's all I have," Sayfullah said. He showed his empty fingers and examined them himself from all sides to see whether a bill had not got stuck somewhere.

Then the widow began to cry, brandishing her big red hands, complaining that everyone came to her and later denounced her in the newspapers, and that only her wretched lot compelled her to make a living from all the good-for-nothings in Cheremshansk. Although this wide-browed young fellow was not visiting her for the first time, just to be on the safe side she mentioned her deceased husband, crushed between two cars that were being coupled, and her constant risk of being deported together with her children to some cold uninhabitable land. . . . Sayfullah listened to the dull slapping of a sheet on the wash-line and kept turning away from her lest she unwittingly stick a finger in his eye. He recalled a rumor that Medvedeva accepted payment in objects; he drew his father's watch out of his pocket. It was going, marching in a soldierly step in the cold air. The widow liked it, the crossed guns embossed on its lid somehow reminded her of her youth. In general she liked objects of the time of Tsar Nicholas. Her high-cheek-boned, insensitive face grew more human. She examined the watch with almost motherly interest, put it to her ear, breathed on it and then wiped it with her tattered sleeve. The hands showed half-past one, and she decided to give twenty-five rubles for it: a whole quart of that special brew flavored with birch buds which, if you drank it, made you cough, and then laugh out, as though a whole flock of vernal birds had fluttered from a green grove into your soul. . . .

They went into the house. Two emaciated twin girls were reading a story aloud in a singsong voice as if it were a poem. Accustomed to everything, they bent down further over their page and fell silent. Sayfullah impatiently crumpled his cap; swearing, the widow dug into a closet; St. Nicholas, dark-faced as an Indian, leered at the Tartar from the scratched wooden icon. After the custom of all tavern-keepers, Medvedeva poured a first glass for herself and put it to her lips to show that the liquor was not poisoned. Then her swollen eyelids dropped. "It's eighteen rubles a quart," she said. "I have no change, and anyhow you'd lose it. You still have some money . . . when you give it to me you'll get another quart!" She did not want to cheat the Tartar who had given her such a valuable thing. "When you come, knock twice at the window-frame. I'll know who it is!"

Sayfullah tore his purchase out of her hands and ran away. For a long time he roamed around the woods, seeking a comfortable spot; it seemed to him, all the time, that the girl who had pinned a flower on his chest during the memorable night of his promotion would emerge from behind a corner. (And surely there had never been such an expressive dance of a first youthful despair!) The bottle was gluey, its chipped neck cut his tongue, the brew was a troubled tea-color. He took two swallows to deaden his thick, animal grief and kept stroking his chest where the fiery draught got caught. . . . Then he buried the remainder in the snow, thinking he would come back for it later, and with his head on fire set out to find a just and warm-hearted man who would arbitrate his old litigation with the baleful Mariam. . . .

An hour later, gloomy and lonely, he sat in Abdurakhman's den, and a flock of dark-skinned boon-companions surrounded him. As though blinded by drunkenness, looking straight ahead, he told them all about himself, and treated everyone, because he fancied that his only salvation lay in spending his money. And so they had drinks on him in honor of his fiancée, tapped and shook his shoulder, had fun, called him by the insulting name of *chaplashka* and dropped ashes from their cigarettes into his cup to see what his reaction would be. And one of them kept asking him whether it was true that his parents tied ribbons from his undergarments around their necks, and the others——

"Come on, tell us about your 'shaven one,'" enthusiastically yelled the others, "our Grinia Kashechkin slept with her last week!" And Grinia himself, the young leader of the Cheremshansk ruffians, unconcernedly picked the petals from a paper flower in the vase, making guesses about his own beloved, she loves me, she loves me not, she loves me. . . .

Then a huge fist in an armor of unwashable soot made its way through the company, and all of them stared at it with nearsighted curiosity which passed into sober and alarmed surprise. The blow fell on the nearest brawler. His weak body tipped over with his chair, and even Abdurakhman, always ready to give his life for the order of his beloved "Red East," laughed with pleasure like a child. He ran toward them, painstakingly raised the stricken man from the floor, put him back on his chair and even straightened out his necktie. "Ai, it's not good to fall like that," he told him with an exaggerated accent and much feeling, as though speaking to a child. Then he stepped to one side to see whether the effect was good and shook his head reproachfully. "One can break in two like that. Say 'mersse' to the citizen for not having killed you . . . offer him a cigarette!" But the gay drinker of a moment ago was silent and sat as if hypnotized.

Near the table tottered a man of impressive appearance, black-faced, with all the bands of his padded jacket torn so that the soot penetrated even to his grey undershirt: only at the railroad yard could one become so dirty. His gesture was hardly didactic in intention, it was rather a natural reaction to vileness. . . . Everything was very quiet, sharp and exciting in the bar. Suddenly Grinia drummed with his knuckles on the table, and everyone jumped up, noisily moving the chairs, and Grinia himself, with a very pale face, jerking as though on springs, began to walk around the offender; he held his hands behind his back. The gang shouted in one voice, and in the tobacco smoke there gleamed the metallic rainbow of a knife. . . . One minute later the chieftain lay quietly under the table with outspread hands, and, as though a full-blown rose had been scattered over his face, red petals flowed from Grinia's thin lips.

"Let's get out of here, Tartar, . . ." thundered the conqueror of Grinia Kashechkin. "What's your name . . . Mirgalim? Hassan? It's not beasts who will understand your cry of pain, you nomad . . . it's people!"

Sayfullah looked dejectedly at his rescuer. He had often seen him, but he was giddy and was unable to recall any special detail that would help to identify him. He seemed now to be the only man who genuinely liked him. And because neither of them had any money left, they went to enjoy themselves together for the rest of the day. Their arms around each other, they dragged themselves from snowdrift to snowdrift, and it would have been impossible to relate all the variations of their man-to-man and garrulous talk. And indeed Sayfullah's part was only that of confidant to the heartfelt ramblings of a drunk.

"I remember you, you're Ziganshin. We're related, I fought under your uncle. Ha, harnessed to one yoke we plowed those devilish deserts! And I app . . . appro . . ." He was unable to pronounce the polysyllabic word, he spat it out and laughed. "It's stubborn! . . . I was there when you were put on the engine. Eh, don't be sad, that's often the case with us: a man is put on a pedestal, and he makes a bad job of it. You were cheated by a locomotive, and I by a woman. She was a devil, a *shaitan* in your language. Eh, you wouldn't believe if I described her to you. . . ." Then followed the story that many in Cheremshansk knew of how a certain Zoska had thrown him out, calling him a camel for farewell; how he allegedly drew a red circle on his chest and cried to her: "Shoot me, bitch"; how he took a swing at her, how she indifferently turned her back to him, and her back was firm and white like cream. "And so, Tartar, six months have passed, and I still don't know whether she's an angel, or just a slut. . . ."

He felt the need to confide his vision to everyone he met, to be told whether he should kill, forgive or forget her. He shook his fists when he spoke of her, in the hope that at least the wind would convey to her his animal and base despair.

"Talk quietly . . . you mustn't yell!" Sayfullah admonished him, thinking that he would be glad to change places with him.

"Shut up. . . . What's your name? Hassan? Mirgalim? Skuriatnikov told us that the son of a bitch insulted you. How? Did he hit you or did he just make as if to hit you? Where? In your cheek . . . your head . . . your teeth?" And he struck the wind with his fist. "Never mind, I'll help you. Go to Protoklitov right now, mention my name. Tell him loudly that Kormilitsin sent you. And look him in the eyes, so you can see how they grow soft toward you. Ha-ha, I'm giving you a talisman against this fellow . . . take it and perform miracles!" He shouted hoarsely, the road was not wide enough for him; and, because Russia had always respected drunks, carriages that met them passed around them.

Sayfullah only blinked his eyes; in his position the only thing one could count on was a miracle. He had overcome many things in himself, but he still had a superstitious hope for some ancient powerful word that was known to men of the old generation. It was enough to pronounce it at a propitious hour, and it would break out in a blue flame, singeing his throat, and his grief would turn to ashes, and fate would present him with another chance to make the Sarzan pass. And somehow he firmly believed that Kormilitsin knew that secret word; and that he would blurt it out at any moment. . . . But he was still beating around the bush. Then the shrewd young Tartar brought the enormous hulk containing the secret to the sacred place in the woods where he had buried his bottle.

Until nightfall no one saw them. At twilight Katia and Peresypkin happened to pass the cooperative store. They noticed a crowd of all kinds of people who were standing in a circle watching a not very edifying spectacle. Peresypkin peered in from behind someone's shoulders. "Aha, my boy," he said with a harsh smile, "so in addition to everything else you're drunk!" And he beckoned Katia with his finger to admire her chosen one. . . . In the center, all covered with snow, and with a cut eyebrow, Sayfullah was dancing; but this was no longer the dashing *apipà* with its restrained and furious rhythm, but the disorderly convulsions of a poisoned man. He threw up one hand, and it fluttered like a wounded bird, then he grasped something, and threw it violently to the ground. (Kormilitsin was no longer with him.) The spectators observed these spasms with gloomy interest. And one tiny old woman, probably an engineer's mother, expressed loudly her pity for this fellow who had gone astray: here was another one who had been baptized into the locomotive faith. . . .

Katia broke into the crowd that obediently made way. She grasped Sayfullah by his hand, looked him into the eyes, and he began to tremble; she dragged him after her, and there was such a furious imperiousness in her gesture that not even the wives of engineers, envious of other people's secrets, dared to condemn her. (And although he was happy, happy because she had found him here, he tried to free himself. "*Ky mun nan* . . . leave me alone!"

She brought him to a water hydrant, made him bend down, and washed his face. He obeyed, full of admiration for her strength. Thirst burned him; he broke an icicle off the spigot and crunched it like glass. They went on, Katia biting her lips, slightly ahead of him. She decided to take him to an inspection booth and keep him in hiding until his human countenance was restored. A friend of hers was on duty at the switch; he would keep the secret. The place was dark and small, with only room for two. The switchman had dropped in to get warm, but he stamped for a moment in confusion, grumbled something and left, with the characteristic tact of the common people. Crossing her arms and swaying, Katia stared at the sitting Sayfullah. Engines passed by outside the little window, and Sayfullah shrank at the approach of their slow, creeping, all-seeing lights. The poison had evaporated through his temples. He was completely master of himself. From a distance came a dull whistle: the night train for Aldermesh was leaving. The young man rushed to the door, and Katia mockingly made way for him, but Sayfullah's own hands clinging to the edge of the wooden cot would not let him out. After all he could go to Aldermesh later, when he saved up some more money for gifts; Mariam would wait, she was used to waiting!

"I fell, . . ." he said, touching his swollen eyebrow. "Why are you silent! . . . Bawl me out!"

"What's the matter with your hands?"

"I burned them. . . ."

She was silent, waiting for him to invent justification; she of course would have thrown him out if he had dared to say even one word. Suddenly he jumped up and raised his hands. "*Betiun*, all Tatarstan is watching me. And even worse, you're watching me. . . ."

She stamped her foot to stop him from talking; then she asked with disgust: "Is it true that he hit you?" and a warmth spread over her cheeks as though the shame of Protoklitov's blow also affected her.

He cried out, protecting himself from her eyes with his hands: "That is not true, not true!"

Katia lowered her head and ran her fingers over the edging of her kerchief. "What am I to do with you?" her lips whispered. She went outside, having ordered him to stay there. The cold of the night did not calm her, the station seemed too small for her. She walked around it twice, and still no decision was born in her. Near the club there was a throng of people, and in their midst a tall drunk was shouting things that made people laugh and nudge each other. Katia listened for a moment; she felt disgusted that such a vile life still existed! In a backyard she struck her face against a fence, wept from annoyance and drummed with her fists on the hard, rough boards. ". . . What shall I do now?"

To drop Sayfullah meant to lose him forever. Nor could he remain at Cheremshansk: the older people working in the yard would have revolted. It occurred to her that a mistake was only the shadow of a crime, that there were extenuating circumstances in the accident with the engine (she had learned the details from her brother) and that one's own man is more precious than any machine. She was frightened by this thought and hastened to forget it. . . . Then she recalled Martinson—his Diesel car was still on a side track. This man had the right to make decisions even when they went counter to the regulations. She went straight to the dead-end siding behind the control post where stood the *nachpodor's* car. She was already on the footboard when she realized that she was doing all this for herself. And while she stood there hesitating and pondering, the door opened, and Peresypkin almost fell on her from above.

He had hardly ever before been in such a state; he had lost all self-command and was oblivious of everything in the world. He rushed through the snowdrift, childishly pressing his cap over his mouth, but some savage force brought him back to the car. And although Katia did not know what had happened up there, her own grief made her approach him, call him, and stroke his elusive shoulders.

"What has happened, Alexei?" Unwittingly she touched his wet cheeks and drew back. Her former tough and business-like comrade was unrecognizable. "You're crying?"

He shuddered from this uninvited closeness, groaned and freed himself from her hands: "I'm so sorry for Aliosha. . . ." (And Katia did not realize at first that he was referring to Kurilov.)

Her unexpected caress sobered him up; he tried to explain to Katia what kind of man was now sitting alone with his horrible pain in a closed compartment, how carefully this "father and gardener of many people like me" had brought him up and how vile it was that he had not yet succeeded in repaying Kurilov with any great joy for what he had done for him. Katia listened and she regretted her own momentary weakness. . . . They went away from the car. (Thus Alexei Nikitich never learned perhaps the most essential episode in the story of a certain anonymous couple whom he had observed at various periods of his life.)

Aliosha walked first, discussing in a level-headed fashion the Cheremshansk events, but suddenly sat down, almost falling over the iron casing of the switch and, with his head between his knees, burst into tears. His pity for Kurilov was stronger even than his shame before this girl, and she was delicate enough not to try to comfort him. Then he rose, gradually getting accustomed to the idea that Alexei Nikitich would not always be there to direct his thoughts and actions; sometimes human maturity begins with such a realization. "Let's go, the Bureau meeting isn't over yet," he said, pulling his cap over his eyebrows. "Turn away, I'll rub my face with snow. . . ." And as though to justify himself for his sentimentality, he added that he had seen the old age of a great man. (The scene with Liza that he had unwittingly come upon in the Borschnia woods now appeared to him in a different, a human light.)

At an uncovered table, amid clouds of tobacco smoke, the Bureau of the cell was holding a meeting. They were Sayfullah's comrades, the strictest of all judges. More than forty people crowded into a room intended for five. Everyone was upset, and it was hard to maintain order. Once again, only one word, fiery as before, was on the agenda: the locomotive. Katia looked for Martinson, but he had not yet returned from Kulla; she caught Protoklitov's questioning eyes staring at her, and shrugging her shoulders, turned away.

They were discussing the verdict independently of the decision concerning Sayfullah's case. Reshotkin was eliminated from the Bureau and sent to work as a mechanic; Skuriatnikov was dismissed altogether. Protoklitov, summoned to testify, was given the floor, and although the Komsomol disaster was a trump in his game, he even now succeeded in preserving the bored impassivity of an expert. He spent a long while folding a newspaper, and kept glancing at Katia, in whose face one could see some lurking secret. His appearance here could be interpreted as a call for agreement, and he was paying generously those whom he had invited as accomplices. What he was saying struck one by the reasonableness of its arguments and simultaneously aroused suspicion because everyone felt that anything he said was part of a complicated and shrewd manoeuvre. According to Protoklitov a severe punishment might ruin the young engineer. "Don't forget, my friends, that he has no place to go from here; his village will receive him as a renegade; and the boy is every inch one of our own!" Sparing the feelings of Sayfullah's countrymen (and at the same time flattering them, for they did not miss a word of his speech), he hinted in passing at the cultural backwardness of this honest and industrious people; he emphasized that a snowstorm as violent as the one of the day before would have confused even experienced engineers, and not without humor cited an example from his own past that was listened to with tense sympathy. (The incident he related had actually taken place, with a White armored train, the very same night that Gleb had decided to flee to a "new" life; he passed over these details in silence, as they had no direct relation to the matter under discussion.)

"But as for the little musician, . . ." he concluded referring to Skuriatnikov, "I'd give him a hard blow." He began to roll a cigarette, and this time he dropped tobacco untidily on his knees, revealing his fatigue.

His proposal was bound to win support; the honorable conditions of the peace found favor in the eyes of many of the boys. "Let the organization repair the engine in the shortest possible time, and Sayfullah will take it to Sarzan!" But after Protoklitov, Katia took the floor, and because her face expressed indignation, the noise instantaneously abated. She walked to the table.

"Are you asking for the floor?" the secretary asked her. "You're late, Victor's case has been discussed."

"No, I want to speak about Sayfullah."

The judges exchanged glances; they felt awkward for Katia, who ventured to defend the guilty man singlehanded. No one looked at her, and even Peresypkin, biting his nails, lowered his eyes with an incorruptible expression. His fingers were trembling.

"Why didn't he come here himself?" he asked. "Is he chewing over his experience?"

"I picked him up in a bad state. It was your duty to support a comrade in need. . . ."

The secretary laughed. "Well, we had enough to do without him," he said, significantly stroking a bleeding callus on his palm. "There is a rumor that the yard master struck him. What do you know about it?"

"I asked him, but he denies this."

"Is he afraid that his confirmation would be interpreted as a complaint? In his position this would, of course, be ridiculous. . . ."

She shrugged her shoulders. "Well, I'm not his wife yet, and he has no need to lie to me."

Peresypkin smiled with approval. This girl walked with her head high and she disliked gossip! . . . She began by angrily denouncing the references made to Sayfullah's nationality, and jeered at the formulas of comradely complaisance: ". . . He does not in any way differ from any of us and for that reason does not need exaggerated praise or milder punishment. Too many eyes, friendly and hostile, are today directed at Cheremshansk, comrades. It will be better for our cause if we remember them, even when we quarrel or love!" The boys rewarded with applause the tone of her speech rather than its meaning; everyone there was obscurely aware that any indulgence toward the guilty engineer would cause a bad impression in the yard. And although all of them without exception felt sorry for this comrade, each of them tried to speak more harshly and severely, as though this implied harshness toward himself. Thus Sayfullah's fate was decided. (No doubt Katia knew with certainty that she would find means to keep him from returning to Aldermesh.)

Ironically smiling at their youthful ardor, Protoklitov rose from his seat. He inquired whether his continued presence was needed; he was not detained. But Katia Reshotkina stopped him on his way out. "Just wait a minute," she said across the whole room, and waited until the noise subsided. "I'd almost forgotten, Protoklitov. . . ."

He slowly turned around with an attentive and motionless face. They confronted each other as in a duel. Katia seemed taller and paler than usual; Peresypkin gazed at her with unconcealed admiration.

". . . When you go past the club," Katia said, biting her lips, "pick up your Kormilitsin. He's shouting there that you are a well-known White officer . . . people around him are laughing, and the result is not very nice. . . ."

She said this in her ordinary voice without emphasizing a word, but the assembly suddenly rose, someone dropped a stool, and it was as though the number of people in the room doubled. One quarrelsome little fellow jumped out to the center, and made hurried gestures asking her to go on, to finish . . . but she herself did not know any more.

Still nothing stirred in Protoklitov's face. He nodded his head negatively.

"I don't employ professional bouncers, my dear lady, to pick up *all* the drunks in Cheremshansk. But if there's room in your booth for this rather well-preserved bachelor. . . ." He squinted encouragingly in the direction of Katia, as though recommending Kormilitsin to her attentions.

There was a moment of disorder; no one knew exactly what to do. Then Peresypkin jumped onto the table and with raised fists rushed after Protoklitov, who was moving toward the door. Peresypkin was caught and held by all his leather straps; he hit out at his comrades' arms, trying to reach the door that was slowly closing.

"You boor, you boorish vermin!" he cried in a breaking, childish voice, and the combined efforts of all there were required to keep him in the room.

# CHAPTER 46

# Before Leaving Home

WHILE WAITING TO BE TAKEN to Moscow, Kurilov lived in his successor's Diesel car. Martinson had returned late the day before and found the Cheremshansk doctor talking loudly in Kurilov's compartment. A doctor's knowledge of his patient's disease undoubtedly creates a closer bond than does a twenty-year-old friendship. The red-haired physician now called Kurilov "little father," initiated him into the secrets of the human organism and, although he deprecated the value of medicine, brought along a whole collection of little phials to show that he was the boss of all illness in Cheremshansk. Martinson smiled; his guests were talking about the merits of sudden abstinence from liquor.

". . . Now imagine, little father, a most responsible engine, which for the space of thirty years has been working on high-grade fuel. And suddenly it's fed tea and lemon, let's say, eh-eh!" (That was the way he laughed.) "What's the result? A catalysis, and *mauvais* in the highest degree. I don't have to go far to illustrate this. . . . Once I had a comrade: a man in excellent health, well educated, a good son, husband, father and so forth . . . do you get the picture? He stopped drinking, got involved in an embezzlement case and now, completely sober, sits in prison, eh-eh-eh!"

"So what? . . . I don't grasp the mechanism of this case. . . ." Kurilov asked curiously, and it was clear that anyone now would be able to alleviate his loneliness.

"Why, it's obvious, little father! Abrupt change of conditions. Suppose a man was called Ivan Rebrov, and then became Semyon Samsonov, eh-eh-eh-eh! . . ."

A sleepy employee with catlike whiskers brought them tea. Martinson refrained from interrupting this familiar and interesting talk, and went to the Komsomols' meeting. Protoklitov was no longer in the room with them. The boys were sitting there very subdued; in the presence of the new chief no one even hinted at the scandal of an hour ago. Just as they suspected Sayfullah, so the *nachpodor* might suspect the organization of trying to place the responsibility for the disaster on a stranger. The murdered locomotive loomed threateningly in everyone's mind. And nothing could be done about Katia's sensational revelation until Kormilitsin was questioned in a sober state. There was no evidence against Protoklitov except a drunkard's slip of the tongue; an ill-considered step might only spoil the whole thing. By silent agreement they decided to surround Kormilitsin with attentions and friendship in order to discover a passage to the rotten, human hollow of the tree where the secret nested like an owl.

Although Martinson did not return until midnight, he knocked at the door of Kurilov's compartment: the ill chief was not yet asleep. The younger comrade asked the older whether he needed anything. Alexei Nikitich asked him to tuck in his blanket on the side near the window. "I'm shivering all over, it must be from fatigue!" Actually there was a tropical heat in the car; the conductors were doing their best. Then the station's light signals began to move over the curtains, and the Diesel car plunged into the boundless expanse of the winter night.

"Well, how are things with them?" Kurilov asked, raising himself on his elbows.

"See here, lie down, old man. The boys burnt out a locomotive ... and now they're cast down. Real maturity always has to be paid for. I remember what my own cost. . . ." He did not finish the sentence; this clear-sighted man, carved out of one block as it were, disliked useless lyrical emotions. "Snow is falling ... lots of it!"

"It's winter," Kurilov said slowly; he let himself down on the pillow, carefully, first one shoulder blade, then the other. (In his Oceanic capital, too, a cold rain must be splashing in the sleepy streets, and the lighthouse high in the air blinks at dirigibles arriving from fraternal continents.)

"And how do you feel?" It would have been tactless not to inquire about Kurilov's illness.

"I think it's subsiding." The chief was referring to his last attack. "Of course, this wretched condition is unpleasant: to be lying ... while people pass over you. . . ."

In the last analysis Kurilov had no grievance against his fate. Once he had seen an apple tree being cut up for wood. It did not spatter sappy splinters, but fell apart in whole pieces. Yet this tree too had worked all its life; then it got tired and died, and people cleared its place in order to plant another one. Thus the river is never the same! ... Still it was possible to spend the remainder of one's life in a more intelligent way. And he regretted that he was not fated to screen a great leader with his body, or fall before a firing squad so that his death might serve as an example to others. How many times he had provoked death and escaped it, only to see it suddenly lurking behind his back . . . or perhaps in his back!

"There was a warrior in the Middle Ages, a man named Corydal, . . ." Kurilov began pensively.

"I don't remember anyone by that name. . . ."

"Very few people remember him. In 1422, during the siege of Karlstein, he hurled human corpses from a catapult into the enemy's citadel. A clever fellow . . . he used his soldiers to the very end. . . ."

Martinson understood that Kurilov was being poisoned by his own idleness. "You'd better go into dry dock and get thoroughly repaired, old man!" he said with severe tenderness, and Alexei Nikitich agreed that the reconditioning of a warship is indeed a serious business. "Illness, comrade, is an abnormal state!" Martinson remarked.

"You're right, you're absolutely right," Kurilov echoed with feeling.

Thus the variation once imagined by Marina in a Moscow side-street was coming true. And it required great skill on the part of both of them to make this conversation last until Moscow. . . . Next morning an automobile awaited them at the station. Kurilov's driver listened to Martinson's order to take them straight to the office. On the way there the two men exchanged only a few insignificant words.

They climbed up to the office, and the rumor spread among the workers that Alexei Nikitich was turning over all his affairs to his successor. Later, they went out to lunch together: Martinson wanted to consult Kurilov as to whom he should send to the forthcoming railroad conference. Sashka Tiutchev, whom they met in the restaurant, walked home with Kurilov. This time he was not as boisterous as usual and was exaggeratedly attentive. Alexei Nikitich had not succeeded in reading Sashka's secret thoughts in his face, and night was already falling. They found themselves at Kurilov's door before they had had time to discuss everything.

Finally Tiutchev said in a guiltily facetious tone: "And so you're going to the hospital?"

"Yes, they've told me I have to have my belly opened. . . . An annoying interruption in my work . . . and in my life. And it's a vile disease, treacherous, attacks you from the back. . . ."

That day the roofs were cleared in Moscow. Icy lumps fell from above, and Alexei Nikitich no sooner tried to examine one of them than it disintegrated into many dirty pieces.

"It's a pity you have to undergo all that," Tiutchev said, trying to find words of comradely encouragement.

And now, spurred on by the events which moved so rapidly, Kurilov spoke hurriedly: "If any of your people goes abroad, tell him to buy me a good pipe. Look, I'll show you exactly what I want. . . ." And in great detail he described the shape, the make, the quality of the wood, especially emphasizing its solidity. "You see I had one, a very good one, for fifteen years, almost a friend . . . but someone stole it. I'll make a drawing for you."

He made a drawing in Tiutchev's notebook, and they separated with manly and intelligent restraint. He wanted to hold Sashka's warm hand in his for another minute, but the janitor who knew all the tenants had already opened the door. As he entered the elevator, Kurilov recalled that he had forgotten to mention that the mouthpiece of the pipe should be straight, but it was too late now; the iron box was on its way up, clicking at every floor. He had barely touched the bell, when his sister opened the door. Thus throughout this day he had never been able to stop for even an instant the flow of events marked on the timetable of his life. . . . When she saw her brother, Frosia rushed away, but changed her mind, returned to the entrance hall and in her fright even forgot to hold out her hand. The apartment smelt of medicines. As he removed his coat Alexei Nikitich noticed a dirty, frayed jacket on the peg. A three-flapped cap, which looked as if it had been gnawed by dogs, lay beside a pair of galoshes (and that was perhaps its proper place). A stranger was in his apartment and this explained Frosia's confusion.

"So you have a guest, little sister?" remarked Alexei Nikitich in a surprised tone.

"My husband." Her face expressed expectation that now her brother would be angry and put all of them out into the cold. "Luka was sick, and I had to postpone my departure."

"What's the matter with Luka?" asked Alexei Nikitich, alarmed. "Have you had the doctor? . . . You mustn't take chances with a sick child!"

"Oh, he is on his way to recovery now. And I couldn't throw Pavel out: after all he is his father. How he found out that I was here with Luka is beyond me. . . ."

Kurilov glanced at the peg. "The janitor didn't stop him?"

"I telephoned downstairs and told them to admit him. Forgive us all, Alioshka!" And she bowed deeply, touching the floor with her hand.

He drew her to him and, holding her by the chin, looked reproachfully into her guilty, tearful eyes until they smiled. "You should be ashamed of yourself, Frosia. Is Pavel Stepanych here?"

"He is with Luka . . . he stayed up all night. He'll go . . . I told him not to dare to come here for a second night . . . to get out. After all, it's *your* apartment! I locked all the drawers myself, don't be afraid. . . ." She lowered her eyes and her brother realized that Frosia had overheard his conversation with Klavdia about the need for vigilance.

"Well, that's fine. Put the tea kettle on the fire and give us something to nibble on. You can give me meat, it's all right! Now, march, le-eft turn!"

He looked in at the doorway without trying to conceal himself. A lamp wrapped in a newspaper was burning on the table; apparently the lampshade had got broken somehow in the confusion. The room smelt more of singed paper than of medicine. A special disorder characteristic of sick-rooms struck one's eyes. Frosia's boy, very long, as though he had grown only during the last three weeks, lay on the leather sofa. Beside him sat Omelichev, who had not changed much since the meeting at Sakonikha. He was leaning forward with his elbows on his knees; black hair with sparse streaks of grey showed between his fingers; motionless, poised to act, he watched his ill-starred son sleeping and in sleep moving his fingers. The rustle of Kurilov's step made him raise his head. He stared into the darkness, then rose, respectfully holding his hands down along the seams of his trousers.

Kurilov stood beside him and gazed at Luka. Every few moments the boy turned over and threw his covers onto the floor. A morbid blue color spread around his deep-sunken, ill-looking eyes; children with such eyes rarely survived. . . . Everything was now clear. Alexei Nikitich felt nothing except a desire to see Ziamka as soon as possible.

"Here you find me like a thief, uninvited," Omelichev said and, uncertain of what the man whose apartment this was would do, did not hold out his hand. "Shall I go, or what?"

Kurilov remained silent for a minute. What could this tamed, embittered and, most important, completely harmless man tell him? Yet, as he moved further and further into the future, perhaps Kurilov yearned to touch for the last time this prehistoric antiquity, which reminded him of his youth, his hand-to-hand fights with the past, his self-denial born of a great richness that had not been spent in vain.

"Why should you hurry away at this late hour? Sit down. Frosia will make some tea for us . . . I remember that you liked tea. . . ."

Yes, he adored that ancient Russian leisure pastime—drinking tea. At his estate on the Kama they used to consume seven pounds of it a month. Omelichev respectfully coughed into his palm and from this distance was amazed at the fantastic figures of his former prosperity.

After Alexei Nikitich had changed and washed they went into the adjoining room in order not to disturb the patient. Because of his fatigue from a sleepless night Omelichev asked Kurilov not to turn on a bright light. However, Kurilov had realized of his own accord that it would be foolish to confuse his guest by too much politeness. This man was going down, and although aware of the inevitability of his fate, he was still unaccustomed to his new position. He hardly sat down, but walked this way and that all the time, so that Kurilov could not examine him; during the conversation he left the room three times to cast a glance at Luka. His hands were empty, but the keys of his lost kingdoms and of the future still tinkled in them. And these hands of his had not lost their old habits; he would take an object and examine it anxiously as though trying to recognize it, and would find in it a different purpose and a novelty no longer accessible to him; he would be angry and would not put it back but seem to reject it. ("No, nothing new has been invented since the time of his defeat!") He still wore the same things that had been given him two years earlier at the military store, and at that time government clothes were not beautiful. . . They sat down; Frosia brewed the tea strong and remained with Luka.

For some time the conversation did not go well, only half an hour later did their old frankness assert itself. "You've grown shaggy, Pavel Stepanych. You've stopped taking care of yourself. Did you leave the railroad of your own will?" said Kurilov.

"No, I got a furlough. I went to the Kama to have a last look at my beautiful river. . . . It's like a mother!"

"It's a good thing that you haven't forgotten your mother. Well, is life on the Kama easier than it used to be?"

Omelichev shrank together, as from cold: "Those who have simple brains fare better."

"And what kind of brains do you think you have, Omelichev?"

He did not answer, but sat with closed eyes. Finally he said: "I met Anatolyi, a muzhik whom I used to employ to look after my samovar. So many years have gone by, yet he recognized his old employer. Apparently he was afraid to ask questions, but he stuck three rubles into my hand, without looking back at me. I felt very much like asking him whose samovar he attended now, but I refrained. I don't know whether he is an official or not . . . he had a briefcase . . . he was cleanly dressed, and his eyes were frightened, but sharp. He must have sensed at once what gift I had in store for him. . . . In my house he took care of the samovar!"

"Your observation is correct: people are growing. Did you take the three rubles?"

"Why not? . . . He got enough pleasure for five: think whom he gave them to!"

There was on the table a jar of filled candy, which was popular just then. Omelichev crushed a piece between his fingers, examined it, threw it into his mouth, chewed it pensively and smiled: the color, the taste were the same as in old times. . . . "Then why, why has life changed so much?"

"You didn't go to the Kama at the right time, Pavel Stepanych. In winter the beauty can't be seen, it's asleep."

"Oh, I saw what I wanted. An official can be seen a long way off."

"Don't slander, merchant. Not everyone is an official!"

"Don't be offended, I'm not thinking of you. You're a saint . . . but so far as I remember no undertaking has ever flourished on saints. I've never believed in that kind of leaven. People stole from me a great deal; those who weren't lazy made profits. . . . But I had more confidence in the best-fed thief than in the most starving saint."

"That's true: it was a time of plunder!"

"But he gave all his heart to the steamship business. His left eye was asleep, but his right eye stayed on the job. I've raised whole generations of people on my business. And with you—a fool who does a dirty job on land is sent to work on the river. . . . You don't mind my frankness? Just tell me when you want me to stop."

"What you say isn't very interesting, Pavel Stepanych. I expected something sharper . . . something that would prick my heart!"

Omelichev shrivelled up: he no longer had an instrument that could prick Kurilov's heart. He raised his head and listened: his boy was making sounds and tossing in the fever; then came Frosia's soothing whisper, and everything was quiet again.

". . . And what sort of merchant was I, Alexei Nikitich? I had an enormous business, many barges and steamships—Lord, the number of my shares in various enterprises was four thousand—but did I use them? My only pleasure was to drive in a two-wheeled cart in the Chuvash woods. Oh, my groves, orange-colored in the dusk, and the nameless little streams. . . ."

"Don't be such a fake, you yourself cut down those groves!"

"You too cut them, and you're paid for ruling us. And I rejoiced in the bustle. I looked at my hands, my all-powerful hands, and rejoiced. In 1918 the Whites burned my ships to prevent them from falling into the hands of the Reds . . . my warriors have fallen . . . have you seen my tears?"

"No, but I can hear your words, Omelichev. They're wet words! You're still sorry for yourself. . . ."

"Eh, even today I should have been able to multiply my investments sevenfold. Give me back my Kama!" He leaned with his whole body on the table, the glasses tipped over, the tablecloth slipped to one side, and Omelichev's voice had a strange, cracked sound. "I'd sweep it every day with a broom! . . . I'd take you from ship to ship, without wetting your feet, to Piany Bor where my fleet lies buried. My water on the Kama would not have rested night and day. Make me a good offer, buy these hands from Omelichev!"

Kurilov laughed open-heartedly at his greediness and sincerity. "I'd be glad to buy them . . . but first I'd have to tear them off their head." He recalled his conversation with Klavdia and tried to test this man. "But if you agree, I'll speak with the proper person. Let your hands go to the Kama and get busy. . . . What do you say?"

Omelichev shook his head mockingly. "For whom? I don't count on this planet, in your statistics! I had Egorka, but he died too."

"And what about Luka?"

"Don't laugh at such a thing, Alexei Nikitich!" And he ominously raised his finger as though prophesying disaster.

Kurilov felt bored; he was sorry he had started the tea party. He had hardly any time for a good sleep and to telephone a few friends before leaving for the hospital. Moreover, although Alexei Nikitich wanted to listen to the enemy's malicious and intelligent criticism, this mirror was too small, it was cracked and broken; Kurilov could not find room there. (And he could have spent an excellent evening with Ziamka!)

"Well, you must admit that the freight turnover on the Kama is higher than before the war."

But this man's mind was poisoned by his injury. "Oh, you're clever . . . you always compare things with what they were before the war. Yet what about me? . . . Would I have been asleep during these sixteen years? Do you imagine that only you were born to grow? No, this tree was cut, it did not dry up. Look, fifteen years ago there was no man child in my house, now he is lying there suffering." And again he was moved to the point of tears, and one could see how the dried wick in vain licked the empty bottom of the lamp: the flame was dying, it gave neither light nor heat.

Omelichev lowered his head, and his hands hung down limply. "I can see that our conversation in the attic has stayed in your head. Much time has passed. Here we sit opposite each other, and how many human bones and heads are between us! Recently I ran into that little officer who came to look for you on the Kama. So many years have passed, yet he has changed very little . . . just as in former times, he raises his eyebrows like a saber!"

"You should have taken him by the coat-sleeve and brought him to the authorities. . . ."

"Why should I ruin him? I never touched you either. . . ."

(You're lying, lying, Pavel Stepanych, Kurilov thought. You just wanted to remind me of my debt. . . .) "I still don't understand," he said, "why you didn't give me away. Were you taking revenge on someone through me, or did you hope to survive the Soviet regime . . . or was it just because we are related?"

"We're not related: you are a nomad, and I am settled. You treat even the nomad Mordvins as your own, while for me they only dug ditches. . . . They're not sacred, after all!"

He himself was frightened by the confession that had slipped off his tongue, he muttered something about the revolution being a "warning" to other "nations," but his manoeuvre was clumsy and false. Alexei Nikitich expected Omelichev to ask him for protection and money and, in an effort to put an end to this fruitless conversation, inquired with an air of indifference whether he did not need anything. . . . No— except a few shirts! (He wanted to make sure that the insignificance of his demand was appreciated, but once again his offended feeling broke through: "There was a time when a whole company left my house in clothes I had given them!") Soon afterward Frosia asked him to stay with Luka for a while, and when he returned, Kurilov was asleep with his head on the table. Two hours later, after Omelichev had gone, Frosia woke her brother and put him to bed.

Next morning he got up early. The tea kettle was hissing on the table as though it had stayed there all night. Wrapped in a blanket Luka sat on the sofa; Frosia was feeding him with a spoon. Alexei Nikitich was shaving when Klavdia called him on the telephone. First she reproached him for not having taken the trouble to inform her of his arrival. Her voice, fresh in the morning, had a metallic ring in the receiver.

"I had a telephone call from . . . well, from *your* Tiutchev. You've got very unpleasant friends, Aliosha. Wait a moment, let me get a chair." She went away, and Kurilov patiently listened to the crackling of the soap bubbles on his cheeks. "What did you say?"

"I said, Klasha, that you should gather together a complete set of friends for me. But please avoid moralizing women and all non-drinking people, if possible!"

"You wisecrack like a provincial lawyer, Alexei! And to think that you're the chief of the Political Bureau of the Railroad!"

"Well, I'm only the former chief of the Political Bureau. And I'm in a hurry; I'm all soapy, and Luka is making faces at me. I'm going to have my tea. Then, after I've had my tea, I'll leave. . . ."

"Won't I have time to take you to the hospital?"

"My dear sister, I'm not setting out on a tiger hunt. You can visit me tomorrow. And don't forget to bring Ziamka . . . please! Good; I press your hands with all my strength. . . ."

He hung up, but five minutes later Klavdia telephoned again. "I wanted to remind you, Aliosha, to take handkerchiefs and tooth powder. Do you have your car?"

"Thanks, I'll go on foot. It's a beautiful morning, and I don't get enough exercise."

"It's a rather overcast morning," his sister contradicted him sharply. "Why don't you have your windows cleaned?"

She was silent for a while; then she asked him about the thing that was the real purpose of her second call: ". . . Are you frightened?"

"No-o!" And now he no longer felt like playing the clown. "To tell the truth, I don't very much like the idea of going. It's a rather ticklish business. . . ."

She asked to speak to Frosia, who listened to all her sister's instructions with a sad face. Half an hour later Kurilov started to get ready, but he had to put his papers in order and did not leave home before noon. . . . However, he did not get to the hospital that day. All at once he saw the same young couple he had seen before, or so it appeared to him. Yes, there they were, and he had long since got accustomed to the idea that the world was full of reflections of them. He met them frequently, everywhere—at all the great construction projects, or at May First demonstrations (hand in hand they passed the reviewing stands), or at his station (perhaps on their way to the mysterious city of Komsomolsk, which is halfway on the road to the Ocean). There was a high rate of occurrence in their appearing. . . . Laughing, swaying, as though welded together at the elbows, the young people now ran into a movie theatre. Lured by the colorful poster (a blue silhouette was diving into a conventional lavender sea painted in geometric circles), Alexei Nikitich also bought a ticket to the movie. The other buyers peered curiously at the man with a bundle who looked as though he were going to a bathing establishment. (Catherine had always intended to buy him a small suitcase!) He sat to the end, listening to the whisper of the couple in front of him, and he liked it very much . . . it still was not too late to go to the hospital if he took a trolley car. But the cars were crowded, and this gave him the moral right to postpone the hospital until the next day. All in all, he had won a whole day from fate, a fi-irst rate January day, with a fizz-water sharpness in the air, even a little longish, like all idle days. . . . He considered going to see Ziamka; but he decided against it lest he be overtaken there by the next attack.

Then he started to wander about at random. He went to government institutions, and with a new feeling, as an outsider, watched the busy, bustling people; he dropped into the empty courtyards of many-storeyed houses and with the air of an amateur examined the sooty plaster of the walls, the dirty windows, food on the sills (in the dark vaulted gateways the icy draft flapped like a sail); he tried all the time to imagine what human dwellings would look like, not tomorrow, but after ten Five Year Plans. (Time intervals were now a matter of indifference to him.) He walked in the street, mentally abolishing whole blocks and replacing them with buildings the very sight of which aroused proud and dizzying rapture. He stood in front of bookshops, where the evening sun flowed and thawed upon the gilded backs of beautiful and wise works of antiquity, and was horrified at the number of books he had not had time to read (and he firmly decided to obtain, immediately after his recovery, a two-month furlough in order to catch up with learning that he had missed). He went as far as the outskirts of the city, felt with his hands the uneven winter skin of the trees, and then examined his hands or, scooping up some snow in his palm, watched the dirty lump give birth to a living and frisky little stream which tried to trickle down his sleeve. He talked to children, seeing in them future engineers, flyers, warriors and leaders, and they answered him as though they were talking to themselves. He behaved very strangely. He was not in a hurry to get anywhere.

He returned home when it seemed to him that his agitated contemplation of other people's lives was becoming almost a debauch. "My nose is terribly cold, Frosia. Won't you give me a glass of vodka, under the circumstances?" His sister could not get over his young and vigorous appearance, Alexei Nikitich told her that it was the hospital's day off and that all the doctors were lying around drunk. Frosia's face reflected an incomprehensible confusion . . . of which the explanation was simple. Taught by poverty to be economical, she had prepared dinner just for two, not expecting the presence of a third person, a stranger.

Alexei Nikitich was becoming this stranger.

# CHAPTER 47

# Fear

LIZA WOULD NOT have written that letter if she had been able to confide her feelings to anyone else. She would not have sent those four
sheets written in a small hand if she had known the impression they
would make upon her uncle. He did not even read them to the end, as
soon as he realized that they referred to a living Taniechka. Everything became confused in his mind, and he no longer recognized a
single card in the deck with which he had played all his life.

The letter arrived late at night. Fearing even to think about what
had happened, he hurried to bed. He removed his *tolstovka*, brushed
it outside the door, and carefully hung it on a chair. He placed his
trousers beside his *tolstovka* and put his shoes underneath the chair, as
he had done for the last forty-five years. He put all that was left of
himself into bed and covered it with a blanket. . . . Sleep refused to
come, and never before had the yellow, crumpled pillows been so
touzled.

He imagined that he was sitting in his chair, looking at himself and
laughing. For the sole purpose of ending this tormenting dualism he
turned on the light and got dressed. He again took up the letter, but
again did not dare to read it to the end. The lines got mixed up before
his eyes. Taniechka was alive! He wanted air, he felt as though any
minute he would stop breathing. He covered his face with his hands
and parsimoniously, drop by drop, evoked everything that was still
intact in his memory. . . . There could be no doubt: the deceased
woman had never died. He recalled that Taniechka had always been
very strong; she loved to get wet in a storm, she loved the Christmas
holiday drives enlivened with little bells, she loved to outstrip the
rushing cavalcades and, during all of Arkadyi Hermogenovich's stay
in Borschnia, had never been ill a day. (Even in her pensive moments,
which seemed attractive in the eyes of the young Pokhvisnev, was she
not pondering over her next athletic exploit?) And so Taniechka was
alive, pining away, and perhaps more than once remembering the
young man who had not dared to touch her. ("How wonderful that
you're still alive!")

. . . Everything was born anew, and even the objects in his room

looked fresher. The imaginary graveyard at which he had become a
constant visitor vanished as though it had been merely painted on
paper, folded up and thrown into the fire. His solitude was at last
coming to an end. Rivals no longer existed. Now that he still had un-
fulfilled obligations it was worth while to go on living. His joy rejuvenated him. A last warm reflection of youth was falling on his
hands that had begun to grow cold. . . . Yes, she existed; she had
existed in the past, too, and this was just as certain as that the worm-
eaten chair under him had once been a tree saluting the sun and
storms!

At daybreak he somehow fell asleep, tied up in a bundle in his
chair. That morning his pharmacists waited for him in vain. What
could he have taught them except Seneca's verses:

> *Eternal darkness I have escaped at last!*
> *And the gloomy vault of the prison underground*
> *Is blinded by the long-yearned-for day.* . . .

He dressed in his Sunday best. Sauntering leisurely in a senile
fashion he set the table for coffee for two and mentally questioned her,
as if she were sitting opposite him, about how she had been living all
these years. No, nothing could darken her deep and radiant eyes. She
must have grown younger while he aged. With time she had even lost
the defects that accompany man as signs of his earthly existence.
Vergil was right, a thousand times right: "Let him survive who will
confide my ashes to the earth!" Next, he went to buy flowers and put
three penny pots on the table. The large-windowed room now looked
twice as clean and pleasant. . . . Later on in the day, when quite unexpectedly the gloomy Protoklitov appeared at his home, the old man
met him with solemnity and behaved as though a third person were
actually present in the room.

Aha, so the haughty Ilya had not enough strength to bear the six-
months' ordeal! He put his fur coat on a chair and sat beside Pokhvisnev with the air of a supplicant. Arkadyi Hermogenovich smirked in
silence, leaving the initiative of the conversation to his visitor. Ilya
Ignatyich for a long time stroked the reddish mark on his forehead
left by his cap.

"Ha, I see you're celebrating today?"

Arkadyi Hermogenovich nodded in confirmation. "Yes . . . someone
has turned up who had vanished from my life for . . ." he could not
even figure out the length of the separation and said at random, ". . .
more than ten years."

"A relative of yours?"

"More than a relative, a friend." And with an air of sly superiority he added: "You have of course some purpose in coming here?"

They maintained a pause indispensable for the transition to the object of Protoklitov's visit.

"Hasn't Liza returned yet? . . . Or nas she gone away again? I saw her performance announced on a poster."

"Oh, she's been away for three weeks now. She is well, she is taking a rest, she feels fine. After all the unpleasantness of her married life, she is entitled to a little enjoyment. . . ."

Ilya Ignatyich had not known this. He was perceptibly disappointed and worried. He tried to remove a little stain from his sleeve, but it refused to go. He was angry and tormented, he hated him, this little. . . .

"You don't have to answer me if my question seems indiscreet. Did she go alone?"

Arkadyi Hermogenovich ambiguously shrugged his shoulders. "Eh, n-not quite. It's very, eh . . . very far from here!"

"But still . . . do you know her address?"

"She asked me not to give it to anyone. And even I myself. . . ."

"The devil take it, you correspond with her, don't you?" Ilya Ignatyich's face displayed a mixture of fury and bewilderment, as though he had diagnosed himself and learned that his disease was incurable. "Ha, I beg you . . . I beg you urgently to inform her that . . . in spite of everything she is still dear to me. Her room is locked and no one occupies it. And if she wishes to return. . . ." He suddenly interrupted himself. "She didn't go with that worthless man, what's his name? . . . oh, yes, Victor Agrafenovich, devil take it! That would be horrible. . . ."

Arkadyi Hermogenovich playfully raised all nine, long grey hairs of his right eyebrow. Let this important and haughty man suffer for half an hour over the same thing that had lacerated him for half a century!

"My dear friend, a woman's secret is even more sacred than a patient's secret!" Arkadyi Hermogenovich lectured him, touching the drooping, frozen petals of his plants. "That's what Bakunin always said."

This name, uttered by Pokhvisnev at such a moment, put his visitor almost into a frenzy. He looked with a sneer into the old man's self-satisfied face. "Ha, were you really that man's friend?" he asked.

"Oh, I was the last companion of his martyr's life," Arkadyi Hermogenovich answered easily with respectable pride.

"But he died abroad and at that time (I have calculated this carefully) you were only twenty-two years old!"

Pokhvisnev shook his head for a long time. "I beg your pardon, but he died on Basmannaya Street, in my brother's house. You must be confusing him with someone else. *My* Bakunin, Sergey Petrovich, was a teacher of cosmography and natural science. Dudnikov hated this worthy man no less than myself. I recall one memorable day. . . ."

Shaking with silent laughter, Ilya Ignatyich rose, crawled into his fur cave and, like Atlas, put it on. The doors were too narrow for him and under his weight the floor, made for slight people, creaked. The bewildered Arkadyi Hermogenovich followed his guest into the entrance hall. "Today I've made more coffee than one person can drink. Won't you have breakfast with me, dear friend?" Protoklitov was leaving, he was in a hurry: the spectacle of a surgeon beating up a helpless old man would have been disgusting! . . . Arkadyi Hermogenovich returned to Taniechka, invisibly present here. "How good that you're alive! . . ."

For three whole days he remained in this state of marvellous agitation, comparable only to rolling on a high ocean wave. Out of a secret drawer he took an old battered photograph which he had once stolen from the family album in Borschnia. It showed a dark girl standing near a flower table; from under her pleated dress, which was finished with a ruching, narrow lace pantalettes showed. With a bit of bread pap, vinegar and a chip of glass he tried to erase an inscription on the back, which he had made himself so many years before: "For the shores of your distant fatherland you left the foreign land. . . ." Later, somewhat accustomed to his joy, he took up his niece's letter: he had some time to read it to the end! . . . But this time every line of the letter stunned him.

". . . And so we found here an old woman whose age is that of your Taniechka (if she had been alive). The muzhiks around here for some reason call her Arestantovna and maintain that she is indeed the sister of the last owner of the Borschnia estate, who was killed here in 1918. Kurilov and I went to see her. There is no path from the house to her cabin; we had to cut it ourselves. In the woods near her dwelling there are many tree stumps; we trampled on the snow, sat down on one of them and waited. Then Alexei Nikitich nudged me. Something was moving. The old woman was returning from an inspection of her domain. At first sight it was difficult to determine whether she was a man or a woman (doubtless nature needs that difference only in young people). I don't even remember how she was dressed, so strange did she seem to me. On her head there was something furry, wrapped in colored rags. She barely moved her feet, although she held herself fairly straight. A beggar's satchel hung from her neck like a nose-bag from a horse. We kept quiet. Kurilov whispered to me that such longevity is worse than death. Have you ever seen wrinkles that seam a face vertically like fissures in a rock? The past era was moving before us. She did not look at us and crawled through the low door to the cabin. . . . Strunnikov, the director of the sovkhoz, hinted yesterday that the old woman would be moved out of here because the site of her cabin is needed for a new building. . . ."

Liza also reported Strunnikov's story to the effect that two years before several very old men from neighboring villages had led Arestantovna to the edge of the woods to "bow to the earth," to implore it "not to torment her with the fierce torment of life, to accept her and to give her a little place in which to sleep until Judgment Day. . . ." A tall old man, the local soothsayer, who was apparently familiar with mysterious forces, had pushed her lightly on her hump, saying: "Bow to her, the mother . . . bow to her deeply, to the beloved!" And she nodded obediently and gloomily. And perhaps it was spring then, and fragrant flabby catkins were falling from the birches. "This of course shows how strong pagan superstitions still are in certain remote corners of the U.S.S.R. and how difficult is the task of the local schools," Liza added.

Only now did Arkadyi Hermogenovich see Taniechka as she really was. It was as though he had been awakened by the same woman whose name he had repeated as he fell asleep half a century earlier. An impressive-looking owl appeared before him, with a mustache like a sergeant's, and fur protruded from her ears; she had definitely acquired the features of the forest monster whose life she had lived for so many decades. This lovely vision irrupted into his mind, not alone, but accompanied by other unforgettable phantoms: Dudnikov blinked with a dead eye, Spirka walked toward him with his hands tied behind his back, and Blankenhagel swung his stick at him. ("How terrible that you're still alive!") And suddenly an incredible idea completed all this history (which, in passing, should be read with the inner rather than with the physical eye.) Arkadyi Hermogenovich felt chilly inside as though he had swallowed too large a portion of ice cream.

The rest had probably come about all by itself. Out of curiosity Liza went to the cabin to see the Borschnia monster for a second time. They sat down together, and the old woman told the young one about the interesting people of her century, about the burdens of immortality, about her forthcoming eviction into nowhere. . . . But no one can tell what two women really talk about—Taniechka might have mentioned Pokhvisnev, and Liza might have confirmed to her that he was still alive and repeated her name with the same tenderness as of old. Liza might also have blurted out her secret mission for her uncle, and then Taniechka would have become animated, seized Liza's hand and stroked it, stroked it with her own hand rough as a grater, thankful and unable to speak. Perhaps she asked Liza to write his address on a piece of paper; of course, the old woman merely intended to write him a letter as sad as the last handshake of a friend.

But the next morning Director Strunnikov comes to communicate to her the decision of the local authorities. The old Blankenhagel woman is not at home, she has gone for some food. He pastes the paper on the door and two hours later returns. The old woman prepares quickly. She leaves with a bundle of which the contents are ash-grey in color. For the moment her only wish is to get to the nearest ditch. She leaves the boundaries of the estate; a minute-long fright before the unaccustomed expanse makes her dizzy. Then she grows adjusted. . . . Some impulse inexplicable at her age compels her to straighten herself, and now she knows whither to go! She walks on foot over the road along the frozen river where she had so often been driven in a high-wheeled, lacquered carriage with a liveried coachman in front of her. There are no landmarks to guide her, so much has everything changed. But she advances without deviating from the right path, led on by animal instinct. As she goes forward, the January snow that has already grown pink fades around her; she is gone and it is as though a birthmark had vanished from Borschnia. The skies are bluer, and the number of birds in the woods has perceptibly increased.

"Don't come to me, die magnanimously outside my door!" Arkadyi Hermogenovich whispered, mentally tossing in his room. . . .

During the days that followed he locked himself up and sat completely crushed. A boy who lived in the same house brought Arkadyi his dinner from a restaurant. As a reward the old man stroked the boy's head a fixed number of times and after thus petting him put back his cap. All the rest of the time, equipped with a map and a self-made compass, he carefully followed the old woman's route. This was just an exercise in elementary arithmetic. At her age the old woman could not possibly advance more than seven miles a day. Assuming that she had been evicted two days after Liza's letter had been posted, she should now have travelled one-third of the distance from Borschnia. Actually, this calculation was correct only if she followed a straight course, like a witch or a crow; however, her path was blocked by her own weakness, the winter frost and even by police regulations. Thus the date of her arrival was indefinitely postponed. On the other hand, the devilish woman might have hidden certain family jewels, a ruby ring or some relic made of precious metals with which to raise enough money to buy a railroad ticket. If so, she might barge in at any minute.

More and more distinctly he saw details that took his breath away. At this time she is asleep on the hay in an unlocked barn. In her half-open eye shimmers a reflection of the twilight; vapor steams from her furry nostrils. She is alive; ghosts do not freeze! Dawn comes, the winter birds quarrel, Tania walks on further, dragging her skirts along the smooth, shining road. Now her feet lag, now her crutch. . . . She saunters through a bazaar. She is attracted by the hissing of blood-sausage cooking and stretches out her hands to the brazier. Then, escorted by gaping street urchins, she is led to the police station. She smiles, industriously chewing what she has stolen, and remains silent. There is no place in which to lock up such a creature, so, with a shrug of the shoulders, they release her. She crawls on further, seeking the promised hospitality, and every step she takes echoes thunderously in Arkadyi Hermogenovich's heart. . . . Sometimes he awakes in the dark of the night with a foreboding that she is about to push open the door. Unconquerable senile fear paints fantastic pictures of the threatened punishment; for instance, the old woman would come in and beat him up with an umbrella, unless she discovered some more unusual and insulting weapon! . . . He had to concentrate, prepare his defense; he thought and thought, losing his beneficent sleep in all sorts of ruses. As never before Vergil's admonition resounded in his memory:

> . . . *How can you sleep 'midst such events?*
> *Or do you not see the dangers rising around you?*
> *Why do you not flee while you can yet struggle?*

Surely, in the silence of night the creak of her crutch and her low panting cough will suddenly resound. He will open the door even before she has knocked, hushing her in the darkness so as not to waken his neighbors. He will see an unfamiliar being in an ancient cloak sprinkled with round black spangles and, to make her more terrible, an enormous Swiss straw hat crowned with a rotten little bird. He will see an unfamiliar being whom he would know in any crowd by the tormenting and guilty pounding of his heart. . . . "It" will come in, "it" will sit down in the center of the room, filling the place with the piercing cold of the grave. "It" would be silent. Then it would ask quietly: "Do you mind if I weep?"

He will be surprised at the absence of tears and the usual spasms—is this how she cries? However, he will bow to her very punctiliously, urging her to take courage, and will stealthily adjust his lustrine coat suitably for the awesome occasion.

"Don't you recognize me? . . . Have you forgotten me, Arkadyi? . . . Didn't you send for me?"

He would bow again, mute with terror and sticking one hand under the hem of his jacket. Then in her agitation she would speak in a bass voice, incoherently; she would remind him of everything, including the salted mushrooms he had liked so much, gourmet that he was! In her talk there are more punctuation marks than words. Meanwhile he would examine her hands in their tattered gloves, her cheek, her familiar dimple through which the earth can already be seen, her mouth like a ruined pipe organ. . . . (Once it sang in a heavenly voice, now it is just a hole for taking in food!) He will open her bundle and take out her only identification paper, carefully wrapped in a grey kerchief; it is a certificate drawn up by the local soviet concerning her eviction, with a seal and an illegible signature as if traced by a fly that had crawled out of an inkpot. "If I could only live out my last days in peace. . . ."

Arkadyi Hermogenovich would severely shake his head, surprised at such persistence and angry at this protracted, useless conversation. "And what about Dudnikov, Madam?" he would bellow suddenly, no longer fearing that that person too might irrupt into the room with clenched fists. . . . In short, to strengthen his resolution he would remind her of all the insults she had dealt out, even to others than himself. ("And do you remember, my lady, how once upon a time you beat up your coachman with your own hands?") Crushed, he would try to appear offended. In a vile, cocky voice he would say that he was not a Tenants' Association for assigning shelter. And with lowered head Taniechka would close her eyes before this man's insufferable timidity. For the sake of decorum and dignity she would stay a little while, ask about one Anton Feofilaktovich, whether he was still alive or had been killed; then she would rise to go. He would not stop her, although she would take with her all that he had painstakingly hoarded in his soul during those years; perhaps he would only quote aloud this exclamation of Seneca:

> *. . . Oh, this encounter*
> *Fully worthy of one escaped from hell!*

He would remain alone, all sweating, ashamed of his nakedness; the same books that had once been his friends, his companions, almost his accomplices in the great secret, would now become his judges. Impelled by a momentary repentance he would run after his guest, and Taniechka would return. Then would arise the great uproar, caused in the house by his having taken on a new tenant without permission. Even before this, he had suffered from the continuous persecutions of the House Committee and from the hostility of his pharmacists; he foresaw a letter of denunciation from his neighbor, describing the acquaintances of this receiver-of-a-pension, and a threatening resolution underlined in red pencil. The old man would be chased from every place in succession until finally granted the beggars' right to wander hand-in-hand with Taniechka and drink with her the sorrow he deserved.

So that was whom fate had chosen to be his executioner!

# CHAPTER 48

# Gleb Goes into Action

THE DEFEAT AT Sarzan Pass did not end the war in Cheremshansk. Protoklitov seemed willing to accept any conditions in order to obtain harmony. It would have been unfair to accuse him of desiring merely to hush up the whole affair; he even wrote a newspaper article in defense of Sayfullah, in which, quoting Katia Reshotkina almost literally, he reproached his enemies for callousness toward a comrade who had met with misfortune. He adduced dozens of proofs of the young engineer's innocence, admitted his own insufficient concern with the young people's initiative and promised to make up in the immediate future for his past negligence. Reading these solemn words Skuriatnikov poked Peresypkin in the sides, "What vermin! . . . And you say I can't control myself! If I weren't controlling myself, do you know what I'd do to him for this infamy?"

This article, which later became famous as an example of the basest hypocrisy, was correctly appraised at Cheremshansk as an attempt to create a split among the young people. All of them shared the feeling of guilt. And Protoklitov's frantic efforts at reconciliation perhaps united the Young Communists just as firmly as did their efforts to put the Komsomol locomotive on the road again. The first big test of their brotherhood had strengthened it sufficiently to permit them to pass to the attack. A few days before the decisive engagement (the date when Protoklitov was to pass through the party cleansing), Peresypkin went with Katia to Ulgan-Urmansk, where Sayfullah now worked as a mechanic. From their conversation he gathered that their forced separation had only heightened Katia's love for the guilty engineer. Peresypkin saw before him a new person; Sayfullah's grief had given his face an expression of concentrated earnestness and independence. Not a trace remained of the adolescent of yesterday; this young man would scarcely have shown him the letter about Mariam. On this occasion Peresypkin learned that to Sayfullah also Kormilitsin had hinted at some special secret which, if only it were spoken aloud, would make the manager "softer than grass." But it still was unclear whether this was a drunken boast or an echo of some unknown fact.

Naturally enough Kormilitsin now became the hero and center of attention of all the socially conscious elements in Cheremshansk. This man, as Peresypkin remarked at one closed meeting, possessed an invaluable treasure, the security of the state. Acutely regretting the fact that he could not receive any advice from Kurilov, Peresypkin invented a system of secret espionage; Kormilitsin's every gesture and tone of voice were subjected to thorough scrutiny. Whereupon, frightened by this abundance of attentive eyes and ears, the laborer drew into his shell and answered all questions with the same quickly muttered sentence, to the effect that Protoklitov was a good, a very good man. His questioners might have decided to give up the game had not the reticent Kormilitsin abruptly turned to another extreme: he began to invent obvious lies about his friendship with Protoklitov, contradicted himself, became confused and thus reawakened the curiosity of his pursuers.

Gleb carefully followed the course of these attacks, but he did not interfere and never showed that he understood the meaning of this game. Outwardly nothing had changed in his relations with Kormilitsin, but from time to time the hulking fellow caught the yard master's lazy, scrutinizing glance fixed upon him, so that he was compelled to drop his head and interrupt himself. At such moments he experienced the vile repentance of a guilty dog anxiously awaiting chastisement. . . . In the end, Kormilitsin began to avoid Protoklitov. He did not believe in his old friend's studied indifference, but neither did he have the strength to vanish from Cheremshansk. He was conscious with all his being that if he left this place he would immediately fall under the domination of his old ghosts and would set out to kill the woman who still tortured him from a distance. That week he abstained from drinking, displayed greater efficiency in his work and, when off duty, did not show himself in public; perhaps all this constituted his defense against Protoklitov.

Gleb's amazing self-control, which always distinguished him from other gamblers of his type, now seemed to be ebbing away; more and more often he thought of taking strong measures to put an end to the suspicions that surrounded him. But although the chain of incriminating evidence against him was growing longer, good luck as usual accompanied all his undertakings. For example, he found a pretext for visiting the Cheremshansk doctor. They sat down to a glass of vodka, and after an hour or so Protoklitov broached the subject of Kurilov. Out of boredom the host told his guest the gist of his talk with Alexei Nikitich. It seemed that the chief had asked him which one of all the heart-warming liquors he liked best, and the physician had found the courage to answer that he was inclined to all of them in a noble and successive gamut, but that in his heart he preferred plain vodka: "It seizes you faster, holds you for a longer space and, most important of all, does not tickle your throat! . . . He's a charming man. It's really sad to see such a man in that condition, eh-eh!" the doctor barked with genuine regret.

Gleb showed an interest in the last remark, and the doctor, having touched upon the nature of Kurilov's illness, took a burnt match and made a drawing of this hypernephroma on a cigarette box to show his guest what it looked like, how it developed in the kidney and how it knocked a vigorous man off his feet. Protoklitov listened with a licking of his dry lips; everything was developing in the most favorable way, but he could not hurry the sequence of events. That same night, out of motives inexplicable at first sight, Gleb again prepared an extensive and well-phrased declaration to the party, in which with the utmost frankness he confessed one crime: the concealment of his social origin —in order to mask his other and principal crime. He did not date it and did not send it anywhere, but hid it in his basket, just to be on the safe side and to be able to produce a document proving his repentance. Without waiting for the moment when Kurilov's successor would enter the game with fresh forces, he next thought of making Kormilitsin harmless as speedily as he could.

This gloomy man with the eyes of a widower still remained the focus of all conceivable accidents, because he had nothing to lose except his long hair and his hatred for Zoska. There were several possible methods of getting rid of him; the simplest and most satisfactory for Gleb's soul would have been to take him into the woods under some plausible pretext and there carry out his own passionate and inflexible resolution. Wisdom, however, made him ponder over the details of the undertaking with greater care. Its complexity did not frighten him: if he executed it in a subtle way it would be harder to unravel his motives; in addition, Gleb had never forgotten his father's admonition: no matter how many enemies you have, always destroy them one by one!

The extent of Kormilitsin's agitation soon became obvious. Unable to bear his ambiguous position, he made up his mind to have it out with Gleb. One day during lunch hour he broke into the yard master's office without knowing whether he would fall at his feet and implore him to mete out the well-deserved punishment or hit him from behind with a monkey wrench in order to end his own torture at one stroke. . . . He did neither of these things, for they could be seen together through the glass door. He simply burst in, and although their conversation might have been going to last long, Kormilitsin did not sit down.

Stroking the back of the chair he looked dully at the shaven neck of his accomplice and friend of yesterday who was bent over his desk.

Finally Gleb wrenched himself away from his reports. "Oh, it's you?" he said without looking up. "You applied for a suit of working clothes. I have given orders that they be issued to you. You may go."

Temporary unskilled laborers had no right to working clothes; by violating regulations Gleb deliberately challenged the yard bureaucrats and fooled Kormilitsin's vigilance.

"Thanks . . . I have received them!" And he kept gazing at the hollow of Protoklitov's neck with a martyrized expression. "Tell me the truth, are you very angry at me? I don't myself know how the thing happened. I became sober immediately afterwards, but it was too late. I feel ashamed and disgusted with myself. . . . It was a lousy way to repay your kindness. Haven't you anything to say to me?"

"Nothing except that you are keeping me from my work! Be kind enough to say what you have to say briefly!"

"I don't know what's happening to me, Glebushka. You must know that Kurilov was here on his way to Moscow. I couldn't restrain myself from going to have a look at him. . . ."

"You're the limit, Evgenyi. But you must have been drunk. . . . What did you do that for?" asked Gleb, turning violently in his chair.

"I felt an irresistible craving to have a look at the man whom we wanted to destroy that time. I couldn't help it. I wanted to test fate. He might have sensed my thoughts, and everything would have been revealed at once. Clarity! . . . Glebushka, I'd have paid any price for clarity. But I didn't see him and I kept watch near his car for nothing. What is more, a horrible cry cut me to the quick, it came through the double window (or so it seemed to me). Is he very sick—do you know anything about it?"

"It isn't he that's sick, you fool. . . ." Protoklitov suddenly kicked at the door to see whether someone was squatting behind it and eavesdropping on them; he was losing his self-command; he almost lost his breath in the presence of this man. "You're spoiling things, not only for me, Evgenyi."

"Yes, I know. I've even toyed with the idea of poison, but . . . Peresypkin once hinted that any attempt to run away on my part would only arose new suspicions. Does it mean anything, the fact that he is constantly watching me, talking to me? Yesterday he invited me to have a drink with him at Abdurakhman's . . . I refused. Was that right, Glebushka: I didn't tell him anything, I only praised you. Why don't you speak? . . . You're a great man, Glebushka. Tell me what to do!"

With a grey, contorted face Gleb observed him from under lowered eyelids. He had not known that the affair had gone so far. "A drinking bout with Peresypkin, eh? Only that was lacking!" He had to master a fit of almost overpowering nausea before stroking his friend's trembling hand.

"First of all I advise you not to drink," he said distinctly. "Next time I'll have to fire you. All right, get out now!"

The situation required decisive action. While he amicably pushed Kormilitsin out of the door, he had already made up his mind in rough outline. Actually, his plan had been born more than a month before, during an inspection of the yard, as an unaccountable and monstrous fantasy arises suddenly in a weary mind and does not vanish without leaving some trace. Gleb had had to stop near a big locomotive. It had served its time, and the foreman's diagnosis consisted in the enumeration of the usual diseases of an aged engine. The manometer was inaccurate, the pipes were leaky, the steam began to rattle at a pressure of eight atmospheres. The yard master listened absent-mindedly to the chatter of this locomotive surgeon, and his eyes watched the mechanic who was removing the bearings. It was obvious that a thorough overhauling was required in this case, including the dismantling of the boiler jacket. Protoklitov had thought it unfair that this mechanic earned higher wages than the unskilled laborer who would have to work in the narrow and cramped space of the firebox.

This boiler jacket, semi-circular in form, was composed of fire-resistant bricks; its function was both to help regulate the fire and to protect the boiler from the cold air coming from the pipes. Usually, the clay of this arc is baked into a compact, silicate mass of a dullish yellow color; it had to be broken up with a hammer. The job requires particularly sturdy people, capable of spending two hours in a cloud of thick and corrosive silica dust. The laborers were reluctant to do this work. And if, while the task was in progress, the ash-pan and the firebox door were closed simultaneously. . . . At that time he did not think through to the end, and only now did it occur to him that Kormilitsin might be the guinea pig for the experiment. The thorough isolation of an engine such as one of the ESH series precluded every possibility of a cry for help reaching the outside. Soberly appraising the physical condition of his intended victim, Gleb estimated at exactly half an hour the time necessary to finish him off in there.

In these technical calculations Gleb actually started from the other end—as though he were being severely cross-examined by the investigating judge. . . . Yes, Kormilitsin was a newcomer, a drunk; moreover, the competition with the Ulgan-Urmansk shock workers was approaching, and the victim of the "accident" had long looked for an opportunity to earn a bonus. The judge might also suppose that indirect responsibility for this death fell upon the fitter who would have to remove the manometer for checking. To reach this round brass box he would inevitably have to stand on the handle of the fire door after having hermetically locked the firebox. Directly responsible for the accident would be only the foreman of the unskilled laborers' crew and the senior foreman of the engine house—and, even so, only to the extent that they had not together arranged for the whole overhauling job. Kormilitsin's sudden death would unavoidably give rise to an abundance of false interpretations, but any consequences would be less dangerous than if Kormilitsin were opened like a safe with a secret lock. Thus all the unpleasantness involved in the affair would be richly compensated by its result. And with luck, Kormilitsin's respectable death on the job would free him from all suspicion, serve as a silent reproach to his enemies and consequently help Protoklitov too.

In two days the stage was set. The engine suitable for the execution of the plan was discovered in the last shed, to the right of the engine house. The engine placed next to it there for cleaning would serve as an excellent screen for the crime. Protoklitov studied the situation and decided that it would be senseless to await another opportunity as favorable as the present one. The deed would have to be done during the lunch hour in order to avoid witnesses at the moment when the yard master would climb onto the engine. . . . But at noon on January 22 Protoklitov revised his plan. He was overtaken by doubts as he entered his office. Finding himself in danger, Kormilitsin might attract attention by knocking his hammer against the boiler wall. A better way of getting rid of the fool had to be found, and the new variation was born with almost lightning speed, as most great inventions are born if all that is necessary for them has been prepared in advance. . . .

Protoklitov was about to enter his office and had his hand on the doorknob, when the man on duty, in a voice that reached across the whole section, asked the foreman for an unskilled laborer to work at the cleaning pit. The two regular firebox cleaners had not come to work that day, and people like Kormilitsin were always used as reserves when labor was short. Protoklitov heard the foreman call out Kormilitsin's name, and this fact excited him to the point of frenzy, although he did not yet know how he would exploit the trifling event. Very slowly he took some tobacco and began to roll a cigarette; the paper tore, but he kept twisting it in his fingers, rubbing into dust the remaining grains of tobacco. From above, pigeon droppings fell on his back; Gleb jerked and kept waiting for his moment. . . . Three minutes later he saw Kormilitsin's reflection on the glass of the door: he was walking outside with spade and shovel over his shoulders. This was the busiest time in the yard; the workers had just finished their lunch and, as usual at the end of the shift period, they were trying to make their quota.

He went out ten minutes later; by that time the mechanic would, according to his calculation, have handed the engine over to the cleaner, after calling his attention to the fact that the control plugs were in good order and that a given amount of steam was in the manometer. Kormilitsin would have crawled under the engine and begun to work. . . . Gleb entered the shed and looked about him. The engine being cleaned was a shunting engine, a CN with a low ash-pan, constructed in the old-fashioned style, which Gleb now intended to use as the instrument of a murder. This type of iron drayhorse has a small firebox and devours enormous quantities of fuel; so much slag piles up in such engines that the whole cleaning operation would last at least an hour. This moment marked the beginning of Gleb's new plan. The place beside the CN was unoccupied, but the cleaning pit was never empty for long, and it was absolutely certain that within the next hour another engine would be brought there. All the technical conditions favored Protoklitov's design. The engine stood over the pit, its tender turned toward the shed, and the tender itself was on a complete roadbed; as a result, Kormilitsin working under the engine was leaning his back against the wall of the pit. Gleb imagined distinctly how Kormilitsin, covering his face with his mittens and being careful not to burn himself, was furiously digging the redhot melted slag out of the firebox and toward himself.

Then, as though in answer to his wishes, a powerful passenger locomotive moved over the pit; its front buffers stopped only half a yard from the CN. A cold sweat of impatience covered Protoklitov's body when he visualized what would happen if this monster were suddenly shifted forward. He almost saw before him Kormilitsin's pale face, his lips bitten to death and his chest torn by the bolt of the ash-pan. Thus the second half of his decision was taken. . . .

A grey-mustached black-faced man got off the engine cab and timidly saluted the yard master. His locomotive was exceptionally dirty; Protoklitov inquired with a sneer whether it had been lying drunk somewhere in a dung pit. The mechanic recoiled as though scalded; the yard master's tone foreboded no good. Burdened with a numerous family, not very alert, he obeyed the slightest intonations of Protoklitov's voice. And because every man who is at fault usually looks for someone more at fault than himself, he began to complain of the overhauling, of the bad quality of the babbitt washers, of the untidiness of the shaft crew, in fact of everyone who could conceivably share the responsibility.

"Just look, Gleb Ignatyich, look at what's going on! For instance, these things here are shaking like a tongue in a bell. It's like driving to music. . . ." And he shook the bearings with his hand. "Believe it or not, the whole way over we tried to fasten them. . . ."

"That's only because your assistant isn't any better than you are. Do you at least manage to run your wife all by yourself . . . or do you also throw responsibility for her onto your neighbors?" Gleb observed gloomily, sticking his hands into his pockets; he was sure that Kormilitsin under the engine had no mind for eavesdropping!

"Gleb Ignatyich. . . ." the mechanic said imploringly, taking his cap off.

"Your work is bad, too non-partisan, my dear friend. How many years have you been on an engine?"

"At Intercession Day it will be ten years. . . ." He was about to give some additional information about himself, but again Protoklitov stopped him, and it was not clear whether he was joking or meant business.

"All this is an oversight on the part of the administration . . . no wonder we're defeated. You should be a housewife, tending a Primus stove!"

Protoklitov wanted to push him to the extreme limit, to make him lose his head. So he pushed; but it was still not enough, and he could not find the words necessary to blind and paralyze this man's mind. The image of Kormilitsin did not leave him for a moment; it seemed that one more effort of his will would make the wheels turn forward. And the engineer had committed faults before, too: he had refused to subscribe to the government loan, citing his large family; only a month before, after the disaster at Sarzan, his train had stopped during a run. Now he was losing countenance; if he were fired he would forfeit his cozy berth, his little house and garden, a thousand small comforts to which he had become accustomed. The safety pin on his pocket pricked his fingers, but he kept rummaging there and finally shoved into the manager's hands two scraps of paper that certified to his useful activity in the past. . . .

"Put those back," Protoklitov ordered him in a dull voice. "We'll see. . . . Move to the center!"

This necessitated displacing the engine in such a way that the bearings of the piston shaft would be above the center of the crosshead guide. The engineer clambered insanely onto his engine. A second followed, which was entirely saturated with the clank of metal. The buffers of the passenger locomotive energetically struck the shunting engine with a sound resembling the closing of gigantic scissors. Protoklitov straightened out as though at a salvo, and lowered his eyes. . . . Kormilitsin no longer existed. The action of the scissors must have been instantaneous, but he still strained his ears, trying amidst the chaotic rattle to distinguish at least a groan confirming the event. His conversation with the driver ended by itself. Almost without realizing what he was saying, Gleb promised to think over the man's case and turned away. At that moment he perhaps felt a little pity for the big fool who had remained under the locomotive, but this was only a momentary reaction to an excessive nervous shock. In addition, he knew from experience that the role of fools in history is to pay for the deeds of the clever. . . . But a shadow of doubt made him turn around. What he saw forced him to lean against a wall in search of some sort of material support.

No mistake was possible. Behind him stood Kormilitsin, smiling, intact, somehow immaterial, like a hallucination. With a crooked finger he beckoned to Protoklitov to come near; there was a faint hope that even now he did not realize what had happened. Gleb remained motionless; he had not the strength to approach him. Then Kormilitsin himself, staggering like a drunk, as though uncertain whether he was still alive, came toward him. What in the distance had looked like a smile, at close quarters turned out to be a grimace of utter fury. (An accident had saved Kormilitsin. He had dropped one of his mittens and bent to pick it up at the very moment when the iron box of the ash-pan rushed over his head. Through the gap between the wheels he must have recognized Gleb's buckskin boots. . . . It was not for nothing that for the whole past week he had been expecting Protoklitov's hard blow, calculated to the last detail.)

He was all white from ashes, like a miller. Even his goggles pushed up over his cap were covered with a thin layer of ash. He was shaking, and his chin was hanging loose; he seemed about to burst into sobs of anger, frenzy and disgust. . . . His nose itched, his mouth was still full of bitter slag dust. He wanted to weep, but a spasm choked him and he was unable to. He was still unsteady on the earth, this Cheremshansk Lazarus, and kept spitting out a grey saliva that appeared on the snow to be faintly covered with blood. It was absurd to try to defend oneself against him. "Hear me to the end, Evgenyi. . . ."

Kormilitsin interrupted him. "You beast, . . ." he muttered, and chewed his lips. "Now I recognize the real Protoklitov!"

And he ran away, clumsily jumping over snowdrifts and slag piles, falling, hastening, as though he might be overtaken by some burning word, as though Protoklitov had the redoubtable ability to turn even human hatred to his own advantage.

# CHAPTER 49

# The Professor Lectures in Unusual Surroundings

THAT SAME NIGHT Kormilitsin vanished from Cheremshansk. A man in his state might take extremely dangerous steps, and the most logical thing for him was to disclose everything to Kurilov. Of course, he could have made his denunciation in Cheremshansk, but this would have involved his detention until the affair was cleared up and would have prevented him from carrying out his other plans. Kurilov would think of some clever way of repaying his frankness. But although their common guilt before Kurilov was somewhat abstract—they had failed to find him in those early years—Kormilitsin could hardly have forgotten those of Kurilov's companions-in-arms whom they had discovered. . . . Without yet knowing exactly how to prevent Evgenyi from acting, Protoklitov rushed to his pursuit, although he realized that any flight without reasonable justification would under the circumstances immediately outlaw him. . . . He failed to make the train that night, which thus became the worst and most barren of all his nights. By morning he had still not invented anything, beyond a plausible excuse for going to Moscow.

Following one salutary impulse, he examined his basket once again. His revolver was not there. Kormilitsin had stolen it at an opportune moment, and this fact permitted Gleb to hope that the tormented fool would satisfy his jealousy before he vented his rage against his former friend. Of course, the little man-killing machine had to be fired some time . . . and if only Zoska were the first to atone for everything! . . .

When Gleb took the morning train from Cheremshansk his purpose was to have a complete explanation with Kurilov. He intended to admit only to that part of his biography which he had committed to paper in the document that remained at his home. His conversation with the chief would surely be an anguishing dispute about man's right to a new life, about one's alleged responsibility for one's father's crimes and, finally, about whether the proletarian regime was strong enough to include magnanimity among its other lofty qualities. He knew, however, that the first part of his argument did not necessarily involve the second, that no one was entitled to give a man a certificate establishing his second birth except that man himself, that Kurilov would not be impressed by this reasoning, which was more sentimental than rational. Gleb was motivated by despair, and in his mind his capitulation was to be simply a means of achieving a respite in this fierce war. . . .

Naturally Kurilov would smile at him, would take him into his study, offer him good tobacco and observe his enemy's miserable wriggling, from behind a thick curtain of smoke.

"Do you want to destroy me?"

"I want to make you harmless, Protoklitov. The new epoch is only beginning, you are sufficiently literate to know that. It would be a mark of little faith in the creative program of the proletariat to think that it intends to limit itself to the Dnieprostroy or the introduction of compulsory education. We are looking far ahead, and what we see out there, on the Ocean, compels us to be vigilant. That's why we check on everything that can possibly be checked on. . . ."

"You don't trust me. But if I had spent all these years in prison, wouldn't I have acquired the right, if not to your friendship, at least to your indifference?"

And Kurilov would smile at his stratagem.

. . . Gleb telephoned the chief's home from the station to make an appointment. He hoped to determine from Kurilov's tone whether Kormilitsin's fatal confession had been made the day before. . . . An artless and melancholy female voice informed him that Alexei Nikitich had been in the hospital for two days. The woman named the hospital: it was the same one in which Ilya worked. Protoklitov was deeply agitated by this piece of news, and once again was at a loss as to how he should play the new trump card fate had put into his hand. He had enough presence of mind to inquire whether the patient might be visited; Kormilitsin might have asked the very same question. Efrosinia said that the best time for a visit was after the operation, which was to take place within the next few days. She asked who was speaking, and, as Kurilov had done when telephoning Ilya, Gleb gave a fictitious name.

Now his conversation with Kurilov could not come off: Gleb sighed with relief. Although he needed so sorely an accomplice and indeed a direct agent of his wishes, he had always underestimated the importance of Kurilov's sickness as an asset to him. It would be useful to obtain some details about it. . . . Then he recalled his brother. Ilya could give him complete information about Kurilov's fate . . . thus his seemingly futile trip turned out to be worth while.

He rang at the door with the name plate. The cook was out market-ing. Ilya opened it in person. This little success encouraged Gleb. "It's lucky you're home," he said, embracing his brother. "Why are you in your dressing-gown?"

"I've had the grippe, but I intend to go out tomorrow. Come into my wigwam and make yourself at home. Ha, aren't you in a hurry this time? You're always so full of plans and plans. Of course you've come on some business?"

"Not this time . . . I just dropped in to make sure that you were still alive, still cutting up patients and still cheerful."

"Thanks, I'm not used to such kindness. Ha, you shall be rewarded with coffee. I make it myself, and connoisseurs praise it."

Ilya was in a good mood. He looked fresh and serious, his cheek-bones were pink; Gleb even fancied that his brother smelled of the morning river. . . . He now seemed younger than his age. Long-armed, in a flowing, picturesque wrap, his broad and vigorous gait reminded one of a boxer climbing up to the ring with assurance. One could see that he had spent the first half of his life storing up experience, that he was satisfied with it but knew with certainty that he had not yet accomplished the most essential thing. His was the intelligent and mature youth of a scientist. . . . With a boyish gesture Ilya pushed his brother into the study. Gleb remarked jokingly that he would like to give his coffee a solid material basis. He was accustomed to dining early.

Ilya winked slyly at his brother. "You see," he said, "my cook tries to save me money. Ha, I wouldn't be surprised if she chopped the grey paper bag up with the meat it contains. The result tastes some-thing like mortar."

"Why don't you revolt?"

"I bear up with it. Aside from myself, she is perhaps the only per-son in the world who is devoted to my wife." Then he decided he had been indiscreet and frowned. "In brief, I've never had any luck with old women. I have to feed myself extra rations in secret. Do you want some excellent sausage?"

"I want a great deal of excellent sausage!" Gleb warned him, rub-bing his hands. "And how about your wife? I remember that a certain Enoch said: The wife is bound to take care of her husband. . . ."

Ilya grimaced. "Well, she hasn't read the Bible. Open the upper drawer of my desk. There's a package . . . have you found it? Ha, go at it, I'll be back in a minute."

And while the younger brother fell ferociously upon three enormous pieces of meat, the elder went to the kitchen with a coffee pot. One could hear the screech of the coffee-grinder handle and the tinkle of dishes carelessly shoved aside on the range. Ilya had never been known for talent as a cook. His guest looked for other changes in the apartment, but all he could make out was that the older Protoklitov's life was now concentrated in his study. It was as bare as a desert, a real bachelor's cave; fantastic piles of books and magazines played the part of stalagmites. Of course the dirty coffee cups, and in a corner the pile of clothes just delivered from the laundry, might be accidental. But there was an unaccustomed silence in the apartment. Then Gleb realized that a fundamental change had taken place. It seemed that Ilya's enthusiasm for his famous clock collection had cooled.

Outwardly everything was as of old, but not one mechanism was in motion. Some of the clocks, as though ready to be sent away, stood haphazardly on the floor. The pendulums did not tick, the little bells did not ring, the antique dials had a dead and dull look. Unwound stood the elegant French toy clock with a bronze Cupid, created for counting the moments of amorous pleasure; silent also was the black Masonic instrument in a marble frame, destined for marking the years as they approached eternity. Yesterday's favorites were reduced to the role of old furniture, and Gleb marvelled at the sight, thinking how much all this was Ilya!

Soon the surgeon returned and began hurriedly to serve the coffee; a delicately oscillating, oblong reflection of the window swam in the curved black stream. He lifted the coffee pot, and the window was magically lengthened into a thread. The cups were enormous. A thick festive aroma pervaded the room. Ilya's nostrils widened as he inhaled the blissful fragrance. And for some reason the room at once acquired a coziness that favored an amicable and leisurely conversation. Gleb took one swallow and felt hot as from wine.

"You should open a café and become famous!"

"Oh, I have a scientific approach to this concoction. I drink it like water, and . . . ha, I work like a river!" He folded up and shoved himself into the leather cushions of his chair. "You look rather tired . . . but you have the expression of a skier approaching his goal. How's your work . . . does our father's shadow still disturb you?"

Gleb hastened to change the subject. "Oh, that's over and done with. . . . But what's happening to your collection?"

"I'm giving it to a museum. They're coming for it today. All this is no longer mine."

"Fed up? You have some rare items from which I'd hate to part."

"Ha, they're too much trouble . . . you've got to wind them up all the time. Unwound clocks are like a burial vault, don't you think? My fondness for these things became a disease, and we surgeons are a resolute kind of people. If something is diseased, it must be cut out and thrown away. Don't you agree?"

Gleb narrowed his eyes and refrained from asking whether this surgical attitude also extended to one's devotion to a runaway wife.

"Yes ... this passion was too 'non-partisan' for the time we're living in. You're mobilizing at the right moment, Ilya. A feverish period is approaching, but we're still unprepared for it. Strange people, they want trains to go on enthusiasm, while normally they go on coal and hard work well done. Enthusiasm is a too costly and uncertain fuel ... I'd like to save it in hermetically sealed vessels. It might come in handy later. . . ."

Ilya pondered for a while. "What do you propose in its place?"

"What I have in mind is cultural. Material well-being without culture is philistinism, and there's no master key to culture! By the way, you should at least get a starling here, to make a little noise in your desert!"

"Oh, starlings are dirty and quarrelsome. But go on, I'm interested to hear such ideas from you. . . . Culture, you know, cannot be made to order. It can't be manufactured like galoshes or tractors. Just remember how America developed her motley but first-class cadres— courageous flyers, gangsters, speculators in human flesh, great scientists. . . ."

"It's a long story, Ilyusha! We'll have to wait many years before that imponderable and powerful thing is formed, the thing that by some secret sign is transmitted from generation to generation."

"But one must grant that your party has succeeded in setting an enormous, many-peopled monolith into motion, whose kinetic energy is today beyond all calculation. The acceleration of their production is enormous. I think it's a great honor to have been part of it from the very start. . . ."

Gleb laughed clumsily. "If that's the way you feel, be logical," he said coldly. "Put in your application for admission. . . . *They'll* think it over. But I can tell you in advance, they'll think for a long time. And, anyway, they won't let you get any farther than the waiting room. You'll get tired waiting."

"You think badly of your own party. But I'm sure they won't refuse to admit me!"

". . . Why not? . . . How can you prove your loyalty? . . . By your work? But you're paid for it. All this stuff here costs money." He picked up several objects from the table, brandished them and put them back. "These things are very fine, first-rate . . . engravings, furniture. Even when you retire in seclusion you want to make your surroundings attractive. . . ."

Ilya began to stir, his chair creaked. "Eh, better not stick your dirty fingers into me, Gleb. There are teeth in there!"

Gleb was silent; he had to be on guard against blurting out everything. It was not for nothing that old Ignatyi Protoklitov had said that Ilya was to be feared even when he said yes, and he would begin to say yes as soon as he grasped Gleb's secret intentions. "Obviously you're making progress, Ilya!" The last object Gleb happened to pick up was a leather-framed photograph. He glanced at it; it was Ilya's dissolute, unfaithful, but beautiful wife—Liza. The lens had taken her by surprise, so to speak; she had not had time to set her face and was smiling with the naïve interest of a child amazed at the wide expanse of the world.

Apparently Gleb looked for too long a time at the picture of this woman.

"Put it back," said Ilya with a frown.

"Oho, you're jealous of my relative! . . . You know, she has a striking and intelligent face. When are you going to introduce me to her?"

"Please put that thing down," Ilya reiterated, blushing perceptibly.

"Aha, he still loves her, no matter what she does. He still has a youthful tenderness toward her. It isn't hard to preserve one's essential nature in small things, but even in great things he has remained Ilya Protoklitov!" This discovery interested Gleb; he hoarded such discoveries, just as a self-educated inventor collects all kinds of little wheels while waiting to find a use for them. . . . The silence lasted until the point beyond which Ilya would begin to be angry. "You must be very much attached to her," Gleb remarked with pretended envy, replacing the picture. "Does she requite your feelings?"

"Oh, yes!" replied Ilya emphatically.

And having lied, he at once began to fidget with a martyrized expression, reddened like a boy caught doing something forbidden, and his shirt collar grew too tight for him. On top of everything else he upset his cup in order to hide his confusion. His brother indifferently and ruthlessly observed his hand-to-hand combat with himself. "Of course, you can't admit that your wife ran away from you . . . but do you know *with whom?*" And because every advantage he gained could prove useful later on, he resolved upon a piece of insolent frankness that at any other time he would have considered risky.

He slowly walked around the table and familiarly tapped his brother's shoulder. "You haven't forgotten how to blush, Ilyushka? . . . Where is your professional callousness? And I thought that all urologists are cynics because of their trade. They begin their acquaintances with man in his most shameful and most sacred spot."

Ilya struggled, trying to free himself from his brother's strong and somehow humiliating embrace. "Ha, the urologists you know must specialize in the treatment of gonorrhea."

(They continued this facetious struggle in the style of their childish quarrels. But this time it concealed a stark, realistic significance, and the victor was bound to dominate the forthcoming duel; at bottom this was a fight for seniority rights.)

"There's a difference, Gleb, between these two kinds of urologists, a difference that people like you are apparently unable to grasp! The ones you have in mind use a bougie, we use a knife. . . ."

"Oho, you're trying to revenge yourself, you jealous egoist!" Gleb smiled, but he grew pale and released Ilya. "You're showing the old Protoklitov claws. . . ."

Ilya himself thought that his harshness had been excessive (but he was unable now to soften his tone). "One must know everything, comrade. You're not talking with a locomotive!"

Gleb continued casting stealthy glances at Liza's picture. ". . . There's something wrong with your life if even an innocent question embarrasses you so much. Judging by her childlike face, the fault is of course yours, Ilya. Don't family quarrels interfere with your work? And you must have quite a lot of work!"

"Yes, I get very tired." (And he thought that Gleb had easily had the better of him as a child.) "All my colleagues are away just now. The old man came back from Barcelona and collapsed . . . an acute heart attack. And Zemel is about to be transferred to the Ukraine. . . ."

Gleb returned to his chair, finished drinking his coffee and, comfortably stretching his legs, unhurriedly pondered his next move.

"That reminds me . . . do you often come across hypernephroma in your practice?"

Ilya was breathing heavily; he cast a suspicious glance at his brother and did not answer. ("So that's what Gleb's business is today!")

"Tell me, is it a serious disease?"

"And . . . why do you want to know?"

"Oh, I'm all right myself! . . . I intend to live until I get disgusted with living, until I have tasted everything . . . and I have a voracious appetite. I am thinking of a friend, to whom I owe a great deal. I see you don't say anything . . . is it bad?"

"Yes," said Ilya heavily.

". . . And very painful, isn't it?"

"Unfortunately it isn't. So *they* always come to us too late. Does your friend have pains?"

"He is a man of unusual will power . . . but recently I happened to go by his window and I heard him scream through a double door."

Ilya frowned, and now it was a physician who sat opposite Gleb (there even seemed to be a smell of ether in the room).

"It's possible that his tumor is combined with stones. They distend the kidney pelvis and . . . well, I've almost never met a man capable of standing that pain. However, there are sometimes other obstructions that act like a stone. Send him to me one of these days. I'll take him out of turn whenever he comes. . . ."

"I suppose there is no time to lose?"

"The stone might travel from the pelvis into the ureter and . . . unless it is pushed farther . . . there will follow aneuria, uremia . . . and death."

Gleb blinked his eyes, figuring something out in his mind; he fidgeted, as though trying the disease on himself. "Very well then! . . . Sooner or later he'll have to be cut open, is that right?"

"Well, that can't be determined offhand. Why don't you go to a star-gazer?" And Ilya watched his brother, sure that there was some cleverly concealed lie behind all these questions. "I must see, touch. I need much additional data. . . ."

". . . For instance?"

"Ha, I must make sure whether the other kidney functions, whether there are no dysuric phenomena. . . ."

"Oh, tuberculosis is out of the question. No Koch bacilli were found in the urine. Only blood and pains! The last attack was accompanied by vomiting. And although I know this isn't enough for a diagnosis. . . ."

Ilya became animated. "Oh, so you've studied the question! Do you intend to take the bread out of your brother's mouth?"

He certainly had studied the question! It was not for nothing that he had spent a whole evening with the Cheremshansk physician listening to his wife's musical exercises and sharing a bottle with her husband. He had read all the medical books he had found on the half empty shelves of the infirmary. He had memorized the formulas and now wanted to see their application in real life. And the coffee he had just drunk stimulated him to carry on the conversation in a tone of acute and ambiguous frankness.

"This man plays an important part in my life. He is like an enormous planet, and I am his insignificant satellite. For fifteen years I've been turning in his orbit, unable to wrench myself away. . . ."

"Ha, that must be an unpleasant feeling!"

"No . . . to be fair. I have improved, lest I appear unworthy in his eyes. To lose him would be as serious an event for me as to lose you. However, all these are personal matters. . . . But I'll send him to you with a note. His name is, let us say, Postnikov—yes, his name is Postnikov. But tell me, will he live?"

"Some of them survive, . . ." Ilya muttered vaguely.

Gleb's eyes worriedly roamed around the walls; a dull sound broke through his clenched teeth, which Ilya had every reason to interpret as an expression of impotent sympathy for his dying friend.

"Have you some cognac, Ilya? I'd gladly drink with you now. . . ."

"Why are you nervous? . . . Perhaps there's no danger!"

However, he did not have to be asked twice, and he held the bottle with both hands as though warming it.

"Pour me a lot," said the visitor.

"All right." And Ilya poured out a long drink.

Gleb must have become tired from his fright and constant ruses; his usual self-possession was abandoning him. How hard it was for him not to spill some of his brother's precious liquor. In vain did he attempt to give his cry for help a prosaic ring. "You see," he began, "we've been acquainted for a long time, dear brother, but we've become friends only now. I don't believe too much in friendship: a friend is one's first candidate for enmity. And yet nothing strengthens genuine friendship so much as common enemies. So let's have our enemies in common, from now on! You'll help me, won't you?"

"Don't be upset. . . . I'll do anything I can."

Gleb, on his feet, drank his brandy in four big gulps. With a hand pressed to his forehead, he seemed to be listening to himself.

"Take it away, I don't want to drink any more. Now sit down, over here . . . and tell me everything about this disease, from the very beginning!"

Ilya approached him slowly. "Well, take your clothes off, let me examine you."

"Oh, Ilyushka! . . . Just look at me: do I look like a patient?"

The feverish gleam of his eyes, his voice raised to the pitch of hoarseness, the sharpened angularity of his whole body, from his jaws to his clenched fingers—all this, better than words, proved that his brother's suspicion was unfounded. Gleb's mind was clear, too, and every sentence rang in it like a musical phrase. His sight was as though multiplied many times; his reason penetrated the tiniest folds and sinuosities of the world; in every grain of being he divined the marvellous and harmonious proportions of its elements. Only now did he fully understand everything, as though he dominated everything he saw: Ilya, the books, the greyish snow on the window-sill, the old woman who had just closed the door with a rumbling noise, the coming day, the very destiny of the world. His was a magnificent and bestial feeling of physical well-being, strengthened by unfailing success. . . . While Ilya took the coffee pot to the kitchen, Gleb stealthily, like a thief, scrutinized Liza's portrait; and he felt that he had already held her in his arms and been satiated by her, and had cast her away for the sake of a pure, almost mathematical contemplation of the world. . . . Ilya returned, having almost forgotten what his conversation with his brother had been about. Gleb had to ask him again to continue his description of hypernephroma.

He spoke as though giving an ordinary introductory lecture, adapted to an audence of one lay listener. Within the space of an hour he tried to expound a whole branch of his complex clinical experience. Gleb kept bringing him back to his subject, and at one point Ilya in a tone of irritation asked him to keep quiet if he did not want him to heal this Postnikov to death. He began with a general description of tumors, touched briefly upon their structure and development, then dwelt in somewhat greater detail on the methods of diagnosis; this part would be most useful to Gleb. At the same time he avoided technical terms and tried without sacrificing accuracy to give a graphic picture of the process as a result of which a man begins to hate his whole body because of one diseased part. He even showed Gleb a few typical X-ray pictures (the shadows of oxalic stones stood out blacker than the ribs), and the yard master fervently touched them with his fingers, scrutinizing these murderous bits of fog that piled up one on another. He had never listened with so much attention . . . and although Ilya mentioned only in passing the names of the classical pioneers of surgery, he felt almost physically the presence of those fearless and ruthless old men with their sleeves rolled up, as he had always imagined them. With a shudder of aversion he saw fragments of half-dead tissue, lumpy, crumpling up in one's fingers, now yellow like amber and no bigger than a pea (but there are so many of them!), now in the form of heavy, flabby capsules of a burnished but dead color. Worst of all was the fact that although the body resists this unexplained affliction with all its strength, the disease grows, coloring everything around it, the flesh and the mind, bubbling up and spreading to adjacent organs, sending out its putrid poison in all directions and finally causing its host to founder, like a tall tree that in vain clings with its branches to its neighbors in order to avoid crashing.

Once Gleb succeeded in interrupting the lecturer. ". . . But if this

thing spreads even to the blood stream, then in a year or two . . . I
don't set a fixed period . . . it will recur?"

"Judging by your description. . . . Ha, memorize your friend as
well as you can, Gleb!"

Walking back and forth in the room, Ilya continued his lecture. He
spoke of the methods of medical intervention: almost all of them were
surgical. He also spoke of the different methods of cutting out the
affected kidney, of the sequence of the incisions and of the percentage
of mortality with regard to each. And it was now as though Ilya were
working, and Gleb from behind his back were watching the master's
quick and accurate hands. He saw Kurilov lying on his side on a
pillow, the faces of the assistants made impersonal by gauze masks,
and finally, the nimble, almost invisible surgeon's knife cutting through
the abdominal wall from the twelfth rib to the edge of the *rectus
abdominis*. The incision was enormous—the invasion monstrous. It
seemed to Gleb that even with a favorable outcome this could no
longer be the former Kurilov, the great hunter, the seeker after
human happiness, the man-mountain, from the summit of which we
see the future.

Absorbed in his thoughts, he almost ceased hearing Ilya. Only separate sentences slipped into his consciousness. ". . . In twenty seconds
I'll see the kidney . . . the yellow cellular tissue. Then I draw out the
kidney, downward and outward, and my assistant distends the edges
of the wound. I palpate the pulse of the *renal* artery, squeeze it,
bandage it and cut. . . ."

"Wait a minute, you mean you take it in your fingers? . . ."

"Of course. . . . Well?" And he impatiently awaited a question.

"Does it pulsate?"

"What?"

"That *vein* you mentioned!" Gleb reminded him, and broke one
match after another into little pieces; he hurried, prompted his brother,
almost suggested to him how the thing should be done.

"Yes, it pulsates. Now calm down . . . I respect you for caring so
much about someone! But don't be afraid: your friend is in no danger
as long as he is on my table."

"One more question," Gleb asked in a voice that was dead in spite
of himself. "Would you be upset if you knew that the man you operated upon was your enemy?"

"Ha, a bagatelle! You don't know surgeons. . . . Once I even had to
operate on General Yudenich's aunt. I had disliked him since the
time he visited father . . . do you remember how father beat up the
coachman Fedka for some trifling offense? I worshipped that simple

fellow: he knew how to catch lizards, launch kites with little lanterns, make Pan pipes; the old woman was fat, I sweated over her . . . and really she can't complain of what I did for her. A week later she was run over by a trolley car. Ha, I was sorry for her. Some innovations were used in her case for the first time, and I wanted to follow the metastasis. . . ."

He did not finish the lecture until he had completed his imaginary operation. And as soon as Ilya had sewed up the motionless body before him, Gleb was ready to go. Despite his experience in matters of this sort, he felt oppressed, as though he had sat in a dank morgue for an hour; he was as weak as a gambler who has staked everything on his unfailing success. Now he was almost frightened by the ease and rapidity with which the separate little wheels of his mechanism were rolling toward one another. Oh, Ilya would get a good role in this tragic drama! And although they had just drunk to their friendship, in Gleb's eyes any kind of behavior was justified with regard to his brother. So, like all your kinsmen, pay the full price, Ilya, for the right to breathe deeply in this epoch. . . .

In the foyer Ilya touched his brother's shoulder in an embarrassed fashion. "I feel guilty," he began in a grumbling voice, kneading his forefinger, "because I lied to you about my wife. I resent the fact that my lie seems to have been successful this time. You see, Liza's left me. I believed for a long time that good sense would triumph and that she would return. . . ."

"What a queer duck you are; after all you could have left my question unanswered!" said Gleb, laughing—and he thought of how tactless it would be to ask this man to lie deliberately. "Forgive my curiosity, but after all you brought up the subject yourself. . . . Who is your lucky rival?"

"I suspect that she was seduced by a stage manager. Ha, in a velvet coat and leggings . . . can you picture the type?"

"Challenge him to a duel and gloat over your revenge. . . . But, joking aside, I'm sorry for you, brother! You were so attached to her. What happened . . . did she stop loving you?"

"You see, Gleb, no textbook tells us anything about a woman's heart. It's a more ancient and obscure question even than your Postnikov's tumor. Well, run along . . . drop in now and then."

Never before had their separation had this character of warmth and sincerity. It was hard for Ilya to get accustomed to his solitude; after Liza left him, all his former experience as a bachelor proved useless. The door slammed. . . . On the way downstairs Gleb ran into three people carrying boxes and old blankets. They were preceded by a gloomy young man in pince-nez and a soft hat. In a polite but toneless voice he asked where was Professor Protoklitov's apartment. "We have to get a collection of clocks from him," he explained sadly.

"Rub yourself . . . if you don't want to spoil your beauty forever," Gleb said sternly, pointing to the fellow's frost-bitten ear, which was the color of wax, and then stalked by,

# CHAPTER 50

# Guests

Outside the window, in the depths of the hospital courtyard, stood a tree, and beyond it a street lamp. At night the shadows of its branches slid along the walls of Alexei Nikitich's room, on the coarse greyish sheets and on the pages of the book he was reading. When he raised his hand, the shadows swayed over his palm, and when he sat up to rearrange his blanket on his feet, he felt them on his neck. Nothing he read remained in his memory. His eyes unwittingly followed only the play of the shadows, immaterial and somehow swollen in a way that evoked spring. At such moments it seemed to Alexei Nikitich that he had been lying here for a long time. A chain of subtle, intermediate links in his imagination always led him to the identical picture of the kindly Russian spring. . . . Outside the city, four o'clock in the afternoon. The trees have recovered their flexibility of last year. Wind . . . if you hold out your hand, the wind licks it, wet, strong, fervent, like a big dog. A flock of rooks is circling overhead. Like ships in a storm on some oceanic bay they try to cast anchor on a birch tree, but the whole harbor is swaying, and they are unable to detect the mighty breath of the waves and sail with it. . . . Thus every gust outside the window diverted him from his page. It was impossible to read. Moreover, his cot was placed in such a way that the scanty light from the ceiling did not fall on his book.

Kurilov's neighbor moved his book also down onto his knees. He was a provincial inventor, and apparently the authorities had good reasons for sending him to be treated in the capital. Alexei Nikitich never understood the nature of this man's disease; he had some kind of internal growth; much bad abnormal tissue had been cut out, but he had not recovered and once again was awaiting his turn on the operating table. The nurses considered him the most capricious and unmanageable patient in the hospital. No one ever came to visit him.

His book slipped to the floor; he did not pick it up. "How much would a *livre* be in our money?" he asked Kurilov.

"A certain amount of rubles, I don't remember exactly. What are you reading?"

"Oh, some trash. Imagine, Kurilov . . . a silly young thing is married

456

to a divisional general. She is trying to *procure* (vile word, isn't it?) the blue ribbon for him, yet she cohabits with his nephew. Meanwhile the general's sister. . . . No, I can't go on! Can you picture the ignoble snout of this author, Kurilov?"

"Why don't you read something else?"

The inventor began to fidget, hung his hand down and squeezed the leg of his bed. "Eh, I'm fed up with your lives of the saints," he said. "I'm a saint myself. I have ten prizes and an inventor's diploma . . . but I'm dying. I want stories about sinners, about beauties with blue-black curls, about extraordinary things. . . . Do you understand that, Kurilov?"

"Why do you grumble all the time, you queer duck?" asked Kurilov, laughing.

"Eh, you're lucky. . . . You're a *walking* patient! And I . . . do you know what I could have constructed if I'd been as healthy as you?"

It seemed strange to Kurilov that he was still capable of arousing envy in anyone. But this was not much of a comfort; the conversation was unpleasant to him. . . . He rummaged for his radio ear-phones, and his neighbor at once imitated the gesture. It took just as much time to get accustomed to this sonorous chaos as to enter a concert hall, remove one's coat, check it and climb the marble staircase to the auditorium. . . . The first part of the concert had just ended, the second was beginning. The public was noisy, the instruments were being tuned, and from the solemn musical rumble one could imagine the dimensions of the concert hall. Everything was quiet for a moment as though to make the applause that followed more sudden. Probably the visiting conductor had appeared or the skilful pianist whose virtuoso playing the whole orchestra was to enhance. In vain did someone try to outshout the ovation and quiet the audience. The applause subsided only to break out again with new force . . . and a low feminine voice, almost touching the microphone, dully, almost as if chanting, kept repeating the artist's name.

". . . Can you see her, Kurilov? She is very pretty and knows it. She doesn't have to shout to attract attention. And she doesn't know that we are watching her as the old men watched Susanna . . . Look, look how *he* bows to everything—to the people, the chandeliers, the marble pillars. And he is applauded because he is famous, austere, clean-shaven and wears good black tails. . . ."

"And also because wealth is being accumulated in this country, and the people, freed from want and, having learnt to appreciate beauty, are becoming increasingly generous yet exacting toward their artists!" Kurilov thought to himself.

". . . Look how pink he is, how fresh! He has taken a good nap before his appearance, hasn't he? Now he is kneading a handkerchief in his hands and gazing at the woman. Turn away, Kurilov . . . don't embarrass them."

"And he has healthy, intact kidneys. . . ."

But he liked this solemn celebration, because he had an invisible share in the success of the undertaking, and he forgave them for not thinking of Oshkurov and his anonymous victims, not once during this evening. . . . The conductor tapped on his desk, and the woodwinds quietly intoned a melody unfamiliar to Kurilov; his work had always kept him too busy to go to concerts. And because everyone interprets music as best he can, Alexei Nikitich again saw snowy patches on the fields, flocks of sailing crows, and with all his body felt the damp, sweetish cold of ravines in thaw.

The door opened. The nurse admitted Klavdia and Ziamka, who energetically wriggled out of her dry, ruthless hands. No sooner was he freed from his guardian than he approached Kurilov, knitting his brows and looking very solemn. From the frost, or from confusion at being at this unusual place, his cheeks were burning. "It's too early, too early to dream about spring!" All three of them greeted one another in silence. There was only one chair. Klavdia put the boy on it and sat beside him, holding him by the shoulder. Only fifteen minutes were allowed for the visit, and none of them knew how to spend this little eternity.

With her free hand Klavdia adjusted the lace bow on her blouse. "Well, how do you feel here, Aliosha?"

"Not bad, you know. I'm resting . . . only they don't give me much to eat. Suggest to them that they shouldn't be so stingy!"

He sat up, intending to introduce his companion in misfortune to his famous sister and thus give him an opportunity of taking part in the conversation. (Since his imprisonment, Alexei Nikitich had been accustomed to sharing all his belongings with the inmates of his cell.) But the inventor had hidden himself: he had turned his back and pretended to be asleep.

"I received your apples, Klavdia, thanks. . . . No, I'm fine here! Look at the flowers on this partition. From here souls go immediately to register for Paradise. . . ."

He asked her whether she had not come directly from the plenum. No, the plenary session of her organization began the next day at noon. Alexei Nikitich calculated that by then his torment would be over, and he repeated that everything was fine. He got an apple from under his pillow and put it in Ziamka's hand. Klavdia drew back her sleeve and looked at her watch. A minute and a half had passed, one-tenth of their time.

"What do the doctors say?"

"They say that the left kidney is gone, but that the right one can be saved."

"Of course, this operation is the best thing for you, Alexei. Where do you want to go to recuperate?"

The presence of the boy moderated the adults' agitation. Casting alternate glances at both of them, he did not miss a word, and Klavdia with an austere and restrained caress touched his forehead. "Did you want to say anything, Izmail?"

"No, I just, . . ." Ziamka stammered, remembering all sorts of things he had been told not to do.

"Never mind, say it . . . if it's sensible."

"Nothing thpecial. . . . Our *dvornik* got married. It's funny! . . . and our yard hasn't been cleaned. The milithiaman came to fine him . . . and tho he got married!" Ziamka finished up, choking with laughter.

Kurilov shook his head, casting a significant glance at Klavdia. "You see, sister, how bad it is to marry at the wrong time. And why don't you eat the apple, parachutist?"

"I lost an apple in a bet with Shanka. Now I can pay him."

"I have many apples, tormentor. . . . Did you pick him up at his home?" he asked his sister.

No, Marina had brought him. She was waiting downstairs; the physician on duty refused to admit a third person, and Klavdia thought it better not to insist. (Even she had had to obtain permission for the visit in violation of the regulations and through the prestige of her name.)

"Well, shall I tell you a story, Izmail? All right . . . a friend of mine, an author, made up the beginning of it, but I made up the end. Shall I tell you about the elephant?"

Ziamka had bitten off a piece of his apple and, holding it in his cheek, maintained an alert silence. From his eyes it was clear that he would be interested to hear about the elephant at any time. And Kurilov began without hurrying: ". . . Once upon a time a wandering German was travelling in Asia with a menagerie. He travelled past Tibet, through mountains and white deserts. . . ."

"And did he also go where the Chinese Red Army is?" Ziamka asked suddenly.

"A little bit to one side of it, . . ." said Alexei Nikitich, again exchanging a glance with his sister. "He showed his animals: pay a nickel and come in! He had a tent, something like a circus. The spec-

tators were given folded chairs. Then the German would come out—
*guten Tag, guten Tag!*—and the program began. He made the tigers
bow to the audience, put a boa constrictor around his neck and then
tied him in a knot so that he could not crawl away during the intermission. . . . And a dog, dear Ziamka, did such tricks that it was often
taken for a monkey. But the people who live there are poor, they are
plundered by foreigners. All of them tried very hard to tear a picture
off the wagon as a souvenir! A wagon is a big box on wheels, it creaks
a lot. . . . The German's business went very badly. Sometimes he would
go to the biggest cage and eat a jelly sandwich with a cup of tea; and
the animals looked so sad because he had only one sandwich. He
would have released them to get their food by themselves, but he was
afraid of the police. And then he was sorry for his elephant. The name
of this beast was Ali; he was white, intelligent, with a black spot on
his forehead. Do you find this story interesting, Ziamka?"

"Go on, go on!" Ziamka nodded with a tense and sympathetic face.

". . . But then his wife came in, she had been selling tickets at the
window. 'Everything's sold,' she said. 'Begin!' He put down his cup
and rang the third bell at once. But when he came out he was amazed:
there was no audience, only one fellow in a checked suit and a bowler
hat sitting there, fanning himself with all the tickets to keep cool. The
German shrugged his shoulders: '*Guten Tag*, shall I begin?' The fellow
answered: '*Guten Tag*, begin at once with the second part, only don't
hurry your elephant!' The wife turned a barrel organ, counting up in
her mind how much food they had left. . . . Then came the number
with the elephant. He was pretty starved, and when he came out to
show his tricks, the German supported him with his shoulder, just to
be on the safe side. At the end the fellow said: 'Seeing your success,
I want to try my luck, too. I'll buy your elephant!' The circus owner
resisted: 'How can you think of such a thing! An elephant like this one
. . . to a stranger!' But he had only one choice left: to feed the rest of
the menagerie with the price of his elephant, until they got to China
or. . . . He struggled against the thought, but finally gave in. And together with his wife he watched the stranger leading the elephant
away on a string in the direction of the unknown mountains. . . ."

Klavdia again looked at her watch. This was the ninth minute. They
had not discussed the most important things, and precious time was
being wasted on trifles. But she had not the courage to interrupt her
brother's fantasy now. Alexei Nikitich looked slyly at his sister. Her
shoulders had grown sharper, her left eyebrow was sorrowfully raised
in a high arc. He suddenly understood why she had not clipped her
hair when she was young. She was very old now—yellow bones pushed

through her temples; her hair was growing perceptibly sparse, and it took great skill to make it suffice for any kind of hair-do. He stretched out his hand and stealthily, without Ziamka's being aware of it, patted his sister's knees. She jerked, became confused, rose and went to the window.

". . . And about two hundred miles to the south there was a ridiculous kingdom. The people paid taxes and worked for foreigners, too; they starved and lived in a disgraceful fashion. When all the other tricks for deceiving them failed, the priests made up a legend. They said that a saviour would come in the shape of a white elephant with a spot on his forehead and then everyone would be well fed for a hundred years. A legend is just a fancy lie, you know! Do you understand now why that scoundrel in a bowler hat had come to the circus? . . . Well, the elephant was unloaded from the freight car. They put a big box on him, and on the box there was a label with inscriptions: Careful . . . Don't turn upside down . . . Don't drop. (They did this, because they did not want the people to know that the elephant had come in a train.) The box with elephant feet went through the streets and bazaars. He reached his destination, the boards were removed from him, he was fed, and he, the god, began to realize that he had got himself into a pretty pickle. But elephants, Ziamka, rarely weep. . . . Soon there was a holiday, a lot of people came from the villages. They burned colored fires, the priests danced till their shoes wore out, awaiting the appearance of the god. They took him out of the darkness into the light, they led him by golden cords . . . but he disliked the whole business. And when drums began to beat and long trumpets sounded, the god got scared. He broke his reins and rushed headlong, crushing everything in his path. Yes, Ziamka, with his tusks! . . . Then he was driven into a big barn and for a long time they shot at him with arrows. Soon the god looked like a folded tarpaulin dirigible when it is inflated with gas. . . ."

"Aliosha, we have only four minutes left!" Klavdia said in a hopeless voice, without turning away from the window.

"I hear you, Klasha." He saw out of the corner of his eye how she was fidgeting, but his story was the only way of avoiding the pitiful words of farewell. He went on, watching Ziamka's frowning face: " . . Then a telegram was sent to the mechanic. '*Guten Tag?*'—'*Guten Tag!*' Can you fix up this thing?'—'I can . . . do you want it to talk or only to move? If you want it to talk, it's twenty per cent more.'—'No, we only want it to move. God has nothing to say.'—The mechanic worked for two months. He removed the elephant's insides with a shovel, stretched out his skin on supports, put in a mechanism, regulated it and fixed the belly so that it could open with a zipper—you know, like the one your mother has on her galoshes! If anything goes wrong in the mechanism, zip, the belly is opened, it can be fixed! . . . The next year when the holiday came again the elephant travelled as though nothing had happened. He waggled his trunk, his ears flopped, his eyes blinked. He was very well balanced, thicker and even more beautiful than before. His skin was oiled, so it would not crack in the heat, and was painted to cover up the patches. Unfortunately the wheels creaked—this was an oversight on the part of the mechanic. Thus the dark-peopled kingdom set up a new god. That's all, Ziamka. . . . Did you want to tell me anything special, Klasha?"

"No . . . but we must go now, Aliosha!"

"Well, that's fine. Give my regards to Marina! . . . I'll tell you the other half of the story later, Ziamka. I'll have time to think over what happened to the elephant. . . ."

The eighteenth minute was ending. A nurse appeared in the doorway. Very erect and calm, Klavdia kissed her brother on the forehead. Ziamka was silent; his eyes were red and he was frowning. Alexei Nikitich called his sister back from the doorway and asked her to give Ziamka the toy locomotive that was on his desk at home.

"Thank him, Izmail," said Klavdia in a low and solemn voice.

Still knitting his brows, Ziamka returned to the bed. "And what will you have then?"

"I don't need such things! . . . I'm big, too old for toys."

"Perhaps you'll recover, . . ." said the boy, austerely hopeful, and suddenly he drew his head into his shoulders, and his whole face became wrinkled, as though he were a little old man.

Quite agitated, Alexei Nikitich reached out for him, but Klavdia dragged him by his hand as if he were a frisky little dog.

A minute later Kurilov again picked up his earphones. The concert was still going on, and for a whole half hour he persuaded himself that he was listening to it. A sudden thought made him sit up: he had completely forgotten about Luka. He distinctly imagined the scene of handing over his gift. Klavdia would come in with Ziamka while Luka was rolling that marvellous locomotive along the floor. Ziamka's eyes would begin to shine, but he would remain silent. His sister would bend down for the toy, but Luka would cling to it, refusing to give it up. "It's bad to be so set on ownership, boy!" Klavdia would say harshly, forgetting about Luka's deafness. "You've had it a long while, now give it to someone else. . . ." And Ziamka would undoubtedly say: "Never mind, I'll wait . . . you finish playing!"—and would turn away. It was too late for Kurilov to stop this obvious injustice.

Once again he pictured Ziamka in his imagination. Of course he would not be given that toy to play with, he might break it, and it was too precious for a street urchin. It would be placed on a chest of drawers, on a lace doily, amidst paper tulips and beside the photograph of Aunt Anfisa's late husband. Ziamka's guests, boys from the same poor street, would examine this too generous and incomprehensible gift with respectful seriousness. And the most unhappy among them would be Ziamka . . . (then perhaps, in his unsatisfied desire to handle the locomotive, his childish friendship with Alexei Nikitich would dissolve without a trace).

Suddenly the inventor turned in his bed. "But you're not a bit of an atheist, Kurilov," he said with an unpleasant laugh. "I'm referring to your elephant. Atheism means ignoring God. But you negate him, fight against him, disrespectfully take the universe away from him. . . . I'm not speaking of myself. I'm dying and am enraged at everything that might be responsible for the vile thing that has been done to me. Therefore, I'm ready to recognize everything that might cure me or become an object of my hatred. But you! . . . After all, one can't be angry at something that is not! Am I right?"

Kurilov remained silent for a while. "Next time she comes you must make my sister's acquaintance. Try to expound your philosophy to her . . . she simply adores such discussions!" This man who clung to his shadow on earth seemed pitiful to him.

# CHAPTER 51

# A Denunciation to the Wrong Authorities

JUST THEN A SCANDAL TOOK PLACE in the vestibule of the hospital. An orderly had gone out to get a newspaper for the physician on duty. Upon his return he found near the first-aid room a tall, dishevelled citizen, so dirty that the hospital attendant's soul, conditioned by five years of scrubbing and sterilizing, was horrified. Refusing to answer any questions, the stranger tried to enter the nearest ward, and an impressive display of strength was required to force him downstairs. Then he tried to break into the clinical laboratory, and the attendant, fearing for the safety of the test tubes, called for help. The physician on duty found this brawler, whose hands were covered with unwashable soot, in an almost hysterical state; finally they sat him on a chair, and two tall attendants held him by the shoulders. Their white smocks bore the marks of hand-to-hand fighting. In view of the extraordinary demands made by this man, the altercation was reported to the senior surgeon.

It was by sheer accident that Protoklitov happened to be at the hospital. He had dropped in to visit one of his women patients, a young worker who had fallen under a circular saw four days before. Its edge had cut her from the neck almost to the bridge of the nose and uncovered the cerebral cortex, and Protoklitov, who liked to defeat death when it had almost succeeded in extinguishing the eyes of its victim, could be justly proud of his work. Sitting beside her bed, his elbows on his knees, and face to face with her, he alternately looked at the girl's shaven head where one could divine a long purple seam through the bandages, and at her lifeless eyes; now it was the faintly colored strip on the gauze, now the barely perceptible blinking of her eyelashes that indicated the return of consciousness. He spoke her name and waited patiently for her to smile. Her smile was now only a mechanical movement of some facial muscle; it expressed neither pain nor joy, nor even the awareness of her misfortune. But the primitive clay in the myths of the creation of man must have smiled just like that, when, as it changed color and acquired flexibility, it felt for the first time the warmth of the sun's rays.

The same smile was reflected much more broadly and earthily in the master's face. "Ha, don't forget to invite me to your wedding, my girl. . . ." He spoke caressingly and insinuatingly, as one speaks to a child one wishes to awaken from sleep. He did not turn to the physician who had come up behind him, until the girl's trembling eyelashes had closed. "We know little about man's potentialities. Look, a piece of iron sawed through this girl's head . . . and she smiles. . . . I find that pleasant. Now, what's on your mind?"

The physician related the incident in the vestibule for the second time, this time more emphatically. No, the man who had broken in was hardly drunk, despite his incoherent speech; he seemed exhausted by sleeplessness and threatened to complain to the authorities if he were not given a hearing. Protoklitov asked to have him brought to his office. Five minutes later, having given the necessary instructions concerning his patients, he went there. He walked along the corridor, humming some march and experiencing the satisfaction of the creator certain of his power. . . . The attendants respectfully took their places at the entrance to his office. The visitor sat slouching in a chair. He had been dressed in a white hospital uniform. Poor Don Quixote's soul would have looked like him if it had been blackened for a week in the central flue of hell. The man was tall and unkempt; under his short, worn-out trousers one could see his cheap socks which had fallen down. Upon seeing Protoklitov, he jumped up in a melodramatic manner, pushing the chair aside. Apparently he intended to make an official declaration. His pinpoint pupils were disagreeably piercing. From the very first moment Protoklitov felt a physical aversion to him.

Without offering him a seat, the surgeon inquired who he was and what he wanted.

"Take your policemen away!" the man said, gesticulating abruptly as though in a fit. "This hospital not only treats sick people, but also breaks the bones of healthy ones!"

"Very well," said Protoklitov and he made a sign to the men to go. "Calm yourself, they won't come back."

"I've got to see Kurilov. He is lying here somewhere. I refuse all your objections in advance!" And he smiled imperiously. "Lead me to him."

This was impossible. Visitors were no longer admitted to see patients. No one could penetrate to Kurilov's room now, even if it were to communicate to him a joy capable of healing. Their interview would have to be postponed (the doctor calculated the probable period of recovery) for at least two weeks. Then the visitor displayed extreme excitement; he shouted that he had urgent business with the railroad chief, a piece of "dynamite," that he was about to leave for a long trip to a distant place and that no one had the right to delay him; he ran around in circles and loops, twice mentioned a certain Zoska (and when he spoke her name he picked up everything that was on the desk before him, in order to test its weight or sharpness); he was in a hurry; his hatred never died down or lost its force. Ilya found his convulsions unbearable. He remarked: "If your news is so important, you can tell it to me. I shall give your message to the sick comrade as soon as possible. If you wish, sit down and write him a note, but . . . ha, let's be brief!"

"Eh, your appearance doesn't inspire any confidence in me!"

Protoklitov lowered hs eyes, changed a thick pencil from one groove to another, and again cast a calm glance at the visitor. "I am an official, and we are speaking in my office."

The visitor meditated, kneaded his unshaven chin with his fingers, jerked as though he were being bitten by insects everywhere, and all the time kept looking at the physician's white cuffs with solid links in them. Finally he seemed to have made up his mind to tell this stranger his secret, when suddenly he pushed back the table, which he had gripped again. "No! . . ." And with a tormented expression he rubbed his temples, trying to remember something. "I'd still prefer to see Kurilov himself. Enough! . . . You have aristocratic hands . . . and I don't like the way you stick yourself forward as a mediator."

Toying with a colored pencil, Protoklitov said that he did not claim any rights to someone else's secret, but that he refused to agitate his patient on the eve of an operation; in addition, that he was too tired himself to waste time on nonsense. This ruse proved ineffective, and in disgust he asked his visitor to come in another time when he was in a more balanced and trusting state. The visitor seemed about to leave, but at once changed his mind as though discounting his possible early return; he quieted down, again burst into a contagious nervous trembling, looked for his cap and, having found it, plucked hairs out of it in confusion—on one side the fur was completely gone. They had a few more exchanges, in which the visitor's excited distrust alternated with a minute-long, hesitant consent, and his flabby submissiveness with a stubborn, even defiant refusal to say a single word. "I don't know what it is . . . but I have the feeling that he is spying on me through you!" he whispered almost inaudibly. . . . Suddenly the thick pencil broke in Protoklitov's fingers with a dry crackle, and this outward sign of real fury convinced the visitor better than all his arguments.

"You're angry . . . that man is never angry. No, I'm mistaken." He uneasily picked up the fragments of the pencil from the floor; he seemed to be struck by the fact that the two halves were of different colors. Then, without looking, he moved the chair under him. "Very well then, you're responsible for everything . . . or else, you understand what can happen to you? Well, my name is Kormilitsin. Maybe you'd better take it down? Kurilov should know this: on his railroad a scoundrel is hiding. He has the job of yard master at the station of. . . ." He suddenly jumped up, and the chair rolled from under him. "Aha, you're frowning? . . . Do you guess whom I am going to betray to you?"

"You're really an insufferable person!" Protoklitov said quietly, and although not all yard masters were his brothers, he felt his ears beginning to burn.

"He has many victims on his conscience. (By the way, he once said that conscience is only lack of habit!) I don't know whether it's ten or a hundred . . . I met him later. He always did everything efficiently. And he is not after easy fame . . . that's why he's survived. But ghosts wouldn't dare to visit a man of his kind. . . . Oh, he'd have shot them a second time! In brief, he is *indifferent*. Now let me see what you've written. . . ."

And he had enough assurance to reach out for the sheet of paper with Protoklitov's rapid notes, made to calm his visitor rather than with any other purpose, but Ilya Ignatyich pushed the hand away and leaned across the table with a furious air. However, the mention of the yard contained a remote allusion to Gleb, whom Ilya had always suspected of something underhanded and dirty (the sharp lid of the inkpot pressed into his palm); he lowered his eyes and no longer felt that he had the right to throw out this decaying creature.

"I suppose abuse isn't indispensable for *our* document," he remarked judiciously. "We'll let Kurilov evaluate this case!"

A pause followed, during which their eyes met; Protoklitov's long practice as a physician helped him to endure the suspicious, wandering look of the maniac.

"It's . . . it's good that you don't shout at me. You mustn't. You're only the paper on which I'm writing my last note . . . get it? I am betraying a man whom I once loved. I was his armor-bearer and his shadow. I repeated religiously his words about Russia, the Slavs and immortality. Why do you laugh . . . have you forgotten? It's funny now, but then those ideas fired guns!"

"Ha, stop talking about immortality," Protoklitov said impatiently (he almost added that for his visitor the only form of immortality was to be a dummy in some saloon near a graveyard). "We've piled up enough for an introduction. Kurilov will certainly want to know whether there are witnesses . . . of what I believe was your common activity."

"I myself!"

"Ha, that's not enough! Judging by your state of mind you have reasons, not only for telling the truth, but also for lying! . . . And what is in question is a human life, isn't that so?"

Kormilitsin was bewildered; the denunciation on which he was spending all of himself might pass in this place as a delirious fiction. Now it was Protoklitov's turn not to believe what he heard.

". . . But you must understand that in this case no witnesses are any longer alive!" Kormilitsin defended himself in an insinuating nasal voice and grimaced a smile. "Otherwise they would have come with me, he-he. They'd have found this place rather cramped . . . if they all tried to get in!"

"The facts!" cried Protoklitov.

Kormilitsin shuddered; now he was submissive, as though this imperious and stern man were holding him with his fist. A minute passed, during which Kormilitsin rummaged in his memory for the most convincing proofs. Then followed an impetuous enumeration of provinces and cities through which the hero of his tale had passed. Yes, Kormilitsin could point out the place where, one on top of the other, were buried the same Gerasimov and Farafontov in whose honor villages had even been renamed. Yes, together they had looked for Kurilov on the Kama, and if their search had been successful this conversation would never have taken place!

"Oh, of course, of course," Kormilitsin confirmed feverishly. "That's what I want . . . all of us want it," he cried excitedly, spreading his hands toward the dark empty corners of the office. "Let the dead have some fun!"

Protoklitov's hand unhurriedly grasped the telephone receiver, but his visitor was beside him in two jumps; pressing the lever with the whole weight of his body, he pulled the cord out of the plug.

"What . . . what do you intend to do?" Torpid stupefaction flowed from his now completely dimmed pupils.

"You came to the wrong address with this information. I wanted to correct a mistake."

". . . You mustn't!" Kormilitsin whispered, both threateningly and imploringly.

"Ha, you're a coward!" Protoklitov said with disgust.

"No . . . but I still have some business to settle."

Protoklitov attentively studied him with the eyes of a physician. It was clear that this failure was responsible equally with the man whose head he had by stealth dragged to Kurilov. His time for rampaging and consuming himself was short too; aside from his hatred, which had already evaporated, certain other poisonous fumes filled this skin bag. Protoklitov removed his hand from the receiver. "Have you no other information to communicate to Kurilov?"

". . . Perhaps some details about this scoundrel?"

"Well . . . did he do the killing himself?" (This question was a personal one.)

Kormilitsin shrivelled up. "I don't think that is indispensable, . . ." he snapped back.

For another ten minutes he continued listing episodes incoherently and without any regard for chronological order. When the explanation was over, Kormilitsin sat leaning with his back against the enamelled door to the cupboard, completely exhausted, as though everything had flowed out of him. "How white everything is here," he muttered, looking at his hands; he seemed to be coming to. . . . Ilya Ignatyich rose behind his desk. "In your confusion, ha . . . you have forgotten to mention the man's name."

From his childhood he had felt disgust at any kind of tale-bearing. And even though there had been no indication that his brother was involved here, because of his physical and constantly growing hostility to this hysterical organism, Ilya felt a previously unfamiliar consanguine warmth toward Gleb, as a courageous man who had uncomplainingly earned his right to live and to have his errors forgotten. Nothing changed his expression when his brother's name was uttered aloud. Very slowly he folded the sheet of paper half covered with writing.

"I guarantee that Kurilov . . . one way or another . . . will receive this information. . . . For my part"—and here the Protoklitov teeth gleamed in a smile—"I must inform you that my name is also Protoklitov. . . ."

Kormilitsin remained seated, but his unshaven jaw dropped somewhere to the side. Clinging to the back of his chair he stared at his go-between and recognized what was concealed under his white cloak. So that was why he had unconsciously resisted him! . . . Oh, he might have thrown his denunciation into a garbage can with the same results. The promise that it would be conveyed to Kurilov now sounded almost a mockery. It seemed to him that he was losing his mind. . . . A hundred-handed Gleb aiming at him with guns was following him everywhere. The door might open, and not one, but seven Protoklitovs, flexible, clever, and noiseless as though made of rubber, would surround him, after the last of them had turned the key in the lock. In a daze he stared at the door, which actually did move. (This was an ordinary occurrence: when a door was slammed downstairs the air rushed upwards and other doors moved. . . .) Stepping backward and without listening to what was being said to him, he began to retreat from the office. He tore open the door, one could hear impetuous footsteps rushing down the stairs, and again a faint gust of fresh air rushed into Protoklitov's face. He went out into the corridor, stood for a while, smoothed a corner of the strip of carpet that his visitor had rumpled in his flight, and then went home.

All his plans for the evening were automatically cancelled. . . . He turned on all the lights in his apartment, as though this would give his mind greater clarity. He was confused, and hated Kormilitsin for having thrown into his lap this vile "gutter" secret. His friendly feeling for Gleb was disintegrating into fragments of pity and dubious sympathy, in which condemnation began to emerge. And next to him, so cautious, never caught, large as life, arose the obscure Farafontov, a courageous sailor or Red Guard. . . . (The older Protoklitov had seen a good deal of these anonymous apostles of socialism crisscrossed with machine-gun cartridge belts, who irrupted like lions into the dark history of mankind.) This comparison did not result in his brother's favor. . . . And after an hour of idle walking back and forth, just as he realized with relief that Gleb's fate was passing by without grazing him and as he was ready to content himself with the role of a spectator and stranger in this dubious affair, he caught sight of a note from Gleb that had been brought to his home while he was out. Unfamiliar with his brother's handwriting, Ilya Ignatyich recognized the author only after he had read it. Gleb had forgotten to sign it; apparently he had been in a hurry. The envelope contained two hundred rubles in payment of his old debt. In facetious, slippery words Gleb thanked his brother for this old favor and promised to send the rest in a few days.

From the very beginning Ilya had disliked the light, buffoonish style of the note. At any other time it would not have occurred to him that all this tomfoolery was introduced for the sake of the last ten lines. He read them over and over until he knew them by heart: . . . "You were wrong to suspect the theatrical Adolf of seducing your lovely and fickle wife. I've happened to learn accidentally that she was taken on a trip by a certain Kurilov. He has a job at our railroad . . . I've met him. He is a soldier of the period of the military committees, who was suddenly endowed with great power: coarse, self-willed, a lover of drink . . . all this with a Shakespearian nuance, but can you imagine Shakespeare on the Russian model? There are rumors about him . . . an incurable disease . . . in the kidneys, and as a urologist you'll understand his belated hunt for pleasure. At present it appears they're living together at Borschnia. . . ."

And now Ilya Ignatyich began to recognize his brother's features in the portrait sketched by Kormilitsin. "Yes, this man never misses!" And even details intensified through the megaphone of the civil war, and for that reason seemingly invented, could now no longer be doubted. Ilya Ignatyich had time to be amazed at his brother's adroitness. In order to be able to aim without missing he had penetrated the subtleties of a science that was alien to him and hinted that Kurilov's intensified erotic activity might be a consequence of his intoxication by the secretions of the affected kidneys—what is known in medicine as a *local tonus*. More than that, from distant Cheremshansk, Gleb had found out exactly who was going to operate on his enemy; all he wanted was that Ilya slightly remember Liza while digging around in Kurilov. He used Ilya's indestructible, almost morbid attachment for this defenseless actress as a control relay through which from a distance he could direct another man's hand armed with a knife. The device was calculated to arouse and satisfy the coarsest, lowest instincts, and this constituted its motive force. Thus, what the old and infamous Ignatyi, their father, had not been able to do, Gleb now bequeathed to the surgeon's reliable hands.

Ilya Ignatyich tried to imagine Kurilov as he had been at the examination. But there was nothing memorable in their conversation; that time Alexei Nikitich had had no mind for talking. Having folded the crumpled sheet of paper, which had aged in his hands, in two and then in four, Ilya Ignatyich went to the telephone. But halfway there he changed his mind. And what made him change it was not at all the fact that it was late and that the colleague who might have replaced him was doubtless already in bed.

CHAPTER 52

# The Operating Table

IT APPEARS THAT Kurilov's neighbor was still asleep when someone came in and said that it was time to start.

Alexei Nikitich put aside the newspaper he was reading. That day it was full of the most wonderful reports he had ever seen. He rose from his cot and cast a worried glance around him to see whether he had not forgotten anything, but not one of his accustomed objects would be needed *there*. He went with an oppressive feeling of empti- ness, and was much more agitated than he had been when Oshkurov, just for the fun of it, had led him out of his cell over and over again, assuring him each time that he was going to be shot. However, after only a few steps down the hospital corridor his agitation yielded to normal human confusion. The tall, grey-mustached man dressed only in his underwear was walking along on the arm of a very pretty nurse. Kurilov was tormented by the suspicion that mocking glances were following them. . . . But it was an ordinary day; the convalescents were playing checkers or learning how to walk again. Something was led by in a little truck. This something was alive, it was covered with sheets, and its condition was such that to fix it was tantamount to adding a new man to one remaining healthy finger.

"It's fine, all this is fine, . . ." Alexei Nikitich said shudderingly, in an almost chanting voice.

He did not notice the distance to the sterilizing room, and there, too, he failed to notice anything except the walls covered with glazed tiles —on their varnished surface moved distorted and seemingly striped reflections of people. Only the perfectly commonplace window im- pressed his mind and remained solidly fixed in it. Having decided that it was the last one before the darkness he had to enter now, he looked attentively at it and the cool (fi-i-rst rate!) day outside.

This was a typical error, explainable by the depressed condition of the patient. For the operating room had three huge windows into the world. In the blue enamel frame of the middle one, stood a little tree covered with a thin snowy down. The old plaster on the hospital walls across from it had a faded vernal color. These deceiving colors of spring, timid and as though slightly surprised, greenish and pale yellow, passed through the clean panes and were distributed in the tiniest doses to the phials and bowls, the brass plugs and marvellous pieces of apparatus of whose existence one learns only at the very last moment. . . . There was also enough color for the legs of the high operating table, with the wide dome of the operating lamp above it, the marble wash-basin and the white smocks of the doctors and nurses. There were six of these. Alexei Nikitich did not succeed in counting them all at once, but subconsciously he was glad there were so many of them. . . . Their presence had a calming effect upon him. The same nurse as before, it seemed to him, gave him water to rinse his mouth. He went through this procedure with a feeling of respectful amazement, and thanked her with embarrassment. Apparently everything was ready, they were waiting only for the sign to begin. Three persons at three wash-basins washed their hands with identical motions. Then the tallest of them, who stood at the extreme right, asked without turning around why the patient was not yet on the table. Alexei Nikitich was led to it.

"You're treating me like a bishop, . . ." he tried to joke.

"Lie down, lie down!" the nurse whispered quickly and sternly.

He climbed up from the stool and felt bored to be sitting so high. He was again told to lie down, and someone began to tie his hands to something cold. He looked at the multitude of scattering prisms in the cone of the lamp and thought tenderly of that lover of all technology, Ziamka.

He waited in vain to see this magic device lit up. Everything went very fast. A mat aluminum globe with a rubber ring was placed over him; it lay tightly around his lips, pressing down his mustache. "Aha, this is put on one's face. A fi-irst-rate thing, . . ." thought Alexei Nikitich in the words of Arsentyich, whom he never forgot in his life. Without waiting to be told, he energetically inhaled the cold sweetness of the anaesthetic, coughed and began to pull at his straps. It seemed to him that he had to remember something of the utmost importance, but his mind stopped functioning, his chest curved high, his body grew long and narrow. Then, completely disembodied, it slipped downward with a merry ringing into the moving spheres of the unknown.

. . . I learned later than everyone else that Kurilov was to be operated upon by Protoklitov. On that day Klavdia Nikitichna asked me to accompany her to the hospital; the request had the form of a military order, as always with this woman. We arrived in time. I left her downstairs with Marina and went up to see a young doctor whom I knew. One of Protoklitov's disciples and an old friend of mine, who secretly dabbled in literature, he had long since promised me to show me this rising star at work. A month before he had obtained Ilya Ignatyich's consent to my visit, having ascribed to me an irresistible desire to write an article on the occasion of the hospital's centenary. I donned a gown and entered the operating room to find Protoklitov with his mask on standing in his place at the table. The patient lay on his side on a pillow, in the position required for kidney operations. His whole body was covered with sheets, except for the field of operation. Kurilov's skin, reddened by the frequent use of hot water bottles, had a marble hue; out of ignorance I ascribed this to the effect of the lamp. Eight people watched the iodine growing blue and dry. I heard the clang of metal against glass. At the same moment the knife swung, and Kurilov's body opened from the right inguinal region to the hardly perceptible birthmark on his back.

I was still waiting for the gleam of the scalpel, but instead I saw at once the spongy layer of subcutaneous tissue and the pulsating, severed muscles. They contracted, retreating to the edges of the enormous ellipsoid wound. There in the violet depth stirred and breathed organs that I could not identify; they had looked different in the books I had read the day before. I had an approximate idea of the operational procedure, but I found it strange that Alexei Nikitich did not cry out. . . . And only two days before, this now subdued man had asked me with a somewhat embarrassed air what was a caravel, and I had hurriedly told him about the one-decker ships of Columbus' time, realizing that even now his thoughts were on the Ocean. The other Kurilov was closer to me and more understandable, but this one was more truthful and convincing. In vain did the good Sergei Petrovich whisper some general information about the peritoneum and the gigantic dimensions of the tumor. I automatically freed myself from his hand that held me by the elbow and stepped aside.

"The chyle!" said one of the assistants at that moment.

An unbearably red little fountain bubbled up from the depths of the wound, and the opening was at once flooded with blood. Apparently the metallic clamp had slipped off the largest kidney artery. A lively stream ran down among the yellow protruding vertebrae. Immediately many fingers rushed into the wound; there were perhaps thirty of them, and the little fountain was one, but for two whole minutes it twisted among them with the flexibility of a worm. . . . Then again Protoklitov's slow and imperious hands entered my field of vision. I tried to look at the reddish hair on his arm so as not to see this silent struggle. He caught the base of the vessel and, squeezing it with his finger, uttered a word that I had encountered only in books of prosody. This time, that two-faced word' signified an instrument for arresting a hemorrhage: *Péan's forceps.*

I do not know how much time I spent there. The complex odor of the operating room almost poisoned me, but this was because I examined the physical body of my hero for too long a time and at excessively close quarters. I went toward the exit, and my fairly new shoes creaked indecently in the dry and somehow sterilized silence. I did not succeed in finding out whether it is true that all surgeons use obscene language during operations. No one noticed my departure, but Sergei Petrovich followed me. He caught up with me in the corridor and with his usual politeness asked me my impressions.

"I'm really sorry I have to go," I answered rudely, averting my eyes (but of course it had been an even greater breach of professional tact to visit Alexei Nikitich at that hour).

. . . A stooping old woman sat alone near the door, like a petitioner. Clouds of cold coming from the outer door surrounded her each time someone went by. (Marina had gone out to walk in the courtyard; it seems that she was more nervous than anyone else. Indeed, Klavdia sent me out twice to bring her in to get warm.) I was met by the old woman's inquisitive, worried eyes. I repeated Sergei Petrovich's words that everything was going well, and I must have sounded sufficiently convincing. Her hand gratefully squeezed mine, as though it depended upon me whether Kurilov would recover. I told her this. She smiled with bewilderment and stroked her grey temples with her fingers.

"Have you a cigarette?" she asked harshly, so as not to betray her confusion.

I gave her one, together with some matches. The flame swayed in her fingers, as though seven people were blowing on it. Because she puffed at it too often it became charred and did not burn. This was the second cigarette of her life. (The stub of the first, which she had apparently obtained from a nurse, was lying under her chair.) Klavdia Nikitichna demanded details, and with the air of a schoolboy I reported on outward and secondary matters because the others had escaped my attention.

Then, squinting from the smoke and shaking the non-existent ashes off her cigarette every minute, she asked me: "Have you been Alexei's friend for a long time?"

"Two years."

"That is not enough to know him well."

"But I knew him before we met."

I meant to say that I had had several occasions to observe Kurilov's characteristics in his companions-in-arms. She understood me differently: "Yes . . . he is only a rank-and-file worker in our party, and that is good!"

Klavdia Nikitichna had never before talked so much. She was nearly unembarrassed by Marina's and my presence, and for the space of half an hour I had a full opportunity to observe the austere human interior of this old woman. All her life she had probably followed her brother's career from a distance. We learned a number of episodes, told with stenographic dryness, which we had not known before. In Marina's face I read the regret that her brief and incomplete work about Alexei Nikitich had already been published. (Alexei Nikitich was always reticent when his positive deeds were in question. I had also only a very vague knowledge of his relations with the younger Protoklitov; later Peresypkin helped me to find my way among some of the details. But at that moment I vividly evoked Gleb, whose portrait had begun to form in my mind earlier. Now he enters his engine house and looks at the clock: a quarter past ten! So it's a whole hour that Ilya has been "working" on his enemy. And sadly smiling, he lowers his eyes.)

After Sergei Petrovich came down to tell the three of us that Kurilov had been taken back to his room, Klavdia Nikitichna hastened to the plenum. The meeting was to begin twenty-five minutes later. Marina said goodbye and went to her office. Klavdia Nikitichna suggested that I accompany her. "You're a writer, and it's good for you to see everything!" she reminded me with icy clarity.

We went off together. The hall was full. At the entrance people unknown to me surrounded her. She dropped out of sight, but a few minutes later I saw her on the platform. She was sorting her notes, patiently bearing up with the applause that greeted her; this applause lasted for a longer time than usual and seemed to include some sympathy on account of her misfortune, which was already known. One had to have something very close to courage to begin with the same phrase that all her contemporaries—great and small, honest and dishonest, blind and clear-sighted—overworked in every one of their speeches; yet on her lips this phrase sounded like the guiding formula of the century: "Comrades, we are called to work in a joyous and beautiful time. . . ."

Her silhouette, straining forward, expressed an inflexible will to soar to the heavens. The calm hardness of her dispassionate marble face was striking. Never had I known that the late and clear-sighted youth of old people could be so beautiful.

# CHAPTER 53

# An Actor's Overcoat

BEFORE LEAVING CHEREMSHANSK, Liza received an incoherent letter from her uncle. He spoke of matters inaccessible to people of her age —of irretrievable errors of the heart, of the sorrowful clarity of disappointment and finally of the dream that kills its creator. Something had happened to the old man during Liza's absence. In the course of the four pages, teeming with Latin quotations, corrections and marginal additions, Arkadyi Hermogenovich in his agitation twice called his niece Taniechka; he wrote that he had no significance in the contemporary world and was powerless to do anything useful; he enumerated the troubles that her unprepared arrival would bring in its train, troubles all the more intolerable because they pertained to the fundamental material basis of existence! Finally, he asked her to refrain from any impulsive moves, to be expected in her situation. Had he imagined that Liza would read these pages to all the inhabitants of Borschnia, until the letter reached the real addressee? . . . Liza interpreted this letter as Arkadyi Hermogenovich's opposition to her return to her room in Moscow.

But the letter was not all in one tone; it expressed a long and complicated process. The initial confusion was followed by open rebellion, both of which were resolved in the subsequent reconciliation. From the beginning of the third page the lines were much more even. Arkadyi Hermogenovich confessed that he had not enough courage to taste the dream that had been preserved in the depths of the grave for half a century. Then Arkadyi Hermogenovich capitulated. His cry for mercy was suddenly replaced by a lyrical summons to come at once. "And if not much has remained at the bottom of the cup that many had taken to their lips, let us at least taste together the poisonous bitterness of the dregs!" This sentence definitely convinced Liza that the old man had gone stark mad. . . . Otherwise, taking the old man's metaphors as referring to herself, she interpreted them as her uncle's consent to her returning to what was her own.

The most important thing in this whole chaotic epistle was a passing reference to a visit from Pakhomov. Of course, Arkadyi Hermogenovich told him about Liza's expected arrival, and Pakhomov had

promised to drop in again, but did not explain what he had come for.
. . . Liza's first guess was a timid hope that her company wanted her
back. Had she not been too hasty in her promise to Shamin? . . . She
blushed from shame and annoyance with herself, yet she was unable
to resist her imperious and unrealizable illusions. In her mind she returned to that gloomy den of art; respectable and conceited old women
kissed her; the new young people of the company sought her friendship. . . . But their cordiality would find little response. The former
Liza, the madcap giggler, so quick to join in every joke, was no longer
alive. . . . In fact she went to Moscow with the firm intention of refusing Pakhomov's offer, and she did not wish to see Alexei Nikitich
before winning the first victory over herself. His steady, knowing eyes
would have asked her what was new with her, and she was now fed up
with the role of a guilty and repentant little girl.

Her personal business was settled in two days; a week and a half
later her unwritten agreement with Shamin would begin to operate,
and Pakhomov still did not show himself. She lived on vague hopes
that something would inevitably happen, but nothing did happen, except small clashes with her uncle. He became bustling and restless
and made enough trouble for a dozen old men. He created the impression that several bats were constantly piercing the narrow space of the
room. He kept running away somewhere and upon his return he filled
the apartment with the noise of his incomprehensible exclamations,
sighs and regrets. Having decided not to throw out Taniechka when
she arrived, he took a concomitant decision, which, in his opinion, was
absolutely necessary: he would renounce his pension. . . . And he
dragged himself to all kinds of offices in search of a man who would
listen to his motives for this renunciation. At first his written declarations—sufficiently foggy to cover his heart wounds—were a source of
entertainment to the office girls. The case was simply incredible in the
annals of the People's Commissariat for Social Insurance. Then Arkadyi
Hermogenovich decided to approach the higher rungs of the official
ladder. The directors shrugged their shoulders; they simply tried to
avoid the old man. One of them, who wore a military tunic, went so
far as to compare him to a break-through tank designed to operate in
the most heavily fortified enemy zone. . . . In brief, within the shortest
possible time Arkadyi Hermogenovich managed to make himself a
nuisance to the whole department.

He worked out tactics all his own for his campaign. He caught the
director he wanted at the door of his office and tried to explain his
business in one salvo, while the official walked along the corridor with
a worried and busy air. "I want to be honest, you understand?"

Arkadyi Hermogenovich kept repeating while advancing upon him from the side.

"But it would be easier for you simply not to cash your pension checks!" the official would remark with irritation. "Furthermore, I'm in a hurry. . . ."

But no, the old man considered it desirable to have an official understanding about this matter! "Give me only half an hour of your time . . . I understand that I happen to be living not in my own century, and this is like . . ."

"But can't you see . . . but can't you see . . . oh, the devil take it!" the official would say in a reproachful bass.

The narrow door slammed before the old man's nose and, sitting on the bench reserved for the messenger girl, he listened attentively to the crackling paper behind the door and the snapping buckle of the belt. . . . These sorties took all his time. He definitely abandoned his pharmacists. His books began to vanish from the shelves. What once served as food for his reason, now went in lumps to feed his body. He sold them. As he separated from his books, it was as though he were undressing himself. His much-praised politeness vanished, and now the plumber's wife no longer dared be noisy behind his door! Traits of unsociability, querulousness and sometimes even superstitiousness, which had never existed before, began to appear in his character.

"You're losing your last traces of charm, uncle!" Liza once blurted out, and she thought with fear that this respectable old man would chew her up entirely before Pakhomov came to visit her.

. . . But this visit was bound to take place. Finally he came—very polite and even a little sad; he was dressed shabbily, in black, and looked somewhat languid. Seconds in duels must have been like that, and inviters to funerals will be like that until the end of time. Liza was packing her belongings into her suitcase, preparing to leave for Cheremshansk.

"I'm listening, go ahead, . . ." she said, without interrupting her work.

Her dresses were all packed. Now came the turn of her shoes. Frowning, Liza took up one of them. In its heel gleamed a little brass wheel tarnished and rubbed from walking. Its steel pin had penetrated into the leather, and her attempt to tear it out with her fingernail proved futile. Then she tried with a knife, but it slipped and scratched her finger.

"I don't know what you will think of my proposal, and I won't be surprised if you refuse," Pakhomov began solemnly.

"Oh, I'm very much interested to hear it."

She carried on the conversation and all the time kept wondering how this little thing had got into the shoe. Suddenly she saw before her Protoklitov's Caron clock, smashed the night of her break with him, and the mechanism scattered on the floor. . . . She also recalled her unstable and flaunting wealth at that time, and the ambiguous respect it had won her from her theatrical friends. Thus she was strengthened in her intention of refusing Pakhomov's proposal.

"I've come to you to speak about Ksaveryi."

Now everything was different. Surely they had not once remembered her in the theatre! . . . Liza impatiently shrugged her shoulders. What did that restless old man want of her? After all, she was not a sepulchre for cinerary urns with the ashes of her past life! . . . Or wasn't he yet satisfied? . . . Had he any claims? . . . Did he seek revenge? The fact that Pakhomov referred to Ksaveryi by his first name, intimately, seemed insulting to her. She remarked, sucking her scratched finger: "All right! . . . How is he?"

Oh, Zakurdaev's days were long and full of deep experience. He was alive, was undergoing energetic medical treatment, and more than that, he needed a winter coat very badly. "Oh, no, this is not a collection campaign! Zakurdaev would refuse any charity!" But his friends had decided to organize a benefit performance for him. True, there was no anniversary to celebrate, but one might truly consider that his theatrical career had begun at the moment he graduated from dramatic school or even at the moment when in his childish soul there awoke an inclination for the boards. In brief, the occasion for the performance was a minor matter! What was more important was that the biggest actors in the capital had promised to take part in the performance. Some of them had even agreed to play the leading parts. The varied and attractive cast assured the financial success of the enterprise—Pakhomov knew how to influence Liza.

He proceeded to describe the aim of this undertaking. The overcoat they wished to buy Zakurdaev was to be padded, the top material was to be Russian cheviot and there was to be an inexpensive but decent-looking fur collar. The old man was freezing in his jacket. Quite recently one end of his *bashlyk* [1] had fallen under the wheel of a trolley car, but Providence had been satisfied with the loss of its gilded tassel. What would remain of the proceeds was to be given to Zakurdaev's landlady, who would feed him hot meals as long as the money lasted.

"You knew Ksaveryi . . . and we'd like you to play in this!"

She fancied it was some trap. Her name would hardly serve as an

[1] Caucasian hood.

adornment for a striking poster! . . . And would not Zakurdaev resent her very presence? She said so.

"Quite the contrary, he gave me to understand that he wanted to play his last performance with his friends. He remembers you all too intensely. . . . But I don't dare betray other people's secrets. We have chosen Ostrovsky's *It's a Family Affair—We'll Settle it Ourselves!* I am sure that with two rehearsals you can master the part of Lipochka!" This time Pakhomov's tone was almost friendly.

Liza had grown thin, subdued and somehow matured in these years that pretended to be only months. Her poor old dress finally reconciled him to her. He preserved his former conviction that only grief gives a person real humanness, and was satisfied that to the measure of his strength he had secretly, behind the scenes, worked on this girl. And having obtained Liza's consent, he hurriedly and boorishly tried to finish his cigarette, so as not to waste it for nothing.

". . . But what's going on in the theatre, Pakhomov?"

Everything was going on as before, although the idea of staging *Mary Stuart* had been abandoned upon the insistence of the Artistic Council. There was talk of moving to a new building. Victor Adolfovich had the part of a priest in a film and had had his head tonsured. The toilets upstairs had been repaired, they did not leak any more. Vasiliev had been ill with the grippe for two weeks and now as a result of complications was, in his own words, "a cripple." Pakhomov soon became insipid, left his address on a piece of paper, a cigarette stub on the window-sill, a notebook with the part, and departed. . . . Liza rushed to the bookshelves. Ostrovsky had not been sold yet, although he was already tied up—he was to be the next to go. She undid the package and found the play. A shrewd merchant's daughter threw out her father after having pocketed his money. It went without saying that the actor whose jubilee was being celebrated would play the part of the deceived father. Liza thought with distress of his thunderous lamentations, calculated to shake inveterate and deaf scoundrels. The choice of the play had hardly been dictated by any aggressive intention with regard to Liza: this would have been too much of an honor; anyhow she found no similarity between herself and Lipochka, or between Ksaveryi and the merchant Bolshov.

The play was not even rehearsed once; the prominent actors participating in the performance thought it beneath their dignity to waste time on exercises for the sake of a cheviot overcoat. Even Liza was not asked to do more than read her part twice to Pakhomov; in the hope of finding some employment, he was trying his talents as a stage manager for the first time. He praised Liza and pointed out her mistakes with fatherly gentleness; what made him so compassionate was Liza's hands, red and swollen from laundering, an occupation she had been engaged in all morning. And, of course, only he could succeed in making those sharp thin shoulders shake with genuine grief. . . . By right of age and his aroused sympathy he again addressed her in a familiar tone: "Eh, Liza . . . try to make yourself unhappy at any cost. A great poet once cut the chest of his hero and put in a piece of live coal in the place of the heart." He laughed bitterly, as realistic thinkers possessing the absolute truth must laugh at the unrealizable fantasies of dreamers. "Unfortunately this angelic surgery is punishable according to our earthly Soviet laws!"

"It seems to me that youth is a defect so easily remedied that. . . ."

He did not listen to her; people do not appreciate the favors done them! "I would throw you into an ice hole, and when your heart grows numb. . . ."

Liza felt bored. "You know, everyone has known such ice holes," she said politely.

Pakhomov became angry. "You don't understand me! What I have in mind is a comprehensive disaster . . . when the artist enters it completely, as in a Gothic cathedral, he loses himself amidst the columns supporting the stony sky. A new music lacerates his hearing, the coldness of the ancient walls penetrates his soul; and one must grow up a great deal, my dear, to contemplate the green meadows through the high vaulted windows." Apparently he was still torn by visions—visions of the unfortunate Rachel or of Asenkova, of the beautiful Adrienne poisoned and thrown out of her grave because of her love, or of the more modern Isadora Duncan whom fate strangled with her own scarf, after having robbed her of her children and her lover. In his eyes all of them were blood-sisters of his own Ellen, and on an impulse of real generosity he was ready to introduce Liza into their tragic family. "Yes, I, a miserable provincial comedian, envy your future, your purification . . . even your future disappointments!"

All this was unnatural, expressed in tasteless and inflated phrases, not without the shedding of tears, and, most distressing of all, demanded immediate refutation from Liza: the hearts of teachers feed on gratitude. Pakhomov was forgetting that nothing had come of Pakhomov, no matter how much life had thrown him into its miriest places. But Liza's own meditations on the same subject agitated her . . .

The following night, when Arkadyi Hermogenovich came to sit on her bed, she was not asleep.

"It seems to me I heard you crying, Liza?"

"No . . . but you've been heating the place so during the last few days!"

"Spring is coming; this is the most dangerous period for people like me. Nature looks over everything living, to find out who is ready for melting and reforging. . . . Look how everything is in a hurry! (And for whose sake, for whose sake?)" He passed his hand over the thick green growth of his window-boxes. "I've become so involved in my troubles that I haven't had time to question you properly. You've been in Borschnia. . . . Well, what do the groves say now when they rustle?"

"But it's winter, uncle, everything is covered with snow."

He was dumfounded: winter! . . . He, who had gone to Borschnia only during the summer vacations, had thought Borschnia was the land of unfading summer! "But you've seen a woman whom I thought dead," he said apprehensively. "You've resurrected her for me. Tell me about her!"

Liza sat up. "Why is it decent to speak of this old woman only at night, when one cannot see the expression in the other person's eyes?" With a sleepy tongue she repeated the contents of her letter. He listened greedily; he had not enough to disturb him. Those who are hungry imagine that all the granaries in the world would not be enough to satisfy them.

"You talked to her, didn't you?"

"I was scared. She's frightening. If you saw her . . . one could plant a tree in her. . . . She's earth!"

"Don't hurry, I want to see the whole picture!"

"I mean that she has acquired the color and quality of crumbly ploughed earth. She shows all her visitors a chair covered with a Gobelins tapestry . . . and stains, bad glossy stains on the cloth. It seems that her relative . . . the last Borschnia landlord, was killed in it."

"Was that her brother? . . . Was his name Edmond Orestovich?"

Liza did not know whither the old man's questions were leading. "No, uncle. Why didn't you ask me that right away? The old woman's name is Daria Andreevna. . . ."

The robbed must feel like this. . . . Arkadyi Hermogenovich's hand withered and hung lifeless. He staggered to the glass wall that gave on the small garden; he wiped his forehead after having cooled his hands against the glass; he tried to compare certain events scattered haphazardly in his memory. The past grew clearer, and the image of the saucy two-headed Darienka emerged. She was a distant relative of the Blankenhagels, employed as a companion for their daughter; she was in charge of various things in the house . . . and, he recalled, she watched the peasant girls who picked up refuse in the park. Now, she pricked her bare foot, and returned limping along the alley streaked with tree shadows; laughing, oblique stripes of midday sun fell upon her. . . .

The image in the old man's memory was so sharp that he could even distinguish a colored chicken feather on the sunlit terrace, lightly swayed by the breeze. . . . So all his fears of the recent weeks had been in vain. After having wandered in familiar places, the phantom again lay down under its mossy slab. "Ugh, how you scared me, Darienka!" So it was she who had grown into bitter and loathsome deformity, but Taniechka had never withered! (More than that, now he knew with certainty that none the less *she* was moving toward him. And he no longer had to fear that she would throw herself around his neck as a pile of musty earth from a grave. . . .)

More and more distinctly he saw Taniechka's shining face before him—very unlike her former face, because now he too was reflected in it. A warrior maiden, she advanced to extinguish the lump of living clay that was called Arkadyi Hermogenovich. . . . A sharp cold breeze blew from under her eyelashes. Everything around him was now understandable, completely transparent; a plain multiplication table would suffice to comprehend all the secrets of the universe.

# CHAPTER 54

# The Clown

THE DARK, DRY MOSCOW WINTER held on firmly. The snow was carted off as soon as it fell, and poisonous winter dust whirled continually along the streets. But one day the long-awaited crisis in nature broke. . . . At midnight a wind began to blow. The day that followed was feverish; now some snow would fall, now the day was bright, the people waiting at the trolley-car stops grew more sociable and trusting; some of them, secretly expecting a miracle, looked up. . . . And a glazier walked on the illuminated side of the street, he walked and kept winking at everyone, this light-haired little fellow who knew something special. Suddenly a reflected patch of light from his shoulder darted along the plaster of the houses in the shadows, a restless, frisky, merry little patch that everyone could consider a remote signal for the offensive of spring.

Zakurdaev's friends were unable to find a theatre for their jubilee performance. They had to content themselves with a hall in a recently built club. It was a long distance for Liza to walk, and in addition the play opened with a monologue by Lipochka delivered while she tried on various new dresses. Liza went to the place early. Everything went well, as long as the patch of light on the walls led her; then the glazier turned into a yard, looking for broken window-panes. Immediately everything grew dark, a wintry cloud crept over the street. The wind began to tear along, signs rattled, and at that moment in the gateway of a big hotel Liza saw the old man with a basket. Shivering with cold he was waiting for buyers. Gusts of hard, grainy snow lashed his frozen wares. Marionettes—a whole circus collection of them was in his basket! They were brothers, all made from the same piece of material. Two watchmen even looked out of the artisan's pocket, no doubt to warn him when a militiaman was approaching: the old man was a *chastnik*, a private merchant. From a distance Liza thought he was selling flowers.

She stopped. The old man held them all out to her so that she could choose. Liza hesitatingly took one. Her choice represented a clown. It was a graphic piece of propaganda for turning every piece of junk into something useful. Through his stuffed chest one could feel two

485

unpolished little boards. Tiny rings had been sewn to the legs and arms with a hurried needle: they still bore letters from the tin cans out of which they had been cut. A little bell was on the cap, but the maker had forgotten to put in a clapper: it did not rattle. And although the marionette's head was of clay, its expression was so lively and joyful that one could not help being touched by it. Suddenly Liza thought that if she had had her child he could have enjoyed this artless little object. Her regret for her unsuccessful motherhood was rather furtive, but, more important, Kurilov now occupied Protoklitov's place in her mind. . . . Then she remembered that she herself had never, never had any toys. The low price and elegant braided black jacket of the marionette seduced Liza. Let it hang for some time over her poor cot in Cheremshansk, as a symbol of her bad, unskilful art!

To set the toy going it was necessary to do exactly what Pakhomov advised: to press lightly on the spot where the heart is. Then little tin wheels rattled and the silent frozen wood danced.

". . . Does it have a voice?" Liza asked, disappointed.

The old man knew what a consumer's doubts meant at such a moment. "But that's only because of the cold, miss. Otherwise, all of them sing. When he warms up he'll begin to make so much noise—you won't be able to stop him!"

Liza liked the way he spoke of the marionette—as of a living being. The merchant had no wrapping paper, so Liza stuck her purchase in her pocket. And true enough, he began to squeak there, and when the check-room attendant put Liza's fur coat on a peg, the marionette seemed to utter a whole coherent sentence. He was indignant that he, an actor, should be left in the lobby. . . .

The blaring poster for Zakurdaev's benefit proved justified. The success was tremendous. Benefit performances of the old days, which were remembered in small towns like earthquakes, came to mind. A large audience had gathered, and all the members turned out to know one another, all of them spoke loudly; and the curtain went up an hour later than scheduled. The hero was greeted with an ovation; everyone felt flattered at taking some part in the fate of an insignificant stranger. Moreover, these fastidious spectators liked the sharp, deliberate provincialism of the show. But Zakurdaev took all this seriously, grew sentimental, and from the second act on bowed with the airs of a matinee idol. . . . Originally an introductory skit about Zakurdaev's forty years on the stage had been planned, but he had no social merits, in fact some things were discovered in his life that were rather the opposite of merits, and even Pakhomov could not bring himself to praise him for his creative achievements. Moreover, the purpose of the

whole affair had been fulfilled. The new overcoat hung very decora-
tively on a nail in Zakurdaev's small dressing room. During intermissions an endless file of guests went there, not so much to shake
Zakurdaev's sweaty hand as to have the pleasure of examining the
quality of the much-praised collar and, incidentally, to smoke their
fill. For some unknown reason the smoking room had been put somewhere in the basement, in a room pierced by a great number of heating pipes covered with clay.

These intermissions, long to the point of absurdity, were doubtless
the most important part of the celebration. The table in the center of
the foyer was adorned with a somewhat burnt cabbage pie, a pot of
hydrangeas with the flower crown somehow askew, and a harmless-
looking decanter. The more distinguished guests, the stars and the
main attractions of the performance, sat on chairs. They wore their
make-up just as when they had left the stage. Boyishly sentimental
like all old actors, who become soft or angry with equal ease, they
were glad to help a colleague in need, but now strove to preserve a
decent distance between him and themselves; carried away by his
own cordial feelings, Zakurdaev called them simply Vasil, Ivan or
Nikolai—and even that was too much! . . . The others milled around at
random, and among them, terrifically busy, deafeningly noisy, with
his unpasted beard in his hand, moved Ksaveryi himself. He had had
time to drink a good deal. He offered vodka immediately to every new
guest, without of course forgetting himself. It was obvious that by the
end of the show he would be completely tipsy.

"A little glass, my precious one!" he shouted enthusiastically; everyone shook his head in reproachful surprise at the phenomenal volume
of his voice. "Well, well . . . ugh, it's gone down!"

"Eat something, eat something with it, you clown!" prompted Pakhomov, who did not leave him for a second.

But the old man repulsed every attempt at guidance by violence or
tutelage. He was enjoying his own celebration. He thirsted for attention, public love, favorable criticism, as though his fame were being
born only now. He did everything to clinch his success. He appeared
simultaneously in four places to say a warm word to someone important, smackingly kissed imprudent visitors, gave drinks to theatrical
workers, praised their children, shook hands by the dozen, questioned
everyone about his impressions, although he could not hear their answers—and publicly, in every intimate detail, related the tricks he had
put over with Pakhomov thirty years ago on a tour to Voronezh. He
was already hated for his excessive vitality and for his former decep-
tive appearance of helplessness. Someone even dubbed him a "papillon"

out of gear, and another said that people like him should be kept on a leash. . . . Finally, this unspontaneous and wearisome bustle was interrupted by the bell, and the noisy stream of visitors returned to their seats. They emerged from the grey masses of tobacco smoke like gods from the clouds.

The show rolled on like most shows of its kind. In the beginning there was the pompous and boring parade of stars who felt uncomfortable in such a narrow space; later, each of them went more or less his own way. But the play had four long acts, and after the third, the leading actors played so as to make the thing funny and not to tire themselves too much. Ksaveryi alone tried with all the strength of his whipped-up organism and confused his colleagues by his impetuous manner, so that some of them perceptibly got out of his way to avoid being knocked off their feet by such intensive creative fury. Unable to feel the rhythm of the lines because of his deafness, acting from memory a play that he had acted in all the minor towns of Russia, he jealously tried to outshout everyone else. His droll tricks amused the audience less than his lamentations that sounded like animal bleats. The spectacle assumed the character of a family affair; the box-attendants borrowed from a good theatre shook their heads. One of Zakurdaev's ancient boon-companions roared to him in the middle of the act from a box: "Go at it, old Ksaveryi!" (and from his throat emitted an extremely interesting sound that reminded one of the uncorking of a bottle.) And Ksaveryi went at it as best he could, in every conceivable style, so that everything foamed around him, and it was not his fault that fate had not swallowed him before into its putrid and rainbow-colored waters.

Liza sadly watched this wretched, inexcusable buffoonery. Fundamentally the whole affair was the funeral of a mediocre and unintelligent actor. The deceased appeared on the stage for the last time. He was applauded for the very reason that he was dying with ease, gaily, without burdening anyone with the necessity of feeling sorry for him. He knew himself that the next day he would be left without friends or fame, and he now gluttonously devoured his pretended success as a starved man chokes on a meal he dreams of. . . . At certain moments Liza fancied that he was about to be stricken by apoplexy and that he would be carried out, his head covered with his new overcoat, of which the cheviot sleeves would drag along the steps of the back staircase.

To congratulate him, she chose an opportune moment when Zakurdaev was dashing along the corridor, holding the sacred decanter. She touched his sleeve; with unexpected soberness he leered at her and waited. "All I want to say is that I am glad for you, Ksaveryi," she whispered in his ear.

He diffidently drew his head into his shoulders when her warm curls touched his cheek. "Thanks, little daughter, thanks," and although he did not believe that an intelligent person could be sincere at this moment, he shook her hand with feeling. "It's nonsense all this, smoke! Now I've earned an overcoat. I've played this part a thousand times and every time in a drunken state. Today for the first time I'm sober, and . . . it doesn't come off. What do you think? Well, that's fine, fine! . . . And how about you, you've left your doctor? I once dropped in to see him, and he acted sort of strange, as though I had come to be cut up by him. 'Sit down and tell me how you feel. . . .' It's not for nothing, Lizushka, that I've always been afraid of motors and doctors. . . ."

At this point the tall, sad and certainly once handsome man, whom Liza had noticed from the stage, came to greet Zakurdaev. Liza imagined that he must be an engineer engaged in some responsible construction work. He spoke words that are usually offered on such occasions to old men, softening the insincerity by friendly facetiousness. Ksaveryi looked up questioningly, was about to embrace his well-wisher so that he too might remember him for a week, but his hand dropped from his victim's neck, and his grotesque gesture did not come off. . . . However, his confusion did not last long. Suddenly, with renewed strength, he seized the guest by his hand and dragged him along. "How about a little glass to celebrate, ah? . . . Would you mind, with an invalid? What an audience . . . nationally famous names, all of them. If a bomb fell here no newspaper would have enough space for the obituaries. Get acquainted: my pupil, Liza . . . Not bad, Zakurdaev's school!" He could not refrain from the pleasure of casting a glance at her at that moment. "For the time being she is called just Lizushka, if you receive her permission. In old times she'd deserve a contract; I don't know how it is now. Well, thanks, thanks for the honor. And the people still remember Ksaveryi, honor him, eh . . . and how about a little glass with the old man?"

Here he began to stammer a little; generally speaking his talents became less and less apparent as the play wore on. Furthermore, the walls were still damp; the future club building had been heated particularly generously that day; the air was steamy. The old man was exhausted, spent, and among the audience one heard voices saying that the play ought to be finished some other day. Liza's new acquaintance took the first opportunity to leave Zakurdaev. She accompanied him.

"Daddy's a bit inebriate!" she said, quoting a line from the play, as though apologizing for Ksaveryi.

Her companion supported her. "Yes, it's a sad day. The old story of the clown, only read in a new manner. . . ."

"Nevertheless, he did what he could," Liza said evasively. "Even tower clocks, my husband told me, break in the end."

Her companion laughed. "Don't defend him, Liza! The dead need only justice. Your name is Liza, isn't it?" They turned back into the corridor. "You acted well today . . . with excellent and fresh clarity. It's not quite mature, but incompleteness of color is pleasant in the morning. That old man never had a morning. . . ."

She did not answer at once. She did not know whether she had acted well or badly, but in this role she did not repent, she only asserted her right to live under all circumstances. Later she said: "But you, too, congratulated him!"

"Well, that means I've not yet mastered my old actor's tendencies. I was a bad actor myself, but I was drawn into the revolution, and. . . . Where do you work now?"

She wanted to cry: nowhere, nowhere. . . . She said in a low voice: "I'm going to the periphery, to a town of which no one has ever heard: Cheremshansk."

"I'm sorry . . . I was about to ask you to come to my theatre."

Liza started and blushed. "Forgive me, but I didn't hear your name when we were introduced."

"I am Tiutchev."

"Ah, you're the same. . . ." She straightened out, half closed her eyes; she felt hot. "Yes, I've heard your name."

They had to move toward the over-heated radiator. A group of people was moving past them, and in the center the tireless Zakurdaev was bustling. His half-empty decanter danced over his head, and Ksaveryi's present victim had an angry and embarrassed expression. The affair threatened to end in a riot, but at this point the bell rang, and the whole witches' cauldron disintegrated.

"Yes . . . I have promised to go to Cheremshansk." She extended her hand. "Well, it's time for me to go on, comrade Tiutchev!"

So that was the price of every victory over oneself! . . . Her refusal had almost exhausted her. For a moment it seemed to her that her commitment in Cheremshansk was imaginary, fictitious, completely unnecessary. Who wanted her to miss her chance? She felt a desire to run after the director and to repeat to him a hundred times that she would come to his company. . . . But it was inconvenient in her make-up to look for him among the whole audience, and in the fourth act she was busy from the first scene on. Moreover, she recalled a passing remark of Kurilov's that she had not understood when he made it, about the necessity of mastering oneself every minute, and for the sake of his high praise she would have accepted an even greater grief. She finished the act in a state of great excitement and immediately rushed to the check room.

Her clown squeaked in her pocket, and people around smiled at her. She ran into the street with her coat unbuttoned. A strong ground wind was blowing, and the snow turned into mire the moment it touched the dusty pavement. As never before she wanted to see Alexei Nikitich—to boast childishly of her double success and to listen to his simple, intelligent, fatherly "Good!" She was in a hurry and yet she went on foot; she now liked to hold her fate dangerously, elusive as a bird, in her hands; this gave her a feeling of near equality with Kurilov. She was sure that on holidays Alexei Nikitich stayed home until dinner time. At that moment she felt filial tenderness toward the first man on her path who had been kind to her not for his own sake.

In the elevator, while the Roman numerals marking the floors slipped by, she freed her clown from his wadded surroundings. "You haven't lost anything, silly, by not having seen Ksaveryi!" The toy had perceptibly faded during that half-day, but it seemed to have more voice. And so they went to Kurilov's together. . . . She rang the bell, holding the marionette behind her back, but for a long time no one opened, and she rang for a second time. Then a swarthy, emaciated boy, his head and chest wrapped in a scarf, appeared in the doorway. He was followed by a woman dressed smoothly and warmly, as though for travelling. She dragged a big basket tied with straps behind her. The door slammed before Liza had had time to enter.

This woman's eyes emanated the sadness of departure. Liza asked her whether Alexei Nikitich was at home. The woman moved aside and examined her from top to toe with bitter and incredulous sympathy. "No. What's the matter with you!" she said sternly and shook her head. "Alexei Nikitich is dead."

Liza stared wildly at Frosia's old-fashioned, grey mother-of-pearl buttons adorned with little stars. It seemed to her that she had mistaken the number and rung the wrong bell. . . . But then how did this woman *know*?

"He died after an operation . . . lean against the wall, you'll fall!" the woman whispered, anxiously bustling about her. In her confusion it did not occur to her to ask Liza to sit on the basket. "I'm his sister. . . ."

"Oh—h—h," Liza gasped with an open mouth, and everything, the walls and door, began to whirl around her.

Efrosinia was in a hurry to make a train; this was her last attempt to begin life again. She quickly explained the details of the disaster. It had happened four days ago as a result of a sudden hemorrhage. It was at daybreak, he was all alone, no one could come to his aid. In her hasty story important things alternated with trifles, but Liza was struck only by the name of her own former husband, which was for some reason mentioned in passing. . . . Frosia's train was leaving in forty minutes. For a farewell Frosia simply and in peasant fashion embraced Liza and kissed her on the mouth. All that time little Luka had sat gloomily on the basket and did not take his eyes off the clown, which now and then gleamed in Liza's wilted hands.

"Let's go, Luka," said Frosia.

Their steps died away; soon a radio began to play somewhere. With wrinkled brows, Liza went away from Kurilov's apartment. She recalled how, as he left life, he had summoned everyone who could to live. No other loss, neither that of her mother, nor of the theatre, had so devastated her. Her fear in the face of her approaching maturity came a little later and lasted until she had reached the salvation of Cheremshansk. For long years she was to grow and hoard within herself the realization through which Kurilov had become so close to her. . . .

After a few steps, something made her look down the stairwell. Growing smaller and then vanishing, the storeys descended in a spiral. Somewhere in the last circle she caught a glimpse of Frosia's reed basket; then it disappeared. Liza bent over the banister and lost her will to go on. Far below a bulb burned in a glass tulip and a yellow stony square shone dimly under it. This enormous funnel with a diffuse star at the bottom attracted her, and her body of itself bent toward it; there was no one beside her to drag Liza away from the vacuum. For a moment her consciousness was dimmed. . . .

But something greater happened to her, for she was allowed to watch herself from without. Whether her hands opened involuntarily, or whether the emptiness wrenched the marionette from her grip—it slipped down evenly and strongly like a detached drop of liquid. Biting her lips, leaning with her side against the banister, Liza unblinkingly followed its flight. It fell, destroying itself and, as it were, thawing in the perspective of the staircase, and its whole fall took no more time than one deep sigh. She closed her eyes before the object had touched the stone, but she felt the shock at the same time. And suddenly a terrible and heavy curiosity seized her. In a great hurry, two steps at a time, burning her hands on the polished wood of the hand-rail, she ran down. She broke a heel before she had passed all twelve storeys. "So that is the way it happens."

The clown lay with a broken head. One of his glass eyes had fallen out of the clay and rolled for a yard, the socket of the other eye was surrounded with little black cracks. He no longer had any voice—he was not built for such ordeals. Liza mechanically dropped on her knees, and as she had once done with Protoklitov's clock, hurriedly picked up the scattered fragments. . . . Her head was still turning a little, but a sober sensation of reality was already returning. She smelt the odor of dust and fresh oil paint. She raised her head to look for her heel and saw many unknown people around her. None of them said anything.

"You see . . . it fell from upstairs!" Liza said, perplexed and still on her knees.

Then she rose, shook the dust off her dress and with arms hanging empty went out of the circle. People made room for her, and though knowing nothing, they looked after her, as she limped out, with severe and censuring sympathy, such as one accords unsuccessful suicides.

Thus passed the day of Liza's coming of age.

# CHAPTER 55

# The Broom Raises Dust in Cheremshansk

AND SO THE BEGINNING of the century resembled a stormy day. A hot sultriness hung in the air—and an angry silence and a haze of sham prosperity. At such times all things flourish. Clouds accumulated, matured and disintegrated, but each was more threatening than its predecessors (even the most stubborn reason guessed behind them the blue, sorrowless sky of the future). They passed majestically overhead, setting in motion everything alive beneath them. And it seemed that the continents wrenched from their original places drifted like blocks of ice on a river, into beautiful and terrible necessity. . . . All the attention of my contemporaries was directed toward them. For that reason, even on the railroad, the news of Kurilov's death did not arouse an echo commensurate with the size of the event. Only within a very small circle was the catastrophe fully appreciated.

Here they are all before me, the companions of Alexei Nikitich's last years: the mournful and still more reserved Klavdia; the shaken Liza, with her nails bitten off; Arsentyich—come to boast about his decoration to his former pupil who had gone further than his teacher; Tiutchev, who for a long time lost his usual smile; Aliosha Peresypkin, who pressed his eyes close together from grief; and, finally, Marina.

On the morning of the fourth day after the operation, upon Ziamka's request, she took him to visit Kurilov. The boy was very agitated while they travelled in the trolley car. But the hospital was surrounded by a police cordon, and no one was admitted. Some young girl expressed the opinion that pictures were being taken for a film. They decided to wait until all this was finished. There was a great deal of sun in the suburbs that day. Ziamka's attention was attracted by a frozen puddle with a thin crust of ice—so alluring. The frost had drunk it during the night; it would have been interesting to crush it through with one's felt boot. . . . But then a black boot stepped into that tiny hole, and Ziamka lost count trying to find out how many times this happened; a half company of Red Army men with fixed bayonets entered the cordon. . . . Funeral music played, the procession moved out, and although Marina did not know any of Kurilov's friends personally, she interpreted this

494

drunkenness, and even more as a result of his attempts to invent
[ne]w methods of treatment, he was dismissed from the provincial hospi-
[ta]l. His family patiently bore up with discomfort, hoping that in the
[en]d God would grow tired of persecuting the same people with mis-
[fo]rtune. . . . The last invention of the debased old man was some sort
[of] boots on metallic spiral springs which he called by the strange and
[a]luring name of "universals." He maintained that they made possible
[a] tremendous saving of energy and increased the length of each step
[b]y one hundred and eighty-six per cent. He wanted the Tsarist gov-
[e]rnment to apply his invention in all spheres of life, from children's
skates to infantrymen's boots and horseshoes. He was ignored by the
authorities. . . . Finally he decided to go to Petersburg in person in
these miraculous boots in order to sell his invention and obtain justice.
. . . Gleb was then four and a half years old.

"Well, did he find justice in Petersburg?" One of the members of
the commission who was following the mood of the audience asked
sarcastically, with a view to making a little subtle propaganda.

"He did not reach Petersburg. He was killed by a night train near
Saratov," Gleb answered sadly; then he added facetiously that this
disaster indirectly determined to some extent the profession of his son.
"In short, my papa, so to speak, jumped to his end. . . ."

He discreetly watched with bated breath those who were listening
to his every word. His patronizing irony toward this unlucky original
—but with all the outward signs of filial respect—found favor among
the simple-hearted audience. They also approved Protoklitov's silence
about the old man's other inclinations, although everyone realized that
he must have been a frightful drunkard. The fable about horses and
soldiers walking on springs put them in a definitely friendly mood.
The performance was a success, and the most far-fetched details,
veiled by the utmost impudence, acquired full plausibility. It was
necessary to maintain this tone to the very end. . . . Gleb saw that Sayfullah, after having whispered with Katia, moved toward the door, and
he recalled that the time to send the freight train to Porozhensk was
approaching. All these circumstances were fortunate; but Gashin maintained a sneering and incorruptible silence. . . .

. . . After Gleb's father's death, his mother made a living by laundering. He had no brothers or sisters. He and the old woman lived in the
insignificant part of the basement that was left by the enormous wash-
tub. The washerwoman had many customers; mother and son did not
starve. However, a broad stinking river of slops flowed through Gleb's
childhood; clouds of suffocating chlorine steam were reflected in it.
Thus from his earliest years Gleb had learned the true odors of man's

encounter as a bad omen. The real meaning of the austere red coffin
was revealed half an hour later, when she, together with Ziamka, succeeded in penetrating the building.

Gleb Protoklitov received the news at almost exactly the same moment. It might seem that all his fears were now at an end; he had
heard nothing from Kormilitsin. And if the maniac had not wasted a
bullet on himself on the way, somewhere the obscure Zoska was probably lying in a pool of blood; she had paid for everything now. . . .
His victory did not give Gleb any direct joy. He experienced a feeling,
inexplicable at first, not only of freedom, but also of loneliness. This
feeling derived from his deep and intelligent admiration for Alexei
Nikitich. . . . Gleb's alarm grew greater as the cleansing of the railroad party organization approached. However, the months did not go
by without bringing him some profit.

Barely perceptible changes affected the whole station. Reasons were
found for transferring Sayfullah to Cheremshansk; this was a result of
Gleb's attempt to win over Katia Reshotkina. Peresypkin was urgently
summoned to Moscow and was hardly likely to return soon. The cell
secretary, a witness to all these events, was transferred to Siberia with
a promotion. The spring bustle began; the massive freight loads of
spring grain for sowing moved along the line. And, above all, the
Komsomol locomotive again, and this time successfully, went on the
road. Protoklitov actively helped the young people to win this belated
victory. It seemed that the old quarrel was being forgotten, and Gleb's
cleverness consisted in his having given the reconciliation a reasonable
and unhurried gradualness. Everything was returning to normal, and
even the indices of work at the yard went up perceptibly.

Gleb had only Gashin to watch now. This man had a habit of pretending to be unhappy only in order to sting his victim, disarmed by
pity, with a barbed word. His body constantly moved and jerked, as
though his shirt was smouldering in many places. His knowledge of
another man's secret gave him courage and intelligence. This mechanic
happened once to be fined a trifling sum for having lost a monkey-
wrench. Three rubles were to be deducted from his wages, but Gashin
had the insolence to contradict the direct evidence. "You, Gleb Ignatyich, wrote for a penny, but I'll have to work half a day for it!" he
argued hotly and humbly. Gleb did not wish to take his part, both
because he felt disgusted and because the moment had at last come
to discover Gashin's secret. Gashin left with a smile that boded no
good: "Just hold on, old friend! . . . The iron broom is rustling!" And
Gleb did not have the strength to call him back and buy him for a
three-ruble bribe.

Then it became known that the commission had been in Cheremshansk for two days. No one had any idea of its composition, except perhaps that it was headed by the People's Commissar for Public Health of one of the national republics. Scrupulous, indefatigable despite his age, he wandered about the surrounding territory, questioning everyone, including housewives, invited declarations, dropped in at the yard shops and among other things constantly expatiated on hygiene as the principal factor in efficient railroad traffic. He preserved strict incognito but did not mind being silently recognized. Protoklitov had an opportunity to ascertain that this chairman of the commission was not a very redoubtable judge. "The terrain around your yard, Protoklitov, is in a rather neglected state. The best proof of it is that your locomotives often have to be checked over. Ay, ay, why do you stare like that?" he remarked to Gleb one day.

Gleb answered in a military tone: "The station master is under the division superintendent, not under me."

"Excuses!" And he threatened him with his finger. "Rather than put the blame on others you should send some men. It's as if a poisoned man were lying in the street, and you passed by. Of course, that is the doctor's business! . . . But we haven't got enough doctors, and everybody should be attended to. Isn't that true? . . . After all this man is your brother, eh? Have you got any shovels? Give me a shovel right away!"

"All right, I'll send you one."

The meetings took place in the evening hours, so that at least two shifts could take part in the discussions. The cleansing began with the locomotive yard, and Protoklitov was the third on the list. A mass of people gathered as on Doomsday, and everyone expected a surprise. Everyone had prepared a little stone to hurl at Protoklitov, and everyone wondered what would happen if all of these were hurled at once. Gashin, too, told someone confidentially and obscurely: "Now all of us together will pull out that rotten tooth!" Protoklitov entered while the examination of one of the Cheremshansk party organizers was drawing to an end. He was a simple kind of fellow, and it was no wonder that he had missed the true significance of the incident with the Komsomol locomotive.

". . . And these were my jobs," he said in agitation. "At a glass works I was employed carrying boxes, then I was a bricklayer at an open-hearth furnace, a loader on freight trains, a secretary of a people's university cell, a tutor in a children's home, a member of the bureau of a regional trade union, and so on and so on. I was fined twice: for leav-

ing without permission—my wife got sick—and for ha much with a football team. . . ."

"We've heard about that," the chairman said, noddin ill?"

"During the civil war I had a slight case of typhus. . . .

The chairman then asked a few questions about the dec last party congress and the social roots of the Rightist de This candidacy was discussed only briefly; next came t Protoklitov. No sooner had this name been uttered than the was filled to bursting; everyone began to stand up, as though never seen Protoklitov before, and Gashin silently moved back rows to the edge of the platform—there, covered with bunting, was the control commission's table. Gleb came out platform, and everyone watched sharply as he picked up the de they expected that he would spill some water (but he did not that he would drop his glass (but he did not). Gashin rose, his head, and everyone heard him say with admiring hatred: what a wolf!"

"I was not born in a working-class family, although I have n known great prosperity," Gleb began in a very low voice, as tho regretting this fact. "But I am thirty-nine years old. That is more t half a life. And those who say that I have not accomplished enou will be right. However, if my milieu is taken into account, this r proach will be considerably weakened."

At this point his cap dropped to the floor, having slipped from th edge of the table. And while he picked it up, everyone hastened to take the most comfortable position so as not to have to move afterwards. Then followed Gleb's biography, told in a matter-of-fact way and too scantily to satisfy the curiosity that the yard master had for some time aroused in Cheremshansk. Apparently this man refused to boast of his poor childhood; only once in a while a bitter memory won the upper hand, and then one detail developed in the proper way would have satisfied the most captious examiner. Enviable courage was required to indulge in such a risky enterprise before this audience especially sensitive to the description of poverty. During the preceding years Gleb must have convinced himself of the truth of his inventions, and more than that, he had almost fallen in love with his fantasy mother, a sturdy old woman maddened by misery, chosen from among the filthy populace he in truth despised.

And so Gleb had become an orphan at an early age. His father, an unlucky assistant physician, fancied himself a misunderstood inventor.

birth, his love, his sickness, his old age. . . . From that period of his life Gleb had preserved only one vivid memory. At Christmas in 1904 his mother brought him a great quantity of preserves. This joint gift from the newborn God and the local official Chestnokov had come from a broken glass jar and was wrapped in old newspapers containing communiqués of the Russo-Japanese war. (Gleb could read by now.) Chestnokov adored this kind of preserve, made from barberries, and had separated from it only because he feared to cut his insides with a chip of glass. The washerwoman and her son had preserves for a long time.

". . . Everything ended well, but I recall how industriously we spat those prickly icicles out into our hands!" Gleb concluded, and he stopped to let everyone in the audience feel the invisible glass sting his tongue.

He had been standing in public view for twenty-six minutes and had not yet made one false move. The deep social meaning of Protoklitov's short story about the Christmas preserves struck even Gashin. He no longer tried to catch the speaker in a contradiction, but sat gloomily stroking his shiny knees hardened by oil. The yard master continued his tale; the frank although not very cheerful tone he used when speaking of his childhood seemed to penetrate the very hearts of his listeners. At one point Gashin even cried out in agitation that "if one closed one's eyes, one would believe him!" No less striking details were contained in the rest of Protoklitov's Odyssey, which he had once tested on Kurilov—his flight from the basement, his life in saloons, the philanthropic Irkutsk official—and it was clear that on his path he had met, not people, but only beasts of various colors, teeth and faces. . . . Finally, as though throwing off a burdensome verbal load, the chairman asked Gleb about his activities during the civil war. Gleb answered evasively, but the chairman insisted: "Still it's somewhat unclear; did you do any fighting or did you spend all your time eating preserves or watching cabbage? . . . Were you carried away by the upsurge of the revolutionary spirit?"

Gleb slowly wiped the sweat off his forehead. This was the climax. With the conviction of utter despair he named certain regiments, certain momentary fronts, which had not left their mark on history, certain cavalry raids, and all this was so unusual that no one interrupted him even with a breath. Luckily for him, no one among the audience had taken part in the engagements he mentioned. . . . The cleansing was nearing its end; he was now cross-examined, but after half an hour of gleaming sabers and stamping partisan horses all these questions seemed trifling and cavilling. The dejected Gashin sat silent, listening to the sounds that came from outside. The room was filled with smoke, and someone had opened a window. One could hear a drunken switchman walking on the tracks and blowing his horn—his inexcusable mooing was absolutely meaningless. And somewhere from a distance the arrival of the seven o'clock train from Moscow was being signalled. The train was scheduled to arrive at 7:12, and it was obvious that the clock in the club was fifteen minutes late.

And because his recent hostility toward the yard master was now dulled, Gashin rose to speak without particular enthusiasm. ". . . Everyone is putting on an act, everyone shouts 'the proletarian element.' . . . At Kulla they shouted about the dispatcher that he was a hero of emancipated labor, but then he turned out to be a mullah. So is Protoklitov: he keeps saying that he's a worker, but he's a pure-blooded bureaucrat! What are you staring at, Protoklitov? . . . Are you frightened?"

And true enough, violently pressing the edge of the table, Gleb seemed to await the *coup de grâce*, as everyone else awaited it. All remembered Gashin's mysterious hints.

". . . And so one day I went to see him, uninvited, and there was a book on his table . . . he had had no time to hide it. A foreign book about electric locomotives. I've got good eyes, I see everything at once! And tell me, if you're a worker, how do you happen to know a foreign language? You work all day, you come in in the morning, you leave at night . . . you eat without sitting down, you sleep without removing your shoes. . . ."

The last danger had passed. . . . There, in the first row, sat a five-year-old girl. Her grandmother, who did not want to leave her child alone at home, had tied her pigtails with a pink ribbon and brought her along. This faded ribbon of washed-out silk lent a note of coziness to the general grey and sooty color of the gathering. Suddenly the little girl burst out laughing at some amusing gesture of Gashin's, and following the example of the child, the grown-ups, too, were amused. And when his secret failed to cause an explosion, Gashin became confused and in disgrace ran away from the red table.

"So I've given you the floor for nothing," the chairman thundered in a facetious voice. "You don't make sense. It's like when a patient needs, say, three grains of aspirin, and you give him salol. It won't do any harm, but it's a waste of time. . . . N-no, my friend, the party doesn't forbid its members to study foreign languages. That will be very useful to us. Foreign nations have things to tell us. Sit down, don't make a laughing stock of yourself!" And he demonstrated with his hand exactly how he should do so.

Gleb was at last sailing on smooth waters. With embarrassment he admitted that he actually did spend some time on self-education, because he intended to work independently as a constructor; the late Kurilov, he said, had more than once insisted upon his leaving the railroad, but his feeling of duty toward it, as toward his mother, had prevented him from giving up his yard. The chairman asked a last question, then leaned forward with his whole body; and at once everyone started to get up from their seats. Although the hall was overcrowded, a passage was immediately formed from the entrance to the red table. Gashin, who had been making his way toward the exit, again came closer, giving everyone to understand that the game was not yet lost, was only approaching its dénouement.

Very broad, with an alert expression, wearing an enormous fur coat, appeared Ilya Protoklitov, who had been unable to come earlier because of the extremely inconvenient schedule of the trains to Cheremshansk.

# CHAPTER 56

# The Curtain Falls

A SEAT WAS IMMEDIATELY FOUND for him in the front row. He sat beside the little girl: her ribbon was a little above her elbow. . . . Some
speakers continued taking the floor, but the very presence of this
stranger changed the previous style of the gathering. First, the change
affected the chairman. The audience no longer heard any of his jokes,
and all of them tried to act as though the appearance of such a man
was completely natural. Indeed, everyone was allowed to come to a
cleansing and express his opinion concerning a party man who was being
checked upon. Ilya Ignatyich was as though unnoticed. He felt increasingly hotter and more uncomfortable, but there was no space for
his fur coat, and he kept on sitting, bathed in sweat, very stern and
very lonely, with a wet handkerchief in his hand. . . . The questions
now concerned current politics; the chairman tried to show off the
ideological level of the gathering. This took much time and of course
would have been the easiest part of the ordeal for Gleb, had it not
been for Ilya's presence. Trying to unravel the meaning of his arrival,
his brother cautiously winked at him, but the older Protoklitov left
his greeting unanswered. . . .

Ilya wrote a note, and the little girl took it to the red table: "From
the little uncle. . . ." In the silence her voice sounded as though a glass
dish had dropped on the floor. From that moment on no one listened to
Gleb; his words vanished, did not reach anywhere; in the end he
stopped completely. The chairman made an imperceptible sign to the
older Protoklitov, and he rose, leaving his cap on the chair. (While
he spoke, the little girl stealthily stroked this cap, as though it were
a warm and marvellous cat.)

"State briefly, very briefly, who you are and what is your work. I
know you, but this is for the comrades. . . . And please don't hurry!"
the chairman declared considerately and stroked his mustache, unable
to conceal his normal human curiosity.

The club had been preparing to give a play, and the stage-set that
had been left at the back of the platform represented a merchant's
private chapel with a mass of icons painted on canvas. (A cheerless
woman with a halo, holding a baby, looked from behind the chair-

man's massive shoulders.) At first this shocked the eyes of the audience, later everyone got accustomed to it, and as soon as Ilya had climbed to the platform no one noticed it. . . .

However, I know this final episode, when Gleb's activity, dark and abounding in evil, was suddenly revealed, only from Victor Reshotkin's description of it. An intelligent and capable fellow when his locomotives were in question, he unfortunately proved completely helpless when it came to describing the commotion that followed Ilya's appearance. Moreover, he sat in the next-to-the-last row, and in the noise that broke out after Ilya Ignatyich's very first words he could only guess the bare meaning of what was afterwards said. It appears that the older Protoklitov contented himself with reporting his conversation with Kormilitsin and refrained from expressing any opinion of his own. Thus everything that had been intended for Kurilov reached its true destination, without passing through all the proper intermediate stages.

However, the surgeon's revelations were so unexpected that at first, not Gleb's fictitious biography, but Ilya's report was felt to be a monstrous accumulation of slander and lies. In the first moments of the tumult, Gleb was somehow forgiven all the former insults and persecutions that he had dealt the workers, for the sole reason that the frayed familiar coat of one brother was closer and more understandable to the gathering than the rich coat, lined with expensive fur, of the other. The chairman himself was affected by this mirage and subjected the witness to thorough questioning; and now he was no longer the former comedian who built his speeches upon all kinds of medical allusions! Everything was tied into a knot, everyone wanted to see Gleb at close quarters; suddenly even the most insignificant details of his behavior became understandable. (Reshotkin remembered distinctly that Liza's name was not mentioned. Ilya Ignatyich's position was made more difficult because, when describing Gleb's infamous role in Kurilov's death, he did not wish to bring in the name of his runaway wife.)

"In brief it was a terrible uproar!" Victor said. "The little girl screamed, the member of the commission who sat at the right put the burning end of the cigarette into his mouth, and Gashin yelled: 'Where were your eyes, you devils!' . . . A general bedlam! And the one in the fur coat stood there like a monument. Only his eyebrows—remember when I showed you a manometer?—well, his eyebrows moved like the hands on the manometer. The yard master was of course very gloomy; he took his cap from the table, put it on, and sat . . . as calmly as if he were about to go away somewhere on a trip! And there was some crowd—everyone came from the shift. No, there was no chance for him to run away. . . ."

All these were not the details I wanted. Reshotkin did not tell me whether the audience was glad to give up the skilfully constructed myths about the extravagant father, about mankind walking on springs and the preserves dotted with glass. But he gave a sufficiently exact description of Dr. Protoklitov's departure. "He went to the door . . . and now no one any longer looked at his fur coat, but at his face. Such an oblong face . . . and as though stung by bees. And what a silence, man! . . . One could hear Fedka dropping a file in the yard." And there was another detail which at first seemed completely inexplicable to me. It seems that Skuriatnikov came that night to the yard and sat in a corner and played all the time on his tin toy as though asking it to give him advice. (And surely it must have told him that everything was well and would be even better!)

Ilya had a whole three hours and one half before the departure of his train. He went to Cheremshansk. A dashing sleigh overtook him, and the driver, a fellow from the cooperative, leaning back on his seat, stared for a long time at the silhouette, rare in these parts. Night was falling, the kerosene lights multiplied in the windows, as Ilya crossed the town limits. The night promised to be frosty, and the road creaked in an appetizing way. The bells of Lent flowed into the silence, drop by drop. Ilya walked, the dogs gathered in packs behind him, fearing to attack him single-handed. He was trying to get to the address that Arkadyi Hermogenovich had given him before he left. . . .

It was a little one-storey house; the curtains were pulled to each side as artisans arrange their hair; the entrance was from the yard. Two little boys were busy attaching a starling-house to a tree. One of them asked the little uncle to hold the pole while he himself climbed the tree holding the plywood box. As a reward for Ilya's help, they led him to the proper wing of the building. "He must have come to see the new tenant!" one of the boys surmised aloud. Ilya pulled the string of the wooden latch and walked in. A pail with water had been near the entrance to trip any uninvited visitors. No one came out at the noise. . . . The second door was very much like the opening of the boy's birdhouse. The lamp smoked, a black thread spun above the glass. On a garden cot made of wood, Liza slept, completely dressed. She was covered with her short coat. Ilya knew her habit of taking a nap anywhere.

He turned the wick, and the thread broke. A dingy, lazy man had long been living in this room; Liza had not yet had time to leave her mark upon it. Ancient postcards with young brides in tinfoil frames were surrounded with a rim of bedbug stains; there was a paunchy chest of drawers with a mass of phials, so tall that you had to stand on the stool to reach the mirror. . . . The rustle awakened Liza. She swung her legs down, and with her little fists childishly and painstakingly rubbed her eyes.

"Ah, it's you again!" There was neither fright nor the former bitterness in her voice, flabby, indifferent and still sleepy.

Ilya Ignatyich removed his cap. "I was very much afraid that I wouldn't find you at home."

"Have six months passed already?"

"I came before the term because I love you, Liza."

She squinted at him, as he screened the light from her, and carefully adjusted her dress over her knees.

"Thank goodness you're at least not offering to save me from poverty."

This woman had never loved him. And worst of all, he had never found a minute to ask her about her feelings in former times. He saw a stack of books on the window-sill and did not dare open one of them so that he might understand in what direction Liza was travelling away from him.

"Well, it's a good thing you woke me up, Ilya. I must leave now. I have an evening class."

"Are you studying . . . or teaching?"

"Oh, both together! What can one do? There are some who know even less than I do. And the younger one is, the more one wants to act the part of Hamlet and Romeo and even Mary Stuart. . . ."

"If I may, I'll accompany you, Liza."

"Will your patients wait this time?" (And he had no reason to interpret her calm joke as a reproach.)

Liza put on her outer clothes. . . . It happened that the mirror could be taken down from the wall and put on the table. Ilya Ignatyich found his height useful. The short coat was somewhat too big for Liza, it hung down from her shoulders, but when tightened with a belt it was very becoming. In this unfamiliar wrapping she had a special and mysterious attractiveness. The smell of sheepskin made his nostrils distend.

They went out. Idlers at a lodge gate fell silent as Liza passed with her companion.

"And so you're happy?"

"I've never thought about it. But when one makes one's fate oneself, even mistakes are pleasant. Everything, everything can be found in one's own self . . . and you know, Ilya, a human heart is deeper than any mine in the world!"

He had not known such self-assurance in her in former times, even at her most boastful moments. It would have been tactless now to offer her money or naïvely to ask her to return.

"You've changed a great deal, Liza."

"Yes!" And she laughed. "For instance, I used to be ticklish, but I'm not any more. I wanted to play Mary, and now I don't. I must have learned too much about her. Moreover, I had a great grief." And he knew that she was not referring to their child. "Tell me, nevertheless, how *he* died."

An unmistakable note of command sounded in her voice. She was fully entitled to this. In detail, as though reading his surgical record, Ilya expounded the circumstances of the misfortune, and the dead, porous snow creaked under his feet. . . . The operation itself had been successful, but two days later, at night, the ligature cut through a bandaged artery. The hemorrhage caused an increased weakening, a comatose state, and death. Liza demanded precise details, and he did not spare medical terms which explained the impotence of the physicians.

". . . But why did it cut this artery?"

"Apparently the tissue had been destroyed by the pathological process. It had lost its elasticity. . . ."

"I believe you, Ilya."

"Were you very much attached to this man?"

"I don't know . . . but he never reproached me for my youth!"

They walked down long streets, and it seemed to her that they were the same ones in which she had run barefoot. Provincial towns seem made on a conveyor belt! . . . In this house where a giant's boot is on the fence, her mother had died. There was a light at Aunt Shura's: she was doubtless correcting children's dictations, the funny little old woman. In an illuminated window, near which Zakurdaev liked to sit, there was a bottle; apparently this room was traditionally occupied by drunks. At the left there was a small ramshackle church; near it pigskins were delivered. And here, at last, was the famous ravine! . . . The landslide reached the very bench; Liza stopped at the edge. A young moon, with its horns upwards, as though lying on its back, endowed the landscape with a penetrating newness. An indistinct mound of snow gleamed at the bottom of the violet-colored abyss. The silence was like an icicle; even a whisper could break it. And the old bitterness of the half-forgotten turnip suddenly burned Liza's tongue. The second act of her life was finished, and how good it was that the most important part was still ahead of her!

"That's all, Ilya. Now we have to separate. I don't want us to be seen together *there*. Apparently, I haven't yet reached the stage when one is indifferent to what people say. . . ." And she left forever, very light and transparent, without shaking his hand, without having let him say anything, without looking back.

Ilya Ignatyich returned to the station. He recalled how he himself at first had *not known* anything. (He performed operations while mentally looking things up in his books. . . . And only the war had given the young surgeon an enormous and terrible practice.) He thought of himself, but only at the end of his road did he begin to understand that he had missed the most precious thing that had ever been his to hold—the youth of a woman.

# CHAPTER 57

# Epilogue

ONE SUMMER NIGHT, after a long interruption, Peresypkin came to see me, and I was glad as though Alexei Nikitich himself, alive and rejuvenated, had come. We had already met through Kurilov, and Aliosha's first visit to me had taken place at a time when he was only beginning to expound the causes and circumstances of the creation of his railroad. Hurried, quarrelsome, he had broken in on me, the thorns of boyish contradiction sticking out all over him. .   . This time he came silently, self-absorbed, and nothing could stir him up. It seemed to me that he had fallen in love again.

"I'm being transferred to the oil industry. I think!" he finally told me.

Unless it was his imminent separation from his friends that was bothering him, he must have been upset by the necessity of abandoning his literary work. His new field of activity inevitably implied new preoccupations. I reminded him that the rivers of oil, like the cars of the Volga-Revizan line, like all the streams of commodities, nations and ideas, necessarily flowed into the same Ocean that Kurilov had tried to reach. He understood my hint without additional explanation . . . and his very work on the history of the railroad had turned out to be a kind of university for Aliosha. Apparently he began to feel uncomfortable within the boundaries of the Volga-Revizan alone. Having understood the mechanism of small crimes, he now wanted to give mankind a developed epic of the world railroad business, richly illustrated with the stories of the Spiridon Matochkins of all lands and ages.

"I want to call it: An Inheritor Looks Back at the Past," he confessed with embarrassment.

I began to question him about Kurilov's companions in life, and he told me of the second, nearly epic visit of Bibi-Kamal to her son's wedding, of the amusing metamorphoses of Ziamka, to whom Klavdia Nikitichna had transferred her last affection, of the long-legged Shamin's unsuccessful wooing, of Liza's refusal and of the arrest of the Cheremshansk yard master. . . . He also touched upon the subject of Pokhvisnev, whom Aliosha had wanted to meet for such a long time.

His story put me in an embarrassing position with regard to those of my friends who have agreed to read this book to the end.

After the return from Cheremshansk the youthful historian finally set out to visit his principal witness. He did not want to indict or to question him, but only to have a look at his faded eyes, to see whether at their bottom some reflection of the Psnia incident had not been preserved. . . . He found the house, entered it and rang the bell; he was admitted by the plumber, who had soap on his cheeks. Aliosha asked for Pokhvisnev, and the plumber said that a man by that name had *never* lived there. Anxiously Aliosha described all his features, but the tenant kept shaking his head. "There's one Gulkin here, also a former pensioner, but he used to be a cashier. And there was never anyone by the name of Pokhvisnev!" The numbers of the house and of the apartment were the same that Peresypkin had noted. The plumber was angry, the soap was drying on his cheeks. Greatly upset, Aliosha left without having accomplished anything. The inconspicuous old man must have just as inconspicuously vanished from life into trackless non-being.

We spent the rest of the time in a walk, such as I had often taken in the company of Alexei Nikitich. My young visitor, too, sometimes liked to peer behind that tightly drawn curtain—and we went out of the boundaries of the narrow, smoke-filled room and the rainy July night. Actually, there were three of us; Alexei Nikitich was there, because, once we left the presence, his reality was no less than our own. . . . We passed hundreds of indistinct events, barely sketched on the screen of the future; we visited dozens of historically remarkable towns that do not exist as yet. Frolicking like boys, Aliosha and I romped through that immense expanse of the universe, and Kurilov's shade, like a mountain, rose above us. We went up on escalators to a high tower, where dwelt a grey-haired original with an archaic electronic telescope. We hindered him from rummaging in the abysses with his magic sheaf of rays, disturbing his waves, and he comically ascribed this fact to an intensification of cosmic radiation. With a sudden knock at his window we awakened a schoolboy who had fallen asleep over his lesson about the Battle of Shanghai; the child was bored from having to cram lessons about the age of the capitalists, whom he imagined to be something like the Lestrigonian cannibals (an obvious invention, Ziamka would have said). We climbed up to a hanging airport just when a flying apparatus was taking off for the Southern Hemisphere. This machine cannot be described in words: it had neither gas sausages nor wings nor noisy propellers. Busy people were preparing for the night, and we were ashamed of making fun of them. And finally, by silent agreement, we paid a visit to our second homeland: the mother of gay earthly cities, Ocean.

It was a night of bad weather when we entered. This was the rainy season on these shores. The planet was shivering. Overhead, in the tops of tall trees, hard, almost metallic leaves scraped one another. From the port came the roar of the siren calling nocturnal ships. I heard the breath of ancient ages in the combined noise of the surf and the wind. Everything was asleep. . . . Suddenly the rain grew more violent, and we were compelled to seek the shelter of trees. Somewhere beside us a young couple was hiding; the same girl that Kurilov had met countless times reached out her lips toward someone in the darkness, and now, against the phosphorescent stream of a fountain I distinguished her slender, tense and virginal silhouette. . . .

But as though having felt our jealous glance upon them, *they* interrupted their whispering. We were disturbing them. . . . Aliosha sternly nudged me, inviting me to leave. I looked back for the last time, but I now saw no one in the shadows. Lovers have always possessed the magic property of dissolving into the rustle of trees, into moonlight, into the odor of nocturnal flowers, when they want to hide from a stranger's curiosity. . . . And although our Moscow coats were soaked to the very shoulders, we left our shelter and silently went along the path that anyone must take who leaves home in stormy weather.

THE END